OF

LOVE

AND

LIFE

OF LOVE AND LIFE

Three novels selected and condensed
by Reader's Digest

The Reader's Digest Association Limited, London

The Reader's Digest Association Limited
11 Westferry Circus, Canary Wharf, London E14 4HE

www.readersdigest.co.uk

ISBN 0-276-42872-2

CONTENTS

PHILIPPA GREGORY

the Queen's Fool

In Tudor England it is a crime to follow
the Jewish religion, and from an early
age Hannah Green has learned to hide
her faith. She also has the troubled gift
of second sight. Both things make her
vulnerable to accusations of heresy
and witchcraft.
In the treacherous world of the Tudor
court, Hannah desperately needs to find
a protector.

SUMMER 1548

THE GIRL, GIGGLING and overexcited, was running in the sunlit garden, running away from her stepfather, but not so fast that he could not catch her. Her stepmother, seated in an arbour with Rosamund roses in bud all around her, caught sight of the fourteen-year-old girl and the handsome man chasing round the broad tree trunks on the smooth turf and smiled, determined to see only the best in both of them: the girl she was bringing up and the man she had adored for years.

He snatched at the hem of the girl's swinging gown and caught her up to him for a moment. 'A forfeit!' he said, his dark face close to her flushed cheeks.

Like quicksilver she slid from his grasp and dodged to the far side of an ornamental fountain; Elizabeth's excited face was reflected in the water as she leaned forward to taunt him. 'Can't catch me!'

''Course I can.'

She leaned low so that he could see her small breasts at the top of the square-cut green gown. She felt his eyes on her and the colour in her cheeks deepened. He watched, amused and aroused, as her neck flushed rosy pink.

'I can catch you any time I want to,' he said.

'Come on then!' she said, not knowing exactly what she was inviting, but knowing that she wanted to hear his feet pounding the grass behind her, to feel his arms round her, pulling her against the fascinating contours of his body. She gave a little scream and dashed away again down an *allée* of yew trees, where the Chelsea garden ran down to the river.

The queen, smiling, looked up from her sewing and saw her beloved stepdaughter racing between the trees, her handsome husband a few easy strides behind. She looked down again at her sewing and did not see him catch Elizabeth, whirl her round, and put her back to the red papery bark of the yew tree.

Elizabeth felt the smooth sweep of his moustache against her lips. She closed her eyes and tipped back her head to offer her neck to his mouth. When she felt his sharp teeth graze her skin, she was no longer a giggling child, she was a young woman in the heat of first desire.

Gently he loosened his grip on her waist, and his hand stole up the firmly boned stomacher to the neck of her gown, where he could slide a finger down inside her linen to touch her breasts. Her nipple was hard and aroused; when he rubbed it she gave a little mew of pleasure that made him chuckle at the predictability of female desire.

Elizabeth pressed herself against the length of his body, feeling his thigh push between her legs in reply. She had a sensation like an overwhelming curiosity. She longed to know what might happen next.

All at once he caught at the hem of her brocade skirt and pulled it up and up until he could get at her, sliding his practised hand up her thighs, underneath her linen shift. At his teasing touch, she melted and he could feel her almost dissolve beneath him. She would have fallen if he had not had a firm arm round her waist, and he knew at that moment that he could have the king's own daughter, Princess Elizabeth, against a tree in the queen's garden. The girl was a virgin in name alone. In reality, she was little more than a whore.

A light step on the path made him quickly turn, dropping Elizabeth's gown and putting her behind him, out of sight. He was afraid it was the queen, his wife, whose love for him was insulted every day that he seduced her ward under her very nose: Queen Catherine, who had been entrusted with the care of her stepdaughter the princess, who had sat at Henry VIII's deathbed but dreamed of this man.

But it was not the queen who stood before him on the path. It was only a girl, a little girl of about nine years old, with big, solemn dark eyes and a white Spanish cap tied under her chin. She carried two books strapped with bookseller's tape in her hand.

'How now, sweetheart!' he exclaimed, falsely cheerful. 'You gave me a start. I might have thought you a fairy, appearing so suddenly.'

She frowned at his rapid, over-loud speech, and then she replied, very slowly with a strong Spanish accent. 'Forgive me, sir. My father told me to bring these books to Sir Thomas Seymour.'

She proffered the package of books, and Tom Seymour was forced to step forward and take them from her hands. 'You're the bookseller's daughter,' he said cheerfully. 'The bookseller from Spain.'

She bowed her head in assent, not taking her scrutiny from his face.

'What are you staring at, child?' he asked, conscious of Elizabeth hastily rearranging her gown behind him.

'I was looking at you, sir, but I saw something most dreadful.'

'What?' he demanded, afraid she would say that she had seen him with a princess of England backed up against a tree like a common doxy.

'I saw a scaffold behind you,' said the surprising child, and then she turned and walked away.

Tom Seymour whirled back to Elizabeth. 'Did you hear that?'

The princess was trying to comb her disordered hair with fingers still shaking with desire. 'No,' she said silkily. 'Did she say something?'

'She only said that she saw the scaffold behind me!' He was more shaken than he wanted to reveal.

At the mention of the scaffold Elizabeth was suddenly alert. 'Why?' she snapped. 'Why should she say such a thing?'

'God knows,' he said. 'Probably mistook the word—she's foreign. Probably meant throne! Probably saw the throne behind me!'

But in Elizabeth's imagination the throne and the scaffold were always close neighbours. The colour drained from her face. 'Who is she?' Her voice was sharp with nervousness.

He turned to look for the child but the *allée* was empty. At the distant end of it he could see his wife, Catherine, walking slowly towards them, her back arched to carry the pregnant curve of her belly.

'Not a word,' he said quickly to the girl at his side. 'Not a word of this, sweetheart. You don't want to upset your stepmother.'

He hardly needed to warn her. The girl was always conscious that she must play a part. She might be only fourteen, but she had been trained in deceit for twelve long years since the death of her mother. She might feel desire, but she was always more alert to danger or ambition than to lust.

He took her cold hand and led her up the *allée* towards his wife. He tried for a merry smile. 'I caught her at last!' he called out. He glanced around. He could not see the child. 'We had such a race!' he cried.

I was that child, and that was the first sight I ever had of the Princess Elizabeth: panting with lust, damp with desire, rubbing herself like a cat against another woman's husband. But it was the first and last time I saw Tom Seymour. Within a year, he was dead on the scaffold, charged with treason, and Elizabeth had denied three times having anything more than the most common acquaintance with him.

WINTER 1552–3

'I REMEMBER THIS!' I said excitedly to my father, turning from the rail of the Thames barge as we tacked our way upstream. 'Father! I remember these gardens running down to the water, and the great houses, and the day you sent me to deliver some books to the English lord, and I came upon him in the garden with the princess.'

He found a smile for me, though his face was weary from our long journey. 'Do you, child?' he asked quietly. 'That was a happy summer for us. She said . . .' He broke off. We never mentioned my mother's name, even when we were alone. At first it had been a precaution to keep us safe from those who had killed her and would come after us, but now we were hiding from grief as well as from the Inquisition.

'Will we live here?' I asked hopefully.

'Nowhere as grand as this,' he said gently. 'We will have to start small, Hannah, in just a little shop. We have to make our lives again. And when we are settled then you will come out of boy's clothes, and dress as a girl again, and marry young Daniel Carpenter.'

'And can we stop running?' I asked, very low.

My father hesitated. We had been running from the Inquisition for so long that it was almost impossible to hope that we had reached a safe haven. We ran away the very night that my mother was found guilty of being a Jew—a false Christian, a 'Marrano'—by the Church court, and we were long gone when they released her to the civil court to be burned alive at the stake. First over the border to Portugal, then overland to Paris, all the way pretending to be something that we were not: a merchant and his young apprentice lad, pilgrims on the way to Chartres, a scholar and his tutor going to the great university of Paris.

We met my mother's cousins in Paris, and they sent us on to their kin in Amsterdam, where they directed us to London. We were to hide our race under English skies; we were to become Protestant Christians. We would learn to like it. I must learn to like it.

The kin—the People whose name cannot be spoken, whose faith is hidden, the People who are condemned to wander, banned from every country in Christendom—were thriving in secret in London as in Paris, as in Amsterdam. We all lived as Christians and kept the Sabbath in secret, and then, the very next day, went to Mass with a clean conscience. Our family helped us to London with letters of introduction to the d'Israeli family, who went by the name of Carpenter, organised my betrothal to the Carpenter boy, financed my father's purchase of a printing press and found us rooms over a shop off Fleet Street.

In the months after our arrival my father set up his print shop with a determination to survive and to provide for me. At once, his stock of texts was much in demand, especially his copies of the gospels that he had brought inside the waistband of his breeches and now translated into English. He bought the books and manuscripts which had once belonged to the libraries of religious houses—destroyed by Henry, the king before the young king, Edward. My father went out daily and came back with something rare and precious, and when he had tidied it, and indexed it, everyone wanted to buy. At night, even when he was weary, he set print and ran off short copies of the gospels and simple texts for the faithful to study, all in English, all clear and simple. We sold them cheaply, at little more than cost price, to spread the word of God. We let it be known that we believed in giving the Word to the people. We could not have been better Protestants if our lives had depended on it.

Of course, our lives did depend on it.

I ran errands, read proofs, helped with translations, set print. On days when I was not busy in the print shop I stood outside to summon passers-by, still dressed in the boy's clothes I had used for our escape.

As I lounged against the wall of our shop, drinking in the weak English sunshine, I heard the ring of a spur against a cobblestone and I snapped my eyes open and leapt to attention. Before me, casting a long shadow, was a richly dressed young man, a tall hat on his head, a cape swinging from his shoulders, a thin silver sword at his side. He was the most breathtakingly handsome man I had ever seen.

Behind him was an older man, near thirty years of age, with the pale skin of a scholar, and dark, deep-set eyes. He was a writer—I saw the ink stain on the third finger of his right hand—and he was something greater even than this: a thinker, a man prepared to seek out what was hidden. He was a dangerous man, a man not afraid of heresies, not afraid of questions, a man who would seek the truth behind the truth.

I had been so interested in these two, the young man like a god, the older man like a priest, that I had not looked at the third. This third man was all dressed in white, gleaming like enamelled silver. I could hardly see him for the brightness of the sun on his sparkling cloak. I blinked, but still I could not see his face. Then I realised that the men were looking in the doorway of the bookshop next door.

Cursing myself for an idle fool, I jumped into their path and said clearly, in my newly acquired English accent, 'Good day to you, sirs. Can we help you? We have the finest collection of pleasing and moral books you will find in London, at the fairest of prices and—'

'I am looking for the shop of Oliver Green,' the young man said.

At the moment his dark eyes flicked to mine, I felt myself freeze, as if all the clocks in London had suddenly stopped still. I wanted to hold him: there, in his red slashed doublet in the winter sunshine, for ever. I wanted him to look at me and see me, me, as I truly was: not an urchin lad with a dirty face, but a girl, almost a young woman. But his glance flicked indifferently past me to our shop, and I came to my senses and held open the door for the three of them.

'This is the shop of the scholar and bookmaker Oliver Green. Step inside, my lords,' I invited them, and I shouted into the inner dark room: 'Father! Here are three great lords to see you.'

I heard the clatter as he pushed back his high printer's stool and came out, wiping his hands on his apron. 'Welcome,' he said. 'I am Oliver Green. And I will serve you in any way that I can do. Any way that is pleasing to the laws of the land, and the customs—'

'Yes, yes,' the young man said sharply. 'We hear that you are just come from Spain, Oliver Green.'

My father nodded. 'I am just come to England indeed, but we left Spain three years ago, sir.'

'Your name? It is a very English name?'

'It was Verde,' he said with a wry smile. 'It is easier for Englishmen if we call ourselves Green.'

'And you are a Christian? And a publisher of Christian theology and philosophy?' the young man asked.

I could see the small gulp in my father's throat at the dangerous question, but his voice was steady when he answered. 'Most certainly, sir.'

'And are you of the reformed or the old tradition?'

My father did not know what answer they wanted to this, nor could he know what might hang on it. Actually *we* might hang on it, or burn for it, or go to the block for it, however it was that they chose this day to deal with heretics in this country under the young King Edward.

'The reformed,' he said tentatively. 'Though christened into the old faith in Spain, I follow the English church now.'

I could smell the sweat of his terror, acrid as smoke. 'It's all right,' I said in a quick undertone in Spanish. 'I'm sure they want our books, not us.'

14

My father nodded to show he had heard me. But the young lord was onto my whisper at once. 'What did the lad say?'

'I said that you are scholars,' I lied in English.

'Go inside, *querida*,' my father said quickly to me. 'You must forgive the child, my lords. My wife died just three years ago and the child is a fool, only kept to mind the door.'

'The child speaks only the truth,' the older man remarked pleasantly as I hovered in the doorway. 'For we have not come to disturb you; there is no need to be afraid. I am a scholar, not an inquisitor. I only wanted to see your library.' He turned to me. 'But why did you say three lords?' he asked. 'There are only two of us, lad. How many can you see?'

I looked from the older man to the handsome young man and saw that there were, indeed, only two of them. The man in white had gone.

'I saw a third man behind you, sir,' I said to the older one. 'Out in the street. I am sorry. He is not there now.'

'She is a fool but a good girl,' my father said, waving me away.

'No, wait,' the young man said. 'Wait a minute. I thought this was a lad. A girl? Why d'you have her dressed as a boy?'

'And the third man?' his companion asked me. 'What was he like?'

'All in white,' I said through half-closed lips. 'And shining.'

'What did he wear?'

'I could only see a white cape.'

'And on his head?'

'I could only see the whiteness.'

'And his face?'

'I couldn't see his face for the brightness of the light.'

'D'you think he had a name, child?'

I could feel the word coming into my mouth though I did not understand it. 'Uriel.'

The man looked into my face as if he would read me like one of my father's books. 'Uriel?'

'Yes, sir.'

The younger man turned to my father. 'When you say she is a fool, d'you mean that she has the Sight?'

'She talks out of turn,' my father said stubbornly. 'Nothing more.'

'She has the Sight,' the older man breathed. 'Praise God, I come looking for manuscripts and I find a girl who sees Uriel and knows his holy name.' He turned to my father. 'Does she have any knowledge of sacred things? Has she read your books?'

'Before God, no,' my father said earnestly, lying with every sign of conviction. 'I swear to you, my lord, I have brought her up to be a good ignorant girl. She knows nothing, I promise you. Nothing.'

The older man shook his head. 'Please,' he said gently to my father, 'do not fear me. You can trust me. This girl has the Sight, hasn't she?'

'No,' my father said baldly, denying me for my own safety. 'She's nothing more than a fool. She's not worth your attention . . .'

'Peace,' the young man said. 'We did not come to distress you. This gentleman is John Dee, my tutor. I am Robert Dudley.'

At their names my father grew even more anxious, as well he might. The handsome young man was the son of the greatest man in the land: Lord John Dudley, protector of the King of England himself. If they took a liking to my father's library then we could find ourselves supplying books to the king, a scholarly king, and our fortune would be made. But if they found our books seditious or blasphemous or heretical, then we could be thrown into prison or into exile again or to our deaths.

'May I see your library?' John Dee asked.

I saw my father's reluctance to let the man browse the shelves and drawers of his collection. I knew that the books of secret wisdom in Greek and Hebrew were always hidden, behind the sliding back of the bookshelf. But even the ones on show might lead us into trouble.

'Of course, my lord,' he surrendered. 'It will be an honour to me.' He led the way into the inner room and John Dee followed him.

The young lord, Robert Dudley, took a seat on one of the stools and looked at me with interest. 'Twelve years old?'

'Yes, sir,' I lied promptly, although in truth I was nearly fourteen.

'And a maid, though dressed as a lad.'

'Yes, sir.'

'No marriage arranged for you?'

'Not straight away, sir.'

'But a betrothal in sight?'

'Yes, sir.'

'And who has your father picked out for you?'

'I am to marry a cousin from my mother's family when I am sixteen,' I replied. 'I don't particularly wish it.'

'You're a maid,' he scoffed. 'All young maids say they don't wish it.'

I shot a look at him which showed my resentment too clearly.

'Oho! Have I offended you, Mistress Boy?'

'I know my own mind, sir,' I said quietly. 'And I am not a maid like any other.'

'Clearly. So what is your mind, Mistress Boy?'

'I don't wish to marry.'

'And how shall you eat?'

'I should like to have my own shop, and print my own books.'

'And do you think a girl, even a pretty one in breeches, could manage without a husband?'

'I am sure I could,' I said. 'Widow Worthing has a shop.'

'A widow has had a husband to give her a fortune; she didn't have to make her own.'

'A girl can make her own fortune,' I said stoutly. 'I should think a girl could command a shop.'

'And what else can a girl command?' he teased me. 'A ship? An army? A kingdom?'

'You will see a woman run a kingdom better than any in the world before,' I fired back, and then checked at the look on his face. I put my hand over my mouth. 'I didn't mean to say that,' I whispered.

He looked at me as if he would hear more. 'Do you think, Mistress Boy, that I will live to see a woman rule a kingdom?'

'In Spain it was done,' I said weakly. 'Once. Queen Isabella.'

He nodded and let it go, as if drawing us both back from the brink of something dangerous. 'So. D'you know your way to Whitehall Palace, Mistress Boy?'

'Yes, sir.'

'Then when Mr Dee has chosen the books he wants to see, you can bring them there, to my rooms. All right?'

I nodded.

'How is your father's shop prospering?' he asked. 'Selling many books? Many customers coming?'

'Some,' I said cautiously. 'But it is early days for us yet.'

'Your gift does not guide him in his business, then?'

I shook my head. 'It is not a gift. It is more like folly, as he says.'

'You speak out? And you can see what others cannot?'

'Sometimes.'

'And what did you see when you looked at me?'

I took a quiet breath. 'I think that you would trouble a young woman who was not in breeches.'

He laughed out loud at that. 'Please God that is a true seeing. But I never fear trouble with girls; it is their fathers who strike me with terror.'

I smiled back, I could not help myself. There was something about the way his eyes danced when he laughed that made me want to laugh too.

'And have you ever foretold the future and it came true?' he asked, suddenly serious.

The question itself was dangerous in a country that was always alert for witchcraft. 'I have no powers,' I said quickly.

17

'But without exerting powers, can you see the future? It is given to some of us, as a holy gift, to know what might be. My friend here, Mr Dee, believes that angels guide the course of mankind and may sometimes warn us against sin, just as the course of the stars can tell a man what his destiny might be.'

I shook my head at this dangerous talk, determined not to respond.

He looked thoughtful. 'Can you dance or play an instrument? Learn a part in a masque and say your lines?'

'Not very well,' I said unhelpfully.

He laughed at my reluctance. 'Well, we shall see, Mistress Boy. We shall see what you can do.'

Next day, carrying a parcel of books and a carefully rolled scroll of manuscript, I walked to Whitehall Palace, my cap pulled over my ears against the icy wind. I had never been inside a royal palace before, and I had thought I would just give the books to the guards on the gate, but when I showed them the note that Lord Robert had scrawled, with the Dudley seal of the bear and staff at the bottom, they bowed me through as though I were a visiting prince, and ordered a man to guide me.

Inside the gates, the palace was like a series of courtyards, each beautifully built, with a great garden in the middle set with apple trees and arbours and seats. The soldier led me across the first garden and gave me no time to stop and stare at the finely dressed lords and ladies who, wrapped in furs and velvets against the cold, were playing at bowls on the green. Inside the door, swung open by another pair of soldiers, there were more fine people in a great chamber, and behind that great room another, and then another. My guide led me through door after door until we came to a long gallery, and Robert Dudley was at the far end.

I was so relieved to find him that I ran a few steps towards him and called out: 'My lord!'

The guard hesitated, as if he would block me from getting any closer, but Robert Dudley waved him aside. 'Mistress Boy!' he exclaimed. He got to his feet and then I saw his companion. It was the young king, King Edward, fifteen years of age and beautifully dressed in plush blue velvet but with a face the colour of skimmed milk.

I dropped to my knee, holding tight to my father's books and trying to doff my cap at the same time, as Lord Robert remarked: 'This is the girl-boy. Don't you think she would be a wonderful player?'

I did not look up but I heard the king's voice, thinned with pain. 'You take such fancies, Dudley. Why should she be a player?'

'Her voice,' Dudley said. 'Such a voice, very sweet, and that accent, part Spanish and part London, I could listen to her for ever. And she holds herself like a princess in beggar's clothes.'

I kept my head down so that he should not see my delighted beam.

The young king returned me to the real world. 'It's against Holy Writ for a girl to dress as a boy.' His voice tailed away into a cough which shook him like a bear might shake a dog.

I looked up as the king took his handkerchief from his mouth and I saw a glimpse of a dark stain. Quickly, he tucked it out of sight.

'It's no sin,' Dudley said soothingly. 'She's no sinner. The girl is a holy fool. She saw an angel walking in Fleet Street. Can you imagine it?'

The younger man turned to me at once, his face brightened with interest. 'Did you see an angel?'

I nodded, my eyes downcast. I could not deny my gift. 'Yes, sire. I—'

'What can you see for me?' he interrupted.

I looked up. Anyone could have seen the shadow of death on his face, in his waxy skin, in his swollen eyes, in his bony thinness, even without the evidence of the stain on his handkerchief. I tried to tell a lie but I could feel the words coming despite myself. 'I see the gates of heaven opening.'

The young king was not angry. He smiled. 'This child tells the truth when everyone else lies to me,' he said. He gestured to me. 'Stay at court. You shall be my fool.'

'I have to go home to my father, Your Grace,' I said as quietly and as humbly as I could, ignoring Lord Robert's glare. 'I only came today to bring Lord Robert his books.'

'You shall be my fool and wear my livery,' the young man ruled. 'Robert, I am grateful to you for finding her for me. I shan't forget it.'

It was a dismissal. Robert Dudley bowed and snapped his fingers for me, turned and went from the room. I hesitated, wanting to refuse the king, but there was nothing to do but bow to him and run after Dudley like some pet greyhound scampering at his master's heels. He went down a long gallery, towards double doors guarded by soldiers with pikes, who flung them open as we approached. Finally we came to a great pair of doors where the soldiers wore the Dudley livery, and we went in.

'Father,' Dudley said, and dropped to one knee.

There was a man at the fireplace of the great inner hall, looking down into the flames. He turned and made an unemotional blessing over his son's head with two fingers. I dropped to my knee too, and stayed down even when I felt Robert Dudley rise up beside me.

'How's the king this morning?'

'Worse,' Robert said flatly. 'Cough bad, he brought up some black bile, breathless. Can't last, Father.'

'And this is the girl?'

'This is the bookseller's daughter, dresses like a lad but certainly a girl. Has the Sight, according to John Dee. I took her into the king as you ordered, begged her for a fool. She told him that she saw the gates of heaven opened for him. He liked it. She is to be his fool.'

'Good,' the duke said. 'And have you told her of her duties?'

'I brought her straight here.'

'Stand, fool.'

I rose to my feet and took my first look at Robert Dudley's father, the Duke of Northumberland, the greatest man in the kingdom. I took him in: a long bony face like a horse, dark eyes, balding head half hidden by a rich velvet cap with a big silver brooch of his coat of arms: the bear and staff. I looked into his eyes and saw—nothing. This was a man whose face could hide his thoughts.

'What's your name?' he asked of me.

'Hannah Green, my lord.'

'Listen, Hannah the Fool, you have been begged for a fool and the king has accepted you. D'you know what that means?'

I shook my head.

'You become his, like one of his puppies. Your job is to be yourself. Speak as your gift commands you. Say the first thing that comes into your head. It will amuse him. You will be paid to be his fool.'

I waited.

'Do you understand, fool?'

'Yes. But I don't accept.'

'You can't accept or not accept. You were your father's property, now you are ours. And we have begged you for a fool to the king. He owns you. D'you understand?'

'My father would not sell me,' I said stubbornly.

'He cannot stand against us,' Robert said quietly behind me. 'And I promised him that you would be safer here than out on the street. I gave him my word and he accepted. The business was done while we ordered the books, Hannah. It is finished.'

'Now,' continued the duke. 'Not like a puppy, and not like a fool, you have another task. You are to be our vassal.'

At the strange English word I glanced at Robert Dudley.

'Servant to command, servant for life,' he explained.

'Everything you hear, everything you see, you tell me, or Robert here. You are our eyes and our ears at his side. Understand?'

'My lord, I have to go home to my father,' I said desperately. 'I cannot be the king's fool. I have work to do at the bookshop.'

The duke raised one eyebrow at his son. Robert leaned towards me and spoke very quietly.

'Mistress Boy, I think your father is not a good Christian from a good Christian family at all, but a Jew.'

I opened my mouth to deny it, but I could not speak for fear.

'Now, luckily for you, your Sight has won you the safest and highest place that you might dream of. Serve the king well, serve our family well and your father is safe. Fail us in any one thing and he is tossed in a blanket till his eyes fall backwards in his head, and you are married to a red-faced chapel-going Luther-reading pig herder. You can choose.'

There was the briefest of moments. Then the Duke of Northumberland waved me away. He did not even wait for me to make my choice. He did not need the Sight to know what my choice would have to be.

'And you are to live at court?' my father confirmed.

We were eating our dinner, a small pie brought in from the bake-house at the end of the street.

'I am to sleep with the maidservants,' I said glumly. 'And wear the livery of the king's pages. I am to be his companion.'

'It's better than I could have provided for you,' my father said, trying to be cheerful. 'We won't make enough money to pay the rent on this house next quarter, unless Lord Robert orders some more books.'

'I can send you my wages,' I offered. 'I am to be paid.'

He patted my hand. 'You're a good girl. Never forget that. Never forget your mother, never forget that you are one of the children of Israel.'

I nodded. 'I am to start tomorrow,' I whispered. 'Father . . .'

'I will come to the gate and see you every evening,' he promised. 'Have courage, daughter. You are one of the Chosen.'

'How will I keep the fast days?' I demanded in sudden grief. 'They will make me work on the Sabbath. They will make me eat pork!'

He met my gaze and then he bowed his head. 'I shall keep the law for you here,' he said. 'God is good. He understands. I will pray for you, Hannah. And even if you are praying on your knees in the Christian chapel God still sees you and hears your prayer.'

'Father, Lord Robert threatened me. He knows we are Jews and he said that he would keep our secret as long as I obey him.'

'Daughter, we are safe nowhere. And you at least are under his patronage. He swore to me that you would be safe in his household.'

'Father, how could you let me go? Why did you agree that they could take me away from you?'

'Hannah, how could I stop them?'

In the lime-washed room under the eaves of the palace roof I turned over the pile of my new clothes and read the inventory from the office of the Master of the Household: *One pageboy livery in yellow. One pair of hose, dark red. One pair of hose, dark green. One surcoat, long. Two linen shirts. Two pairs of sleeves, one pair red, one pair green. One black hat. One black cloak for riding. One pair of slippers for dancing. Two pairs of boots, one pair for riding, one pair for walking. Everything used but clean and darned and delivered to the king's fool, Hannah Green.*

'I shall look a fool indeed,' I said to myself.

That night I whispered an account of my day to my father as he stood at the postern gate and I leaned against the doorway. 'There is a fool at court already, a man called Will Somers. He was kind to me, and showed me where I should sit. He is a witty man; he made everyone laugh.'

'And what do you do?'

'Nothing as yet. I have thought of nothing to say.'

My father glanced around. 'Won't they want you to think of something?'

'Father, I cannot command the Sight.'

'Did you see Lord Robert?'

'He winked at me.' I leaned back against the cold stone and drew my warm new cloak round my shoulders.

'The king?'

'He was not even at dinner. He was sick, they sent his food to his rooms. The duke took his place at the head of the table.'

'And does the duke have his eye on you?'

'He did not seem to see me at all.'

'Has he forgotten you?'

'He doesn't have to look to know who is where, and what they are doing. He will not have forgotten me. He is not a man who forgets.'

The duke had decided that there was to be a masque at Candlemas and gave it out as the king's command, so we all had to wear special costumes and learn our lines. Will Somers, the king's fool who had come to court twenty years ago when he was a boy, was to introduce the piece and recite a rhyme, the king's choristers were to sing, and I was to recite a poem, specially composed for the occasion. My costume was to be a new livery, specially made for me in the fool's colour of yellow.

The Master of the Revels gave me a little sword and ordered that Will and I should prepare for a fight, which would fit somewhere into the story of the masque.

We met for our first practice in one of the antechambers off the great hall. I was awkward and unwilling; I did not want to learn to fight with swords like a boy. No man at court but Will Somers could have persuaded me to it, but he treated our lesson as if he had been hired to improve my understanding of Greek. He behaved as if it was a skill I needed to learn, and he wanted me to learn well.

He started with my stance. Resting his hands on my shoulders, he gently smoothed them down, took my chin and raised it up. 'Hold your head high, like a princess,' he said. Then he showed me the swordsman's stance, hand on my hip for balance, how to slide forward with my leading foot always on the floor so that I should not trip or fall, how to move behind the sword and to let it retreat to me. Then we started on the feints and passes. Will commanded me to stab at him.

I hesitated. 'What if I hit you?'

'Then I shall take a splinter, not a deadly cut,' he pointed out. 'It's only wood, Hannah.'

'Get ready then,' I said nervously, and lunged forward.

To my amazement Will sidestepped me and was at my side, his wooden sword to my throat. 'You're dead,' he said. 'Not so good at foresight after all. Try again.'

The next time I lunged with a good deal more energy and caught the hem of his coat as he flicked to one side.

'Excellent,' he said breathlessly. 'And again. We have to plan how you are going to murder me amusingly by Candlemas.'

We had our sword dance planned in good time and it did seem very funny. At least two practices ended in us both having fits of giggles as we mistimed a lunge and cracked heads together. But one day the Master of the Revels put his head into the room and said: 'You won't be needed. The king is not having a masque.'

I turned with the play-sword still in my hand. 'But we're all ready!'

'He's sick,' the Master said dourly.

'And is the Lady Mary still coming to court?' Will asked.

'Said to be,' the Master said. 'She'll get better rooms and a better cut of the meat this time, don't you think, Will?'

He shut the door before Will could reply, and so I turned and asked, 'What does he mean?'

'He means that those of the court who move towards the heir and away from the king will be making their move now.'

'Because?'

'Ah, child. Lady Mary is the heir. She will be queen if we lose the king, God bless him, poor lad.'

'But she's a heret—'

'Of the Catholic faith,' he corrected me smoothly.

'And King Edward . . .'

'His heart will break to leave the kingdom to a Catholic heir but he can do nothing about it. It's how King Henry left it. God bless him, he must be rolling in his shroud to see it come to this. It makes you think, doesn't it? Is England ever to get any peace? Two young lusty kings: Henry's father, Henry himself, handsome as the sun, each of them, lecherous as sparrows, and they leave us with nothing but a lad as weak as a girl, and an old maid to come after him?'

'And what will happen to us?' I demanded. 'If the young king dies and his sister takes the throne?'

Will grinned. 'Then we shall be Queen Mary's fools,' he said simply. 'And if I can make her laugh it will be a novelty indeed.'

My father came to the side gate that night and he brought someone with him, a young man dressed in a worsted cape, dark ringlets of hair falling to his collar, dark eyes and a shy, boyish smile. It took me a moment to recognise him; he was Daniel Carpenter, my betrothed.

He was twenty years old, training to be a physician like his father, who had died only last year. I had seen Daniel only once before, when he and his mother welcomed us to England with a gift of bread and some wine, and I knew next to nothing about him.

'Daniel asked to see you alone,' my father said awkwardly, and he stepped back a little, out of earshot.

'I heard that you had been begged for a fool,' Daniel said. At first glance he looked more Portuguese than Jewish, but the heavy-lidded eyes would have betrayed him to one who was looking.

I slid my gaze from his face and took in a slight frame with broad shoulders, narrow waist, long legs: a handsome young man.

'Yes,' I said shortly. 'I have a place at court.'

'When you are sixteen you will have to leave court and come home again,' he said.

I raised my eyebrows at this young stranger. 'Who gives this order?'

'I do.'

'I don't believe you have any command over me.'

'When I am your husband . . .'

'Then, yes.'

'I am your betrothed. You are promised to me. I have some rights.'

I showed him a sulky face. 'I am commanded by the king, I am commanded by the Duke of Northumberland, I am commanded by his son

Lord Robert Dudley, I am commanded by my father; you might as well join in. Every other man in London seems to think he can order me.'

He gave a little gulp of involuntary laughter and clipped me gently on my shoulder as if I were his comrade. I found I was smiling back at him. 'Oh, poor maid,' he said. 'Poor set-upon maid.'

I shook my head. 'Fool indeed.'

'When I have served my apprenticeship and I am a physician I will make a home for us.'

'And when will that be?' I asked him.

'Within two years,' he said stiffly. 'I shall be able to keep a wife by the time you are ready for marriage.'

'Come for me then,' I said unhelpfully. 'Come with your orders then, if I am still here.'

'In the meantime, we are still betrothed,' he insisted. 'I have waited for you and your father to come from Amsterdam. When you finally came to England I thought you would be glad of . . . be glad of . . . a home. And then I hear you and your father are to set up house together, you are not coming to live with Mother and me, and you have not put aside your boy's costume. Then I hear you are working for him like a son. And then I hear you have left the protection of your father's house. And now I find you at court.'

It was not the Sight that helped me through all of this, but the sharp intuition of a girl on the edge of womanhood. 'You thought you would rescue me, that I would be a fearful girl longing to cling to a man!'

The sudden darkening of his flush and the jerk of his head told me that I had hit the mark.

'Well, learn this, young apprentice physician, I have seen sights and travelled in countries that you cannot imagine. I have been afraid and I have been in danger, and I have never for one moment thought that I would throw myself at a man for his help.'

'You are not . . .' He was lost for words, choking on a young man's indignation. 'You are not . . . maidenly.'

'I thank God for it.'

'You are not . . .' His temper was getting the better of him. 'You would not be my first choice!'

That silenced me, and we looked at each other in some sort of shock.

'Do you want another girl?' I asked, a little shaken.

'I don't know another girl,' he said sulkily. 'But I don't want a girl who doesn't want me.'

'It's not you I dislike,' I volunteered. 'It's marriage itself.'

My father glanced over curiously and saw the two of us, face to face, aghast in silence. Daniel turned away from me and took two paces to one side, I leaned against the cold stone of the doorpost and wondered if this would be the last I would see of him.

Daniel mastered himself, and came back to me. 'You do wrong to taunt me, Hannah Green,' he said, his voice trembling with his intensity. 'Whatever else, we are promised to one another. We can make a home here. You and I can be married and have children who will be English children. They will know nothing but this life. We need not even tell them of your mother, of her faith. Nor of our own.'

'Oh, you'll tell them,' I predicted. 'You say you won't now, but once we have a child you won't be able to resist it. And you'll find ways to light the candle on Friday night and not to work on the Sabbath. You'll be a doctor then, you will circumcise the boys in secret and teach them the prayers. You'll have me teach the girls to make unleavened bread and to keep the milk from the meat and to drain the blood from the beef. And so it goes on, like some sickness that we pass on, one to another.'

'It's no sickness,' he whispered passionately. 'It is our gift, we are chosen to keep faith.'

I would have argued for the sake of contradicting him, but it went against the deeper grain of my love for my mother and her faith. 'Yes,' I admitted. 'It is not a sickness, but it kills us just as if it were. My grandmother and my aunt died of it, my mother too. And this is what you propose to me. A lifetime of fear, not Chosen so much as cursed.'

'If you don't want to marry me, then you can marry a Christian and pretend that you know nothing more,' he pointed out. 'You can deny the faith that your mother and your grandmother died for. Just say the word and I shall tell your father that I wish to be released.'

I hesitated. I wanted to be free. I did not want to be cast out. 'I don't know,' I said, a girl's plea. 'I'm not ready to say . . .'

'Then be guided by those who do,' he said flatly. He saw me bridle at that. 'Look, you can't fight everyone,' he advised me. 'You have to choose where you belong and rest there.'

'It's too great a cost for me,' I whispered. 'For you it is a good life. For me it is to lose everything I might be and everything I might do, and become nothing but your servant.'

'This is not being a Jew; this is being a girl,' he said. 'Would you deny your sex as well as your religion?'

I said nothing.

'You are not a faithful woman,' he said. 'You would betray yourself.'

'That's a dreadful thing to say,' I whispered.

'But true,' he maintained. 'You are a Jew and you are a woman and you are my betrothed, and all these things you would deny. Who do you work for in the court? The king? The Dudleys? Are you faithful to them?'

I thought of how I had been begged as a fool and appointed as a spy. 'I just want to be free,' I said. 'I don't want to be anybody's anything.'

I saw my father looking towards us. I saw him make a little tentative move as if to interrupt us, but then he waited.

'Shall I tell them that we cannot agree and ask you to release me from our betrothal?' Daniel asked tightly.

Wilfully, I was about to agree, but his silence, his patient waiting for my reply made me look at Daniel Carpenter more closely. The light was going from the sky and in the half-darkness I could see the man he would become. He would be handsome, he would have a dark mobile face, a quick observing eye, a sensitive mouth, thick black hair like mine. And he would be a wise man; he was a wise youth, he had seen me and understood me and contradicted my very core, and yet still he stood waiting. He would be a generous husband.

'Leave me now,' I said feebly. 'I can't say now. I have said too much already. I am sorry for speaking out. I am sorry if I angered you.'

But his anger had left him as quickly as it had come, and that was another thing that I liked in him.

'Shall I come again?'

'All right.'

'Are we still betrothed?'

I shrugged. '*I* haven't broken it,' I said.

He nodded. 'I shall need to know,' he warned me. 'I shall want to marry within two years—you, or another girl.'

My father came up beside Daniel before I could reply, and put a hand on his shoulder. 'And so you two are getting acquainted,' he said hopefully. 'What d'you make of your wife-to-be, Daniel?'

I expected Daniel to complain of me to my father, but he gave me a small rueful smile. 'I think we are coming to know each other,' he said gently. 'We have overleapt being polite strangers and reached disagreement very quickly, don't you think, Hannah?'

'Commendably quick,' I said, and was rewarded by his smile.

Lady Mary came to London for the Candlemas feast, as had been planned; it seemed that no one had told her that her brother was too sick to rise from his bed. She rode in through the palace gate of Whitehall with a great train behind her, and was greeted at the very threshold of the palace by the duke, with his sons, including Lord Robert, at his side, and the council of England bowing low before her.

As I watched her seated high on her horse, looking down at the sea of humbly bowing heads, I thought I saw a smile of pure amusement cross her lips before she put down her hand to be kissed.

I had heard so much about her, the beloved daughter of the king who had been put aside on the word of Anne Boleyn, the whore. The princess who had been humbled to dust, the mourning girl who had been forbidden to see her dying mother. I had expected a figure of tragedy, but what I saw was a stocky little fighter with enough wit about her to smile at the court, knocking their noses on their knees because, suddenly, she was the heir with formidable prospects.

The duke treated her as if she were queen already. She was helped from her horse and led in to the banquet. The king was in his chamber, coughing and retching in his little bed, but they had the banquet anyway, and I saw the Lady Mary look round at the beaming faces as if to note that, when the heir was in the ascendant, a king could lie sick and alone, and no one mind at all.

There was dancing after dinner but she did not rise from her seat, though she tapped her foot and seemed to enjoy the music. Will made her laugh a couple of times, and she smiled on him as if he were a familiar face in a dangerous world.

I looked her over, as did the court: this woman who might be my next mistress. She was a woman in her thirty-seventh year, but she still had the pretty colouring of a girl. She wore her hood set back off her square, honest face and showed her hair, dark brown with a tinge of Tudor red. Her smile was her great charm; it came slowly, and her dark eyes were warm. But what struck me most about her was her air of honesty. She looked as if she said nothing that she did not mean.

She had a great jewelled cross at her throat as if to flaunt her religion in this most Protestant court, and I thought that she must be either very brave or very reckless to insist on her faith when her brother's men were burning heretics for less. But then I saw the tremor in her hand when she reached for her golden goblet, and I imagined that like many women she had learned to put on a braver face than she might feel.

When there was a break in the dancing, Robert Dudley was at her side, whispering to her, and he beckoned me forward.

'I hear you are from Spain, and my brother's new fool,' she said in English.

I bowed low. 'Yes, Your Grace.'

'Speak Spanish,' Lord Robert commanded me, and I bowed again and told her in Spanish that I was glad to be at court.

When I looked up I saw the delight in her face at hearing her mother's language. 'What part of Spain?' she asked eagerly in English.

'Castile, Your Grace,' I lied at once. I did not want any enquiries made of us and of my family's destruction in our home of Aragon.

'And why did you come to England?'

I was prepared for the question. My father and I had discussed the dangers of every answer and settled on the safest. 'My father is a scholar,' I said. 'He wanted to print books from his library of manuscripts, and he wanted to work in London, which is such a centre of learning.'

'And you are my brother's holy fool,' she said. 'D'you have any words of wisdom for me?'

I shook my head helplessly. 'I wish I could see at will, Your Grace. I am much less wise than you, I should think.'

'She told my tutor, John Dee, that she could see an angel walking with us,' Robert put in.

The Lady Mary looked at me with more respect.

'This is a good little maid,' he continued, 'and I think she does have a true gift. She has been a great comfort to your brother in his illness. She has a gift of seeing the truth and speaking true, and he likes that.'

'That alone is a rare gift to find at court,' the Lady Mary said. She nodded kindly to me and I stepped back and the music started up again. I kept my eye on Robert Dudley as he led out one young lady and then another to dance before the Lady Mary, and I was rewarded when he glanced over to me and gave me a hidden approving smile.

The Lady Mary did not see the king that night but the chambermaids' gossip was that when she went into his room the next day she came out again, white as a winding sheet. She had not known till then that her little brother was so near to his death.

After that, there was no reason for her to stay. She rode out as she had come, with a great retinue following behind, and all the court bowing low, praying silently that, when she came to the throne, she would be blessed with forgetfulness and overlook the priests they had burned at the stake, and the churches they had despoiled.

I was watching this charade of humility from one of the palace windows when I felt a gentle touch on my sleeve. I turned, and there was Lord Robert, smiling down at me.

'My lord, I thought you would be with your father, saying goodbye to the Lady Mary.'

'No, I came to find you to ask if you would do me a service?'

I felt my colour rise to my cheeks. 'Anything . . .' I stammered.

He smiled. 'Just one small thing. Would you come with me to my tutor's rooms, and see if you can assist him in one of his experiments?'

I nodded and Lord Robert took my hand and, drawing it into the crook of his arm, led me to the Northumberland private quarters.

John Dee was seated in the library overlooking an inner garden. He raised his head as we came into the room. 'Ah, Hannah Verde.'

It was so odd for me to hear my real name, given in full, that for a moment I did not respond, and then I dipped a little bow. 'Yes, sir.'

'She says she will help. But I have not told her what you want,' Lord Robert said.

Mr Dee rose from the table. 'I have a special mirror,' he said. 'I think it possible that one with special sight might see rays of light that are not visible to the ordinary eye, d'you understand?'

I did not.

'Just as we cannot see a sound or a scent, but we know that something is there, I think that the planets and the angels send out rays of light, which we might see if we had the right glass to see them in.'

'Oh,' I said blankly.

The tutor broke off with a smile. 'No matter. You need not understand me. I was only thinking that since you saw the angel Uriel that day, you might see such rays in this mirror.'

'I don't mind looking, if Lord Robert wishes it,' I volunteered.

He nodded. 'I have it ready. Come in.' He led the way to an inner chamber. The window was shielded by a thick curtain, all the cold winter light blocked out. A square table was placed before it, the four legs standing on four wax seals. On top of the table was an extraordinary mirror of great beauty. I stepped up to it and saw myself, reflected in gold, looking not like the boy-girl I was, but like a young woman.

'I want you to close your eyes,' Dee said, 'and listen carefully to the prayer that I am going to read. When you say "amen" you can open your eyes again and tell me what you see. Are you ready?'

I closed my eyes and I could hear him softly blowing out the few candles illuminating the shadowy room. 'I am ready,' I whispered.

It was a long prayer in Latin; I understood it despite Mr Dee's English pronunciation of the words. It was a prayer for guidance and for the angels to come and protect the work we would do. I whispered 'amen' and then I opened my eyes.

The candles were all out. The mirror was a pool of darkness, black reflected in black, I could see nothing.

'Show us when the king will die,' Mr Dee whispered from behind me.

I watched, waiting for something to happen, my eyes staring into the blackness. I could see nothing. I waited. Nothing came to me. I stared into the darkness until I knew that far from being a holy fool I was a fool pure and simple, looking at a reflection of nothing.

I had to say something. They knew who I was. They had bought me and now they expected some benefit for their bargain.

'July,' I said quietly, as good a reply as any.

'Which year?' Mr Dee prompted me, his voice silky and quiet.

Common sense alone suggested that the young king could not live much longer. 'This year,' I said unwillingly.

'The day?'

'The sixth,' I whispered in reply.

'Tell the name of the next ruler of England,' Mr Dee whispered.

I was about to reply 'Queen Mary', echoing his own tranced tone. 'Jane,' I said simply, surprising myself.

I turned to Lord Robert. 'I don't know why I said that. I am most sorry, my lord. I don't know—'

John Dee quickly grasped my jaw, and turned my head back to the mirror. 'Don't talk!' he ordered. 'Just tell us the king who comes after Jane. Look, Hannah. Tell me what you see. Does Jane have a son?'

I would have said 'yes' but my tongue would not move in my dry mouth. 'I cannot see,' I said humbly. 'Truly, I cannot see.'

'A closing prayer,' Mr Dee said, gripping my shoulders. He prayed again in Latin that the visions should be true, and that no one in this world nor in any other should be harmed by our scrying.

'Amen,' I said, more fervently now that I knew this was dangerous work, perhaps even treasonous work.

'She has the Sight,' Mr Dee said. 'She has it indeed.'

Lord Robert looked at his tutor. 'Will this make a great difference to your work?'

The older man shrugged. 'Who knows? We are all children in darkness. But she has the Sight.' He paused, and then turned to me. 'Hannah Verde, I must tell you one thing.'

'Yes, sir?'

'You have the Sight because you are pure in heart. Please, for yourself and for the gift you bear, refuse any offers of marriage, resist any seduction, keep yourself pure.'

Behind me, Lord Robert gave a snort of amusement.

I felt my colour rise from my neck to my ear lobes. 'I have no carnal desires,' I said in a low whisper. I did not dare to look at Lord Robert.

'Then you will see true,' John Dee said.

'But I don't understand,' I protested. 'Who is Jane? It is Lady Mary who will be queen if His Grace dies.'

Lord Robert put his finger on my lips and at once I was silent. 'Mistress Boy, you must say not a word of this. It is treason to cast the horoscope of a king, and the punishment for treason is death. D'you want to see me on the scaffold?'

'No! I—'

'Do you want to die yourself?'

'No!' I could hear a quaver in my voice. 'My lord, I am afraid.'

'Then never say one word of this to anyone. Not even to your father. Just forget all you saw, forget the mirror, forget the room.' He gave me his sweet seductive smile. 'I ask it of you as your friend. I have put my life in your hands.'

I was lost. 'All right,' I said.

The court moved to Greenwich Palace later that February and it was given out that the king was better. But he never asked for me, nor for Will Somers. He did not ask for music nor for company, nor did he ever come to the great hall for dinner. The physicians, who had been waiting in every corner of the court, talking among themselves and giving guarded replies to all enquiries, seemed to slip away as the days wore on and there was no news of his recovery, and not even their cheerful predictions about leeches cleansing the king's blood and carefully administered poison killing his disease seemed to ring true. Lord Robert's father, the Duke of Northumberland, was all but king in Edward's place.

I said nothing. I was being paid as a fool to say surprising and impertinent things but I could think of nothing more impertinent and surprising than the truth—that the young king was half-prisoner to his protector, that he was dying without companions or nursing, and that this whole court was thinking of the crown and not of the boy, left to die alone. I would be a fool indeed to tell the truth in this court of liars.

I had new work to do. Lord Robert's tutor, Mr Dee, sought me out and asked if I would read with him. His eyes were tired, he said, and my father had sent him some manuscripts that could be more easily deciphered by young sight.

'I don't read very well,' I said cautiously.

He smiled. 'You are a very careful young woman,' he said. 'And that is wise in these changing times. But you are safe with me and with Lord Robert. I imagine you can read English and Latin fluently, am I right?'

I nodded.

'And Spanish, of course, and perhaps French?'

I kept my silence.

Mr Dee came a little closer and bent his head to whisper in my ear.

'Can you read Greek? I need someone who can read Greek for me.'

If I had been older and wiser I would have denied my knowledge. But I was only fourteen and proud of my abilities.

'Yes,' I said. 'I can read Greek and Hebrew.'

'Hebrew?' he exclaimed, his interest sharpened. 'I guessed you had fled Spain as soon as I saw you,' he continued gently. 'I guessed you were Conversos. But it was not for me to say. You go to church, don't you? You believe in Jesus Christ and his mercy?'

'Oh yes, my lord. Without fail.' There was no point in telling him that there was no more devout Christian than a Jew trying to be invisible.

Mr Dee paused. 'As for me, I believe there is a creator, a great creator who has given us a world full of mysteries. I believe that God made this world as a great and glorious mechanical garden, one that works to its own laws and that we will one day come to understand it. Alchemy—the art of change—is how we shall come to understand it, and when we know how things are made, we can make them ourselves, we will have the knowledge of God . . .' He broke off. 'You shall come every morning and read with me for an hour and we shall make great progress.'

'If Lord Robert says I may,' I said.

Mr Dee smiled at me again. 'Young lady, you are going to help me to understand the meaning of all things. There is a key to the universe and we are just beginning to grasp at it. There are rules, unchangeable rules, which command the courses of the planets, the tides of the sea, and the affairs of men, and I know, I absolutely know, that all these things are linked: the sea, the planets and the history of man. With God's grace and with the skill we can muster we will discover these laws and when we know them . . .' He paused. 'We will know everything.'

SPRING 1553

I WAS ALLOWED to go home to my father in April and I took him my wages for the quarter.

'What news of the court?' my father asked.

'Everyone says that the king is growing stronger with the warmer weather.' I did not add that everyone was speaking a lie.

'God bless him and keep him,' my father said piously. He looked at me as if he would know more. 'And Lord Robert. Do you see him?'

I felt myself colour. 'Now and then.' I could have told him to the very hour and the minute when I had last seen Lord Robert. He had been mounted on his horse, about to go hawking for herons along the mud flats of the river shore. He was wearing a black cape and a black hat with a dark feather pinned to the ribbon with a jet brooch. He had a beautiful hooded falcon on his wrist and he rode with one hand outstretched to keep the bird steady. He looked like a prince in a storybook.

'There is to be a great wedding,' I said to fill the pause. 'Lord Robert's father has arranged it.'

'Who is to marry?' my father asked with a gossip's curiosity.

I ticked off the three couples on my fingers. 'Lady Catherine Dudley is to marry Lord Henry Hastings, and the two Grey sisters are to marry Lord Guilford Dudley and Lord Henry Herbert. They say that Lady Jane does not want to marry; she lives only to study her books. But her mother and her father have beaten her till she agreed.'

My father nodded, the forcible ordering of a daughter was no surprise. 'And what else?' he asked. 'What of Lord Robert's father, the Duke of Northumberland?'

'He's very much disliked,' I whispered. 'But he is like a king himself. He goes in and out of the king's bedroom and says that this or that is the king's own wish. What can anyone do against him?'

'They took up our neighbour the portrait painter only last week,' my father remarked. 'Mr Tuller. They said he was a Catholic and a heretic. Took him off for questioning, and he has not come back.'

We both glanced towards the door.

'D'you think we should leave?' I asked, very low.

'Not yet,' he said cautiously. 'Besides, where could we go that was safe? I'd rather be in Protestant England than Catholic France. We are good reformed Christians now. You go to church, don't you?'

'Twice, sometimes three times a day,' I assured him.

'I make sure I am seen to go. And I give to charity, and I pay my parish dues. We can do nothing more. We've both been baptised. What can any man say against us?'

I said nothing. We both knew that anyone could say anything against anyone. In the countries that had turned the ritual of the church into a burning matter, no one could be sure that they would not offend.

'If the king falls ill and dies,' my father whispered, 'then Lady Mary takes the throne, and she is a Roman Catholic. Will she make the whole country become Roman Catholic again?'

'Who knows what will happen?' I asked, thinking of my naming the next heir as 'Jane' and Robert Dudley's lack of surprise.

'Don't worry, *querida*. Everyone in the country will have to change, not just us. Everyone will be the same.'

I glanced over to where the Sabbath candle burned under the upended pitcher, its light hidden but its flame burning for our God. 'But we're not the same,' I said simply.

John Dee and I read together every morning like devoted scholars. Mostly he commanded me to read the Bible in Greek and then the same passage in Latin so that he might compare the translations.

In the afternoons Will Somers and I practised our sword fighting, leaving aside the comical tricks and concentrating on proper fighting, until he told me that I was a commendable swordsman for a fool. Although I was glad to learn a useful skill, we thought that the lessons would have been for nothing since the king continued to be so sick. In May, however, we were commanded to entertain at the great wedding feasts at Durham House in the Strand.

'You would think it a royal wedding,' Will said slyly to me.

'How, royal?' I asked.

He put his finger to his lips. 'Jane's mother, Frances Brandon, is King Henry's niece. Jane and Catherine are royal cousins.'

'Yes,' I said. 'And so?'

'And Jane is to marry a Dudley.'

'Yes,' I said, following this not at all.

'Who more royal than the Dudleys?' he demanded.

'The king's sisters,' I pointed out. 'Jane's own mother. And others too.'

'Not if you measure in terms of desire,' Will explained sweetly. 'In terms of desire there is no one more royal than the duke.'

Our sword fight was preceded by dancers and a masque and followed by jugglers, and we acquitted ourselves well. The guests roared with laughter at Will's tumbles and my triumphant skill, and the contrast between our looks: Will so tall and gangling, thrusting his sword wildly this way and that, and me, neat and determined, dancing round him and stabbing with my little sword, and parrying his blows.

The chief bride was as white as the pearls embroidered on her gold gown. Her bridegroom sat closer to his mother than to his new bride and neither bride nor groom spoke so much as one word to each other. Jane's sister had been married to her betrothed in the same ceremony, and she and he toasted each other and drank amorously from the same loving cup. But when the shout went up for a toast for Jane and Guilford, I could see that it cost Lady Jane an effort to raise her golden goblet to her new husband. Her eyes were red and raw, and there were marks on either side of her neck that looked like thumbprints.

'What d'you think, Hannah the Fool?' the Duke of Northumberland shouted down the hall to me. 'Shall she be a lucky bride?'

My neighbours turned to me, and I felt the old swimming sensation that was a sign of the Sight coming. I tried to fight it off; this court would be the worst place in the world to tell the truth. I could not stop the words coming. 'Never more lucky than today,' I said.

Lord Robert flashed a cautionary look at me but I could not take back the words. I had spoken as I felt, not with the skill of a courtier. My sense was that Jane's luck, at a low ebb when she married with a bruise on her throat, would now run ever more swiftly downhill. But the duke took it as a compliment to his son and raised his goblet.

The court danced until late, as if there were great joy from such weddings, and then the three couples were taken to their bedrooms and put to bed with much throwing of rose petals and sprinkling of rosewater. But it was all show, no more real than Will and I fighting with wooden swords. None of the marriages was to be consummated yet, and the next day Lady Jane went home with her parents to Suffolk Place, Guilford Dudley went home with his mother, and Lord Robert and the duke were up early to return to the king at Greenwich.

'Why does your brother not make a house with his wife?' I asked Lord Robert. I met him at the gateway of the stable yard, and he waited beside me while they brought out his great horse.

'Well, it is not unusual. I do not live with mine,' he remarked.

I saw the roofs of Durham House tilt against the sky, as I staggered and held on to the wall till the world steadied again. 'You have a wife?'

'Oho, did you not know that, my little seer? Oh yes, I have been married since I was a lad. And I thank God for it because if I had not been married already, it would have been me married to Jane Grey and dancing to my father's bidding.'

'Does your wife never come to court?'

'Almost never. She lives in the country; she has no liking for London.'

'What's her name?'

'Amy,' he said casually. 'Why?'

I had no answer. Numbly, I shook my head.

'You don't like the thought of me married, Mistress Boy?'

'I was surprised, only.'

Lord Robert put his gloved hand under my chin and turned my face up to him so that I was forced to meet his dark eyes. 'Tell me the truth. Are you troubled with the desires of a maid, my little Mistress Boy?'

I was too young to hide it. I felt the tears come into my eyes and I stayed still, letting him hold me.

He saw the tears and knew what they meant. 'Desire? And for me?'

Still I said nothing, looking at him through my blurred vision.

'I promised your father that I would not let any harm come to you,' he said gently.

'It has come already,' I said, speaking the inescapable truth.

He shook his head, his dark eyes warm. 'Oh, this is nothing. This is young love, greensickness. The mistake I made in my youth was to marry for such a slim cause. It is not love that matters, Mistress Boy; it is what you choose to do with it. What d'you choose to do with yours?'

'I could serve you.'

He took one of my cold hands and took it up to his lips, a touch as intimate as any kiss on the lips. 'Yes,' he said gently, not raising his head, 'you could serve me. A loving servant is a great gift for any man. Will you be mine, Mistress Boy? Heart and soul? And do whatever I ask of you?'

'Yes,' I said, hardly grasping the enormity of my promise.

'Whatever I ask of you?'

'Yes.'

At once he straightened up, suddenly decisive. 'Good. Then I have a new post for you, new work.'

'You begged me to the king,' I reminded him. 'I am his fool.'

His mouth twisted in a moment's pity. 'The poor lad won't miss you,' he said. 'I shall tell you all of it. Come to Greenwich tomorrow, with the rest of them, and I'll tell you then.'

I clattered into the courtyard of the palace at Greenwich riding astride one of the cart-horses pulling the wagon with supplies. It was a beautiful spring day, the fields were a sea of gold and silver daffodils, and as I paused, feeling the breeze against my face, one of the Dudley servants shouted towards me: 'Hannah the Fool?'

'Yes?'

'Go to Lord Robert and his father in their privy rooms at once.'

I nodded and went into the palace at a run, past the royal chambers to the ones that were no less grand, guarded by soldiers in the Dudley livery. They swung open the double doors for me and I was in the presence room where the duke would hear the petitions of common people. I went through another set of doors, and another, the rooms getting smaller, until the last double doors opened, and there was Lord Robert leaning over a desk with a manuscript scroll spread out before him, his father looking over his shoulder. I recognised at once that it was Mr Dee's writing, and that it was a map that he had made partly from ancient maps of Britain, and partly from calculations of his own based on the sailors' charts of the coastline. Mr Dee had prepared the map because he believed that England's greatest fortune were the seas around the coast, but the duke was using it for a different purpose.

He had placed little counters in a crowd at London, and more in the painted blue sea. A set of counters of a different colour was in the north of the country—Scots, I thought—and another little group in the east of the country. I made a deep bow to Lord Robert and to his father.

'It has to be done at speed,' the duke remarked, 'before anyone has a chance to protest, then we can deal with the north, with the Spanish, and with those of her tenants who stay loyal, in our own time.'

'And she?' Lord Robert asked quietly.

'She can do nothing,' the duke said. 'And if she tries to run, your little spy will warn us.' He looked up at me on those words. 'Hannah Green, I am sending you to wait upon the Lady Mary. You are to be her fool until I summon you back to court. My son assures me that you can keep your counsel. Is he right?'

The skin on the back of my neck went cold. 'I can keep a secret,' I said unhelpfully. 'But I don't like to.'

Robert smiled. 'Hannah will keep our secrets,' he said gently. 'She is mine, heart and soul.'

The duke nodded. 'Well, then. Tell her the rest.'

Lord Robert came round the table and took my hand. He stood close to me and when I looked up from my study of the floor I met his dark gaze. 'Mistress Boy, I need you to go to the Lady Mary and write to me and tell me what she thinks, and where she goes, and whom she meets.'

I blinked. 'Spy on her?'

He hesitated. 'Befriend her.'

'Spy on her. Exactly,' his father said brusquely.

'Will you do this for me?' Lord Robert asked. 'It would be a very great service to me. It is the service I ask of your love.'

'Will I be in danger?' I asked. In my head I could hear the knock of the Inquisition and the trample of their feet over our threshold.

'No,' he promised me. 'I have guaranteed your safety while you are under my protection. No one can hurt you if you are a Dudley.'

'What must I do?'

'Watch the Lady Mary and report to me.'

'You want me to write to you? Will I never see you?'

He smiled. 'You shall come to me when I send for you,' he said. He put his hand into his jacket and brought out a letter. It was from my father to the duke, promising him the delivery of some manuscripts. 'Here is a mystery for you,' Lord Robert said gently. 'See the first twenty-six letters of the first sentence?'

I scanned them. 'Yes.'

'They are to be your alphabet. When you write to me I want you to use these. Where it says "My Lord", that is your ABC. The M for "my" is your A, the Y is your B, and so on. Do you understand? When a letter occurs twice you use it only once. Use the first set for your first letter to me and your second set for your second letter, and so on. I have a copy of the letter and when your message comes to me I can translate it.'

'Will you reply to me?'

'Only if I need to ask you something, and if I do, I will use this almanac also. Burn my letters as soon as you have read them.'

I nodded.

'Do you promise to do this exactly as I ask?'

'Yes,' I said miserably. 'When do I have to go?'

'Within three days,' the duke said from his place behind the table. 'There's a cart going to the Lady Mary with some goods for her. You can ride alongside that. You shall have one of my ponies, girl, and you can keep her at Lady Mary's house for your return. And if something should happen that you think threatens me or Lord Robert, something very grave indeed, you can ride to warn us at once. Will you do that?'

'Yes, sir,' I said obediently.

Lord Robert said that I might send for my father to say goodbye to him and he came downriver to Greenwich Palace in a fishing smack on the ebbing tide, with Daniel seated beside him.

'You!' I said without any enthusiasm, when I saw him help my father from the bobbing boat.

'Me,' he replied with the glimmer of a smile. 'Constant, aren't I?'

I went to my father and felt his arms come round me. 'Oh, Papa,' I whispered in Spanish. 'I have to go to the Lady Mary and I am afraid of the journey, and afraid of living at her house, I am afraid of . . .' I broke off, tasting the many lies on my tongue and realising that I would never be able to tell anyone the truth about myself ever again.

'Daughter, come home to me. I will ask Lord Robert to release you, we can leave England. You are not trapped here . . .'

'Lord Robert himself asked me to go,' I said simply. 'And I already said I would.'

His hand caressed my cropped hair. '*Querida*, I shall be here, and if you send for me I shall come to you. Or Daniel will come and fetch you away. Won't you, Daniel?'

I turned in my father's arms to look at my betrothed. He was leaning against the wooden railing that ran round the jetty.

'I would rather fetch you away now.'

My father released me and I took a step towards Daniel.

'I have agreed to go to serve Lady Mary,' I said quietly to him.

'She is a Papist in a Protestant country,' he said. 'You could not have chosen a place where your faith and practices will be more scrutinised. What are you to do for Lady Mary?'

He stepped closer to me so we could whisper.

'I am to be her companion, be her fool.' I paused and decided to tell him the truth. 'I am to spy for Lord Robert and his father.'

His head was so close to mine that I could feel the warmth of his cheek against my forehead as he leaned closer to speak into my ear.

'And you have agreed?'

I hesitated. 'They know that Father and I are Jews,' I said.

He was silent for a moment. I felt the solidity of his chest against my shoulder. His arm came round my waist to hold me closer to him and I felt the warmth of his grip. A rare sense of safety came over me as he held me, and for a moment I stood still.

'You are a hostage.'

'In a way. It feels more as if Lord Robert knows my secret and trusts me with his. I feel bound to him.'

He nodded. I craned my neck to look up into his scowling face. At first I thought he was angry, then I realised that he was thinking hard.

'Does he know my name?' he demanded.

'He knows I am betrothed, but not your name, and nothing of your family,' I said. 'I have not brought danger to your door.'

'No, you keep it all to yourself,' he said with a brief unhappy smile. 'Hannah, I beg you not to go. This road leads straight into danger.'

'I am in danger whatever I do. This way, Lord Robert will protect me.'

'But only while you do his bidding.'

I nodded. I could not tell him that I had volunteered to walk into this danger, and I would have risked worse for love of Lord Robert.

'This is a burden that you shouldn't have to bear alone,' he said. 'If you are in danger, send for me and I will help you escape.'

'I promise that I will.'

Gently he kissed me, full on the lips, and I felt the warmth of his mouth on mine. He released me and stepped back to the boat.

I found I was slightly dizzy, as if I had gulped down strong wine. 'Oh, Daniel!' I breathed, but he was climbing into the boat and did not hear me. I turned to my father and caught him hiding his smile.

'God bless you, daughter, and bring you home safe to us,' he said quietly. I knelt on the wooden pier for my father's blessing and felt his hand come down on my head in the familiar, beloved caress. He took my hands and raised me up. 'He *is* an attractive young man, isn't he?' he demanded, a chuckle behind his voice. Then he wrapped his cape around himself and went down the steps to the fishing smack.

SUMMER 1553

LADY MARY WAS at her house at Hunsdon, in the county of Hertfordshire. It took us three days to get to her, riding northwards out of London, on a winding road through muddy valleys and then climbing arduously through hills called the North Weald. We stayed overnight on the road, once at an inn, once at a grand house that had been a monastery and was now in the hands of the man who had cleansed it of heresy at some profit to himself. These days they could offer us no rooms better than a hayloft over the stable, and the carter complained that in the old days this had been a generous house of good monks where any traveller might be sure of a good dinner and a comfortable bed. It was the same story all round the country. All the monasteries and abbeys were now in the possession of the great lords, the men of court who had made their fortunes by advising that the world would be a better place if wealth was stripped from the English church and poured into their own pockets.

'If the poor king dies then Lady Mary will come to the throne and turn it all back,' the carter said. 'She will be a queen for the people. A queen who returns us to the old ways.'

Since I had not known the England that he said was lost, I could not feel as he did. I rode ahead of the cart, and it was such an adventure to travel so freely in a strange country that I was sorry when the carter whistled to me and called out, 'Here's Hunsdon now.' I realised that these carefree days were over, that I had to return to work, and that now I had two tasks: one as a holy fool, and the other as a spy.

Lady Mary was in her chamber sewing blackwork, the famous Spanish embroidery of black thread on white linen, while one of her ladies read aloud to her. The first thing I heard, on reaching her presence, was a Spanish word, mispronounced, and she gave a merry laugh when she saw me wince.

'Ah, at last! A girl who can speak Spanish!' she exclaimed and gave me her hand to kiss. 'If you could only read it!'

'I can read it,' I said, considering it reasonable that the daughter of a bookseller should be able to read her native tongue.

'Oh, can you?' She turned to her maid in waiting. 'You will be pleased to hear that, Susan! Now you will not need to read to me in the afternoons.'

Susan did not look at all pleased, but she took herself off to the bay window with the other ladies and took up some sewing.

Lady Mary gestured that I should sit on a cushion at her feet. 'Tell me the news of the court. Do you have a message from my brother the king?'

'No, Lady Mary,' I said, and saw her disappointment.

'I was hoping he would have thought of me more kindly, now he is so ill,' she said. 'When he was a little boy I nursed him through half a dozen illnesses. I hoped he would remember that and think that we . . .' She tapped her fingertips together as if to draw herself back from memories. 'No matter,' she said. 'Any other messages?'

'The duke asked me to give you this letter.'

She took it and broke the seal and smoothed it out. I saw her smile and then I heard her warm chuckle. 'You bring me very good news, Hannah the Fool,' she said. 'This is a payment under the will of my late father which has been owed to me since his death. I thought I would never see it, but here it is, a draft on a London goldsmith. I can pay my bills and face the shopkeepers of Ware again.'

'I am glad of it,' I said awkwardly, not knowing what else to say.

'Yes,' she said, then paused, thoughtful. 'The question which remains is why I am suddenly to be so well treated.' She looked speculatively at me. 'Tell me, child, tell me the truth. Is my little brother dying?'

I hesitated, unsure if it was treason to tell of the death of the king.

She took my hand and I looked into her square, determined face. Her eyes, dark and honest, met mine. She looked like a woman you could trust, a mistress you could love. 'You can tell me. I can keep a secret,' she said. 'I have kept many many secrets.'

'Since you ask it, I will tell you: I am certain that he is dying,' I admitted quietly. 'But the duke denies it.'

She nodded. 'And this wedding of Lady Jane Grey to the duke's son. What do they say about it at court?'

'That she was unwilling, and he not much better.'

'And why did the duke insist?' she asked.

'It was time that Guilford was married?' I hazarded.

She looked at me, bright as a knife blade. 'They say no more than that?'

I shrugged. 'Not in my hearing, my lady.'

'And what of you? Did you ask to come to this exile?' Her wry smile indicated to me that she did not think it likely.

'Lord Robert told me to come,' I confessed. 'And his father, the duke.'

'Did they tell you why?'

I wanted to bite my lips to hold in the secret. 'No, my lady. Just to keep you company.'

'What are you afraid of?' she asked bluntly.

For a moment I was so taken aback I could have told her. I was afraid of arrest, of the Inquisition, of the torture chamber and the heretic's death. I was afraid of betraying others to their deaths, afraid of the very air of conspiracy itself. 'I am just a little nervous,' I said quietly. 'I am new to this country, and to court life.'

She let the silence run and then she looked at me more kindly. 'Poor child, you are very young to be adrift, all alone in these deep waters.'

'I am Lord Robert's vassal,' I said. 'I am not alone.'

She smiled. 'Perhaps you will be very good company,' she said finally. 'There have been days and months and even years when I would have been very glad of a merry face and an uplifted voice.'

'I am not a witty fool,' I said cautiously. 'I am not supposed to be especially merry.'

Lady Mary laughed aloud at that. 'And I am not supposed to be given especially to laughter,' she said. 'Perhaps you will suit me very well.'

The household at Hunsdon turned out to be a melancholy place. Lady Mary was plagued with headaches, which often came in the evening, darkening her face as the light drained from the sky. Her ladies would notice her frown, but she never mentioned the pain and never drooped in her wooden chair. She sat as her mother had taught her, upright like a queen, and she kept her head up, even when her eyes were squinting against dim candles.

The mornings were the best times for her. After she had been to Mass and broken her fast she liked to walk, and often she chose me to walk with her. One warm day in late June she commanded me to walk at her side and to name the flowers in Spanish. I had to keep my steps short so that I did not stride ahead of her, and she often stopped with her hand to her side, the colour draining from her face.

'Are you not well this morning, my lady?' I asked.

'Just tired,' she said. 'I did not sleep last night.' She smiled at the concern on my face. 'Oh, it is no worse than it has always been. I should learn to have more serenity. But not to know . . . and to have to wait . . . and to know that he is in the hands of advisers who have set their hearts . . .'

'Your brother?' I asked when she fell silent.

'I have thought of him every day from the day he was born!' she burst out passionately. 'Such a tiny boy and so much expected of him. So quick to learn and so—I don't know—so cold in his heart where he should have been warm. Poor boy, poor motherless boy! All three of us, thrown together, and none of us with a mother living, and none of us knowing what would happen next.

'I had more care of Elizabeth than I did of him, of course. And now she is far from me, and I cannot even see him. Of course I worry about him: about what they are doing to his body and his soul . . . and about what they are doing to his will,' she added very quietly.

'His will?'

'It is my inheritance,' she said fiercely. 'If you report, as I imagine you do, tell them I never forget that.'

'I don't report!' I exclaimed, shocked. It was true, I had sent no report, there was nothing in our dull lives to report.

'Whether or no,' she dismissed my defence, 'nothing and no one can deny me my place. My father himself left it to me. It is me and then it is Elizabeth. We are three heirs, taking precedence one after another to honour our father. Elizabeth knows that I am the next heir after Edward: he came first as the boy; I come second as the first legitimate princess. And since you promise that you don't report, you can make this reply if anyone asks you: tell them that I will keep my inheritance. I am an English queen-to-be. No one can put me aside.'

Her face was illuminated with her sense of destiny. 'It is the purpose of my life,' she said. 'Nobody will pity me ever again. They will see that I have dedicated my life to being the bride of this country. I will be a virgin queen. I shall have no children but the people of this country. I shall be their mother. I shall live for them. It is my holy calling. I shall give myself up for them.'

She turned from me and strode back to the house, and I followed her at a distance. The morning sun burning off the mist made a lightness in the air all around her, and I had a moment's dizziness as I realised that this woman would be a great queen for England, a queen who would bring back the richness and beauty and charity that her father had stripped out from the churches and from the daily life. The sun was so bright around her yellow silk hood that it was like a crown, and I stumbled on a tussock of grass and fell.

She turned and saw me on my knees. 'Hannah?'

'You will be queen,' I said simply, the Sight speaking in my voice. 'The king will die within a month. Long live the queen.'

In a second she was by my side, holding me up. 'What did you say?'

'You will be queen,' I said. 'He is sinking fast now.'

I lost my senses for a moment and then I opened my eyes again and she was looking down at me, still holding me closely.

'Can you tell me any more?' she asked me gently.

I shook my head. 'I am sorry, Lady Mary, I barely know what I said. It was not said knowingly.'

She nodded. 'It is the Holy Spirit which moves you to speak such news to me. Will you swear to keep it secret between us?'

For a moment I hesitated, thinking of the complicated webs of loyalties that were interwoven around me. I nodded. It was no disloyalty not to tell Lord Robert something he must already know. 'Yes, Lady Mary.'

I tried to rise but I dropped back to my knees with dizziness.

'Wait,' she said. 'Don't get up till your head is clear.' She sat beside me on the grass and gently put my head in her lap. 'Close your eyes.'

I wanted to sleep as she held me. 'I am not a spy,' I said.

Her finger touched my lips. 'Hush,' she said. 'I know that you work for the Dudleys. And I know you are a good girl. Who better than I to understand a life of complicated loyalties? After my father sent my mother away from me there was no one near me who did not try to persuade me that Anne Boleyn was the true queen and her bastard child the true heir. They made me deny my mother, they made me deny my faith, they threatened me with death on the scaffold. I was a girl of twenty and they made me proclaim myself a bastard and my faith a heresy. You need not fear, little Hannah. I understand.'

I felt her soft touch on my hair. I felt my eyes close and the sinews of my back and neck unknot as I realised I was safe with her.

We sat in silence, and then I heard the door of the house bang open. I sat up and saw one of Lady Mary's ladies burst out of the shadowy interior and look wildly around for her. Lady Mary waved and the girl ran over. It was Lady Margaret. As she came close I felt Lady Mary's back straighten, as she steadied herself for the news I had foretold.

'Lady Mary! Oh!'

The girl was almost speechless with her desire to tell, and breathless from her run. 'At church just now . . .'

'What?'

'They didn't pray for you.'

'Pray for me?'

'No. They prayed for the king and his advisers, same as always, but where the prayer says "and for the king's sisters", they missed you out.'

Lady Mary's gaze swept the girl's face. 'Both of us? Elizabeth too?'

'Yes!'

Lady Mary rose to her feet, her eyes narrowed with anxiety. 'Send out Mr Tomlinson into Ware. Tell him to get reports from other churches. See if this is happening everywhere.'

The girl bobbed a curtsy and ran back into the house.

'What does it mean?' I asked, scrambling to my feet.

She looked at me without seeing me. 'It means that Northumberland has started to move against me. First he does not warn me how ill my brother is. Then he commands the priests to leave Elizabeth and me from the prayers. Next he will command them to mention another, the king's new heir. Then, when my poor brother is dead, they will arrest me, arrest Elizabeth, and put their false prince on the throne.'

'Who?' I asked.

'Edward Courtenay,' she said decisively. 'My cousin. He is the only one Northumberland would choose, since he cannot put himself or his sons on the throne.'

I suddenly saw it. The wedding feast, the white face of Lady Jane Grey, the bruises at her throat as if someone had taken her by the neck to shake their ambition into her. 'Oh, but he can: Lady Jane Grey,' I said.

'Newly wed to Northumberland's son Guilford,' Lady Mary agreed. She paused for a moment. 'I would not have thought they would have dared. Her mother, my cousin, would have to resign her claim for her daughter. But Jane is a Protestant, and Dudley's father commands the keys to the kingdom.'

Her pale face suddenly drained even paler and I saw her stagger. 'My God, what of Elizabeth? He will kill us both,' she whispered. 'He will have to. Otherwise there will be rebellions against him from both Protestant and Catholic.' She turned towards the house. 'Come, Hannah!' she threw over her shoulder. 'Come quickly!'

She wrote to warn Elizabeth; she wrote for advice. I did not see either letter, but that night I took the manuscript Lord Robert had given to me and wrote a message, using my father's letter as the base of the code.

'M is alarmed that she is left out of the prayers. She believes Lady J will be named heir. She has written to Eliz to warn her. And to the Sp ambassador for advice.' I paused. It was arduous work, translating every letter into another, but I wanted to write something to remind him of me.

'I miss you,' I wrote, and then I scratched it out, not even troubling to translate it into code.

'When can I come home?' went the same way.

'I am frightened,' was the most honest of all the confessions.

In the end I wrote nothing, there was nothing I could think of that would turn Lord Robert's attention to me, while the boy king was dying and his own young, white-faced sister-in-law was stepping up to the throne of England and bringing the Dudley family to absolute greatness.

There was nothing to do but to wait for news of the death of the king to come from London. Lady Mary had her own private messages coming and going, and optimistic letters from the duke. Then, in the first days of July, one letter made her snatch her breath and put a hand to her heart.

'How is the king, my lady?' I asked her. 'Not worse?'

Her colour burned in her cheeks. 'The duke says that he is better, and that he wants to see me.' She rose to her feet and paced to the window.

'Shall we go?' I asked. I was on my feet already at the thought of returning to London, to court, to see Lord Robert again, to see my father, and Daniel.

I saw her shoulders straighten as she took the decision. 'If he asks for me, of course I have to go. We'll leave tomorrow.'

Next day we were on the road, Lady Mary's pennant before us, her soldiers around us, and the country people tumbling out of their houses to call out blessings on her name.

Riding towards London with the people of England cheering her on, Lady Mary looked like a true princess. She wore a deep red gown and jacket, which made her dark eyes shine. She rode well, one hand in a worn red glove on the bridle, the other waving to everyone who called out to her, her head up, her courage high, her weariness all gone.

We rode hard along the London road, splashing through the fords at their summertime low, cantering where the tracks were soft enough. Just after midday we came into the town of Hoddesdon, weary of the saddle and hoping for a good dinner and a rest before we continued the journey. Without warning, a man stepped out from a doorway and put his hand up to signal to her. Clearly she recognised him: she waved him forward so he could speak to her privately. He was brief, and kept his voice low. Then he stepped back and Lady Mary snapped an order to halt, and tumbled down from her saddle so fast that her Master of Horse could scarcely catch her. She ran into the nearest inn, shouting for paper and pen, and ordering everyone to drink, eat, see to their horses and be ready to leave again within the hour.

'Mother of God, I can't,' Lady Margaret said pitifully as her royal mistress strode past. 'I'm too tired to go another step.'

'Then stay behind,' snapped Lady Mary, who never snapped. That sharpness of tone warned us that the hopeful ride to London, to visit the young, recovering king, had suddenly gone terribly wrong.

When she came out of the parlour she was pale and her eyes were red, but she was not softened by grief. She was sharp with decision, and she was angry.

She sent one messenger flying south down the road to London to find the Spanish ambassador, to beg for his advice and to alert the Spanish emperor that she would need his help to claim her throne. She took another messenger aside for a verbal message for Lady Elizabeth. 'Speak only to her when you are alone,' she emphasised. 'Tell her not to go to London; it is a trap. Tell her to come at once to me for her own safety.'

She sent a further message to the duke himself, swearing that she was too ill to ride to London but would rest quietly at Hunsdon. Then she ordered the main group to stay behind. 'I'll take you, Lady Margaret, and you, Hannah,' she said. She smiled at her lady in waiting and closest friend, Jane Dormer. 'Follow us,' she said, and she leaned forward to whisper our destination in her ear. 'You must bring this company on behind us. We are going to travel too fast for everyone to keep pace.'

She picked six men to escort us, gave her followers a brief leave-taking and snapped her fingers for her Master of Horse to help her into the saddle. She wheeled her horse round and led us out of Hoddesdon, back the way we had come. But this time we took the great road north.

'Where are we going, Lady Mary? It's getting dark,' Lady Margaret asked plaintively. 'We can't ride in the dark.'

'Kenninghall,' Lady Mary crisply replied.

'Where's Kenninghall?' I asked, seeing Lady Margaret's aghast face.

'Norfolk,' she said as if it were the end of the world. 'God help us, she's running away.'

'Running away?' I felt my throat tense.

'It's towards the sea. She'll get a ship out of Lowestoft and run to Spain. Whatever that man told her must mean that she's in such danger that she has to get out of the country altogether.'

It was a punishing ride. We did not check until it was fully night, when we paused at the home of a gentleman, John Huddlestone, at Sawston Hall. I begged a piece of paper and a pen from the housekeeper and wrote a letter, not to Lord Robert, whose address I did not dare to give, but to John Dee.

'My dear tutor,' I wrote, hoping this would mislead anyone who opened my letter, 'this little riddle may amuse you.' Then underneath I wrote the coded letters in the form of a serpentine circle, hoping to make it look like a game that a girl of my age might send to a kind scholar. It simply read: 'She is going to Kenninghall.'

The housekeeper promised to send it to Greenwich by the carter who would pass by tomorrow, and I had to hope that it would find its destination and be read by the right man. Then I lay down on a little truckle bed that they had pulled out beside the kitchen fire.

I woke painfully early, at five in the morning, to find the kitchen lad clattering pails of water and sacks of logs past my head. Lady Mary heard Mass in John Huddlestone's chapel, as if it were not a forbidden ceremony, broke her fast, and was back in the saddle by seven in the morning, riding in the highest of spirits away from Sawston Hall with John Huddlestone at her side to show her the way.

I was riding at the back, the dozen or so horses clattering ahead of me, my little pony too tired to keep pace, when I smelt an old terrible scent on the air. I could smell smoke, the scent of heresy, a fire burning up someone's faith, burning up someone's house . . . I turned in the saddle and saw the glow on the horizon where the house we had just left, Sawston Hall, was being torched.

'My lady!' I called out. She heard me, and turned her head and then reined in her horse, John Huddlestone beside her.

'Your house!' I said simply to him.

He looked beyond me, squinting his eyes to see. He couldn't tell for sure; he could not smell the smoke as I had done.

Lady Mary looked at me. 'Are you sure, Hannah?'

I nodded. 'I can smell it. I can smell smoke.' I heard the quaver of fear in my voice. 'Your house is being burnt out, sir.'

He turned his horse as if he would ride straight home, then he remembered the woman whose visit had cost him his home. 'Forgive me, Lady Mary. I must go home . . . My wife . . .'

'Go,' she said gently. 'And be very well assured that when I come into my own, I will give you another house, a bigger and richer house than this one you have lost for your loyalty to me. I shall not forget.'

He nodded, half deaf with worry, and then set his horse at a gallop to where the blaze of his house glowed on the horizon.

His groom rode up beside Lady Mary. 'D'you want me to guide you, my lady?' he asked.

'Yes,' she answered. 'Can you take me to Bury St Edmunds?'

'Through Mildenhall and Thetford forest? Yes, m'lady.'

She gave the signal to move on and she rode without once looking back. I thought that she was a princess indeed, if she could see last night's refuge burnt to the ground and think only of the struggle ahead of her and not of the ruins left behind.

That night we stayed at Euston Hall near Thetford, and I lay on the floor of Lady Mary's bedroom, wrapped in my cape, still fully dressed, waiting for the alarm that I was sure must come. All night I did little more than doze, waiting for a Protestant mob. I could not close my eyes for fear that I would be wakened by the smell of smoke, so that it was almost a relief near dawn when I heard the sound of a horse's hoofs on cobbles. I was up at the window in a second, my hand outstretched to Lady Mary as she woke, cautioning her to be quiet.

'What can you see?' she demanded from the bed, as she pulled back the covers. 'How many men?'

'Only one horse. He looks weary.'

'Go and see who it is.'

I hurried down the wooden stairs to the hall. The porter had the spyhole opened and was arguing with the traveller, who seemed to be demanding admission to stay the night. I touched the porter on the shoulder and he stood aside.

'And who are you?' I demanded, my voice as gruff as I could make it.

'Who are you?' he asked back.

'You'd better tell me what you want,' I insisted.

He came closer to the spyhole and lowered his voice to a whisper. 'I have important news for a great lady. It is about her brother. D'you understand me?'

There was no way of knowing whether or not he was sent to entrap us. I took the risk, stepped back and nodded to the porter. 'Let him in, and then bar the door behind him again.'

He came in.

'What's the message?' I asked.

'I shall tell it to no one but herself.'

There was a rustle of silken skirts and Lady Mary came down the stairs. 'And you are?' she asked.

It was his response to the sight of her that convinced me that he was on our side, and that the world had changed for us, overnight. Fast as a stooping falcon, he dropped down to one knee, pulled his hat from his head, and bowed to her, as to a queen.

God save her, she did not turn a hair. She extended her hand as if she had been Queen of England for all her life. He kissed it reverently, and then looked up into her face.

'I am Robert Raynes, a goldsmith of London, sent by Sir Nicholas

Throckmorton to bring you the news that your brother Edward is dead, Your Grace. You are Queen of England.'

'God bless him,' she said softly. 'God save Edward's precious soul.'

There was a short silence.

'Did he die in faith?' she asked.

He shook his head. 'He died as a Protestant.'

She nodded. 'And I am proclaimed queen?' she demanded.

He shook his head. 'The king died in much pain on the night of the sixth,' he said quietly.

'The *sixth*?' she interrupted.

'Yes. Before his death he changed his father's will. You are denied the succession, the Lady Elizabeth also. Lady Jane Grey is named heir.'

'And what about me?'

'You are named as a traitor to the throne. Lord Robert Dudley is on his way now to arrest you and take you to the Tower.'

'Lord Robert is coming?' I asked.

'He will go to Hunsdon first,' Lady Mary reassured me. 'I wrote to his father that I was staying there. He won't know where we are.'

I did not contradict her, but I knew that John Dee would send my note on to him this very day and that, thanks to me, he would know exactly where to look for us.

Her concern was all for her sister. 'And Lady Elizabeth?'

He shrugged. 'I don't know. She may be arrested already.'

'And when was the king's death announced? And Lady Jane falsely proclaimed?'

'Not when I left.'

She took a moment to understand, and then she was angry. 'He has died, and it has not been announced? My brother is lying dead, unwatched? Without the rites of the church? Without any honours done to him at all?'

'His death was still a secret when I left.'

She nodded, her eyes suddenly veiled and cautious. 'I thank you for coming to me,' she said. 'You can sleep here tonight. Go back to London in the morning and convey my thanks to Sir Nicholas. He has done the right thing to inform me. I am queen, and I will have my throne.'

She turned on her heel and swept up the stairs, and I followed. As soon as we got into her room she closed the door behind us, and threw aside her regal dignity.

'Get me the clothes of a serving girl, and wake John Huddlestone's groom,' she said urgently. 'Then go to the stables and get two horses ready, one with a pillion saddle for me and the groom, one for you.'

'My lady?'

'You call me Your Grace now,' she said grimly. 'I am Queen of England. Now hurry.'

'What am I to tell the groom?'

'Tell him that we have to get to Kenninghall today. That I will ride behind him; we will leave the rest of them here. You come with me.'

I nodded and hurried from the room. The serving maid who had waited on us last night was sleeping with half a dozen others in the attic bedrooms. I shook her awake, put my hand over her mouth and hissed in her ear: 'I've had enough of this; I'm running away. I'll give you a silver shilling for your gown and cape. You can say I stole them.'

'Two shillings,' she said instantly.

'Agreed,' I said. 'Give them me, and I'll bring you the money.'

She bundled them up for me with her cap and I went light-footed downstairs to Lady Mary's room.

'Here,' I said. 'They cost me two shillings.'

She found the coins in her purse. 'No boots.'

'Please wear your own boots,' I said fervently. 'I've run away before, I know what it's like. You'll never get anywhere in borrowed boots.'

She smiled at that. 'Hurry,' was all she said.

I ran back upstairs with the two shillings and then I found Tom, John Huddlestone's groom, and sent him down to the stables to get the horses ready. I crept down to the bakery just outside the kitchen door, and found, as I had hoped, a batch of bread rolls baked in the warmth of the oven last night. I stuffed my breeches pockets and my jacket pockets with half a dozen of them so that I looked like a donkey with panniers, and then I went back to the hall.

Lady Mary was there, dressed as a serving maid, her hood pulled over her face. The porter was arguing, reluctant to open the door to the stable yard for a maidservant. She turned with relief as she heard me approach.

'Come on,' I said reasonably to the man. 'She is a servant of John Huddlestone. His groom is waiting. He told us to leave at first light.'

He complained, but he opened the door and Lady Mary and I slipped through. Tom was in the yard, holding one big hunter with a pillion saddle on its back and a smaller horse for me.

He got into the saddle and took the hunter to the mounting block. I helped the Lady Mary scramble up behind him. She took a tight grip round his waist and kept her hood pulled forward to hide her face. I mounted my horse from the block too. I had never ridden such a big horse before, but no smaller animal could manage the hard ride ahead.

Tom led the way out of the yard. I turned after him and heard my heart pounding and knew that I was on the run, once again, and afraid, once again, and that this time I was perhaps in a worse case because this time I was running with the pretender to the throne of England, with Lord Robert Dudley and his army in pursuit, and I was his vassal sworn; her trusted servant, and a Jew; but a practising Christian, serving a Papist princess in a country sworn to be Protestant. Little wonder that my heart was in my mouth and beating louder than the clopping of the hoofs of the horses as we went down the road to the east.

When we reached Kenninghall at midday, I saw why we had ridden till the horses foundered to get here. It was a solid moated house, with a drawbridge that could be raised and a portcullis above it that could be dropped down to seal the only entrance. It was built in warm red brick, a deceptively beautiful house that could be held in a siege.

Lady Mary was not expected, and the few servants who lived at the house to keep it in order came tumbling out of the doors in a flurry of surprise. After a nod from Lady Mary I quickly told them of the astounding news from London as they took our horses into the stable yard and a cheer went up as they heard of her accession to the throne.

As they pulled me down, I let out a yelp of pain. The inner part of my legs had been skinned raw from three days in the saddle, and my back and shoulders were locked tight from the jolting ride.

Lady Mary must have been near-dead with exhaustion, after sitting pillion for all that long time, but only I saw the grimace of pain as they lifted her down to the ground. Everyone else saw the tilt of her chin as she heard them shout for her, and the charm of the Tudor smile as she welcomed them all into the great hall and bade them good cheer. She took a moment to pray for the soul of her dead brother, and then she raised her head and promised them that, just as she had been a fair landlord and mistress to them, she would be a good queen.

That earned her another cheer and the hall started to fill with people, workers from the fields and woods and villagers from their homes, and the servants ran about with flagons of ale and cups of wine and loaves of bread and meat. The Lady Mary took her seat at the head of the hall and smiled on everyone as if she had never been ill in her life, then after an hour of good company, she laughed out loud and said she must get out of this cloak and this poor gown, and went to her rooms.

The few house servants had flung themselves into getting her rooms ready and her bed was made with linen. They brought in a bathtub, lined it with sheets to protect her from splinters, and filled it with hot water. And they found some old gowns, which she had left behind when she was last at this house, and laid them out on the bed for her.

'You can go,' she said to me, as she threw the servant girl's cloak from her shoulders, and turned her back to the maid to be unlaced. 'Find something to eat and go straight to bed. You must be tired out.'

'Thank you,' I said, hobbling for the door.

'And, Hannah?'

'Yes, my lady . . . Yes, Your Grace?'

'You have been a good friend to me this day. I will not forget it.'

I paused, thinking of the two letters I had written to Lord Robert that would bring him hard on our heels, thinking what would happen to this determined, ambitious woman when he caught us. It would be the Tower for her, and probably her death for treason. I had been a spy in her household and the falsest of friends.

If I could have confessed to her then, I would have done. I wanted to tell her that I had been put into her household to work against her, but that now that I knew her, and loved her, I would do anything to serve her. I wanted to tell her that Robert Dudley was my lord and I would always be bound to do anything he asked me. I wanted to tell her that everything I did seemed to be always full of contradictions: black and white, love and fear, all at once.

But I could say nothing, and so I just dropped to one knee before her and bowed my head.

She did not give me her hand to kiss, like a queen would have done. She put her hand on my head like my own mother used to do and she said, 'God bless you, Hannah, and keep you safe from sin.'

At that moment, at that particular tenderness, I felt the tears well up in my eyes. I got myself out of the room and into my own small attic bedchamber and into my bed without bath or dinner, before anybody should see me cry like the little girl I still was.

We were at Kenninghall for three days on siege alert, but still Lord Robert and his company of cavalry did not come. The gentlemen from the country all around the manor came pouring in with their servants and their kinsmen, some of them armed, some of them bringing blacksmiths to hammer out spears and lances from the pruning hooks, spades and scythes they brought with them. Lady Mary proclaimed herself as queen in the great hall, despite the advice of the Spanish ambassador. He had written to tell her that Northumberland had sent warships into the French seas off Norfolk, to prevent the Spanish ships from rescuing her. She must surrender to the duke and give up her claim to the crown, and throw herself on his mercy.

'What can you see, Hannah?' she asked me. It was early morning, and she had just come from Mass, her rosary beads still in her fingers.

I shook my head. 'I have only seen for you once, Your Grace, and I was certain then that you would be queen. And now you are. I have seen nothing since.'

'I am queen indeed now,' she said wryly. 'I am proclaimed queen by myself at least. I wish you had told me how long it would last, and if anyone else would agree with me.'

'I wish I could,' I said sincerely. 'What are we going to do?'

'My Spanish kinsmen tell me to surrender,' she said simply. 'They tell me that I will be executed if I continue with this course, that it's a battle I can't win. The duke has the Tower, he has London, he has the country, he has the warships at sea and an army of followers and the royal guard. I have this one castle, these few loyal men and their pitchforks. And somewhere out there is Lord Robert and his troop coming towards us.'

'Can't we get away?' I asked.

She shook her head. 'Not fast enough, not far enough. If I could have got on a Spanish warship then, perhaps . . . but the duke was ready for this, and I was unprepared. I am trapped.'

I remembered John Dee's map spread out in the duke's study and the little counters that signified soldiers and sailors on ships all around Norfolk, and Lady Mary trapped in the middle of them.

'Will you have to surrender?' I whispered.

She smiled as if I had suggested a challenge, a great gamble. 'You know, I'm damned if I will!' she swore. She laughed aloud as if it was a bet for a joust rather than her life on the table. 'I have spent my life running and lying and hiding. Just once, *just once* I should be glad to ride out under my own standard and defy the men who have denied my right and denied the authority of the church and God Himself.'

Lady Mary gathered her rosary beads, tucked them into the pocket of her gown and strode towards the door of the great hall, where her armies of gentlemen and soldiers were breaking their fast. She mounted the dais. 'Today we move out,' she announced, loud and clear. 'We go to Framlingham, no more than a day's ride. I shall raise my standard there. If we get there before Lord Robert we can hold him off in a siege. We can hold him off for months. I can fight a battle from there. I can collect troops.'

There was a murmur of surprise and then approbation.

'Trust me!' she commanded them. 'I will not fail you. I am your proclaimed queen and you will see me on the throne, and then I will remember who was here today. I will remember and you will be repaid many times over for doing your duty to the true Queen of England.'

Mary raised her standard at Framlingham Castle, a fortress to match any in England, and unbelievably half the world turned up on horseback and on foot to swear allegiance to her. I walked beside her as she went down the massed ranks of the men and thanked them for coming to her and swore to be a true and honest queen to them.

We had news from London at last. The announcement of King Edward's death had been made shamefully late. After the poor boy had died, the duke had kept the corpse hidden in his room while the ink dried on his will, and the powerful men of the country considered where their best interests lay. Lady Jane Grey had to be dragged onto the throne by her father-in-law. They said she had cried and said that she could not be queen, and that the Lady Mary was the rightful heir. It did not save her from her fate. They unfurled the canopy of state over her bowed head, they served her on bended knee despite her tearful protests, and the Duke of Northumberland proclaimed her as queen.

The country was launched into civil war, against us, the traitors. Lady Elizabeth had not replied to Lady Mary's warnings. She had taken to her bed when she heard of her brother's death and was too sick even to read her letters. When Lady Mary learned of that, she turned away to hide the hurt in her face. She had counted on Elizabeth's support, the two princesses together defending their father's will. To find that Elizabeth was hiding under the bed covers rather than racing to be with her sister, was a blow to Mary's heart as well as to her cause.

We learned that Windsor Castle had been fortified and provisioned for a siege, the guns of the Tower of London were battle-ready and turned to face inland, and Northumberland himself had raised an army and was coming to root out our Lady Mary, who was now officially named as a traitor to Queen Jane.

But then, in the middle of July, it all fell apart for the duke. His alliances, his treaties, could not hold against the sense that every Englishman had that Mary, Henry's daughter, was the rightful queen. Northumberland was hated by many and it was clear that he would rule through Jane as he had ruled through Edward. The people of England, from lords to commoners, muttered and then declared against him.

The accord he had stitched together to darn Queen Jane into the fabric of England all unravelled. More and more men declared in public for Lady Mary, and Lord Robert himself was defeated by an army of outraged citizens, who just sprang up from the ploughed furrows, swearing that they would protect the rightful queen. Lord Robert declared for the Lady Mary and deserted his father but, despite turning his coat, was captured at Bury by citizens who declared him a traitor. The duke himself, trapped at Cambridge, his army disappearing like the morning mist, announced suddenly that he too was for Lady Mary and sent her a message explaining that he had only ever tried to do his best for the realm.

'What does this mean?' I asked her, seeing the letter shaking so violently in her hand that she could hardly read it.

'It means I have won,' she said simply. 'Won by right, accepted right and not by battle. I am queen and the people's choice.'

'And what will happen to the duke?' I asked, thinking of his son, Lord Robert, somewhere a prisoner.

'He's a traitor,' she said, her eyes cold.

I said nothing. I waited for a moment, a heartbeat, a girl's heartbeat. 'And what will happen to Lord Robert?' I asked, my voice very small.

Lady Mary turned. 'He is a traitor and a traitor's son. What do you think will happen to him?'

Lady Mary took her big horse and, riding sidesaddle, set off on the road to London, a thousand, two thousand men riding behind her, and their men, their tenants and retainers and followers coming on foot behind them. The Lady Mary, in her old red riding habit, with her head held high, rode her big horse like a knight going into battle, a queen going to claim her throne. She had won the greatest victory of her life by sheer determination and courage.

Everyone thought that her coming to the throne would be the return of the good years, rich harvests, warm weather, and an end to the constant epidemics of plague. Everyone thought that she would restore the wealth of the church, the beauty of the shrines and the certainty of faith. Everyone was glad to see her, with her army of men behind her, their bright faces showing the world that they were proud to serve such a princess and to bring her to her capital city, which was ringing the bells in every church tower to make her welcome.

Lady Elizabeth, too sick to rise from her bed during the days of danger, managed to get to London before us. She came riding out from the city to greet us, at the head of a thousand men, all in the Tudor colours of green and white, riding in her pride as if she had never been sick with terror and hiding in her bed. She came out as if she were Lord Mayor of London, coming to give us the keys to the city, with the cheers of the Londoners all around her.

I reined in my horse and fell back a little so that I could see her. I remembered the girl in the garden that I had seen running from her stepfather and making sure that he caught her. I was desperately curious to see how that girl had changed.

She was young, only nineteen years old, yet she was imposing. I saw at once that she had arranged this cavalcade—she knew the power of appearances and she had the skill to design them. The green of her livery had been chosen to suit the flaming brazen red of her hair, which she wore loose beneath her green hood as if to flaunt her youth and maidenhood beside her older spinster sister. Against her radiance, the Lady Mary, drained by the strain of the last two months, faded into second place.

Lady Elizabeth's entourage halted before us and Lady Mary started to dismount as Lady Elizabeth flung herself down from her big white gelding, almost as grand as a man's warhorse, as if she had been waiting all her life for this moment. At the sight of her, the Lady Mary's face lit up, as a mother will smile on seeing her child. Lady Mary held out her arms, Elizabeth plunged into her embrace and Lady Mary kissed her warmly.

Elizabeth welcomed her sister to the city and congratulated her on her great victory. 'A victory of hearts,' she said. 'You are queen of the hearts of your people, the only way to rule this country.'

'Our victory,' Mary said generously at once. 'Northumberland would have put us both to death. I have won the right for us both to take our inheritance. You will be an acknowledged princess again, my sister and my heir, and you will ride beside me when I enter London.'

'Your Grace honours me too much,' Elizabeth said sweetly.

The Lady Mary gave the signal to mount and Elizabeth turned to her horse as her groom helped her into her saddle. She smiled around at us and saw me, riding astride in my pageboy livery. Her gaze went past me, utterly uninterested. She did not recognise me as the child who had seen her with Tom Seymour in the garden, so long ago.

But I was interested in her. From the first glimpse I had of her, up against a tree like a common whore, she had haunted my memory. There was something about her that fascinated me. When I saw her, in her green gown on that huge white horse, I saw a woman who was proud of her beauty and beautiful in her pride, and I longed to grow into a woman like that. I had been an unhappy girl for so long, and then a boy for so long, and a fool for so long that I had no idea how to be a woman—the very idea baffled me. But when I saw Lady Elizabeth, high on her horse, blazing with beauty and confidence, I thought that this was the sort of woman that I might one day become.

I looked from her to Lady Mary, the mistress I had come to love, and I thought that it would be better for her if she made plans to marry off Lady Elizabeth at once, and send her far away. No household could be at peace with this firebrand in its midst, and no kingdom could settle with such an heir burning so brightly beside an ageing queen.

AUTUMN 1553

As LADY MARY became established in her new life as the next Queen of England, I realised that I must speak to her about my own future. I chose my time carefully, just after Mass when the Lady Mary walked back from her chapel at Richmond in a mood of quiet exaltation. It was then that I fell into step beside her.

'Your Grace?'

'Yes, Hannah?' she smiled at me. 'Do you have any words of wisdom for me?'

'I am a most irregular fool,' I said. 'I see that I pronounce very rarely.'

'You told me I would be queen, and I held that to my heart in the days when I was afraid,' she said. 'I can wait for the gift of the Holy Spirit to move you.'

'It was that I wanted to speak to you about,' I said awkwardly. 'I came into the king's service when I was begged as a fool to him by the Duke of Northumberland, who then sent me as a companion to you. You, er . . . you don't have to have me.'

As I spoke, we turned into her private apartments and it was as well, for she gave a most unqueenly gurgle of laughter. 'You are not, as it were, compulsory?'

I found I was smiling too. 'Please, Your Grace. I have been in your household without you ever asking for my company. I just wanted to say that you can release me.'

She sobered at once. 'Do you want to go home, Hannah?'

'Not especially, Your Grace,' I said tentatively. 'I love my father very well but at home I am his clerk and printer. It is more enjoyable at court.'

'Hannah, would you like to stay with me?' she asked sweetly.

I knelt at her feet. 'I would,' I said, speaking from my heart. I thought I might be safe with her. 'But I cannot promise to have the Sight.'

'I know that,' she said gently. 'It is the gift of the Holy Spirit, which blows where it lists, I don't expect you to be my astrologer. I want you to be my little maid, my little friend. Will you be that?'

'Yes, Your Grace, I should like that,' I said, and felt the touch of her hand on my head.

She was silent for a moment, her hand resting gently as I knelt before her. 'It is very rare to find one that I can trust,' she said quietly. 'I know that you came into my household paid by my enemies, but I think your gift comes from God, and I believe that you came to me from God. And you love me now, don't you, Hannah?'

'Yes, Your Grace,' I said simply.

These were not easy days for the Lady Mary. She was preparing for her coronation but the Tower, where the kings of England usually spent their coronation night, was filled with traitors who had armed against her only a few months before. Her advisers told her that she should execute at once everyone who had been involved in the rebellion.

'I will not have the blood of that foolish girl on my hands,' the Lady Mary said.

Lady Jane had written to her cousin and confessed that she had been wrong to take the throne but that she had acted under duress.

'I know Cousin Jane,' the Lady Mary said quietly to Jane Dormer one evening. 'I have known her since she was a girl. She would never have put herself before one of my father's named heirs. The sin was done by the Duke of Northumberland and by Jane's father between them.'

'You can't pardon everyone,' Jane Dormer said bluntly. 'And she was proclaimed queen and sat beneath the canopy of state. You can't pretend it did not happen.'

Lady Mary nodded. 'The duke had to die,' she agreed. 'But there it can end. I shall release Jane's father, the Duke of Suffolk, and Jane and her husband Guilford can stay in the Tower until after my coronation.'

'And Robert Dudley?' I asked in as small a voice as I could make.

She looked around and saw me, seated on the steps before her throne, her greyhound beside me. 'Oh, are you there, little fool?' she said gently. 'Yes, your old master shall be tried for treason but held, not executed, until it is safe to release him. Does that content you?'

'Whatever Your Grace wishes,' I said obediently, but my heart leapt at the thought of his survival.

'It won't content those who want your safety,' Jane Dormer pointed out bluntly. 'How can you live in peace when those who would have destroyed you are still walking on this earth? How will you make them stop their plotting? D'you think they would have pardoned and released *you* if they had won?'

The Lady Mary smiled and put her hand over the hand of her best friend. 'Jane, this throne was given to me by God. I shall show His mercy whenever I can. Even to those who know it not.'

I sent a note to my father that I would come on Michaelmas Day, and I collected my wages and strode out through the darkening streets in my good-fitting boots and with a little sword at my side.

The door of the bookshop was closed, candlelight showing through the shutters. I tapped on the door and he opened it cautiously. It was Friday night and the Sabbath candle was hidden under a pitcher beneath the counter, burning its holy light into the darkness.

He was pale as I came into the room and I knew, with the understanding of a fellow refugee, that the knock on the door had startled him.

'Father, it is only me,' I said gently and I knelt before him, and he blessed me and raised me up.

'So, you are in service to the royal court again,' he said, smiling. 'How your fortunes do rise, my daughter.'

'She is a wonderful woman,' I said. 'I would rather serve her than anyone else in the land.'

'Rather than Lord Robert?'

I glanced towards the closed door. 'Only the Tower guards can serve him and I pray that they do it well.'

My father shook his head. 'I remember him coming here that day, a man you would think could command half the world, and now . . .'

'She won't execute him,' I said. 'She will be merciful to all now that the duke himself is dead.'

My father nodded. 'Dangerous times,' he said. 'Mr Dee remarked the other day that dangerous times are a crucible for change.'

'You have seen him?'

He nodded again. 'He is a most profound student and thinker. A great man. Oh! And I nearly forgot. He has ordered some books to be delivered to Lord Robert in the Tower.'

'Has he?' I said. 'Shall I take them for him?'

'As soon as they arrive,' my father said gently. 'And, Hannah, if you see Lord Robert . . .'

'Yes?'

'*Querida*, you must ask him to release you from your service to him and bid him farewell. He is a traitor sentenced to death. We cannot be associated with him.'

I bowed my head.

'Daniel wishes it too.'

My head came up at that. 'Why, whatever would he know about it?'

My father smiled. 'He is not an ignorant boy, Hannah.'

'He is not at court. He does not know the way of that world.'

'He is going to be a very great physician,' my father said gently. 'He is a thoughtful young man, and he has a gift for study. He comes here twice a week to read. And he always asks for you.'

'Does he?'

My father nodded. 'He calls you his princess,' he said.

I was so surprised for a moment that I could not speak. 'His princess?'

'Yes,' my father said, smiling at my incomprehension. 'He speaks like a young man in love. He comes to see me and he asks me, "How is my princess?"—and he means you, Hannah.'

The coronation of my mistress, Lady Mary, was set for the first day of October and the whole court, the whole city of London and the whole country had spent much of the summer preparing for the celebration that would bring Henry's daughter to his throne at last. There were faces missing from the crowds that lined the London streets. Devoted Protestants had already fled into exile. But the rest of the court, city and country turned out in their thousands to greet the new queen.

It was a fairy-tale coronation, a spectacle like something out of one of my father's storybooks. A princess in a golden chariot, wearing blue velvet trimmed with white ermine, riding through the streets of her city, which were hung with tapestries, past fountains running with wine so that the very air was heady with the warm scent of it, past crowds who screamed with delight at the sight of their princess, their virgin queen.

In the second carriage was Princess Elizabeth and Henry's neglected queen, Anne of Cleves, fatter than ever, with a ready smile for the crowd. And behind that chariot came forty-six ladies of the court and country, on foot and dressed in their best, and flagging a little by the time we had processed from Whitehall to the Tower.

Behind them, in the procession of officers of the court, came all the minor gentry and officials. I walked amongst them with Will Somers, the witty fool, beside me, and my yellow cap on my head and my fool's bell on a stick in my hand. I marched with my head up and thought myself an Englishwoman that day, and a loyal Englishwoman at that, with a proven love for my queen and for my adopted country.

We slept that night in the Tower, and the next day Lady Mary was crowned Queen of England, with her sister Elizabeth carrying her train, and the first to kneel to her and swear allegiance. I could hardly see them; I was crammed at the back of the Abbey, peering round a gentle-man of the court. In any case, my sight was blinded with tears at the knowledge that my Lady Mary had come to her throne, and her lifelong battle for recognition and justice was over at last. God (whatever His name might be) had finally blessed her; she had won.

WINTER 1553

IT WAS AS DARK as midnight, though it was still only six in the evening, the mist peeling like a black shroud off the corpse of the cold river. The smell in my nostrils was the scent of despair from the massive, wet, weeping walls of the Tower of London, surely the gloomiest palace that any monarch ever built. I presented myself to the postern gate and the guard held up a flaming torch to see my white face.

'I've got books to deliver to Lord Robert,' I said.

He withdrew the torch and the darkness flooded over me, then the creak of the hinges warned me that he was opening the gate.

'Let me see them,' he said.

I proffered the books readily enough. They were works of theology defending the Papist point of view, licensed by the Vatican and authorised by the queen's own council.

'Go through,' the guard said.

I walked on the slippery cobblestones to the guardhouse, and from there along a causeway, and then up a flight of wooden steps to the high doorway in the fortress wall of the white tower.

Another soldier was waiting in the doorway. He led me inside and then rapped at an inner door and swung it open to admit me.

At last I saw him, my Lord Robert, leaning over his papers, a candle at his elbow, the golden light shining on his dark head, on his pale skin, and then the slow-dawning radiance of his smile.

'Mistress Boy! Oh! My Mistress Boy!'

I dropped to one knee. 'My lord!' was all I could say before I burst into tears.

He laughed, pulled me to my feet, put his arm round my shoulders, wiped my face, all in one dizzying caress. 'Come now, child, come now. What's wrong?'

'It's you!' I gulped. 'You being here. And you look so . . .' I could not bear to say 'pale', 'ill', 'tired', 'defeated', but all those words were true. 'Imprisoned,' I found at last.

He laughed and led me over to the fire, seated himself on a chair and pulled up a stool so that I was facing him, like a favourite nephew.

'It was a great gamble,' he said softly. 'And we lost, and the price we will pay is a heavy one.'

'Will they . . .?' I could not bear to ask him if it was his own death that he was facing with this indomitable smile.

'Oh, I should think so,' he said cheerfully. 'Very soon. I would, if I were the queen. Now tell me the news. Tell me everything.'

'The queen is considering if she should marry; you'll know that, I suppose,' I said, low-voiced. 'And she has been ill. They have proposed one man after another. The best choice is Philip of Spain. The Spanish ambassador tells her that it will be a good marriage, but she is afraid. She knows she cannot rule alone but she is afraid of a man ruling over her.'

'And Lady Elizabeth?'

I glanced at the thick wooden door and dropped my low voice to an even quieter murmur. 'She and the queen cannot agree these days,' I said. 'Lady Elizabeth is no longer the little girl of the queen's teaching, and she goes to Mass only when she has to. And everyone says . . .'

'What do they say, my little spy?'

'That she is sending out letters to true Protestants, that she has a network of supporters. That the French will pay for an uprising against the queen. And that, at the very least, she only has to wait until the queen dies and then the throne is all hers anyway, and she can throw off all disguise and be a Protestant queen as she is now a Protestant princess.'

'And the queen believes all this slander?'

I looked up at him, hoping that he would understand. 'She thought that Elizabeth would be a sister to her,' I said. 'Elizabeth went with her into London at the very moment of her greatest triumph. She was at her side then, and again at the day of her coronation. She was first to kneel before the new queen and put her hands in hers and swear to be a true and faithful subject. She swore fidelity before God. How can she now plot against her?'

He sat back in his chair and observed my heat with interest. 'Is the queen angry with Elizabeth?'

I shook my head. 'No. It's worse than anger. She is disappointed in her. She is lonely, Lord Robert. She wanted her little sister at her side. She singled her out for love and respect. She can hardly believe now that Elizabeth would plot against her.'

'And yet the queen does nothing against her?'

'She wants to bring peace,' I said. 'She won't act against Elizabeth unless she has to. She says that she won't execute Lady Jane, or your brother . . .' I did not say 'or you' but we were both thinking it. 'She wants to bring peace to this country.'

'Well, amen to that,' Lord Robert said. He rose to his feet and looked out of the window at the dark courtyard below, where his own father had been executed. 'And shall I stay here till I rot?' he asked quietly.

'I once asked her directly. She said that she wanted no blood spilt that could be spared. She won't execute you and she must let you go free when Lady Jane goes free.'

'I wouldn't if I were her,' he said quietly. 'If I were her, I would rid myself of Elizabeth, of Jane, of my brother and of me, and name Mary Stuart as the next heir, French or not. One clean cut. That's the only way to get this country back into the Papist church and keep it there, and soon she will realise it.'

I crossed the room and stood behind him. Timidly I put my hand on his shoulder.

'And you?' he asked gently. 'Safe in royal service now?'

'I am never safe,' I said in a low voice. 'I love the queen and no one questions who I am or where I have come from. I should feel safe, but I always feel as if I am creeping across thin ice.'

He nodded. 'I'll take your secret with me to the scaffold if I go that way,' he promised. 'You have nothing to fear from me, child.'

I nodded. When I looked up he was watching me, his dark eyes warm. 'You've grown, Mistress Boy,' he remarked. 'Soon be a woman. I shall be sorry not to see it.'

I had nothing to say. He smiled as if he knew only too well the churn of my emotions. 'Ah, little fool. I should have left you in your father's shop that day, and not drawn you into this.'

'My father told me to bid you farewell.'

'Aye, he is right. You can leave me now. I release you from your promise to love me. You are no longer my vassal. I let you go.'

It was little more than a joke to him. He knew as well as I did that you cannot release a girl from her promise to love a man. She either gets herself free or she is bound for life.

'I'm not free,' I whispered. 'My father told me to come to see you and to say goodbye. But I am not free. I never will be.'

'Would you serve me still?'

I nodded.

Lord Robert smiled and leaned forward, his mouth so close to my ear that I could feel the warmth of his breath. 'Then do this one last thing for me. Go to Lady Elizabeth. Tell her to study with my old tutor, John Dee. Then find John Dee and tell him to make contact with his old master, Sir William Pickering. Tell him to meet also with James Crofts and Tom Wyatt. I think they are engaged in an alchemical experiment that is near to John Dee's heart. Edward Courtenay can make a chemical wedding. Can you remember all of that?'

'Yes,' I said. 'But I don't know what it means.'

'All the better. They are to make gold from the basest of metal, and cast down silver to ash. Tell him that. He'll know what I mean. And tell him that I will play my part in the alchemy, if he will get me there.'

'Where?' I asked.

'Just remember the message,' he said. 'Tell it back to me.'

I repeated it, word for word, and he nodded. He then put his lips to my neck, just below my ear, a little brush of a kiss, a little breath of a kiss. 'You're a good girl,' he said. 'And I thank you.'

He let me go then, and I stepped backwards from him as if I could not bear to turn away. I tapped on the door behind me, and the guard swung it open. 'God bless you and keep you safe, my lord,' I said.

'God speed, lad,' he replied evenly, to the closing door, and then it was shut and I was in the darkness and without him once more.

As fool to the queen I was expected to be in her chambers every day, at her side. But as soon as I could be absent for an hour without attracting notice, I took a chance, and went to the old Dudley rooms to look for John Dee. I tapped on the door and a man in strange livery opened it and looked suspiciously at me.

'I thought the Dudley household lived here,' I said timidly.

'Not any more,' he said smartly.

'Where will I find them?'

He shrugged. 'The duchess has rooms near the queen. Her sons are in the Tower. Her husband is in hell.'

'The tutor?'

He shrugged. 'Gone away. Back to his father's house, I should think.'

I nodded and took myself back to the queen's rooms, and sat by her feet on a small cushion. Her little dog, a greyhound, had a cushion that matched mine, and dog and I sat, watching with the same brown-eyed incomprehension, while the courtiers came and made their bows and applied for land and places and favours of grants of money, and sometimes the queen patted the dog and sometimes she patted me.

When they were all gone, she walked over to the window and rested her head against the thick pane of glass. The door opened and Jane Dormer beckoned two porters into the room, carrying a frame between them, swathed in linen cloth.

'Something for you, Your Grace!' she said with a roguish smile.

'What is it, Jane? I am weary now.'

In answer, Mistress Dormer waited till the men had leaned their burden against the wall, and then took the hem of the cloth and turned to her royal mistress. 'Are you ready?'

The queen was persuaded into smiling. 'Is this the portrait of Philip?' she asked. 'I won't be taken in by it. You forget, I am old enough to remember when my father married a portrait but divorced the sitter.'

In answer, Jane Dormer swept the cloth aside. I heard the queen's indrawn breath, and then heard her little girlish giggle. 'My God, Jane, this is a man!' she whispered.

Jane Dormer collapsed with laughter, dropped the cloth and dashed across the room to stand back to admire the portrait.

He was indeed a handsome man. He was young, in his mid-twenties, brown-bearded with dark smiling eyes, a full sensual mouth, broad shoulders and slim strong legs. He was wearing dark red with a dark red cap at a rakish angle on his curly brown hair.

'What d'you think, Your Grace?' Jane demanded.

The queen said nothing. I looked from the portrait back to her face again. She was gazing at him. For a moment I could not think what she reminded me of. Then I knew it. It was my own face in the looking glass when I thought of Robert Dudley.

'He's very . . . pleasing,' she said.

Jane Dormer met my eyes and smiled at me.

I wanted to smile back but my head was ringing with a strange noise, a tingling noise like little bells. I put my hands over my ears but the sound echoed louder inside my head.

'And see? A gold cross on a chain,' Jane cooed. 'Thank God, there will be a Catholic Christian prince for England once more.'

It was too much to bear now. I twisted round, trying to shake the terrible ringing out of my ears. Then I burst out, 'Your Grace! Your heart will break!' and at once the noise was cut off short and there was silence, and the queen was looking at me, and Jane Dormer was looking at me, and I realised I had spoken out of turn, shouted out as a fool.

'What did you say?' Jane Dormer challenged me to repeat my words, defying me to spoil the happy mood of the afternoon.

'I said, "Your Grace, your heart will break",' I repeated. 'But I cannot say why.'

Jane turned to the queen. 'Your Grace, pay no heed to the fool.'

The queen's face, which had been so bright and so animated, suddenly turned sulky. 'You can both leave,' she said flatly. She hunched her shoulders and turned away. I knew that she had made her choice and that no fool's words would change her mind.

While the long negotiations about the marriage went on between the queen's council, sick with apprehension at the thought of a Spaniard on the throne of England, and the Spanish representatives, eager to add another kingdom to their sprawling empire, I found my way to the home of John Dee's father, a small house near the river. I tapped on the door and for a moment no one answered. Then a window above the front door opened and someone shouted down: 'Who is it?'

'Mr Dee, it is me. Hannah the Fool,' I called up. 'I was looking for you.'

'Hush,' he said quickly and slammed the casement window shut. I heard his feet echoing on the wooden stairs inside the house and the noise of the bolts being drawn, and then the door opened inwards to a dark hall. 'Come in quickly,' he said.

He slammed the door shut after me and bolted it.

'Did anyone follow you?'

My heart thudded at the question. 'No, sir. I don't think so.'

John Dee nodded, and then he turned and went upstairs without a word to me. I hesitated, then followed him.

At the top of the stairs the door was open and he beckoned me into his room. At the window was his desk with a beautiful strange brass instrument in pride of place.

'Are you a wanted man, Mr Dee? Should I go?'

He smiled and shook his head. 'I'm overcautious,' he said frankly.

'You are sure?' I pressed him.

He gave a little laugh. 'Hannah, you are like a young doe on the edge of flight. Be calm. You are safe here.'

I steadied myself and started to look around. He saw my gaze go back to the instrument at the window.

'What d'you think that is?' he asked.

I shook my head. It was a beautiful thing, made in brass, a ball as big as a pigeon's egg in the centre on a stalk, and around it a brass ring cunningly supported by two other stalks, which meant it could swing and move, a ball sliding around on it. Outside there was another ring and another ball, outside that, another. They were a series of rings and balls and the farthest from the centre was the smallest.

'This,' he said softly, 'is a model of the world. This is how the creator made the world and then set it in motion. This holds the secret of how God's mind works.' He leaned forward and gently touched the first ring. As if by magic they all started to move slowly, each going at its own pace, each following its own orbit, sometimes passing, sometimes overtaking each other. Only the little gold egg in the centre did not move; everything else swung round it.

'Where is our world?' I asked.

He smiled at me. 'Here,' he said, pointing to the golden egg at the very centre of all the others. He pointed to the next ring with the slowly circling ball. 'This the moon.' He pointed to the next. 'This the sun.' He pointed to the next few. 'These are the planets, and beyond them the stars.' He put a hand on one ring to steady it and I watched the instrument slow and stop. Then, as if he suddenly remembered me, 'And you? What did you come here for?' he asked in quite a different tone of voice.

'I have a message. From Lord Robert.'

'What does Lord Robert want?'

'He gave me two tasks. One, to tell Lady Elizabeth to seek you out and ask you to be her tutor, and the other to tell you to meet with some men.'

'What men?'

'Sir William Pickering, Tom Wyatt and James Crofts,' I recited. 'And he said to tell you this: that they are engaged in an alchemical experiment to make gold from base metal and to refine silver back to ash and you should help them with this. Edward Courtenay can make a chemical wedding. And I am to go back and tell him what will come to pass.'

Mr Dee glanced at the window as if he feared eavesdroppers on the very sill outside. 'These are not good times for me to serve a suspect princess and a man in the Tower for treason, and three others whose names I may already know, whose plans I may already doubt. What is he thinking of, exposing you to such danger?'

'I am his to command,' I said firmly. 'I have given my word.'

'He should release you,' he said gently. 'He cannot command anything from the Tower.'

'He has released me.'

'Hannah, will you look in the mirror again and see for me?' he asked.

I hesitated. I was afraid of the dark mirror, afraid of the things that might come through to haunt us. 'Mr Dee, last time I did not have a true seeing,' I confessed awkwardly.

'You said the date of the king's death. You predicted the next queen would be Jane. Your answers were true,' he observed.

'They were nothing more than guesses,' I said.

He smiled. 'Then just do that again,' he said. 'Just guess for me.'

'Very well.'

'We'll do it now,' he said. He took my hand and led me into a small box-room. The same mirror we had used before was leaning against a wall. He lit two candles and put them before the mirror, so that they seemed like innumerable candles disappearing into infinite distance.

I drew a long breath to ward off my fear and seated myself before the mirror. I heard his muttered prayer and I repeated: 'Amen'. Then I gazed into the darkness of the mirror.

I could hear myself speaking but I could hardly make out the words. I could hear the scratching of his pen as he wrote down what I was saying. I could hear myself reciting a string of numbers, and then strange words, like a wild poetry that had a rhythm and a beauty of its own, but no meaning that I could tell. Then I heard my voice say very clearly in English: 'There will be a child, but no child. There will be a king but no king. There will be a virgin queen all-forgotten. There will be a queen but no virgin.'

'And Lord Robert Dudley?' he whispered.

'He will have the making of a prince who will change the history of the world,' I whispered in reply. 'And he will die, beloved by a queen, safe in his bed.'

When I recovered my senses, John Dee was standing by me with a drink that tasted of fruit with a tang behind it of metal.

'Are you all right?' he asked me.

I nodded. 'Yes. A little sleepy.'

'You had better go back to court,' he said. 'You will be missed.'

It was hard to find a way to speak with the Lady Elizabeth without half the court remarking on it. I could not simply go to her rooms and ask to see her. I would be reported to the queen. But one day, as I was walking behind her in the gallery, she stumbled for a moment. I went to help her, and she took my arm.

'I have broken the heel on my shoe,' she said.

'Let me help you to your rooms,' I offered, and added in a whisper, 'I have a message for you, from Lord Robert Dudley.'

She did not even flicker a sideways glance at me, and in that absolute control I saw at once that she was a consummate plotter.

'I can receive no messages without my sister's blessing,' Elizabeth said sweetly. 'But I would be very glad if you would help me to my chamber; I wrenched my foot when the heel broke.'

She bent down and took off her shoe. I gave her my arm. A courtier passing looked at us both. 'The princess has broken the heel of her shoe,' I explained. He nodded, and went on. He, for one, was not going to trouble himself to help her.

Elizabeth limped slightly on her stockinged foot and it made her walk slowly. She gave me plenty of time to deliver the message that she had said she could not hear without permission.

'Lord Robert asks you to summon John Dee as your tutor,' I said.

'You can tell him that I will not do anything that would displease my sister the queen,' she said easily. 'But I have long wanted to study with Mr Dee and I was going to ask him to read with me.'

We were at the door of her rooms. A guard stood to attention as we approached and swung the door open. Elizabeth released me. 'Thank you for your help,' she said coolly, and went inside. As the door shut behind her I saw her bend down and put her shoe back on. The heel was perfectly sound.

I went home to my father leaving a court humming with gossip, walking through a city seething with rebellion. Rumours of a secret army mustering to wage war against the queen were everywhere. Ballads were sung against the marriage; the braver preachers thundered against the match; chapbooks abused the queen for even considering the Spanish prince. England was not some dowry to be handed over to Spain. The very notion was treason.

My father had company in the bookshop. Daniel Carpenter's mother was perched on one of the stools at the counter, her son beside her. I knelt for my father's blessing, and then made a little bow to Mrs Carpenter and to my husband-to-be.

'I waited to see you and hear the news from court,' Mrs Carpenter said. 'And Daniel wanted to see you, of course.'

The glance that Daniel shot at her made it clear that he did not wish her to explain his doings to me.

'Is the queen's marriage to go ahead?' my father asked.

'Without doubt,' I said. 'The queen is desperate for a helper and a companion, and it is natural she should want a Spanish prince.'

My father glanced at Mrs Carpenter. 'Please God it makes no difference to us,' he said. 'Please God she does not bring in Spanish ways.'

She leaned forward and patted my father's hand. 'We have lived in England for three generations,' she said reassuringly. 'Nobody can think that we are anything but good Christians and good Englishmen.'

'I cannot stay if it is to become another Spain,' my father said in a low voice. 'You know, every Sunday, every saint's day, they burned heretics, sometimes hundreds at a time. And those of us who had practised Christianity for years were put on trial alongside those who had hardly pretended to it. And no one could prove their innocence! I knew one day they would come for me, and I started to prepare. But I did not think they would take my parents, my wife's sister, my wife before me . . .' He broke off. 'I should have thought of it. We should have gone earlier.'

'Papa, we couldn't save her,' I said, comforting him with the same words that he had used to me when I had cried that we should have stayed and died beside her.

'Old times,' Mrs Carpenter said briskly. 'And they won't come here. Not the Holy Inquisition, not in England.'

'Oh yes, they will,' Daniel asserted.

It was as if he had said a foul word. A silence fell at once. His mother and my father both turned to look at him.

'A Spanish prince, a half-Spanish queen—she must be determined to restore the church. How better to do it than to bring in the Inquisition to root out heresy?'

'She's too merciful to do it,' I said. 'She has not even executed Lady Jane, though all her advisers say that she should. I think she will restore this country to the true faith by gentle means. Already, half the country is glad to return to the Mass; the others will follow later.'

'I hope so,' Daniel said. 'But we should be prepared. I don't want to hear a knock on the door one night and know that we are too late to save ourselves.'

'Where would we go?' I asked. I could feel that old feeling of terror in the pit of my belly, the feeling that nowhere would ever be safe for me.

'First Amsterdam, and then Italy,' he said firmly. 'You and I will marry as soon as we get to Amsterdam and then continue overland. We will travel all together. Your father and my mother and my sisters with us. I can complete my training as a physician in Italy, and there are Italian cities that are tolerant of Jews, where we could live openly in our faith. Your father can sell his books, and my sisters could find work. We will live as a family.'

'See how he plans ahead,' Mrs Carpenter said in an approving whisper to my father.

'We are not promised to marry till next year,' I said. 'I'm not ready to marry yet.'

'Oh, not again,' said my father.

'All girls think that,' said Mrs Carpenter.

Daniel said nothing.

I slid down from my stool. 'May we talk privately?' I asked.

'Go into the printing room,' my father told Daniel. 'Your mother and I will take a glass of wine out here.'

He poured wine for her and I caught her amused smile as Daniel and I went into the inside room where the big press stood.

'Mr Dee tells me that I will lose the Sight if I marry,' I said earnestly. 'He believes it is a gift from God, I cannot throw it away.'

'It is guesswork and waking dreams,' Daniel said roundly.

It was so close to my own opinion that I could hardly argue. 'It is beyond our understanding,' I said stoutly. 'There are secrets I cannot tell you,' I said, and then I added: 'And that is another reason that I cannot be your wife. There should not be secrets between man and wife.'

He turned away with an exclamation of irritation. 'Don't be clever with me,' he said. 'You are so full of trickery that you will talk yourself out of happiness and into heartbreak.'

'How should I be happy if I have to be a nothing?' I asked. 'I am the favourite of Queen Mary. I am highly paid. The greatest philosopher in the land thinks I have a gift from God to foretell the future. And you think my happiness lies in walking away from all this to marry an apprentice physician!'

He caught my hands, which were twisting together, and pulled me towards him. His breath was coming as quickly as my own. 'Enough,' he said angrily. 'You have insulted me enough, I think. You need not marry an apprentice physician. You can be Robert Dudley's whore or his tutor's adept. You can think yourself the queen's companion but everyone knows you as the fool. You make yourself less than what I would offer you. You could be the wife of an honourable man who would love you and instead you throw yourself into the gutter for any passer-by to pick up.'

'I do not!' I gasped, trying to pull my hands away.

Suddenly he pulled me towards him and wrapped his arms round my waist. His dark head came down, his mouth close to mine. I could smell the pomade in his hair and the heat of the skin of his cheek. I shrank back even as I felt the desire to go forward.

'Do you love another man?' he demanded urgently.

'No,' I lied.

'Do you swear, on all you believe, whatever that is, that you are free to marry me?'

'I am free to marry you,' I said, honestly enough, for God knew as well as I did that no one else wanted me.

'With honour,' he specified.

I could have spat at him in my temper. 'Of course, with honour,' I said. 'Have I not told you that my gift is dependent on my virginity? Have I not said that I will not risk that?' I pulled away from him but his grip on me tightened. Despite myself, my body took in the sense of him: the strength of his arms, his thighs pressing against me, the scent of him and, for some odd reason, the feeling of absolute safety that he gave me. I realised that I wanted to mould myself around him, put my head on his shoulder, let him hold me against him and know that I was safe—if only I would let him love me, if only I would let myself love him.

'If they bring in the Inquisition, we will have to leave, you know that.'

'Yes, I know that,' I said, only half hearing him, feeling him with every inch of my body.

'If we leave, you will have to come with me as my wife, I will take you and your father to safety under no other condition.'

'Yes.'

'Then we are agreed?'

'If we have to leave England then I will marry you,' I said.

'And in any case we will marry when you are sixteen.'

I nodded, my eyes closed. Then I felt his mouth come down onto mine and I felt his kiss melt every argument away.

He released me, and smiled as if he knew that I was dizzy with desire. 'As to Lord Robert, it is my request that you serve him no longer,' he said. 'He is a convicted traitor, and you endanger yourself and us all by seeking his company.' His look darkened. 'And he is not a man I would trust with my betrothed.'

'He thinks of me as a child and a fool,' I corrected him.

'You are neither,' he said gently. 'And neither am I. You are half in love with him, Hannah, and I won't tolerate it.'

I hesitated, ready to argue, and then I felt the most curious sensation of my life: the desire to tell the truth to someone.

'If I tell you the truth about something, will you help me?' I asked.

'I will give you the best help I can,' he said, drawing me back to him.

'Daniel, this is the truth. I saw that the king would die, I named the day. I saw that Jane would be crowned queen. I saw that Queen Mary would be queen, and I have seen a glimpse of her future, which is heart-break. John Dee says I have a gift of Sight. He tells me it comes in part from me being a virgin and I want to honour the gift. And I want to marry you. And I desire you. And I cannot help but love Lord Robert. All those things. All at once.' I held him close, while he considered the rush of truths I had told him. Moments later he eased me back from him and looked into my eyes.

'Is it an honourable love, as a servant to a master?' he asked.

I felt my lip quiver and the tears come to my eyes. 'It's all muddled up,' I said weakly. 'I love him for what he is . . .' I was silenced by the impossibility of conveying to Daniel the desirability of Robert Dudley; his looks, his clothes, his wealth, his boots, his horses were all beyond my vocabulary. 'I love him for what he might become—he will be freed, he will be a great man, a great man, Daniel. He will be the maker of a Prince of England. And tonight he is in the Tower, waiting for the sentence of death, and I think of him, and I think of my mother waiting, like he is waiting, for the morning when they took her out . . .' I lost my voice, I shook my head.

He held me for a few more seconds and then he coldly put me from him. 'This is not your mother. There is no reason to love a man who has plotted and intrigued his way to treason. He would have put Lady Jane on the throne and beheaded the mistress that you say you love: Queen Mary. He is not an honourable man.'

I opened my mouth to argue but there was nothing I could say.

'And you are all mixed up with him, with his treasonous plans, and with your feeling for him. I won't call it love because if I thought for one moment it was anything more than a girl's fancy I would go out now to your father and break our betrothal. But I tell you this. You have to leave the service of Robert Dudley, whatever future you have seen for him. You have to avoid John Dee and you have to surrender your gift. You can serve the queen until you are sixteen but you have to be my betrothed in word and in every act you take. And in eighteen months' time, when you are sixteen, we will marry and you will leave court.'

'Eighteen months?' I said, very low.

'Eighteen months,' he said flatly. 'Or I swear I will take another girl to be my wife and throw you away to whatever future the soothsayer, the traitor and the queen make up for you.'

It was a cold winter, and not even Christmas brought any joy to the people. The queen held Christmas at Whitehall and appointed a Lord of Misrule and demanded a merry court in the old ways, but it was no good. The missing places at the Christmas feast told their own story: Lady Elizabeth stayed at Ashridge, her house on the Great North Road, ideally placed to advance on London as soon as someone gave the word. Half a dozen of the queen's council were unaccountably missing; the French ambassador was busier than any good Christian should be at Christmastide. It was clear that there was trouble brewing right up to the very throne, and the queen knew it; we all of us knew it.

'It's not very merry, is it, Hannah?' she asked me sadly. 'I have waited for this Christmas all my life, and now it seems that people have forgotten how to be happy.'

'Next year it will be better,' I said. 'When you are married and Prince Philip is here.'

At the very mention of his name the colour rose up in her pale cheeks. 'Hush,' she said, gleaming. 'I would be wrong to expect it of him. He will have to be often in his other kingdoms. There is no greater empire in the world than the one he will inherit, you know.'

Suddenly, there was a sharp knock from the guards outside and the double doors were thrown open. The noise startled me and I was on my feet in an instant, my heart pounding. A messenger stood in the doorway, the Lord Chancellor, Bishop Gardiner, with him, and the veteran soldier Thomas Howard, Duke of Norfolk, beside him, their faces grim.

I fell back, certain that they had somehow discovered who I was, and had a warrant for my arrest as a heretic Jew. Then I saw they were not looking at me. They were looking at the queen.

'Oh, no,' I whispered.

She must have thought it was the end for her, as she rose slowly to her feet and looked from one stern face to another. She knew that the duke could turn his coat in a moment; the council could have mustered a swift plot. But the face she turned to them was as serene as if they had come to invite her to dine. In that moment I loved her for her courage, for her determination never to show fear. 'How now, my lords?' she said pleasantly. 'I hope you bring me good news for all you seem so severe.'

'Your Grace, it is not good news,' Bishop Gardiner said flatly. 'The rebels are marching against you. My young friend Edward Courtenay has seen the wisdom to confess to me and throw himself on your mercy.'

'And Edward tells you?'

'That a plot is in train to march on London, to put you in the Tower and to set the Lady Elizabeth on the throne in your place. We have the names of some of them: Sir William Pickering, Sir Thomas Wyatt in Kent and Sir James Crofts.'

I kept back behind her. These were the very men that my lord had named to me, that he had asked me to name to John Dee. These were the men who were to make a chemical wedding and to pull down silver and replace it with gold. Now I thought I knew what he meant. I thought I knew which queen was silver and which was gold in his metaphor. And I thought that I had again betrayed the queen while taking her wage, and that it would not be long before someone found out.

She took a breath to steady herself. 'Any others?'

'The Duke of Suffolk is not at his house in Sheen, and no one knows where he has gone.'

If the Duke of Suffolk had disappeared then it could mean only one thing: he was raising his hundreds of tenants and retainers to restore the throne to his daughter Jane. We were faced with an uprising for Elizabeth and a rebellion for Queen Jane. Those two names could turn out more than half of the country, and all the courage and determination that Queen Mary had shown before could come to nothing now.

'And Lady Elizabeth? Does she know of this? Is she at Ashridge still?'

'Courtenay says that she was on the brink of marriage with him, and the two of them were to take your throne and rule together. Thank God the lad has seen sense and come over to us in time. She knows of everything; she is waiting in readiness. The King of France will support her claim and send a French army to put her on the throne. She may even now be riding to head the rebel army.'

I saw the queen's colour drain from her face.

The duke stepped forward. 'You must go to Framlingham at once, Your Grace. And we will have a warship standing by to take you out of the country to Spain. This is a battle you cannot win. Once you're safe in Spain perhaps you can regroup, perhaps Prince Philip . . .'

I saw her grip on the back of her chair tighten. 'It is a mere six months since I rode into London *from* Framlingham,' she said. 'The people wanted me as queen then.'

'You were their choice in preference to the Duke of Northumberland with Queen Jane as his puppet,' he brutally reminded her. 'Not instead of Elizabeth. The people want the Protestant religion and the Protestant princess. They won't have you with Prince Philip of Spain as king.'

'I won't leave London,' she said. 'I have waited all my life for my mother's throne; I shan't abandon it now.'

'You have no choice,' he warned her. 'They will be at the gates of the city within days.'

'I will wait till that moment.'

'You are gambling with your life as well as your throne,' the duke almost shouted at her.

'I know that!' she exclaimed.

He took a breath. 'Do I have your command to muster the royal guard and the city's trained bands and lead them out against Wyatt in Kent?'

'Yes. But there must be no sieges of towns and no sacking of villages.'

'It cannot be done!' he protested. 'In battle, one cannot protect the battleground.'

'These are your orders,' she insisted icily. 'I will not have a civil war fought over my wheat fields, especially in these starving times.'

For a moment he looked as if he would argue. Then she leaned towards him. 'Trust me in this,' she said persuasively. 'I know. I am a virgin queen; my only children are my people. They have to see that I love them and care for them. I cannot get married on a tide of their innocent blood. This has to be gently done, and firmly done.'

He shook his head. 'No,' he said. He was too afraid to waste time in flattery. 'Nobody can do it. They are gathering in their hundreds, in their thousands. These people understand only one thing and that is force.

They understand gibbets at the crossroads and heads on pikes. You cannot rule Englishmen and be merciful, Your Grace.'

'You are mistaken,' she said, as determined as he was. 'I came to this throne by a miracle and God does not change his mind. We will win these men back by the love of God. It has to be done as God would have it, or His miracle cannot take place.'

The duke looked as if he would have argued.

'It is my command,' she said flatly.

He shrugged and bowed. 'As you command then,' he said. 'Whatever the consequences.'

The Duke of Norfolk took the apprentice boys from London and the queen's own guard, and marched them down to Kent to meet Wyatt's force in a set-piece battle, which should have routed the men from Kent in a day. But when our forces, who had sworn to protect the queen, faced Wyatt's men and saw their honest faces and their determination, they threw their caps in the air and shouted 'We are all Englishmen!'

Not a shot was fired. They embraced each other as brothers and turned against their commander, united against the queen. The duke hared back to London, having done nothing but add a trained force to Thomas Wyatt's raggle-taggle army, which came onwards, even more determined than before. Swelled by recruits from every village on the London road, they reached the south bank of the Thames on a wave of enthusiasm, and found London Bridge raised against them, and the guns of the Tower trained on the southern bank ready for them.

'They are not to open fire,' the queen ruled.

'Your Grace, for the love of God. The rebels are encamped within range now. We could destroy them in one cannonade.'

'They shall stay there until we can raise an army to drive them away.'

'Your Grace, you have no army.'

She was pale but she did not waver. 'I have no army *yet*,' she emphasised. 'But I will raise one from the good men of London.'

Against her council's advice, the queen put on her great gown of state and went to the Guildhall to meet the Mayor and the people. Jane Dormer, her other ladies and I went in her train.

Of all of the queen's council and certainly of all of her ladies in waiting, only Jane and I had any hopes of getting out of London alive, but Jane and I had seen her at Framlingham, and we knew that this was a queen to back against all odds. She was at her very best when she and her God stood against disaster. With an enemy at the very gates of London, you would want no other queen.

They had set up a throne for her in the Guildhall and half of London came from sheer curiosity, crowding to hear the queen argue for her life. When she stood, a small figure under the weighty golden crown, draped in the heavy robes of state, I thought for a moment that she would not be able to convince them to keep their faith with her.

She opened her mouth to speak and there was no sound. I thought she had lost her voice from fear itself, and Wyatt might as well march into the hall now and claim the throne for the Lady Elizabeth. But then her voice rang out, clear and sweet as if she were a chorister singing in the chapel on Christmas Day.

She told them everything. She told them that she was a king's daughter and she claimed her father's power, and their fealty. She reminded them that she was a virgin without a child of her own and that she loved the people of the country as only a mother can love her child, and that she could not doubt but that they loved her in return.

She was seductive. Our Mary blazed with passion until they caught her fire and were part of it. She swore to them that she was marrying solely to give them an heir, and if they did not think it was the best choice then she would die a virgin for them; that she was their queen— it meant nothing to her whether she had a man or not. What was important was the throne. Nothing else mattered. She would be guided by them in her marriage, as in everything else. She was theirs, they were hers, and there was nothing that could change it.

'And now, good subjects, pluck up your hearts and like true men face up against these rebels and fear them not, for I assure you I fear them nothing at all!'

She was tremendous. They threw their caps in the air, and cheered her as if she were the Virgin Mary herself. And they raced outside and took the news to all those who had not been able to get into the Guildhall. London went mad for Mary. The men volunteered to march against the rebels; the women tore up their best linen into bandages and baked bread for the volunteer soldiers to take in their knapsacks. The battle was won, not when Wyatt's army was defeated just a few days later, but in that single afternoon, by Mary, standing on her own two feet, head held high, blazing with courage.

Once again the queen learned that holding the throne was harder than winning it. She spent the days after the uprising struggling with her conscience, faced with the agonising question of what should be done with the rebels who had been so dramatically defeated. Clearly, God would protect this Mary on her throne, but God was not to be mocked.

Mary must also protect herself. There could be no more mercy from a tenderhearted queen. It did not matter that Jane had not led this rebellion; hers was the head that they would crown, and so hers was the head that must be struck off the body.

'She would do the same to you, Your Grace,' they murmured to her.

'She is a girl of sixteen,' the queen replied.

'Her father joined the rebels for her cause. The others joined for the Princess Elizabeth. Both young women were born to be your enemies. Their existence means that your life is in perpetual danger. Both of them must be destroyed.'

The queen took their hardhearted advice to her prie-dieu. 'Jane is guilty of nothing but her lineage,' she whispered, looking up at the statue of the crucified Christ. 'And You know, as I do, that Elizabeth is guilty indeed. But how can I send my cousin and my sister to the scaffold?'

Jane Dormer shot me a look and the two of us moved our stools so as to block the view and the hearing of the other ladies in waiting. The queen on her knees should not be overheard. She was consulting the only adviser she truly trusted.

We did not live like a victorious court in a victorious city. It was a court hanging on a thread of its own indecision, sick with worry. Every day, after Mass and breakfast, Queen Mary walked by the side of the river, her cold hands dug deep in her muff, her steps hastened by the cold wind blowing her skirts forward.

I knew she was troubled and so I kept silent. I dogged her footsteps two steps behind her because I knew she had taken so many lonely walks, that she liked to know that someone was keeping vigil with her.

The wind coming off the river was too cold for her to walk for long, even with a thick cape and a fur collar at her neck. She turned on her heel and I nearly bumped into her.

'I beg pardon, Your Grace,' I said, ducking a little bow and stepping out of her way.

'You can walk beside me,' she said.

I fell into step, saying nothing, but waiting for her to speak. She was silent till we came to the small garden door where the guard swung it open before her. Inside, a maid was waiting to take her cloak and to offer her a pair of dry shoes. I swung my cloak over my arm and stamped my feet on the rushes to warm them.

'Come with me,' the queen said over her shoulder, and led the way up the winding stone stairs to her apartments. The stairs emerged into a little lobby room, which led to the queen's private chamber. Jane Dormer was sewing in the window seat, half a dozen women working alongside her; one of the queen's ladies was reading from the Book of Psalms. The queen gave a little nod of pleasure. Philip of Spain, when he finally came, would find a sober and devout court.

'Come, Hannah,' she said, taking a seat at the fireside and gesturing to me to sit on a stool nearby.

I sat down, folded my knees under my chin and looked up at her.

'I want you to look at something for me.'

'Look at something?'

'Look with your gift, with your inner eye.'

I hesitated. 'Your Grace, you know it is not at my command.'

'No, but you have seen the future twice with me; once you spoke of my becoming queen and once you spoke to warn me of heartbreak. Now I want you to warn me again.'

'Warn you against what?' My voice was as low as hers. No one in the room could have heard us over the crackle of the logs in the fireplace.

'Against Elizabeth,' she breathed.

'Your Grace, there are wiser heads than mine to advise you,' I said.

'None I trust more. None who comes with your gift.'

I hesitated. 'Is she coming to court?'

Mary shook her head. 'She won't come. She says she is near death with sickness, a swelling of the belly and of her limbs. She is too ill to be moved. It is an old illness of hers, a real one, I believe. But it always comes on at certain times.'

'Certain times?'

'When she is very afraid,' Mary said quietly, 'and when she has been caught out. The first time she was sick like this was when they executed Thomas Seymour. Now I think she fears being accused of another plot. I am sending my doctors to see her, and I want you to go too.'

'Of course.' I did not know what else I could say.

'Sit with her, read to her, be her companion as you have been mine. If she is well enough to come to court, you can travel with her. If she is dying you can comfort her, send for a priest and try to turn her thoughts to her salvation. It is not too late for her to be forgiven by God.'

'Anything else?' My voice was a thread of sound.

'Spy on her,' she said flatly. 'Everything she does, everyone she sees, every name you hear mentioned. Write to me every day and tell me what you have learned. I have to know if she is plotting against me. I have to know if she is my enemy and will stop at nothing till my death. You can tell me that.'

I surrendered to her conviction. 'When do I leave?'

'Tomorrow at dawn,' the queen said.

I rose to my feet and gave her a little bow. She put out her hand to me. 'Hannah,' she said quietly.

'Yes, Your Grace?'

'I wish you could see into her heart and see that she is able to love me, and able to turn to the true faith.'

'I hope I see that too,' I said fervently.

Her mouth was working, holding back tears. 'But if she is faithless, you must tell me, even though it will break my heart.'

'I will.'

It took us three days to travel the thirty miles to Ashridge, heads bowed through a storm of freezing cold sleet. We reached the house by noon and we were glad to see the curl of smoke from the tall chimneys. We clattered round to the stable yard and found no grooms to take the horses. Lady Elizabeth kept only a small staff, and none of them was ready to greet a train such as ours. We trooped round to the front door of the house.

The princess's own cousin, Lord William Howard, hammered on the door and tried the handle. It was bolted and barred from the inside. He stepped back and looked around for the captain of the guard. At that moment I realised that his orders were very different from mine. I was here to look into Elizabeth's heart, to restore her to the affection of her sister. He was here to bring her to London, alive or dead.

'Knock again,' he said grimly. 'And then break it down.'

At once the door yielded, swung open by an unenthusiastic pair of menservants, and we marched into the great hall without invitation.

The place was in silence, extra rushes on the floor to muffle the sound of the servants' feet, a strong smell of mint purifying the air.

A redoubtable woman, Mrs Kat Ashley, Elizabeth's best servant and protector, was at the head of the hall, her hands clasped together under a solid bosom. She looked the royal train up and down as if we were a pack of pirates. 'I shall tell my lady that you are here but she is too sick to see anyone,' she said flatly. 'I will see that you are served such dinner as we can lay before you, but we have not the rooms to accommodate such a great company as yourselves.'

'We will stay at Hillham Hall,' Sir Thomas Cornwallis said helpfully.

Mrs Ashley raised her eyebrow as if she did not think much of his choice, and turned to the door at the head of the hall. I fell into step behind her. She rounded on me. 'And where d'you think you're going?'

I looked up at her, my face innocent. 'To the Lady Elizabeth.'

'She'll see no one,' the woman ruled. 'She is too ill.'

'Then let me pray at the foot of her bed,' I said quietly.

'If she is so very ill she will want the fool's prayers,' someone said from the hall. 'That child can see angels.'

Kat Ashley, caught out by her own story, nodded briefly and let me follow her out of the door, through the presence chamber and into Elizabeth's private rooms.

There was a heavy curtain over the door to shut out the noise from the presence chamber. Candles illuminated the room and showed the princess, red hair spread like a haemorrhage on the pillow, her face white.

At once I could see she was ill indeed. Her belly was as swollen as if she were pregnant but her hands were swollen too, as if she were an old lady. Her lovely face was puffy. Even her neck was thick.

'What is the matter with her?' I demanded.

'Dropsy,' Mrs Ashley replied. 'Worse than she has ever had it before.'

'My lady,' I breathed.

The princess peered at me from under swollen eyelids. 'Who?'

'The queen's fool,' I said. 'Hannah.'

She veiled her eyes. 'A message?' she asked, her voice a thread.

'No,' I said quickly. 'I am come to you from Queen Mary. She has sent me to be your companion.'

'I thank her,' Elizabeth said, her voice a whisper. 'You can tell her that I am sick indeed and need to be alone.'

'She has sent doctors to make you better,' I said.

'I am too sick to travel,' she said, speaking strongly for the first time.

I bit my lip to hide my smile. She was ill; no one could manifest a swelling to escape a charge of treason. But she would play her illness as the trump card it was.

'She has sent her councillors to accompany you,' I warned her.

'Who?'

'Your cousin, Lord William Howard, among others.'

I saw her swollen lips twist in a bitter smile. 'She must be very determined against me if she sends my own kin to arrest me,' she remarked.

'May I be your companion during your illness?' I suggested.

She turned her head away. 'I am too tired,' she said. 'You can come back when I am better.'

I rose from my kneeling position by the bed and stepped backwards. Kat Ashley jerked her head towards the door to send me from the room.

Then we waited. Good God, how we waited. She was the absolute mistress of delay. When the physicians said she was well enough to leave, she could not choose the gowns she would bring, then her ladies could not pack them in time for us to set off before dusk. Then everything had to be unpacked again since we were staying another day, and then Elizabeth was so exhausted she could see no one at all the next day, and the merry dance of Elizabeth's waiting began again.

During one of these mornings, when the big trunks were being laboriously loaded into the wagons, I went to Lady Elizabeth to see if I could assist her. She was lying on a day bed, in an attitude of exhaustion.

'It is all packed,' she said. 'And I am so tired I do not know if I can begin the journey.'

The swelling of her body had reduced but she was clearly still unwell. She would have looked better if she had not powdered her cheeks with rice powder and, I swear, darkened the shadows under her eyes.

'The queen is determined that you shall go to London,' I warned her.

She bit her lip. 'Do you know if she will accuse me when we get there?' she asked, her voice very low.

'She loves you,' I reassured her. 'I think she would take you back into her favour even now, if you would just accept her faith.'

Elizabeth looked into my eyes, that straight honest Tudor look, like her father, like her sister. 'Are you telling me the truth?' she asked. 'Are you a holy fool or a trickster, Hannah Green?'

'I am neither,' I said, meeting her gaze. 'I was begged for a fool by Robert Dudley, against my wishes. I have a gift of Sight which comes to me unbidden.'

'You saw an angel behind Robert Dudley,' she reminded me.

I smiled. 'I did.'

'What was it like?'

I giggled, I couldn't help it. 'Lady Elizabeth, I was so taken with Lord Robert that I hardly noticed the angel.'

She sat up, quite forgetting her pose of illness, and laughed with me. 'He is very . . . he is so . . . he is indeed a man you look at.'

'And I only realised it was an angel afterwards,' I said.

'And do your visions come to pass?' she asked keenly.

'Some things that I see have come to pass,' I said, honestly enough. 'But sometimes the very things I need to know, I cannot tell. Then it is a useless gift. If it had warned me—just once—'

'What warning?' she asked.

'The death of my mother,' I said. I would have bitten back the words as soon as they were spoken.

'I did not know,' she said gently. 'Did she die in Spain? You came from Spain, did you not?'

'In Spain,' I said. 'Of the plague.' I felt a sharp twist of pain in my belly at lying about my mother.

'I am sorry,' she said, very low. 'It is hard for a young woman to grow up without a mother.'

I knew she was thinking of herself, and of the mother who had died on the scaffold with the names of witch, adulteress and whore. She put away the thought. 'But what made you come to England?'

'We have kin here. And my father had arranged a marriage for me.'

'And your betrothed? Do you like him?'

'Well enough as a cousin. Not enough for a husband.'

'And do you have any choice in the matter?'

'Not much,' I said shortly.

She nodded. 'It's always the same for all women,' she said, a hint of resentment in her voice. 'The only people who can choose their lives are those in breeches. You do right to wear them.'

'I'll have to put them aside soon,' I said.

'When I was your age, I thought I would never know how to be a young woman,' she said. 'All I wanted to do was to be a scholar. I hoped that I might become a great and learned lady and be allowed to stay at court. When my father died I thought I would be always at court: my brother's favourite sister, and aunt to his many children, and together we would see my father's work complete.' She shook her head. 'Indeed, I should not want your gift of Sight,' she said. 'If I had known that I would come to this, under the shadow of my sister's displeasure, and my beloved brother dead, and my father's legacy thrown away . . .'

Elizabeth broke off and then turned to me, her dark eyes filled with tears. 'Even if the Vatican named me a saint, Mary would not be happy,' she said. 'And I will tell you why. She will never forgive me for what they did to her mother, and for what they did to her. She will never forgive me for being my father's best beloved daughter. And the last thing she wants at court is a younger sister to show her up.'

I said nothing. It was too shrewd an assessment.

'A younger sister who is prettier than she. A younger sister who looks like a pure Tudor and not like a half-caste Spaniard.'

I turned my head. 'Have a care, Princess.'

Elizabeth laughed, a wild little laugh. 'She sent you here to see into my heart. Didn't she? She has great faith in God working his purpose in her life, telling her what is to be. But her God is very slow in bringing her joy, I think. That long wait for the throne and then a rebellious kingdom at the end of it. And now a wedding, but a bridegroom who is in no hurry to come but instead stays at home with his mistress. What do you see for her, fool?'

I turned my head, afraid that my face might show the sudden vivid image I had in my mind's eye, the dark mirror, and the words spilling out of my mouth, telling of the two queens who would rule England. A child, but no child, a king but no king, a virgin queen all-forgotten, a queen but no virgin. 'Nothing, Your Grace. I cannot see to command.'

She half closed her eyes and smiled. 'Not a fool at all then, Hannah.'

The next day she could resist no longer. The wagons with her trunks, furniture and linens had already gone. The queen's own litter with cushions and rugs of the warmest wool was standing at the door, four white mules harnessed to it. As the doctors bundled her into the litter, she cried out as if in pain, but I thought it was fear that was choking her.

We travelled slowly. At every halt the princess delayed, complaining of the jolting pace. She rose later every morning, too pained with her aching joints to face the litter until midday. Whenever we stopped to dine she sat late at the table and was reluctant to get back into the litter.

'What do you think to gain from this delay, Princess?' I asked her on the third morning, when Lord Howard had sent me into her bedchamber for the tenth time to ask when she would be ready to come.

She was standing stock-still, while one of her ladies slowly wound a scarf round her throat. 'I gain another day,' she said.

'But to do what?'

She smiled at me, though her eyes were dark with fear. 'Ah, Hannah, you have never longed to live as I long to live if you do not know that another day is the most precious thing. Every day we do not reach London is another day that I am alive.'

On the fourth day into the journey a messenger met us on the road, carrying a letter for Lord William Howard. He read it and tucked it into the front of his doublet, his face suddenly grim. Elizabeth waited till he was looking away and then crooked her swollen finger at me. I drew up my horse beside the litter.

'I would give a good deal to know what was in that letter,' she said. 'Go and listen for me. They won't notice you.'

My opportunity came when we stopped to dine. Lord Howard and the other councillors were watching their horses being taken into the stalls. I saw him pull the letter from inside his doublet and I paused beside him to straighten my riding boot.

'Lady Jane is dead,' he announced baldly. 'Executed two days ago. Guilford Dudley before her.'

'And Robert?' I demanded urgently.

Much was always forgiven a fool. 'I have no news of him,' he said. 'I should think he was executed alongside his brother.'

I felt the world become blurred around me and I realised I was about to faint. I plumped down onto the cold step and put my head in my hands. 'Lord Robert,' I whispered into my knees. 'My lord.'

It was impossible that he was dead, that bright, dark-eyed vitality gone for ever. Who could bring themselves to kill bonny Robin? Who could sign such a warrant, what headsman could bear to do it? And it was all the more impossible since I had seen the prophecy in his favour. I had been shown that he would be beloved by a queen, that he would die in his bed. If my Lord Robert was dead then not only was the great love of my life dead, but also I had been taught that my gift was a delusion. Everything was over in one sweep of the axe.

I got to my feet and staggered back against the stone wall.

'Are you sick, fool?' came the cool voice of one of Lord Howard's men. His Lordship glanced over indifferently.

I gulped down the lump that was in my throat. 'May I tell Lady Elizabeth about Lady Jane?' I asked him. 'She will want to know.'

'You can tell her,' he said.

'The charge?' I asked, although I knew the answer.

'Treason,' he said flatly. 'Tell her that. And pretending to the throne.'

Without another word being said, everyone turned to the litter where Lady Elizabeth was laboriously descending.

'So die all traitors,' said her cousin, looking at the white-faced girl who had been a friend to every man who now swung on the gibbet.

I waited till she had dined before I found my way to her side.

'The letter?' she asked me.

'I am sorry to tell you, Lady Elizabeth,' I said, 'that your cousin Lady Jane Grey has been executed and her husband . . . and Lord Robert Dudley too.'

'She has done it then,' she observed quietly. 'The queen. She has found the power of the axe. Thank God I am innocent of any wrongdoing.'

Ten days after we had first set off we arrived at the house of a private gentleman in Highgate, late in the evening.

I was housed with Lady Elizabeth's ladies, and they were up at dawn preparing for her entry into London. As I saw the virginal white gown being brushed and pressed and carried into her chamber I remembered the day that she greeted her sister into the city of London, wearing the Tudor colours of white and green. Now she was driven snow, all in white, a martyr-bride. When the litter came to the door she was ready; there was no delaying when there was a crowd collecting to see her.

'You'll want the curtains closed,' Lord Howard said gruffly to her.

'Keep them back,' she said. 'The people can see what condition I am in when forced out of my house for a fortnight's journey in all weathers.'

'Ten days,' he said gruffly. 'And could have been done in five.'

She did not deign to answer him, but lay back on her pillows and lifted her hand to indicate that he could go. I heard him swear briefly under his breath and then swing into the saddle of his horse. I pulled my horse up behind the litter and the little cavalcade turned out of the courtyard to the London road and into the city.

Elizabeth kept her eyes straight to the front and did not look left or right, but she sensed the dangling bodies on the gallows at every corner; half of them were known to her, and all of them had died in a rebellion that they believed she had summoned.

A few people called out 'God save Your Grace!' to her, and she raised a weak hand to them. She looked like a martyr being dragged to her death and, under this avenue of gallows, no one could doubt her fear.

At Whitehall, Elizabeth straightened up in the litter and looked towards the great steps of the palace. Queen Mary was not there to greet her sister, and neither was anyone of the court. She arrived to silent disgrace. A single gentleman-server was on the steps and he spoke to Lord Howard, not to the princess, as if they were her gaolers.

Lord Howard came to the litter and put out his hand for her. 'An apartment has been prepared for you,' he said shortly. 'You may choose two attendants to take with you.'

'My ladies must come with me,' she argued instantly. 'I am not well.'

'The orders are two attendants and no more,' he said coldly. 'Choose.'

'Mrs Ashley and . . .' Elizabeth looked around and her eye fell on me. I stepped back, as anxious as any other turncoat not to be linked with this doomed princess. But she knew through me she had a chance to reach the queen. 'Mrs Ashley and Hannah the Fool,' she said.

Lord Howard laughed. 'Three fools together then,' he muttered.

I did not wait to see Elizabeth settled in her rooms before I sought out my fellow fool Will Somers. He was dozing in the great hall on one of the benches. I sat beside him, wondering if I might wake him.

Without opening his eyes he remarked: 'A pair of fools we must be: parted for weeks and we don't even speak,' and he sat bolt upright and hugged me round the shoulders.

'I thought you were asleep,' I said.

'I was fooling,' he said with dignity. 'I have decided that a sleeping fool is funnier than one who is awake. The princess has come, has she?'

I nodded.

'Ill?'

'Very. Truly ill, I think.'

'The queen could offer her an instant cure for all pain. She has become a surgeon. She specialises in amputations.'

'Please God it does not come to that,' I said quickly. 'But, Will, tell me—did Robert Dudley make a good death? Was it quick?'

'Still alive,' he said. 'Against all the odds.'

I felt my heart turn over. 'Dear God, I thought he was dead.'

'He should be dead, God knows. He's seen his father and his brother and his poor sister-in-law all taken out and executed underneath his window, and yet he's still there.'

'Could I visit him without trouble?'

Will laughed. 'The Dudleys always bring trouble.'

'I mean without being suspected.'

He shook his head. 'This is a court gone dark,' he said sadly. 'Nobody can do anything without being suspected. That is why I sleep. I cannot be accused of plotting in my sleep.'

SPRING 1554

IN THE DAYS that followed I went between the queen's apartments and Lady Elizabeth's, but in neither place could I be comfortable.

The cold days turned warmer in March and the skies grew pale earlier in the mornings and later at night. The court stayed on tiptoe, watching to see what would happen to the princess. She was examined almost daily by the councillors but the queen would not see her. 'I cannot,' she said shortly, and I knew that she was nerving herself to send Elizabeth to trial, and from there it would be a short walk to the scaffold.

They had enough evidence to hang her three times over but still the queen waited. Just before Easter I was glad to get a letter from my father asking me if I could absent myself from court for a week and come to the shop. He said he was unwell, but I was not to worry, it was just a passing fever and Daniel came every day.

I took the letter to the queen and when she gave me leave, made my way to the princess's apartment.

'I have been given leave to go to my home, to my father,' I said as I knelt before her.

'Going? When will you return?' Elizabeth asked.

'Within the week, your ladyship.'

She nodded, turned away and brushed her eyes with the back of her hand. 'Good God, I am weak as a child losing a nursemaid!'

'What's the matter?' I asked. I had never seen her so low.

'I am frozen to my very bones with fear,' Elizabeth said. 'I tell you, Hannah, if fear is cold and darkness I am living in the wastes of the Russias. My only friends have been exiled, imprisoned or beheaded. I am twenty years old and I am utterly alone. I have no one's love and care. No one comes near me but Kat and you, and now you are leaving.'

'I have to see my father,' I said. 'But I'll come back as soon as he is well.'

The face she turned to me was not that of the defiant princess, the hated Protestant enemy, but that of a young woman trying to find the courage to face a death that must come soon. 'You will come back to me, Hannah? I have become accustomed to you. I ask it of you as a friend, not a princess. You will come back?'

'Yes,' I promised. I took her cold hand. 'I swear I will come back.'

My father's shop had the shutters up though it was only early in the afternoon. Daniel was putting the bolt on the last shutter and he turned round at the sound of my footsteps.

'Good,' he said shortly. 'Come inside.'

I put my hand on his arm. 'Daniel, is he very ill?'

He covered my hand briefly with his own. 'Come inside.'

I went into the shop. The counter was bare of books, the printing room quiet. I went up the rickety stairs at the rear of the shop and looked towards the little truckle bed in the corner of the room, fearing that I would see him there, too ill to stand.

The bed was heaped with papers and a small pile of clothes. My father was standing before it. I recognised at once the signs of packing for a long journey.

'Oh, no,' I said.

My father turned to me. 'It's time for us to go,' he said. 'Did they give you permission to come away for a week?'

'Yes,' I said. 'But they expect me back. I came running down here in terror that you were ill.'

'That gives us a week,' he said, disregarding my complaint. 'More than enough time to get to France.'

'Not again,' I said flatly. 'You said we were to stay in England.'

'It's not safe,' Daniel insisted, coming into the room behind me. 'The queen's marriage is to go ahead, and Prince Philip of Spain will bring in the Inquisition. Already the gallows are up on the street corners, and there is an informer in every village. We cannot stay here.'

'You said we would be English.' I appealed past him to my father. 'And the gallows are for traitors, not for heretics.'

'She will hang traitors today and heretics tomorrow,' Daniel said firmly. He took my hand and led me to the bed, which was covered with rolls of manuscript. 'See these? Every one is now a forbidden book. What are we to do with them? Burn them before they burn us?'

'Keep them safe for better times,' I said, incurably the daughter of a librarian.

He shook his head. 'There is nowhere safe for them, and there is nowhere safe for their owner in a country ruled by Spain. We have to go away and take them with us.'

'But where do we have to go now?' I cried. It was the wail of a child who has been too long travelling.

'Venice,' he said shortly. 'France, then Italy, and then Venice. I shall study at Padua, your father will be able to open a print shop in Venice, and we will be safe there.'

I waited. I knew what was coming next.

'And we will marry,' he said, 'as soon as we arrive in France.'

'And your mother and your sisters?' I asked. It was living with them that I dreaded as much as marriage.

'They are packing now,' he said.

'When do we leave?'

'In two days' time, at dawn. Palm Sunday.'

'Why so soon?' I gasped.

'Because they have come asking questions already.'

I stared at Daniel, filled with horror as my worst fears started to take shape. 'They came for my father?'

'They came to my shop looking for John Dee,' my father said quietly. 'They knew that he sent books to Lord Robert. They knew that he had seen the princess. They knew that he had foretold the young king's death, and that is treason. They wanted to see the books that he asked me to store here.'

I was twisting my hands together. 'Why are you storing forbidden books?' I cried out in frustrated anger.

His face was gentle. 'Because all books are forbidden when a country turns to terror. The scaffolds on the corners, the list of things you may not read. These things always go together. John Dee and Lord Robert and even Daniel here and I, even you, my child, are all scholars steeped in knowledge that has suddenly become against the law.'

'We are not guilty of treason,' I said stubbornly. 'Lord Robert is still alive, John Dee too. The queen is merciful . . .'

'And what happens when Elizabeth confesses?' Daniel snapped at me. 'When she names her fellow traitors, not just Thomas Wyatt but Robert Dudley, John Dee, perhaps even you. Have you never taken a message or run an errand for her? Could you swear to it?'

I hesitated. 'She would never confess.'

'She is a woman.' He dismissed her. 'They will frighten her and then promise her forgiveness, and she will confess to anything. And she is enmeshed with Dudley and Dee and Wyatt and the rest of them. I warned you of this. I told you that if you played a double game at court you would bring danger to our door.'

I was breathless with rage. 'What door?' I demanded. 'We have no door. We have the open road, because you, like a coward, are afraid of your own shadow.'

For a moment I thought Daniel would strike me. His hand flew up and then he froze. 'I am sorry you call me a coward before your father's face.' He spat out the words. 'I am sorry you think so lowly of me, your husband-to-be. But whatever you think of me, I am commanding you to help your father pack and be ready.'

I drew myself up and faced him. 'I will not come.'

'Then our betrothal will be ended.'

My father raised a hand in dissent, but he said nothing.

'So be it,' I said. I felt cold. 'I release you from your promise to me, and I ask you to release me.'

'That's easily done,' he flared. 'I release you, Hannah, and I hope that you never regret this decision.' He turned on his heel and clattered down the stairs. We heard the shop door bang, and he was gone.

Over the next two days we worked in an almost unbroken silence. I helped my father tie his books together, the manuscripts we rolled into scrolls and packed in barrels. He could take only the core of his library; the rest of the books would have to follow later.

'I wish you would come too,' he said earnestly. 'You're too young to be left here on your own.'

'I'm under the protection of the queen,' I said.

We worked all through the last night, and when he would not stop to eat I knew that he was mourning for me as a daughter that he had lost. At dawn I heard the creaking of wheels in the street and I looked out of the downstairs window, and there was the dark shape of the wagon lumbering towards us with Daniel leading a stocky pair of horses.

'Here they are,' I said quietly to my father, and started to heave the boxes of books through the door.

The wagon halted beside me and Daniel gently put me aside. 'I'll do that,' he said. He lifted the boxes into the back of the cart, where I saw the glimpse of four pale faces: his mother and his three sisters.

'Hello,' I said awkwardly, and then went back to the shop. I felt so wretched I could hardly carry the boxes from the rear of the printing shop out to the cart and hand them over to Daniel.

My father did nothing. He stood with his forehead leaning against the wall of the house. 'The press,' he said quietly.

'I will see that it is taken down, sheeted and stored safely,' I promised. 'Along with everything else. And when you decide to come back, it will be here for you and we can start again.'

'We won't come back,' Daniel said. 'This country is going to be a Spanish dominion. How can we be safe here? How can you be safe here? Do you think your names are not on Inquisition records as heretics and runaways? Newly arrived from Spain? Named Verde? Do you really think you will pass as an English girl called Hannah Green? With your speech, and your looks?'

I put my hands to my face. It was unbearable.

'Daughter,' my father said.

'All right,' I said furiously, in anger and despair. 'Enough! I'll come.'

Daniel said nothing in his triumph; he did not even smile. My father muttered, 'Praise God,' and picked up a box as if he were a twenty-year-old porter and loaded it on the back of the wagon. Within minutes everything was done.

'We'll pay the rent for the next year,' Daniel decided. 'Then we can fetch the printing press and the rest of the manuscripts.'

My father climbed in the back of the wagon and held out his hand for me. I hesitated. The three white faces of Daniel's sisters turned to me, blank with hostility. 'Is she coming now?' one of them asked.

'You can help me with the horses,' Daniel said quickly and I left the tailgate of the wagon and went to the head of the nearest horse.

'Where are we going?' I asked.

'To the docks,' he said. 'A ship is waiting on the tide. I have booked our passage to France. I already paid for you. I knew you would come.'

I gritted my teeth at his arrogance and tugged on the reins of the big horse and said, 'Come on then!' as if the horse were to blame, and as it felt the even ground of the street under its hoofs it started a steady walk and I swung up onto the driving box of the wagon.

A few moments later, Daniel joined me. 'I did not mean to taunt you,' he said stiffly. 'I only meant that I knew you could not leave your father and your People, and choose to live among strangers for ever.'

I shook my head. In the cold morning light we entered the city, just stirring to start the day, and I saw the smoke from the ovens uncurling from the bakers' chimneys, past the church of St Paul's scented once more with incense, and then we headed towards the Tower.

Daniel knew I was thinking of Robert Dudley as I looked up, past the wall to where the great white tower pointed like a raised fist.

'Perhaps he'll slither free,' Daniel said.

I turned my head away. 'I'm leaving, aren't I?' I said inconsequentially. 'That should be enough for you.'

I looked at the thickness of the walls and the forbidding gated entrances as we skirted the Tower and came back to the riverside.

One of Daniel's sisters poked her head up from the back of the wagon. 'Are we nearly there?' she asked, her voice sharp with fear.

'Nearly,' Daniel said gently. 'Greet your new sister, Hannah. This is Mary.'

'Hello, Mary,' I said.

She nodded, and stared as if I were some freak show at Bartholomew's fair. She took in the richness of my cloak and the fine quality of my linen, then her eyes went down to my embroidered hose and breeches. Without another word she dropped down to the body of the wagon and whispered to her sisters, and I heard their muffled laughter.

'She's shy,' Daniel said. 'She doesn't mean to be rude.'

I was certain that she was determined to be rude but there was no point in telling him. Instead I watched the dark flow of the water as we plodded down the road to the dockside.

I glanced back upriver and then I saw a sight that made me put my hand out to Daniel. 'Stop!'

He did not tighten the rein. 'Why? What is it?'

'Stop, I say!' I said abruptly. 'I have seen something on the river.'

He paused then, and I could see the royal barge, but with no standard flying, the drumbeat keeping the rowers in time, a dark figure at the front of the boat, two hooded men, one at the rear, one at the prow, scanning the banks in case of trouble.

'They must have Elizabeth,' I guessed.

'You can't possibly tell,' Daniel said. 'And if they do have her? It's nothing to do with us. They'd be bound to arrest her now that Wyatt . . .'

'If they turn into the Tower then they have her on board and they are taking her to her death,' I said flatly. 'And Lord Robert will die too.'

He went to flick the reins to make the horse move on, but I clamped my hand on his wrist. 'Let me see, damn you,' I spat at him.

He waited for a moment. As we watched, the barge turned, struggled against the onrush of the tide and then headed towards the Tower. The dark water gate—a heavy portcullis that protected the Tower from the river—rolled up; this visit was prearranged to be secret and silent. The barge went in, the water gate came down, there was utter silence.

I slipped down from the wagon and I leaned back against the forewheel, closing my eyes. I could see her in her room, looking down on the green where her mother had her head swept from her body with the sharpest French sword they could find, and I could see her watching them build the scaffold that would be her own death place.

Daniel was by my side. 'I have to go to her,' I said. I opened my eyes as if I had wakened from a dream. 'I have to go. I promised I would go back to her, and I cannot betray a promise to a dying woman.'

'You will be identified with her and with him,' he whispered passionately. 'When they come to hang the servants you will be among them.'

I did not even answer him, something nagged in my mind. 'What was that you said about Wyatt?'

He flushed. I had caught him out. 'He has been tried and found guilty and sentenced to death. They have his confession to convict Elizabeth.'

'You knew this? And kept it from me?'

'Yes.'

I drew my cloak round my dark breeches, and went round to the back of the wagon.

'Where are you going?' He grabbed me at the elbow.

'I am getting my bag, I am going to the Tower, I am going to Elizabeth,' I said simply. 'I will stay with her till her death and then I will come to find you.'

'You cannot defy me like this,' he said in sudden rage. 'You are my betrothed. I have told you what we are doing. See, my sisters, my mother, all obey me. You have to do the same.'

I gritted my teeth and squared up to him as if I were in truth a young man and not a girl in breeches. 'See, I do not obey you,' I said bluntly. 'See, I am not a girl like your sisters. See, even if I were your wife you would not find me biddable. Now take your hand off my arm!'

My father climbed out of the wagon and Daniel's sister Mary tumbled out after him, her face bright with excitement.

'What is happening?' my father asked.

'The Lady Elizabeth has just been taken to the Tower,' I explained. 'We saw the royal barge go in by the water gate. I am certain she was on board. I promised I would go back to her. I was going to break that promise to come with you. But now she is in the Tower and under sentence of death, I am honour bound to go to her.'

My father turned to Daniel, waiting for his decision.

'It is nothing to do with Daniel,' I went on, trying to keep the rage from my voice. 'There is no need to look to him. This is my decision.'

'We will go to France as we planned,' Daniel said steadily. 'But we will wait at Calais for you. We will wait for Elizabeth's execution, and then you will come to us.'

I hesitated. Calais was an English town, part of the remaining English settlement in France. 'Don't you fear the Inquisition in Calais?' I asked. 'If they come here, their writ will run there too.'

'If it comes, we can get away to France,' he said. 'And we should have warning. Do you promise you will join us?'

'Yes,' I said, feeling my rage and my fear roll away from me. 'Yes, I can promise I will come when it is over, when Elizabeth is safe or dead.'

'I shall come back for you when I hear that she is dead,' he said. 'We can collect the printing press and the other papers at the same time.'

My father took my hands in his. 'You will come, *querida*?' he asked. 'You won't fail?'

'I love you, Father,' I whispered. 'Of course I will come to you. But I love Lady Elizabeth too, and I promised to stay near her.'

'What is she doing now?' one of Daniel's sisters demanded in a delighted hiss from the rear of the wagon. Mary stepped up to the side, and I heard their scandalised whispers.

'Give me my bag and let me go,' I said shortly to Daniel. I stepped up to the rear of the wagon and said, 'Goodbye,' to the lot of them.

Daniel dropped my bag on the cobbles. 'I will come for you,' he reminded me.

'Yes, I know,' I said, with as little warmth in my voice as in his.

My father kissed my forehead, and put his hand on my head to bless me, then he turned without another word and got back into the wagon. Daniel waited till he was seated inside, and then he reached for me, pulled me close and kissed me fiercely on the mouth. It was a kiss so full of desire and anger that I flinched away from him and only when he abruptly let me go and swung onto the driver's box did I realise that I wanted that kiss from him, and that I wanted more. But it was too late to say anything, too late to do anything. Daniel flicked the reins and the wagon rolled past me, and I was left in the cold London morning with nothing but a small bag at my feet, a hot bruised mouth and a promised duty to a traitor.

SUMMER–AUTUMN 1554

THOSE DAYS and then weeks in the Tower with the princess were the worst ones of my life in England, the worst days for Elizabeth too. She went into a sort of trance of unhappiness and fear which nothing could lift. She knew that she was going to die. Philip of Spain had sworn that he would not come to England while the Protestant princess was alive.

In the middle of May, the proposed month of the queen's wedding, as the weather grew warmer, still the scaffold was not built for Elizabeth; still Philip of Spain did not come. Then, one day, there was a sudden change at the Tower. A Norfolk squire and his blue-liveried men marched into the Tower to make it their own. Elizabeth went from door to window in a frenzy of fear, craning her head at the arrow slit, peering through the keyhole of the door trying to see what was happening.

Finally, she sent me out to ask if he had come to oversee her execution. 'I have to prepare,' she said. 'I am not ready to die tomorrow.'

I nodded, and went out. The green was empty; there were no sawn planks awaiting a carpenter. She was safe for another day. I stopped at the water gate and fell into conversation with one of the blue-liveried men. The gossip he told me sent me flying back to the princess.

'You're saved,' I said briefly, coming in through the door of her cramped room. Kat Ashley looked up and made the sign of a cross, the old habit forced out of her by her fear.

Elizabeth, who had been kneeling up at the window, looking out at the circling gulls, turned round, her face pale, her eyelids red. 'What?'

'You're to be released to Sir Henry Bedingfield,' I said. 'And to go with him to Woodstock Palace.'

There was no leap of hope in her face. 'And what then?'

'House arrest,' I said.

'I am not declared innocent? I am not received at court?'

'You're not on trial and you're not executed,' I pointed out. 'And you're away from the Tower.'

'They will bury me at Woodstock,' she said. 'This is a trick to get me away from the city so I can be forgotten. They will poison me when I am out of sight and bury me far from court.'

'If the queen wanted you dead she could have sent for a swordsman,' I said. 'This is your freedom, or at least a part-freedom. I should have thought you would be glad.'

Elizabeth's face was dull. 'D'you know what my mother did to Mary's mother?' she asked in a whisper. 'Queen Catherine died in poverty and hardship while her daughter was a servant in my nursery, waiting on me. Don't you think that daughter remembers that? Don't you see this is Mary's revenge?'

'But, Lady Elizabeth,' I pleaded with her. 'You said to me, every moment you have is a moment you have won. When you leave here, you have won yourself another moment.'

'When I leave here I go to a secret and shameful death,' she said flatly.

I knew I could not leave the Tower without trying to see Lord Robert. I was searched before I was allowed to his door, and I was not left alone with him. My service to Elizabeth had tainted my reputation of loyalty to the queen.

When they swung open the door he was at his desk at the window, reading. He turned in his seat as the door opened and looked to see who was coming in. When he saw me he smiled, a world-weary smile. I stepped into the room and took in the difference in him. He was heavier, his face puffed up with fatigue and boredom, his skin pale from his months of imprisonment, but his dark eyes were steady and his mouth twisted upwards in what had once been his merry smile.

'It is Mistress Boy,' he said.

'The queen commanded me to bear the Lady Elizabeth company,' I said, coming into the room, awkwardly conscious of the guard behind me. 'So I have been in the Tower with you all this time.'

His dark glance flared with interest. 'And is she well?' he asked.

'She has been ill and very anxious,' I said. 'I came to see you now because tomorrow we leave. She is to be released under house arrest to Sir Henry Bedingfield and we are to go to Woodstock Palace.'

'Released,' he said quietly. 'Why would Mary be merciful?'

'She has a tenderness for Elizabeth even now,' I volunteered. 'Not even to please her new husband can she send her sister to the scaffold.'

'Elizabeth was always lucky,' he said.

'And you, my lord?' I could not keep the love from my voice.

He smiled at me. 'I am more settled,' he said. 'Whether I live or die is beyond my command, and I understand that now.'

'My lord,' I whispered earnestly. 'You cannot die. Your tutor and I looked in the mirror and saw your fortune. He said that you are to die safe in your bed, and that you will be the beloved of a queen and the making of a prince who will change the history of the world.'

He frowned. 'Are you sure? What d'you mean?'

The guard cleared his throat. 'Nothing in code.'

Lord Robert shook his head at the idiocy of the man but curbed his impatience. 'Well,' he said. 'It's good to know that you think I will not follow my father out there.' He nodded at the green beyond the window.

There was a tap on the door behind us. 'I can't go yet!' I exclaimed, turning, but it was not another guard who stood there; it was a woman.

She was a pretty brown-haired woman with a creamy skin and soft brown eyes. She was dressed richly; I noticed the embroidery on her gown and the slashing of velvet and silk on her sleeves. She took in the scene, me with my cheeks flushed and my eyes filled with tears, my master Lord Robert smiling in his chair, and then she stepped across the room and he rose to greet her. She kissed him coolly on both cheeks.

'And who is this?' she asked. 'Ah! You must be the queen's fool.'

There was a moment before I replied. I had never before minded my title. But the way she said it gave me pause. 'And you must be Lady Dudley,' I said bluntly.

She nodded. 'You can go,' she said, and turned to her husband.

He stopped her. 'I have not yet finished my business with Hannah Green.' He seated her in his chair at his desk and drew me to the other window, out of earshot.

'Hannah, if anything changes between the princess and the queen, if you should chance to meet with our friend John Dee, I should be glad to know of everything.'

I smiled at his touch on my hand, at his words that told me that he was alive and yearning for life again.

'I shall write to you,' I promised him. 'I shall tell you everything that I can. I cannot be disloyal to the queen—'

'Nor now to Elizabeth either?' he suggested with a smile.

'She is a wonderful young woman,' I said.

He laughed. 'Child, you want to love and be loved so much that you are always on all sides at once. I've known Elizabeth all her life. I taught her to jump with her first pony. She was a most impressive child,' he said fondly. 'Give her my love and my loyalty. Tell her that if I could have dined with her I would have done.'

I nodded.

'You had better go,' he said quietly. 'Do not forget me, Hannah.'

I nodded again and went to the door. The guard swung it open for me. I bowed to Lady Dudley and she gave me a brief, dismissive nod.

Woodstock turned out to be a crumbling old palace that had been neglected for years. It was better than the Tower but Elizabeth was still undoubtedly a prisoner. At first she was allowed access to only the four rooms of the gatehouse, but she extended her parole until she could walk in the gardens, and then in the orchard.

She became increasingly confident that she would not be assassinated by Sir Henry, and instead of fearing him she became contemptuous of him. He, poor man, was worn thin by her peremptory demands.

Then, one day in early summer, a messenger came from London, with a bundle of business for Elizabeth and a letter for me, addressed to 'Hannah Green, with Lady Elizabeth at the Tower of London'.

Dear Hannah,

This is to tell you that your father is safely arrived in Calais. We have rented a house and a shop and he is buying and selling books and papers. My mother is keeping house for him and my sisters are working, one at a milliner's, one for a glover and one as a housekeeper. I am working for a surgeon, and I am learning much from him.

I am sorry that you did not come with us, and I am sorry that I spoke to you in such a way that did not convince you. I understand that you will not do as I command; I understand that you do not see why I should command. It is unmaidenly, but it is the truth of you.

Let me be clear with you. I cannot become a cat's-paw. I cannot do as you desire and hand over the mastery of our family. It is my duty and responsibility; it cannot be yours. But I will make a good husband to you. I regret that I released you from our betrothal and this letter is to ask you to promise yourself to me once more. I wish to marry you, Hannah.

I think about you all of the time. I want to see you, to touch you. When I kissed you goodbye I am afraid I was rough with you and you did not want my kiss. I felt anger and desire, all mixed up at that moment, and had no care what you might be feeling. I hope the kiss did not frighten you. You see, Hannah, I think I am in love with you.

I tell you this because I do not know what else to do with this hot stir of feelings in my heart and in my body. I cannot sleep and I cannot eat. Forgive me if this offends you, but what am I to do? Surely I should tell you? If we were married we would share this secret in the marriage bed—but I cannot even think about being wedded and bedded with you; it heats my blood to think of you as my wife.

Please write back to me as soon as you read this and tell me what you want. I wish to God you would write to me soon. I wish to God I could make you understand the fever that I am in.

Daniel

A woman ready for love would have replied at once. A girl ready for womanhood would have at least sent some sort of reply. I read it through very carefully, and then I put it at the back of a fire and burned it, as if I would burn my desire to ashes, along with his letter. At least I had the honesty to recognise my desire. I had felt it when he had held me in the shadowy press room; it had blazed up when he had crushed me to him when we parted at the wagon. But I knew that if I replied to him he would come to fetch me, and then I would be his wife, and I was not yet ready to be an obedient wife.

Besides, I had no time to think about Daniel, or about my future. The messenger from London had brought papers for Elizabeth as well as me. When I entered her rooms I found her wound up to breaking pitch at the prospect of her sister's marriage, and her own disinheritance. She was stalking the room like a furious cat. She had received a cold message from the queen's chamberlain that Philip of Spain had left his country and was sailing for England, that the court would meet him at Winchester—but Elizabeth herself was not invited. And to add insult to her hurt pride, she was to send me to join the queen and the court at once. The fool was valued more than the princess.

'This is to insult me,' she spat. 'She does not dare to meet Philip of Spain with me at her side! She knows he will look from the old queen to the young princess and prefer me!'

'He is betrothed to her,' I said quietly. 'It's not a matter of desire.'

'Then why am I not summoned to court? It's all right for you,' she said nastily. 'You're not a prisoner. You're not even my servant. You can come and go as you please. She wants you at her side. You will be able to see all your friends again when you meet them at Winchester for the wedding feast. No doubt you will be in the queen's train.'

'Perhaps.'

'Hannah, you can't leave me,' she said flatly.

'Lady Elizabeth, I have to go. The queen commands me.'

'She said you were to be my companion.'

'And now she says I am to leave.'

'Hannah!' She broke off, near to tears. 'I am ruined. If she bears a son to him, I am ruined. A son,' she muttered, cautious even in her chagrin to keep her voice low. 'A damned Spanish son. A damned Catholic Spanish son. And England an outpost of the Spanish empire, England, my England, a cat's-paw of Spanish policy. And the priests back, and the burnings beginning, and my father's faith and my father's legacy torn out of English earth before it has time to flower. Damn her. Damn her to hell and her misconceived child with her.'

'Lady Elizabeth!' I exclaimed. 'Don't say that!'

She rounded on me, her hands up, her fists clenched. 'Damn her, and damn you too for standing her friend.'

'You must have thought it might happen,' I started. 'The marriage was agreed; he would not delay for ever . . .'

She let out a wail at that and dropped to the floor.

I knelt beside her and took her hands. They were icy. 'Lady Elizabeth,' I said soothingly. 'Be calm. It is a marriage which is bound to take place and there is nothing you can do about it.'

'But not even invited . . .' She gave another little wail.

'It is hard. But she has been merciful to you.' I paused. 'Remember, he would have had you beheaded.'

'And I am to be grateful for that?'

'You could be calm. And wait.'

The face she turned up to me was suddenly glacial. 'If she bears him a son then I will have nothing to wait for but a forced marriage to some Papist prince, or death.'

'You said to me that any day you could stay alive was a victory,' I reminded her.

She shook her head. 'Staying alive is not important,' she said quietly. 'It never was. I was staying alive for England. Staying alive to be England's princess. Staying alive to inherit.'

'You must do that,' I said soothingly. 'Stay alive for England. Wait.'

I could not see much of the actual wedding service. I had a glimpse of Prince Philip as he stepped towards the blaze of gold of the altar of Winchester Cathedral, heard the soaring voices of the queen's choristers singing the wedding mass, and then the soft gasp as Bishop Gardiner raised the couple's clasped hands to show that the wedding was completed and England's virgin queen was now a married woman.

I thought I would see the prince clearly at the wedding feast, but as I was hurrying on my way to the hall I heard the rattle of the weapons of the Spanish guard and I stepped back into a window embrasure as the men at arms marched down, and after them the bustle of his court with the prince himself at the centre. And then, amid all this hustle of excitement, something happened to me. I could see the flurry of silks and velvets, hear the tap of swords against the stone walls, smell the pomade they wore in their hair and beards, and I stumbled back, feeling for the cold wall behind me to steady me, almost fainting, overwhelmed with a homesickness and a longing for Spain. I think I even cried out, and one man turned dark familiar eyes and looked towards me.

'What is it, lad?' he asked, seeing my golden pageboy suit.

'It's the queen's holy fool,' one of his men remarked in Spanish. 'Some toy that she affects. A boy-girl, a hermaphrodite.'

'Good God, a wizened old maid served by no maid at all,' someone quipped. The prince said 'Hush,' but absent-mindedly, as if he was not defending a new wife but reprimanding a familiar offence.

'Are you sick, child?' he asked me in Spanish.

One of his companions stepped forward and took my hand. 'The prince asks are you sick?' he demanded in careful English.

'I am not sick,' I said in English, hoping that no one would hear the vestiges of my accent. 'I was startled by the prince.'

'You startled her only,' he laughed, turning to the prince and speaking in Spanish. 'God grant that you may startle her mistress.'

'She's more likely to startle him,' someone remarked. 'God save us, how are we to put our prince to bed with such an aged dame?'

'And a virgin,' someone else replied. 'Not even a willing widow.'

'And she's so dull,' the first one persisted.

'Enough,' the prince said clearly, speaking in Spanish, thinking that only they would understand. 'I have wedded her, and I shall bed her, and if you hear that I cannot do it you can speculate then as to the cause.'

I had not forgotten Daniel Carpenter and his letter to me for all that I had thrown it in the fire after one reading. I might as well have folded it and kept it, close to my heart, for I remembered every word that he had written, as if I reread it like a lovesick girl every night.

I found that I was thinking of him more frequently since the arrival of the Spanish court. No one could have thought badly of marriage who could see the queen; from the morning that she rose from her married bed, she looked like a woman who has found a safe haven at last. She was a woman in love, a beloved wife; she had a councillor she could trust, a powerful man devoted to her well-being. I thought that if a woman as fiercely virginal and as intensely spiritual as the queen could find love, then so perhaps could I. A woman might blossom into being a wife, not be trimmed down to fit. And this made me think that Daniel might be the man I could turn to, could trust. Daniel, who loved me.

He also came to my mind for his fears and his cautions, even though I had scoffed at them at the time. Though the Spanish court drew me in, I knew that Daniel had been right to take his family and my father out of the country. These were early days, but there were signs that the queen's fabled mercy—so generous to those who challenged her throne—might not extend to those who insulted her faith.

I thought I should write to Daniel, and to my father, and send the letter by some of the many soldiers who were going to Calais to refortify the town against the French, now doubly our enemy since we had a Spanish king.

Dear Daniel,

I did not reply to you earlier because I did not know what to say. Besides, I have been with the princess at Woodstock and could not have got a letter to you. I am now with the queen at Winchester and we will soon go to London when I can send you this letter.

I am very glad that your business took you to Calais, and I propose to join you and my father when matters change here for me, just as we agreed. I think you judged rightly when you should leave and I am ready to join you in good time.

I read your letter very carefully, Daniel, and I think of you often. To answer you with honesty, I am not eager for marriage as yet, but when you speak to me as you did in your letter, and when you kissed me on parting, I felt a delight I cannot name. You did not frighten me, Daniel; I liked your kiss. I would have you as my husband, when I am released from court, when the time is right and we are both equally ready. I accept your proposal that we should be betrothed but I need to see my way clear to marriage.

I do not want to turn you into a cat's-paw in your own home; you are wrong to fear that and to reproach me with a desire I do not have. I do not want to rule over you, but I do not want you to rule over me. I need to be a woman in my own right, and not only a wife. I have travelled far and lived according to my own means, and I seem to have adopted a lad's pride along with breeches. I would not mislead you in this, Daniel. I cannot be a servant to a husband; I would have to be his friend and comrade. I write to ask you if you could have a wife like this.

I enclose a letter for my father. He will tell you the rest of my news. I do not forget that I went from you only to bear the princess company in the Tower. She is now released from the Tower but she is still a prisoner. I know if I were an ordinary betrothed girl I would have no obligations but to you—but, Daniel, I am not a girl like that. I want to complete my service to the princess and to the queen and then, and only then, come to you. I hope you can understand this.

But I should like to be betrothed to you, if we can agree . . .
Hannah

I folded the letter up and put it away, ready to send to Daniel when the court moved to London in August.

The queen and her new husband settled into the Palace of Whitehall and started to establish the routines of a joint court.

I was in her chamber early one morning, waiting for her to come to Mass, when she emerged in her nightgown and knelt in silence before the prie-dieu. Something in her silence told me that she was deeply moved, and I knelt behind her, bowed my head and waited. Jane Dormer came from the queen's bedroom where she slept when the king was not with his wife and knelt down too, her head bowed. After a good half-hour of silent prayer, the queen still rapt on her knees, I shuffled cautiously towards Jane and whispered in a voice so low that it could not disturb the queen. 'What's happening?'

'She's missed her course,' Jane said, her voice a tiny thread of sound.

'She is with child?' I could hardly believe it. And I did not feel the joy I would have expected at the prospect of Mary's dreams coming true. 'Really with child?'

She heard the doubt in my voice and turned a hard gaze on me. 'What is it you doubt, fool? My word? Hers?'

'I doubt no one,' I said quickly. 'Please God it is so. And no one could want it more than I.'

Jane shook her head. 'No one could want it more than she,' she said, nodding towards the kneeling queen, 'for she has prayed to carry a son for England since she was old enough to pray.'

The queen said nothing to the king nor to the court, but Jane watched her with the devotion of a mother and next month, in September, when the queen did not bleed, she gave me a small triumphant nod and I grinned back. The queen told the king in secret, but anyone seeing his redoubled tenderness towards her must have guessed that she was carrying his child.

Their happiness illuminated the palace, and for the first time I lived at a royal court that was alive with flirtation and music and dancing and parties and in the heart of it all was the queen, serene and smiling, with her young husband always lovingly at her side. We were the richest, most elegant court in the whole of Christendom, and we knew it.

In October the queen was informed that Elizabeth was sick again.

'She can see my doctors if she insists,' she said absently to me. 'Would you go with them, Hannah? And see if she is as bad as she claims? I don't want to be unkind to her. If she would just admit her part in the plot I would release her. I am carrying an heir to the throne, an heir for England and for the whole Spanish empire. This will be the greatest prince the world has ever known. Elizabeth can admit her fault and I will forgive her. And then she should be married; the king has suggested his cousin, the Duke of Savoy. Tell Elizabeth that this time of waiting and suspicion can be at an end; tell her I am with child. Tell her I shall have my baby in early May. Any hopes she had of the throne will be over by next summer. Make sure she understands, Hannah. There has been bad blood between us but it can be over as soon as she consents.'

I knelt to her and bowed my head. 'I shall miss being with you,' I said honestly. 'Especially now that you are so happy.'

She put her hand on my head. 'I shall miss you too, my little fool,' she said. 'But you shall come back in time for the Christmas feast, and after that you shall bear me company when I am confined.'

'Your Grace, I shall be so pleased to bear you company.'

'A spring baby,' she said dreamily. 'A little spring lamb of God. Won't that be wonderful, Hannah? An heir for England and for Spain.'

At Woodstock I found Elizabeth very ill. No one could have doubted her frailty. She was in bed, exhausted and fat, and looked years older than twenty-one. With her jowls bloated by illness Elizabeth bore a startling resemblance to the portraits of her father in his later years.

I waited till the physicians had seen her and bled her and she had rested before I went into her bedchamber.

'Lady Elizabeth,' I said and dropped to my knees by the bed.

'Faithless,' she said, hardly opening her eyes.

I had to choke back a giggle at her tendency to drama. 'Oh, my lady,' I said reproachfully. 'You know I have to go where I am bid.'

'I know you went dancing off to Winchester for the wedding and I have not seen you since.' Her voice rose to match her temper.

'The queen commanded me to go with her to London and now she has sent me to you. And I bring a message.'

She raised herself a little on her pillows. 'I am almost too sick to listen, so tell me briefly. Am I to be released?'

'If you will admit your fault.'

Her dark eyes flared under the puffy eyelids. 'Tell me what she said.'

I recited to her what the queen had offered. I spared her nothing, not the news of the pregnancy, her sister's willingness to be friends again.

I thought she would rage when she heard the queen was with child, but she did not even comment. 'I will think about what you have told me,' she said, following her usual instinct to buy time. 'Are you to stay with me? Or take an answer back to her?'

'I am not to go back to court until Christmas,' I said. Temptingly, I added: 'If you were to beg her forgiveness perhaps you could be at the court for Christmas. It's very gay now, Princess, the court is filled with handsome grandees and there is dancing every night. And you would be the virgin princess in England, at the greatest court in the world.'

'I'm not a child to tempt with toys,' she said with quiet dignity. 'And I am not a fool. You can go now, Hannah, you have served her and done her bidding. But for the rest of your stay here you shall serve me.'

WINTER 1554–SPRING 1555

CHRISTMAS CAME AND WENT and Elizabeth would not confess. There was no joy for me either, as I was ordered to stay with her until she begged for forgiveness. Woodstock was a malevolent house in winter, freezing cold and damp. I had been in good health when I arrived, and yet even I could feel myself growing weak. For Elizabeth, it was a nightmare.

But to everyone's surprise, the queen weakened first. As the bitter winter melted into a wet spring, Elizabeth was bidden to court, without having to confess, and I was ordered to ride in her train. It was not the return she might have wanted; she was brought in almost as a prisoner. We skirted the city—the queen had ordered that Elizabeth should not ride down the great roads of London—but as we went through the little lanes I felt my heart skip a beat in terror, and I pulled up my horse in the middle of the lane and made the princess stop.

'Go on, fool,' she said ungraciously. 'Kick him on.'

'God help me, God help me,' I babbled.

'What is it?'

Seeing me stock-still, Sir Henry Bedingfield's man turned his horse and came back. 'Come on now,' he said roughly, taking the bridle and pulling my horse forward. 'Orders are to keep moving.'

'My God,' I said again. It was all I could say.

Elizabeth came up alongside. 'Look, she's white as a sheet and shaking. Hannah? What is it?'

'Smoke,' was all I could say. 'Fire.'

'Oh, it's the Smithfield fires,' the soldier said. 'That's upset the lass. It's that, isn't it, bairn?'

At Elizabeth's quick look of enquiry he explained. 'New laws. Heretics are put to death by burning. They're burning today in Smithfield.'

'Burning?' Elizabeth demanded. 'Burning heretics? You mean Protestants? In London? Today?' Her eyes were blazing black with anger.

'Aye,' he said briefly. 'It's a new world. A new queen on the throne, a new king at her side, and a new law to match. We've had nothing but foul weather and bad luck since King Henry broke with the Pope. But now the Pope's rule is back and the Holy Father will bless England again and we can have a son and heir and decent weather.'

Elizabeth said not one word. She took her pomander from her belt, put it in my hand and held my hand up to my nose so I could smell the aromatic scent of dried orange and cloves.

We rode to Hampton Court in an icy silence and we were greeted as prisoners with a guard. They bundled us in the back door as if they were ashamed to greet us. But once the door of her private rooms was locked behind us, Elizabeth turned and took my cold hands in hers.

'I could not smell smoke,' she said. 'Nobody could. The soldier only knew that they were burning today; he could not smell it.'

Still I said nothing.

'It was your gift, wasn't it?' she asked curiously.

'Yes,' I admitted.

'You were sent by God to warn me that this was happening,' she said.

I nodded, though I knew that it was my own terror she had seen, the horror I had felt as a child when they had dragged my own mother from our house to tie her to a stake and light the fire under her feet.

Princess Elizabeth went to the window, knelt and put her bright head in her hands. 'Dear God, thank you for sending me this messenger with this vision,' I heard her say softly. 'I understand it, I understand my destiny today as I have never done before. Bring me to my throne that I may do my duty for you and for my people. Amen.'

She rose to her feet. 'You have given me a vision today, Hannah. I knew it before, but now I have seen it in your eyes. I have to be queen of this country and put a stop to this horror.'

In the evening, before dinner, I was summoned to the queen's rooms and found her in conference with the king and with the new arrival and greatest favourite: the archbishop and papal legate, Cardinal Reginald Pole. I was in the presence chamber before I saw him, for if I had known he was there I would never have crossed the threshold. I was immediately, instinctively afraid of him.

He glanced up as I came into the room and his gaze flicked indifferently over me, but the queen held out her hands in greeting. I ran to her and dropped to my knee at her feet.

'Your Grace!'

'My little fool,' she said tenderly.

I looked up at her and saw at once the changes in her appearance made by her pregnancy. Her belly was a proud curve only partly concealed by the loosened panel of her stomacher and the wider cut of her gown, and I thought how proudly she must be letting out the lacing every day to accommodate the growing child.

With her hand resting on my head in blessing she turned to the two other men. 'This is my dear little fool Hannah, who has been with me since the death of my brother. She is a faithful, loving girl and I use her as my little emissary with Elizabeth, who trusts her too.' She turned to me. 'She is here?'

'Just arrived,' I said.

She tapped my shoulder to bid me rise and I warily got to my feet and looked at the two men.

'You see visions?' the cardinal asked. 'Hear voices?'

'Very rarely,' I said shortly, trying to keep my accent as English as possible. 'And unfortunately, never at times of my choosing.'

'She saw that I would be queen,' Mary said. 'And she foretold my brother's death. And she came to the attention of her first master because she saw an angel in Fleet Street.'

The cardinal smiled at the king. 'Can you advise us, holy fool? We are about God's business as it has not been done in England for generations. We are bringing the country back to the church. We are making good what has been bad for so long.'

I hesitated. It was clear to me that this was more rhetoric than a question demanding an answer. But the queen looked to me to speak.

'I would think it should be done gently,' I said. 'But that is my opinion, not the voice of my gift. I just wish that it could be done gently.'

'It should be done quickly and powerfully,' the queen said. 'The longer it takes the more doubts will emerge.'

'One should never offend more men than one can persuade,' her husband, ruler of half of Europe, told her.

I saw her melt at his voice, but she did not change her opinion. 'These are a stubborn people,' she said. 'Given a choice they are like children who will go from apple to plum and take a bite out of each, and spoil everything.'

The cardinal nodded at the king. 'Her Grace is right,' he said. 'Best that we should root out heresy, destroy it, and have the country at peace and in the old ways in one move.'

The king looked thoughtful. 'We must do it quickly and clearly, but with mercy,' he said. He turned to the queen. 'You have to be a gentle mother to your people. They have to be persuaded, not forced.'

Sweetly, she put her hand on her swelling belly. 'I want to be a gentle mother indeed,' she said.

He put his hand over her own. 'I know it,' he said. 'Who should know better than I? And together we will make a holy Catholic inheritance for this young man of ours so that when he comes to his throne, here, and in Spain, he will be doubly blessed with the greatest lands in Christendom and the greatest peace the world has ever known.'

SPRING–SUMMER 1555

AT HAMPTON COURT they made the room ready for the queen's confinement. The privy chamber behind her bedroom was hung with tapestries especially chosen for their holy and encouraging scenes. The windows were bolted shut so that not a breath of air should come into the room. They tied the posts of the bed with straps that she might cling to while her labour tore her thirty-nine-year-old body apart. The bed was dressed with a magnificent counterpane which the queen and her ladies had been embroidering since her wedding day. There were great log piles beside the fireplace so that the room could be heated to fever pitch. They shrouded the floors with carpets so that every sound should be muffled and they brought in the magnificent royal cradle with a 240-piece layette for the boy who would be born within the next six weeks.

In the first week of May, the queen said farewell to the court and went through the doors of her privy chamber to the darkened interior where she must stay until the birth of her boy, and for six weeks after that, before being churched. The only people to see her would be her ladies; the queen's council would have to take their orders from the king, acting in her stead.

The baby was a little late; the weeks came and went with no sign of him. The midwives predicted a stronger baby for taking his own time and an easier labour when it started. But as May went by they started to remark that it was an exceptionally late baby.

While the long hot dull weeks of waiting dragged on, I sat with

Queen Mary in the shrouded room. Sometimes I read to her from the Bible in Spanish, sometimes I gave her little pieces of news about the court, or told her Will Somers's latest nonsense. I took flowers in for her, hedgerow flowers like daisies, and then the little roses in bud.

She took them with a smile of pleasure. 'What, are the roses in bud already?'

'Yes, Your Grace.'

'I shall be sorry to miss the sight of them this year.'

As I had feared, the darkness and quietness of the room was preying on her spirits. I had seen her unhappy and fearful before and I recognised the gauntness of her face as the shine was rubbed off her.

Elizabeth, in contrast, was now free to go where she would, and grew more and more confident as the summer drew on. She had lost the fleshiness that had come with her illness; she was filled with energy and zest for life. The Spanish adored her—her colouring alone was fascinating to them. When she rode her great grey hunter in her green riding habit with her copper hair spread out on her shoulders, they called her Enchantress, and Beautiful Brass-head. Elizabeth would protest at the fuss they made, and so encourage them even more.

King Philip never checked them, though a more careful brother-in-law would have guarded against Elizabeth's head being turned by the flattery of his court. Nor did he speak now of her marrying and going away from England. Indeed, he made it clear that Elizabeth was an honoured member of the court and heir to the throne.

I thought this was mostly policy on his part, but then one day I was looking from the palace window to a sheltered lawn on the south side of the palace and I saw a couple walking, heads close together, half hidden and then half revealed by the dark strong yew trees. I smiled as I watched this clandestine courtship.

But then the girl turned her head and I saw a flash from under her dark hood, the unmistakable glint of copper hair. The girl was Elizabeth, and the man walking beside her, close enough to touch but not touching, was Prince Philip.

I put myself outside Elizabeth's door that night and waited for her and her ladies to go to dinner.

'Ah, fool,' she said pleasantly as she came out of her rooms. 'Are you dining with me?'

'If you wish, Princess,' I said politely, falling into her train. 'I saw a curious thing today in the garden.'

'In which garden?' she asked.

'The summer garden,' I said. 'I saw two lovers walking side by side.'

'Not lovers,' she said easily. 'You lack the Sight if you saw lovers, my fool. That was the king and I, walking together.'

'You looked like lovers,' I said flatly, 'from where I was standing. You looked like a courting couple. And if the queen had seen you and her husband today, she would banish you to Woodstock in a moment.'

Elizabeth gave a dizzy laugh. 'Oh no, for he would not let her.'

'He? He does not give the orders here.'

'He is king,' she pointed out. 'He told her I should be treated with respect, and I am. He told her that I should be free to come and go as I wish, and I am. He will tell her that I am to stay at court, and I will. And, he will tell her that I shall be free to meet whom I choose, and talk with whom I choose, and, in short, do anything at all that I choose.'

I gasped that she could leap so far in her confidence. 'You will always be under suspicion.'

'Not I,' she said. 'Not any more. I could be caught with a dozen pikes in my laundry basket tomorrow, and I would not be charged. He will protect me.'

'Princess, this is the most dangerous game you are playing,' I warned her. 'I have never heard you so reckless before.'

'If he loves me then nothing can touch me,' she said, her voice very low. 'And I can make him love me.'

'He cannot intend anything but your dishonour, and her heartbreak,' I said fiercely.

'Oh, he intends nothing at all.' She was gleaming with pleasure. 'He is beyond intentions. I have him on the run. D'you not know the pleasure of turning a man's head, Hannah? Let me tell you, it is better than anything. And when the man is the most powerful man in Christendom, the King of England and Prince of Spain, and the husband of your icy, arrogant, tyrannical ugly old sister, it is the greatest joy that can be had!'

In mid-June the queen, still pregnant, broke with convention to release herself from the confinement chamber. The physicians could not say that she would be any worse for being outside. In the cool of the morning or in the shadowy evening she would stroll slowly in her private garden, attended only by her ladies and the members of her household.

'Your Grace.' I dropped to one knee as I met her in the privy garden one day. She had been looking at the fast flow of the river past the boat pier. She turned an unseeing dark gaze to me. 'Oh, Hannah.'

'Are you well, Your Grace?'

She tried to smile. 'No, my child. I am not very well.'

'Are you in pain?'

She shook her head. 'I should be glad of pain, of labour pains. No, Hannah. I feel nothing, not in my body, not in my heart.'

I drew a little closer. 'Perhaps these are the fancies that come before birth,' I said soothingly.

She shook her head. 'No, I don't think so.' She held out her hands to me, as patient as a sick child. 'Can't you see, Hannah? With your gift? Can you see, and tell me the truth?'

Almost unwillingly I took her hands, and at her touch I felt a rush of despair as cold as if I had fallen into the river that flowed beneath the pier. She saw the shock in my face, and read it rightly at once.

'He's gone, hasn't he?' she whispered. 'I have somehow lost him.'

'I wouldn't know, Your Grace,' I stumbled. 'I'm no physician. I wouldn't have the skill to judge . . .'

She shook her head, the bright sunlight glinting on the rich embroidery of her hood, on the gold hoops in her ears, all this worldly wealth encasing heartbreak. 'I knew it,' she said. 'I had a son in my belly and now he is gone. I feel an emptiness where I used to feel a life.'

'Oh, Your Grace!' I cried out. 'There can be another child. Where one has been made you can make another.'

She did not even seem to hear me. She let her hands lie in mine and she looked towards the river as if she would want it to wash her away.

'Your Grace?' I whispered, very quietly. 'Queen Mary? Dearest Mary?'

When she turned her face to me her eyes were filled with tears. 'It's all wrong,' she said, and her voice was low and utterly desolate. 'It has been going wrong since Elizabeth's mother took my father from us and broke my mother's heart, and nothing can put it right again. It's been going wrong since Elizabeth's mother won my father to sin and led him from his faith so that he lived and died in torment. It's all wrong, Hannah, and I cannot put it right though I have tried and tried. It is too much for me. And now Elizabeth has taken my husband from me, the only joy of my life, the only person I have ever loved since I lost my mother. She has taken him from me. And now my son has gone from me too.'

I gripped her hands as if she were a drowning woman. 'Mary!'

Gently she pulled her hands from me, and walked away, alone again, as she always had been, as now she thought she always must be. I knew that she was walking with the tears streaming down her cheeks. She could not ask for help; she could not receive help. The pain in her heart was that of loss. She had lost the love of her father; she had lost her mother. Now she had lost her child, and every day, in full view of the court, she was losing her husband to her pretty younger sister.

113

In July the court should have been on progress, travelling round the great houses of England, enjoying the hunting and the parties and the pleasures of the English summer, but our setting out had been delayed, waiting for the birth of the prince, and now, twelve weeks late, nobody truly believed that the prince would come.

Nobody said anything to the queen—that was the worst of it. She had lost a child which meant more to her than the world itself, and nobody comforted her. She was surrounded by a wall of polite silence, but they smiled when she had gone by, and some of them laughed behind their hands and said that she was an old and foolish woman and that she had mistaken the drying up of her courses for a pregnancy! and what a fool she was! and what a fool she had made of the king!

She must have known how they spoke of her, and the bitter twist of her mouth showed her hurt, but she walked with her head high through a summertime court that was buzzing with malice and gossip, and she still said nothing. At the end of July, the midwives packed up their dozens of bandages, put away the embroidered white silk layette, packed away the bonnets, the little bootees, the petticoats and the swaddling bands and finally carried the magnificent wooden cradle from the birthing room. The servants took down the tapestries from the windows and the walls, the thick Turkish rugs from the floor, the straps and the rich bedding from the bed. Without any word of explanation the matter was closed. The court moved in an almost silent procession to Oatlands Palace and took up residence so quietly that you would have thought that someone had died in hiding, of shame.

I had a letter from my father in August, asking me when I would join them at Calais. Indeed, I was anxious to go. I wanted to be with my father. I wanted to be far from the smoke of Smithfield.

I went to Elizabeth first. 'Princess, my father asks me to join him in Calais. Do I have your permission to go?'

Her pretty face scowled at once. 'Hannah, I have need of you.'

'God bless you, Princess, but I think you are well served,' I said with a smile. 'And you did not give me a very warm welcome when I came to you at Woodstock.'

'I was ill then,' she said irritably. 'And you were Mary's spy.'

'I have never spied on anyone,' I said, conveniently forgetting my work for Lord Robert. 'The queen sent me to you, as I told you. Now I see that you are respected at court, I can leave you, you don't need me.'

'I shall decide what service I need and what I can do without,' she said at once. 'Not you.'

'Please, Princess, let me go to my father and my betrothed.'

She was diverted by the thought of my marriage, as I knew she would be. She smiled at me, the true Tudor charm shining through her irritability. 'Is that what you are after? Do you think you are ready to be a woman, little fool? Have you studied me enough?'

'You would not be my study if I wanted to be a good wife,' I said.

She gave a ripple of laughter. 'Thank God, no. But what have you learned from me?'

'How to torment a man to madness, how to make a man follow you without even turning your head, and how to get down from your horse so you press against every inch of him.'

She threw back her head and laughed. 'You've learned well,' she said. 'I only hope you get as much joy from these skills as I do.'

'But what profit?' I asked.

The glance Elizabeth shot me was one of acute calculation. 'Some amusement,' she conceded. 'And real profit. You and I have slept safer in our beds because the king is in love with me, Hannah. And my path to the throne has been a little clearer since the most powerful man in the world swore he would support me.'

'You have his promise?' I asked, amazed at her.

She nodded. 'Oh, yes. My sister is betrayed more deeply than she knows. Half her country is in love with me, and now her husband too. My advice to you, as you go to your husband, is never to trust him and never love him more than he loves you.'

I shook my head, smiling. 'I mean to be a good wife,' I said.

'Ah, you can't be that,' she said bluntly. 'You're not a woman grown yet. You're afraid of his desire. You're afraid of your own desire. You're afraid of being a woman.'

I said nothing, though it was the truth.

'Oh, go then, little fool. But when you are bored, and you will be bored, you can come back to me again. I like having you in my service.'

I bowed and took myself off to the queen's rooms.

The moment I opened the door I knew that there was something wrong. Queen Mary was crouched on the floor, doubled up, folded over her knees, her forehead pressed on the cold hearthstone at the empty fireside. Only Jane Dormer was with her, seated in the shadows behind her, in stubborn silence. When I went to the queen and knelt before her I saw her face was wet with tears.

'Your Grace!'

'Hannah, he is leaving me,' she said.

'Leaving you?'

Her eyes were sightless, filled with tears, fixed on the empty hearth. 'He is going to the Low Countries. Hannah, he is leaving me . . .'

I went over to Jane Dormer, who was stabbing her needle into a linen shirt in the window seat. 'How long has she been like this?'

'Since he told her his news, this morning. He has broken her heart, as you predicted,' she said flatly. 'Don't you remember it? I do. When I brought her the portrait and I was so hopeful and she was so taken with him. You said he would break her heart and he has done so. Him with his baby that was there and then gone. Now he has told her he is going to war against the French and she cries as if she would die of grief.'

I went to the queen and knelt beside her where she keened, soundlessly, her forehead knocking against the hearthstone as she rocked forward and back. 'Your Grace, I'm going down to the kitchen. Can I bring you anything to eat or drink?'

She sat back on her heels but did not look at me. Her gaze remained fixed on the empty hearth, but she put out her cold little hand and took mine. 'Don't leave me,' she said. 'Not you as well. He's leaving me, Hannah. He's leaving me, and I don't know how I can bear to live.'

Dear Father,

Thank you for your blessing in your letter to me. I am glad that you are well and that the shop in Calais is doing so well. I should have been glad to obey your command and come to you at once but when I went to the queen for permission to leave her service I found her so ill that I cannot leave her, at least for this month. The king has set sail for the Lowlands, and she is quite desolate without him. We have come to Greenwich and it is like a court in mourning. I will stay with her until he returns, which he has promised, on his word of honour, will be very soon. When he comes back I shall come to you without delay.

I send you my love and duty and hope to see you soon—
Your Hannah

Dear Daniel,

Forgive me, I cannot come yet. The queen is in a despair so great that I dare not leave her. The king has left and she is clinging to all her other friends. She is so bereft that I fear for her mind. Forgive me, love, I will come as soon as I can. He has sworn it is a brief absence, merely to protect his interests in the Low Countries and so we expect him back within the month. September or October at the latest, I will be able to come to you. I want to be your wife, indeed I do.
Hannah

AUTUMN–WINTER 1555

THE QUEEN RETREATED into a private world of silent misery in the palace that had been the happiest of them all: Greenwich. The king had hidden from her despair in the elaborate formality of leave-taking. Once he was gone she kept to her darkened rooms and would be served only by Jane Dormer or me, and the court became haunted by her unhappiness. She hid her face from us, deep in despair and filled with shame at how low she had been brought by love.

When she emerged to sit on her throne in the empty room it was to find that the Spaniards were openly rebelling against being forced to stay, and all the English men and women of the court were angry too. Life in the queen's service was not what it had been when the king had arrived, not what a court should be. It was like a nunnery ruled by a mortally sick abbess. No one spoke above a whisper, no feasts ever took place, there were no entertainments or gaiety, and the queen sat on her throne with a face of blank misery and retired to her rooms to be on her own whenever she could. Life at court had become long days of hopeless waiting for the king to return. We all knew that he never would.

With no man to torment, and no chance of making the queen more miserable than she was already, Princess Elizabeth took the opportunity to go to her palace at Hatfield. The queen let her go without a word.

I went down to the great gate to bid the princess farewell. She gave me a roguish wink as she put her boot in a stablelad's cupped hands and let him throw her up into the saddle.

'I wager you'd rather come with me,' she said wickedly. 'I don't see you having a very merry Christmas here, Hannah.'

'I will serve my mistress in good times and bad,' I said steadily.

'You're sure your young man will wait for you?' she teased me.

I shrugged my shoulders. 'He says he will.'

'Well, you can come to me, at any time, if you wish,' she said.

'Thank you, Princess,' I said and was surprised by my pleasure in her invitation, but nobody could resist Elizabeth's charm.

'Don't leave it too late,' she warned me with mock seriousness.

'Too late?'

'When I am queen they will all be rushing to serve me. You want to be at the head of that queue,' she said frankly.

'It could be years yet,' I rejoined.

She shook her head. She was supremely confident on this crisp autumn morning. 'Oh, I don't think so,' she said. 'The queen is not a strong woman and she is not a happy woman. In King Philip's absence I think my poor sister will fade away of grief. And when that happens they will find me, studying my Bible, and I will say—' She broke off for a moment. 'What did my sister plan to say when they told her she was queen?'

I hesitated. I could remember vividly her words in those optimistic days when Mary had promised she would be the virgin queen and restore the England of her mother to its true faith and happiness. 'She was going to say: "This is the Lord's doing; it is marvellous in our eyes", but in the end they told her when we were on the run and she had to fight on her own for her throne, rather than be granted it.'

'I say, that's good,' Elizabeth said with appreciation. '"This is the Lord's doing; it is marvellous in our eyes." That's excellent. I'll say that. You'll want to be with me when that happens, won't you?'

I glanced around to make sure we were not overheard but Elizabeth knew there was no one in earshot. She never put herself at risk—it was always her friends who ended up in the Tower.

The small cavalcade was ready to go. Elizabeth looked down at me, her smiling face bright under her black velvet hat. 'So you'd better come to me soon,' she reminded me.

'If I can come, I will. God keep you, Princess.'

She leaned down and patted my hand as a gesture of farewell. 'I shall wait,' she said, her eyes dancing. 'I shall survive.'

King Philip wrote frequently, but his letters were no reply to Mary's tender promises of love and demands that he should come back to her. They were brisk letters of business and instructions as to how the council should decide one matter or another, and the queen was forced to go to council meetings with his letter in her hands and lay before them the orders of a man who was king only in name, and force them through on her own authority. They did not welcome her as she came red-eyed into the chamber, and they were openly doubtful that a prince of Spain, fighting his own wars, had English interests at heart.

In October I was looking for Jane Dormer before dinner, and failing everywhere else I put my head round the door to the queen's chapel in case the lady in waiting had taken a few moments for prayer. To my surprise I saw Will Somers, kneeling before a statue of Our Lady, lighting a candle at her feet, his fool's peaked hat crumpled in his hand.

I had never thought of Will as a devout man. I stepped back and waited for him at the doorway. With a heavy sigh, he got to his feet and came down the aisle, looking older than his thirty-five years.

'Will?' I said, coming to meet him.

'Child.' His habitual sweet smile came readily to his lips but his eyes were still dark.

'Are you in trouble?'

'Ah, I wasn't praying for me,' he said shortly.

'Then who?'

He glanced around the empty chapel and then drew me into a pew. 'D'you have any influence with Her Grace, d'you think, Hannah?'

I thought for a moment, then honestly, regretfully, I shook my head. 'She listens only to the king,' I said. 'And to her own conscience.'

'If you spoke from your gift, would she listen to you?'

'She might,' I said cautiously. 'But I cannot command it to serve me, Will. You know that.'

'I thought you might pretend,' he said bluntly.

I recoiled. 'It's a holy gift! It would be blasphemy to pretend!'

'Child, this month there are three men of God in prison charged with heresy, and if I am not mistaken they will be taken out and burned to death: poor Archbishop Cranmer, Bishop Latimer and Bishop Ridley.'

I waited.

He looked at me and he put his arm round my shoulder and hugged me. 'Tell her that you have had a gift of Sight and that they must be sent into exile,' he urged me. 'Hannah, if these men die then the queen will make an enemy of every man of compassion. They must not die on the queen's order. She will be shamed for ever if she does this.'

I hesitated. 'I dare not, Will. You told me yourself never to meddle,' I whispered. 'Your master beheaded two wives, never mind bishops, and you didn't stop him.'

'And he'll be remembered as a wife-killer,' Will predicted. 'And they will forget that he brought peace and prosperity to the country, that he made an England that we could all love. All they will remember of him will be that he had six wives and beheaded two of them. And all they will remember of this queen is that she brought the country floods and famine and fire. She will be remembered as England's curse when she was to have been our virgin queen, England's saviour.'

I rose up from the pew and found my knees were shaking. 'I am afraid, Will,' I said in a small voice. 'I cannot have her accusing me. I cannot have anyone asking where I came from, who my family is . . .'

He fell silent. 'Jane Dormer will not speak with her,' he said. 'I already tried her. The queen has no other friend but you.'

I paused, I could feel his will and my conscience pressing against my head, forcing me to do the right thing despite my fears. 'All right. I'll speak with her,' I burst out. 'I'll do the best I can.'

I waited till the queen was going to bed that evening and was kneeling before her prie-dieu in the corner of her bedroom. I knelt beside her but I did not pray. I was going over in my mind what I could say to persuade her not to do this dreadful thing.

Finally she rose from her knees and went to her chair at the fireside. I drew the poker from the embers where it had been heating, and thrust it into the mug of ale to warm it for her. When I put it in her hands her fingers were icy-cold.

'Your Grace, I have something to ask you,' I said very quietly.

She looked at me as if she hardly saw me. 'What is it, Hannah?'

'I have heard that your prisons are holding three good men on charges of heresy: Bishop Latimer, Bishop Ridley and Archbishop Cranmer.'

'Yes. It is true that those men are charged.'

'I want to ask you to show mercy,' I said simply. 'It is an awful thing to put a good man to death. And everyone says that these are good men. Just mistaken men, just disagreeing with the church's teaching. But they were good bishops to your brother, Your Grace, and they are ordained bishops in the Church of England.'

She said nothing for a long time. I did not know whether to press the case or to leave it. The silence started to frighten me a little. I sat back on my heels and waited for her to speak and I could feel my own danger coming towards me.

When she turned to me, she was not like the Mary I loved at all. Her face was like a mask of snow. 'They are *not* good men, for they deny the word of God and the rule of God, and they win others to their sin,' she hissed at me. 'It is men like them that have brought down the wrath of God on England. God must be appeased. Only when this sin is rooted out of the country will I be able to conceive a child and be able to give birth. No holy prince could come to a country such as this. The wrong that my father started, which my brother continued, has to be reversed. It all has to be turned back.'

She broke off, panting. I said nothing; I was stunned by her passion.

'Sometimes I don't think I have the strength to do it,' she went on. 'But God gives me the strength. He gives me the resolution to order these dreadful judgments, to send sinners to the fires so that the land may be cleansed. And then you—who I have trusted!—you come here to me when I am praying, to tempt me into error, into weakness, asking me to deny God and my holy work for Him.'

'Your Grace . . .' My voice caught in my throat. She rose to her feet and I jumped up. I had cramp in my right leg from kneeling for so long and it gave way beneath me so I sprawled on the floor.

She looked at me as if God Himself had struck me down. 'Hannah, my child, you are halfway to mortal sin yourself to ask this of me. Don't take one step further, or I shall send for the priests to wrestle with your soul.'

I could smell the smoke. I tried to tell myself it was from the fire in the grate, but I knew it was the smoke of my mother burning, the smoke of the other English men and women burning in the market-places up and down the countryside. I scrabbled at the queen's feet like a cripple and she pulled her skirts away from me as if she could not bear me to touch her, and she went from the room without another word, leaving me on the floor, smelling smoke and crying for sheer terror.

Christmas was celebrated at court with much weighty ceremony but no joy, just as Elizabeth had predicted. Everyone remembered that last year Queen Mary had swirled around the court with her stomacher unlaced and her big belly carried proudly before her. Last year we had been waiting for our prince. This year we knew that there could not be one, for the king had left the queen's bed and her red eyes and thin body attested to the fact that she was sterile and alone. All autumn there had been rumours of plots and counterplots. It was said that the English people could not tolerate to be ruled by a Spanish king. Philip's father was going to hand over the empire to his son and then most of Christendom would be under his command. People muttered that England was an outlying island to him, that he would rule it through the barren queen, who did not cease to adore him though everyone knew he had taken a mistress and would never come home to her again.

The queen must have heard at least half of this gossip; the council kept her informed of the threats that were made against her husband, against herself, against her throne. She grew very quiet and withdrawn and determined. She held to her vision of a peaceful religious country where men and women would be safe in the church of their fathers, and she tried to believe that she could bring this about if she did not waver from her duty, however much it might cost her. The queen's council passed a new law which said that a heretic who repented on the stake had changed his mind too late—he should still be burned to death. Also, anyone who sympathised with his fate would be burned too.

SPRING 1556

THE COLD WET WINTER turned to a wetter spring. The queen waited for letters which came infrequently and brought her little joy.

One evening in early May she announced her intention of spending the whole night in prayer and sent me and all her ladies away. I was glad to be excused from yet another long, silent evening when we sewed by the fireside and tried not to notice when the queen's tears drenched the linen shirt that she was stitching for the king.

I was walking briskly to the chamber that I shared with three of the other maids when I saw a shadow by a doorway in the gallery. I did not hesitate. I would never pause for someone waiting to speak to me, and he had to fall into step beside me and keep to my rapid pace.

'You must come with me, Hannah Verde,' he said.

Even at the sound of my full name I did not pause.

'I only obey the queen.'

He held before me a rolled scroll and dropped one end to let it fall open. Almost despite myself I felt my feet slow and stop. I saw the seals at the bottom and my name at the top: Hannah Verde, alias Hannah Green, alias Hannah the Fool.

'What is this?' I asked, though I knew.

'A warrant for your arrest, for heresy,' he said.

'Heresy?' I breathed, as if I had never heard the word before, as if I had not been waiting for this moment every day since they took my mother.

'Yes, maid, heresy,' he said, taking my arm in a grip that I could not have fought even if my strength had not been bleeding away in my terror.

'The queen will intercede for me!' I whimpered, hearing my voice as weak as a child's.

'This is a royal warrant,' he said simply. 'You are to be arrested for questioning and she has given her authority.'

They took me to St Paul's in the city and they kept me overnight in a prison room with a woman who had been racked so badly that she lay like a rag doll in the corner of the cell, her arm and leg bones broken. With us also was a woman whose nails had been pulled from her fingers.

She nursed her broken hands in her lap and did not look up when they turned the key in the door and thrust me inside. Her mouth was pursed in a funny little grimace, and I realised they had also cut out her tongue.

I hunkered down like a beggar on the threshold, my back to the door. In my terror, I watched the moonlight stroll across the floor, illuminating first one woman then the other. The night passed in the end, though I thought that it would last for ever. In the morning the door swung open and neither woman raised her head.

'Hannah Verde,' the voice outside said.

I tried to rise to my feet in obedience but my legs buckled beneath me from sheer terror. I knew that I could not have my fingernails torn out without screaming for mercy, telling everything I knew. I could not be tied to the rack without betraying my lord, Elizabeth, John Dee, every name I had ever heard whispered.

The guard dragged me along, my feet scrabbling like a drunkard's on the stones behind us.

'Where?' I said faintly.

'Bishop Bonner,' he said. 'God help you.'

'Amen,' I said promptly, as if accurate observation now would save me. 'Dear God, amen.'

I knew I was lost. I could not speak, let alone defend myself. I thought what a fool of a girl I had been not to go with Daniel when he would have saved me. What an arrogant child I had been to think that I could weave my way through these plots and not attract notice. Me, with olive skin and dark eyes, and a name like Hannah?

We came to a panelled door, monstrous with hammered nails. He tapped on it, opened it at a call from within, and walked in, arms tight around me as if we were mismatched lovers.

The bishop was sitting at a table facing the door; his clerk had his back to the door. A chair was set at a distance facing both table and bishop. The gaoler dumped me roughly into it and stood back, closed the door and set himself before it.

'Name?' the bishop asked wearily.

'Hannah Verde,' the gaoler answered, while I searched for my voice and found it was lost in terror.

'Age?'

He reached forward and prodded my shoulder.

'Seventeen,' I whispered.

'What?'

'Seventeen,' I said, a little louder. I had forgotten the meticulous record-keeping of the Inquisition, the bureaucracy of terror. They would take my name, my age, my address, my occupation, the names of my father and mother, their address, their occupations, and only when they had everything named and labelled would they torture me until I spilled out everything I knew, everything I could imagine.

'Occupation?'

'Fool to the queen,' I said.

There was a splashing noise in the room, a childish damp warmth in my breeches and a shameful stable smell. I had pissed myself for fear. I bowed my head, mortification overlaying my terror.

The clerk raised his head as if alerted by the warm, sharp smell. He turned and observed me. 'Oh, I can vouch for this girl,' he said as if it were a matter of very little interest.

It was John Dee.

I was beyond wondering how he came to be the bishop's clerk. I just met his neutral look with the blank eyes of a girl too frightened to think for herself.

'Can you?' asked the bishop doubtfully.

John Dee nodded. 'She is a holy fool,' he said. 'She once saw an angel in Fleet Street.'

'That must be heretical,' the bishop maintained.

John Dee considered it for a moment, as if it were not a matter of life and death to me. 'No, a true vision I think, and Queen Mary thinks the same. She will not be best pleased when she discovers we have arrested her fool.'

That gave the bishop pause. I could see him hesitate. 'The queen's orders to me are to root out heresy wherever I find it, and to show no favour. The girl was arrested with a royal warrant.'

'Oh well, as you wish,' John Dee said negligently.

I opened my mouth to speak but no words came. I could not believe that he would defend me so halfheartedly. Yet here he was, turning his back to me once more and copying my name into the Inquisition's ledger.

'Details,' Bishop Bonner said.

'Subject was seen to look away at the elevation of the Host on the morning of 27 December,' John Dee read in a clerkly mutter. 'Subject asked the queen to show mercy to heretics. Subject is a familiar to Princess Elizabeth. Subject has a knowledge of learning and languages unbecoming in a woman.'

'How d'you plead?' Bishop Bonner asked me.

'I did not look from the elevation of the Host . . .' I started, my voice weary and hopeless.

'Oh! This is nothing but malice,' John Dee exclaimed impatiently.

'Eh?' the bishop said.

'Malicious complaint,' John Dee said briskly and pushed the ledger away. 'We are supposed to be rooting out heresy here, and they bring us the quarrels of waiting maids.'

The bishop glanced at the paper. 'Sympathy with heretics?' he queried. 'That's enough for burning.'

John Dee raised his head and smiled confidently at his master. 'She's a holy fool,' he said, laughter in his voice. 'It's her task in life to ask the questions that no sane man would ask.'

'Let her go?' the bishop asked, his eyebrows raised.

'Sign here,' John Dee said, sliding a paper across the desk. 'Let's get rid of her and get on with our work. The child is a fool; we would be fools to question her.'

I held my breath.

The bishop signed.

'Take her away,' John Dee said wearily. He swung round in his seat to face me. 'Hannah Verde, also known as Hannah the Fool, we are releasing you from an inquiry into heresy. No charge to answer. D'you have wit enough to understand that, child?'

'Yes, sir,' I said very quietly.

John Dee nodded to the gaoler. 'Release her.'

I pushed myself up from the chair. My legs were still too weak to hold me. The guard slid a hand round my waist and kept me on my feet.

I bowed my head to the bishop, and to the man I had once been honoured to know, and I left them with their bloodstained hands to interrogate innocent people and send them out to be burned.

When they turned me roughly out into the dirty street, I wandered around at the back of St Paul's and stumbled blindly until I felt I had put a safe distance between the tower's ominous reaching shadow and my frightened weaving steps. Step by step I found my way to our little shop off Fleet Street and hammered on our neighbour's door.

'Dear God, what has become of you?'

I managed a twisted smile. 'I have a fever,' I said. 'I forgot my key, and lost my way. Would you let me in?'

He stepped back from me. In these times of hardship everyone was afraid of infection. 'Do you need food?'

'Yes,' I said, too low for pride.

'I will leave you something on the doorstep,' he said. 'Here's the key.'

I took it wordlessly, and staggered to the shop. It turned in the lock and I stepped into the shuttered room. At once the precious scent of printers' ink and dry paper surrounded me. I stood, inhaling it, the very perfume of heresy, the familiar beloved odour of home.

I heard the scrape and clink of a dish on the doorstep and went to fetch a pie and a little mug of ale. I ate sitting on the floor behind the counter, hidden from the shuttered windows.

As soon as I had eaten, I put the bowl back on the doorstep and locked the door. Then I went into my father's print shop and storeroom, cleared the volumes from the bottom shelf of his book collection and put myself to sleep on the shelf. I tucked a couple of folio volumes under my cheek for a pillow, curled up in the shape of a G and closed my eyes and slept.

In the morning, when I woke, I was determined on my future. I found a piece of manuscript paper and wrote a letter to Daniel, a letter I thought I would never write.

Dear Daniel,
 It is time for me to leave the court and England. Please come for me and the printing press at once. If this letter miscarries or I do not see you within a week, I shall come on my own.
 Hannah

When I sealed it up I was certain, as I had known in my heart for the last few months, that there was no safety for anyone in Queen Mary's England any more.

There was a tap at the door. My heart plunged with the familiar terror, but then I could see, through the shutters, the silhouette of our next-door neighbour.

I opened the door to him. 'Slept well?' he demanded.

'Yes,' I said. 'Thank you.'

'Ate well? They are a good baker's.'

'Yes. Thank you.'

'Are you going back to court today?'

For a moment I hesitated, then I realised that there was nowhere else for me to go. If I went missing from court it was tantamount to a confession of guilt. I had to go back and act the part of an innocent woman rightly freed, until Daniel came for me.

'Yes, today,' I said brightly.

'Would you see this gets to the queen?' he asked, abashed but determined. He handed me a trade card, an illustrated label which assured the reader that he could supply all the books that were moral and improving and approved by the church.

'I will put it in her hands,' I lied to him. 'You can depend upon it.'

I put Daniel's letter in the hands of a shipmaster who was sailing to Calais that morning, and came back to a subdued court. The maids in waiting had thought I had gone to my father's shop. The queen had not missed me. Only Will Somers cocked an enquiring eyebrow at me when I came in to dinner. He made his way to my bench and sat down beside me.

'Are you well, child? You're white as a sheet.'

'I've just got back,' I said shortly. 'I was arrested.'

Any other person in the court would have found an excuse to move elsewhere to take his dinner. Will planted both elbows on the table. 'Never!' he said. 'How come you got out again?'

A little unwilling giggle escaped me. 'They said I was a fool, and could not be held responsible.'

His crack of laughter made all the neighbouring tables turn their heads and smile. 'You! Well that's good news for me. I shall know what to plead. And that's what they truly said?'

'Yes. But, Will, it is no laughing matter. I was most afraid.'

His warm big hand took my cold fingers in a gentle grasp. 'Child, we are all of us afraid. Better times coming, eh?'

'When will they come?' I whispered.

He shook his head without saying anything, but I knew that he was thinking of Elizabeth and when her reign might begin. And if Will Somers was thinking of Elizabeth with hope, then the queen had lost the love of a man who had been a true friend indeed.

I counted the days, waiting for Daniel's arrival. I decided that if I heard nothing from him within seven days I would go to the shop, pack the most precious books and manuscripts in as large a box as I could manage and take a passage to Calais on my own.

In the meantime I had to wait. I attended Mass in the queen's train; I read the Bible to her in Spanish in her room every day after dinner; I prayed with her at her bedtime. I watched her unhappiness turn to a solid-seated misery, a state that I thought she would live and die in.

One morning, as we were coming out of Mass, the queen leading the way and her ladies behind her, one of the queen's newest maids in waiting fell into step beside me.

'Have you heard? Have you heard?' the girl whispered to me as we turned into the queen's presence chamber. The gallery was crowded with people who had come to see the queen, most of them to ask for clemency for people on trial for heresy.

'Heard what?' I asked.

'The Princess Elizabeth is accused of treason!' the maid in waiting hissed at me. 'Her servants are all arrested. They're tearing her London house apart, searching it.'

Despite the heat of the crowd, I felt myself freeze, right down to my toes in my boots. 'Elizabeth? What treason?' I whispered.

'A plot to kill the queen,' the girl said in a breath of ice.

'Who else with her?'

'Nobody knows! Kat Ashley, for certain. Perhaps all of them.'

I nodded. I knew somebody who would know. I extricated myself from the train that was following the queen into her presence chamber. She would be in there for at least two hours. She would not miss me while I ran down the gallery to the great hall.

Will was not there. A soldier directed me to the stable yard and I found him in a loose box, playing with one of the deerhound puppies. The animal, all long legs and excitement, clambered all over him.

'Will, they're searching the Princess Elizabeth's London house.'

'Aye, I know,' he said, lifting his face away from the puppy, which was enthusiastically licking his neck.

'What are they looking for?'

'Doesn't matter. What matters is what they found.'

'What did they find?'

'Letters and pamphlets and all sorts of seditious nonsense in Kat Ashley's box. A May Day plot cooked up between her and the princess's new Italian lute player and Dudley—' He broke off as he saw my aghast face. 'Oh, not your lord. His cousin, Sir Henry.'

'Lord Robert is not under suspicion?' I demanded.

'Should he be?'

'No. How could he do anything? And anyway, he is loyal to the queen.'

'As are we all. Even Tobias the hound, here. Well, Tobias is more loyal because he can't say one thing and think another. He gives his love where he eats his dinner, which is more than others I could mention.'

I flushed. 'If you mean me, I love the queen and I always have done.'

His face softened. 'I know you do. I meant her pretty little sister who has not the patience to wait her turn, but has been plotting again.'

'She's guilty of nothing,' I said at once, my loyalty to Elizabeth as reliable as my love of the queen.

Will laughed. 'She's an heir in waiting. She'd attract trouble like a tall tree attracts lightning. So Kat Ashley and the lute player are for the Tower.'

I said nothing, my throat tightening with fear.

'What's the matter, child?' Will's tone was kindly. 'You're white as snow.'

'I have not been well this last week. A touch of fever.'

'Let's hope it doesn't spread,' Will said wryly.

I held to my lie of fever and took to my bed. I thought of Elizabeth, who seemed to be able to summon ill health as an alibi when she needed one, and I knew the pangs of a terror that made me sweat so much that I would have passed for a sick girl indeed.

I heard the news from the maids in waiting. Cardinal Pole headed the inquiry into the conspiracy and every day another man was arrested and taken for questioning. Kat Ashley's box in Elizabeth's London house held the first draft of a pamphlet urging Englishmen to rise up against the Catholic queen and put the Protestant princess on the throne.

Cardinal Pole started to look around Elizabeth's friends for who might have a press that would have printed such a pamphlet in secret. I thought of the sheeted press in the printer's shop off Fleet Street and wondered how soon it would be before they came for me.

I spent three days in bed, staring at the white ceiling, shivering with fear though the sunshine was bright on the lime-washed walls and bees bumbled against the glass of the window. Then in the evening of the third day, I got up from my bed. I knew the queen would be preparing to walk into the great hall and sit before a dinner that she could not bear to eat. I got myself to her rooms as she rose from her prie-dieu.

'Hannah, are you better now?' The words were kind but her eyes were dead. She was trapped in her own world of grief.

'I am better, but I have been much distressed by a letter which came to me this day,' I said. The strain on my white face supported my story. 'My father is ill, near to death, and I would like to go to him.'

'Is he in London?'

'In Calais, Your Grace. He has a shop in Calais, and lives with my betrothed and his family.'

She nodded. 'You can go to him, of course. And come back when he is well again, Hannah. You can go to the Household Exchequer and get your wages to date; you will need money.'

'Thank you, Your Grace.' I felt my throat tighten at the thought of her kindness to me when I was running from her.

She reached out to me and I knelt and kissed her fingers. For the last time, her gentle touch came on my head. 'God bless you, Hannah, and keep you safe,' she said with all her old sweetness. She gave me a weary little smile as she went to the double doors and they threw them open for her, and then she went out, her head high, her face drained, her eyes dark with sadness, to face the court that no longer respected her.

As soon as I heard the court settle to their dinner, I put on my dark green livery, my new riding boots, my cape and my cap. I took my little knapsack from my box and put in the wages I had from the Exchequer.

I crept down the side stairs and hesitated at the entrance to the great hall. I could hear the familiar sound of the household at dinner. It was the sound of my life for the past three years. I could not believe that this was no longer my home, my haven. I could not believe that this was increasingly the most dangerous place for me to be.

I turned on my heel and dashed out of the door, careless of who saw me. I headed for the river, as my quickest and least noticeable route into the city, and made my way to our shop at a dawdle. I wanted to see that the place was untouched before I approached it. Suddenly, I came to an abrupt standstill. To my horror, as I turned the corner I could see that it had been broken and entered. The door was thrown wide open; the dark entrance was lit with a flickering light as two men, three men moved about inside. Outside waited a wagon with two horses. The men were taking away great barrels of goods. I recognised the packed manuscripts that we had stored away when my father left, and I knew they would be evidence enough to hang me twice over.

I was just about to slide backwards into the alley when one of the shadows inside the shop came out with a big box and loaded it into the wagon. Something about the profile was familiar: the scholar's bend of the shoulders, the thinness of his frame below his worn cape.

I felt my heart thud with hope and fear but I did not step out until I was sure. Then the two other men came out, carrying a well-wrapped piece of the printing press. The man in front was our next-door neighbour, and the man carrying the other end was my betrothed, Daniel.

'Father! My father!' I cried out softly, and sprang from the dark doorway into the shadowy street.

His head jerked up at the sound of my voice and his arms opened wide. I was in his embrace in a moment, feeling his warm, strong arms wrapped around me, hugging me as if he would never let me go again.

'Hannah, my daughter, my girl,' he said, kissing the top of my head.

I looked up into his face, worn and older than I remembered, and saw him too tracing my features. We both spoke at once:

'I got your letter. Are you in danger?'

'Father, are you well? I am so glad . . .'

We laughed. 'Tell me first,' he said. 'Are you in danger? We have come for you.'

I shook my head. 'Thank God,' I said. 'They arrested me for heresy, but I was released.'

At my words, he glanced quickly around. I thought anyone in England would have known him for a Jew now, that furtive ever-guilty glance of the People with no home and no welcome among strangers.

Daniel crossed the cobbled street, strode over the drain and came to an abrupt halt before us.

'Hannah,' he said awkwardly.

I had summoned him to save me. By rights he should have something more from me than a down-turned face and a mumbled: 'Hello, Daniel.'

'Hello,' he said, equally inadequate.

'Let's go into the shop,' my father said, casting another cautious glance up and down the street. He shut the door behind us. 'We were packing up here and then Daniel was going to fetch you. Why are you here?'

'I was running away from court,' I said. 'I didn't dare wait for you to come. I was coming to you.'

'Why?' Daniel asked. 'What has happened?'

'They are arresting men for plotting to overthrow the queen,' I said.

Daniel's glance at me was acute. 'Were you involved in the plot?'

'No,' I said.

He gave me a hard, sceptical look, then asked, 'Have you dined?'

'I'm not hungry,' I said. 'I can help to pack.'

'Good, for we have a ship that leaves on the one o'clock tide.'

I set to work with Daniel, my father and our next-door neighbour, carrying the boxes and barrels and pieces of the press to the wagon.

It was near ten o'clock at night by the time we had finished, and a late spring moon was lighting the street. My father swung himself into the back of the wagon; Daniel and I rode on the box. Our neighbour shook hands all round and bade us farewell. At Daniel's signal, the horses leaned against the traces and the wagon eased forward.

'This is like last time,' he remarked. 'I hope you don't jump ship again.'

I shook my head. 'I won't.'

'No outstanding promises?' Daniel smiled.

'No,' I said sadly. 'The queen does not want anyone but the king, and I think he will never come home to her. And though the Princess Elizabeth's household is charged with treason, she has the favour of the king. She might be imprisoned but she won't be killed now. She is determined to survive and wait.'

He took my hand and brought it to his lips. The touch of his mouth on my fingers was warm, I could feel his breath on my skin, and for a moment I could think of nothing but his touch.

'I cannot go on living without you,' he said softly.

Our road took us past the Tower. I felt, rather than saw, Daniel stiffen as the lowering shadow of Robert Dudley's prison fell on us.

'You know, I could not help loving him,' I said in a small voice. 'When I first saw him I was a child, and he was the most beautiful man I had ever seen in my life and the son of the greatest man in England.'

'Well, now you are a woman and he is a traitor,' Daniel said flatly. 'And you are mine.'

I shot a sideways smile at him. 'As you say, husband,' I said meekly.

The ship was waiting as Daniel had arranged and we had a few hours of hard work loading the pieces of the dismantled press and the barrels and boxes of books and papers before finally we were all aboard and the sailors cast off, the barges took us in tow, and the ship went slowly downriver, helped by the ebbing tide. My father had brought a hamper of food and we sat on the deck and ate cold chicken with a strange, strong-tasting cheese and a hard, crunchy bread.

Daniel laughed at me. 'This is Calais food. You'll have to get used to it.'

'Shall we stay in Calais?' I asked.

He shook his head. 'It's not safe for us for ever,' he said. 'Soon Queen Mary will turn her attention there too. The place is riddled with all sorts of heretics.' Daniel smiled at me and put his hand over my own. 'I have found a home for us. We are going to go to Genoa.'

'Genoa?'

'They are making a community of Jews there,' he said, his voice very low. 'They want the trade contacts and the gold and trustworthy credit that the People bring with them. We'll go there. A doctor can always find work, and a bookseller can always sell books to the Jews.'

'And shall we live as Jews or Gentiles?' I asked.

His smile at me was infinitely warm. 'We shall live as suits us,' he said. 'I won't have the Christian rules that forbid my learning; I won't have Jewish rules that forbid my life. I shall accept no prohibitions on my thoughts or my actions except those that make sense to me.'

'And shall I?' I asked.

'Yes,' he said simply. 'Everything you have ever said makes sense to me only if I see you as my partner in this venture. Yes. You shall find your own way and I hope we will agree.'

My father, seated a little away from us and carefully not listening to our conversation, enacted an unconvincing yawn. 'I'm for sleep,' he said. He put his hand on my head. 'Bless you, child. It is good to have you with me once more.' He wrapped his cape round himself and laid down on the cold deck.

Daniel stretched out his arm to me. 'Come here and I will keep you warm,' he said.

I was not in the least cold but I did not tell him that as I went into the circle of his arm and let myself stretch out against the mystery of his male body. I felt him gently kissing my cropped hair and then I felt and heard his breath against my ear.

'Oh, Hannah,' he whispered. 'I have dreamed of having you for so long I could cry like a girl for desire.'

I giggled. 'Daniel,' I said, trying the unfamiliar name on my lips. I turned my face up towards him and felt the warmth of his mouth on mine, a kiss that melted the very marrow of my bones. Under his cape his hands caressed my back and then fumbled under my jerkin and linen and stroked my breasts, my throat, my belly, and I stretched out like a petted cat and whispered 'Daniel' once more. This time it was an invitation. Gently, his hands explored the contours of my body. Shyly but with gathering curiosity I let my fingers explore the soft fine hair of his chest, the warmth of his skin beneath his breeches.

Under Daniel's cloak we slid our breeches down and coupled with an easy confident delight that started breathless and became ecstasy. I had not known that it could feel like that. Watching other women and men court, even trembling beneath Lord Robert's touch, I had not known that such pleasure was possible. We parted only to doze and within an hour we woke and moved together again. Only when we saw the sky lighten through the ropes to our left did I drift from arching desire and satisfaction into exhausted sleep.

I woke to a cold morning, and had to scramble into my clothes before the sailors could see what we had been about. At first I could see nothing but the dark outline of the land, and then slowly it became clearer to me. A solid fort guarded the entrance to the harbour.

'Fort Risban,' Daniel said, standing behind me. 'Do you see the port beyond? The canals flow from it all round the city, so it is a moated city as well as a walled one.'

As the ship came into port I stayed at the side, watching the features of this town where I would make my home. The cobbled streets between the high houses would be my routes to and from the baker, from the market, to my house. This strange smell of a working port: old fish, the tarry odour of drying nets, the clean tang of salt wind, all this would become the familiar taste on my lips and the perfume of my woollen cape. In a little while I would cease to wonder how the queen was this morning, how Elizabeth was faring, and how my lord was, watching the sun rise from the arrow-slit window of his prison. All of those thoughts and loves and loyalties I must put behind me. Now I would live for my husband and my father and I would learn to belong to this new family: a husband, three sisters and my mother-in-law.

'My mother is waiting for us.' Daniel's breath was warm against my hair as he leaned against me at the rail of the ship. I looked to where he was looking and saw her, scrutinising the deck of the ship as if to see whether her reluctant daughter-in-law had arrived this time.

'Welcome to Calais,' she said to me as we came down the gangplank. Daniel she wordlessly enfolded into an adoring embrace.

He struggled to be free. 'I have to see to them unloading the press,' he told her, and went back on board and swung down into the hold. Mrs Carpenter and I were left alone in awkward silence on the quayside.

'He found you then,' she said eventually, with no great pleasure.

'Yes,' I said.

'And are you ready to marry him now?'

'Yes.'

'You'll have to get out of those clothes,' she said. 'They're respectable people in Calais; they won't like the sight of you in breeches.'

Daniel appeared and looked pleased that we were talking. 'I think I have everything unloaded,' he said. 'Your father is going to stay here with the things while I fetch a wagon.'

'I'll wait with him,' I said hastily.

'No,' he said. 'Go home with Mother. She can show you our house and you can get warm.'

He wanted to ensure that I was comfortable. He did not know that the last thing I wanted to do was to go home with his mother and sit with his sisters and wait for the men to finish their work and come home. 'I'll get the wagon with you then,' I said. 'I'm not cold.'

At a glance from his mother he hesitated. 'You can't go to the carter's yard dressed like that,' she said firmly. 'You will shame us all. Wrap your cloak around you and come home with me.'

Home was a pretty enough little house in London Street, squashed in beside others in a row near the south gate of the town. The top floor was divided into three bedrooms; Daniel's three sisters shared the big bed in the room that faced the back of the house, his mother had a tiny room all to herself, and my father had the third. Daniel mostly lived with his tutor, but would sleep on a truckle bed in my father's room when he stayed overnight. The next floor served as a dining room and sitting room for the family, and the ground floor was my father's shop facing the street, and at the back a little kitchen and scullery. In the yard behind, Daniel and my father had built and thatched a roof, and the printing press would be reassembled and set up in there.

All three of Daniel's sisters were waiting to greet us in the living room at the top of the stairs. I was acutely conscious of my travel-stained clothes and dirty face and hands, as I saw them look me up and down and then glance in silence at each other.

'Here are my girls,' their mother said. 'Mary, Sarah and Anne.'

The three of them rose and dipped a curtsy as one, and sat down again. In my pageboy livery I could not curtsy; I made a little bow to them and saw their eyes widen.

'I'll put the kettle on,' Mrs Carpenter said.

'I'll help,' Anne said and dived out of the room. The other two and I regarded each other with silent dislike.

'Did you have a good crossing?' Mary asked.

'Yes, thank you.' The tranced night on the deck and Daniel's insistent touch seemed to be a long way away now.

'And are you going to marry Daniel now?'

'Yes, I am,' I said.

'You've left court then?'

'Yes.'

'And will you not go back?' the other one, Sarah, asked.

'No,' I said, keeping the regret from my voice.

'Won't you find it awfully dull here, after living at court?'

'I shall help my father in the shop, I expect,' I said.

'Where are you and Daniel going to sleep?' Mary asked.

'Mary! Really!'

'Well, they can hardly bed down on the truckle bed,' she pointed out reasonably. 'And Mother can't be asked to move. And we have always had the best back bedroom.'

'Daniel and I will decide,' I said with an edge to my voice. 'And if there is not enough room for us here we will set up our own house.'

Mary gave a little scream of shock as her mother came up the stairs.

'What is it, child?' she demanded.

'Hannah has not been in the house five minutes and already she says she and Daniel will live elsewhere!' Mary exclaimed, halfway to tears. 'Already she is taking Daniel away from us! Just as I knew she would! Just as I said—she will spoil everything!' She leapt to her feet, tore open the door and ran up the stairs leading to her room.

'Oh, really!' her mother exclaimed in indignation. 'How could you upset Mary on your very first day? You will have to learn to mind your tongue, Miss Hannah. You are living with a family now. You have not the right to speak out like a fool any more.'

For one stunned moment I said nothing to defend myself. Then: 'I am sorry,' I said through my teeth.

SUMMER 1556

IT WAS A LONG HOT SUMMER, that first summer in Calais. I loitered in the squares, and dawdled at the fish quay to see the dazzle of sunlight on the ripples of the harbour. They called it *le Bassin du Paradis*, and in the bright sunlight I thought it was paradise indeed. But it was a breathtakingly tedious season. Daniel and I were under the same roof, but we had to live as maid and suitor; we were hardly ever left alone together. I longed for his touch, for his kiss, and for the pleasure that he had given me on the night that we sailed to France. But he could hardly bear to come near me, knowing that he must always step back, knowing that he must never do more than kiss my lips or my hand.

I was out of my breeches and into a gown in the first week and soon experiencing a constant tuition in how a young lady should behave. Daniel's mother had awarded herself the task of 'taking me in hand'.

She found a sulky and unwilling pupil. I was not naturally gifted at housekeeping. I did not want to know how to scour a brass pan with sand so that it glittered. I did not want to take a scrubbing brush to the front step. I did not want to peel potatoes so that there was no waste at all. I wanted to know none of these things, and I did not see why I should learn them.

'As my wife you will need to know how to do such things,' Daniel said reasonably enough. I had slipped out to waylay him before he entered the house and we both fell under his mother's rule.

'Why should I know? You don't do them.'

'Because I will be out at work and you will be caring for our children and preparing their food,' he said.

'I thought I would keep a printing shop, like my father.'

'And who would cook and clean for us?'

'Couldn't we have a maid?'

He laughed. 'Perhaps, later on. But I couldn't afford to pay wages for a maid at first, you know, Hannah. I am not a wealthy man. When I set up in practice on my own we shall have only my fees to live on.'

'And will we have a house of our own then?'

He drew my hand through his elbow as if he were afraid that I might pull away at his answer. 'No,' he said simply. 'We will find a bigger house, perhaps in Genoa. But I will always offer a house to my sisters and to my mother, to your father too. Surely you would want nothing less?'

I hesitated. 'I don't get on very well with your sisters, and your mother does not approve of me,' I said quietly.

He nodded, I was telling him nothing he did not know. 'They'll come round,' he said warmly.

'I hope so,' I said and watched him smile.

We were married in late June, as soon as all my gowns were made and my hair long enough for me to be—as Daniel's mother said—passable, at l'Eglise de Notre Dame, the great church of Calais. It was a Christian wedding with a mass afterwards and every one of us was meticulous in our observation of the rituals in church. Afterwards, in the privacy of the little house in London Street, Daniel's sisters held a shawl as a chuppah over our heads as my father repeated the seven blessings for a wedding, as far as he could remember them, and Daniel's mother put a wrapped glass at Daniel's feet for him to stamp on. Then we drew back the shutters, opened the doors and held a wedding feast for the neighbours with gifts and dancing.

The vexed question of where we would sleep as a married couple had been resolved by my father moving to a bunk alongside the printing press in the little room created by thatching the back yard. Daniel and I slept in Father's old room on the top floor, a thin plaster wall between us and his sleepless mother on one side, and his curious sisters, awake and listening, on the other side.

On our wedding night we fell upon each other as a pair of wanton lovers, longing for an experience too long denied. They put us to bed with much laughter and jokes and pretended embarrassment, and as soon as they were gone Daniel bolted the door, closed the shutters and drew me into the bed. Desperate for privacy we put the covers completely over our heads and kissed and caressed in the hot darkness, hoping that the blankets would muffle our whispers. But the pleasure of his touch overwhelmed me and I gave a breathy little cry. At once, I stopped short and clapped a hand over my mouth.

'It doesn't matter,' he said, prising my fingers from my lips to kiss them again.

'It does,' I said, speaking nothing but the truth.

'Kiss me,' he begged me.

'Well, very quietly . . .'

I kissed him and felt his mouth melt under mine. He rolled underneath me and guided me to mount him. At the first touch of his hardness between my legs I moaned with pleasure and bit the back of my hand, trying to stay silent. He turned me so that I was underneath him.

'Put your hand over my mouth,' I urged him.

He hesitated. 'It feels as if I am forcing you,' he said uncomfortably.

I gave a little breathy laugh. 'If you were forcing me I would be quieter,' I joked, but he could not laugh. He pulled away from me, dropped onto his back and pulled me to lie beside him, my head on his shoulder.

'We'll wait till they are all asleep,' he said.

We waited and waited but his mother's heavy tread did not come up the stairs until late, and then we heard, with embarrassing clarity, her sigh as she sat on the side of her bed, the 'clip, clop' as she dropped one wooden clog then another on the floor. Then we heard with a sharpness that showed us how thin the walls must be, the rustle of her undressing and then the creak of the bed as she got under the covers.

After that it was impossible. If I even turned the bed creaked so loud that I knew she would hear it. I pressed my mouth to his ear and breathed, 'Let us make love tomorrow when they are all out,' and I felt the nod of his silent assent. Then we lay, sleepless with lust, not touching, not even looking at each other, on our bridal night.

They came for the sheets in the morning, and would have flown them like a bloodstained flag from the window to prove the consummation of the marriage but Daniel stopped them. 'There's no need,' he said. 'And I don't like the old ways.'

The girls said nothing but they raised their eyebrows at me as if they well knew that we had not bedded together at all, and suspected that he could not feel desire for me. His mother, on the other hand, looked at me as if it proved to her that I was not a virgin and that her son had brought a whore into her home.

Within a few days I had learned to lie like a stone beneath my husband, and he had learned to take his pleasure as quickly as he could in silence. Within a few weeks we made love as seldom as possible. The early promise of our night of lovemaking on the boat that had left me dizzy with satisfied desire could not be explored or fulfilled in a bedroom with four nosy women listening.

As the summer wore on and Daniel's mother gave me the pick of the food, the breast of the scrawny French chickens, the fattest sweetest peaches, I realised that she was waiting for me to speak to her. In the last days of August she could not bear to wait any longer.

'Have you got something to tell me, daughter?' she asked. 'A little news that would make an old woman very, very happy?'

I realised what she was after. 'No,' I said shortly.

'Not yet sure?'

'Sure I am not with child, if that is what you mean,' I said flatly.

'Well, what is the matter with you?' she demanded. 'Daniel has had you at least twice a week ever since your wedding day. No one can doubt him. Are you ill?'

'No,' I said through cold lips. She would, of course, know exactly how often we made love.

'Then what is the matter?' she repeated. 'I have been waiting for you to tell me that you are with child any day these last two months.'

'Then sorry I am, to so disappoint you,' I said, as cold as Princess Elizabeth in one of her haughty moods.

'You're not taking something?' she hissed. 'You've not got some draught to take to stop a child coming? Some slut's trick?'

'Of course not!' I said, roused to anger. 'Why would I?'

'God knows what you would or would not do!' she exclaimed in genuine distress. 'Why would you go to court? Why would you not come with us to Calais? Why be so unnatural, so unwomanly, more like a boy than a girl? Why come now, too late, when Daniel could have had his pick of any girl in Calais? Pretty girls and fertile girls too. A girl who has a baby in the cradle this summer and knows her place, and would be glad enough to be in my house, and proud to call me mother.'

I felt very cold, like fear, like a dreadful uncertainty. 'I thought you were talking in general,' I said. 'D'you mean that Daniel has a woman he likes, here in Calais?' I asked.

'He never offered her marriage,' she said grudgingly. 'He always said that you and he were betrothed and that he was promised.'

'Is she Jew, or Gentile?' I whispered.

'Gentile. But she would take our religion if Daniel married her.'

'Married her?' I exclaimed. 'But you just said he always said he was betrothed to me!'

'It was nothing,' she said, trying to slide away from her own indiscretion. 'Only something she once said to me.'

'You spoke to her about Daniel marrying her?'

'I had to!' she flared up. 'She came to the house, her belly before her, wanting to know what would be done for her.'

'Her belly?' I repeated numbly. 'She is with child?'

'She has his son,' Daniel's mother said. 'And a fine healthy boy, the very picture of him as a baby.'

I sank to the stool at the table and looked up at her in bewilderment. 'Why did he not tell me?'

She shrugged. 'Why would he tell you? Did you tell him everything in all these long years when you made him wait for you?'

I thought of Lord Robert. 'I did not lie with another and conceive a child,' I said quietly.

'Daniel is a handsome young man,' she said. 'Did you think he would wait like a nun for you? Or did you not think of him at all, while you played the fool and dressed like a whore and ran after who knows who?'

I said nothing, listening to the resentment in her tone, observing the rage in her flushed cheeks.

'Does he see his child?'

'Every Sunday at church,' she said. I caught her quickly hidden smile of triumph. 'And twice a week, when he tells you he is working late, he goes to her house to dine with her and to see his child.'

I rose up from the table.

'Where are you going?' she asked, suddenly alarmed.

'I am going to meet him as he walks home,' I said.

'Don't upset him,' she said. 'Don't tell him that you know of this woman. Better women than you have turned away and seen nothing.'

I thought of the look of blank pain on Queen Mary's face when she heard Elizabeth's lilting laugh at the king's whisper in her ear.

I stormed from the house and across the marketplace, not seeing the stalls and the usual traders. I came to the door of the physician's house in a rush and then realised that I could not hammer on it and demand to see Daniel. I would have to wait. I hitched myself up onto a low stone wall of the opposite house and settled down to wait for him.

I did not plan what I might say or do. I just waited.

I heard the clock strike four and then half past before the side door opened and Daniel came out, calling a farewell and closing the door behind him. At once I crossed the road and ran up to him. 'Daniel!'

'Hannah!' His pleasure in seeing me was unfeigned. But after one glance at my white face he said: 'Is there something wrong? Are you ill?'

'No,' I said, my lip trembling. 'I just wanted to see you.'

'And now you do,' he said. He drew my hand through his arm. 'Shall I walk you home round the city walls, m'lady? Get a breath of sea air?'

I tried to smile at him but I was too heartsore. I let him lead me to the end of the street and then along a lane. At the very end of the lane was the towering wall of the town, shallow stone steps running up the inside. We climbed them until we got to the ramparts and could look north towards the horizon where England lay—England, the queen, the princess, my lord: all a long way away. It seemed to me in that moment that I had known a better life as a fool to a queen than I had being a fool to Daniel and to his stone-hearted mother and his poisonous sisters.

'Now,' he said, matching his steps to mine as we walked along the wall. 'What is the matter, Hannah?'

I did not turn the conversation round and round. I went straight to the heart of it, as if I were still a troubled pageboy and not a betrayed wife. 'Your mother tells me that you have got a Calais woman with child,' I said bluntly. 'And that you see her and her child three times a week.'

I could feel his stride falter, and when I looked up at him he had lost the colour from his cheeks. 'Yes,' he said. 'That's true.'

'You should have told me.'

He nodded, marshalling his thoughts. 'I suppose I should have done. But if I had told you, would you have married me?'

'I don't know. No, probably not.'

'Then you see why I did not tell you.'

'You cozened me and married me on a lie.'

'I told you that you were the one great love of my life, and you are. I told you that I thought we should marry to provide for my mother and for your father, and I still think that we did the right thing. I told you that we should marry so that we might live together, as the Children of Israel, and I could keep you safe.'

'You lied to me,' I said again.

'Yes,' he said simply. 'I had to.'

'Do you love her?' I asked. I could hear the pitiful note in my own voice and I pulled my hand from his arm, filled with resentment that love should have brought me so low that I was whimpering at betrayal.

'No,' he said bluntly. 'But when we first came to Calais, I was lonely and she was pretty and warm and good company. If I had any sense I would not have gone with her, but I did.'

'More than once?' I asked, wounding myself.

'More than once.'

'And I suppose you didn't make love to *her* with a hand over her mouth so your mother and sisters couldn't hear?'

'No,' he said shortly.

'And her son?'

His face warmed at once. 'He is five months old. Strong and lusty.'

'Does she take your name?'

'No. She keeps her own.'

'Does she live with her family?'

'She is in service.'

'They allow her to keep her child?'

'They have a kindness for her, and they are old. They like to have a child about the house.'

141

'They know that you are the father?'

He nodded his head.

I rocked with shock. 'Everyone knows? Your sisters, the priest? The people who came to our wedding feast and wished me well? Everyone?'

Daniel hesitated. 'It's a small town, Hannah. Yes, I should think everyone knows of it.'

'Does she know you are married?'

'Yes, she knew I was betrothed when we first met, and I told her I was going to England to fetch you and we would marry when we returned.'

'Did you not want to marry her when you knew she was carrying your child?'

'She is not one of the People,' Daniel said simply. 'And, in any case, I wanted to marry you. When I knew she was with child I was ashamed of what I had done, but she knew I did not love her, and that I was promised to you. She did not expect me to marry her. So I gave her money for a dowry and I pay her every month for the boy's keep.'

'What's the child named?'

He took a breath. 'Daniel,' he said and saw me flinch.

'I am sorry,' he said again. 'But we can overcome this. She makes no claims against me. I will support the child but I need not go and see her. I shall miss the boy; I hoped to see him grow up, but I will understand if you cannot tolerate me seeing her. I will give him up. You and I are young. You will forgive me, we will have a child of our own, we will find a better house. We will be happy.'

'No,' I said shortly.

'What?'

'I said, "No". Tomorrow I shall buy a boy's suit and my father and I will find new premises for the bookshop. I shall work as his apprentice again. I shall never trust a man again, as long as I live. You have hurt me, Daniel, and betrayed me and I will never forgive you.'

He went very white. 'You cannot leave me,' he said. 'We are married in the sight of God, our God. You cannot break an oath to God. You cannot break your pledge to me.'

I rose to it as if it were a challenge. 'I care nothing for your God, nor for you. I shall leave you tomorrow.'

We spent a sleepless night. There was nowhere to go but home and we had to lie side by side, stiff as bodkins in the darkness with his mother alert behind one wall, and his sisters agog on the other side. In the morning I took my father out of the house and told him that my mind was made up and that I would not live with Daniel as his wife.

'Hannah, what will you do with your life?' he said anxiously. 'I cannot be always with you. Who will protect you when I am gone?'

'I shall go back to royal service. I shall go to the princess or to my lord,' I said.

'Your lord is a known traitor and the princess will be married to one of the Spanish princes within the month.'

'Not her! She's not a fool. She would not marry a man and trust him! She knows better than to put her heart into a man's keeping.'

'She cannot live alone any more than you can live alone.'

'Father, my husband has betrayed me and shamed me. I cannot take him back as if nothing had happened. I cannot live with his sisters and his mother all whispering behind their hands every time he comes home late. I cannot live as if I belonged here.'

'My child, where do you belong if not here? If not with me? If not with your husband?'

I had my answer: 'I belong nowhere.'

My father shook his head. A young woman always had to be placed somewhere. She could not live unless she was bolted down in one service or another.

'Father, please let us set up a little business on our own, as we did in London. Let me help you in the printing shop. Let me live with you and we can be at peace and make our living here.'

He hesitated for a long moment, and suddenly I saw him as a stranger might see him. He was an old man and I was taking him from a home where he had become comfortable.

'What will you wear?' he asked finally.

I could have laughed out loud, it mattered so little to me. But I realised that it signified to him whether he had a daughter who could appear to fit into this world or whether I would be eternally out of step with it.

'I will wear a gown if you wish,' I said to please him. 'But I will wear boots underneath it. I will wear a jerkin and a jacket on top.'

'And your wedding ring,' he stipulated. 'You will not deny your marriage.'

'Father, he has denied it every day.'

'Daughter, he is your husband.'

I sighed. 'Very well. But we can go, can we? And at once?'

He rested his hand on my face. 'Child, I thought that you had a good husband who loved you and you would be happy.'

I gritted my teeth so the tears did not come to my eyes and make him think that I might soften, that I might still be a young woman with a chance of love. 'No,' I said simply.

AUTUMN 1556

THE FIRST MONTH in our little shop at the south city gate, I rejoiced in my escape from the Carpenter household. Every morning I awoke with an utter exultation that I need not fit myself to someone else's pattern.

Most Sundays at church I would glimpse Daniel, meticulously observant to every movement of the Mass. In their pew his mother and his sisters stole little glances at me, and once I saw them with a pretty, vapid-looking, fair-haired young woman with a baby on her hip and I guessed that she was the mother of Daniel's child.

I turned my head away from their curious glances but I felt an odd swimmy feeling that I had not known for years. I leaned forward and gripped the smooth, time-worn wood of the pew and waited for the sensation to pass. But it grew stronger. The Sight was coming to me.

The last thing I wanted was to make a spectacle of myself in church, especially when the woman was there with her child, but the waves of darkness seemed to engulf me.

I could hear the sound of a battle and someone screaming: 'Not my baby! Take him! Take him!' and at that moment there was a dreadful crash like a forest falling, and a rush of horses and men and danger, and I wanted to run but there was nowhere to run, and I cried out with fear.

'You're all right now,' came a voice and it was Daniel's beloved voice and I was in his arms, and the sun was shining warmly on my face, and there was no darkness, nor terror, nor the clatter of hoofs on stones.

'I fainted,' I said. 'Did I say anything?'

'Only "I can't take him",' he said. 'Was it the Sight, Hannah?'

I nodded. I should have pulled away from him but I rested against his shoulder and felt the seductive sense of safety that he always gave me.

'A warning?' he asked.

'Something awful,' I said. 'But I don't know what. That's what it's like, I see enough to feel terror but not enough to know.'

'I had thought you would lose the Sight,' he said quietly.

'It seems not. It's not a vision I would want.'

'Hush then,' he soothed. He turned his face to one side and said, 'I will take her home. You can leave us. She needs nothing.'

At once I realised that a small circle of people had gathered behind him to see the woman who had cried out and fainted in church.

My father appeared beside Daniel. 'Could you walk if we both helped you?' he asked. 'Or shall I fetch a litter?'

'I can walk,' I said. 'I am not ill.'

The two of them helped me to my feet and we went down the narrow path to the lane that led to the city gate and our shop. At the corner I saw a knot of women waiting, Daniel's mother, his three sisters, and the woman with a baby on her hip. She was staring at me just as I stared at her, each of us measuring the other. She gave me a smile, a shy smile, half apologetic, half hopeful. The baby she held against her was a true Jewish boy, dark-haired, dark-eyed, solemn-faced, with sweet olive skin. I would have known him for Daniel's child the moment I had seen him, even if Mrs Carpenter had not betrayed the secret.

As I looked at her I saw a shadow behind her, a shadow that was gone as quickly as I turned my gaze to it. I had seen something like a horse-man, riding behind her, bending low towards her. I blinked. There was nothing there but this young woman, her baby held close, and Daniel's womenfolk looking at me, looking at them.

'Come on, Father,' I said, very weary. 'Get me home.'

WINTER 1556–SPRING 1557

WITHIN DAYS THE WORD was out that I had fainted in church because I was pregnant, but by winter they had to acknowledge that they were wrong and that the bookseller's daughter had not yet received her come-uppance. By Christmas it was all but forgotten, and by the long, cold spring I was almost accepted as yet another eccentric in this town of runaways, vagabonds, ex-pirates and chancers.

The spring storms kept ships in port and made news from England late and unreliable. I was not the only person who waited every day on the quayside and called to incoming ships: 'What's the news? What's the news in England?' We had learned that King Philip's long desire to drag his wife's country into war against France had finally triumphed over her better sense, and England and France were declared enemies.

The spring gales threw rain and salt water against the tiles and windows of the house and chilled my father to his very bones. Some days he was too cold and weary to get out of bed at all and I would kindle a little fire in the grate in his bedroom and sit by his bed and read to him in Hebrew from the precious scraps of our Bible. He smiled to hear the old words that promised the land to the People, and safety at last.

In March, as the town went mad for King Philip, who travelled through the port on his way to Gravesend, I paid little attention to the rumours of his plans for war and his intentions towards the Princess Elizabeth. I was growing very anxious for my father, who did not seem to be getting any stronger. After two weeks of worry, I swallowed my pride and sent for the newly licensed Dr Daniel Carpenter, who had set up an independent practice at a little shop on the far side of the quay. He came the moment that the street urchin delivered my message.

'How long has he been ill?' he asked me.

'He is not really ill. He seems tired more than anything else,' I said, taking his wet cape from him and spreading it before the little fire to dry. 'He doesn't eat much, just soup and dried fruit. He sleeps day and night.'

'His urine?' Daniel asked.

I fetched the flask that I had kept for his diagnosis and he took it to the window and looked at the colour in the daylight.

'Is he upstairs?'

'In the back bedroom,' I said, and followed him up the stairs.

I waited outside while Daniel took my father's pulse and laid his cool hands on my father's forehead, and asked him gently how he did.

When Daniel came out, his face was grave and tender. He ushered me downstairs and did not speak until we were in the shop once more.

'Hannah, I could cup him, and physic him, and torment him a dozen different ways, but I don't think I or any other doctor could cure him.'

'Cure him?' I repeated stupidly. 'He's just tired.'

'He is dying,' my husband said gently.

For a moment I could not take it in. 'But, Daniel, that's not possible! There's nothing wrong with him!'

'He has a growth in his belly which is pressing against his lungs and his heart,' Daniel said quietly. 'He can feel it himself; he knows it.'

'He is just tired,' I protested.

'And if he feels any worse than tired, if he feels pain, then we will give him physic to take the pain away,' Daniel assured me.

'I thought he was just tired,' I said again, stupidly.

'I know,' Daniel said.

'How long d'you think?' I thought he would say months, a year.

'Days,' he said quietly. 'Perhaps weeks. But no more, I don't think.'

'Days?' I said uncomprehendingly. 'How can it be days?'

He shook his head, his eyes compassionate. 'I am sorry, Hannah. But he is in no pain. And he is not afraid. He is prepared for his death. He is only anxious about you.'

'Me!' I exclaimed.

'Yes,' he said steadily. 'You should assure him that you are provided for, that you are safe.'

I hesitated.

'I myself have sworn to him that if you are in any difficulty or in any danger that I will care for you before any other. I will protect you as my wife for as long as you live.'

I held on to the door handle so that I did not pitch myself into his arms and wail like a bereaved child. 'That was kind of you,' I managed to say. 'I don't need your protection, but you were kind to reassure him.'

'You have my protection whether you need it or not,' Daniel said. 'I am your husband, and I do not forget it.' He took up his cape from the stool before the fire and swung it round his shoulders. 'I shall come tomorrow, and every day at noon,' he said. 'And I shall find a woman to sit with him so that you can rest.'

I nodded; I could not trust myself to speak. Then he went out of the door into the rain and I went upstairs to my father.

As Daniel had predicted, my father slipped away very quickly. True to his word, Daniel brought a night nurse, Marie, so that my father was never alone. In the day I found a lad to mind the shop while I sat with my father and read to him in Hebrew. In April I found a new volume which had a small surviving snippet of the prayers for the dead. I saw his smile of acknowledgment. He raised his hand. I fell silent.

'Yes, it is time,' was all he said. His voice was a thread. 'You will be well, my child?'

I put the book on the seat of my chair and knelt at his bedside. Effortfully he put his hand on my head for a blessing. 'Don't worry about me,' I whispered. 'I will be all right. I have the shop and the press; I can earn a living, and Daniel will always look after me.'

He nodded. Already he was drifting away, too far to give advice, too far to remonstrate. 'I bless you, *querida*,' he said gently.

'Father!' My eyes were filled with tears. I dropped my head to his bed.

'Bless you,' he said again and lay quietly.

I levered myself back to my chair and blinked my eyes. Through the blur of tears I could hardly see the words. Then I started to read.

'"Magnified and sanctified be the name of God throughout the world which He has created according to His will. May He establish His kingdom during the days of your life and during the life of all of the house of Israel, speedily, yea soon; and say ye, Amen."'

Daniel cared for me as he had promised he would. As son-in-law, all my father's goods became his by right, but he signed them over to me in the same day and he asked Marie to stay on for the next few months. She could sleep downstairs in the kitchen, and would keep me safe at nights. Mrs Carpenter frowned her disapproval but held her peace.

She made the preparations for the requiem mass and then the secret Jewish ceremony, done the same day, behind our closed door. When I thanked her she waved me away. 'These are the ways of our People,' she said. 'We have to remember them. If we forget them, we forget ourselves. And now you know how it is done, you can teach your children, and the way of our People can be handed down.'

Daniel did not ask me if I would forgive him and if we could start again as man and wife. He did not ask me if I was longing for a touch, for a kiss, longing to feel alive like a young woman in springtime and not always like a girl fighting against the world. He did not ask me if I felt, since my father was dead, that I was terribly alone in the world, and that I would always be Hannah alone, neither of the People, nor a wife, and now, not even a daughter. He did not ask me these things; I did not volunteer them. And so we parted kindly on my doorstep, with a sense of sadness and regret, and I imagine he went home and called on the way at the house of the plump fair-haired mother of his son, and I went into my house and closed my door and sat in darkness for a long time.

SUMMER 1557

BY EARLY SUMMER the streets were filled with the sound of recruiting officers marching along, drumming and whistling for lads to volunteer for the English army to fight the French. The harbour was a continual bustle of ships coming and going, unloading weapons and gunpowder and horses. In the fields outside the city, a little camp had sprung up and soldiers were marched here and there, and bawled at, and marched back again. All I knew was that the extra traffic through the city gate did not bring much extra trade. The town became unruly with the hundreds of extra men coming through and I took to wearing a pair of dark breeches, tucked my hair up under my cap, and donned a thick jerkin, despite the summer heat. I carried a dagger in my boot and I would have used it if anyone had come against me or broken into the shop. I kept Marie, my father's nurse, as my lodger and she and I bolted the door at six o'clock every night and did not open it until the morning, blowing out our candles if we heard brawling in the street.

By midsummer the English army, half trained and wholly wild for a fight, moved out of Calais, led by King Philip himself. They launched an attack on St Quentin, and in August stormed the town and won it from the French. It was a resounding victory against a hated enemy. The citizens of Calais, ambitious to reclaim the whole of the lost English lands in France, went mad with joy at this first sign, and every returning soldier was laden with flowers and had a horn of wine pressed into his willing hand and was blessed as the saviour of his nation.

I saw Daniel at church on Sunday when the priest preached the victory of God's chosen people over the treacherous French, and then, to my amazement, he prayed for the safe delivery of the queen of a son and heir to the throne. For me, it was better news even than the taking of St Quentin, and for the first time in long months I felt my heart lift. When I thought of Mary carrying a child in her womb again I felt my down-turned face lift up and smile. I knew how glad she must be, how this must bring her back to the joy she had felt in early marriage, how she must think now that God had forgiven the English and she might become a gentle queen and a good mother.

When Daniel came up to me after church he saw the happiness on my face and smiled. 'You did not know of the queen's condition?'

'How could I know?' I said. 'I see nobody. I hear only the most general of gossip.'

'There is news of your old lord too,' he said levelly. 'Have you heard?'

'Robert Dudley?' I felt the shock of his name. 'What news?'

'Good news,' Daniel said quietly, though I could see it brought little joy for him. 'He and half a dozen other men accused of treason were released some time ago and fought with the king.'

'He came through the town? And I didn't know?'

'He fought at St Quentin and was mentioned in dispatches for bravery,' Daniel said shortly.

I felt myself glow with pleasure. 'Oh! How wonderful!'

'Yes,' Daniel said without enthusiasm. 'You won't try to find him, Hannah? The countryside is unsafe.'

'Will he go home through Calais, when the French sue for peace?'

'I should think so.'

'I will try to see him then. Perhaps he'll help me return to England.'

Daniel went pale, his face even graver than before. 'You cannot risk going back while the rules against heresy are so strong,' he said quietly.

'If I were under my lord's protection I would be safe,' I said with simple confidence.

It cost him a good deal to acknowledge Lord Robert's power. 'I suppose so. But please, talk to me before you take a decision. His credit may not be so very good. It is only one act of bravery in a long life of treason.'

I let the criticism go.

'Can I walk you to your door?'

He offered me his arm and I took it and fell into step beside him. For the first time in months I felt a little of my own darkness lift and dissolve. The queen was with child, Lord Robert was free and honoured for his bravery, England and Spain in alliance had defeated the French army. Surely things would start coming right for me too.

'Mother tells me that she saw you in the marketplace in breeches,' Daniel remarked.

'Yes,' I said carelessly. 'When there are so many soldiers and rough men and women on the streets I feel safer like that.'

'Would you come back to my house?' Daniel asked. 'I would like to keep you safe. You could keep the shop on.'

'It's making no money,' I conceded honestly. 'I don't stay away from you for the sake of the shop. I can't come back to you, Daniel. I have made up my mind and I will not change it.'

We had reached my door. 'But if you were in trouble or danger you would send for me,' he pressed me.

'Yes.'

'And you wouldn't leave for England, or meet with Lord Robert, without telling me?'

I shrugged. 'I have no plans, except I should like to see the queen again. She must be so happy now, expecting her child.'

'Perhaps when the peace treaty is signed,' he suggested, 'I could take you to London for a visit and bring you back, if you would like that.'

I looked at him attentively. 'Daniel, that would be kind indeed.'

'I would do anything to make you happy,' he said gently.

I opened my door. 'Thank you,' I said quietly and slipped away from him before I should make the mistake of stepping forward into his arms.

WINTER 1557–8

THERE WERE RUMOURS that the defeated French army was regrouping on the borders of the English Pale and every stranger who came into Calais for the Christmas market was regarded as a spy. The French must come against Calais in revenge for St Quentin, but the French must know, as we all knew, that the town could not be taken.

Then in the night, without warning, Fort Nieulay fell. It was one of the eight forts that guarded Calais, and as such was only a small loss. But Nieulay was the fort on the River Hames that controlled the sea gates, which were supposed to flood the canals round the town so that no army could cross. With Nieulay in French hands we had nothing to defend us but the other forts and the great walls. We had lost the first line of defence.

The very next day we heard the roar of cannon and then a rumour swept through the town. Fort Risban, the fort that guarded the inner harbour of Calais, had fallen too, even though it was newly built and newly fortified. Now the harbour itself lay open to French shipping.

'What shall we do?' Marie asked me.

'It's only two forts,' I said stoutly, trying to hide my fear. 'The English army will know we are under siege and come to rescue us.'

But it was the French army that drew up in lines before the walls of Calais, and it was the French harquebusiers who flung a storm of arrows that arched over the top of the walls and killed people at random as they ran through the streets, desperate to get inside their houses.

'The English will come,' I said. 'Lord Robert will come and attack the French from the rear.'

We bolted the shutters on the shop and shrank inside to the back room, in a terror that the great south city gate, so close to our little shop, would be a focus for attack. The French brought up siege engines. Even hidden in the back room of the shop I could hear the pounding of the great ram against the barred gates.

Then the clatter of hundreds of horses' hoofs was in the street outside our door, and I realised that the English army, garrisoned inside the town, was gathering for a counterattack. They must think that if they could dislodge the French from the city gates, the surrounding country-side could be retaken and the pressure relieved from the town defences.

We could hear the horses go by and then the silence while they assembled at the gate. I realised that, for them to get out, the gate would have to be thrown open, and for that time my little shop would be right in the centre of the battle.

It was enough. I whispered to Marie in French, 'We have to get out of here. I am going to Daniel. D'you want to come with me?'

'I'll go to my cousins. They live near the harbour.'

I crept to the door and opened it a crack. The sight as I peered through was terrifying. The street outside was absolute chaos, with soldiers running up the stone steps to the ramparts laden with weapons, wounded men being helped down.

I threw open the door and almost at once heard a most dreadful cry from the walls immediately above the shop as a hail of arrows found an unprotected band of men. Marie and I fled into the street. Behind us, and then all around us, came a dreadful crash. The French siege engine had catapulted a great load of stone and rubble over the wall. It rained down on our street like a falling mountain.

'I'm off!' Marie shouted to me, plunging down a lane to the fish quay.

I could not even shout a blessing; the smell of the smoke—the very scent of my nightmares—filled the air, filled my nostrils, my lungs, even my eyes, so that I could not breathe and my eyes were filled with tears so that I could not see.

From the ramparts above me I heard a high shriek of terror and I looked up to see a man on fire, the burning arrow still caught in his clothing, as he dived to the floor and rolled, trying to extinguish the flames, screaming like a heretic as his body burned.

I ducked from the doorway and started to run, anywhere to get away from the smell of a man burning. I wanted to find Daniel. He seemed like the only safe haven in a world turned into a nightmare.

I pressed myself back against the walls of the houses as a company of horse mustered in the street. Then I found the courage to dart round the dangerous hoofs and duck into a refuge further down the street as a great charge of horsemen came thundering by. I looked up and saw the standard they were carrying before them—the bear and staff embroidered on the bright ground—and I called out: 'Robert Dudley!'

A man looked over at me. 'At the head, where he always is.'

I pushed my way back, afraid of nothing now, turning horses' heads to one side, sliding between their big flanks. 'Let me by, let me by, sir. I am going to Robert Dudley.'

It became like a dream. The great horses with the men mounted as high as centaurs above me. Their heavy armour shining in the sunshine, clashing when they brushed one against another, sounding like cymbals when they hammered their halberds on their shields.

I found myself at the head of the square and there was his standard-bearer, and beside him . . .

'My lord!' I yelled.

The helmeted head turned slowly towards me, the visor down so he could not see me. I pulled the cap from my head, my hair tumbled down and I lifted my face towards the dark knight, high on his horse.

'My lord! It's me! Hannah the Fool.'

His gauntleted hand lifted the false face of metal, but the shadow of the helmet left his face in darkness and still I could not see him. His head was turned towards me. I could feel his eyes on me, sharp under the sharp points of the helmet. 'Mistress Boy?'

It was his voice, coming from the mouth of this man-god, this great man of metal. But it was his voice, as intimate and warm and familiar as if he had come from dancing at King Edward's summer feast.

The horse sidled. I stepped back on a doorstep; it raised me up four inches, nothing more. 'My lord, it is me!'

'Mistress Boy, what the devil are you doing here?'

'I live here,' I said, half laughing and half crying at seeing him again. 'What of you?'

'Released, fighting, winning—perhaps losing at the moment. Are you safe here?'

'I don't think so,' I said honestly. 'Can we hold the town?'

He pulled the gauntlet from his right hand, twisted a ring from his finger, threw it towards me. 'Take this to the *Windflight*,' he said. 'My ship. Go now, get aboard. We are to make a charge.'

'My lord . . .'

'It's an order!' he shouted at me. 'Go!'

I gasped, pushing the ring on my finger. It had been on his little finger, it fitted my third, just above my wedding ring.

'My lord!' I cried out again. 'Come back safe.'

The bugle played so loud that no one could be heard. They were about to charge. He dropped his visor over his face, pulled his gauntlet back on his hand, lifted his lance from its place, tipped it to his helmet in a salute to me, and wheeled his horse round to face his company.

'A Dudley!' he shouted. 'For God and the queen!'

'For God and the queen!' they roared back at him. 'For God and the queen! Dudley! Dudley!'

They moved towards the city walls, out of the square, and like a camp follower, disobedient to his order, I moved after them. The roar of the siege grew louder as they got near to the gate, and at the sound of French rage I shrank back, looked behind for the way to the harbour.

Then I saw her. Daniel's woman, bedraggled with her pretty dress half dragged from her shoulder, exposing her breast. Her child was on her hip, clinging to her, his dark eyes wide. Her hair was tumbling down, her eye blacked, her face anguished, running like a hunted deer, skipping and stumbling on the cobbles of the street.

She recognised me at once. She had watched me, as I had watched her, every Sunday at Mass.

'Hannah,' she called out to me. 'Hannah!'

'What is it?' I shouted irritably. 'What d'you want with me?'

She showed me her child. 'Take him!'

At once I remembered the intensity of my vision in church, the first time I had seen her. Then as now there was a screaming and a thundering noise. Then, in my nightmare, she had called out 'Take him!' As she cried out the sky suddenly grew dark with a hail of missiles and I ducked into a doorway, but on the other side of the street she came on, dodging through the falling rocks. 'Hannah! Hannah! I need your help.'

'Go home,' I shouted unhelpfully. 'Go to a cellar or somewhere.'

The last of the horses was moving out of the square. We heard the groan of the counterweights as they pulled back the gate for Lord Robert and his cavalry to charge out, and the great roar of rage as they thundered out to meet the French army.

'They are leaving us?' she screamed in horror. 'Running away?'

'No, going out to fight. Find yourself a refuge . . .' I yelled impatiently.

'God save us. They need not go out to fight them; they are in the town already! We are lost!' Daniel's woman shouted. 'It was them . . .'

Her words suddenly penetrated my mind, and I whirled round to look at her again. At once I realised the significance of her black eye and her torn gown. The French were in the city, and they had raped her.

'They came in through the harbour! Ten minutes ago!' she screamed at me, and as she shouted the words I saw coming down the street behind her a tide of French cavalry, in the streets and behind my lord, cutting off him and his men from the harbour. The first rank was on us in a moment, a lance plunging down towards me, and without thinking I snatched the dagger from my boot and with the short blade I parried the thrust. The shock of the blow jarred my blade from my hand, but saved my life as it threw me back against the door of the house behind me. I felt it yield and I fell back into the darkness of an unknown house as I heard Daniel's woman scream: 'Save my baby! Take him! Take him!'

Even as she ran towards me with him held out before her, even as she thrust him into my hands, and he came all warm and soft and heavy, I heard myself say: 'I can't take him.'

I saw the lance run her through, spearing her spine, as she cried out again: 'Take him! Take him!' and at that moment there was a dreadful crash like a forest falling down all at once and a rush of horses and men and danger, and I stumbled back into the dark interior of the house with the boy held tight against me, and the door swung shut on the street with a bang like a thunderclap.

I turned to thank whoever had saved me, but before I could speak there was a roar of flames and a sudden blast of hot smoke, and someone pushed past me and threw open the door again.

The thatched roof of this temporary refuge was alight, blazing up like kindling in seconds. Everyone who had been hidden in the house was pushing past me to the street outside, and I, smelling smoke, dashed out after them, the child tight against my shoulder.

Mercifully, the streets were clear for the moment. The French horsemen had chased after Lord Robert's troop in one mad, dangerous dash. But Daniel's woman was where they had left her with two great lance thrusts through her body.

At the sight I snatched her child closer to me and started to run down the street, down the stone steps to the harbour. I could not wait to look for Daniel; I could not do anything but take the chance I had been given with Lord Robert's ring.

The boats were tied by just one rope, all sails furled ready to go at a moment's notice. I looked desperately around for Lord Robert's standard and saw it, at the prime position, at the very end of the pier where it would be easiest to slip away. I ran down the pier, my feet thudding on the wooden boards, and skidded to a halt when a sailor leapt from the ship and stood before the gangplank with a shining cutlass out of its scabbard, pointing at my throat. 'No further, lad,' he said.

'Lord Robert sent me,' I panted.

He shook his head. 'We could all say that. What's happening in town?'

'Lord Robert led his company out in a charge but the French are in the town already, at his back.'

'Can he turn?'

'I don't know. I didn't see it.'

He shouted an order over his shoulder. The men on deck stood by the ropes for the sails and two men vaulted ashore and held the rope ready to cast off.

I held out my hand to show Lord Robert's ring gripped tight on my finger, above my wedding ring.

The sailor looked at it carefully. 'His ring,' he said.

'His own. He gave it me himself. He saw me before he led them out. I am his vassal. I was Hannah the Fool before I came here.'

'I'd not have recognised you,' he said. 'And this? Your son?'

'Yes.' The lie was said before I had time to think, and then I would not have recalled it.

He stepped to one side and nodded me up the narrow gangplank, then positioned himself square at the foot again.

The winter afternoon grew dark and no one could tell us whether Lord Robert had broken the French ranks or whether they had entered the town behind his back and cut him down. Then we saw the town lit up from one point to another as the French besieging army broke through the walls and fired one thatched roof and then another.

Suddenly there was a rush of men and horses down to the quayside and a flurry as they flung themselves from the saddle, threw off their armour and hared up to the waiting ships.

Then I saw my lord. I would have recognised him in any crowd. He was walking, broadsword in one hand, helmet in the other, trailing his feet like a defeated man. Behind him came a train of men, limping, bleeding, heads bowed. He led them to the ship and stood aside as they went up the gangplank and threw themselves down on the deck.

'That's enough, sir,' the sailor said to him quietly when we were fully loaded. My lord looked up, like a man newly wakened from sleep, and said: 'But we have to take the rest. I promised they would serve me and I would take them to victory. I can't leave them here now.'

'We'll come back for them,' the sailor said gently. He put one strong arm round my lord's shoulders and drew him firmly up the gangplank. 'We'll come back for the rest of them and then we'll retake Calais. Never doubt it, sir. Never doubt it.'

Lord Robert went to the stern of the boat, scanning the harbour, seeing the disorderly retreat. We could smell the smoke drifting in a pall across the water from the burning buildings. We had lost. The English had lost. It was as simple and as brutal as that, and the path of a true man was to consider how to win the next battle.

He spent the whole voyage gazing over the stern towards the coast of France. I knew, because I was watching him, as I sat on a coil of rope at the mast, just behind him. We made an odd trio: a renegade Jew with a Gentile bastard on her hip, and a newly released traitor who had led his men to defeat.

I had not expected his wife Amy at the quayside, but she was there, hand over her eyes, scanning the deck for him. I saw her before she saw him and said, 'Your wife,' in his ear.

He went quickly down the gangplank to her. He did not take her in his arms nor greet her with any sign of affection, but he listened intently to her and then he turned to me.

'I have to go to court to explain to the queen what has happened at Calais,' he said briefly. 'Heads will have to roll for this, perhaps mine.'

'My lord,' I breathed.

'Yes,' he said savagely. 'I don't seem to have done much to advance my family. Hannah, you go with Amy. She is staying with friends in Sussex. I shall send for you there.'

'My lord.' I went a little closer. 'I don't want to live in the country,' was all I could say.

Robert Dudley grinned at me. 'I am sure, sweetheart. I cannot stand it myself. But you must endure it for a month or two. If the queen beheads me, then you can make your own way where you please. All right? But if I survive this, I will open my London house and you shall come back to my service. Whatever you wish. How old is the child?'

I hesitated. 'He's nearly two,' I said.

'You married his father?' he asked.

I looked him in the face. 'Yes.'

'And named him?'

'Daniel, for his father.'

He nodded. 'Amy will take care of you,' he said. 'She likes children.' A snap of his fingers summoned his wife to his side. I saw her shake her head in disagreement, and then lower her eyes when she was overruled. When she shot me a look of pure hatred, I guessed that he had ordered her to care for me and my son.

She had brought his horse. I watched him swing up into his saddle, his men mount up around him. 'London,' he said succinctly and rode his horse north towards whatever fate had for him.

I could not get the measure of Amy Dudley as we rode through the icy countryside of England in those cold days of January 1558. She was a good rider but she seemed to take little pleasure in it, even on the days when the sun rose like a red disc on the horizon and when a few robins hopped and hid in the leafless hedgerows. I thought it was the absence of her husband that made her so sulky, but her companion, Mrs Oddingsell, did not try to cheer her; they did not even speak of him. They rode in silence, as women accustomed to it.

I had to ride behind them, all the way from Gravesend to Chichester, with the baby strapped on my back, and every evening I was aching from my buttocks to my neck with the strain. The extraordinary child had barely made a noise from the moment that his mother had half flung him at me as the French cavalry rode her down. Sleeping, he had rested against me, nestled in as if he were my own; awake, he sat on my lap or on the floor at my feet, or stood, one hand holding firmly on to my breeches. He said not one word, not in French, nor in English. He regarded me with solemn dark eyes and said nothing.

I was not a naturally maternal woman, yet I could not help but admire this small person's tenacity. I started to like the feeling of his fat little hand stretching trustfully up for mine. I started to sleep well with him nestled against my side.

I went down the empty roads with my eyes on the country that was bleak and so cursed, but my mind was on my husband and the town I had left. Now that our flight was over and we had arrived in a comparative safe haven, I was sick with fear for Daniel. I did not even know if he was alive. I knew that worrying about him helped neither of us, but it was impossible to stop myself. I could not get a letter into Calais until some sort of peace was declared, and that would not be for months. Worse, I could not expect to hear from him; he would have no idea where I had gone or even if I were alive. When he went to my shop in the city wall to look for me, as he surely would do, he would find the place sacked or burnt out, and not even Marie, supposing she had survived, would be able to tell him where I was. And then he would find that little Daniel's mother was dead and that the boy was missing too. He would have no reason to guess that I and his son were together in safety in England. He would think that he had lost his wife and his child in one dreadful battle.

I could not enjoy my safety when I knew that he might still be in danger. There could be no happiness for me until I knew that he was alive. Somewhere on the road—in Kent, I think—it came to me with the simple brightness of the wintry sun lying on the horizon and shining blindingly into my eyes. I could not settle without Daniel, because I loved him. I had loved him perhaps from the moment I had seen him at the gates of Whitehall Palace where we had quarrelled at our meeting, and I had loved his steadiness and his fidelity and his patience with me ever since. I felt as if I had grown up with him. He had seen me begged as a fool to the king, devoted to the queen and entranced by the Princess Elizabeth. He had seen my schoolchild adoration of my master, and he had seen me struggle with myself to become the woman I now was. The only thing he had not seen was the resolution of this inner battle: the moment when I could say, 'Yes, I am a woman, and I love this man.'

Everything that had happened in Calais melted away before this one fact. The intrusion of his mother, the malice of his sisters, his own innocent stupidity. Nothing seemed to matter but that I knew now that I loved him, and that it might be too late for me ever to tell him.

If he were dead then it did not seem to matter very much that he had lain with another girl; the greater loss quite concealed the smaller betrayal. As I mounted my horse in the morning and dismounted wearily at night, I realised that I was indeed the widow I announced myself to be. I had lost Daniel, and only now did I have the sense to find that I had loved him all along.

We were to stay in a great house, north of Chichester, and I was glad to clatter into the stable yard at midday and hand over my tired horse to one of the grooms. I was weary as I followed Lady Dudley up the steps to the great hall, and apprehensive. I followed Mrs Oddingsell with Danny on my hip, and there was our hostess, Lady Philips, with a hand held out for Lady Dudley and a deep curtsy.

'You shall have your usual room overlooking the park,' she said, and then she turned to Mrs Oddingsell and me with a smile.

'This is Mrs Carpenter. She can share with your housekeeper,' Lady Dudley said abruptly. 'She is a woman known to my lord, that he rescued from Calais. I dare say he will let me know what she is to do, shortly.'

Lady Philips raised an eyebrow at Amy's abrupt tone, which all but named me as Robert Dudley's whore. Mrs Oddingsell curtsied and went to the stairs, but I did not immediately follow her.

'I need some things for the child,' I said uncomfortably.

'There are some clothes in the paupers' cupboard,' Lady Philips said.

I curtsied. 'It was very kind of his lordship to give me a place on his ship from Calais,' I said clearly. 'The more so since he had not seen me for so long, since I had been in royal service to the queen. But I am a married woman now, my husband a doctor in Calais, and this is my husband's son.'

I saw that they both understood me and had heard the reference to royal service.

'My lord is always good to his servants, however lowly,' Amy Dudley said unpleasantly, and waved me away.

'And I need proper clothes for my son,' I said, standing my ground. 'Not from the paupers' cupboard.'

Both women looked at me with renewed attention.

'I need clothes for a gentleman's son,' I said simply.

Lady Philips, not at all sure now what cuckoo she had welcomed into her house, gave me a cautious smile. 'I have some things put by,' she said carefully. 'My sister's boy wore them.'

'I am sure they will suit the purpose excellently,' I said with a pleasant smile. 'And I thank you, your ladyship.'

Within a week I was desperate to leave. The bleak countryside of Sussex in winter seemed to press on my face like a pane of cold glass. The sky above the hills was iron grey, filled with snow.

Amy Dudley was a welcome and regular guest here. There was some debt between Sir John Philips and my lord that was repaid by his hospitality to Lady Dudley.

'Does she not have a house of her own?' I demanded of Mrs Oddingsell in frustration.

'Not one that she chooses to use,' she said shortly.

Without a house to command or lands to farm, Lady Dudley was a woman of complete idleness. There was nothing that brought her alive. She was in a state of obedient waiting. Then I realised what she was waiting for. She was waiting for a sign from Robert.

But there was no sign of him, though January went into February. No sign of Robert, though he clearly had not been arrested by the queen. Whatever the blame for the loss of Calais, it was not to be laid at his door.

In the absence of any work to do in the household, I found that I spent all my time with the child, Danny, and all my thoughts were with his father. I decided to write to Daniel and address the letter to my father's old shop in London. If Daniel came looking for me, or sent anyone to seek me, that would be one of the places he would visit first. I would send a copy of it to my lord and ask him to forward it to Calais. Surely there must be emissaries going to the city?

> Dear husband,
>
> It is strange that after all we have been through we should once more be separated, and once again I am in England and you in Calais, but this time I think you are in greater danger than I. I pray every night that you are safe and well.
>
> I had the good fortune to be offered a place on the English ship belonging to Lord Robert and in the hurry of battle I thought it best to take it. I wish now I had found my way to you, but, Daniel, I did not know what to do. Also, I had another life to consider. The mother of your child was killed by a French horseman before me, and her last act was to put your

son in my hands. I have him with me now and I am caring for him as my own. He is safe and well though he does not speak yet. He is eating well and growing well, and learning to walk more strongly.

We are living at Chichester in Sussex with Lord Dudley's wife until I can find myself a place. I am thinking of going to court or to the Princess Elizabeth, if she will have me.

I pray that you are safe, Daniel, and I tell you now, as I should have told you before, that I never stopped loving you, even when I left your home. I loved you then, I love you now. If God ever grants me another chance with you, Daniel, I would want to be your wife once more.

Your wife (if you will let me call myself that)
Hannah Carpenter

I sent the letter to my lord, with a covering note.

My lord,
Your wife has been very kind to me but I am trespassing on her hospitality here. Please give me permission to come to court or to see if the Princess Elizabeth will take me into her service.
Hannah Green

I heard nothing from Daniel, and I had hardly hoped for it, though I could not tell if it was the silence of distance or the silence of death.

But, at last, a note came from court.

I shall be with you next week. RD

Amy Dudley reacted with great dignity. She saw that the silver plate and the pewter trenchers were given an extra polish, and that the best linen was laid out for her bed, but other than that, she made no special provision for the return of the lord. Only I saw that she was waiting like a dog waits for his master's step on the threshold. No one else would have noticed the tension in her body every day, from daybreak, when he might come early, till dusk, when he might arrive late.

Finally, on Friday, when there was nothing to put before him but carp from the moat, we saw his train coming down the lane, his standard at the head of a trotting column of riders, smartly in step, two by two, all bright in his livery, and Robert before them all, like a young king. Riding behind him—I squinted my eyes against the low winter sun shining towards me—was John Dee, the reverend and respected Catholic chaplain to Bishop Bonner.

I stepped up to the window of the upper gallery where I had been playing with Danny, so that I could see Robert Dudley's welcome. The front door of the house was torn open and Amy Dudley was on the top step, her hands clasped before her, the picture of demure self-control, but I knew she was raging to be with him.

Lord Robert pulled up his horse, jumped from the saddle, threw the reins to a waiting groom, tossed some remark over his shoulder to John Dee and bowed and kissed his wife's hand as if he had been away for a couple of nights and not for most of their married life.

I picked up Danny, who came to me eagerly with his beaming smile but saying nothing, and made my way down the great stairs to the hall. The household was assembled, lined up as if they were an army for inspection, Sir John Philips and his lady at the head. My lord stood illuminated in the doorway, his broad shoulders brushing the door frame, his smile confident and challenging.

The years of imprisonment had scarred him with nothing worse than a deep groove on either side of his mouth and a hardness at the back of his eyes. Apart from that shadow, he was the same young man whom I had seen walking with an angel in Fleet Street five years ago.

'I'm very glad to be with you,' he said to them all. 'And I thank you all for the good service you have done to me and mine while I have been away.' He paused. 'You will be anxious for news of the queen.' He glanced up the stairs and saw me dressed as a woman, for the first time ever. His amazed stare took in the cut-down gown that I had sewn with the help of Mrs Oddingsell, my dark hair smoothed back under my hood, the dark-headed child on my hip. Comically, he looked and then looked again at the sight of me, recognised me despite the gown, and then shook a baffled head, but continued his speech.

'The queen is in her confinement chamber and expecting to give birth to a son. The king will return to England when the baby is born. In the meantime he is protecting the borders of his Spanish lands in the Low Countries, and has sworn to retake Calais for England. The Princess Elizabeth has visited her sister and wished her well. The princess is in good health, good spirits and great beauty, praise God. She has told the queen that she will not marry any Spanish prince, nor anyone of the king's choosing. She will remain a bride of England.'

There was a little murmur at the news and the servants began to disperse. Robert shook John Philips warmly by the hand, kissed Lady Philips on her cheek and then turned to me.

'Hannah? Is that really you?'

I came down the stairs slowly, conscious of his wife behind him, still standing in the doorway.

'My lord,' I said. I reached the bottom step and dropped him a curtsy.

'I would never have known you,' he said incredulously. 'You are more than a girl, Hannah. You are a woman grown, and out of your breeches at last! And a babe in your arms? This is a transformation!'

I smiled but I could feel Amy's eyes boring into me. 'This is my son,' I said. 'I thank you for saving us from Calais.'

His face clouded over. 'I wish I could have saved them all.'

'Have you any news from the town?' I asked him. 'My husband and his family may still be there. Did you send my letter onward?'

'I gave it to my pageboy and told him to give it to a fisherman who goes out deep into the French seas and ask him to pass it to a French ship if he met with one, but I could do no more for you. We have heard nothing of the men who were captured. King Philip will keep us at war with France for as long as he can, and the queen is in no position to argue. There will be some exchange of prisoners, and men sent home, but God knows when.' He shook his head as if to dislodge the memories of the fall of the infallible castle. 'I have never seen you in a gown before. You are transformed!'

I tried to laugh but I could see Amy coming to claim her husband.

'You will want to wash and change out of your riding clothes,' she said firmly. 'There is hot water in your bedchamber.'

'Then I'll go up.' He glanced over his shoulder. 'And someone must show Dee where he is to lodge.' I shrank back, but my lord did not notice. He called out: 'Here, John—look at who we have here!'

John Dee came forward and I saw that he was more changed than Robert. His hair was greying at the temples, his eyes were dark with fatigue. But his confidence and inner peace were as strong as ever.

'Who is this lady?' he asked.

'I am Hannah Carpenter, Mr Dee,' I said guardedly. I did not know whether he was going to acknowledge that we had last met in the most terrible place in England when I was on trial for my life and he was my judge. 'I was Hannah Green. The queen's fool.'

He looked quickly at me again and then a slow, sweet smile spread from his eyes to his lips and I knew he would never speak of it. 'Ah, Hannah, I would not have known you in your gown.'

'And he is Dr Dee now,' my lord said. 'Bishop Bonner's chaplain.'

'Oh,' I said guardedly.

'And is this your son?' John Dee asked.

'Yes. This is Daniel Carpenter,' I said proudly, and John Dee reached forward and touched my little boy's fingers with his own.

'How old is he?'

'Nearly two.'

'And his father?'

I frowned. 'I parted from my husband at Calais. I don't know if he is safe,' I said.

'You have no . . . sense of him?' John Dee asked me, his voice low.

I shook my head.

'Dr Dee, Hannah will show you to your chamber,' Amy's voice broke in abruptly, speaking of me as if I were her servant.

I led the way up the stairs to one of the small bedchambers on the first floor, John Dee following me. Lord Robert sprang up the stairs two at a time behind us. We heard the door bang as he went into his room.

I had barely showed John Dee where he was to sleep, the cupboard where he could put his clothes, and poured hot water for him to wash, when the chamber door opened and Lord Robert came in.

'Hannah, don't go,' he said. 'I want to hear your news.'

'I have none,' I said coolly. 'I have been here, as you know, all this long while, with your wife, doing nothing.'

He gave a short laugh. 'Have you been bored, Mistress Boy? It cannot be worse than married life, surely?'

I smiled. I was not going to tell Lord Robert that I had parted from my husband within a few months of our marriage.

'And have you kept your gift?' John Dee asked quietly. 'I always thought that the angels would only come to a virgin.'

'It comes so rarely that it is hard to tell,' I said, my voice very small. 'But I had a true seeing in Calais, after my wedding: I foresaw the horsemen riding through the streets.' I shut my eyes against the memory.

'You saw the French coming into Calais?' Lord Robert asked incredulously. 'Dear God, why didn't you warn me?'

'I would have done if I had known what it was,' I replied.

Robert shook his head and turned to look out of the window. 'I wish to God I had been warned,' he said moodily.

'Will you scry for me again?' John Dee asked. 'So that we can see if your gift remains true?'

I looked at him in utter disbelief. 'Are you seeking the advice of angels?' I asked the Inquisitor's chaplain. 'You? Of all men?'

John Dee was not at all perturbed by the sharpness of my tone. 'I do not change my beliefs. And we need guidance all the more, in these troubled times. But we must ask discreetly. There is always danger for those who seek knowledge. But if we could know that the queen will give birth to a healthy child we would be better able to plan for the future. If she is to be blessed with a son, then Princess Elizabeth should change her plans.'

'And I should change mine,' Lord Robert remarked wryly.

'I don't know if I can do it,' I said. 'I have seen the future only once, in all the time I was in Calais.'

'Shall we try this evening?' Lord Robert asked. 'Will you try and see if it comes easily, Hannah? For old times' sake?'

'If you will ask a question for me,' I bargained.

'What is it?' John Dee asked.

'If my husband is alive or dead,' I said. 'It's all I want to know. I don't even ask the future, if I shall see him again. I would be happy just to know that he is alive.'

'You love him so much?' Lord Robert asked sceptically.

'I do,' I said simply. 'I cannot rest until I know that he is safe.'

'I shall ask the angels and you shall scry for me,' John Dee promised. 'Tonight?'

'When Danny is asleep,' I said.

'At eight o'clock?' Lord Robert asked. 'Here?'

John Dee glanced around. 'I will ask the men to bring up my table and my books.'

Amy had hoped to sit up late with her husband, or to go to bed early together, but at eight o'clock he made excuses and he and John Dee and I gathered in John Dee's room with the door closed, the shutters across the window and only one candle lit and glowing in the mirror.

'Are you happy to do this?' John Dee asked.

'What are you going to ask?'

'If the queen will have a boy child,' Robert said. 'There is nothing more important to know than this. And if we can win back Calais.'

I looked towards John Dee. 'And if my husband lives,' I reminded him.

'We will see what is given us,' he said gently. 'Watch the flame and tell us what you hear or what you see.'

The candle flame bobbed in a little draught; its brightness filled my mind. It was like the summer sunshine of Spain, and I thought I heard my mother calling me, her voice happy and filled with confidence that nothing would ever go wrong. Then abruptly I heard a tremendous banging that made me gasp and leap to my feet, jolted out of my dream with my heart thudding in fear of arrest.

John Dee was white-faced. We were discovered and ruined. Lord Robert had his sword from his belt and a knife from his boot.

'Open up!' came the shout from the barred door and there was a great blow against the wood which made it rock inwards. I was certain that it was the Inquisition. I crossed the room to Lord Robert. 'Please, my lord,'

I said rapidly. 'Don't let them burn me. Run me through, before they take me, and save my son.'

In one fluid movement he was up on the window seat, pulled me up beside him and kicked out the windowpane. 'Jump out,' he advised me. 'And run if you can. I'll hold them for a moment.' There was another terrible blow on the door. He nodded at John Dee. 'Open up,' he said.

John Dee flung open the door and Lady Amy Dudley fell into the room. 'You!' she exclaimed as soon as she saw me, half out of the window. 'As I thought! Whore!'

A servant behind her raised a mace in a half-apologetic gesture. The Philipses' elegant linenfold door panels were splintered beyond repair. Robert slammed his sword back into the scabbard, and gestured to John Dee. 'Please, John, do shut what is left of the door,' he said wearily.

'What are you doing here?' Amy demanded, her eyes taking in the table, the candles, the holy symbols. 'What foul lechery?'

'Nothing,' Robert said wearily.

'What is she doing here with you? And him?'

He stepped forward and took her hands. 'My lady, this is my friend and this my loyal servant. We were praying together for my prosperity.'

She broke from his grasp and struck at him, her hands clenched into fists, pounding against his chest. 'She is a whore and he is a dealer in black arts!' she cried. 'And you are a false deceiver who has broken my heart too many times to count!'

Robert caught her hands. 'She is a good servant of mine and a respectable married woman,' he said quietly. 'And Dr Dee is chaplain to one of the most important churchmen in the land. Madam, I beg you to compose yourself.'

'I hate you!' she suddenly screamed. With a wail she tore herself from his grip and threw herself face down on the bed. She was screaming with grief, quite beside herself. John Dee and my lord exchanged an aghast look. There was a little tearing noise and I realised she had bitten the counterpane and was ripping it with her teeth.

'Oh, for the sake of God!' Robert took her shoulders and pulled her up from the bed. At once she went for his face with her nails. Robert grabbed her hands and bore her down till she fell on the floor, kneeling at his feet, her wrists in his grip.

'I know you!' she swore up at him. 'If it is not her, then it is another. There is nothing about you but pride and lust.'

His face, suffused with temper, slowly calmed, but he kept a tight hold of her hands. 'I am a sinner indeed,' he said. 'But thank God, *I* at least am not crazed.'

Her mouth trembled and then she let out a wail, looking up into his flinty face, the tears pouring from her eyes, her mouth drooling sobs. 'I am not crazed. I am ill, Robert,' she said despairingly. 'I am sick of grief.'

He met my eyes over her head. 'Fetch Mrs Oddingsell,' he said briefly. 'She knows what to do.'

I nodded and went from the room. Half the household was busy on the landing outside the chamber. 'Go to your work!' I said abruptly, and then I ran down the long gallery to find Mrs Oddingsell seated before a mean fire at the cold end of the chamber.

'Her ladyship is crying, and his lordship sent for you,' I said baldly.

She got to her feet at once, without surprise, and went quickly down the room. I half ran beside her. 'Has this happened before?' I asked.

She nodded.

'Is she ill?'

'Easily distressed by him.'

I took that in, made allowances for a servant's loyal lies. 'Was she always like this?'

'When they were young and in love it passed for passion. But she was only at peace when he was in the Tower—except for when the princess was imprisoned too.'

'What?'

'She was ill with jealousy, then.'

'They were prisoners!' I exclaimed.

Mrs Oddingsell nodded. 'In her mind they were lovers. And now, he is free to come and go. And she knows that he is seeing the princess. He will break her heart. It is no figure of speech. She will die of this.'

We were at Dr Dee's door. I put a hand on her arm. 'Are you her nurse?' I asked.

'More like her keeper,' she said and quietly went in.

Lady Amy Dudley kept to her room for the next three days while Robert and John Dee rode out hunting, read in the library, gambled small sums of money, and talked, at dinner and at play, of what the future of the country might be, what shape the nobility and the parliament should take, how far the borders might extend overseas.

On the evening of the third day of their visit, my lord had a message from Dover, and left me and John Dee alone in the library. John Dee had drawn a map of the world after the model of his friend Gerardus Mercator and tried to explain to me that I must think of the world as round, and think of this map as the skin of the world peeled off, like the skin peeled off an orange and laid flat.

He struggled to make me see it until he laughed and said that I must be content to see angels; I clearly could not see longitude. He took up his maps and went with them to his room as Lord Robert came into the library with a piece of paper in his hand.

'At last I have news of your husband. He is safe,' he said.

I jumped to my feet and found I was trembling. 'My lord?'

'He was taken by the French who suspected him as a spy, but they are holding him with other English soldiers,' he told me. 'I dare say I can arrange for him to be exchanged for other prisoners of war, or ransomed, or something.'

'He is safe?' I asked. 'Not sick, nor injured?'

'See for yourself,' he said, handing over the three scrawled lines on the sheet of paper.

'Thank you,' I said. I read and reread the letter. It said nothing more than he had already told me, but somehow in words of black ink on travel-stained paper it seemed more true. 'Thank God.'

'Thank God indeed,' said my lord with a smile.

Impulsively I took his hand. 'And thank you, my lord,' I said fervently. 'You are kind to take the trouble for me. I know it. I am grateful.'

Gently he drew me in, put a warm hand on my waist. 'Sweetheart, you know I would do anything in my power to make you happy.'

I hesitated. His hand was light, I could feel the heat of his palm through the fabric of my gown. I felt myself lean towards him. He stole a quick glance up and down the empty gallery and then his mouth came down towards mine. He hesitated, he was such a practised seducer that he knew the power of delay to increase desire. Then he bent a little lower and he kissed me, tenderly and then with increasing passion until my arms were round his neck and he had me pressed against a wall, my head tipped back, my eyes closed, quite given up to the delicious sensation of his touch.

'Lord Robert,' I whispered.

'I'm for bed. Come with me, sweetheart mine.'

I did not hesitate. 'I am sorry, my lord, no.'

'You are sorry, my lord, no?' he repeated comically. 'What d'you mean, Mistress Boy?'

'I shall not lie with you,' I said steadily.

'Why not? Don't tell me it is not your desire, for I shan't believe you. I can taste it on your lips. You want me as much as I want you. And that is a good deal, tonight.'

'It is my desire,' I admitted. 'And if I were not a married woman I would be glad to be your lover.'

'Oh, Hannah, a husband such a long way away and safely in prison need not concern you. A word from you to me, and he can stay there until there is a general amnesty. Come to bed with me, now.'

Steadfastly I shook my head. 'No, my lord. It is not that he might catch me,' I said. 'It is that I do not want to betray him.'

'You betray him in your heart,' Robert said cheerfully. 'You lean back against my arm, you tip your head, you open your mouth for my kisses. He is betrayed already, Mistress Boy. The rest is just enacting the desire.'

I smiled at his persuasive, self-serving logic. 'Perhaps, but it is wrong. My lord, I tell you true, I have adored you since the day I first saw you. But I love Daniel with a true and honourable love, and I want to be a good wife to him, and faithful to him.'

'But you would so enjoy a night with me, you know,' he said, partly from vanity, partly as a final attempt.

'I am very sure of it,' I said, as shameless as he. 'And if I cared for nothing but pleasure then I would be begging you for tonight and every night after. But I have fallen in love, my lord, and no one but my lover will do for me.'

He stepped back and swept me a beautiful courtly bow, as low as if for a queen. 'Mistress Boy, you always exceed my expectations. I knew you would make a wonderful woman but I never expected you would make a surprising and honourable woman. I hope your husband is worthy of you, I do indeed. And if he is not . . .'

I laughed. 'If he breaks my heart a second time then I will come back to you as heartless as you are yourself, my lord,' I said.

'Oh well, it is agreed,' he said with a laugh, and went to his bed alone.

SPRING 1558

WITHIN A FEW DAYS his lordship and John Dee returned to court. I waited for news, but heard nothing except common gossip. The baby, which was due in March, was late, and by April people were starting to say that the queen had made a mistake again, and there was no child. I could not imagine how she would be able to bear it if she were to be once more disappointed. I knew her for a courageous woman, but to come out of confinement for a second time and tell the world that there was no baby—I could not see how any woman could bear the humiliation of it, least of all the Queen of England. Then I received word from my lord.

Mistress Boy,
    The queen is to come out of her confinement soon, and I need you here to advise me. You may bring me my blue velvet missal which I left in the chapel at my seat and come at once. Robt.

I went to the chapel, with Danny walking before me. I had to stoop low so that he could hold my fingers with both his hands, and walk with my support. My back ached by the time we got to the chapel and I sat in Robert's chair and let Danny make his way down one of the pews, steadying himself on the seat. I would never have believed that I would have stooped till my back ached for the amusement of a small boy, and yet when I had the missal and we walked back to our chamber I bent low again to let Danny hold on to my fingers. I prayed in silence that perhaps, even now, the queen might have a son and might know joy like this, such a strange, unexpected joy—the happiness of caring for a child whose whole life was in my hands.

He was not an ordinary child. Even I, who knew so little about children, could tell that. Like a house with shuttered windows the child had shielded himself, and had shut himself away from the life of the world outside. I felt that I was standing outside, calling for a response that might never come. But I was determined to go on calling to him.

The court was at Richmond, and the moment I arrived I knew that something had happened. There was an air of suppressed excitement in the stables. Everyone was gossiping in corners and there was no one to take our horses, not even the Dudley grooms.

I threw the reins to the nearest young man, and with Danny on my hip strode up the path to the garden entrance of the palace, to the inner hall, looking for someone I could trust. At the back of the hall, Will Somers was sitting all alone. I went up to him and touched him on the shoulder.

His dull gaze went first to Danny and then to me. He did not recognise me. 'Mistress, I can do nothing for you,' he said shortly, and turned his head away. 'I have no spirits for jests today.'

'Will, it's me.'

He looked at me more closely. 'Hannah? Hannah, the Invisible Fool?'

I nodded at the implied reproach. 'Will, what has happened?'

He did not remark on my clothes, on my child, on anything. 'It's the queen,' he said.

'Oh, Will, she's not dead?'

He shook his head. 'Not yet. But it can only be a matter of time.'

'The baby?' I asked with a swift sure painful knowledge.

'It's happened again,' he said. 'There was no baby. Again. And again she is the laughing stock of Europe.'

Without thinking I stretched out my hands to him for comfort and he gripped them tightly. 'Is she ill?' I whispered after a moment.

'Her women say that she will not rise up from the floor,' he said. 'She sits, hunched on the floorboards like a beggar woman. I don't know how it can have happened, Hannah . . . What will happen next?'

'Why? What will happen next?' I repeated, aghast.

He hunched a shoulder and gave me a crooked sad smile. 'Nothing much here,' he said dismissively. 'It's at Hatfield that it will all happen. There is the heir; clearly, we can't make one here. *She'll* have her speech ready, I don't doubt. She'll be all prepared for the day when they tell her that the queen is dead and she is the new queen.'

'You're right.' I shared his bitterness. 'And she has her speech ready. She's going to say: "This is the Lord's doing; it is marvellous in our eyes".'

Will gave a bitter crow of laughter. 'How d'you know that?'

'Oh, Will! She asked me what the queen was going to say at her accession, and when I told her she thought it so good she would use it herself.'

'Well, why not?' he asked, suddenly bitter again. 'She will have taken everything else. Queen Mary's own husband, the people's love, the throne, and now the very words out of her sister's mouth.'

I nodded. 'Do you think I can see the queen?'

He smiled. 'She won't recognise you. You've become a beautiful woman. Is it just the gown? Was it your dressmaker that transformed you?'

I shook my head. 'Love, I think.'

'For your husband? You found him, did you?'

'I found him, and then I lost him almost at once, Will, because I was a fool, filled with pride and jealousy. But I have his son, and he has taught me to love without thinking of myself. I love him more than I thought possible. More than I knew I could love anyone. This is my son, Danny. And if we ever see his father again I will be able to tell him that I am a woman grown at last, and ready for love.'

Will smiled at Danny, who shyly dipped his head and then looked into Will's kindly creased face and smiled back.

'Can you hold him for me, while I ask if I may see the queen?'

Will held out his arms and Danny went to him with the easy trust that Will inspired in everyone. I went up the sweep of stairs to the queen's presence chamber and then to the closed door of her private rooms. My name got me as far as her privy chamber, and then I saw Jane Dormer standing at the closed door.

'Jane, it is me,' I said. 'Hannah.'

It was a sign of the depth of the queen's grief and Jane's despair that she did not remark on my unexpected return, nor on my new costume.

'Perhaps she'll speak to you,' she said quietly, alert for eavesdroppers. 'Be careful what you say. Don't mention the king, nor the baby.'

Jane opened the door for me with one hand and thrust me into the room with the other. I stumbled in and dropped to a curtsy and heard the door close softly behind me.

The room was in deep shade, still shuttered for confinement. I looked around. The queen was not seated on any of the looming chairs nor crumpled in the great bed. She was not on her knees before her prie-dieu. I could not see her anywhere.

Then I heard a little noise, a tiny sound, like a child catching her breath after a bout of sobbing.

'Mary,' I whispered. 'Where are you?'

As my eyes grew accustomed to the darkness I finally made her out. She was lying on the floor amid the rushes, face turned towards the skirting board, hunched like a starving woman will hunch over her empty belly. I crawled on my hands and knees across the floor towards her, and gently touched her shoulders.

She did not respond. I don't think she even knew I was there. She was locked in a grief so deep and so impenetrable that I thought she would be trapped in that inner darkness for the rest of her life.

I stroked her shoulder as one might stroke a dying animal. Since words could do nothing, I thought a gentle touch might help, but I did not know if she could even feel that. Then I lifted her shoulders gently from the floor, put her head in my lap and took her hood from her poor weary head and wiped the tears as they poured from her closed eyelids down her tired, lined face. I sat with her in silence until her deeper breathing told me that she had fallen asleep. Even in her sleep the tears still welled up from her closed eyelids and ran down her wet cheeks.

When I came out of the queen's rooms, Lord Robert was there.

'You,' I said, without much pleasure.

'Aye, me,' he said. 'And no need to look so sour. I am not to blame.'

'You're a man,' I observed. 'And men are mostly to blame for the sorrow that women suffer.'

He gave a short laugh. 'I am guilty of being a man, I admit it. You can come and dine in my rooms. Your boy is there too. Will has him.'

I went with him, his arm round my waist.

'Is she ill?' he asked, his mouth to my ear.

'Brokenhearted,' I said shortly.

He nodded at that and swept me into his rooms. As we went in Danny looked up from Will's lap and made a little crow, the greatest noise he ever made, and stretched up for me. I took him in my arms.

'Thank you,' I said to Will.

'He was a comfort to me,' he said frankly.

'You can stay, Will,' Robert said. 'Hannah is going to dine with me.'

'I have no appetite,' Will said. 'I have seen so much sorrow in this country that my belly is full of it. I am sick of sorrow. I wish I could have a little joy for seasoning.'

'Times will change,' Robert said encouragingly. 'Changing already.'

'You'd be ready for new times, for one,' Will said, his spirit rising up. 'Since in the last reign you were one of the greatest lords and in this one you were a traitor waiting for the axe. I imagine change would be very welcome to you. What d'you hope from the next, my lord? What has the next queen promised you?'

'Nothing but good for the country,' Robert said easily with a pleasant smile. 'Come and dine with us, Will. You're among friends.'

'All right,' he said, seating himself at the table. I hitched Danny onto the chair beside me so that he could eat from my bowl and I took a glass of wine that Lord Robert poured for me.

'Here's to us,' Robert said, raising his glass in an ironic toast. 'A heartbroken queen, an absent king, a lost baby, a queen in waiting and two fools and a reformed traitor. Here's health.'

'Three fools together,' Will said, raising his glass.

SUMMER 1558

ALMOST BY DEFAULT, I found myself back in the queen's service. She was so anxious and suspicious of everyone around her that she would be served only by people who had been with her from the earliest days. She hardly seemed to notice that I had been away from her for more than two years, and was now dressed like a woman. She liked to hear me read to her in Spanish, and she liked me to sit by her bed while she slept. The deep sadness that had invaded her with the failure of her second pregnancy meant that she had no curiosity about me. I told her that my father had died, that I had married my betrothed, and that we had a child. She was interested only that my husband and I were separated: he in France—safe, I hoped—while I was in England.

'How can you bear not to be with your husband?' she asked suddenly, after three long hours of silence one grey afternoon.

'I miss him,' I said, startled at her suddenly speaking to me. 'But I hope to find him again. I will go to France as soon as it is possible. I will go and look for him. Or I hope he will come to me.'

She turned towards the window and looked out at the river. 'I keep a fleet of ships ready for the king to come to me,' she said. 'And horses and lodgings all along the road from Dover to London. They are all waiting for him. A small army of men does nothing but wait for him. I, the Queen of England, his own wife, wait for him. Why does he not come?'

There was no answer that I could give her. There was no answer that anyone could give her. When she asked the Spanish ambassador, he bowed low and murmured that the king had to be with his army. She must understand the need of that—the French were still threatening his lands. It satisfied her for a day, but the next day, when she looked for him, the Spanish ambassador had gone.

'Where is he?' the queen asked. I was holding her hood, waiting for her maid to finish arranging her hair. Her beautiful chestnut hair had gone grey and thin now. When it was brushed out it looked sparse and dry. The lines on her face and the weariness in her eyes made her seem far older than her forty-two years.

'Where is who, Your Grace?' I asked.

'The Spanish ambassador, Count Feria?'

I handed her hood to her maid, then I gritted my teeth and told her the truth. 'I believe he has gone to see the princess.'

The queen turned round to look at me, her eyes shocked. 'Why? Hannah? Why would he do that?'

I shook my head. 'How would I know, Your Grace? Does he not go to present his compliments to the princess now and then?'

'No. He does not. For most of his time in England she has been under house arrest, a suspected traitor, and he himself urged me to execute her. Why would he go to pay his compliments now?'

None of us answered. She took the hood from the waiting woman's hands and put it on, meeting her own honest eyes in the mirror. 'The king will have ordered him to go.'

She was silent for a moment, thinking what she should do. I kept my gaze down. I could not bear to look up and see her, facing the knowledge that her own husband was sending messages to her heir, to her rival, to his mistress.

When she turned back to us her expression was calm. 'Hannah, a word with you, please,' she said, extending her hand.

I went to her side and she took my arm and leaned on me slightly as we walked from the room to her presence chamber. 'I want you to go to Elizabeth,' she said quietly, as they opened the doors. There was hardly anyone outside waiting to see her. They were all at Hatfield. 'Just go as if for a visit. Tell her you have recently come back from Calais and wanted to see how she did. Can you do that?'

'I would have to take my son,' I stipulated.

'Take him,' she nodded. 'And see if you can find out from Elizabeth herself, or from her ladies, what Count Feria wanted with her. It may be that the king is pressing her to marry the Prince of Savoy. She has sworn to me that she will not have him but Elizabeth has no principles, only appearances. If the king promised to support her claim to be my heir, she might think it worth her while to marry his cousin. I have to know.'

'When d'you want me to go?' I asked unwillingly.

'At first light tomorrow,' she said. 'And don't write to me; I am surrounded by spies. I will wait for you to tell me what she is planning when you come back to me.'

It was a merry ride to Hatfield for Danny and me. He rode the horse astride before me until he grew too tired, and then I strapped him to my back and he slept, rocked by the jolting.

The old palace at Hatfield had been the royal nursery for generations, chosen for its clean air and proximity to London. It was an old building, small-windowed and dark-beamed, and the escort of two men led the way to the front door so that Danny and I might dismount and go inside while they took the horses away.

There was no one in the hall to greet us but a boy bringing in logs for the fire, which was kept going, even in midsummer. 'They're all in the garden,' he said. 'Acting a play.'

His gesture directed me to a door at the rear of the hall, and with Danny in my arms I opened it, followed the stone corridor to another door and then stepped out into the sunshine.

What play-acting there had been was clearly over, and what was left was a romp. Veils of cloth of gold and silver and overturned chairs were scattered around the orchard, and Elizabeth's ladies were running in all

directions from a man in the centre of the circle with a dark scarf over
his face to blindfold him. As I watched he caught a flying skirt and drew
a girl to him, but she wriggled free and ran away laughing. They gathered round him and with much giggling and cooing they turned him
round and round until he was dizzy and then they retreated. Again he
dashed and lunged, while they ran this way and that, giggling with that
heady mixture of girlish playfulness and female arousal. Among them,
her red hair flying loose, her face flushed and laughing, was the
princess. She was not the Elizabeth I had seen white-faced with terror.
She was not the princess I had seen bloated on her bed, sick to her very
bones with fear. She was a princess coming into the midsummer of her
life, coming into her womanhood, coming to the throne. She was a
fairy-tale princess, beautiful, powerful, wilful, infallible.

As I watched she tapped the blindfolded man on the shoulder and
made to run back again. This time he was too quick for her. As his hand
flashed out, she sprang back just too slowly; he snatched her at the
waist and though she struggled he held her close.

'I have caught you!' he called out. 'Who is it?'

'You have to guess! You have to guess!' the ladies cried.

He ran his hand over her forehead, her hair, her nose, her lips. 'A
beauty,' he said certainly.

Impertinently, he let his hand stray down over her chin, down her
neck, he took her throat in his hand. I saw the colour flame into
Elizabeth's cheeks and I realised she was on fire with desire at his touch.
She did not step back from him or move to check him. She was ready to
let him finger her all over, watched by all her court.

He held her firmly, and there was a little whisper as he gripped her
with one hand at the waist, and with the other traced the border of the
neck of her gown, his fingertips brushing the tops of her breasts. Slowly,
tantalisingly, he slid his hand down the front of her gown over the
embroidered stomacher, past the girdle at her waist, over the thick skirt
of her gown at the front, and then round the back to take hold of her
buttocks, as if she were his own woman.

Elizabeth gave a little soft moan and twisted from his grip, almost
falling back among her ladies. 'Who was it? Who was it?' they chanted,
relieved that she had freed herself from his embrace.

'I give up,' he said. 'I cannot play some foolish game. I have touched
the very curves of heaven.'

He pulled the blindfold from his eyes and I saw his face. His eyes met
Elizabeth's. He knew exactly who it had been in his arms. He had
known from the moment he had caught her, as he had intended to do,

as she had intended him to do. He had caressed her in front of all the
court, caressed her as an accepted lover, and she had let him stroke her
as if she were a whore. She smiled at him, her knowing, desirous smile,
and he smiled back.

Of course, the man was my lord Robert Dudley.

'And what are you doing here, child?' he asked me before dinner, walking on the terrace.

'Queen Mary sent me to pay her compliments to Elizabeth.'

'Oho, my little spy, are you at work again?'

'Yes, and most unwillingly.'

'And what does the queen want to know?'

'She wants to know what Count Feria was doing here,' I said simply.
'Is he here?'

'Left yesterday.'

'What did he want?'

'He brought a message from the king. Queen Mary's own beloved
husband. A faithless dog, isn't he, the randy old Spaniard?'

'Why d'you say that?'

'Mistress Boy, I have a wife who does me no service, and shows me no
kindness, but not even I would court her own sister under her nose and
shame her while she was still living.'

'He is courting Elizabeth?'

'The Pope has been approached to give permission for their marriage,' he said flatly. 'If the queen lives then it's my guess that Philip will
apply for an annulment of their marriage and marry Elizabeth. If the
queen dies, then Elizabeth is heir to the throne and an even richer plum
for the picking. He will snap her up within the year.'

I looked at him, my face quite blank with horror. 'This cannot be,' I
said, appalled. 'It's a betrayal. It's the worst thing he could do to her.'

'It's an unexpected move,' he said. 'Disagreeable for a loving wife.'

'The queen would die of grief and shame. To be put aside, as her
mother was put aside? And for Anne Boleyn's daughter?'

He nodded. 'As I said, a faithless Spanish dog.'

'And Elizabeth?'

He glanced over my shoulder. 'You can ask her yourself.'

I slid into a curtsy, and then came up. Elizabeth's black eyes snapped
at me. She did not like to see me with Robert Dudley.

'Princess.'

'I heard you were back. My lord said that you had become a woman. I
did not expect to see you quite so . . .'

I waited.

'Fat,' she said.

Instead of being insulted, as she intended, I giggled out loud at the childish jealous rudeness of her.

At once her eyes danced too. Elizabeth never sulked.

'Whereas you, Princess, are more beautiful than ever,' I said smoothly.

'I hope so. And what were you talking about with your heads so close together?'

'About you,' I said simply. 'The queen sent me to find out how you did. And I was glad to come and see you.'

'I warned you not to leave it too late,' she said, her gesture taking in the waiting women, the courtiers from London.

'I see your ladyship keeps a merry court,' I said evenly. 'As you should. And I cannot join you, even if you would condescend to have me. I have to serve your sister. She does not have a merry court; she has few friends. I would not leave her now.'

'Then you must be the only person in England who has not deserted her,' she said cheerfully. 'I took on her cook last week. Does she get anything to eat at all?'

'She manages,' I said drily. 'And even the Spanish ambassador, Count Feria, her trusted councillor, was missing from court when I left.'

She shot a quick look at Robert Dudley and I saw him nod permission for her to speak.

'I refused his request,' she said gently. 'I have no plans to marry anyone. You can assure the queen of that, for it is true.'

I gave her a little curtsy. 'I am glad not to have to take her any news that would make her yet more unhappy.'

The next day we rode back to the queen, and I found her walking by the river, no more than a handful of courtiers behind her, one being faithful Will Somers, who called himself a fool but had never, in my hearing, said a foolish word.

'Your Grace,' I said, and swept her my curtsy.

The queen took in my appearance, the mud on my cloak, the child at my side. 'You have come straight from Hatfield?'

'As you commanded.'

'Can someone take the child?'

Will stepped forward and Danny beamed. I set him down and he gave his quiet little gurgle of pleasure and toddled towards Will.

'I am sorry to bring him to Your Grace. I thought you might like to see him,' I said awkwardly.

She shook her head. 'No, Hannah, I do not ever want to see him.' She gestured for me to walk beside her. 'Did you see Elizabeth?'

'Yes.'

'And what did she say of the ambassador?'

'I spoke to one of her women.' I was anxious not to identify Lord Robert as the favourite at this treacherous alternative court. 'She said that the ambassador had visited to pay his compliments.'

'And what else?'

I hesitated. My duty to be honest to the queen and my desire not to hurt her seemed to be in utter conflict. I could not bring myself to tell her that her own husband was proposing marriage to her own sister.

'He was pressing the suit of the Duke of Savoy,' I said. 'Elizabeth herself assured me that she would not marry him.'

'The Duke of Savoy?' she asked.

I nodded.

The queen reached out her hand and I took it and waited, not knowing what she would say to me. 'Hannah, you have been my friend for many years, and a true friend, I think.'

'Yes, Your Grace.'

She lowered her voice to a whisper. 'Hannah, answer me a question and then I will never think of this again. But answer me truly.'

I gulped, wondering what terror was opening up beneath my feet. 'I will, Your Grace.' Inwardly I promised myself that if the question endangered me, or Danny, or my lord, I would allow myself to lie.

'Was there any suggestion that the king was pressing his own suit?' she whispered, so low that I could hardly hear her. 'Even though he is my husband, even though he is forsworn before God, the Pope, and our two kingdoms? Please tell me, Hannah. I know that it is the question of a madwoman. I know that I am his wife and he could not be doing this. But I have become filled with the thought that he is courting her, not as a flirtation, but for his wife. I have to know. I am tortured by this fear.'

I bit my lip, and she needed nothing more. With the quick apprehension of a woman seeing her worst fear, she knew it at once.

'Dear God, it is so,' she said slowly. 'I thought that my suspicion of him was part of my illness, but it is not. I can see it on your face. He is courting my sister for marriage. My own sister? And my own husband?'

I clasped her cold hand between my own. 'Your Grace—'

'Dearest God, this is the very worst thing that could ever have happened to me,' she said quietly. 'I saw my mother pushed from her throne and shamed by a younger woman who took the king from her and laughed as she did it. And now this woman's bastard daughter does just the same thing to me.' She broke off and looked at me. 'No wonder I couldn't believe it. It is the thing I have feared all my life. Ending up like my own mother, neglected, abandoned, with a Boleyn whore in triumph on the throne.'

I gave her hand a little tug. 'Your Grace, don't give way. Not here. Not here before all these people.'

I was thinking of her, and I was thinking of Elizabeth's court who would laugh till they cried if they heard that the queen had broken down because she had heard at last what all of Europe had known for months—that her husband had betrayed her.

She shook from head to toe with the effort, but she drew herself up, she blinked back the tears. 'You are right,' she said. 'I will not be shamed. I will say nothing more. I will think nothing more. Walk with me, Hannah.'

I glanced back at Danny. Will was seated on the ground with the boy astride his knees, showing him how he could wiggle his ears. Danny's chuckle was delighted. I took the queen's arm and matched my stride to her slow pace. The court fell in behind us, yawning.

'You know,' the queen whispered to me, 'you know, Hannah, I loved him from the moment I first saw his portrait. D'you remember?'

'Yes,' I said, remembering my warning that he would break her heart.

'I adored him when I met him. D'you remember our wedding day, when he looked so handsome and we were so happy?'

I nodded again.

'I worshipped him when he took me to bed. He gave me the only joy I had known in my life. Nobody will ever know how much I have loved him. And now he is planning to marry my worst enemy when I am dead. He is looking forward to my death and his life after it.'

She stood quietly for a few moments as her court halted aimlessly behind her, looking from her to me and wondering what fresh bad news I had brought. Then I saw her stiffen, and her hand went to her eyes, as if she had a sudden pain. 'Unless he does not wait for my death,' she said quietly.

A quick glance at my white face told her the rest of the story. She shook her head. 'No, never,' she whispered. 'Not this. He would never divorce me? Not as my father did to my mother? With no grounds except lust for another woman?'

I said nothing.

She did not cry. She was Queen Mary who had been Princess Mary, who had learned as a little girl to keep her head up and her tears back. She just nodded, as if she had taken a hard knock to the head.

AUTUMN 1558

IN SEPTEMBER WE MOVED to Hampton Court in the hopes that the fresh air would clear the queen's breathing, which was hoarse and sore. The doctors offered her a mixture of oils and drinks, but nothing seemed to do her any good. She was reluctant to see them, and often refused to take her medicine. I thought she was remembering how her little brother had been all but poisoned by the physicians who tried one thing and then another, but then I realised that she could not be troubled with physic; she no longer cared for anything, not even her health.

I rode to Hampton Court with Danny in a pillion saddle behind me for the first time. He was old enough and strong enough to ride astride and to hold on tightly to my waist for the short journey. He was still mute, but he was as peaceful and as smiling as he had always been. I could tell by the tight grip on my waist that he was excited at the journey and at riding properly for the first time. The horse was steady and we ambled along beside the queen's litter down the damp dirty lanes between the fields where they were trying to harvest the wet rye crop.

Danny looked around him, never missing a moment of this, his first proper ride. He waved at the people in the field; he waved at the villagers who stood at their doorways to watch as we went by. I thought it spoke volumes for the state of the country that a woman would not wave in reply to a little boy, since he was riding in the queen's train. The country had turned against Mary and would not forgive her.

She rode with the curtains of the litter drawn, in rocking darkness, and when we got to Hampton Court she went straight to her rooms and had the shutters closed so that she was plunged into dusk.

Danny and I rode into the stable yard, and a groom lifted me down from the saddle. I turned and reached up for Danny. For a moment I thought he would cling and insist on staying on horseback.

'Do you want to pat the horse?' I tempted him.

His face lit up at once and he reached out his little arms for me and came tumbling down. I held him to the horse's neck and let him pat the warm, sweet-smelling skin. The horse, a handsome big-boned bay, turned its head to look at him. Danny, very little, and horse, very big, stared quite transfixed by each other, and then Danny gave a deep sigh of pleasure and said: 'Good.'

It was so natural and easy that for a moment I did not realise he had spoken. When I did realise, I hardly dared to take a breath in case I prevented him speaking again.

'He *was* a good horse, wasn't he?' I said with affected nonchalance. 'Shall we ride him again tomorrow?'

Danny looked from the horse to me. 'Yes,' he said decidedly.

I held him close to me and kissed his silky head. 'We'll do that then,' I said gently. 'And we'll let him go to bed now.'

My legs were weak beneath me as we walked from the stable yard, Danny at my side, his little hand reaching up to hold mine. I could feel myself smiling, though tears were running down my cheeks. Danny would speak, Danny would grow up as a normal child. I had saved him from death in Calais, and I had brought him to life in England. I had justified the trust of his mother, and perhaps one day I would be able to tell his father that I had kept his son safe for love of him, and for love of the child. It seemed wonderful to me that his first word should be: 'good'. Perhaps it was a foreseeing. Perhaps life would be good for my son Danny.

For a little while the queen seemed better, away from the city. She walked by the river with me in the mornings or in the evenings; she could not tolerate the brightness of midday. But Hampton Court was filled with ghosts. It was on these paths and in these gardens where she had walked with Philip when they were newly married. It was here that she had whispered to him that she was with child, and gone into her first confinement, certain of her happiness, confident of having a son. And it was here that she came out from her confinement, childless and ill, and saw Elizabeth growing in beauty and exulting in her triumph, another step closer to the throne.

'I feel no better here at all,' she said to me one day as Jane Dormer and I came in to say good night. She had gone to bed early again, almost doubled up with pain from the ache in her belly and feverishly hot. 'We will go to St James's Palace next week. We will spend Christmas there. The king likes St James's.'

Jane Dormer and I exchanged one silent glance. We did not think that King Philip would come home to his wife for Christmas when he had not come home when she had lost their child, when he had not come home when she wrote to him that she was so sick that she did not see how to bear to live.

As we had feared, it was a depleted court at St James's Palace. My Lord Robert had bigger and better rooms, not because his star was rising but simply because there were fewer men at court. I saw him at dinner on some days, but generally he was at Hatfield, where the princess kept her merry circle about her.

Lord Robert saw me only rarely, but he had not forgotten me. He came looking for me, one day in September. 'I have done you a great favour, I think,' he said with his charming smile. 'Are you still in love with your husband, Mrs Carpenter? Or shall we abandon him in Calais?'

'You have news of him?' I asked. I put my hand down and felt Danny's hand creep into my own.

'I might have,' he said provocatively. 'But you have not answered my question. Do you want him home, or shall we forget all about him?'

'I cannot jest about this, and especially not before his son,' I said. 'I want him home, my lord. Please tell me, do you have news of him?'

'His name is on this list.' He flicked the paper at me. 'Soldiers to be ransomed, townspeople who are to be returned to England. The whole of the English Pale outside Calais is to come home. If the queen can find some money in the treasury we can get them all back.'

I could feel my heart thudding. 'There is no money in the treasury,' I said. 'The country is all but ruined.'

He shrugged. 'There is money to keep the fleet waiting to escort the king home. There is money for his adventures abroad. Mention it to her as she dresses for dinner tonight, and I will speak with her after dinner.'

I waited until the queen had dragged herself up from her bed and was seated before her mirror, her maid behind her brushing her hair. Jane Dormer, who was usually such a fierce guardian of the queen's privacy, had taken the fever herself, and was lying down. It was just the queen and I and some unimportant girl from the Norfolk family.

'Your Grace,' I said simply. 'I have had news of my husband.'

She turned her dull gaze on me. 'I had forgotten you are married. Is he alive?'

'Yes,' I said. 'He is among the English men and women hoping to be ransomed out of Calais.'

She was only slightly more interested. 'Who is arranging this?'

'Lord Robert. His men have been held captive too.'

The queen sighed. 'Are they asking very much?'

'I don't know,' I said frankly.

'I will speak with Lord Robert,' she said, as if she were very weary. 'I will do what I can for you and your husband, Hannah.'

I knelt before her. 'Thank you, Your Grace.'

When I looked up I saw that she was exhausted. 'I wish I could bring my husband home so easily,' she said. 'But I don't believe he will ever come home to me again.'

The queen was too ill to transact the business herself—the fever was always worse after dinner and she could barely breathe for coughing—but she scrawled an assent on a bill on the treasury for money and Lord Robert assured me that the business would go through. We met in the stable yard. He was riding to Hatfield and in a hurry to be off.

'Will he come to you here at court?' he asked casually.

I hesitated. I had not thought of the details of our meeting. 'I suppose so,' I said. 'I should leave a message for him at my old shop in Fleet Street.'

I said nothing more, but a deeper worry was starting to dawn on me. What if Daniel's love for me had not grown, like mine, in absence? What if he had decided that I was dead and that he should make a new life elsewhere in Italy or France as he had so often said? Worse than that: what if he thought I had run away with Lord Robert and chosen a life of shame without him? What if he had cast me off?

'Can I get a message to him as he is released?' I asked.

Lord Robert shook his head. 'You will have to trust that he will come and find you,' he said cheerfully. 'Is he the faithful type of man?'

I thought of his years of steady waiting for me, and how he had watched me come to my love of him, and how he had let me go and return to him. 'Yes,' I said shortly.

Lord Robert sprang up into the saddle. 'If you see John Dee, would you tell him that Princess Elizabeth wants that map of his?' he said.

'Why would she want a map?' I asked, immediately suspicious.

Lord Robert winked at me. He leaned from his horse and spoke very low. 'If the queen dies without naming Elizabeth as her heir then we may have a battle on our hands.'

His horse shifted and I stepped back quickly. 'Oh, not again,' I said.

'No fight with the people of England,' he assured me. 'They want the Protestant princess. But with the Spanish king. D'you think he'd let such a prize slip away if he thought he could come claim it for himself?'

'You are arming and planning for war *again*?' I asked.

'Why else would I want my soldiers back?' he demanded. 'Thank you for your help with that, Hannah.'

I choked on my shock. 'My lord!'

He patted the horse's neck and tightened the rein. 'It's always a coil,' he said simply. 'And you are always in it, Hannah. You cannot live with a queen and not be enmeshed in a dozen plots. You live in a snake pit and I tell you frankly, you have not the aptitude for it. Now go to her. I hear she is worse.'

'Not at all,' I said stoutly. 'You can tell the princess that the queen has rallied and is better today.'

He nodded. He did not believe me at all. 'Well, God bless her anyway,' he said kindly. 'For whether she lives or dies she has lost Calais, she has lost her babies, lost her husband, lost the throne and lost everything.'

Lord Robert was gone for more than a week and so I could have no news of the release of the English captives. I went to our old print shop and pinned a note on the door. The times were so bad and rents so poor in London that still no one had taken the shop, and many of my father's books and papers would still be stacked, untouched, in the cellar. I thought that if Daniel did not come to me, and if the queen did not recover, then I might set up as a bookseller once again.

When I got back to court there was a scurry around the queen's apartments. She had collapsed while dressing for dinner and been put to bed. The doctors had been called and were bleeding her. Quietly, I handed Danny to Will Somers, who was in the privy chamber, and I went inside the guarded doors to the queen's bedchamber.

Jane Dormer, white as a sheet and visibly ill herself, was at the head of the bed, holding the queen's hand as the physicians were picking fat leeches off her legs and dropping them back into their glass jar. The queen's thin legs were bruised where their vile mouths had been fixed on her. The maid twitched down the sheet. The queen's eyes were closed in shame at being so exposed, her head turned away. The doctors bowed and got themselves out of the room.

'Go to bed, Jane,' the queen said weakly. 'You are as sick as I am.'

'Not until I have seen Your Grace take some soup.'

The queen shook her head and waved her hand to the door. Jane curtsied and went out, leaving the queen and me alone.

'Is that you, Hannah?' she asked without opening her eyes.

'Yes, Your Grace.'

'Will you write a letter for me, in Spanish? And send it to the king without showing it to anyone?'

'Yes, Your Grace.'

I took some paper and a pen from the table, drew up a little stool and sat beside her bed. She dictated to me in English and I translated it into Spanish as I wrote. The sentences were long and fluent. I knew that she had been waiting a long time to send him this letter. In all the nights when she had wept for him, she had composed this letter to be sent from her deathbed. She wrote him a letter like the one her mother wrote to her father from her deathbed: a letter of love and constancy to a man who had offered nothing but heartache.

Dearest Husband,

Since it has pleased you to stay far from me in my illness and my sorrow, I write to you these words which I wish I might have said to your beloved face.

You could not have had and never will have a more loving and faithful wife. The sight of you gladdened my heart every day that we were together. My only regret is that we spent so much time apart.

It seems very hard to me that I should face death as I have faced life: alone and without the one I love. I pray that you may never know the loneliness that has walked step by step with me every day of my life.

This may be my last chance to bid you farewell and to send you my love. May we meet in heaven, though we could not be together on earth, prays

Your wife

Mary R.

The tears were running down my cheeks by the time I had written this to her dictation, but she was calm.

'You will get better, Your Grace,' I assured her.

'No,' she said simply. There was not a trace of self-pity in her tone. It was as if she were weary of the world. 'No. I don't think so.'

WINTER 1558

LORD ROBERT CAME TO COURT with the queen's council to press her to sign her will and name her heir. Every man in the council had been at Hatfield the previous month. All their advice for Queen Mary had been dictated by the queen in waiting.

'She is too sick to see anyone,' Jane Dormer said truculently.

She and I stood shoulder to shoulder in the doorway to the queen's apartments. Lord Robert winked at me but I did not smile back.

'This is her duty,' said the Lord Chancellor. 'She has to make a will.'

'She made one,' Jane said abruptly. 'Before she went into confinement last time.'

He shook his head and looked embarrassed. 'She named her child as heir, and the king as regent,' he said. 'But there was no child. She has to name the Princess Elizabeth now, and no regent. She has a duty to her country and you should not stand in her way.'

We wavered, and they saw it. 'Stand aside,' said the duke, and Jane and I stood unwillingly back and let them walk in to the queen.

They did not take very long, and when they were gone I went in to see her. She was lying propped up on her pillows, a bowl at her side to catch the black bile that spewed from her mouth when she coughed, a jug of squeezed lemons and sugar to take the taste from her lips, a maid in attendance but no one else. She was as lonely as any beggar coughing out her life on a stranger's doorstep.

'Your Grace, I sent your letter to your husband,' I said quietly. 'Pray God he reads it and comes home to you and you have a merry Christmas with him after all.'

Queen Mary did not even smile at the picture I painted. 'He will not,' she said dully. 'And I would rather not see him ride past me to Hatfield.' She coughed and held a cloth to her mouth. The maid stepped forward and took it from her, offered her the bowl, and then took it away.

'I have another task for you,' she said when she could speak again. 'I want you to go with Jane Dormer to Hatfield.'

I waited.

'Ask Elizabeth to swear on her immortal soul that if she inherits the kingdom she will keep the true faith,' she said, her voice a tiny thread but the conviction behind the words as strong as ever.

I hesitated. 'She will not swear,' I said, knowing Elizabeth.

'Then I will not name her my heir,' she said flatly. 'Mary Stuart in France would claim the throne with French blessing. Elizabeth has the choice. She can fight her way to the throne if she can find enough fools to follow her, or she can come to it with my blessing. But she has to swear to uphold the faith. And she has to mean it.'

'How will I know if she means it?' I asked.

She was too weary to turn her head to me. 'Look at her with your gift, Hannah,' she said. 'This is the last time I will ask you to see for me. Look at her with your gift and tell me what is the best for my England.'

I would have argued, but simple pity for her made me hold my tongue. This was a woman clinging on to life by the thinnest thread.

I bowed and went from the room.

Jane Dormer, still recovering from her own fever and exhausted from nursing the queen, riding in a litter, and I, with Danny astride before me, made our way north to Hatfield and noted sourly the number of fine horses that were going in the same direction as us, from the ailing queen to the thriving heir.

The old palace was ablaze with lights. There was some sort of banquet in progress as we arrived. 'I cannot break bread with her,' Jane said shortly. 'Let us ask to see her, and leave.'

'Of course we can dine,' I said practically. 'You must be starving. I am, and Danny needs to eat. You go and eat in the kitchen if it pleases you. I am going in to dine.'

I could have laughed at her astounded face. I lifted Danny up onto my hip and, braced against his weight, I walked into the dining hall at Hatfield.

Elizabeth had the trappings of queenship already, as if she were an actor practising a part in full costume. She had a gold canopy over a wooden chair so thickly carved and heavy it might almost have been a throne. On her right hand she had the Spanish ambassador, as if to flaunt that connection; on her left hand was seated the most favoured lord at this court, my Lord Robert. Beside him was the right-hand man of the Grand Inquisitor of London, the scourge of Protestantism, Dr John Dee; on the other side of the Spanish ambassador was the princess's cousin, who had once arrested her, now dearly beloved to his kin. Beyond him was a quietly ambitious man, a staunch Protestant: William Cecil. I looked at Elizabeth's table and smiled. Nobody would be able to guess which way this cat might jump, judging by those honoured with seats beside her. She had put Spanish and English, Catholic and Protestant advisers side by side. Who could deduce what was in her mind?

John Dee, looking down the hall, caught my smile and raised his hand to me in greeting. Lord Robert followed the direction of his gaze, saw me, and beckoned me forward. I threaded my way through the court and dropped a curtsy to the princess, who shot me a gleaming smile from her eyes like a jet arrow.

'Ah, it is the girl who was so afraid of being a woman that she first became a fool, and then became a widow,' she said acidly.

'Princess Elizabeth,' I said, curtsying as the words hit home.

'Have you come to see me?'

'Yes, Princess.'

'Have you a message for me from the queen?'

'Yes, Princess.'

There was a little ripple of attention all along the table.

'Is Her Majesty in good health?' The Spanish ambassador, Count Feria, leaned forward, taking the heat from the exchange.

'You would surely know better than I,' I said with a sourness that came easily to me, seeing him at Elizabeth's table. 'Since she writes intimately to only one person, since she loves one man in all the world, and he is your master.'

Elizabeth and my lord exchanged a hidden smile at my rudeness. The count turned his head away.

'You may take a seat with my ladies and see me privately after dinner,' the princess ruled. 'Did you come alone with your son?'

I shook my head. 'Jane Dormer came with me. She is dining alone. She did not want to keep this company.'

'I see you are not so choosy,' Elizabeth taunted me.

I met her bright black gaze without shrinking. 'Dinner is dinner, Princess. And both of us have gone hungry in the past.'

She laughed at that and nodded at them to make a space for me. 'She has become a witty fool,' she said to Lord Robert. 'I am glad of it. I never had much faith in seeings and predictions.'

'Once she told me a pretty vision,' he said, his voice very low, his eyes on me but his smile for her.

'Oh?'

'She told me I would be adored by a queen.'

They both laughed, that low-voiced chuckle of conspiring lovers, and he smiled down the hall at me. I met his gaze with a face like flint.

'What is the matter with you?' Elizabeth demanded of me after dinner. We were standing in an alcove in the gallery at Hatfield.

'I don't like Count Feria,' I said bluntly.

'You made that clear enough. Do you really think I will allow you to come into my dinner and insult my guests? You took off a fool's livery; you will have to behave like a lady.'

I smiled. 'Since I carry a message that you want to hear, I think you will listen to it before you have me thrown out of the gates, whether I am a fool or a lady.'

She laughed at my impertinence.

'And I doubt that you like him either,' I said boldly. 'First he was your enemy, now he is your friend. There are many such as him around you now, I should imagine.'

'Most of this court. And you among them.'

I shook my head. 'I have always admired you both.'

'You love her more than you love me,' she insisted jealously.

189

I laughed aloud at her childishness, and Lord Robert, standing near, turned to look at me with a smile.

'But, Princess, she loves me,' I said, 'and you have never done anything but abuse me and accuse me of being her spy.'

Elizabeth laughed too. 'Yes. But I don't forget that you came to serve me in the Tower. And I don't forget that you brought me a true vision. When you smelt the smoke from the burnings I knew then that I must become queen and bring peace to this country.'

'Well, amen to that,' I said.

'And what is your message?' she asked more soberly.

'Can we talk in your privy chamber? And can I bring Jane Dormer to you?'

'With Lord Robert,' she stipulated. 'And John Dee.'

I bowed my head and followed her as she walked down the gallery to her chamber. The court billowed into bows as she went past as if she were queen already. I smiled, remembering a day when she had limped with her shoe in her hand and no one had offered her an arm. Now they would lay down their cloaks in the mud to keep her feet dry.

We went into her chamber and Elizabeth took a small wooden chair by the fireside. She gestured that I could pull up a stool and I took it to the other side of the fire, put Danny on my knee and leaned back against the wooden panelling. The queen wanted me to advise her if Elizabeth would keep the true faith. I had to listen through the words to the meaning behind them. I had to look through the mask of her smiling face and into her heart.

The door opened and Jane came into the room. She swept Elizabeth a scant curtsy and stood before her. Elizabeth gestured her to sit.

'I will stand, if it please you,' Jane said stiffly.

'You have business with me.' Elizabeth invited her to begin.

'The queen has asked Hannah and me to come to you and put a question to you. The queen requires you to make your answer in very truth. She would want you to swear on your soul that the answer you give is the truth and the whole truth.'

'And what is this question?'

'The queen bid me tell you that she will name you as her heir, her one true heir, and you will be queen on the throne of England without a word of dissent if you will promise her that you will cleave to the true faith,' Jane said quietly.

John Dee drew in a sharp breath, but the princess was absolutely still.

'And if I do not?'

'Then she will name another heir.'

'Mary Stuart?'

'I do not know and I will not speculate,' Jane replied.

The princess nodded. 'Am I to swear on a Bible?' she asked.

'On your soul,' Jane said. 'On your immortal soul before God.'

It was a solemn moment. Elizabeth glanced towards Lord Robert and he took a little step towards her, as if he would protect her.

'And does she swear to name me as heir in return?'

Jane Dormer nodded. 'If you are of the true faith.'

Elizabeth took a deep breath. 'I will swear,' she said.

She rose to her feet. I did not rise as I should have done; I stayed completely still, my eyes fixed on her pale face as if I would read her like a clean page of text, fresh off the press, with the ink still drying.

Elizabeth raised her hand. 'I swear, on my immortal soul, that I shall keep this country in the true faith,' she said. Her hand trembled slightly. She brought it down and clasped her hands together before her, and turned to Jane Dormer.

'Did she ask for anything more?'

'No more,' Jane said, her voice very thin.

'So you can tell her I have done it?'

Jane's eyes slid towards me, and the princess was onto her at once.

'Ah, so that is what you are here for.' She rounded on me. 'My little seer-spy. You are to make a window into my soul and see into my heart and tell the queen what you imagine you saw.'

I said nothing.

'You will tell her that I swore her oath,' she commanded me.

I rose to my feet, Danny's little head lolling sleepily against my shoulder. 'If we may, we shall stay here tonight, and return to the queen tomorrow,' I said, avoiding answering. 'We shall leave at dawn,' I said, thinking of the frailty of the queen's health. I knew she would be hanging on to hear that England was safe within the true faith, that whatever else was lost, she had restored England into grace.

'Then I will bid you good night and God speed now,' Elizabeth said sweetly. She let us get to the door and Jane Dormer to go through ahead of me, before she said, so quietly that only I, listening for her summons, could have heard it: 'Hannah.'

I turned.

'I know you are her loyal friend as well as mine,' she said gently. 'Do this last service for your mistress and take my word as true, and let her go to her God with some comfort. Give her peace, and give peace to our country.'

I bowed to her and went out.

I thought we would leave Hatfield without another farewell, but when I went for my horse on a frosty cold morning with the sun burning red like an ember on the white horizon, there was Lord Robert looking handsome and smiling, wrapped in a dark red velvet cloak with John Dee at his side.

'The men are to be released from Calais within a week,' Robert said. 'They will be collected by a ship which will bring them into Gravesend.'

I felt my heart beat faster. 'Do you think he will have had my letter, that I sent when I first came home?' I asked.

Lord Robert shrugged. 'He may have done. But you can tell him yourself, soon enough.'

I drew a little closer to him. 'You see, if he did not receive it then he will not know that I escaped out of Calais. He might think I am dead. He might not come to England, he might go to Italy or somewhere.'

'Someone would have looked for you,' he said. 'If you had been killed they would have found your body.'

I shifted awkwardly. Daniel came to me and stretched out his arms. 'Dan'l up!' he commanded.

'Wait a moment,' I said absently. I turned back to Lord Robert. 'You see, if someone told him that I left with you . . .'

'Then he would know that you are alive, and where to find you,' he said logically. Then he checked and slapped his forehead. 'Mistress Boy, you have played me for an idiot all along. You are estranged from him, aren't you? And you fear that he will think you ran away with me? And he won't come for you because he has cast you off? And now you don't want me, but you've lost him, and all you've got is his son . . .' He broke off, struck with sudden doubt. 'He *is* your husband's son, isn't he?'

'Yes,' I said staunchly.

'Is he yours?' he said, some sense warning him that there was a lie hidden away somewhere near.

'Yes,' I said without wavering.

Lord Robert laughed aloud. 'My God, girl, you are a fool indeed. You did not love him till you lost him.'

'Yes,' I admitted through gritted teeth.

'Well, more a woman than a fool,' he said fairly. 'I would say women love men most when they have lost them, or cannot get them. Well-a-day, my pretty fool. You had best get a ship and set sail for your Daniel as soon as you can. Otherwise he will be out of prison and free as a bird flying away, and you will never find him at all.'

'Can I get a ship to Calais?' I asked blankly.

He thought for a moment. 'Not very readily, but you could go over with the ship that is going to fetch my soldiers home. I'll write you a note.'

He snapped his fingers to a stableboy and sent him running for a clerk with pen and paper. When the lad came he dictated three lines to give me a free pass on the boat for myself and my son.

I curtsied low to him in genuine gratitude. 'Thank you, my lord,' I said. 'I do thank you very deeply.'

He smiled his heart-turning smile. 'My pleasure, dearest little fool. But the ship sails within a week. Will you be able to leave the queen?'

'She's sinking fast,' I said slowly. 'That's why I was in such a hurry to leave at once. She was holding on for Elizabeth's answer.'

'Well, thank you for that information,' he said.

I bit my lip as I realised that to tell him was to tell Elizabeth, and those planning her campaign.

'No harm done,' he said. 'Half of her doctors are paid by us to let us know how she is.'

John Dee drew closer. 'And could you see into the princess's heart?' he asked gently. 'Could you tell if she was sincere in her oath for keeping the true faith? Do you believe she will be a Catholic queen?'

'I don't know,' I said simply. 'I shall pray for guidance on the way home.'

Robert would have said something, but John Dee put a hand on his arm. 'Hannah will say the right thing to the queen,' he said. 'She knows that it is not one queen or another that matters; it is not one name of God or another. What matters most is to bring peace to this country so that a man or woman in danger of cruelty or persecution can come here and be certain of a fair hearing.' He paused, and I thought of my father and me, coming to this England and hoping for a safe haven.

'What matters is that a man or woman can believe what they wish, and worship how they wish, to a God whom they name as they wish. What matters is that we make a strong country here which can be a force for good in the world, where men and women can question and learn freely. This country's destiny is to be a place where men and women can know that they are free.'

He stopped. Lord Robert was smiling down at me.

'I know what she will do,' Lord Robert said sweetly. 'Because she is my tenderhearted Mistress Boy still. She will say whatever she has to say to comfort the queen in her final hours. God bless her, the poor lady.'

I leaned down and scooped Daniel up into my arms. The grooms brought my horse from the stables and Jane Dormer came from the house and got into the litter without a word to either man.

'Good luck in Calais,' Robert Dudley said, smiling. 'Few women succeed in finding the love of their life. I hope you do, little Mistress Boy.'

It was a cold long ride back to St James's palace, but Danny's little body was warm as he rode before me, and every now and then I could hear a delighted little carol of song from him.

When we got to the palace the hall was subdued, the few guards playing cards, the firelight flickering, the torches burning low. Will Somers was in the queen's presence chamber, with half a dozen others, mostly paid court officials and physicians. There were no friends or beloved kin waiting to see the queen, praying for her in her illness. She was not England's darling any more, and the chamber rang with emptiness.

Danny spotted Will and sprang towards him.

'You go in,' Will said. 'She has been asking for you.'

'Is she any better?' I asked hopefully.

He shook his head. 'No.'

Cautiously I opened the door to her privy chamber and went in. Two of her women were seated at the fireside, enjoying a gossip when they should have been watching her. They jumped up guiltily as we went past them into the queen's bedchamber.

Mary was curled up in the bed like a little girl, her hair in a cloud around her face. She did not turn her head at the sound of the opening door, so deep was she in her grief.

'Your Grace?' Jane Dormer said, her voice cracking. 'It is I. And Hannah the Fool. We have come back from Princess Elizabeth.'

The queen sighed deeply and turned her head wearily towards us.

'She took the oath,' Jane said. 'She swore she would keep the country in the true faith.'

I stepped to the bedside and took Queen Mary's hand. It fluttered in mine like a dying bird.

'I saw Elizabeth take the oath,' I started. I was about to tell her the kindest lie that I could form. But gently, irresistibly, I told her the truth, as if the Sight was speaking the truth through me. 'Mary, she will not keep it. But she will do better than keep it, I hope you can understand that now. She will become a better queen than she is a woman. She will teach the people of this country that each man and woman must consider his or her own conscience, must find their own way to God. And she will bring this country to peace and prosperity. You did the very best that you could do for the people of this country, and you have a good successor. Elizabeth will never be the woman that you have been, but she will be a good queen to England, I know it.'

She raised her head a little and her eyelids fluttered open. She looked at me with her straight honest gaze once more, and then she closed her eyes and lay still.

I did not stay to watch the rush of servants to Hatfield. I packed my bag and took Danny by the hand and took a boat down the river to Gravesend. I had my lord's letter to show to the ship's captain, and he promised me a berth as soon as they sailed. We waited a day or two, and then Danny and I boarded the little ship and set sail for Calais.

Danny was delighted by the ship, the moving deck beneath his feet, the slap and rush of the waves, the creaking of the sails and the cry of the seagulls. 'Sea!' he exclaimed, over and over again. He took my face in both of his little hands and gazed at me with his enormous dark eyes, desperate to tell me the significance of his delight. 'Sea. Mamma! Sea!'

'What did you say?' I said, taken aback. He had never spoken my name before; I had expected him to call me Hannah. I had never thought he would call me mother.

'Sea,' he repeated obediently, and wriggled to be put down.

Calais was a different place with the walls breached and the sides of the castle smeared with black oil from the siege, the stones darkened with smoke from the fire. The captain's face was grim when we came into the harbour and saw the English ships, which had been fired where they were moored, like so many heretics at the stake. He tied up with military smartness and slapped down the gangplank like a challenge. I took Danny in my arms and went with the captain and the armed guard up to the castle under our white pennant of truce.

We were expected; the commander came out civilly enough and spoke to the captain in rapid French. The captain bridled, understanding perhaps one word in three, and then leaned forward and said very loudly and slowly: 'I have come for the English men, as has been agreed, and I expect them forthwith.'

When he had no response, he said it again, pitched a little higher.

'Captain, would you like me to speak for you? I can speak French,' I offered.

He turned to me with relief. 'Can you? That might help.'

I stepped forward a little and said to the commander in French: 'Captain Gatting offers his apologies but he cannot speak French. I can translate for you. I am Madame Carpenter. I have come for my husband who has been ransomed and the captain has come for the other men. We have a ship waiting in the harbour.'

He bowed slightly. 'Madame, I am obliged to you. The men are mustered and ready. The civilians are to be released first and then the soldiers will march down to the harbour. Their weapons will not be returned. It is agreed?'

I translated for the captain and he scowled at me. 'We ought to get the weapons back,' he said.

I shrugged. All I could think of was Daniel, waiting somewhere inside the castle for his release. 'We can't.'

'Tell him very well, but tell him that I'm not best pleased,' the captain said sourly.

'Captain Gatting agrees,' I said smoothly in French.

'Please come inside.' The commander led us over the drawbridge and into the inner courtyard. Another thick curtain wall with a portcullis doorway led to the central courtyard where about two hundred men were mustered, the soldiers in one block, the civilians in another. I raked the ranks for Daniel but I could not see him.

'Commandant, I am seeking my husband, Daniel Carpenter, a civilian,' I said. 'I cannot see him, and I am afraid of missing him in the crowd.'

'Daniel Carpenter?' he asked. He turned and snapped an order at the man guarding the civilians.

'Daniel Carpenter!' the man bawled out.

In the middle of one of the ranks a man came forward. 'Who asks for him?' said Daniel, my husband.

I closed my eyes for a moment as the world seemed to shift all around me.

'I am Daniel Carpenter,' Daniel said again, not a quaver in his voice, stepping forward on the very brink of freedom, greeting whatever new danger might threaten him without a moment's hesitation.

The commander beckoned him to come forward and moved to one side so that I could see him. Daniel saw me for the first time and I saw him go very pale. He was older-looking, a little weary, thinner, but nothing worse than winter-pale and winter-thin. He was the same. He was my beloved Daniel with his dark curling hair and his dark eyes and his kissable mouth and that particular smile which was my smile: it only ever shone on me; it was at once desiring, steadfast and amused.

'Daniel,' I whispered. 'My Daniel!'

'Ah, Hannah,' he said quietly. 'You.'

Behind us, the civilians were signing their names and marching out to freedom. I did not hear the shouted orders or the tramp of their feet. All I could see, all I could know, was Daniel.

'I ran away,' I said. 'I am sorry. I was afraid and I did not know what to do. Lord Robert gave me safe passage to England and I went back to Queen Mary. I wrote to you at once. I would not have gone without you if there had been any time to think.'

Gently, he stepped forward and took my hand. 'I have dreamed and dreamed of you,' he said quietly. 'I thought you had left me for Lord Robert when you had the chance.'

'No! Never. I knew at once that I wanted to be with you. I have been trying to get a letter to you. I have been trying to reach you. I swear it, Daniel. I have thought of nothing and no one but you, ever since I left.'

'Have you come back to be my wife?' he asked simply.

I nodded. At this most important moment I found I lost all my fluency. I could not speak. I could not argue my case, I could not persuade him in any one of my many languages. I could not even whisper. I just nodded emphatically, and Danny on my hip, his arms round my neck, gave a gurgle of laughter and nodded too, copying me.

I had hoped Daniel would be glad and snatch me up into his arms, but he was sombre. 'I will take you back,' he said solemnly. 'And I will not question you, and we will say no more about this time apart. You will never have a word of reproach from me, I swear it, and I will bring this boy up as my son.'

For a moment I did not understand what he meant, and then I gasped. 'Daniel, he *is* your son! This is your son by your woman. This is her son. We were running from the French horsemen and she fell, she gave him to me as she went down. I am sorry, Daniel. She died at once. And this is your boy; I passed him off as mine. He is my boy now. He is my boy too.'

'He is mine?' he asked wonderingly. He looked at the child for the first time and saw, as anyone would have to see, the dark eyes that were his own, and the brave little smile.

'He is mine too,' I said jealously. 'He knows that he is my boy.'

Daniel gave a little half-laugh, almost a sob, and put his arms out. Danny reached for his father and went confidingly to him, put his plump little arms round his neck, looked him in the face and leaned back so he could scrutinise him. Then he thumped his little fist on his own chest and said, by way of introduction: 'Dan'l.'

Daniel nodded, and pointed to his own chest. 'Father,' he said.

Danny's little half-moon eyebrows raised in interest.

'*Your* father,' Daniel said.

He took my hand and tucked it firmly under his arm, as he held his son tightly with the other. He walked to the dispatching officer and gave his name and was ticked off their list. Then together we walked towards the open portcullis.

'Where are we going?' I asked, although I did not care. As long as I was with him and Danny, we could go anywhere in the world, be it flat or round, be it the centre of the heavens or wildly circling round the sun.

'We are going to make a home,' he said firmly. 'For you and me and Daniel. We are going to live as the People, you are going to be my wife, and his mother, and one of the Children of Israel.'

'I agree,' I said, surprising him again.

He stopped in his tracks. 'You agree?' he repeated comically.

I nodded.

He drew a breath. 'Hannah, in all my dreams, I did not dream of this.'

I pressed against his side. 'Daniel, I did not know what I wanted when I was a girl. And then I was a fool in every sense of the word. And now that I am a woman grown, I know that I love you and I want this son of yours, and our other children who will come. I have seen a woman break her heart for love: my Queen Mary. I have seen another break her soul to avoid it: my Princess Elizabeth. I don't want to be Mary or Elizabeth; I want to be me: Hannah Carpenter.'

'And we shall live somewhere that we can follow our beliefs without danger,' he insisted.

'Yes,' I said, 'in the England that Elizabeth will make.'

PHILIPPA GREGORY

Philippa Gregory lives in Hartlepool, but I managed to catch up with her in London on her publicity tour for *The Queen's Fool*. As we sat chatting over mouth-watering Italian risotto, I asked her how long it took to research her novels. 'Usually about two and a half years,' she told me, 'but a little less time for this novel because, obviously, I used a lot of the research from *The Other Boleyn Girl*. At that time I had come across accounts of a network of Jewish families living undercover in Europe and was interested in pursuing that—which gave me extra research to do! Amazingly, I came across a book written in 1932 called *A History of the Marranos* and in the foreword the Jewish researcher had written: "Well, at least now in 1932 we have a Europe that is safe for Jewish people and we can live at peace with our neighbours at last." It was so poignant to read that and I found it so very moving. Anti-Semitism is still a live issue and that, in a sense, is why I love history so much. The past gives you an added insight into the world today.'

Philippa Gregory had also chanced upon a reference in a historical document about a woman who had been fool to both Queen Mary and Queen Elizabeth. 'I read up about fools and discovered that there were two different sorts,' Philippa explained. 'One type was comical like Will Somers in the book, and the other type was what they called holy fools, or innocent fools—people who were perhaps even mentally ill—who either had "the sight", or visions. So I made Hannah both Jewish and a holy fool. When you are writing a historical novel you have to first ground yourself in the facts, then answer the question: "If I was her, at that time, how would I react to this situation? The historical records never tell you *why* people do things, only what they do. The novelist can go further than the historian by attempting to explain the human motives.'

To keep track of the wealth of research she gathers, Philippa Gregory keeps a large time-chart in her study, detailing the events of every week and every day during the period covered by the novel. The walls, too, are plastered with portraits of the characters she is writing about, the plans of their houses, and the details of their daily lives—even the weather. 'Readers want accurate historical fiction. This is a wonderful thing to write and should be equally wonderful to read. One of the nice things people say is that reading my books is a very intense, real experience. For me it's got to be like that too.'

Philippa's next project, alongside writing her next historical novel, is the renovation her new home, a farmhouse on the North Yorkshire Moors. 'And for relaxation?' I asked her. 'Spending time with my family and walking my Great Dane, Peaches,' she replied.

Jane Eastgate

Kristin Hannah
Between Sisters

Meghann Dontess is a woman haunted by heartbreak. Twenty-five years ago she was forced to make a terrible choice; one that cost her everything and, most importantly, the love of her sister, Claire.

Now, Meghann is a successful divorce lawyer, with everything she could want in life—everything except love.

Chapter One

DR BLOOM WAITED PATIENTLY for an answer.

Meghann Dontess leaned back in her seat and studied her fingernails. It was time for a manicure. 'I try not to feel too much, Harriet. You know that. I find it impedes my enjoyment of life.'

'Is that why you've seen me every week for four years? Because you enjoy your life so much?'

'I wouldn't point that out if I were you. It doesn't say much for your psychiatric skills. It's possible, you know, that I was perfectly normal when I met you and you're actually *making* me crazy.'

'You're using humour as a shield again.'

'You're giving me too much credit. That wasn't funny.'

Harriet didn't smile. 'Let's talk about the day that you and Claire were separated.'

Meghann shifted uncomfortably in her seat. She knew what Harriet was poking around for, and Harriet knew she knew. If Meghann didn't answer, the question would simply be asked again. 'Separated. A nice, clean word. Detached. I like it, but that subject is closed.'

'It's interesting that you maintain a relationship with your mother while distancing yourself from your sister.'

Meghann shrugged. 'Mama's an actress. I'm a lawyer. We're comfortable with make-believe.'

'Meaning?'

'Have you ever read one of her interviews?'

'No.'

'She tells everyone that we lived this poor, pathetic-but-loving existence. We pretend it's the truth.'

'You were living in Bakersfield when the pathetic-but-loving pretence ended, right?'

Meghann remained silent.

Harriet went on, 'Claire was nine years old. She was missing several teeth, if I remember correctly, and having difficulties with maths.'

'Don't,' Meghann said, curling her fingers round the chair's sleek wooden arms.

Harriet stared at her. Small, round glasses magnified her eyes. 'Don't back away, Meg. We're making progress.'

'Any more progress, and I'll need an aid car. We should talk about my practice. That's why I come to you, you know. It's a pressure cooker down in Family Court these days. Yesterday I had a deadbeat dad drive up in a Ferrari and then swear he was flat broke. Didn't want to pay for his daughter's tuition. Too bad I videotaped his arrival.'

'Why do you keep paying me if you don't want to discuss the root of your problems?'

'I have issues, not problems. And there's no point in poking around in the past. I was sixteen when all that happened. Now I'm a whopping forty-two. It's time to move on. I did the right thing. It doesn't matter any more.'

'Then why do you still have the nightmare?'

Meghann should have seen that coming. She glanced down at her platinum and gold watch. 'Too bad, Harriet. Time's up. I guess we'll have to solve my pesky neuroses next week.' She stood up.

'Do you like your life, Meghann?' Harriet asked.

That wasn't what she'd expected. 'What's not to like? I'm the best divorce attorney in the state. I live—'

'Alone.'

'In a kick-ass condominium above the Pike Place Public Market and drive a brand-new Porsche.'

'Family?'

Maybe it was time to get a new therapist. Harriet had ferreted out all of Meghann's weak points. 'My mom stayed with me for a week last year. If I'm lucky, she'll come back for another visit just in time to watch the colonisation of Mars on MTV.'

'And Claire?'

'My sister and I have problems, I'll admit it. But nothing major. We're just too busy to get together.' When Harriet didn't speak, Meghann rushed to fill the uncomfortable silence. 'OK, she makes me crazy, the way she's throwing her life away. She's smart enough to do anything, but she stays tied to that loser campground they call a resort.'

'With her father.'

'I don't want to discuss my sister. And I *definitely* don't want to discuss her father.'

Harriet tapped her pen on the table. 'OK, how about this: When was the last time you slept with the same man twice?'

'I like variety.'

'The way you like younger men, right? Men who have no desire to settle down.'

'I don't want a house with a picket fence in suburbia. I'm not interested in family life but I like sex.'

'And the loneliness, do you like that?'

'I'm not lonely,' she said stubbornly. 'I'm independent. Men don't like a strong woman.'

'Strong men do.'

'Then I'd better start hanging out in gyms instead of bars.'

'And strong women face their fears. They talk about the painful choices they've made in their lives.'

Meghann actually flinched. 'Sorry, Harriet, I need to scoot. See you next week.'

She rushed from the office.

Outside, it was a gloriously bright June day. Early in the so-called summer. Everywhere else in the country, people were swimming and barbecuing and organising poolside picnics. Here, in good ole Seattle, people were methodically checking their calendars and muttering that it was June, damn it.

Only a few tourists were around this morning, out-of-towners recognisable by the umbrellas tucked under their arms. Meghann crossed the busy street and stepped up onto the grassy lawn of the waterfront park. In front of her the deep blue Puget Sound stretched along the pale horizon. She wished she could take comfort from that view; often she could. But today her mind was caught in the net of another time and place.

If she closed her eyes, which she dared not do, she'd remember it all: the dialling of the telephone number, the stilted, desperate conversation with a man she didn't know, the long drive to that little town up north. And, worst of all, the tears she'd wiped from her little sister's flushed cheeks when she said, *I'm leaving you.*

Her fingers tightened round the railing. Dr Bloom was wrong. Talking about Meghann's painful choice and the lonely years that had followed it wouldn't help.

Her past wasn't a collection of memories to be worked through; it was like an oversized Samsonite with a bum wheel. Meghann had learned that a long time ago. All she could do was drag it along behind her.

Claire Cavenaugh stood on the bank of the Skykomish River, her work boots almost ankle-deep in the soft brown mud. Beside her an out-of-gas Weed Eater lay on its side. She smiled, wiped a gloved hand across her sweaty brow. The amount of manual labour it took to get the resort ready for summer was unbelievable.

Resort.

That was what her dad called these sixteen acres. Sam Cavenaugh had come across this acreage almost forty years ago, back when Hayden had been nothing more than a gas-station stop on the rise up Stevens Pass. He'd bought the parcel for a song and settled into the decrepit farmhouse that came with it. He'd named his place River's Edge Resort and begun to dream of a life that didn't include hard hats and ear-plugs and night shifts at the paper plant in Everett.

At first he'd worked after hours and weekends. With a chain saw, a pick-up truck, and a plan drawn out on a cocktail napkin, he began. He hacked out campsites and cleaned out a hundred years' worth of under-brush and built each knotty-pine riverfront cabin by hand. Now River's Edge was a thriving family business. There were eight cabins in all, each with two pretty little bedrooms and a single bathroom and a deck that overlooked the river.

In the past few years they'd added a swimming pool and a game room. Plans for a miniature-golf course and a Laundromat were in the works. It was the kind of place where the same families came back year after year to spend their precious vacation time.

Claire still remembered the first time she'd seen it. The towering trees and rushing silver river had seemed like paradise to her. Her childhood memories before coming to River's Edge were grey: ugly towns that came and went; uglier apartments in run-down buildings. And Mama. Always on the run from something or other. Mama had married repeat-edly, but Claire couldn't remember a man ever being around for longer than a carton of milk. Meghann was the one Claire remembered. The older sister who took care of everything . . . and then walked away one day, leaving Claire behind.

Now, all these years later, their lives were connected by the thinnest of strands. Once every few months she and Meghann talked on the phone. Then Meghann would invariably 'get another call' and hang up. Her sister loved to underscore how successful she was and how Claire had sold herself short. 'Living on that silly little campground, cleaning up after people' was the usual wording. Every single Christmas she offered to pay for college. As if reading *Beowulf* would improve Claire's life.

For years Claire had longed to be friends as well as sisters, but Meghann didn't want that, and Meghann always got her way. They were what Meghann wanted them to be: polite strangers who shared a blood type and an ugly childhood.

Claire reached down for the Weed Eater. As she slogged across the spongy ground, she noticed a dozen things that needed to be done before opening day. Roses that needed to be trimmed, moss that needed to be scraped off the roofs, mildew that needed to be bleached off the porch railings. She made a mental note to ask George, their handyman, to scrub out the canoes this afternoon.

She tossed the Weed Eater in the back of the pick-up. It hit with a clanging thunk that rattled the rusted bed.

'Hey, sweetie. You goin' to town?'

She turned and saw her father standing on the porch of the registration building. He wore an old pair of overalls and a flannel shirt.

He pulled a red bandanna out of his hip pocket and wiped his brow as he walked towards her. 'I'm fixing that freezer. Don't you go pricing new ones.'

There wasn't an appliance made that he couldn't repair, but Claire was going to check out prices, just the same. 'You need anything from town?' she asked.

'Smitty has a part for me. Could you pick it up?'

'You bet. And have George start on the canoes when he gets here, OK?'

'I'll put it on the list. You here for dinner?'

'Not tonight. The princess has a Tee Ball game at Riverfront Park, remember? Five o'clock.'

'Oh, yeah. I'll be there.'

Claire nodded, knowing that he would. He hadn't missed a single event in his granddaughter's life. 'Bye, Dad.'

She wrenched the truck's door handle and yanked hard. The door screeched open. She climbed up into the seat.

Dad thumped the truck's door. 'Drive safely. Watch the turn at milepost seven.'

She smiled. He'd been giving her that exact bit of advice for almost two decades. 'I love you, Dad.'

'I love you, too. Now, go get my granddaughter. If you hurry, we'll have time to watch *SpongeBob SquarePants* before the game.'

Chapter Two

THE WEST SIDE of the office building faced the Sound. A wall of floor-to-ceiling windows framed the beautiful view.

Meghann sat alone at a long, kidney-shaped conference table. The glossy cherry-and-ebony-wood surface bespoke elegance and money. When a person sat down at this table and looked at that view, the point was clear: Whoever owned this office was damn successful.

It was true. Meghann had achieved every goal she'd set for herself. When she'd started college as a scared, lonely teenager, she'd dared to dream of a better life. Now she had it. Her practice was among the most successful and most respected in the city.

She glanced down at her watch: four twenty. Her client was late.

You would think that charging well over $300 an hour would encourage people to be on time.

'Ms Dontess?' came a voice through the intercom.

'Yes, Rhona?'

'Your sister, Claire, is on line one.'

'Put her through. And buzz me when May Monroe gets here.'

Meghann pushed the button on her phone and forced a smile into her voice. 'Claire, it's good to hear from you.'

'The phone works both ways, you know. So how's life in Moneyland?'

'Good. And in Hayden? Everyone still sitting around waiting for the river to flood?'

'That danger's passed for the year.'

'Oh.' Meghann stared out of her window, casting for something to talk about. Huge orange cranes loaded multicoloured containers onto a tanker. She had no idea what to say to her sister. They had a past in common, but that was pretty much it. 'So how's that beautiful niece of mine? Did she like the skateboard?'

'She loved it.' Claire laughed. 'But really, Meg, someday you'll have to ask a salesperson for help. Five-year-old girls don't generally have the coordination for skateboards.'

'You did. We were living in Needles that year.' Meg immediately wished she hadn't said that. It always hurt to remember their past together. For a lot of years Claire had been more of a daughter to Meghann than a sister. Certainly, Meg had been more of a mother to Claire than Mama ever had.

'Just get her a Disney movie next time. You don't need to spend so much money on her. She's happy with a Polly Pocket.'

Whatever that was. An awkward silence fell between them. Meghann looked down at her watch, then they both spoke at once.

'What are you—'

'How's work going—'

'Good. And the camp?'

'Resort. We open in two weeks. The Jeffersons are having a family reunion here with about twenty people.'

'A week without phone access or television reception? Why am I hearing the *Deliverance* theme music in my head?'

'Some families like to be together,' Claire said in that crisp you've-hurt-me voice.

'I'm sorry. You're right. I know you love the place. Hey,' she said, as if she had just thought of it. 'Why don't you borrow some money from me and build a nice little spa on the property? Better yet, a small hotel. People would flock there for a good body wrap. God knows you've got the mud.'

Claire sighed heavily. 'You just have to remind me that you're successful and I'm not. Damn it, Meg.'

'I didn't mean that. It's just . . . that I know you can't expand a business without capital.'

'I don't want your money, Meg. *We* don't want it.'

There it was: the reminder that Meg was an *I* and Claire was a *we*. Meg refused to feel stung by the remark. That jealousy should have gone away years ago. 'I'm sorry if I said the wrong thing. I just want to help.'

'I'm not the baby girl who needs her big sister's protection any more, Meg.'

'Sam was always good at protecting you.' Meg heard a tiny flare of bitterness in her voice.

'Yeah.' Claire paused, drew in a breath. Meghann knew what her sister was doing. Regrouping, climbing to softer, safer ground. 'I'm going to Lake Chelan soon.'

'The yearly trip with the girlfriends,' Meghann said, thankful for the change in subject. 'What do you call yourselves? The Bluesers?'

'Yeah.'

'You all going back to that same place?'

'Every summer since high school.'

Meghann couldn't imagine still being friends with people she'd gone to high school with. 'Well, have fun.'

'Oh, we will. This year, Charlotte—'

The intercom buzzed. 'Meghann? Mrs Monroe is here.'

'Damn. Sorry, Claire, I've got to run.'

'Oh, right. I know how much you love to hear about my college-dropout friends.'

'It's not that. I have a client who just arrived.'

'Yeah, sure. Bye.'

'Bye.' Meghann disconnected the call just as her secretary showed May Monroe into the conference room.

'Hello, May,' Meghann said, walking briskly towards her client. 'Thank you, Rhona. No calls, please.'

Her secretary nodded and left the room, closing the door.

May Monroe stood in front of a large oil painting, a Nechita original entitled *True Love*. Meghann had always loved the irony of that; here, in this room, true love died every day of the week.

May wore a serviceable black jersey dress and black shoes that were at least five years out of date. Her wedding ring was a plain gold band. Looking at her, you would never know that her husband drove a jet-black Mercedes and had a regular Tuesday game at the Broadmoor Golf Course. May probably hadn't spent money on herself in years. Not since she'd slaved at a local restaurant to put her husband through dental school.

'Please, May, sit down.'

May jerked forwards like a marionette who'd been moved by someone else. She sat in one of the black suede chairs.

Meghann took her usual seat at the head of the table. Spread out in front of her were several manila file folders with bright pink Post-it notes fanned along the edges of the paperwork. Meghann looked at her client. 'As I told you at our last meeting, I hired a private investigator to check into your husband's financial affairs.'

'It was a waste of time, right?'

'Not exactly.'

May stared at her for a long moment, and then she stood up and went to the silver coffee service set out on the cherry-wood sideboard. 'I see,' she said. 'What did you find out?'

'He has more than six hundred thousand dollars in an account in the Cayman Islands, which is under his own name. Seven months ago he took almost all of the equity out of your home. Perhaps you thought you were signing refinance documents?'

May turned round. She was holding a coffee cup and saucer. The porcelain chattered in her shaking hands as she moved towards the conference table. 'The rates had come down.'

'What came down was the cash. Right into his hands.'

'Oh, my,' she whispered.

'It gets worse,' Meghann went on, trying to be gentle with her words but knowing how deep a cut she'd leave behind. 'He sold the practice to his partner, Theodore Blevin, for a dollar.'

'Why would he do that? It's worth—'

'So you wouldn't be able to get the half you're entitled to.'

At that, May's legs seemed to give out on her. She crumpled into her chair. The cup and saucer hit the table with a clatter. Coffee burped over the porcelain rim and puddled on the wood. May immediately started dabbing the mess with her napkin. 'I'm sorry.'

Meghann touched her client's wrist. 'Don't be.' She got up, grabbed some more napkins, and blotted the spill.

'Do any of those documents say why he did this to me?'

Meghann reached into the file and pulled out a photograph. Very gently she pushed it towards May. 'Her name is Ashleigh.'

'Ashleigh Stoker. I guess I know why he always offered to pick Sarah up from piano lessons.'

Meghann nodded. It was always worse when the wife knew the mistress, even in passing. 'Washington is a no-fault state; we don't need grounds for a divorce, so his affair doesn't matter.'

May looked up. She wore the vague, glassy-eyed expression of an accident victim. 'It doesn't matter?' She closed her eyes. 'I'm an idiot.' The words were more breath than sound.

'No. You're an honest, trustworthy woman who put a selfish man through ten years of college so *he* could have a better life.'

'It was supposed to be *our* better life.'

'Of course it was.'

Meg reached out, touched May's hand. 'You trusted a man who told you he loved you. Now he's counting on you to be good ole accommodating May, the woman who puts her family first and makes life easy for Dr Dale Monroe.'

May looked confused, maybe even a little frightened. 'What should we do? I don't want to hurt the children.'

'He's the one who's hurt the children, May. He's stolen money from them. And from you.'

'But he's a good father.'

'Then he'll want to see that they're provided for, and he'll hand over half of the assets without a fight.'

'And if he doesn't?'

'Then we'll make him.'

'He'll be angry.'

Meghann leaned forwards. 'You're the one who should be angry, May. This man lied to you, cheated on you, and stole from you.'

'He also fathered my children,' May answered. 'I don't want this to get ugly. I want him . . . to know he can come home.'

Oh, May. Meghann chose her words carefully. 'We're simply going to be fair, May. I don't want to hurt anyone, but you sure aren't going to be left destitute by this man. Period. He's a very, very wealthy orthodontist. I won't let him hurt you any more.'

'You think a few rounds of paperwork and a pile of money in the bank will protect me from that?' She sighed. 'Go ahead, Ms Dontess, do what you need to do to protect my children's future. But let's not pretend you can make it painless, OK? It already hurts so much I can barely breathe, and it has just begun.'

Across the blistered expanse of prairie grass, a row of windmills dotted the cloudless horizon. Their blades turned in a slow and steady rhythm. Sometimes, when the weather was right, you could hear the creaking *thwop-thwop-thwop* of each rotation. Today it was too hot to hear anything except the beating of your own heart.

Joe Wyatt stood on the poured-concrete slab that served as the warehouse's front porch, holding a now-warm can of Coke, all that was left of his lunch.

He stared at the distant fields. The heat was getting to him, and it was only the second week of June. There was no way he could handle summer in the Yakima Valley. It was time to move on again.

The realisation exhausted him.

He wondered how much longer he could do this, drift from town to town. Loneliness was wearing him down, whittling him away to a stringy shadow. Once—it felt long ago—he'd hoped that one of these places would feel right, that he'd come into some town, think, This is it, and rent an apartment instead of a seedy motel room. He no longer harboured such dreams. He knew better. After a week in the same room he started to feel things, remember things. If he settled in, got comfortable, he invariably dreamed about Diana.

That was OK. It hurt, of course, because seeing her face—even in his dreams—filled him with an ache that ran deep in his bones, but there was pleasure, too; a sweet remembrance of how life used to be, of the love he'd once been capable of feeling. If only the dreams stopped there, with memories of Diana sitting on the green grass of the quad in her college days or of them cuddled up in their big bed in the house on Bainbridge Island.

He was never that lucky. The sweet dreams invariably soured and turned ugly. More often than not he woke up whispering, 'I'm sorry.' The only way to survive was to keep moving.

He'd learned in these vagrant years how to be invisible. If a man cut his hair and dressed well, people saw him. But if a man let himself go, if he forgot to cut his hair and wore a faded Harley-Davidson T-shirt and carried a ratty backpack, no one noticed him.

Three years ago, when he'd first run away, he'd carried an expensive suitcase. He still remembered standing in his bedroom, packing for a trip without destination or duration, wondering what a man in exile would need. He'd packed khaki slacks and merino wool sweaters and even a black Joseph Abboud suit.

By the end of his first winter alone, he'd understood that those clothes were the archaeological remains of a forgotten life. All he needed in his new life were two pairs of jeans, a few T-shirts, a sweatshirt and a rain slicker. Everything else he'd given to charity.

He closed his eyes, and Diana came to him. 'I'm tired,' he said to her.

It's no good, what you're doing.

'I don't know what else to do.'

Go home.

'I can't.'

You break my heart, Joey.

And she was gone.

Claire stood at the kitchen sink, thinking about the phone conversation she'd had with Meg yesterday.

'Mommy, can I have another Eggo?'

'How do we ask for that?' Claire said absently.

'Mommy, may I *please* have another Eggo?'

Claire turned away from the window and dried her hands on a towel. 'Sure.' She popped a frozen waffle into the toaster. While it was warming, she looked around the room for more dirty dishes—and saw the place through her sister's eyes.

It wasn't a bad house, certainly not by Hayden standards. Small, yes: three tiny bedrooms tucked into the peaked first floor; a single bathroom on each floor; a living room; and a kitchen with an eating space that doubled as a counter. In the six years Claire had lived here, she'd painted the once moss-green walls a creamy French vanilla and replaced

213

the orange shag carpeting with hardwood floors. Her furniture, although mostly secondhand, was all framed in wood that she'd stripped and refinished herself.

Meg would see it differently, of course. Meg, who'd graduated from high school early and then breezed through seven years of college, who never failed to mention that she had buckets of money and had the nerve to send her niece Christmas gifts that made the others under the tree look paltry by comparison.

'My waffle's up.'

'So it is.' Claire took the waffle from the slot, buttered and cut it, then put the plate in front of her daughter. 'Here you go.'

Alison immediately stabbed a piece and popped it into her mouth, chewing in that cartoon-character way of hers.

Claire couldn't help smiling. She stared down at the miniature version of herself. Same fine blonde hair, same eyes, same heart-shaped face. Alison's father had left no genetic imprint on his daughter. It was fitting. The minute he'd heard Claire was pregnant, he'd reached for his running shoes.

'You're in your jammies, Mommy. We'll be late if you don't hurry.'

'You're right about that.' Claire thought about all the things she had to do today: recaulk the showers and bathroom windows; unblock the toilet in cabin five; and repair the canoe shed. It was early yet, not even eight o'clock, on the last day of school. Tomorrow they'd be leaving for a week of rest and fun at Lake Chelan. Claire glanced around. 'Have you seen my work list, Alison?'

'On the coffee table.'

Claire picked up her list from the table, shaking her head. She had absolutely no memory of leaving it there. Sometimes she wondered how she'd get by without Alison.

'I want ballet lessons, Mommy. Is that OK?'

Claire smiled. 'I wanted to be a ballerina once.'

'How come you're a worker bee instead?'

'Worker bee is just what Grampa calls me. Really, I'm an assistant manager.'

It had happened a long time ago, her choosing this life. Like most of her decisions, she'd stumbled across it without paying much attention. First she'd flunked out of Washington State University—one of the many casualties of higher education. Without a degree, or a dream, Claire had found herself back in Hayden. But she loved this place, this job. She was, in that and in so many things, her father's daughter. There was something about these gorgeous sixteen acres along the river that filled her soul. She knew her job wasn't much in the great scheme of things, just managing a few campsites and a couple of cabins, but she never felt like a failure, never felt that her life was a disappointment.

Except when she talked to her sister.

Twenty-four hours later Claire was ready to leave on vacation. She took a last pass through the house, looking for anything forgotten or left undone. She was straightening the shower curtain when she heard footsteps in the living room.

'What in the name of a frog's butt are you still doing here?'

She smiled and backed out of the minuscule bathroom.

Her father stood in the living room, dwarfing the small space. Big and broad-shouldered, he made every room seem smaller by comparison. But it was his personality that was truly oversized.

She'd first met him when she was nine years old. *Well,* he'd said as he looked down at her, *you must be my daughter, Claire. You're the prettiest girl I've ever seen. Let's go home.*

Home.

It was the word she'd waited for, dreamed of. It had taken her years—and more than a few tears—to realise that he hadn't offered the same welcome to Meghann. By then, of course, by the time Claire understood the mistake, it was well past the time to rectify it.

'Hey, Dad. I was making sure everything was ready for you to move in here.'

His grin showed a row of white dentures. 'You know damn well I ain't moving in here. I *like* my mobile home. I got my fridge and my satellite TV. That's all I need.'

They'd been having this discussion ever since Claire had moved back to the property and Dad had given her use of the house. He swore up and down that the mobile home hidden in the trees was room enough for a fifty-six-year-old single man.

'Now dance on over here and give your old man a hug.'

Claire did as she was told.

His big, strong arms enfolded her, made her feel safe and adored.

'I'll leave in an hour,' she said. 'The toilet in cabin—'

He spun her round and pushed her gently towards the door. 'Get going. This place isn't going to fall apart without you.'

Claire couldn't help smiling. 'OK.'

'Take as long as you want, Claire. Take three weeks. Really. You're only thirty-five. You and Alison should kick up your heels a bit. You're too responsible.'

'I'm a thirty-five-year-old single mother who has never been married. That's not too responsible, and I *will* kick up my heels in Chelan. But I'll be home in a week.'

He thumped her shoulder. 'You've always done exactly what you wanted, but you can't blame a guy for trying. Have fun.'

Claire walked out of the house and into the steely grey day. A drizzling rain fell like a beaded curtain in front of the trees.

'Come on, Mommy!' Alison's small face poked through the car's open window.

Dad hurried ahead of her and kissed his granddaughter's cheek.

Claire got into the car and started the engine. 'Are we ready, Ali Kat? Do you have everything?'

Alison bounced in her seat, clinging to her lunch box. 'I'm ready!'

'We're off to see the Wizard, then,' Claire said, shifting into drive as she yelled a final goodbye to her father.

Claire loved Lake Chelan's Blue Skies Campground. She and her girlfriends had first vacationed there a few years after high school. There had been five of them; time and tragedy had whittled their number down to four. At first they'd been young and wild and driven to pick up local boys. Gradually, as they'd started dragging carry-cots and car seats with them, the vacation had settled down a bit. Now that the kids were old enough to swim and play on the playground alone, the girls— women—had refound a slice of their previous freedom.

'Mom*my*, you're spacing out.'

'Oh. Sorry, honey.'

'I *said*, we get the honeymoon cabin this year, remember?' She bounced even harder in her seat. 'Yippee! We get the big bathtub. Did you bring my skateboard, Mommy?'

'No. You're too young to ride it.'

'How come Aunt Meg never comes to visit us?'

'Aunt Meg is so busy, she hardly has time to breathe.'

'Eliot Zane turned blue when he didn't breathe.'

'I just meant Meg is superbusy helping people.'

'Oh.'

Claire slid a Disney audiotape into the cassette player. The miles flew by. In no time they were speeding across the flat, arid land on the eastern side of the state.

'Is this the desert already?'

Claire nodded. Her daughter always called eastern Washington the desert. It was easy to see why. After the lush green of Hayden, this yellow and brown landscape seemed desolate and scorched. The black ribbon of asphalt stretched for ever through the prairie.

'There's the water slide!' Alison said at last. She leaned forwards, counting out loud. When she got to forty-seven, she yelled, 'There's the lake!'

Lake Chelan filled their view to the left, a huge crystal-blue lake tucked into a golden hillside. They drove over the bridge that led into town.

Two decades ago this town had been less than three blocks long. But, over time, word of the weather had spread west to those soggy coastal towns that so prized their plate-sized rhododendrons and car-sized ferns. Gradually, Seattleites turned their attention eastwards. It became a summer tradition—the trek across the mountains towards the flat, scorched plains. As the tourists came, so did the development. It had become a thriving vacation destination, with all the kiddy-required amenities—pools, water-slide parks and jet-ski rentals.

The road curved along the lakeshore. They passed dozens of condominium complexes. Then the shore became less inhabited again. They saw the sign: BLUE SKIES CAMPGROUND, NEXT LEFT.

'Look, Mommy, look!'

The sign showed a pair of stylised trees bracketing a tent with a canoe in front.

'This is it, Ali Kat.' Claire turned left onto the gravel road. A mile later, the road took a hairpin turn and spat them out in a grassy field dotted with trailers and motor homes. They drove past the open field and into the trees, where the few, coveted cabins sat in a cluster along the shore. They parked in the gravel lot.

Claire helped Alison out of her car seat, then took her hand. Together, they walked towards the lake.

For a split second, Claire was eight years old again, a girl at Lake Winobee, standing at the shoreline, wearing a pretty pink bikini. She remembered splashing into the cold water, shrieking as she went deeper and deeper.

Don't go in past your knees, Claire, Meghann had hollered out, sitting up on the dock.

Quit bein' such an old fuddy-duddy, Meggy. Mama's voice. *Go on in, sweetums*, she'd yelled to Claire, laughing loudly, waving a menthol cigarette. *It won't do to be a scaredy-cat.*

And then Meghann was beside Claire, holding her hand, telling her there was nothing wrong with being afraid. *It just shows good sense, Claire-Bear.*

'Mommy!' Alison's voice pulled Claire into the present. 'Hurry up.'

After checking in at the lodge, Claire handed Alison the key to the honeymoon cabin. 'Here you go, Ali Kat. You're in charge. Show us the way.'

With a yelp Ali was off, and Claire hurried along behind her. They raced across the expanse of lawn, past the boat-rental shed, and plunged into the trees. The ground here was hard-packed dirt, carpeted with a hundred years' worth of pine needles.

Finally they came to the lake. A silvery wooden dock floated on the wavy blue water, tilting from side to side in a rocking motion.

'Clara Bella!'

Claire tented a hand over her eyes and looked around.

Gina sat at the shoreline, waving. Even from here Claire could see the size of the drink in her friend's hand. Usually Gina was the conservative one, the buoy that held everyone up, but she'd finalised her divorce a few months ago, and she was adrift. Last week her ex-husband had moved in with a younger woman.

'Hurry up, Ali!' That was Gina's six-year-old daughter, Bonnie.

Alison dropped her Winnie-the-Pooh backpack and peeled off her clothes to show off her yellow bathing suit. 'I'm ready.'

'Don't go in past your bellybutton,' Claire said, dropping their suitcases right there, in the sand.

'Aw, Mommy,' Alison whined, then ran for the water.

Claire sat down beside Gina. 'What time did you get here?'

Gina laughed. 'On time, of course. That's one thing I've learned this year. Your life can fall apart, but you're still who you are. I'm the kind of woman who gets somewhere on time.'

'There's nothing wrong with that.'

'Rex would disagree. He always said I wasn't spontaneous enough. I thought it meant he wanted sex in the afternoon. Turns out he wanted to skydive.' She shook her head, gave Claire a wry smile. 'I'd be happy to shove him out of the plane now.'

'I'd rig his parachute for him.'

They laughed, though it wasn't funny. 'How's Bonnie doing?'

'That's the saddest part of all. She barely seems to notice. Rex was never home anyway.'

They were silent for a long moment. The only sound between them was the slapping of the water against the dock and the girls' high-pitched laughter. Gina turned to her. 'How have you done it all these years? Been alone, I mean.'

Claire hadn't thought much about her solitude since Alison's birth. Yes, she'd been alone—in the sense that she'd never been married or lived with a man—but she rarely felt lonely.

Claire looked out at Alison, who was standing up to her bellybutton in the water and jumping up and down. The sight made Claire's chest tighten. She knew she loved her daughter too much; it was dangerous to need another human being so desperately, but Claire had never known any other way to love. That was why she'd never been married. Men who loved their wives unconditionally were few and far between. In truth, Claire wondered if that kind of true love existed.

'You get past being lonely. And you live for your kids,' she said.

'Ali shouldn't be your whole world, Claire.'

'It's not like I didn't *try* to fall in love. I've dated every single guy in Hayden.'

'None of them twice.' Gina grinned. 'And Bert Shubert is still in love with you. Miss Hauser thinks you're crazy for letting him go.'

'It's sad when a fifty-three-year-old plumber with Coke-bottle glasses and a red goatee is considered an eligible bachelor just because he owns an appliance store.'

Gina laughed. 'Yeah. If I ever tell you I'm going out with Bert, please shoot me.' Slowly, her laughter turned to tears.

'You'll be OK, Gina,' Claire said, stroking her friend's back. 'I promise you will.'

'I don't know,' Gina said quietly, and something about the way she said it, maybe the softness in her voice that was usually as hard as steel, made Claire feel empty inside. Alone.

Absurdly, Claire thought about the day her life had changed—when she'd learned that love had a shelf life, a use-by date that could pass suddenly and turn everything sour.

I'm leaving, Meg had said, and she hadn't even been crying. Meg, who until that moment had been Claire's best friend, her whole world. More of a mother than Mama had ever been.

And then Claire was crying, too.

Gina sniffed. 'Ten seconds in my company, and perfectly happy people start to weep.'

Claire wiped her eyes. There was no point in crying about the past. It surprised her, actually, that she had any tears left. She thought she'd made peace with Meghann's abandonment long ago. 'Remember the year Charlotte fell off the dock because she was crying so hard she couldn't see?'

'Bob's midlife crisis. She thought he was having an affair.'

'And it turned out he was secretly getting hair-plug treatments.'

Gina embraced Claire. 'Thank God for the Bluesers. I haven't needed you all this much since I was in labour.'

Chapter Three

LIKE SUNSHINE, night brought out the best in Seattle. The highway—a bumper-to-bumper nightmare at morning rush hour—became, at night, a glittering red-and-gold Chinese dragon that curled along the blackened banks of Lake Union. Meghann stood at her office window. It was eight thirty. Time to head home. She'd bring the Wanamaker file with her. Get a jump on tomorrow.

Meghann was almost to the elevator when her cellphone rang. She pulled it out of her bag. 'Meghann Dontess,' she said.

'Meghann?' The voice was panicky. 'It's May Monroe.'

Meghann was instantly alert. 'What's going on?'

'It's Dale. He came by tonight and said something about the papers he got today. He was crazy. What did you send him?'

'We talked about this, May. I notified Dale's lawyer that we'd be contesting the fraudulent transfer of his business and demanding an accounting of the Cayman Islands accounts. I also told his attorney that we were aware of the affair with the child's piano instructor and that such behaviour might threaten his suitability as a parent.'

'You threatened to take away his children?'

'The kids are a game with guys like your husband. Pretend to want custody, and you'll get more money.'

'You think you know my husband better than I do.'

'I don't have to know him,' Meghann answered, using the canned speech she'd perfected long ago. 'Protecting you is my job. If I upset your husband in the process, that's an unfortunate necessity. He'll calm down. They always do.'

'You don't know Dale,' she said again.

Meghann's senses pounced on some nuance. Something wasn't right. 'Are you scared of him, May?'

'Scared?' May tried to sound surprised by the question.

'Does he hit you, May?'

'Sometimes when he's drinking, I can say just the wrong thing.'

Oh, yeah. It's May's fault. 'Are you OK now?'

'He didn't hit me. And he never hits the children.'

Meghann didn't say what came to mind. Often if a man would hit his wife, he'd get around to hitting his children.

'We need to make sure he understands that I'm not going to take his children from him. Otherwise he'll go crazy,' May said. There was the barest crack in her voice.

'May, say it's three months from now. Dale's living with Dance Hall Barbie, and they come home drunk one night. When they get home, the baby sitter has let the kids demolish the house. I'm guessing that you've always been a buffer between your husband and kids. You probably learned how to calm him down and deflect his attention away from the children. Will Barbie know how to protect them?'

'Am I so ordinary?'

'Sadly, the situation is. The good news is, you're giving yourself—and your children—a new start. Don't weaken now. Don't let him bully you.'

'So what do I do?'

'Lock the doors and turn off the phone. If you don't feel safe, go to a relative's or friend's house. Tomorrow we'll get together and come up with a new game plan. I'll file some restraining orders.'

'You can keep us safe?'

'You'll be fine, May. Trust me. Bullies are cowards. Once he sees how strong you can be, he'll back down.'

'OK. When can we meet?'

Meghann dug through her bag for her palm pilot, then checked her schedule. 'How about a late lunch—say, two o'clock—at the Judicial Annex Café by the courthouse?'

'OK.'

'Good. I'll see you there.' Meghann flipped the phone shut and dropped it in her handbag, then pushed the elevator button. When the door opened, she stepped inside. As always, she studied her reflection in the mirrored walls. She was forty-two years old, and since it felt as if she'd been thirty a moment ago, she had to assume it would be a blink's worth of time before she was fifty.

That depressed her. She imagined herself at sixty. Alone, working from dawn to dusk, talking to her neighbour's cats, and going on singles cruises.

She left the elevator and strode through the lobby, nodding at the night doorman as she passed. Outside, the night was beautiful; an amethyst sky gave everything a pink and pearlised glow. She walked briskly down the street, bypassing people without making eye contact. At her building she paused and looked up.

There was her balcony. The only one in the building without potted trees and outdoor furniture. The windows behind it were black; the rest of the building was a blaze of light. Friends and families were in those lit spaces, having dinner, watching television, making love. Connecting with one another.

Meghann didn't want to go up there, put on her old sweats, eat raisin bran for dinner, and watch a rerun of *Third Watch*. Instead, she walked past her building and went into the Public Market. At this hour pretty much everything was closed up.

She turned into the Athenian, the old-fashioned tavern made famous in *Sleepless in Seattle*. Meghann had perfected the art of scoping out a bar without being obvious. She did that now. There were five or six men at the bar. Fishermen, she'd guess, getting ready to head up to Alaska for the season.

'Hey, Meghann,' yelled Freddie, the bartender. 'Your usual?'

'You bet.' She moved past the bar and found a place at one of the old-fashioned varnished wooden tables.

'Here ye be,' Freddie said, setting a martini glass down in front of her. He shook the steel shaker, then poured her a cosmopolitan. 'You want an order of oysters and fries?'

'You read my mind.'

Freddie grinned. 'Ain't hard to do, Counsellor.' He leaned down towards her. 'The Eagles are coming in tonight.'

'The Eagles?'

'The minor-league ball team outta Everett.' He winked at her.

Meghann groaned. It was bad when bartenders started recommending whole ball teams.

She closed her eyes, reminding herself that this was the life she wanted. She'd tried marriage. It had ended exactly as she'd feared—with his betrayal and her broken heart.

Meghann began drinking. When her first cosmo was gone, Meghann ordered a second. By the time she saw the bottom of the glass again, she'd almost forgotten her day.

'May I join you?'

She looked up and found herself staring into a pair of dark eyes. She could tell by the look of him—young, blond, sexy as hell—that he was used to getting what he wanted. And what he wanted tonight was her. The thought was a tonic.

'Of course.' She didn't offer a half-smile or bat her eyes. 'I'm Meghann Dontess. My friends call me Meg.'

He slid into the seat. His knees brushed hers, and at the contact he smiled. 'I'm Donny MacMillan. You like baseball?'

'I like a lot of things.' She flagged down Freddie, who nodded at her.

A moment later he brought her another cosmopolitan. 'I suppose you're a baseball player.'

He grinned, and she felt the first twinge of desire. Sex with him would be great; she knew it. And it would make her forget.

Their first gathering at Lake Chelan had been in 1989, the year they all turned twenty-one. There had been five of them then. Best friends since grade school.

That first get-together had happened by accident. The girls had pooled their money to give Claire a weekend in the honeymoon cabin for her birthday. At the time—in March—she'd been head over heels in love. By mid-July, on the designated weekend, Claire had been out of love, alone, and more than a little depressed. Never one to waste money, she'd gone on the trip by herself, intending to sit on the porch and read.

Just before dinnertime of the first day, a battered yellow Ford Pinto had pulled into the yard. Her best friends had spilled out of the car and run across the lawn, laughing, holding two big jugs of margarita mix. They'd called their visit a love intervention, and it had worked.

Every year since then, they'd managed to come back for a week. Now, of course, it was different. Gina and Claire each had a daughter; Karen had four children, aged eleven to fourteen; and Charlotte was trying desperately to conceive.

In the past few years their parties had quietened. Instead of getting dressed up and going to Cowboy Bob's Western Roundup to slam tequila and line-dance, they put the kids to bed early, drank glasses of white wine, and played hearts at the round wooden table on the porch of the lodge. They kept a running score for the week. The winner got the keys to the honeymoon cabin for the next year.

They spent their days by the lake, stretched out on red-and-white-striped beach towels. On hot days, like this one, they spent most of their time in the lake, standing neck-deep in the cool water, their faces shielded by floppy hats and sunglasses. Talking. Always talking.

Today the weather was perfect. The sky was a bright seamless blue, and the lake was like glass. The older kids were inside, playing crazy eights and listening to Karen's son Willie's earsplitting music. Alison and Bonnie were pedalling a water bike.

Karen sat in her chair, fanning herself. Charlotte, protected from the sun by a floppy white hat and three-quarter-sleeved cover-up, was reading the latest book club choice and sipping lemonade.

Gina leaned sideways and opened the cooler, rooting noisily through it for a Diet Coke. 'My marriage ends, and we're drinking Diet Coke and lemonade. When Karen's first husband left, we slammed tequila and danced at Cowboy Bob's.'

'That was my second husband, Stan,' Karen said. 'When Aaron left, we went skinny-dipping in the lake.'

'My point remains,' Gina said. 'My crisis is getting the *Sesame Street* treatment. You got *Animal House*.'

'Cowboy Bob's,' Charlotte said. 'We haven't been there in years.'

'Not since we started dragging around these undersized humans,' Karen said. 'It's hard to rock'n'roll with a kid on your back.'

Claire pushed herself up on her elbows. The scratchy cotton of her beach towel seemed to bite into her sunburnt forearms.

'Willie's fourteen this year, right?'

Karen nodded. 'He's starting high school in September.'

'Why couldn't he baby-sit for an hour or two?'

Gina sat up. 'Why didn't we think of that before? He's fourteen.'

Karen frowned. 'With the maturity of an earthworm.'

'We all baby-sat at his age,' Charlotte said. 'Hell, I was practically a nanny that summer before high school.'

'He's a responsible kid, Karen. He'll be fine,' Claire said.

'I don't know. Last month his fish died. Lack of food.'

'They won't starve to death in two hours.'

Karen looked back at the cabin. 'Yeah,' she said finally. 'We'll leave a cellphone with him.'

'And a list of numbers.'

Gina smiled for the first time all day. 'Ladies, the Bluesers are going to leave the building.'

It took them two hours to shower, change their clothes, and make the kids' dinner. It took them another hour to convince the kids that their plan was possible.

Finally, Claire took firm hold of Karen and led her outside. As they walked down the long, winding driveway, Karen paused and looked back every few feet. 'Are you sure?' she said each time.

'Just keep walking.' Gina leaned close to Claire and said, 'She's like a car in the ice. If she stops, we'll never get her going again.'

They were standing across the street from Cowboy Bob's when it hit them. Claire was the first to speak. 'It's not even dark out.'

'As party animals, we've lost our touch,' Charlotte said.

Claire refused to be thwarted. So what if they looked like sorority girls amid the professional drinkers that populated a place like this in the early evening? They were here to have a good time. 'Come on, ladies,' she said, storming forwards.

Her friends fell in line behind her. Heads held high, they marched into Cowboy Bob's as if they owned the place.

Claire led the way to a round table near the empty dance floor. From here they would have an unobstructed view of the band, which was noticeably absent. A whiny Western song played on the jukebox. Gina ordered a round of margaritas and onion rings.

'God, it feels good to get *out*,' Karen said. 'I can't remember the last time I went out without having to do enough preplanning to launch an air strike.'

Claire raised her glass. 'To us,' she said in a firm voice. 'To the Bluesers. We made it through junior high and high school, through labours and surgeries, weddings and divorces. Two of us have lost our marriages, one hasn't been able to get pregnant, one of us has never been in love, and a few years ago one of us died. But we're still here. We'll *always* be here for one another. That makes us lucky women.'

They clinked their glasses together.

Gradually, the conversation turned to the old days, and everything made them laugh. At some point they ordered a plate of nachos. By the time the second order of food came, the band had started. The first song was a loud rendition of 'Friends in Low Places'.

By the time the band got round to Alan Jackson's 'Here in the Real World', the place was wall-to-wall people. A group was line-dancing in a thigh-slappin' way.

'Did you hear that?' Claire leaned forwards and put her hands on the table. 'It's "Guitars and Cadillacs". We *gotta* dance.'

'Dance?' Gina laughed. 'The last time I danced with you two, my butt hit an old man and sent him flying.'

Karen shook her head. 'Sorry, Claire. I danced until I hit a size sixteen. Now I consider it wise to keep as still as possible.'

Claire stood up. 'Come on, Charlotte. You want to dance?'

'I'd love to.' She plopped her bag onto her chair and followed Claire to the dance floor.

The minute Claire started to move in time with the music, to swing her hips and stamp her feet and clap her hands, she remembered how much she loved this. She couldn't believe that she'd let so many quiet years accumulate. By the time the band took a break, she was out of breath. A tiny headache had flared behind her right eye; she stuck a hand in her pocket and found an Excedrin.

Charlotte pushed the hair out of her eyes. 'That was *great*. Come on. I'm so dehydrated, I feel like a piece of beef jerky.'

Claire started to head for the table and then remembered the aspirin.

She went to the bar instead and asked for a glass of tap water.

The water came, and as she swallowed the single pill, she saw a man walk onto the stage. He carried a guitar—a regular, old-fashioned guitar that didn't plug in or amp out.

He sat down easily on a rickety barstool. One black cowboy boot was planted firmly on the floor; the other rested on the stool's bottom rung. He wore a pair of faded, torn jeans and a black T-shirt. His hair was almost shoulder length and shone blond in the overhead lighting. He was looking down at his guitar, and though a black Stetson shielded most of his face, Claire could make out the strong, high bones that defined his cheeks.

'Wow.' She couldn't remember the last time she'd seen a man who was so good-looking. Not in Hayden, that was for sure.

The man leaned towards the microphone. 'I'm gonna fill in while the band takes a short break. I hope y'all don't mind.'

Claire pushed through the crowd to the edge of the dance floor.

He strummed a few notes on the guitar and started to sing. At first his voice was too soft to be heard above the raucous din.

'Be quiet.' Claire was surprised to hear the words spoken out loud; she'd meant only to *think* them. She felt ridiculously conspicuous, standing there in front of the crowd, but she couldn't move, couldn't look away.

He looked up. In the smoky darkness, with a dozen people crammed in beside her, Claire thought he was looking at her. Slowly, he smiled.

Once, years ago, Claire had been running along the dock at Lake Crescent behind her sister. One minute she'd been laughing and upright; the next second she was in the freezing-cold water, gasping for breath and clawing her way to the surface. That was how she felt now.

'I'm Bobby Austin,' he said softly, still looking at her. 'This song is for The One. The one I've been lookin' for all my life.'

His long fingers strummed the guitar strings. Then he started to sing. His voice was low and smoky, seductive as hell. Claire found herself swaying in time to the music, dancing all by herself.

When the song ended, he set down the guitar and stood up. The crowd clapped politely, then headed back to their pitchers of beer.

He walked towards Claire. She couldn't seem to move.

Directly in front of her he stopped. When he didn't say anything, she said, 'I'm Claire Cavenaugh.'

A smile hitched one side of his mouth. 'I don't know how to say what I'm thinking without sounding like an idiot.'

Claire's heart was beating so fast, she felt dizzy. 'What do you mean?'

He closed the distance between them, small as it had been. Now he was so near, she could see the gold flecks in his green eyes and the tiny half-moon-shaped scar at the edge of his upper lip.

'I'm The One,' he said softly.

'The one what?' She tried to smile. 'The way? The light? There is no way to heaven but through you?'

'No joking. I'm the one you've been looking for.'

She ought to have laughed at him, told him she hadn't heard that corny a pick-up line since the year she tried shaping her eyebrows with a Lady Bic. She was long past believing in love at first sight. All of that was what she meant to say, but when she opened her mouth, she heard her heart speak. 'How do you know that?'

'Because I've been lookin' for you, too.'

Claire took a step backwards—just far enough so that she could breathe her own air. She wanted to laugh at him. She really did.

'Come on, Claire Cavenaugh,' he said softly. 'Dance with me.'

Chapter Four

SOME MARRIAGES ENDED with bitter words and ugly epithets, others with copious tears and whispered apologies; each proceeding was different. The one constant was sadness, and it was a fact, well known in Family Court, that no woman who'd gone through a divorce ever saw the world—or love—in quite the same way again.

'Are you OK?' Meghann asked May Monroe.

Her client sat rigidly upright, her hands clasped tightly in her lap. 'I'm fine,' she said.

'Let's go next door and get something to eat, OK?'

In the front of the courtroom the judge stood up. She smiled at Meghann, then at George Gutterson, the opposing counsel; then she left the courtroom. Meghann helped May to her feet. She held on to her arm to keep her steady as they headed towards the door.

'You *bitch*!' Dale Monroe surged forwards. His face was a deep, purply red. A blue vein throbbed down the middle of his forehead.

'Dale,' George said, reaching for his client, 'don't be stupid.'

Dale shook his lawyer's arm away and kept coming.

Meghann sidestepped easily, putting herself between Dale and May. 'Step back, Mr Monroe.'

'That's *Doctor* Monroe, you avaricious bitch.'

'Excellent word usage. You must have gone to a good liberal arts college. Now, please, step back.'

'You took my children away from me,' Dale said to Meghann.

'Are you suggesting *I* was the one who fraudulently transferred assets out of my wife's reach . . . or that *I* stole money and equity from my family? Maybe you're suggesting that *I* was the one who banged my daughter's piano teacher every Tuesday afternoon.'

He paled and tried to make eye contact with his ex-wife.

'May, come on,' he said, 'I didn't do all of those things. I would have given you everything you asked for. But the kids . . . I can't see them only on weekends and two weeks in the summer.'

He sounded sincere, actually. If Meghann hadn't seen the ugly truth in black and white, she might have believed him.

She spoke quickly, so May wouldn't have to. 'The separation of your assets was entirely fair and equitable, Dr Monroe. The custody issues were also fairly resolved and, when you calm down, I'm sure you'll agree. We all read the depositions that reflected your lifestyle. You were gone in the morning by six a.m.—before the children woke up—and you rarely returned home before ten p.m.—after they were in bed. You'll probably see your children more now than you did while you resided at the family home.'

'Who do you think you are?' Dale whispered harshly, taking a step towards her. At his sides his fingers curled into fists.

'You going to hit me, Dale? Go ahead. Lose what custody you have.'

Meghann slipped her arm round May's waist. Together they walked out of the courtroom.

'You'll pay for this, you bitch,' Dale screamed to their backs.

Meghann kept a steadying hand on May's waist and led her into the elevator. The moment the door closed, May burst into tears.

Meghann held May's hand, squeezing it gently. 'I know it seems impossible now, but life will get better. I promise.'

She led May down the courthouse steps and outside. The sky was heavy and grey with clouds. They walked down Third Street to the Judicial Annex, the favourite lunch spot for the Family Court gang.

'Hey, Meg,' said a few colleagues as she walked through the restaurant to a table at the back. Within moments a waitress was beside them. 'Is this a champagne or a martini day?' she asked.

'Definitely champagne. Thanks.'

May looked across the table at her. 'We aren't really going to drink champagne, are we?'

'May, you are now a millionaire. Your children can get Ph.D.'s from Harvard if they want. You have a beautiful waterfront home and no mortgage. And you got full custody. Hell, yes, we're celebrating.'

'What happened to you?'

'What do you mean?'

'My life has been hit by a Scud missile. The man I love is gone. My children will have to live all their lives knowing that families break, that love is impermanent and, most of all, that promises get broken. They'll go on, of course. That's what children and women do—we go on. But we won't ever be quite whole again.' May looked down at her hand. At the wedding ring on her finger. 'I feel like I'm bleeding. And there you sit, ordering champagne.' She looked up again. 'What's wrong with you?'

'This can be a harsh job,' Meghann answered truthfully. 'Sometimes the only way I can get through it is—'

A commotion broke out in the restaurant. Glass shattered. A table crashed to the floor. A woman screamed.

'Oh, no,' May breathed. Her face was pale.

Meghann frowned. 'What in the—' She turned in her chair.

Dale stood in the open doorway, holding a gun in his left hand. He appeared to be crying.

'Put down the gun, Dale.' Meghann was surprised to hear the calmness in her voice.

'You ruined my life.'

'Put the gun down. You don't want to do something stupid.'

'I already did something stupid.' His voice broke. 'I had an affair and got greedy and forgot how much I love my wife.'

May started to get to her feet. Meghann grabbed her, forced her down, and then stood up herself.

'Come on, Dale. Put the gun down. We'll get you some help.'

'Where was all your help when I tried to tell my wife how sorry I was?' Tears rolled down his cheeks.

'Dale,' Meghann said in a calm voice, 'I know how—'

'Shut *up*. It's your fault, you bitch. You're the one who did all of this.' He raised the gun, aimed, and pulled the trigger.

Joe woke with a fever and a stinging throat. A dry, hacking cough brought him upright before he'd even fully opened his eyes. When it was over, he sat there, bleary-eyed.

A glittering layer of frost coated his sleeping-bag, its presence a testament to the altitude. Though the days in this part of the state were as hot as hell, the nights were cold.

He coughed again, then climbed out of the sleeping-bag. His fingers were trembling as he dug the toothbrush, soap and toothpaste out of his pack. Squatting by the rushing rapids of Icicle Creek, he readied himself for the day.

Today was his birthday. His forty-third. In another time—another life—this would have been a day for celebration, for family. Diana had always loved a party. The year he'd turned thirty-eight, she'd rented the Space Needle and hired a Bruce Springsteen impersonator to sing the soundtrack of their youth. The place had been packed with friends. Everyone wanted to celebrate Joe's birthday with him.

Then.

With a sigh he pushed to his feet. A quick check of his wallet and pockets revealed that he was nearly broke again. Slinging his backpack into place, he hiked out of the National Forest. By the time he reached Highway 2, his forehead was on fire. He knew he had a fever—one hundred degrees, at least.

He stared at the black river of asphalt that flowed down to the tiny town of Leavenworth. It was only a mile or so away.

By the time Joe got there, his headache was almost unbearable. At a Chevron station he spent his last two dollars on aspirin.

He was standing outside the minimart, trying to will the aspirin to take effect, when the first raindrop hit.

'Damn.' Before he finished the word, the storm hit. A pounding rain that seemed to nail him in place. And suddenly he couldn't live like this any more. He was sick and tired of being sick and tired.

Home.

He closed his eyes and thought of the small town where he'd been raised, where he'd played shortstop for the local ball team and worked at a garage after school and every summer until he went away to college. If any town would still accept him after what he'd done, it would be that one.

Moving slowly, his emotions a convoluted mixture of fear and anticipation, he went to the phone booth and stepped inside its quiet enclosure. Now the rain was only noise; it was like his heartbeat: fast, breathless. He let out a long breath, then picked up the phone, punched 0, and placed a collect call.

'Hey, little sister,' he said when she answered. 'How are you?'

'Oh my *God*. I've been worried sick about you, Joey. You haven't called in—what?—eight months.'

'I know. I'm sorry. How's my beautiful niece?'

'She's great.'

He heard something in her voice. 'What's the matter?'

'Nothing,' she said. Then more softly, 'I could use my big brother right about now, that's all. Has it been long enough?'

There it was, the question upon which everything rested. 'I don't know. I'm tired—I know that. Have people forgotten?'

'I don't get asked so much any more.'

He didn't know if he was strong enough to stand up to his past. He hadn't been when it was his present.

'Come home, Joey. You can't hide for ever. And . . . I need you.'

He heard the sound of her crying; it was soft and broken, and it pulled something out of him. 'Don't cry. Please.'

'I'm not. I'm chopping onions for dinner.' She sniffed. 'Your niece is going through a spaghetti phase.' She tried to laugh.

Joe appreciated the attempt at normality, however forced.

'Make her some of Mom's spaghetti. That should end it.'

She laughed. 'Gosh, I'd forgotten. Hers was awful.'

'Better than her meat loaf.'

After that, a silence slipped through the lines. Softly she said, 'You've got to forgive yourself, Joey.'

'Some things are unforgivable.'

'Then at least come home. People care about you here.'

'I want to. I can't live like this any more.'

'I hope that's what this phone call means.'

'I hope so, too.'

It was that rarest of days in downtown Seattle. Hot and humid. A haze hung over the city. If it was hot outside, it was sweltering in the courthouse. Meghann stared at the yellow legal pad in front of her. She hadn't written a word. Her right hand started to tremble.

'Ms Dontess. Ahem. *Ms Dontess.*'

The judge was speaking to her.

She blinked slowly. 'I'm sorry.' She got to her feet.

The judge—a thin, heronlike woman—was frowning. 'Approach the bench,' she said.

Meghann tried to look confident. At the bench she stopped and looked up. 'Yes, Your Honour?'

The judge leaned forwards to say softly, 'We all know what happened last week, Meghann. That bullet missed you by inches. Are you certain you're ready to be back in a courtroom?'

'Yes.' Meghann's hand was still trembling.

The judge cleared her throat and nodded. 'Step back.'

Meghann went back to the table, slid into her seat.

Her client, a Mercer Island housewife, stared at her. 'What's going on?'

Meghann shook her head. 'Don't worry.'

'I'll restate, Your Honour,' John Heinreid said. He and Meghann had tried dozens of cases against each other. 'My client would like to stay these proceedings for a time so that he and Mrs Miller can obtain counselling. There are, after all, small children involved.'

Meghann heard her client whisper, 'No way.'

Then Meghann planted her hands on the table and slowly rose. Her mind went blank. She couldn't think of a single argument. When she closed her eyes, trying to concentrate, she saw the gun pointed at her, heard an echoed blast. When she opened her eyes, everyone was looking at her.

Meghann turned to her client. 'It's a reasonable request, Celene. You won't look good if we fight this battle in front of the judge.'

'Oh. I guess . . .' Celene frowned.

Meghann returned her attention to the bench. 'We'd ask for a time limit and a follow-up court date to be set now.'

'That's acceptable to us, Your Honour.'

Meghann stood there as the details were worked out. On autopilot, she packed up her briefcase.

'Wait. What just happened?' Celene whispered.

'We agreed to counselling. A few months or so. No more.'

'Counselling? We've tried counselling—or did you forget that? It didn't work. Mr Computer Software likes men, remember?'

Meghann had forgotten all of that. 'I'm sorry, Celene.'

'Sorry? *Sorry.* My children and I need to start over.'

'You're right. I'll fix this. I promise I will.' And she could. A phone call to John Heinreid that threatened to reveal Mr Miller's preferred sex partners, and it'd be handled instantly. Quietly.

Celene sighed. 'Look, I know what happened last week. I feel sorry for that lady—and for you. But I need to worry about myself.'

'You *should* be taking care of yourself. I screwed up in here. But I'll fix it, and you won't be paying a dime for this divorce. OK?'

Celene tried valiantly to smile. 'OK.'

Meghann put a hand down on the desk to steady herself as she stood there, watching her client walk out of the courtroom. A hand pressed against her shoulder. 'Meg?'

It was Julie Gorset, her partner.

'Hey, Jules. Tell me you weren't in the courtroom today.'

Julie looked at her sadly. 'I was. And we need to talk.'

The Pike Place Public Market was wall-to-wall people on a sunny summer's day. Now, at night-time, it was quiet.

Meghann stood outside the Athenian's open door. She could go in there and find someone to spend time with her. But suddenly all she could think about was what would really happen. She'd meet some guy whose name wouldn't matter . . . and then be left more alone than when she'd started. A tic began in her left eye.

She reached into her handbag and pulled out her cellphone. She punched in a number, biting down on her lip as it rang. She was just about to hang up when a voice answered.

'Hello?' Then, 'Meghann, I recognise your cellphone number.'

'I'm going to sue whoever invented caller ID.'

'It's eight thirty. Why are you calling me?' Harriet asked.

'My left eyelid is flapping like a flag on the Fourth of July. I need a prescription for a muscle relaxant.'

'We talked about a delayed reaction, remember?'

'Yeah. Post-traumatic stress.'

'I'll be in my office in thirty minutes.'

'If you could just call in a prescription—'

'My office. Thirty minutes.'

'I'll be there.'

Meghann hung up the phone and put it back in her bag. It took her less than fifteen minutes to get to Harriet's office.

At precisely nine o'clock Harriet showed up, looking rushed and poorly put together. Her hair had been drawn back in a thin headband, and her face shone pink without make-up. 'If you make a crack about the headband, I'll charge you double.'

'Me? Be judgmental? You must be joking.'

Harriet unlocked the door and pushed it open.

Meghann walked through the reception area and went into Harriet's large corner office. Harriet took her usual seat.

'Sit down, Meghann.'

'Do I have to?'

'Sit.'

Meghann did as she was told. The comfortable chair enfolded her. 'I remember when I hated this chair. Now it seems made for me.'

Harriet steepled her fingers and peered at Meghann over her short, clear-polished nails. 'It was a week ago today, wasn't it? When your client's husband tried to shoot you.'

Meghann's left foot started to tap. 'Yes.'

'I told you you needed to deal with it.'

'Yes, you did.'

'Are you sleeping?'

'No. Every time I close my eyes, I see it all again. The gunshot whizzing past my ear . . . the way he dropped the gun afterwards and sank to his knees . . . May rushing to him, holding him, telling him everything would be all right, that she'd stand behind him . . . the police taking him away in handcuffs. Today, I relived it in court.' She looked up. 'That was lovely, by the way.'

'It's not your fault. He's the one to blame.'

'I know that. I also know that I handled their divorce badly. I've lost my ability to really *feel* for people.' She sighed. 'I don't know if I can do this job any more. Today I completely screwed a client. My partner has asked me—ordered me, really—to take a vacation.'

'That might not be a bad idea.'

'Will I feel better in London or Rome . . . alone?'

'Why don't you call Claire? You could go stay at her resort for a while. Maybe try to relax. Get to know her.'

'That's a funny thing about visiting relatives. You need an invitation.'

'Are you saying Claire wouldn't want you to visit?'

'Of course I'm saying that. Claire and I can't talk for more than five minutes without getting into an argument.'

'You could visit your mother.'

'I'd rather contract the West Nile virus.'

'So what you're saying is you have nowhere to go and no one to visit.'

'All I said was where would I go?' It had been a mistake to come here. Harriet was making her feel worse. 'Look, Harriet'—her voice was softer than usual, and cracked—'I'm falling apart. It's like I'm losing myself. All I want from you is a drug to take the edge off. You know me. I'll be fine in a day or two.'

'The Queen of Denial.'

'When something works for me, I stick with it.'

'Only denial isn't working any more, is it? That's why your eyelid is spasming, your hands are shaking, and you can't sleep. You've handled a lot of trauma in your life but you can't keep running away from your own past. Someday you're going to have to settle the tab with Claire.'

'A client's husband tries to blow my brains out, and you manage to make my breakdown about my family. This isn't about Claire, damn it.'

'Sooner or later, Meg, it's always about family. The past has an irritating way of becoming the present.'

'I once had a fortune cookie that said the same thing.'

'You're deflecting again.'

'No. I'm rejecting.' Meghann got to her feet. 'Does this mean you won't write me a prescription for a muscle relaxant?'

'It wouldn't help your tic.'

'Fine. I'll get an eye patch.'

Harriet slowly stood up. Across the desk they faced each other. 'Why won't you let me help you?'

Meghann swallowed hard. She had asked herself the same question a hundred times.

'What do you want?' Harriet asked finally.

'I don't know.'

'Yes, you do.'

'Well, if you know the answer, why ask the question?'

'You want to stop feeling so alone.'

A shudder passed through Meghann, left her chilled. 'I've always been alone. I'm used to it.'

'No. Not always.'

Meghann's thoughts spooled back to those years, so long ago now, when she and Claire had been inseparable, the best of friends. Then Meg had known how to love.

Enough. This was getting Meg nowhere.

She grabbed her bag off the floor and headed for the door. 'Send tonight's bill to my secretary. Charge whatever you want. Goodbye, Harriet.' She said goodbye instead of good night because she didn't intend to come back.

She was at the door when Harriet's voice stopped her.

'Be careful. Especially now. Don't let loneliness consume you.'

Meghann kept walking, right out of the door and into the elevator and across the lobby. Outside, she looked down at her watch: nine forty.

There was still plenty of time to go to the Athenian.

In the passenger seat of an eighteen-wheeler, Joe sat slumped against the window. The driver, a long-hauler named Erv, hit the brakes and shifted gears. The truck groaned and shuddered and began to slow down. 'There's the Hayden exit.'

Joe saw the familiar sign and didn't know how to feel. He hadn't been here in so long.

Home.

No. It was where he'd grown up; home was something else—or, more accurately, someone else—and she wouldn't be waiting up for him to return.

The slip road looped over the freeway and flattened out onto a tree-lined road. On the left side was a small, shingled gas station. Erv pulled up in front of the pump and came to a creaking stop. The brakes wheezed loudly and fell silent. Erv opened his door and got out.

Joe wedged the handle down and gave the door a good hard push. It creaked wearily open, and he stepped down onto the roadside of western Washington for the first time in three years.

He looked at Erv, who was busy pumping gas. 'Thanks for the ride.'

Erv nodded. 'You sure you don't want to go to Seattle? It's only an hour and a half away. There ain't much here.'

Joe looked down the long, tree-lined road. 'You'd be surprised,' he said softly. His sister was just down that road, waiting for him. The thought galvanised him.

'Bye, Erv.' He slung his backpack over his shoulder and started walking. In no time he came to the small green sign that welcomed him to HAYDEN, POPULATION 872. HOME OF LORI ADAMS, 1974 STATE SPELLING BEE CHAMPION. The town where he'd been born looked precisely as he remembered: a pretty little collection of Western-themed buildings dozing peacefully beneath this warm June sun.

The buildings all had false fronts, and there were hitching posts stationed here and there along a wooden boardwalk. The stores were mostly the same—the Whitewater Diner and the Basket Case Florist Shoppe, then Mo's Fireside Tavern and the Stock 'Em Up grocery store. Every sign sparked some memory; every doorway had once welcomed him. Now . . . who knew?

He let out a long sigh and kept walking, past the four-way stop sign that introduced the start of town, past the Loose Screw Hardware Shop and the family-owned bakery.

He felt people looking at him; it beat him down, those looks that turned into frowns of recognition. Whispers followed him.

'Is that Joe Wyatt?'

'Did you see that, Myrtle? It was Joe Wyatt.'

He tucked his chin close to his chest and kept moving. On Azalea Street he veered left, and then on Cascade he turned right. Here, only a few blocks from Main Street, the world was quiet again. Quaint wood-framed houses sat on impeccably trimmed lawns.

By the time he reached Rhododendron Lane, the street was almost completely deserted. He walked past Craven Farms, quiet this time of year before the fall harvest, and then turned into the driveway. Now the mailbox said TRAINOR. For years it had read WYATT.

The house was a sprawling log-built A-frame that was set amid a perfectly landscaped yard. His father had built this house by hand, log by log. One of the last things Dad had said to them was, 'Take care of the house. Your mother loved it so.'

Joe felt a sudden sadness almost too sweet to bear. His sister kept the house looking exactly as it always had. Mom and Dad would be pleased. He climbed the steps, hearing the familiar creaking of the boards underfoot. After a long pause he knocked on the door.

For a moment there was no sound within, then the clattering of heavy-soled shoes and the called-out 'Coming!'

The door swung open. Gina stood there, dressed in baggy black sweats and green rubber clogs, breathing hard. Her chestnut-brown hair was a bird's nest of disarray. She took one look at him, mouthed 'Oh,' then burst into tears. 'Joey . . .'

She pulled him into her arms. For a moment he was dazed. He hadn't been touched in so long, it felt wrong somehow.

'Joey,' she said again, putting her face in the crook of his neck. He felt her warm tears on his skin, and something inside him gave way. He brought his arms round her and held on. The whole of his childhood came back to him then, drifted on the baking-bread smell of the house and the citrusy scent of her shampoo. He remembered baby-sitting her on Saturday mornings and walking her home from school. Though they were seven years apart in age, they'd always been a pair.

She drew back, wiping her red-rimmed eyes. 'I didn't think you'd really come back.' She patted her hair and made a face. 'I look like the undead. I was planting flowers in the back yard.'

'You look beautiful,' he said, meaning it.

'You look sick.' She dragged him into the sunlit living room, sat down on a beautiful butter-yellow sofa and pulled him down beside her.

'I am. My head is pounding.'

Gina popped up and hurried from the room. 'Some water,' she called as she went, 'and aspirin.'

He started to say something—he had no idea what—when he saw the photo on the mantelpiece.

He got slowly to his feet and walked towards it.

The photograph was of five women crowded together; four of them wore matching pink dresses. They were all smiling. Gina, front and centre, was in white. Diana was beside her, laughing.

'Hey, Di,' he whispered. 'I'm home.'

'That's one of my favourite pictures,' Gina said, coming up behind him.

'At the end,' he said softly, 'she talked about you guys. The Bluesers. She must have told me a hundred Lake Chelan stories.'

Gina squeezed his shoulder. 'We all miss her.'

'I know.'

'Did you find it out there . . . whatever you were looking for?'

He thought about that. 'No,' he said at last. 'But now that I'm here, I want to be gone again. Everywhere I look, I'll see her.'

'Tell me that wasn't true out there, too.'

He sighed. His sister was right. It didn't matter where he was. Diana filled his thoughts, his dreams.

'I'm lost, Gigi. I don't know how to start over.'

She touched his cheek. 'You already have. You're here.'

He placed his hand over hers and tried to think of something to say. Nothing came to mind, so he smiled instead. 'Where's my beautiful niece? And my brother-in-law?'

'Bonnie's over at River's Edge, playing with Ali.'

'And Rex? He doesn't work on Sundays.'

'He left me, Joey. Divorced me.'

She didn't say, 'While you were gone,' but she could have. His baby sister had needed him, and he hadn't been there for her. He pulled her into his arms. She burst into tears. He stroked her hair and whispered that he was here, that he wasn't going anywhere.

For the first time in three years it was the truth.

Meghann couldn't get over the sight of her desk. It was clean for the first time in more than a decade. All her pending cases had been portioned out to the other attorneys. She'd promised Julie that she'd take at least three weeks of vacation, but already Meghann was having second thoughts. She hadn't taken a vacation in a decade. What in the hell would she do with all the hours that made up an ordinary day?

She retrieved her briefcase and handbag from the bottom drawer of her desk and headed for the door. She allowed herself a last look at the room that was more of a home to her than her apartment and quietly closed the door.

Outside, night was closing in, drawing the warmth from a surprisingly hot day. As she neared the Public Market, the crowds increased. Tourists stood in front of flower shops and outside bakery windows.

In the lobby of her building, she waved at the doorman and went up to her apartment. She'd forgotten to leave the radio playing. The place was jarringly silent. She tossed her keys on the entrance table. They clanged into a floral-carved Lalique bowl.

Her place was beautiful and neat, with not so much as a paperclip out of place. Without the books and folders and papers piled everywhere, it had the look of an expensive hotel room. A pair of brocade sofas faced each other, with an elegant black coffee table in between. The west-facing walls were solid glass. The view was a blue wash of sky and Sound.

Meghann opened the black and gold lacquered cabinet in the television room and grabbed the remote. As sound blared to life, she slumped into her favourite chair and planted her feet on the ottoman. It took less than five seconds to recognise the theme music.

It was a rerun of her mother's old television show—*Starbase IV*. Mama hurried onscreen wearing that ridiculous lime-green stretch suit with black thigh-high boots.

'Captain Wad,' Mama said, 'we've received an emergency message from the boys in the dehydratin' pod.'

Dehydratin'.

As if a microbotanist on a Martian space station had to be from Alabama. Meg hated the fake accent. And Mama had used it ever since. Said her fans expected it of her. Sadly, they probably did.

'Don't think about it,' Meghann said aloud. But it was impossible. When she was weak, the memories took over. She closed her eyes and remembered. They'd been living in Bakersfield then . . .

Hey, girls, Mama's home.

Meghann huddled closer to Claire, holding her baby sister tightly. Mama stumbled into the trailer's living room, wearing a clinging red-sequinned dress with silver fringe.

I've brought Mr Mason home with me. You girls be nice to him now, she said in that boozy voice that meant she'd wake up mean.

Meghann knew she had to act fast. With a man in the trailer Mama wouldn't be able to think about much else, and the rent was long past due. She reached down for the wrinkled copy of *Variety* that she'd stolen from the local library. *Mama?*

Mama lit up a menthol cigarette. *What is it?*

Meghann thrust out the magazine. She'd outlined the ad in red ink. It read, 'Mature actress sought for small part in science-fiction television series. Open call.' Then the address in Los Angeles.

Mama read the ad out loud. Her smile froze in place at the words 'mature actress'. After a long, tense moment she laughed and gave Mr Mason a little shove towards the bedroom. When he went into the room and closed the door behind him, Mama knelt down and opened her arms. *Give Mama a hug.*

Meghann and Claire flew into her embrace. They waited days for a moment like this, sometimes weeks, but when Mama turned on the heat of her love, it warmed you to the bone.

Thank you, Miss Meggy. I don't know what I'd do without you. I'll surely try out for that part. Now, you two scamper off and stay out of trouble. I've got some entertaining to do.

Mama read for the role. To her—and everyone else's—amazement she nailed the audition. Instead of winning the small part she'd gone up for, she won the starring role of Tara Zyn, the space station's microbotanist.

Meghann sighed. She didn't want to think about the week Mama had gone to Los Angeles and left her daughters alone in that dirty trailer—or the changes that had come afterwards. Meghann and Claire had never really been sisters since.

Beside her, the phone rang. Meghann pounced on it, eager to talk to *anyone*. 'Hello?'

'Hey, Meggy, it's me. Your mama. How are you, darlin'?'

Meg rolled her eyes at the accent. She should have let the answering machine pick up. 'I'm fine, Mama. And you?'

'Couldn't be better. The Fan-ference was this weekend. Lordy, I signed s'many autographs, my fingers ache.'

'Well, your fans love you.'

'Thank God for small miracles. It surely is nice to talk to you, Meggy. Y'all should come down and visit me.'

Mama always said that, but Meghann couldn't sit alone in this apartment for three weeks. 'I'm taking a vacation,' she said in a rush. 'Maybe I could come stay with you.'

'Oh. That would be . . . fine. Maybe this Christmas—'

'Tomorrow.'

'Tomorrow?' Mama laughed. 'Honey, I've got a photographer from *People* magazine comin' over at three o'clock, and at my age I wake up lookin' like one o' those hairless dogs. It takes ten women all day to make me beautiful.'

Meghann wanted to hang up, say forget it, but when she looked around her empty, photo-free apartment, she felt almost sick. 'How about Monday, then? Maybe we could go to a spa.'

'Don't you *ever* watch the E! channel? I'm leavin' for Cleveland on Monday. I'm doin' Shakespeare in some park with Pamela Anderson and Charlie Sheen. *Hamlet.*'

'*You? You're* doing Shakespeare?'

'I'm gonna forget I heard that tone in your voice.'

'Cut the accent, Mama. It's me. I know you were born in Detroit. Joan Jojovitch is the name on your birth certificate.'

'Now you're just being rude. You always were a prickly child. It's a big break for me.'

For me. Mama's favourite words. 'Well, good luck. You better get a good night's sleep before the magazine shoot.'

'That's the God's honest truth.' Mama exhaled heavily. 'Maybe y'all could come down when I'm not so busy. Claire, too.'

'Sure. Bye, Mama.'

Meghann hung up the phone. For the next hour she paced the apartment, trying to formulate a plan that made sense.

The phone rang. She dived for it. 'Hello?'

'Hi, Meg.'

'Claire? This is a nice surprise.' And for once it was. 'I talked to Mama today. You won't believe this. She's doing—'.

'I'm getting married.'

'Shakespeare in— *Married?*'

'I've never been so happy, Meg. I know it's crazy, but that's love, I guess.'

'Who are you marrying?'

'Bobby Jack Austin. I met him ten days ago in Chelan. I know what you're going to say, but—'

'Ten days ago? Claire! Sometimes you sneak away for a wild weekend with men you just met. What you don't do is marry them.'

'I'm in love, Meg. Please don't ruin it for me.'

Meg wanted to give advice so badly, she had to curl her hands into fists. 'What does he do for a living?'

'He's a singer-songwriter. He was singing in Cowboy Bob's Western Roundup when I first saw him. My heart stopped for a second. Have you ever felt that way?'

Before Meghann could answer, Claire went on, 'He's a ski instructor in the winter, and he travels around in the summer, playing his music. He's two years older than I am and so good-looking, you won't believe it. Better than Brad Pitt. He's going to be a star.'

Meghann let it all soak in. Her sister was marrying a thirty-seven-year-old ski bum who dreamed of being a country-and-western singer. And the best gig he could get was at Cowboy Bob's.

'Does he know what the campground is worth? Will he sign a prenuptial agreement?'

'Damn you, Meg. Can't you be happy for me?'

'I want to be,' she said, and it was true. 'When's the wedding?'

'Saturday, the 23rd.'

'Of *this* month?' This was crazy. 'I need to meet him.'

'Of course. The rehearsal dinner—'

'No way. I need to meet him *now*. I'll be at your house tomorrow night. I'll take you guys out to dinner.'

'Really, Meg, you don't have to do that.'

'I have to meet the man who stole my sister's heart, don't I?'

'OK, I'll see you tomorrow.' Claire paused, then said, 'It'll be good to see you.'

'Yeah. Bye.' Meg hung up, then punched in her office number and left a message for her secretary. 'I want everything we've got on prenuptial agreements delivered to my house by ten o'clock tomorrow morning.' As an afterthought she added, 'Thanks.'

Then she headed for her computer to do some checking up on Bobby Jack Austin. *This* was what she'd do on her idiotic vacation. She'd save Claire from making the biggest mistake of her life.

Claire hung up the phone. In the silence that followed, doubt crept into the room. She and Bobby *were* moving awfully fast . . .

'Damn you, Meg.'

But even as she cursed her sister, Claire knew the doubt had been there all along, a little seed inside her, waiting to sprout and grow. She was too old to be swept away by passion.

She had a daughter to think about, after all. Alison had never known her biological father. It had been easy so far, bubble-wrapping Ali's world so that none of life's sharp edges could hurt her. Marriage would change everything.

The last thing Claire wanted to do was marry a man who had itchy feet. She knew all about men like that. She had had four stepfathers before she'd turned nine. That number didn't include the men she'd been asked to call Uncle, the men who'd passed through Mama's life like shots of tequila. There and gone, leaving nothing behind but a bitter aftertaste.

Claire walked to the window. Outside, the sun was just beginning to set. The camp lay bathed in a rose-gold light.

Dad and Bobby strolled into view. Bobby carried a Weed Eater in one hand and a can of gasoline in the other. In the days he'd been here, he had pitched in with the work. He was good at it, though she knew he wouldn't be happy at River's Edge for ever. Already he'd mentioned going on the road for a few weeks this summer. The three of them. 'The

Austins' road trip,' was how he put it. Claire hadn't broached the idea with her father, but knew he'd be all for it.

Dad and Bobby stopped in front of cabin number five. Dad pointed up towards the eaves, and Bobby nodded. A minute later they were both laughing. Dad put his hand on Bobby's shoulder. They moved away, towards the laundry room.

'Hey, Mommy.' Claire turned round. Ali stood at the bottom of the stairs. 'Grandpa's taking me to Smitty's Garage. We're gonna get the truck fixed.'

As Claire watched her daughter run out of the front door, she felt the pressing weight of responsibility. What if the marriage didn't work? She needed to talk to someone about this.

Not her sister, of course. A friend. She dialled Gina's number.

Gina answered on the first ring. 'Hello?'

Claire slumped back into the oversized chair. 'It's me. The Insta-Marry Queen. Meghann thinks I'm being an idiot.'

'Since when do we care what *she* thinks? She's an attorney, for goodness' sake. That's below invertebrates on the evolutionary chain.'

Claire smiled. 'I knew you'd put it in perspective. Just tell me I'm not being a selfish bitch who is going to ruin her daughter's life by marrying a stranger.'

'Oh, so it's your mother we're talking about.'

'I don't want to be like her.' Claire's voice was suddenly soft.

'I've known you since all five of us showed up for the first day of school in the same blue shirt. You've never been selfish. And I've never seen you this happy. God has finally given you the gift of love and passion. Don't return it unopened.'

'I'm scared. I should have done this when I was young.'

'Of course you're scared. A smart person is afraid of marriage. If you're not ready to marry him, wait. But don't wait because your big sister made you question yourself. Follow your heart.'

'What would I do without you?'

Gina laughed. 'The same thing I'd do without you—drink too much and whine to strangers.'

'How are you doing?'

She sighed. 'Not good. Rex came by last night. The son of a bitch has lost about ten pounds and dyed his hair. Pretty soon he'll ask me to call him the Rexster again.' She paused. 'He wants to marry that woman.'

'Ouch.'

'Ouch with a blowtorch. It hurts like hell. But you haven't heard the real news: Joey's back.'

'You're kidding. Where's he been?'

Gina lowered her voice. 'Here and there, he says. He looks bad. Older. He got home yesterday. He's been asleep for almost thirteen hours. I hope I never love anyone as much as he loved Diana.'

'What's he going to do?'

'I don't know. I said he could stay here, but he won't. This house brings back a lot of memories. He stared at the picture of my wedding for almost an hour. Honest to God, I wanted to cry.'

'Give him my love.'

'You got it.'

They talked for a few more minutes about ordinary, everyday things. By the time they hung up, Claire felt better. She looked down at her left hand, at the engagement ring she wore. It was a strip of silver foil, carefully folded and twisted round her finger. She refused to think of what her sister would say about it and remembered instead how she'd felt when Bobby put it there.

Marry me, he'd said on bended knee. His eyes had been filled with the kind of love she'd only dreamed of.

Gina was right. This love was a gift she'd been given. She wouldn't turn away from it because she was afraid. One thing motherhood had taught her—love required boldness.

She grabbed her sweater off the sofa and slipped it over her shoulders, then went outside. Night had almost completely fallen now; darkness enveloped the salmon-hued granite peaks. Claire made her nightly rounds slowly, stopping to talk to several of their guests.

It was completely dark by the time she reached the small row of cabins on the property's eastern edge. At first, she thought the sound she heard was crickets, gearing up for a nightly concert. Then she heard the sweet sound of strings being strummed.

Cabin four had a pretty little porch that faced the river. They had taken the cabin off the market this summer because of rain damage to the roof; the vacancy had given Bobby a place to stay until the wedding. *Destiny*, Dad had said when he gave Claire the key.

Now destiny sat on the edge of the porch, crosslegged, his body veiled in shadows, a guitar across his lap. He stared out at the river, plucking a slow and uncertain tune.

Claire eased into the darkness beneath a giant Douglas fir. Hidden, she watched him. The music sent shivers along her flesh.

Almost too quietly to hear, he started to sing. 'I've been walkin' all my life . . . on a road goin' nowhere. Then I turned a corner, darlin' . . . and there you were.'

Claire stepped out of the shadows. Bobby looked up and saw her. A smile crinkled the suntanned planes of his face.

He began to sing again, his gaze never leaving her face. 'For the first time in my life . . . I believe in God Almighty . . . in the Lord my grandpa promised me . . . 'cause, honey, I see heaven in your eyes.' He strummed a few more chords, and then he thumped his hand on the guitar and grinned. 'That's all I've written so far. I know it needs work.' He put down the guitar and moved towards her.

With every footstep, she felt her breathing shorten, until, by the time he was standing in front of her, she couldn't draw a full breath. It was almost embarrassing to feel this much.

He took her left hand in his, looked down at the strip of foil that was supposed to be a diamond ring. 'Pathetic,' he whispered. 'Not every woman would accept a ring like this.'

'I love you, Bobby. That's all that matters.'

'I'm no prize, Claire. You know that. I've made mistakes in my life. Three of 'em, to be exact.'

'I'm a single mother who never married. I know about mistakes.'

'I've never felt this way before,' he said softly.

'What way?'

'As if my heart doesn't belong to me any more, as if it can't beat without you. You're inside me, Claire, holding me up. You make me want to be more than I am.'

'I want us to grow old together.' She whispered the words.

'I want to hear our kids fight about who's touching who in the smelly back seat of a minivan.'

Claire laughed. It felt so good to dream with someone.

He pulled her into his arms, danced with her to the music of the river and the crickets.

Finally, Claire said, 'My sister, Meghann, is coming tomorrow. She was predictably underwhelmed by our decision to get married.'

Taking her hand, he led her to his porch. They sat down in the swing-seat and rocked gently. 'I thought you said she'd boycott the wedding.'

'Wishful thinking.'

'Does her opinion matter?'

'It shouldn't.'

'But it does.'

Claire felt like a fool. 'It does.'

'She won't be able to change your mind about me, will she?'

'She's never been able to change my mind about anything. It's what makes her foam at the mouth.'

'As long as you love me, I can take anything.'

'Well, Bobby Austin . . .' She put her arms round him and leaned over for a kiss. Just before their lips touched, she whispered, 'Then you can take anything. Even my sister.'

Chapter Five

'IT'S STUPID TO MARRY a man you just met.'

'Stupid is not a good word choice.'

'It's inadvisable to—'

'You're her sister, not her lawyer.'

Meghann had been carrying on this demented conversation with the rearview mirror throughout the entire drive from Seattle. How was it that she came up with closing arguments that would bring a jury to tears and she couldn't find a simple, compelling way to warn her sister of impending doom?

At the last stop on the highway before Hayden, a run-down tavern— the Roadhouse—sat huddled beneath a blinking neon sign that recommended Coors Light. Honest to God, she wanted to pull over, walk into that crowded tavern and lose herself in the smoky darkness. It would certainly be better than saying to Claire after being separated all these years, 'You're making a mistake.' But she didn't slow down. Instead, she continued on for another nine miles before turning off the freeway onto a two-lane road bordered by towering evergreens.

The small green sign welcomed her to Hayden.

Meghann slowed down. It still looked like the kind of place that welcomed newcomers, where women brought homemade tuna casseroles to the families who moved in. But Meghann knew better. She'd lived here long enough to know how cruel these nice-looking people could be to a girl who ran with the wrong crowd. Sure, a small town could comfort a person; it could also turn cold fast.

Meghann came to the one and only traffic light. When it turned green, she hit the gas and sped through town.

A few miles later she came to the sign.

RIVER'S EDGE RESORT. NEXT LEFT.

She turned onto the gravel road. The trees on either side were gigantic. At the first driveway she slowed again. A cute mailbox, painted to look like a killer whale, read: C. CAVENAUGH.

The once-wild yard had been tamed; it now looked like an English country garden. The house had a pale butter-yellow siding and glossy white trim, and a pretty white wraparound porch decorated with hanging pots of geraniums and lobelia.

She parked and got out of the car. Lugging gifts, she walked up to the front door and knocked. No one answered. After a long wait she walked back to the car and drove the 500 or so yards to the campground's main office. She walked past the swimming pool towards the long, narrow log building that served as the registration office. A bell tinkled overhead as she opened the door.

Sam Cavenaugh stood behind the desk. At her entrance he looked up. His ready smile faded slowly, then reinforced itself. 'Hey, Meg. It's good to see you. It's been too damn long.'

'Yeah. I'm sure you missed me.' As always, Meghann felt uncomfortable around Sam; angry. She still remembered the day he told her, 'Go. Just leave.' He'd thought she was a bad influence on his daughter. But what she'd really hated, the one that stayed with her was, 'Just like your damn mother.'

They stared at each other. 'You look good,' he said at last.

'You, too.' Meghann glanced down at her watch. The last thing she wanted to do was stand around not talking with Sam.

'Claire told me to watch out for you. The Ford family, over in campsite seventeen, had a little emergency with their stove, but she should be back any minute.'

'Good. I'll wait for her at the house, then.'

'She should be there any minute.'

'You just said that.'

'You're still tough, aren't you, Meghann?' he said, his voice soft, a little tired even.

'I had to be, Sam. You know that better than anyone.'

'I didn't kick you out, Meghann, I—'

She turned and walked away, let the door slam shut behind her. She was halfway to the car when she heard his voice again.

'She's happy, you know. With this fella,' he said.

Meghann turned round. 'If I remember correctly, you were happy when you married Mama.'

Sam walked towards her. 'Your mama is a piece of work, that's for sure, but I'm glad I married her.'

'You must be on drugs.'

'Claire,' was all he said.

'Oh.' Meghann felt a pinch of jealousy. There it was again—the Claire father-daughter thing.

'Be careful with her,' he said. 'You're her sister.'

'I know I'm her sister.' Once again she walked away. She got into her car and drove to Claire's house.

This time when she knocked on the front door, she heard the patter of feet from inside. The door burst open. Alison stood there, dressed in daisy-festooned denim overalls and a pretty yellow eyelet blouse.

'You can't be Alison Katherine Cavenaugh. She's a baby.'

Ali beamed at that. 'I'm a big girl now.'

'Yes, you are. Can you give your aunt Meg a hug?'

Alison moved forwards and gave her a lukewarm hug. When she stepped back, Meg said, 'I brought you a present.'

'Let me guess.' Claire emerged from the shadows at the end of the hallway. 'A Swiss army knife?'

'No. An air gun.'

'You didn't!'

Meghann laughed. 'The dullest-looking salesperson at the toy store recommended this.' She handed Alison a brightly wrapped box.

Ali ripped it open. 'It's a Groovy Girl, Mommy. A Groovy Girl!' She flung herself at Meghann, this time hugging for real. She showed the doll to Claire, then ran upstairs.

Meghann handed Claire a bottle of wine—Far Niente 1997. 'This is one of my favourites.'

'Thank you.'

They stared at each other. Finally Claire surged forwards, pulled Meghann into a quickie hug, then let her go.

Meghann stumbled back, too surprised by the gesture to respond. 'Dinner smells good, but I wanted to take you out.'

'The Chuck Wagon smorgasbord isn't exactly your style.'

'Oh.'

'Anyway, come in.'

Meghann followed Claire to the sofa and sat down beside her. She couldn't help noticing the ridiculous engagement ring—a band of tin-foil, for God's sake. It was good she'd come up here. There was no point in putting it off. 'Claire, I think—'

Then *he* walked into the room. Meghann knew instantly why her sister had fallen so hard. Bobby might be a loser as a singer, but he was a winner in the looks department. When he smiled, it was with his whole face. A man like this didn't just sweep you off your feet; he twirled you into the air so far and fast there was nowhere to go but down. He and Claire exchanged a look that radiated love.

'I'm Bobby Austin,' he said, smiling.

Meghann rose and shook his hand. 'Meghann Dontess.'

'Claire says folks call you Meg.'

'My friends do, yes.'

He smiled. 'I'm judging by that bite-on-a-lemon look of yours that you'd like me to stick with Miz Dontess.'

'I imagine those mountain girls in Arkansas think you're charming.'

'The Texas girls sure did.' He put an arm round Claire. 'But those days are behind me now. I've found the girl I want to grow old with.' He kissed Claire lightly on the cheek; then he took the wine bottle and walked into the kitchen.

In the few moments he was gone, Meghann stood there, staring at her sister, trying to choose her words with care, but nothing seemed right.

Bobby returned with two glasses of wine and handed one to Meghann. 'I imagine you have some questions for me,' he said, sitting down.

His forthrightness threw Meghann off. Slowly, feeling uncertain, she sat down in the chair opposite the sofa. They were separate entities now: Bobby and Claire versus Meghann. 'Tell me about yourself.'

'I love Claire.'

'Something substantive.'

'I'm thirty-seven years old. Graduated from Oklahoma State. Degree in music appreciation. I've . . . been married.'

Meghann leaned forwards, on alert. 'How many times?'

He glanced at Claire. 'Three.'

Meghann looked at Claire. 'You've got to be kidding.'

He scooted forwards. 'I married Suellen when we were eighteen years old. She was pregnant, and where I come from—'

'You've got kids?'

'No.' His voice grew soft. 'Miscarriage. After that, there wasn't much reason to stay married. We lasted less than three months. I got married again at twenty-one. Unfortunately, it turned out that she wanted a different life than I did. Nice cars, nice jewellery. I got arrested when they busted her for selling cocaine out of our house. I lived with her for two years and never noticed it. I just thought she was moody as hell. Nobody believed I wasn't a part of it. Laura was the only one who counted. She was—is—a paediatrician who loves country music. We were married for ten years. It broke up about a year ago. I could tell you

249

why, but it's none of your business. Claire knows everything, though.'

A three-time loser and a felon. *Perfect.*

And now the bad sister had to break the good sister's heart.

Claire got off the sofa, moved towards her. She sat on the carved Chinese chest that served as a coffee table.

'I know you can't be happy for me, Meg.'

'I want to be.' It was the truth. 'It's just that—'

'He wouldn't get a platinum rating. I know. And you handle divorces for a living. I know that, too. Most of all, I know that you grew up in Mama's house.' She leaned forwards. 'I *know*, Meg.'

Meghann felt the weight of those few words. Her sister had thought of all the same reasons. There wasn't anything Meghann could say that Claire didn't already know.

'It won't ever make sense, and I know it's crazy and risky and—worst of all—Mama-like. But it would mean a lot to me if you'd hug me and say you're happy for me. Even if it's a lie.'

Meghann looked into her sister's pale green eyes and was reminded of their childhood. Whenever Mama had brought a new 'friend' home, Claire had let herself believe that *finally* there would be a daddy in her life. Each stepfather had broken a tiny piece of Claire's heart. And yet, when the next man arrived, her sister found a way to believe again. Of course Claire believed in Bobby Austin.

There was no way she would change Claire's mind or—more important—her heart. Thus she had two choices: pretend to give her blessing or stick to her guns.

'I trust you, Claire,' Meghann said at last. 'If you say Bobby Austin is the man you love, that's good enough for me.'

Claire released a sharp breath. 'Thank you.' She leaned forwards and hugged Meghann, who didn't respond by hugging her back.

Claire pulled away and stood up. She went over to the sofa and sat down by Bobby, who immediately put an arm round her.

Meghann tried to think of what to say in the awkward silence that followed. 'So what's the wedding plan? Justice of the peace?'

'No way.' Claire laughed. 'I waited thirty-five years for this. I'm having the whole enchilada. White dress. Formal church wedding. Cake. Reception with dancing. All of it.'

'There's a consultant in my building,' Meghann said. 'I think she planned Bill Gates's wedding.'

'This is Hayden, not Seattle. I'll rent the community hall, and everyone will pitch in with pot luck. It'll be great.'

'Pot luck? *Pot luck?*' Meghann got to her feet. Apparently there was something of her mother in her after all. She wasn't going to let her sister have a Wal-Mart wedding. 'I'll organise the wedding and reception,' she said impulsively. Once she'd offered, she felt steady again. In control of something.

Claire's smile faded. 'You?'

'I'm not a social moron. I can do this.'

'But—but your job is so hectic. I couldn't ask you to take time out of your busy schedule for this.'

'You didn't ask. I offered. And it so happens that I find myself . . . underutilised at work.' The idea seized her. Maybe it could bring them together. 'This would be perfect, really. I'd *like* to do this for you, Claire.'

'Oh.' Claire sounded underwhelmed. Meghann knew what her sister was thinking—Meghann was a bull in a small-town china shop.

'I'll listen to you and do what you want. It'll be *your* wedding.'

Claire frowned at her sister. 'You never do anything in a small way, Meg.'

Meghann felt awkward suddenly, vulnerable. She wasn't certain why she wanted this so badly. 'I will this time. Honest.'

'OK,' Claire said finally. 'You can help me plan my wedding.'

Meghann grinned and clapped her hands. 'Good. Now, what's the date again—the 23rd? Next Saturday? That's not much time to pull this together.' She headed for the kitchen, where she found a scrap of paper and began a 'to do' list.

'Oh, man,' she heard her sister say. 'I've created a monster.'

By the second night in his sister's house, Joe felt as if he were suffocating. Everywhere he looked he saw glimpses of his old life. He didn't know how he was going to go forwards, but he knew he couldn't stay here.

He waited until Gina left to go grocery shopping, then crammed his things—including several framed photographs of Diana that he'd taken from the house—into the old backpack and headed for the door. He left a note on the kitchen counter: *Can't stay here. Sorry. Hurts too much. I know this is a rough time for you, so I won't go far. Will call soon. Love you, J.*

He walked back to town. There were a few people milling around the streets, and more than one face peered frowningly up at him, but no one approached him. He saw when he was recognised, saw the way old friends lurched at the sight of him, drew back.

He was about to give up on finding a job, when he came to the end of town. He stood opposite Riverfront Park, staring at a corrugated-iron hut that advertised SMITTY'S, THE BEST AUTO SHOP IN HAYDEN.

On the chain-link fence was a sign: HELP WANTED. EXPERIENCE REQUESTED, BUT WHO AM I KIDDING?

Joe crossed the street and headed towards the entrance.

A dog started barking. He noticed the BEWARE OF DOG sign. Seconds later a miniature white poodle came tearing round the corner. 'Madonna, stop that damn yapping.' An old man stepped out from the shadowed darkness of the hut. He wore oil-stained overalls and a Mariners baseball cap. 'Don't mind the dog. What can I do ya for?'

'I saw your "Help Wanted" sign.'

'No kiddin'.' The old man slapped his thigh. 'That thing's been up there pret near on two years now. I—' He paused, stepped forwards, frowning slowly. 'Joe Wyatt?'

Joe tensed. 'Hey, Smitty.'

Smitty blew out a heavy breath. 'I'll be damned.'

'I'm back. And I need a job. But if it'd cost you customers to hire me, I understand. No hard feelings.'

'You want a job *wrenching*? But you're a doctor—'

'That life is over.'

Smitty stared at him, then said, 'You remember my son, Phil?'

'He was a lot older than me, but yeah, I remember him.'

'Vietnam ruined him. Guilt, I think. He did stuff over there . . . Anyway, I've seen a man run before. It isn't good. Of course I'll hire you, Joe. The cabin still comes with the job. You want it?'

'Yes.'

Smitty nodded, then led the way through the hut and out the other end. The back yard was big and well maintained. Flowers grew in riotous clumps along the path. A thicket of evergreens stood clustered behind a small log cabin.

'You were a teenager the last time you lived here.'

'That was a long time ago.'

'Yeah,' Smitty sighed. 'Helga still keeps it spick-and-span clean. She'll be glad to have you back.'

Joe followed Smitty to the cabin.

Inside, it was as clean as always. A red-striped woollen blanket covered an old leather sofa, and a rocking chair sat next to the river-rock fireplace. The kitchen appeared well stocked with appliances and pots and pans, and a single bedroom boasted a queen-sized bed.

Joe reached out and shook Smitty's bear-claw hand. 'Thank you, Smitty,' he said, surprised at how deep his gratitude ran.

'There are a lot of people in this town who care about you, Joe. You seem to have forgotten that.'

'That's nice to hear. Still, I'd be happier if no one knew I was here—for a while, anyway.'

'It's a long road back from something like that, I guess.'

'A very long road.'

After Smitty left, Joe burrowed through his backpack for one of the framed photographs that he'd taken from his sister's house. He stared down at Diana's smiling face. 'It's a start,' he said to her.

Meghann woke up disorientated. She thought a radio was on in a room down the hall. Then she realised that the noise was birdsong. Birdsong, for God's sake.

Claire's house.

She sat up in bed. The beautifully decorated guest room was oddly comforting. Everywhere were handmade trinkets—proof of time spent on the little things—as well as Ali's artwork.

There was a knock at the door, then a hesitantly called out 'Meg?'

She glanced at the bedside clock: ten fifteen. *Oh, man.* She rubbed her eyes, which felt like a sandpit from lack of sleep. As usual, she'd tossed and turned all night.

'I'm up,' she said, throwing the covers back.

'Breakfast is on the table,' Claire said through the closed door. 'We'll leave at about eleven if that's still OK.'

It took Meghann a second to remember. She'd promised to join Claire and her friends in town. Wedding-dress shopping in Hayden with grown women who called themselves the Bluesers.

'I'll be ready.'

'See you then.'

Meghann listened to the footsteps as Claire walked away. How long could she keep up this charade of *I'm your sister, I support your wedding*? Sooner or later, her mouth would open and her opinion would explode, bomblike. *You can't marry him. You don't know him. Be smart.* None of these opinions would sit well.

Meghann got out of bed and hurried down the hallway to the small first-floor bathroom. She brushed her teeth, then took a quick, very hot shower. Thirty minutes later she was ready to go, re-dressed in yesterday's clothes—a white Dolce & Gabbana blouse and a pair of Marc Jacobs jeans.

Outside, the sun shone brightly on the well-tended yard. It was late June, a glorious time of year in the Northwest. Meghann tossed her bag into her Porsche and got inside. The engine growled to life. She drove towards the resort office slowly, careful not to stir up too much dust on the gravel road. It was a short distance, but her high-heeled sandals couldn't handle the loose stone.

She pulled up in front of the registration building and parked. Choosing a careful path through the dewy grass, she went into the building. It was empty.

She went to the desk and found the Hayden phone book. There was one wedding consultant listing: *Royal Event Planning*. In fine print it read, *Pretend you'll only get married once.*

Meghann couldn't help smiling at that. She wrote down the number and put it in her bag.

She went out to her car, put the convertible top down, and waited. At eleven o'clock Claire appeared, wearing a pair of jeans and a River's Edge Resort T-shirt. She tossed her canvas handbag behind the seat and climbed in. 'Now, this is going to town in style.'

Meghann didn't know if Claire intended that remark as a put-down or not, so she kept silent. Actually that was her new mantra: *Shut up and smile.*

'You sure slept late,' Claire said. 'I thought you usually got to the office by seven.'

'I had trouble sleeping last night.'

'Please don't worry about me, Meg. Please.'

Meghann couldn't let her sister think the insomnia was because of the wedding. 'It's not the wedding. I never sleep.'

'Since when?'

'I guess it started in college. Cramming all night for exams. You know how it is.'

'No, I don't.'

Meghann had been trying to protect Claire, to hide the fact that the insomnia had started when their family fell apart, but college had been the wrong tack. 'From what I hear, motherhood causes a few all-nighters, too.'

'You know something about babies. Mama said I was colicky.'

'Yeah, like Mama would know. You didn't have colic. You had ear infections. When you were sick, you wailed like a banshee. I used to carry you, screaming, down to the Laundromat. If I sat on top of the dryer, holding you, you'd eventually fall asleep. Mama always wondered what happened to all her quarters.'

'No wonder I don't mind doing the laundry. Here, this is it.' Claire pointed to an old Victorian house, painted Pepto-Bismol pink, with lavender trim. The white picket fence bore a hand-painted sign that read *Miss Abigail's Drawers. Come on in.*

Meghann looked up at the ridiculously cute house. 'We could zip down to Escada or Nordstrom.'

'Don't be yourself, Meg.'

'OK.' She sighed. 'Lead on. I'll shut my mouth.'

They walked up the rickety stairs and entered the store. There was merchandise everywhere—plastic flowers and seashell picture frames. The fireplace screen was alight with votive candles.

'Hello!' Claire called out.

There was an immediate response—a gaggle of women's voices, then a herd of running footsteps.

A large, older woman, wearing a floral muumuu, barrelled round the corner. 'Claire Cavenaugh, I'm so glad to *finally* be able to show you the first floor.'

'Wedding dresses are on the first floor,' Claire said to Meghann. 'Miss Abigail had given up on me.'

Before Meghann could respond, two other women hurried into the room. One was short and wore a baggy, waistless dress and white tennis shoes. The other was tall, perhaps too thin, and dressed flawlessly in beige silk. Two of the Bluesers. Waistless dress, Meg learned, was Gina, and beige silk was Charlotte.

'Karen couldn't make it today,' Gina said. 'Willie had an orthodontist appointment and Dottie sat on her glasses.'

'In other words,' Charlotte said, 'an ordinary Karen day.'

Claire fell in beside Charlotte and Abigail. They were talking about lace and beadwork and veils.

'So, Meghann,' Gina said, 'I'm surprised you could get away from the office. I hear you're the best divorce attorney in Seattle.'

'I wouldn't miss Claire's wedding.'

'I know a divorce attorney. She's good at breaking up families.'

'That's what we do.'

A look passed through Gina's eyes. Her voice softened. 'Do you ever put them back together?'

'Not often.'

Gina's face seemed to fall; it crumpled like an old paper bag, and Meghann understood. 'You're going through a divorce?'

Gina tried to smile. 'Just finished it, actually. Tell me it'll get better.'

'It will,' Meg said softly. 'But it may take a while. There are several support groups that might help you.'

'I've got the Bluesers to cry with, but thanks. I appreciate the honesty. Now, let's go upstairs and find your sister the perfect dress.'

Gina led Meg upstairs. By the time they got there, Claire was already wearing the first dress. It had huge leg-of-mutton sleeves and a skirt that looked like an upside-down teacup. Meg sat down in a white wicker chair. Gina stood behind her.

'Oh, my. That's lovely,' Abigail said.

Claire stood in front of a three-panelled full-length mirror, turning this way and that.

'It's very princesslike,' Charlotte said.

Claire looked at Meg. 'What do you think?'

Meghann wasn't sure what was expected of her: honesty or support. She took another look at the dress and knew support was impossible. 'It's hideous.'

'My sister is always harsh,' Claire said quietly, walking back into the dressing room.

Meghann sighed. She'd screwed up again, wielded her opinion like a blunt instrument to the back of the head. She hunkered down in her chair and clamped her mouth shut.

The remainder of the afternoon was a mind-wrecking parade of cheap dresses, one after another. Claire zipped in, got opinions, and zipped out. She didn't again ask for Meghann's opinion, and Meghann knew better than to offer it. Instead, she leaned back in her chair and rested her head against the wall.

A jab in the rib cage woke her up. She blinked, leaned forwards. Charlotte, Abigail and Claire were walking away from her into a room marked HATS AND VEILS.

Gina said to her, 'I'd heard you could be a bitch, but falling asleep while your sister tries on wedding dresses is pretty rude.'

'It was the only way I could keep quiet. Did she find one?'

'No.'

Meghann frowned suddenly. 'What do you mean I'm a bitch? Is that what Claire says?'

'No. Yes. Sometimes. You know how it is when you're drinking margaritas on a bad day. Karen calls her sister Susan the Soulless Psychopath. Claire calls you Jaws.'

Meghann wanted to smile but couldn't. 'Oh.'

'I remember when she moved here, you know,' Gina said softly. 'She cried if you looked at her the wrong way. All she'd say for years was that she missed her sister. I didn't find out until after graduation what had happened to her.'

'What I'd done, you mean.'

'I'm not one to judge. My point is this: Claire was wounded by all of that, but it means a lot to her that you're here.'

'I told her I'd plan the wedding.'

'You seem perfectly suited for it.'

'Oh, yeah. I'm a real romantic.' Meghann sighed.

'All you have to do is listen to Claire. When was the last time you sat down for a drink with your sister and just *talked*?'

'Let's put it this way: We wouldn't have been old enough to have wine with our meal.'

'That's what I thought. Go with her now.'

'But Alison—'

'Sam can take care of Ali. I'll let him know.'

'Claire won't want to go with me after I nixed the dresses.'

'And fell asleep. The snoring was especially poignant.'

'You don't pull any punches, do you?'

'Thus the divorce. Take Claire out for dinner. Go see a movie. Do *something* sisterly. It's about time.'

Claire glanced sideways at her sister, who was behind the steering wheel, driving too fast, her black hair flapping behind her like some celebrity starlet's. 'Where are we going?' she asked for the fourth time.

'You'll see.' Always the same answer.

'I need to get back to Ali,' Claire said, also for the fourth time.

'We're here.' Meg tucked the silver Porsche into an empty parking spot on the street. Before Claire could respond, Meghann was out of the car and standing by the meter. 'Come on.'

They were in downtown Seattle now. Her sister's territory. Claire fell into step beside Meghann.

'Here,' Meghann said, stopping suddenly in front of a narrow white door flanked by windows on either side. A small sign read BY DESIGN.

'What *is* this place?'

'You said I could plan your wedding, right?' Meg opened the door and went inside.

Claire hesitated.

'Come on.' Meghann waited for her in front of an elevator.

Claire followed. A second later the elevator pinged, and the doors slid open. They went in; the doors closed.

Meghann said, 'I'm sorry about this morning. I screwed up.'

'Sleeping is one thing. Snoring is another.'

'I know. I'm sorry.'

Claire sighed. 'It's the story of our lives, Meg, but we never—'

The elevator doors opened. Claire gasped.

There were mannequins everywhere, dressed in the most beautiful

257

wedding dresses Claire had ever seen. She stepped forwards. The gown in front of her was an off-the-shoulder creation. Claire peeked at the price tag. It read *Escada $4,200*.

She let go of it suddenly and turned to Meghann. 'Let's go.'

Meg grabbed her wrist. 'I want you to try on dresses *here*.'

'I can't. I know you're just being you, Meg. But this . . . hurts a little. I work at a campground.'

'I don't want to say this twice, Claire, so please listen and believe me. I work eighty-five hours a week, and my clients pay almost four hundred dollars an hour. Money is something I have. It would mean a lot to me to buy you this wedding gown. You don't belong in the dresses we saw this morning. I'm sorry if you think I'm a bitch and a snob, but that's how I feel.'

Before Claire could answer, a woman cried out, 'Meghann Dontess. In a wedding shop. Who would *ever* believe it?'

A tall, rail-thin woman in a navy-blue sheath dress strode forwards. Her hair, a perfect combination of white-blonde and silver, stood out from her face in a Meg Ryan-type cut.

'Hello, Risa,' Meg said, extending her hand.

'And this is the great one's baby sister, yes?'

Claire heard the barest hint of an Eastern European accent, maybe even Russian, then said, 'I'm Claire.'

'And Meghann is letting you marry.'

'She's advised against it, actually.'

Risa threw back her head and laughed. 'Of course she advised against it. I have heard such advice from her twice. Both times I should have listened, yes, but love will have its way.' She took a step back, studying Claire from head to toe.

'You are beautiful,' she said at last. 'Size ten or twelve, I expect. For you I think the classics: Prada, Valentino, Armani, Wang. Come.' She turned and began marching away. Her hand snaked out now and then to grab a dress.

Claire looked at Meghann. 'Armani? Vera Wang?' She shook her head, unable to say, 'You can't do this.'

'We can always leave without buying anything,' Meghann said. 'Try them on. Just for fun.'

A few minutes later Claire stepped into a dressing area that was bigger than her bedroom. Three floor-to-ceiling mirrors fanned out in front of her. A small wooden platform stood in the centre.

'Go on. The dresses are in there.' Risa gave her a gentle shove.

Claire went into the dressing room, where several gowns hung waiting. The first one was a stunning white silk Ralph Lauren with an intricate lace-and-beadwork patterned bodice.

Claire peeled out of her wrinkled jeans and T-shirt. The gown floated over her shoulders like a cloud.

'Come on, honey. Let's see,' Risa said.

Claire opened the door and stepped into the dressing area. There was a gasp at her entrance. Risa shouted, 'Shoes!' and ran off.

Meg stood there, holding an armful of dresses. Her lips parted in a soft sigh.

Claire couldn't help smiling. She stepped up onto the platform and looked at herself in the mirror. No wonder Meghann had hated the gowns this morning.

Risa came back, brandishing a pair of satin pumps. 'Put them on.'

Claire did as she was told, then stood very still. 'I think the fabric is too flimsy, don't you?' she said. Her job was to find a flaw in each dress, a reason her sister shouldn't spend this much money.

Meghann frowned. 'Too flimsy? You look gorgeous.'

After that, Claire tried on a succession of dresses, each one more beautiful than the last. She felt like a princess, and it didn't ruin the day at all that she had to decline each one. She could tell Meghann was getting frustrated. She kept delivering armfuls of gowns.

Risa had long ago gone on to other customers.

Finally Claire came to the last dress of the day. Meghann had chosen it. An elegant white gown with a heavily beaded tank bodice and a flowing taffeta silk skirt. Claire was still fastening the back as she stepped out of the dressing room.

Meghann was completely silent.

Claire looked at her sister. 'You're uncharacteristically quiet.'

'Look.'

Claire lifted the heavy skirt off the ground and stepped up onto the platform. Slowly she faced the trifold mirror.

The woman who stared back at her wasn't Claire Cavenaugh. No. This woman hadn't partied her way out of a state college, she hadn't borne a child out of wedlock, and she certainly didn't manage a campground. This woman arrived in limousines and drank champagne.

Claire imagined the look on Bobby's face when she walked down the aisle. Bobby, who'd knelt on one knee when he asked her to please, please be his wife. If he saw her in this dress . . .

Meghann came up behind her, stood on the platform. There they were, side by side. Mama's girls. Meghann touched Claire's bare shoulder. 'Don't even try to find something wrong with this dress.'

'I didn't look at the price tag, but—'

Meghann ripped the tag in half. 'And you won't.'

Claire looked at her sister. 'You knew. You handpicked it.'

Meg tried not to smile. 'It's Vera Wang. Of course I knew. It means a lot to me that you've included me in your wedding.'

'We're family,' Claire answered after a long pause. It felt awkward, this conversation, and vaguely dangerous. As if they were skating on a frozen pond that couldn't possibly hold their weight. 'Thank you for the dress. It's what'—her voice cracked—'I always dreamed of.'

Meg finally smiled. 'Just because I don't believe in marriage doesn't mean I can't plan a kick-ass wedding, you know.'

Risa had returned and now stepped up to the platform. 'The Wang,' she said softly, looking at Meg. 'You said this would be her choice.'

'A good guess.'

'She is the picture of love, yes?' Risa went to Claire. 'We'll need to take in the bust a little—just to there, don't you think?' She began pinning and pulling. 'It'll be ready in time,' Risa promised when she was finished, then hurried off.

'Now, how about we pick up some takeout from the Wild Ginger and eat at my place?' Meghann said.

'Alison—'

'Is having dinner at Zeke's Drive-In and joining Sam and Bobby for date night at the Big Bowl.'

Claire smiled. 'Bobby is going to date night at the bowling alley? And you don't believe in true love?'

In front of the Wild Ginger, Meghann double-parked, ran into the restaurant, and came out three minutes later with a paper sack. She tossed it in Claire's lap, got into the driver's seat, and drove home.

At her apartment, the view was breathtaking. An amethyst almost-night sky filled every picture window. The Space Needle, decked out in summertime colours, filled one window. Everywhere else it was the midnight-blue Sound, its dark surface broken only by the streamers of city lights along the shore.

'Wow,' Claire said.

'Yeah. It's some view,' Meghann said, plopping the paper sack on the kitchen's black granite counter.

Everywhere Claire looked, she saw perfection. She walked over to a small Biedermeier desk in the corner. On its shiny surface stood a single framed photograph. It was of Claire and Meghann, taken when they were kids—maybe seven and fourteen—sitting at the end of a dock with their arms looped round each other.

Surprisingly, Claire found that it hurt to see them this way. She glanced over at Meg, who was busily dividing up the food. She put the photograph back and made her way to the kitchen.

'Your home is gorgeous.'

'Home.' Meg laughed as she handed Claire a margarita. 'That's funny. I never think of it that way, but it is, of course. Thanks.'

That was it. This wasn't a home. It was a really nice hotel suite—definitely four-star but cold, impersonal.

Meghann set out the plates. 'Here. Let's eat out on the deck.' They carried their plates and drinks outside. 'We'll have to sit on the floor. I had a decorator come in who chose the most uncomfortable outdoor furniture. I returned it all and haven't found the time to buy new stuff.'

'How long have you lived here?'

'Seven years.'

It was a beautiful night. Stars everywhere. As they ate, silence fell between them. Meg said a few awkward things, clearly designed to break the quiet, but like sea water in a rising tide, the silence always returned.

'Did I thank you for the gown?'

'Yes. And you're welcome.' Meg put her empty plate down on the deck and leaned back.

'It's funny,' Claire said. 'It's loud out here at night—between the traffic and the ferry horns and the railroad—but it feels empty. Kind of lonely.'

'The city can be that way.'

Claire looked at Meghann and, for once, she didn't see the harsh, judgmental older sister who was always right. Neither did she see the older sister who'd once loved her so completely. Now, she saw a pale, rarely smiling woman who seemed to have no life apart from work. A lonely woman who'd had her heart broken long ago and now wouldn't allow herself to believe in love.

She couldn't help remembering the old days, when they'd been best friends. For the first time in years, she wondered if that could happen again. If so, one of them would have to make the first move.

Claire took a chance. 'Maybe you'd like to come and stay at my house for a few nights while you're planning the wedding.'

'Really?' Meghann looked up, obviously surprised.

'You're probably too busy.'

'No, actually. I'm between cases right now. And I do need to spend some time in Hayden. I have a meeting there tomorrow, in fact. With the wedding consultant. But I wouldn't want to intrude.'

Big mistake, Claire thought. *Incredible Hulk big.* 'It's settled, then. You'll spend a few nights at my house.'

Chapter Six

MEGHANN PARKED THE CAR and checked her instructions again, then looked up the street. She walked two blocks, then turned right on Azalea Street. Her destination was easy to spot: a narrow Victorian house painted canary yellow with purple trim. A sign hung askew on the white picket fence out front: *Royal Event Planning*. There were glittery roses all around the pink letters.

Meghann almost kept walking. There was no way that someone who painted with glittery paint could plan a classy wedding. But it was Claire's day, and she wanted a small, casual wedding.

Meghann unlatched the picket gate and stepped into a surreal Candy Land yard. A green AstroTurf walkway led her to the porch steps. At the salmon-pink door, she knocked.

The door opened. A tall man with curly bottle-blond hair and a California-dark tan stood there. 'You must be Meghann Dontess. I'm Roy Royal.'

She tried not to smile.

'Go ahead, have a good laugh. I'm just lucky my middle name isn't Al.' He swung one hip out, planted a hand on it. 'Those are some pretty sharp clothes, Ms Dontess. We don't see much Marc Jacobs in Hayden. I can't imagine what brings you here.'

'I'm Claire Cavenaugh's sister. I'm here to plan her wedding.'

He screeched. 'Claire! All right, girl! Well, let's get going. Only the best for Claire.' He ushered her into the sitting room, towards a pink velvet settee. 'Wedding at the Episcopal church, of course. Reception at the Moose Lodge, catering by the Chuck Wagon.'

'That's a wedding in Hayden, huh?'

'Top drawer.'

'And what does a wedding cost around here?'

'A good, solid event? Say . . . two thousand dollars.'

Meg leaned forwards. 'Do you read *In Style* magazine, Roy?'

He laughed. 'Are you kidding? Cover to cover.'

'So you know what a celebrity wedding is like. Especially the kind they call "simple and elegant".'

'Simple in Hollywood just means really, really expensive but no bridesmaids and an outdoor reception.'

'I want the kind of wedding this town has never seen, Roy. But—and this is important—no one but you and I can know that. You have to master the phrase "It was on sale". Deal?'

'No kidding.' He grinned and clapped. 'What's your budget?'

'Money isn't something we should worry about.'

He shook his head, still smiling. 'Honey, that's a sentence I've *never* heard before. OK, let's get to work.'

Joe was elbow-deep in the undercarriage of an old Kubota tractor, changing the oil, when he heard a car drive up. He listened for Smitty's booming voice, but there was nothing.

'Anyone here?' someone called out. 'Smitty?'

Joe rolled out from under the tractor and got to his feet. A florid, heavyset man walked into the garage. Joe recognised him. It was Reb Tribbs, an old-time logger who'd lost an arm on the job.

Joe pulled his cap down low. 'What can I do for you?'

'My truck's dyin'. I just brought the damn thing to Smitty. He said he fixed it. I ain't payin' for it till it runs.'

'You'll have to take that up with Smitty. But if you want to drive into the garage, I'll—'

'Do I know you?' Reb frowned and stepped closer. 'Joe Wyatt.' Reb made a whistling sound. 'It's you, ain't it? You got some nerve comin' back here, boy. Folks around here remember what you done. Hell, I thought you were in prison.'

'No.' Joe stood there, listening. He deserved every word.

'You'd best get a move on. Her daddy don't need to hear that you're back in town.'

'I haven't seen her dad.'

'Course not. You don't have the guts.'

'That's enough, Reb.' It was Smitty's voice. He stood at the open garage door, holding a half-eaten sandwich in one hand and a can of Coke in the other.

'I can't believe you'd hire this piece of garbage,' Reb said. 'I won't bring my truck here if he's gonna work on it.'

'I can lose your business and still survive,' Smitty said.

Reb made a sputtering sound, then turned on his heel and marched out. As he got into his truck, he yelled out, 'You'll be sorry, Zeb Smith. Trash like him don't belong in this town.'

After he drove away, Smitty placed a hand gently on Joe's shoulder.

'He's the trash, Joe. Always has been. Mean as a badger.'

'You'll lose customers when word gets out that I'm here.'

'Don't matter. My house is paid for. My land's paid for. I own a rental house in town that brings in five hundred a month.'

'Still, your reputation is important.'

Smitty squeezed his shoulder. 'Last Helga and I heard about our Philly, he was living in Seattle. Under the viaduct. Heroin. Every day I hope someone offers him a helping hand.'

Joe nodded. He didn't know what to say.

Then Smitty said, 'I gotta make a Costco run. You think you can handle the garage for the next two hours?'

'Not if Reb is any indication.'

'He isn't.' Smitty tossed him the keys. 'Close up any time you want.' Then he left.

Joe worked for the rest of the day, but he couldn't forget the incident with Reb. The old man's words seemed to hang in the garage, poisoning the air. *Trash like him don't belong in this town.*

By the time he closed up shop, he felt empty again. He locked things up for the night and was just about to turn towards his cabin when he happened to glance down the street. The neon REDHOOK sign in Mo's tavern window caught his attention. Suddenly he wanted to sneak into that smoky darkness and drink until the ache in his chest went away.

He pulled his baseball cap low on his forehead and crossed the street. Praying that no one he knew was inside, he pushed through the scarred wooden door.

Meghann hadn't been to a bridal shower in more than a decade. She had no idea how to blend into this small-town crowd, and the last thing she wanted to do was stand out.

Today, after her four-hour meeting with Roy, Meghann had spent another hour in Too Many Cooks, where she bought Claire—and Bobby, although she didn't think of them as a couple, really—a Cuisinart food processor.

She'd been tired by the time she made it back to Claire's house. Pleading a headache, she'd excused herself quickly from the dinner table and ran upstairs. But now, nearly an hour later, she felt better. A quick glance at the bedside clock told her it was six forty.

She opened her closet, deciding on a plain black dress. Armani was never wrong. She added sheer black hose and a pair of heels, then went downstairs. The house was quiet.

'Claire?'

No answer. Then she saw the note on the kitchen table: *Dear Meg, Sorry you're feeling sick. Stay home and rest, xxoo, C.*

Claire and Bobby had left without her. She glanced at her watch. It was seven o'clock. Of course they'd left. They were the guests of honour.

She dug in her bag for the pale lavender invitation. It read *Couples Shower for Claire and Bobby, 7.00 p.m.* Directions were on the back.

It took her less than ten minutes to find Gina's house. Holding her gift under one arm, she climbed the porch steps and knocked on the door. *You can do this. You can fit in with her friends.*

There was a rush of footsteps, then the door opened.

Gina stood there, her face creased in laughter. Until she saw Meghann. 'Oh'—she stepped back to allow entry—'I'm glad you're feeling better.'

Meghann stared at Gina, who was dressed in jeans and an oversized black T-shirt. *Great.* 'I'm overdressed.'

'Are you kidding? If I hadn't gained fifteen pounds since Rex left, I'd be dressed up, too. Come on. You're my date for the evening.' Gina smiled. 'I thought I'd been stood up.'

She took Meghann by the arm and led her down a wide hallway into a living-room/dining-room combination that overlooked a beautifully landscaped garden. 'Claire, look who made it,' she said over the buzz of conversation.

Claire hurried towards her, smiling. She looked gorgeous in a pair of ice-blue cotton trousers and a white boat-neck cotton sweater. Her long blonde hair had been pulled back from her face. 'I'm so glad you could make it. When I get a headache, I can't move for hours.'

Meghann felt like Jackie O at a barn dance. 'I shouldn't have come. I'll go.'

'Please don't,' her sister said. 'I'm glad you're here. Really.'

They stood there in an uncomfortable silence until Gina said, 'I'll bet you could use a drink.'

Meghann nodded. 'By all means.'

'Come to the kitchen with me,' Gina said. 'We'll get you a jumbo margarita.'

'Hurry back,' Claire said. 'We're going to start the games.'

Meghann actually stumbled.

Games.

Meghann really did have a headache now.

She sat on the edge of the sofa, her knees tucked primly together. The rest of the guests sat sprawled against one another—in pairs, like on

Noah's ark—in a circle on the hardwood floor. They were all talking at once, resurrecting memories from a lifetime Meghann didn't know.

'Remember when Claire fell off the diving board at Island Lake Camp?'

'Or when she hid Mrs Testern's favourite ruler?'

'Or when she called Poison Control because she caught Ali eating the diaper-pail deodorant?'

The junior and senior high school years, the girls-just-want-to-have-fun years, the Alison years. They were all a mystery to Meghann.

'OK, everyone, it's time for the first game,' Gina yelled.

She rushed into the kitchen and came out with a big white bowl. 'This game is called Truth in M&M's. Everybody take as many as you want.' She went round the group, handing out candy.

Meghann could tell that she wasn't the only suspicious person. No one took a handful. Meg chose two.

'For each M&M, you have to tell one thing about the bride or groom and make a prediction for the future.'

A groan moved through the men.

'I'll start,' Charlotte said. 'I have three. Claire has a beautiful smile, and I predict Bobby will keep it on her face. She is a great cook, so I predict he'll be fat by forty. Finally, she hates to do laundry, so I predict Bobby will learn to like the stained, rumpled look.'

Claire laughed the loudest of all of them.

They continued round the circle, and with each comment Meghann felt herself edging towards uneasiness. Even the husbands here seemed to know more about Claire's everyday life than Meghann did, and she was terrified that when her turn came to make a prediction, she'd blurt out, 'I predict he breaks her heart.'

'Meg? Meg?' It was Gina. 'Your turn.'

Meghann looked down into her palm. Sweat had turned the candies into red smudges. 'I have two.' She tried to smile. 'Claire is the best mother I know, so I predict she'll have another child.'

Claire smiled at her, then leaned lovingly against Bobby.

'Another one, Meg.'

She nodded. 'Claire loves well, but not necessarily easily, so I predict'—she barely paused—'that this is the real thing.' When she looked up, Claire was frowning.

Meghann didn't know what she'd said wrong. It had seemed cheery and optimistic to her, but Claire looked ready to cry.

'I'm last,' Gina said in the sudden silence. 'I have only one. Claire is completely tone-deaf. So I predict that Bobby will never let her be his back-up singer.'

That got them all laughing and talking again.

Absurdly, Meghann felt the start of tears. She got to her feet. When no one was looking, she ducked out of the house and ran for her car. She meant to go home, wait up for Claire, and apologise for whatever wrongs she'd uttered.

Then she saw the tavern.

She eased her foot off the accelerator. She knew if she went inside and had a drink—or two or three—she would feel better.

She parked her car and walked in. It was like a hundred other taverns. The bar ran the length of the room on the right side, and the mirror behind it was at least six feet long, veined in strands of gold and aged to a tarnished silver. She saw the people clustered along the bar, seated on wooden stools. Those were the hard-core drinkers.

Scattered throughout the left side of the room were round tables; most of them were full. She walked to the closest empty space at the bar, where a tired-looking man was busily wiping up a spill. On her arrival he said, 'Whaddaya want?'

She smiled. 'A glass of white wine. Vouvray, if you have it.'

'We have Inglenook and Gallo.'

'Inglenook.'

He headed down the other way and returned with a glass of wine.

She slapped her platinum credit card on the bar. 'Open a tab.'

The jukebox clicked, then buzzed. An old Aerosmith song came on. She headed towards the nearest table, where a man was writing on a yellow legal pad, obviously taking notes from a textbook.

She walked over to him. 'May I join you?'

When he looked up, she saw that he was young. Maybe twenty-one or twenty-two. 'I'm sorry, ma'am. What did you say?'

Ma'am.

'Call me Meg.'

'You look familiar. Are you a friend of my mother's?'

She felt like the old lady from *Titanic*. 'No. And I . . . I thought I knew you, but I was mistaken. Sorry.'

She headed towards another table. As she came within range, a woman slipped into the empty chair and kissed the man.

Meghann spun to her left and ran into a shaggy, tramp-like guy who was on his way back from the bar. 'I'm sorry,' she said. 'I should have signalled before I made a turn like that.'

'No harm done.'

He went back to his table and sat down. She saw that he was slightly unsteady on his feet.

She stood there, alone in the midst of the crowded bar. This wasn't going to be her night. She'd have to return to Claire's guest room, climb into bed alone, and spend the night tossing and turning.

She looked at the tramp. His shoulders were broad; his black T-shirt stretched taut along his back. It was him . . . or loneliness.

She went to his table, stood beside him. 'May I sit down?' She pulled out a chair and sat down across from him.

He looked up. Beneath the silvery fringe of hair, a pair of blue eyes stared at her. With a start she realised that he wasn't much older than she was, and he was almost handsome.

'Whatever you're looking for,' he said, 'you won't find it here.'

She started to flirt, to say something funny and impersonal, but before her tongue had even formed the first word, she paused. There was something about him . . .

'Have we met?' she asked, frowning. She prided herself on her memory. Faces, she rarely forgot.

'People say that all the time. Just an ordinary face, I guess.'

No, that wasn't it. She was sure she'd seen him before, but it didn't matter, really. 'Are you from around here?'

'I am now.'

'What do you do for a living?'

'Do I *look* like I make a living? I get by, that's all.'

'That's all any of us do, really.'

'Look, lady—'

'Meghann. Friends call me Meg.'

'Meghann. I'm not going to take you home. Is that clear enough for you?'

That made her smile. 'I don't remember asking to be taken home. You're making quite an assumption.'

'Sorry. I've been alone for a while. Makes a man poor company.'

Poor company. It had the ring of education to it.

She leaned closer, studying him. She liked his face. 'What if I *did* want to go home with you?'

It was an eternity before he answered. 'I'd say it wouldn't mean anything.' His voice sounded tight. He looked scared.

She felt it suddenly—the thrill of the chase. She pressed her forefinger along the back of his hand. 'What if I said that was OK?'

'I'd say that was sad.'

She pulled her hand back, stung by the observation. She felt transparent suddenly, as if those blue eyes could see straight into her. 'Maybe we could just get each other through this one night.'

He stood up so quickly, the chair wobbled and almost fell. 'I live down the street.'

'I'll follow you,' was all she said.

Joe felt her beside him, the warmth of her body, the way her hand brushed accidentally against his every now and then.

Stop this now, he thought. Just turn to her and say, 'I made a mistake, I'm sorry.' But he kept walking. Suddenly he was standing in front of his cabin. Three blocks they'd walked, and they hadn't managed a single word of conversation. He didn't know if he was thankful or not.

'This is where I live right now,' he said—rather stupidly, he thought— as they were standing at the front door.

'Right now, huh?'

He opened the door and stepped aside to let her enter first.

'What's your name?'

'Joe,' he answered, as she walked past him into the darkness.

He followed her, leaving the lights off on purpose. There were photos of Diana everywhere. He didn't want to explain why he lived this way, not to this woman in her designer dress and expensive gold and platinum jewellery. In fact, he didn't want to talk at all.

He went to the kitchen and grabbed some candles. There were dozens, kept on hand for winter storms when the power went out. Wordlessly, he carried them into the bedroom and placed them wherever he could; then, one by one, he lit them. When he was finished, he turned and there she was, standing at the end of the bed.

He released a pent-up breath. She was beautiful. Jet-black hair, pale skin, green eyes. What in the hell was she doing here with him? And what was he doing with her? He hadn't been with a woman since Diana.

She walked towards him, hips swaying slightly.

He meant to say, Go away, but instead he reached for her, pulled her against him. He was trembling.

'Are you OK?' she asked.

He didn't think, didn't speak, just swept her into his arms and carried her towards the bed.

That night, for the first time in years, Joe Wyatt made love to a woman and fell asleep holding her in his arms.

When he woke up, he was alone again.

Claire flopped back onto the pillows. 'You must really love me if you'll kiss me before I brush my teeth.'

Bobby rolled onto his side. His handsome face was crisscrossed with sleep lines. 'You still wonder, don't you?'

'No. Just prove Meg wrong. Nothing will make her crazier.'

'She's trying, you know.'

Claire sat up. 'I can't believe you're defending her. She told me I was stupid to marry you.'

He gave her that slow-growing smile that always made her go weak in the knees. 'Darlin', you can't hold that against her. She's just trying to protect you.'

'Control me is more like it.'

'Come here,' he whispered.

She leaned towards him, and they kissed.

'I'm getting to know you, Claire Cavenaugh-soon-to-be-Austin,' he whispered against her lips. 'You had a headache after the wedding-dress screwup and again last night after she left the party early. When Meghann hurts your feelings, you say you don't care and start chewing aspirin. I've been there, darlin'. I know what matters is that she's your sister. The only one you've got.'

Claire wanted to disagree but knew it was pointless. She *did* want to be close to Meg again. More and more often in the past few days, she'd found herself remembering the old Meg. The way they used to love each other. 'I'm tired of the way we are together,' she admitted.

'Well?'

'No one can push my buttons like Meghann. She has a true gift for saying exactly the wrong thing.'

'Yeah. My dad was like that. We never could quite make it work between us. Now he's gone, and I wish we'd tried harder.'

'OK, Sigmund Freud. I'll try talking to her. Again.'

'No more aspirin.'

She gave him another long, lingering kiss, then walked to the bathroom. By the time she'd finished showering and dressed, he had gone.

Claire went down to start the coffee. When it was ready, she poured herself a cup and went out to the back porch.

The slatted swing welcomed her. She sat there, rocking gently, staring out at the silver curve of water that defined her back property line. The sky was as blue as forget-me-nots and the grass was turning golden from an unexpected week of sunlight.

The screen door screeched open and banged shut. Meghann stepped out onto the porch. She wore a fringed black peasant top and flare-legged jeans. Her hair, unbound, fell down her back in a riot of curls. She looked beautiful. 'Morning.'

Claire tried to hide her legs with the old sweats she'd put on. 'You want some pancakes?'

Meg sat down on the chair opposite the swing. 'No, thanks. I'm still trying to metabolise last night's cake.'

'You sure left the party early.' Claire hoped she sounded casual and not hurt.

'It was a nice party. Gina has a great sense of humour.'

'Yeah, she does.'

'It must be hard on her, watching you plan your wedding so soon after her own divorce.'

Claire nodded. 'She's going through a difficult time.'

'It's always hard to find out you married the wrong man.'

'They were married for fifteen years. Just because they got divorced doesn't mean he was the wrong man to marry.'

Meg looked at her. 'I would say it meant exactly that.'

Claire took a sip of coffee. It occurred to her to drop the whole thing, but then she remembered her conversation with Bobby. Slowly she said, 'You didn't answer my question. How come you left the shower early?'

'It wasn't that early. How were your presents?'

'They were great. Thank you for the Cuisinart, by the way. Now, why did you leave early?'

Meg closed her eyes, then slowly opened them. She looked scared. 'It was the M&M game. I tried to be a good sport and play the game, but I barely know you, so I said something wrong. I still don't know what the hell it was.'

'You said I loved well, but not easily. I don't think it's true, that's all, and it hurt my feelings.'

'It's true for me,' Meg said.

Claire leaned forwards. They were actually circling something that mattered. 'Sometimes it's hard to love you, Meg.'

'Believe me, I know.' She laughed—a bitter, throaty sound.

'You judge people—me—so harshly. Your opinions are like bull-whips. Every one leaves a bloody mark.'

'People, yes. But you? I don't judge you.'

'I flunked out of college. I never left Hayden. I had a child out of wed-lock with a man who, I discovered, was already married. Now I'm mar-rying a three-time loser, and I'm too stupid to protect myself with a prenuptial agreement. Stop me when it sounds familiar.'

Meg frowned. 'Have I hung all that on you?'

'I can't talk to you without feeling like a loser. And, of course, you're rich and perfect.'

'That part is true.' Meg saw that her attempt at humour failed. 'My therapist thinks I have control issues.'

'Well, *duh*. You're a lot like Mama, you know. You both need to run the show.'

'The difference is, she's psychotic. I'm neurotic. But God knows, she handed down bad luck with men.' Meghann looked at her. 'Have you broken the curse?'

Even yesterday, Claire would have been angered by the question. Now, she understood it. Claire's legacy from Mama was a belief that sooner or later love walked out on you. Meg had inherited something else entirely: she didn't believe in love at all. 'I have, Meg. Honestly.'

Meg smiled, but there was sadness in her eyes. 'I wish I had your faith.'

For once, Claire felt like the stronger sister. 'I know love is real. It's in every moment I share with Ali and Dad. Maybe if . . . you'd had a father, you'd be able to believe in it.' Claire saw the way her sister had gone pale; she knew she'd gone too far.

'You were lucky to have Sam,' Meg said slowly.

Claire couldn't help thinking about the summer Dad had tried to be there for Meg. It had been a nightmare. Meg and Sam had had screaming fights about who loved Claire more, who knew what was best for her. It had been Claire herself who'd ended the worst of the battles. She'd cried out to Meg, 'Quit yelling at my daddy'. That was the first time she'd seen her sister cry. The next day Meg had gone.

'He wanted to be there for you, too,' Claire said gently.

'He wasn't my father.'

They fell silent after that. Then Claire leaned towards her sister. 'I'd like you to baby-sit Alison next week. While Bobby and I are on our honeymoon.'

'I thought you weren't taking a honeymoon.'

'Dad insisted. His wedding gift was a week's trip to Kauai.'

'And you want *me* to baby-sit?'

'It would mean a lot to me. Ali needs to know you better.'

Meghann looked nervous. 'You'd trust me?'

'Of course.'

Meg sat back. A tremulous smile curved her lips. 'OK.'

Claire grinned. 'No teaching her to bungee jump.'

'So skydiving lessons are out.'

They were still laughing when the phone started ringing. Claire jumped up and ran inside the house to answer it. 'Hello?'

'Hold for Eliana Sullivan, please.'

Claire heard Meg come up behind her. She mouthed, 'Mama.'

'This should be good,' Meg said.

'Hello?' Mama said. 'Hello?'

'Hey, Mama. It's me, Claire.'

Mama laughed, that throaty, sexy sound she'd cultivated over the years. 'I believe I know which of my own daughters I called.'

'Of course,' Claire answered, although Mama confused the two of them all the time.

'Well, honey, m'houseboy said you left me a message. What's goin' on?'

Claire hated the faux Southern accent. 'I called to tell you I'm getting married.'

'Well, I'll be damned. Who is he?'

'You'll love him, Mama. He's a nice Texas boy.'

'How much money does he make?'

'That isn't important to me.'

'Broke, huh? Well, I'll give you my best advice, honey. It's easier to marry the rich ones, but what the hell. Congratulations. When's the wedding?'

'Saturday, the 23rd.'

'Of June? You mean this comin' Saturday?'

'You would have had plenty of notice if you'd called me back.'

'I was doing Shakespeare in the park. With Charlie Sheen, I might add. Did you see my picture in *People*?'

'I missed that. Sorry.'

'Well, Saturday's difficult for me, honey. How about the first weekend in August?'

Claire rolled her eyes. 'Mama, the invitations have already gone out. It's too late to change the date.'

'What time on Saturday?'

'The wedding is at seven p.m. Reception to follow.'

Mama sighed. 'Saturday. I've been waitin' three months for my hair appointment with José. Maybe he can take me early.'

Claire couldn't take any more. 'I've got to run, Mama. I'll be at the Hayden Episcopal church at seven this Saturday. I hope you can make it, but I'll certainly understand if you're too busy.'

'Tell me straight up, honey. D'you think this one'll last? I'd hate to give up my hair appointment for—'

'I've got to go, Mama. Bye.'

'OK, honey. Me, too. And congratulations.'

'Thanks, Mama. Bye.'

Claire looked up at Meghann. 'Saturday's a bad day for her. A hair appointment with José.'

'We should have sent her the invite after it was over.'

'I don't know why I keep expecting something different from her.'
Meg shook her head. 'Even a mother alligator sticks around the eggs.'
'Mama would make herself an omelette.'
They both laughed at that.

Chapter Seven

'I'VE GOT THE PERMIT for the park, and the tent is reserved from the party rental store. I'll go over the final details of set-up with them tomorrow on my way to Costco.' Roy sat back with a flourish. 'That's it.'

'And the lights?' Meghann asked, checking off the tent from her list.

'Ten thousand white Christmas lights, forty-two Chinese lanterns and twenty hanging lights. Check.'

Meghann marked her list accordingly. That was it. Everything on her list had been taken care of. In the past two days she'd checked and rechecked each detail. It was going to be, Roy declared at least three times a day, the best wedding ever to take place in Hayden.

Meghann didn't think that was much of a standard, but she was learning to keep her cynical thoughts to herself. She'd even been working so hard that she slept at night. The only problem now was her dreams.

They all seemed to be about Joe. When she closed her eyes, she remembered everything about that night. The blue eyes that were so sad . . . the way he'd whispered something—a name, maybe—while they were making love.

Making love.

She'd never thought of it that way, not with anyone.

'Meghann? You're getting that mushy look again. Are you thinking about the hors d'oeuvres?'

She smiled at Roy. 'You should have seen the chef's face when I told her she'd have to do up a tray of pigs in blankets.'

'I hate to admit it, but . . . they are tasty, you know. Little hot dogs wrapped in pastry and dipped in ketchup. Even better dragged in baked beans. They'll probably disappear long before the Brie and pâté.'

'I didn't let Carla do pâté.' Meghann consulted her list again. It was a habit, checking and rechecking everything.

Roy touched her arm. 'Sweetheart, you're done. All you have to do is show up at the rehearsal tonight and then get a good night's sleep.'

'Thanks, Roy. I don't know what I would have done without you.'

'Believe me, it has been an unexpected pleasure to work on this wedding. My next event is a shindig in the Clausens' cow field to celebrate little Todd's acceptance to community college.'

After the meeting, she headed back towards her car. She'd walked several blocks before she realised she was going in the wrong direction. She was just about to turn round when she saw the garage. There, tucked back in a thicket of trees, was Joe's cabin.

She had a sudden urge to walk up to the door, say, 'Hey, Joe,' and follow him to the bedroom. The sex had been great. Hell, it had been better than great. So good that she'd sneaked off in the middle of the night. She'd always been better at goodbye than good morning.

The light in his kitchen went on. She saw a shadow cross the window, a flash of silvery hair.

She almost went to him.

Almost.

The one thing she knew for certain—had learned from hard-won experience—was that anonymous sex was all she could handle.

She turned and walked back to her car.

Friday afternoon turned grey and cold. Rain fell in tiny staccato bursts that were all but invisible to the naked eye.

Claire spent the day pretending to work. Thirty-five was too old to marry for the first time. How could she possibly be doing the right thing? But every time her worries threatened to overwhelm her, she'd turn a corner or open a door and see Bobby. 'Hey, darlin',' he'd say. 'I love you.' Just those few and precious words, and Claire breathed easier again for an hour or so.

At around three in the afternoon her father walked her back to her house. He reached into his pocket, pulled out a small black box, and opened it. Inside was a marquise-cut yellow diamond set on a wide platinum band.

'It's your grandma Myrtle's. She wanted you to have it.' Sam took her hand. 'I couldn't let my baby get married with a tinfoil ring.'

She tried it on. The ring fitted as if it had been made for her. She pulled him into her arms. 'Thanks, Dad.'

After tomorrow she would be a married woman. Another man would be the centre of her life. She would be Bobby's wife from now on, not Sam Cavenaugh's little girl.

When Dad drew back, there were tears in his eyes, and she knew he'd been thinking the same thing.

'Always,' she whispered.

He nodded in understanding. 'Always.'

Meghann wished to God she'd never agreed to let Gina host and plan the rehearsal dinner. Every moment was pure hell.

'Are you here by yourself?'

'Where's your husband?'

'You don't have children? Well, that's lucky. Sometimes I wish I could give mine away.'

Meghann knew that Claire's friends were trying to include her, especially the Bluesers, but the more they tried to make her a part of the group, the more alienated she felt. She could talk about a lot of things— world politics, the situation in the Middle East, Wall Street. What she couldn't talk about were family things. Kid things.

Meghann stood at the fireplace in Gina's house. Across the room Claire stood at the kitchen counter eating potato crisps and laughing with Gina. As Meghann watched, Bobby came up behind Claire and whispered something in her ear. She turned into his arms. They came together like puzzle pieces, fitting perfectly.

'OK, everyone,' Gina said, coming into the room. 'Now it's time for the second part of the evening.'

A hush fell.

Gina smiled. 'Hector is opening the bowling alley just for us! We leave in fifteen minutes.'

Bowling. Rented shoes. Polyester shirts.

Meg walked across the living room and came up beside Claire, gently putting her hand on her sister's shoulder.

Claire turned. She looked so happy right then, it took Meghann's breath away. When she saw Meghann, she laughed. 'Let me guess. You're not a bowler.'

'Oh, I love bowling. Really. I have my own ball.'

'You do, huh?'

'Unfortunately, I have a few last-minute details I need to go over for tomorrow. I have to get up early.'

Claire nodded. 'I understand, Meg. I really do.'

'Well, bye. I'll tell Gina why I'm leaving.'

Fifteen minutes later Meghann was in her car, speeding down the country road. Her sister's well-meaning friends had managed to underscore the emptiness of Meg's life.

She saw the sign for Mo's Fireside Tavern and slammed on the brakes. It was a bad idea to go in, she knew. There was nothing but trouble in there. And yet . . . She parked in the street and went inside.

Men sat on every barstool, at every table. There were a few women scattered throughout the crowd. She made her way through the place, boldly checking out every man.

She had toured the whole place and made her way back to the front door when she realised why she was really here. 'Joe,' she said softly, surprised. She honestly hadn't known that she wanted him.

She left the bar. Out in the street, she took a deep breath of sweet mountain air and stood by her car, looking down the street at his small cabin. Light glowed from the windows.

'No,' she said. She shouldn't do it, but she was walking anyway, crossing the street and entering his yard, which smelt of honeysuckle and jasmine. At the door she paused, wondering what the hell she was doing.

Then she knocked. No one answered.

She twisted the knob and went inside. The cabin was dark. A fire crackled in the hearth. 'Joe?' Cautiously she stepped forwards.

No answer.

A shiver crept along her spine. She sensed that he was here, burrowed into the darkness like a wounded animal, watching her.

She started to turn for the door, when she saw the photographs—on the coffee table, the windowsills, the mantelpiece. Everywhere. Frowning, she walked from place to place looking at the pictures. They were all of the same woman, a lovely blonde with a Grace Kelly kind of elegance. Meghann picked one up.

'Do you always break into other people's homes and paw through their things?'

Meghann jumped back. Her fingers went numb for a second, and the picture crashed to the floor. She turned round, looking for him. 'Joe? It's me, Meghann.'

'I know it's you.'

He was slumped in the corner of the room, with one leg bent and the other stretched out. Firelight illuminated his silvery hair. Sadness clung to him, made her wonder if he'd been crying.

'I shouldn't have come in. Or come here, for that matter,' she said uncomfortably. 'I'm sorry.' She headed for the door.

'Have a drink with me.'

She released a breath, realising then how much she'd wanted him to ask her to stay. Slowly she faced him.

'What can I get you?'

'Martini?'

'I've got Scotch. And Scotch.'

She sidled past the coffee table and sat down on the worn leather sofa. 'I'll have a Scotch.'

He got up, shuffled across the room. She saw now why he'd been so invisible; he had on black jeans and a black T-shirt.

She heard a splash of liquid, then a rattling of ice. As he poured her drink, she looked round the room. All those photographs of the Grace Kelly lookalike made her uncomfortable.

'Here.'

She looked up.

He stood in front of her. 'Thank you,' she said.

He took a drink straight from the bottle, then wiped his mouth with the back of his hand. 'Sure.' He didn't move away, just stood there, staring down at her. He was unsteady on his feet.

'You're drunk,' she said, finally getting it.

'It's June 22nd.' He sat down beside her.

'Do you have something against the 22nd?'

His gaze darted to the photographs clustered on an end table.

'Who is she, Joe?' Her voice was soft, but in the quiet room it seemed too loud, too intimate.

'My wife, Diana.'

'You're married?'

'Not any more. She . . . left me.'

'On June 22nd.'

'How'jou know?'

'I know about divorces. The anniversaries can be hell.' Meghann stared into his sad, sad eyes and tried not to feel anything. It was better that way, safer. But sitting here beside him, close enough to be taken into his arms, she felt . . . needy. Suddenly she wanted something from Joe, something more than sex.

'Maybe I should go. You seem to want to be alone.'

'I've been alone.'

She heard the ache of loneliness in his voice and it drew her in. 'Me too.'

He touched her face. 'I can't offer you anything, Meghann.'

The way he said her name, all sad and drawn out and slow, sent a shiver along her spine. She wanted to tell him that she didn't want anything from him, but she couldn't form the words. 'It's OK.'

'You should want more.'

'So should you.'

She felt fragile suddenly. 'We're talking too much. Kiss me.'

In the fireplace a log fell to the hearth floor with a thud. Sparks flooded into the room.

With a groan he pulled her into his arms.

Chapter Eight

THE NEXT DAY the weather in Hayden was perfect. A bright sun rode high in the cornflower-blue sky. A thin, cooling breeze rustled through the trees, making music on the deep green maple leaves. By five o'clock Claire was showered and ready to begin dressing.

Behind her there was a knock at the door. 'Come in,' she said.

Meghann stood in the doorway, holding a pile of plastic-sheathed dresses. She looked nervous, uncharacteristically uncertain. 'I thought maybe we'd get dressed together.' When Claire didn't answer instantly, Meghann said, 'You probably think it's a stupid idea.'

'Stop. I think it would be great.'

Meghann's hair had been fashioned into a beautiful French twist.

'Your hair looks great,' Claire said.

'I could do yours if you'd like.'

'Really?'

'Sure. I did it all the time when you were little.'

Claire crossed the room and knelt in front of the bed.

Meghann settled in behind her, began brushing her hair.

Claire closed her eyes. It felt so good to have someone brushing her hair.

It came to her then, a memory.

You'll be the prettiest girl in kindergarten, Claire-Bear. I'll put this pink ribbon all through your braids and it'll protect you.

'You *did* do my hair when I was little.'

The hairbrush paused, then began stroking again. 'Yes.'

'I wish I remembered more of those years.'

'I wish I remembered less. There. All done.'

Claire climbed to her feet, then went into the bathroom and looked in the mirror. Her blonde hair had been loosely drawn back from her face and twisted into an elegant roll. The hairstyle emphasised her cheekbones and made her eyes look huge. She'd never looked this pretty. Never.

'I love it,' she said.

Meghann's smile was dazzling. 'Really?'

Claire took a step towards her. 'What happened to us, Meg?'

Meghann's smile faded. 'You know what happened. Please. Let's not talk about it now. Not today.'

'We've been saying "not today" for years. I don't think it's a strategy that's worked, do you?'

Meghann released a sigh. 'Some things hurt too much to talk about.'

Claire knew about that. It was the principle that had guided their whole relationship. Unfortunately, it had kept them strangers to each other. 'Sometimes silence hurts most of all.' She heard the ache in her voice; there was no way to mask it.

Suddenly the door banged open. 'Mommy!' Ali raced into the room, already wearing her ice-blue silk bridesmaid dress. 'Hurry, Mommy, come look.' She grabbed Claire's hand, dragged her towards the door.

Claire and Meghann followed Ali downstairs. Outside in the driveway, Dad, Bobby and Alison stood round an apple-red convertible.

Claire moved towards them, frowning. That was when she noticed the pink bow on the hood. 'What in the world?'

Dad handed her a note. It read, *Dear Claire and Bobby, Best of luck on your big day. I'm still hoping to make it up there. Hugs and kisses, Mama.*

Meg came up beside Claire, laid a hand on her shoulder. 'Let me guess: Mama's wedding gift.'

Claire sighed. 'Leave it to Mama to give me a car with two seats. Am I supposed to have Ali run along behind?'

Then she laughed. What else could she do?

Claire stood in the dressing room at the small Episcopal church on Front Street. The last hour had been nonstop action. The Bluesers had been in and out every few minutes, oohing and aahing over her dress, and Meghann had been busy checking details, clipboard in hand. But now the room was mercifully quiet. Claire stood in front of the mirror, unable to grasp that the woman in the glass was her. The gown fitted perfectly, flowing to the floor in a cascade of white silk.

There was a knock at the door.

It was Meghann. 'The church is packed. Are you ready?'

Claire swallowed hard. 'I am.'

Meghann took her sister's hand and led her out to the area behind the closed church doors. Dad was already there, waiting with Ali.

'Oh, Ali Kat, you look like a princess,' Claire said, kneeling down to kiss her daughter.

Alison giggled. 'I love my dress, Mommy.'

Behind the doors the music started. It was time.

Meghann bent down to Alison. 'Are you ready, sweetie? You walk slow—like we practised, OK?'

Ali hopped up and down. 'I'm ready.'

A second later the organ played 'Here Comes the Bride', and Meghann opened the doors and Ali slipped through and disappeared.

Claire linked her arm through her dad's, and they slowly followed Ali down the aisle. At the end of it, Bobby, dressed in a black tuxedo, waited, smiling broadly.

Dad stopped and turned to Claire. He lifted the veil and kissed her cheek, then eased away from her, and suddenly Bobby was there beside her, taking her arm, leading her up to the altar.

She looked up at him, loving him so much it scared her.

'Don't be afraid,' he mouthed, squeezing her hands.

Father Tim droned on, but Claire couldn't really hear anything except the beating of her own heart. When it came time for her to say her lines, she panicked that she wouldn't remember them. But she did. When she said, 'I do,' it felt as if her heart were actually expanding inside her chest. In that moment, standing in front of her friends and family and staring into Bobby's eyes, she started to cry.

Father Tim smiled down at each of them, then said, 'I now pronounce you husband and—'

The doors to the church banged open.

A woman stood in the doorway, arms out-flung, a cigarette in one hand. She wore a silver lamé dress that showcased her curves. Behind her, there were at least a dozen people: bodyguards, reporters and photographers. 'I can't *believe* y'all started without me.'

A gasp of recognition moved through the church. Someone whispered, 'It's *her*.'

Bobby frowned. Claire sighed and wiped her eyes. She should have expected this. 'Bobby, you're about to meet Mama.'

'I am going to *kill* her.' Meghann sidled out of the pew and stepped into the aisle.

'There's my other girl.' Mama threw open her arms. Again the flashbulbs erupted in spasms of blinding light.

Meghann grabbed her mother by the arm and yanked her back through the doors. The paparazzi followed, all talking at once.

Through the now-closed doors Meghann could hear Father Tim's second attempt to pronounce Bobby and Claire husband and wife. A moment later applause thundered through the church.

Meghann pulled Mama into the dressing room and shut the door behind them.

'What?' Mama whined, obviously unable to frown but wanting to. Too much Botox, no doubt.

A dog barked. Mama looked down at a small travel carrier in her arms. 'It's OK, honey. Meggy's makin' a mountain out of a molehill.'

'You brought your *dog*?'

Mama pressed a hand to her ample breast. 'You know Elvis hates to be left alone. Now, why in the *hell* did you throw me out of my own daughter's weddin'?'

Meghann felt a surge of anger. 'Today was Claire's day to be a star. Can you get that, Mama? *Her* day. And you walked in right at the moment of glory and stole the show. What were you doing out here, *waiting* for the perfect moment to make your entrance?'

Mama looked away for just a second, but it was enough to confirm Meghann's suspicion. 'Oh, Mama,' she said, shaking her head, 'that's a new low. Even for you. And who are all those people? Do you think you need bodyguards at a wedding in Hayden?'

'My fans are everywhere. They scare me sometimes.'

Meghann laughed at that. 'Save the acting for *People* magazine, Mama. Now, you and I are going to walk over to the reception and tell Claire how happy we are for her. You may bring one photographer, no bodyguards, and no dog. These rules are not negotiable.'

They stood there, inches apart, staring at each other.

Then Mama laughed. The real thing this time, not that sexy kitten laugh she used in Hollywood, but the deep tavern sound she'd been born with.

Meghann smiled in spite of herself. How could you stay angry with a woman as shallow as Mama?

She put her arm round Meghann and pulled her close. 'So are we goin' to this reception or not? I have a midnight flight home. I need to be at SeaTac by eleven.'

'That means you need to leave here about eight thirty. So let's go. Claire probably thinks I killed you.'

Claire was the centre of a laughing, talking, congratulatory crowd. She had never felt so special, so completely loved in her life. Bobby slipped an arm tightly round her waist, pulled her close. 'Have I told you how beautiful you look?'

'You have.'

'When you came down that aisle, you took my breath away. I love you, Mrs Austin.'

They kept their arms round each other and followed the wedding guests walking to Riverfront Park. In front of them the crowd stopped; as if on cue, they parted, forming a dark aisle. Around them the guests clapped and cheered them on. A shower of rice seemed to fall from the sky; it sprinkled their faces and crunched beneath their feet.

'Oh my God,' Claire said. She couldn't believe her eyes. A huge white tent had been set up in the park. Thousands of tiny white Christmas lights twined up the poles and across the makeshift ceilings. Claire could see the tables set up within the tent. Silvery, shimmery tablecloths draped each one.

'Wow,' Bobby said.

The band struck up a beautiful rendition of 'Isn't It Romantic?'

'Would you like to dance, Mrs Austin?'

Claire let him take her in his arms and lead her to the dance floor. There, with all her friends and family watching, she danced with her husband.

When the song came to an end, Claire saw her sister. She was tagging after Mama, who was clearly in her meet-and-greet mode.

'Come on, Bobby,' she said, taking his hand and pulling him off the dance floor. They reached the bar, where Mama was regaling a starstruck crowd with stories of life aboard the USS *Star Seeker*.

Mama saw her coming. 'Claire,' she said, reaching for her with both hands, 'I'm sorry I was late, darlin'. A star's life is run by others. But you were the most beautiful bride I've ever seen.'

Their gazes met. In her mother's dark eyes Claire glimpsed a genuine joy, and it touched her.

'Now,' Mama said quickly, 'where's my new son-in-law?'

'Here I am, Miz Sullivan.'

'Call me Ellie. All my family does.' She moved towards him, whistling softly. 'You're good-looking enough for Hollywood.'

It was Mama's highest compliment.

'Thank you, ma'am.'

She took his hand. 'If you sing half as good as you look, you'll be on the radio in no time. Come. Tell me about your career while we dance.'

'I'd be honoured to dance with my new mother-in-law.' Tossing Claire a quick smile, he was off.

Claire turned at last to Meghann. 'Are you OK?'

'Mama brought her dog, plus her entourage of bodyguards.'

'She could be overcome by the hoards of her fans at any moment,' Claire said in her best pseudo-Southern voice.

Meghann laughed. 'She has to leave at eight thirty. I believe a prayer of thanks is in order.'

The band shifted into a soulful version of 'As Time Goes By'.

Claire stared at her sister, trying to come up with words to match her emotions. 'This wedding—' she started, but her voice cracked. She swallowed hard. 'You spent a fortune.'

'No.' Meghann shook her head. 'Almost everything was on sale. They're my Christmas lights. The tent—'

Claire touched her sister's lips, shut her up. 'I'm trying to thank you.'

'Oh.'

'I wish . . .' She didn't even know how to word it, this longing of hers.

'I know,' Meghann said. 'Maybe things can be different now.'

'You were my best friend,' Claire said. 'I missed that when you . . .' *Left.* She couldn't say the harsh word, not now.

'I missed you, too.'

'Mommy! Mommy! Come dance with us.'

Claire twisted round and saw her dad and Alison standing a few feet away. 'I believe it's customary for the bride to dance with her father,' he said, smiling, holding out his calloused hand.

'And her daughter! Grandpa'll carry me.' Alison was hopping up and down with excitement.

Claire gave her champagne glass to Meghann, who mouthed, 'Go.' She let herself be pulled onto the dance floor. As they made it to the centre of the crowd, Dad bent down and scooped Alison up. The three of them clung to one another, swaying gently in time to 'The Very Thought of You'.

All her life Claire would look back on this night and remember how good her life was, how much she loved and was loved in return.

That was what Meghann had given her.

Meghann gazed at the black velvet lawn of Edgar Peabody Riverfront Park. Behind her, the band was breaking down their equipment. Only a few die-hard guests were still here. Mama had left hours ago, as had Sam and Ali.

Everyone else, including the bride and groom, had drifted away at around midnight. Meghann had stayed late, supervising the cleanup, but now that job was done.

She sipped her champagne and looked across the street. Joe was probably sleeping. She knew it was ridiculous to go to him, maybe even dangerous, but there was something in the air tonight. A heady combination of romance and magic. It smelt like roses and made a woman believe that anything was possible. For tonight, anyway.

So she hummed along with the music and walked down the gravel road. At his gate she paused. The lights were on. She debated for another minute or two, then knocked.

Moments later, Joe opened the door. His hair was messed up, as if he'd been asleep; all he wore was a pair of black jeans.

He stared at her, saying nothing.

'I thought maybe we could go out,' she said.

'You want us to go on a *date*? At one o'clock in the morning?'

'Sure. Why not?'

'A better question is why.'

She looked up at him. When their gazes locked, she felt a flutter in her pulse. 'I was in a good mood. Maybe I had too much to drink.' Humiliated, she closed her eyes. 'I shouldn't have come. I'm sorry.' When she opened her eyes, she saw he'd moved closer.

'I'm not much for going out.'

'Oh.'

'But I wouldn't mind if you wanted to come in.'

She felt the start of a smile. 'Great.'

'What I *mind*,' he said, 'is waking up alone. It's OK if you don't want to spend the night, but don't sneak out like a hooker.'

'I'm sorry.'

He smiled. It lit up his whole face, made him look ten years younger. 'OK, come on in.'

She touched his arm. 'That's the first time I've seen you smile.'

'Yeah,' he said softly, maybe sadly. 'It's been a while.'

Joe woke with Meghann in his arms, their naked bodies tangled together. Memories of last night teased him, made him feel strangely light-headed. Most of all, he remembered the hoarse, desperate sound of her voice when she'd cried out his name.

He shifted his weight gently, moved just enough so that he could look down at her. Her black hair was a tangled mess; he remembered driving his hands through it in passion, then stroking it as he fell asleep. Her pale cheeks looked even whiter against the greyed cotton pillowcase. Even in sleep, he saw a kind of sadness round her eyes and mouth, as if she worried her troubles both day and night.

What a pair they were. They'd spent three nights together now and had exchanged almost no secrets about each other.

The amazing thing was, he wanted her again already. Not just her body, either. He wanted to get to know her, and just that—the wanting—seemed to change him. It was as if a light had gone on in a place that had been cold and dark.

And yet it frightened him.

The guilt was so much a part of him. In the last few years it had wrapped around him, bone and sinew. For more nights than he wanted to count, it had been his strength, the only thing holding him together; the first thing he remembered in the morning and the last thing on his mind when he fell asleep.

If he let go of the guilt—not all of it, of course, but just enough to reach for a different life, a different woman—would he lose the memories, too? Had Diana become so intertwined with his regret that he could have both or neither? And if so, could he *really* make a life that was separate from the woman he'd loved for so much of his life?

He didn't know.

But just now, looking down at Meghann, feeling the whisper softness of her breath against his skin, he wanted to try. He reached out, brushed a silky strand of hair from her face. It was the kind of touch he hadn't dared in years.

She blinked awake. 'Morning,' she said, her voice scratchy and raw.

He kissed her gently, whispered, 'Good morning.'

She pulled back too quickly, turned away. 'I need to go. I'm supposed to pick up my niece at nine o'clock.' She threw the covers back and got out of bed. Naked, she yanked a pillow up to cover herself and hurried into the bathroom. By the time she re-emerged, dressed once again in her expensive lavender silk dress, he was dressed.

She picked up her strappy sandals in one hand. 'I've really got to go.' She glanced at the front door and started to turn towards it.

He wanted to stop her, but didn't know how. 'I'm glad you came last night.'

She laughed. 'Me, too. Twice.'

'Don't,' he said, moving towards her. He had no idea what, if anything, was between them, but he knew it wasn't a joke.

She looked at the door again, then up at him. 'I can't stay, Joe.'

'See you later, then. Goodbye.' He waited for her to answer, but she didn't. Instead, she kissed him. Hard. He was breathless by the time she pulled back, whispered, 'You're a good man, Joe.'

Then she was gone.

Joe went to the window and watched her leave. She practically ran to her car, but once she was there, she paused, looking back at the house.

From this distance, she looked oddly sad. It made him realise how little he knew her. He wanted to change that, wanted to believe there was a future for him after all. Maybe even one with her. But he'd have to let go of the past.

He didn't know how to start a life over and believe in a different future, but he knew what the first step was. He'd always known.

He had to talk to Diana's parents.

Meghann was showered, dressed in a T-shirt and jeans, and packed. On her way out, she paused long enough to write Claire a quick note, which she left on the kitchen counter. Then she took one last look at the house that was so much a home. It was unexpectedly difficult to leave. Her apartment was so cold and empty by comparison.

Finally she went to her car and drove slowly through the campground. She came to a horseshoe-shaped yard full of oversized rhododendrons. A grey mobile home squatted on cement blocks.

Meghann parked the car and got out. As always, she felt a tightening in her stomach when she thought about meeting Sam.

She walked up the gravel walkway and onto the porch. She knocked. When no one answered, she tried again.

The door swung open, hinges creaking, and there he was, filling the doorway, dressed in shabby overalls and a pale blue T-shirt that read RIVER'S EDGE. His brown hair was Albert Einstein wild.

'Meg'—he stepped back—'come on in.'

She sidled past him and found herself in a surprisingly cosy living room. 'Good morning, Sam. I'm here to pick up Alison.'

'Are you sure you want to take her? I'd be happy to keep her.'

'I'm sure you would,' she answered, stung.

'I know how busy you are.'

'You still think I'm a bad influence, is that it?'

He took a step towards her, stopped. 'I should never have thought that. Claire's told me how good you were to her. I didn't know about kids back then, and I sure as hell didn't know about teenage girls who—'

'Please. Don't finish that sentence. Do you have a list for me? Allergies. Medications. Anything I should know?'

'She goes to bed at eight. She likes it if you read her a story. *The Little Mermaid* is her favourite.'

'Great.' Meg looked down the hallway. 'Is she ready?'

'She's just telling the cat goodbye. She has a birthday party to go to on Saturday. If you get her here by noon, she'll make it. That way she'll be here when Claire and Bobby get home on Sunday.'

Alison came racing down the hallway, carrying a black cat whose body stretched almost to the ground. 'Lightning wants to come with me, Grandpa. Can I take him with me, Aunt Meg? Can I?'

Meg had no idea whether cats were allowed in her building.

Before she could answer, Sam knelt down in front of Alison and gently eased the cat from her arms. 'Lightning needs to stay here, honey. You know he likes to play with his friends and hunt for mice in the woods. He's a country cat. He wouldn't like the city.'

'I'm not a city girl, either,' she said, puffing out her lower lip.

'No,' Sam said. 'You're an adventurer, though. Just like Mulan and Princess Jasmine. Do you think they'd be nervous about a trip to the big city?'

Ali shook her head.

Sam pulled her into his arms and hugged her tightly. When he finally let her go, he got slowly to his feet and looked at Meghann. 'Take good care of my granddaughter.'

It was not unlike what she'd said to Sam all those years ago, just before she left for good. *Take care of my sister.* The only difference was, she'd been crying. 'I will.'

Alison grabbed her backpack and her small suitcase. 'I'm ready, Aunt Meg.'

'OK, let's go.' Meg took the suitcase and headed for the door.

They were in the car and moving down the driveway when Alison suddenly screamed, 'Stop!'

Meg slammed on the brakes. 'What's wrong?'

Alison climbed out of her seat and ran back into the trailer. A moment later she was back, clutching a ratty pink blanket to her chest. Her eyes glistened with tears.

'I can't go 'venturing without my wubbie.'

The telephone woke Claire up. She sat up fast. 'What time is it?' She looked around the unfamiliar hotel room for the bedside clock, found it: five forty-five. 'Bobby, the phone—'

She scrambled over him and picked it up. 'Hello?'

'Hey, darlin'. How are you?'

Claire released a heavy breath and climbed out of bed. 'I'm fine, Mama. It's five forty-five on Kauai.'

'I thought y'all were the same time zone as California.'

'We're halfway to Asia, Mama.'

'You always did exaggerate, Claire. I *do* have a reason for callin', you know.'

Claire grabbed her robe and slipped it on, then went out onto the balcony. Outside, the sky was just turning pink. The morning smelt of sweet tropical flowers and salt air. 'What is it?'

'I know you don't think I'm much of a mother.'

'That's not true.' She yawned, wondering if there was any chance of falling asleep again. She looked through the windows at Bobby, who was sitting up now, frowning at her.

'No matter what you and your bigmouthed sister remember, or think you do, the truth is that I love you.'

'I know, Mama.' She smiled at Bobby, mouthed 'Mama', then 'coffee'.

'Now put your husband on the phone.'

'Why?'

Mama sighed dramatically. 'It's about a weddin' gift for him.'

'OK, Mama. Whatever. Just a second.' She went back inside. 'She wants to talk to you.'

Bobby got up and took the phone from Claire. 'How's the sexiest mother-in-law in the world?' After a moment his smile faded. 'What?' Then, 'You're kidding me.'

Claire placed her hand on his shoulder. 'What's going on?'

He shook his head. 'That's incredible, Ellie. I don't know how to thank you . . . When?' He frowned. 'You know we're here . . . Oh, yeah. I understand. We'll call right away. And thank you. I can't tell you how much this means . . . . Yes. Goodbye.'

'What did she do?' Claire asked when he hung up the phone.

Bobby's smile was so big, it creased his whole face into pleats. 'She got me an audition with Kent Ames at Down Home Records. I can't *believe* it. I've been waiting ten years for a break like this.'

Claire threw herself at him, holding him tightly in her arms. 'You'll knock 'em dead.'

He twirled her round until they were both laughing. She was still laughing when he eased her back to her feet.

'But . . .' he said, not smiling now. 'The audition is on Thursday. After that, Kent is leaving for a month.'

'This Thursday?'

'This Thursday. In Nashville.'

Claire knew that if she said no, said, 'Our honeymoon won't be over by then,' he'd kiss her and say, 'OK, maybe call your mama back and see if the audition can be rescheduled in a month.'

Her answer was easy. 'I've always wanted to see Opryland.'

Bobby pulled her into his arms, gazed down at her. 'I'd given up,' he admitted quietly.

289

'Let that be a lesson,' she answered happily. 'Now hand me that phone. I better let Dad and Meghann know that we'll probably add a day or two onto the trip.'

The days Meghann spent with Alison as her house guest settled into a comfortable routine. By the third afternoon Meghann had let go of her obsessive need to show her niece every child-friendly venue in Seattle. Instead, they did simple things. They rented movies and made cookies.

The first night, Ali came into her room crying because she couldn't sleep. That night and each night afterwards Meg slept with Ali tucked in her arms, and each morning she woke with an unexpected sense of anticipation. She smiled easier, laughed more often. She'd forgotten how good it felt to care for someone else.

When Claire called to extend the length of her honeymoon, Meg knew she'd shocked her sister by offering—gladly—to keep Alison for a few extra days. Unfortunately, the oh-so-important birthday party back in Hayden ruined that option.

When Saturday finally came, Meghann was surprised by the depth of her emotions. All the way to Hayden she had to work to keep smiling, while Ali chattered nonstop and bounced in her seat. At Sam's house, Ali flew into her grandfather's arms and started telling him about the week. Meg kissed her niece goodbye and hurried out of the trailer. That night she hardly slept at all. She couldn't seem to stave off the loneliness.

On Monday she went back to work.

The hours stacked on top of one another, growing heavier than usual. By the end of the day she was so tired, she could hardly function. She packed up her papers, grabbed her bag and briefcase, and left the office. Outside, it was a balmy, early-summer night. The hustle and bustle of rush-hour traffic clogged the streets.

She pushed away from the doorway and headed home. She didn't want to go to the Athenian to pick up some man she didn't know. She wanted . . . Joe.

At four o'clock Joe was finished for the day. It was a good thing, because he actually had places to go and people to see.

It felt good to look forward to something, even if that something would ultimately cause him pain.

For the next hour, as Joe shaved and showered and dressed in his cleanest worn clothes, he tried to string together the sentences he would need. He tried pretty words, 'Diana's death ruined something inside me'; stark words, 'I screwed up'; painful words, 'I couldn't stand watching her die.' But none of them were the whole of it; none of them expressed the truth of his emotions.

He still hadn't figured out what he would say, when he turned onto their road or, a few minutes later, when he came to their mailbox: DR AND MRS HENRY ROLOFF.

Joe couldn't help touching it. There had been a mailbox in Bainbridge like this one; it read DR AND MRS JOE WYATT.

He stared at his former in-laws' house. It looked exactly as it had on another June day, so long ago, when Joe and Di had got married in the back yard.

He almost turned away, but running didn't help. He'd tried that route, and it had brought him back here—to this house, to these people who he'd once loved so keenly—to say 'I'm sorry'.

He walked up the brick path, towards the white-pillared house. Joe didn't let himself pause or think. He reached out and rang the bell.

A few moments later the door opened. Henry Roloff stood there, pipe in hand, dressed in khaki trousers and a turtleneck. 'Can I—' At the sight of Joe, his smile fell. 'Joey,' he said, his pipe aflutter now in a trembling hand. 'We'd heard you were back in town.'

Joe tried to smile.

'Who is it?' Tina called out from somewhere inside the house.

'You won't believe it,' Henry called, his voice barely above a whisper.

'Henry?' she called again. 'Who is it?'

Henry stepped back. A watery smile spilled across his face, wrinkled his cheeks. 'He's home, Mother,' he yelled. Then, softly, he said it again, his eyes filling with tears. 'He's home.'

'This is the club where Garth Brooks was discovered.'

Claire smiled at Kent Ames, the grand Pooh-Bah of Down Home Records in Nashville. She and Bobby had been in Nashville for two days now. Their room at the Loews Hotel was breathtakingly beautiful. They'd splurged on romantic dinners. They'd toured Opryland and seen the Country Music Hall of Fame. Most important, Bobby had aced his auditions. All four of them.

He'd sung his songs for one executive after another until he'd finally found himself in the big corner office that overlooked the street of country-and-western dreams: Music Row.

Their lives had changed in the last twenty-four hours. Bobby was 'someone'. A guy who was 'going places'.

Now they sat at a front table in a small, unassuming nightclub, Claire and the executives and her husband. In less than an hour Bobby was scheduled to take the stage. It was a chance to 'show his concert stuff' to the executives.

Bobby had no trouble talking to the men. They talked about people and things Claire knew nothing about—demo records and studio time and royalty rates and contract provisions.

She wanted to keep it all straight, but she couldn't seem to concentrate. The endless flight from Kauai to Oahu to Seattle to Memphis to Nashville had left its mark in a dull headache that wouldn't go away. The smoke in the club didn't help. Neither did the thudding music or the shouted conversation.

Kent Ames smiled at her. 'Bobby goes on in forty-five minutes. Usually it takes years to get a spot on this stage.'

Claire felt an odd tingling sensation in her right hand. It took her two tries to reach out for her margarita. When she took hold, she drank the whole thing, hoping it would ease her headache.

It didn't. Instead, it made her sick to her stomach. She slid off the barstool and stood up, surprised to find she was unsteady on her feet.

'Claire?' Bobby got to his feet.

She pulled up a smile. It felt a little weak, one-sided. 'I'm sorry, Bobby. My headache is worse. I think I need to lie down.' She kissed his cheek, whispered, 'Knock 'em dead, baby.'

He put his arm round her. 'I'll walk her back to the hotel.'

Kent frowned. 'But your set—'

'I'll be back in time,' Bobby said. Keeping a close hold, he manoeuvred her out of the club and onto the loud, busy street.

'You don't have to escort me, Bobby. Really.'

'Nothing matters more than you. Nothing. Those guys might as well know my priorities right off the bat.'

They hurried through the lobby and rode the elevator to their floor. In their room Bobby gently put her to bed. 'Go to sleep, my love,' he whispered, kissing her forehead.

'Good luck, baby. I love you.'

'That's exactly why I don't need luck.'

Claire roused herself enough to call home. She tried to sound upbeat as she told Ali and Sam about the exciting day and reminded them that she'd be home in two days. After she hung up, she sighed heavily and closed her eyes.

When Claire woke up the next morning, her headache was gone. She felt sluggish and tired, but it was easy to smile when Bobby told her how it had gone.

'I blew them away, Claire. No kidding. Kent Ames was salivating over my future. He offered me a contract. Can you believe it?'

They were curled up in their suite's window seat, both wearing the ultrasoft robes provided by the hotel. Bright morning sunlight pushed through the window. Bobby looked so handsome, he took Claire's breath away. 'Of course I can believe it. I've heard you sing. How does it all work?'

'They think it'll take a month or so in Nashville. Finding material, putting a back-up band together. They want me to tour through September and October. But don't worry. I told them we'd have to work out a schedule that was good for the family.'

Claire loved him more at that moment than she would have imagined was possible. She grabbed his robe and pulled him close. 'You will *only* have men and ugly women on your bus. I've seen movies about those tours.'

He kissed her, long and slow and hard. When he drew back, she was dizzy. 'What did I ever do to deserve you, Claire?'

'You loved me,' she answered, reaching into his robe. 'Now take me to bed and love me again.'

At six thirty in the morning Meghann rolled out of bed, took a shower, and dressed in a black dress with a lavender silk jacket. One look in the mirror reminded her that she hadn't slept more than two hours the night before. She was at her desk by seven thirty, highlighting a deposition.

Every fifteen minutes she glanced at her phone. It was a weekday. Joe would be at work. *Call him.*

Finally, at ten o'clock, she gave up and buzzed her secretary.

'Yes, Ms Dontess?'

'I need the number for a garage in Hayden, Washington.'

'What garage?'

'I don't know the name or the address. But it's across the street from Riverfront Park. On Front Street.'

'I'm going to need—'

'To be resourceful. Thanks.' Meghann hung up.

Ten long minutes passed. Finally Rhona buzzed on line one. 'Here's the number. It's called Smitty's Garage.'

Meghann wrote down the number and stared at it. Her heart was beating quickly. 'This is ridiculous.' She picked up the phone and dialled. With every ring she had to fight the urge to hang up.

'Smitty's Garage.'

Meghann swallowed hard. 'Is Joe there?'

'Just a sec. Joe!'

The phone clanged down, then was picked up. 'Hello?'

'Joe? It's Meghann.'

There was a long pause. 'I thought I'd seen the last of you.'

'I guess it won't be that easy.' But the joke fell into silence. 'I . . . uh . . . I have a deposition in Snohomish County on Friday. I thought you might like to get together for dinner.'

He didn't answer.

'Forget it. I'm an idiot. I'll hang up now.'

'I could pick up a couple of steaks and borrow Smitty's barbecue.'

'You mean it?'

He laughed softly, and the sound of it released that achy tension in her neck. 'Why not?'

'I'll be there about six. Is that OK?'

'Perfect.'

'I'll bring wine and dessert.'

Meghann was smiling when she hung up. Ten minutes later Rhona buzzed her again.

'Ms Dontess, your sister is on line two. She says it's urgent.'

'Thanks.' Meg pushed the button. 'Hey, Claire. Welcome back. Your flight must have been on time. Amazing. How was—'

'I'm at the airport. I didn't know who else to call.' Claire's voice was shaky; it sounded as if she was crying.

'What's going on, Claire?'

'I don't remember the flight from Nashville. I also don't remember getting my luggage, but it's right here. I don't remember walking through the garage, but I'm sitting in my car.'

'I don't understand.'

'Neither do I, damn it,' Claire screamed; then she started to sob. 'I can't remember how to get home.'

'Oh my God.' Instead of panicking, Meghann took charge. 'Do you have a piece of paper?'

'Yes. Right here.'

'A pen?'

'Yes.' Her sobs slowed down. 'I'm scared, Meg.'

'Write down 829 Post Alley. Do you have that?'

'I'm holding it.'

'Keep holding it. Now, get out of your car and walk to the terminal.'

'I'm scared.'

'I'll stay on the phone with you.'

'Wait. I don't know which way—'

'Is there a covered walkway in front of you, with airlines listed above?'

'Yes. It says Alaska and Horizon.'

'Go that way. I'm right here, Claire. I'm not going anywhere. Take the escalator down one floor. You see it?'

'Yes.'

She sounded so weak. It scared the hell out of Meghann. 'Go outside. Pick up the phone that says TAXI. What's the number above the door you just came through?'

'Twelve.'

'Tell the cab driver to pick you up at door twelve, that you're going downtown.'

'Hold on.'

Meghann heard her talking. Then Claire said, 'OK.'

'I'm right here, Claire. Everything is going to be OK.'

'Who is this?'

Meghann felt an icy rush of fear. 'It's Meghann.'

'I don't remember calling you.'

Meghann closed her eyes. It took an act of will to find her voice. 'Is there a cab in front of you?'

'Yes. Why is it here?'

'It's there for you. Give him the piece of paper in your hand.'

'How did you know I had this paper, Meg? What's wrong with me?'

'It's OK, Claire. Get in the cab. He'll drop you off at my building. I'll be waiting for you.'

The cab pulled along the kerb and stopped. Before Claire could even say thank you, the front passenger-side door opened. Meghann paid the driver, then guided Claire into the cushy interior of a Lincoln cab that was waiting at the kerb. Meg studied her. 'Are you OK now?'

Claire heard the concern in her sister's voice, and it touched her. 'I'm fine now. Really. I guess I had a panic attack or something. Just take me to a quiet restaurant for a cup of coffee. I probably just need to sleep.'

Meg looked at her as if she were a science experiment gone bad. 'Are you kidding me? A panic attack? Believe me, Claire, I know panic attacks, and you don't forget how to get home. We're going to the hospital.'

They exchanged looks then, until Claire turned away. 'Bobby aced the auditions. They offered him a big fat contract.'

'He won't sign it until I review it, right?'

'The standard response is "Congratulations".'

Meghann had the grace to blush. 'Congratulations. That's really something.'

'I believe it belongs in *Ripley's Believe It or Not!* under the headline "Eliana Sullivan Does Good Deed".'

Meg pressed a hand to her breast and said, 'I'm so big-hearted when it comes to family,' in a gooey Southern drawl.

Claire started to laugh. Then she noticed that the tingling in her right hand was back. As she stared down at her hand, her fingers curled into a hook. For a second she couldn't open it. She panicked. *Please, God—*

The spasm ended.

The car pulled up in front of the hospital and let them out.

At the emergency room's reception desk, a heavyset young woman looked up at them. 'Can I help you?'

'I'm here to see a doctor.'

'What's the problem?'

'I have a killer headache.'

Meghann leaned over the desk. 'Write this down: Severe headache. Short-term memory loss.'

'That's right. I forgot.' Claire smiled weakly.

The receptionist shoved a clipboard across the desk. 'Fill that out and give me your insurance card.'

Claire retrieved the card from her wallet and handed it to the receptionist, who said, 'Take a seat until we call for you.'

An hour later they were still waiting. Meghann was fit to be tied. 'They've got a lot of nerve calling this an *emergency* room.'

Claire considered trying to calm her sister down, but the effort was too much. Her headache had got worse.

'Claire Austin,' called out a nurse in a blue scrub suit.

'It's about time.' Meghann helped Claire to her feet.

'You're a real comfort, Meg,' Claire said.

'It's a gift,' Meg said, guiding her towards the tiny, birdlike nurse who stood in front of the double doors of the emergency room.

Claire clung to her sister's hand as they went through the doors. In an examination room she changed into a hospital gown, relinquished her arm for a blood pressure test and her vein for a blood test.

Again they waited. Finally someone knocked and the door opened. In walked a teenage boy in a white coat.

'I'm Dr Lannigan. What seems to be the problem?'

Meghann groaned.

'Hello, Doctor,' Claire said. 'I really don't need to be here. I have a headache, and my sister thinks a migraine is emergency-room-worthy. After a long flight I had some kind of panic attack.'

'Where she forgot how to get home,' Meghann added.

The doctor asked Claire to perform a few functions—lift one arm, then the other, turn her head, blink—and answer some easy questions, like what year it is, who the President is. When he finished, he asked, 'Do you often get headaches?'

'When I get stressed out. More lately, though,' she admitted.

'Have you made any big changes in your life recently?'

Claire laughed. 'Plenty. I just got married for the first time. My husband is in Nashville, making a record.'

'Ah.' He smiled. 'Well, Mrs Austin, your blood work is normal, as is your blood pressure. I'm sure this is all stress. If the headaches persist, however, I'd recommend that you see a neurologist.'

Claire nodded, relieved. 'Thank you, Doctor.'

'Oh, no,' Meghann said to the doctor. 'That's not good enough.'

He blinked at her, stepping back.

'I watch *ER*. She needs a CAT scan or an MRI. Some damn initial test. At the very least she'll take that neurology consult now.'

He frowned. 'Those are costly tests. We can hardly run a CAT scan on every patient who complains of a headache, but if you'd like, I'll recommend a neurologist. You can make an appointment.'

'How long have you been a doctor?'

'I'm in my first year of residency.'

'Would you like to do a second year?'

'Of course. I don't see—'

'Get your supervisor in here. Now. We didn't spend three hours here so that an almost-doctor could tell us that Claire is under stress. I'm under stress; you're under stress. We manage to remember our way home. Get a neurologist in here. *Now.*'

'I'll go get a consultant.' He clutched his clipboard and hurried out.

Claire sighed. 'You're being you again. It *is* stress.'

'I hope it is, too, but I'm not taking the prom king's word for it.'

A few moments later the nurse was back. 'Dr Kensington has reviewed your material. She'd like you to have a CAT scan.'

'She. Thank God,' Meghann said.

The nurse nodded. 'You can come with me,' she said.

Claire clung to Meghann's hand. The walk seemed to last for ever, down one corridor and another, up the elevator, until they arrived at the Center for Nuclear Medicine.

Nuclear. Claire felt Meghann's grip tighten.

'Here we are.' The nurse paused outside a closed door. She turned to Meghann. 'There's a chair right there. You can't come in, but I'll take good care of her, OK?'

Meghann hesitated, then nodded. 'I'll be here, Claire.'

Claire followed the nurse into a room that was dominated by a huge machine that looked like a white doughnut. She let herself be positioned on the narrow bed that intersected the doughnut hole. There she waited. And waited. Periodically the nurse came back, muttered something about the doctor, and disappeared again.

Finally the door opened, and a man in a white coat walked in. 'Sorry to keep you waiting. I'm Dr Cole, your radiologist. You just lie perfectly still, and we'll have you out of here in no time.'

Claire forced herself to smile. She refused to think about the fact that everyone else in the room wore lead aprons, while she lay with only the thinnest sheet of cotton to protect her.

'You're done. Fine job,' he said when it was finally over.

Claire was so thankful, she almost forgot the headache that had steadily increased as she lay in the machine.

In the hallway, Meghann looked angry. 'What happened? They said it would take an hour.'

'And it did, once they corralled a doctor.'

They followed the nurse to another examination room.

'Should I get dressed?' Claire asked.

'Not yet. The doctor will be here soon.'

'I'll bet,' Meghann said under her breath.

Thirty minutes later the nurse was back. 'The doctor has ordered another test,' she said to Meghann. 'An MRI.'

'An MRI?' Meg asked, feeling anxious.

'It's a clearer picture of what's going on. Very standard.'

Claire's one-hour test lasted for two. Finally she was let go, and she and Meghann returned to the nuclear medicine wing, where Claire's clothes were hanging. Then they went to another waiting room. 'Of course,' Meg grumbled.

They were there another hour. At last a tall, tired-looking woman in a lab coat came into the waiting room. 'Claire Austin?'

Claire stood up. At the suddenness of the movement she almost fell. Meg steadied her.

The woman smiled and said, 'I'm Dr Kensington, chief of neurology.'

'Claire Austin. This is my sister, Meghann.'

'It's nice to meet you. Come this way.' Dr Kensington led them to an office that was lined with books and diplomas. Behind her, a set of X-ray–like images glowed against the bright white back-lit boxes.

Claire stared at them, wondering what there was to see.

The doctor sat down at her desk and indicated that Claire and Meghann sit opposite her. 'I'm sorry you had problems with Dr Lannigan. This is a teaching hospital, and sometimes our residents are not as thorough as we would wish. Your demand for a higher level of care was a much-needed wake-up call for Dr Lannigan.'

Claire nodded. 'Do I have a sinus infection?'

'No, Claire. You have a mass in your brain.'

'What?'

'You have a tumour. In your brain.' Dr Kensington rose slowly and went to the X-rays, pointing to a white spot. 'It's about the size of a golf ball and located in the right frontal lobe, crossing the midline.'

Tumour. Claire felt as if she'd just been shoved out of an airplane. She couldn't breathe; the ground was rushing up to meet her.

'I'm sorry to say this,' Dr Kensington went on, 'but I've consulted with a neurosurgeon, and we believe it's inoperable. You'll want second opinions, of course. You'll need to see an oncologist also.'

Meghann was on her feet. 'You're saying she has a brain tumour and that you can't do anything about it?'

'We believe it's inoperable, but I didn't say we can't do anything.'

'Meg, please.' Claire was absurdly afraid that her sister was going to make it worse. She looked pleadingly at the doctor. 'Are you saying I might die?'

'We'll need more tests, but given the size and placement of the mass, it's not a good outlook.'

'Inoperable means *you* won't operate,' Meg said in a growl.

Dr Kensington looked surprised. 'I don't believe anyone will. I consulted with our top neurosurgeon on this. He agrees with my diagnosis. The procedure would be too dangerous.'

Meg looked disgusted. 'Who *will* do this kind of operation?'

'No one in this hospital.'

Meg grabbed her bag. 'Come on, Claire. We're in the wrong hospital.'

Claire looked helplessly from Dr Kensington to her sister. 'Meg,' she pleaded, 'you don't know everything. Please . . .'

Meg went to her, knelt in front of her. 'I know I don't know everything. I even know I've let you down in the past, but none of that matters now. From this second on, all that matters is your life.'

Claire started to cry. She hated how fragile she felt, but there it was. Suddenly she *felt* like she was dying.

'Lean on me, Claire.'

Claire gazed into her sister's eyes and remembered how Meg had once been her whole world. Slowly she nodded.

Meghann helped her to her feet; then she turned to the doctor. 'You go ahead and teach Dr Lannigan how to read a thermometer. We're going to find a doctor who can save her life.'

Outside the hospital, Meghann helped Claire into a cab. 'Are you OK?' she asked, her voice spiked and anxious.

She looked at Meg. 'Do I have cancer? Is that what a tumour is?'

'We don't know what the hell you have. Certainly, those doctors don't know.'

'Did you see the shadow on that X-ray, Meg? It was *huge*.'

Meghann grabbed her, shook her hard. 'Listen to me. You need to be tough now. No getting by, no giving up. Tomorrow we'll start getting second opinions. First we'll go to Johns Hopkins. Then we'll try Sloan-Kettering in New York. There's got to be a surgeon who has some balls.' Meghann's eyes welled up; her voice broke.

Somehow that frightened Claire even more, seeing Meg crack. 'It's going to be OK,' she said automatically. Comforting others was easier than thinking. 'We just need to keep positive.'

'Faith. Yes,' Meghann said. 'You hold on to the faith, and I'll start finding out everything there is to know about your condition. That way we'll have all the bases covered.'

'You mean be a team?'

'Someone has to be there for you through this.'

The whole of their childhood was between them suddenly, all the good times and, more important, the bad.

Claire stared at her sister. 'If you start this thing with me, you have to stick around if things get tough.'

Meg looked at her. 'You can count on me.'

Claire frowned. 'I don't want to tell anyone.'

'Why should we say anything until we know for sure?'

'It'll just worry Dad and make Bobby come home.' She paused, swallowed hard. 'I don't even want to think about telling Ali.'

'We'll tell everyone I'm taking you to a spa for a week.'

'Bobby will believe it. And Ali. Dad . . . I don't know. Maybe if I tell him we need time together. He's wanted us to reconcile for years. Yeah. He'd buy that.'

Meeting Diana's parents had released something in Joe. Their forgiveness, their understanding, had eased his burdens. For the first time since his wife's death, he could stand straight again. He could believe that there was a way out for him. Not medicine. He could never watch death up close again. But something . . .

And there was Meghann. To his disbelief she'd called. Asked him on a date. His first real date with a woman in more than fifteen years. Meghann, perhaps even more so than the Roloffs' forgiveness, had brought Joe back to life.

On his lunch break he got a haircut and bought new clothes. He got back to the garage by one o'clock and worked for the rest of the day.

'That's about the tenth time you've looked at that clock in the past half an hour,' Smitty said at four thirty.

'I've . . . uh . . . got some place to be,' Joe said.

Smitty reached for a wrench. 'No kidding.'

Joe slammed the truck's hood down. 'I thought maybe I'd leave a couple of minutes early.'

'Wouldn't hurt my feelings none.'

'A friend is coming over for dinner,' Joe said.

'This friend drive a Porsche?'

'Yeah.'

Smitty smiled. 'Maybe you want to borrow the barbecue. Cut a few flowers from Helga's garden?'

'I didn't know how to ask.'

'Hell, Joe, you just do. Open your mouth and say please. That's part of being neighbours and coworkers.'

'Thank you.'

'Have a nice night, Joe.'

Joe left the shop and stopped by Smitty's house. He talked to Helga for a few minutes and left carrying a small barbecue. He set it up on the front porch.

Inside the house, he showered and shaved, then dressed in his new clothes and headed for the kitchen. For the next hour he moved from one chore to the next, until the potatoes were in the oven, the flowers were on the table, and the candles were lit. He poured himself a glass of red wine and went into the living room to wait for her.

He sat down on the sofa and stretched out his legs.

From her place on the mantelpiece Diana smiled down at him.

He felt a flash of guilt, as if he'd done something wrong. That was stupid; he wasn't being unfaithful. Still . . .

He set his glass down on the coffee table and collected the photographs, one by one, leaving a single framed picture on the end table. Just one. All the rest he took into the bedroom and carefully put away. Later he'd return a few of them to his sister's house.

When he went back into the living room and sat down, he smiled, thinking of Meghann. Anticipating the evening.

By nine thirty his smile had faded.

He sat alone on the couch, half drunk now with an empty bottle of wine beside him. The potatoes had long ago cooked down to nothing, and the candles had burned themselves out.

At midnight he went to bed alone.

Chapter Nine

IN THE PAST NINE DAYS Meghann and Claire had seen several specialists. It was amazing how fast doctors would see you if you had a brain tumour and plenty of money. Neurologists. Neurosurgeons. Neuro-oncologists. Radiologists. They went from Johns Hopkins to Sloan-Kettering to Scripps. They learned dozens of frightening new words: glioblastoma, anaplastic astrocytoma, craniotomy.

Some of the doctors were caring and compassionate; more were distant and too busy to talk for long. They each said the same thing: inoperable. It didn't matter if Claire's tumour was malignant or benign; either way it could be deadly. Most of them believed the tumour to be a glioblastoma multiforme. A kind they called the terminator. Ha-ha.

Each time they left a city, Meghann pinned her hopes on the next destination, until a neurologist at Scripps took her aside. 'Look,' he said, 'you're using up valuable time. Radiation is your sister's best hope. Twenty-five per cent of brain tumours respond positively to the treatment. If it shrinks enough, perhaps it will be operable. Take her home. Stop fighting the diagnosis and start fighting the tumour.'

So they'd gone home to Seattle. The next day Meghann had taken Claire to Swedish Medical Center, where they'd agreed to begin radiation treatment the day after. Once a day for four weeks.

'I'll need to stay here for the treatments,' Claire said as she sat in Meghann's apartment. 'Hayden's too far away.'

'Of course. I'll take some more time off work.'

'You don't have to do that. I can take the bus to the hospital.'

'I'm not going to dignify that with an answer.'

Claire looked out of the window. 'A friend of mine went through chemo and radiation.' She stared at the sparkling city, but all she really saw was Diana wasting away. In the end, all those treatments hadn't helped at all. 'I don't want Ali to see me like that. She can stay with Dad. We'll visit every weekend.'

'I'll rent a car for Bobby. That way you guys can drive back and forth.'

'I'm not going to tell Bobby . . . yet.'

Meghann frowned. 'What?'

'I am not going to call my brand-new husband and tell him I have a brain tumour. He's waited his whole life for this break. I don't want to ruin it for him.'

'But if he loves you—'

'He *does* love me,' Claire answered fiercely. 'That's the point. And I love him. I want him to have his chance.'

'It sounds to me like you're afraid he won't want to come,' Meghann said. 'I know you're scared, Claire. And I know Mama and I hurt you. But you have to give Bobby the chance to—'

'This isn't about the past. I'm the one who has a tumour. Me. You don't get to organise my choices, OK? I love Bobby, and I am *not* going to ask him to sacrifice everything for me.' Claire stood up. 'We better get going. I need to tell Dad what's going on.'

'What about Mama? You want to call her?'

'I'll call her if I get worse. Now let's go.'

Two hours later Meg turned onto River Road, and they were there. Late-afternoon sunlight drizzled down the sides of the yellow clapboard house; the garden was a riot of colour. A small bicycle with training wheels lay on its side in the overgrown grass.

Claire turned to Meg. 'I need to do this alone.'

Meg understood. This was Claire's family, not hers. 'OK. The doctors are going to make you better.'

Claire looked at Meghann. 'How do I promise that? What if—'

'Promise it, Claire. We'll worry about "what if" later.'

Claire nodded. 'You're right.' Her smile was wobbly.

Meghann saw the way her sister was trembling, and she longed to reach out to her, to hold her as she had when they were kids.

Claire got out of the car and walked haltingly up the path. She turned and glanced back at Meghann. 'Pick me up at six, OK?'

Meg backed out of the driveway and drove away. She didn't even know where she was going until she was there.

The cabin looked dark, unoccupied. She parked in front of it. Leaving her car, she walked up to the front door. She knocked.

He opened the door. 'You have got to be kidding me.'

That was when she remembered their date. Over a week ago. She was supposed to bring the wine and dessert. She looked past him, saw a dying bouquet of flowers on the coffee table, and hoped he hadn't bought them for their date. How long had he waited, she wondered, before he ate his dinner alone? 'I'm sorry. I forgot.'

'Give me one good reason not to slam the door in your face.'

She looked up at him, feeling so fragile she could barely breathe. 'My sister has a brain tumour.'

His expression changed slowly. A look came into his eyes, a kind of harrowing understanding that made her wonder at the dark roads that had traversed his life. 'Oh, Jesus.'

He opened his arms, and she walked into his embrace. For the first time she let herself really cry.

Joe stood on the porch, staring out at the falling night. It had been better, he now understood, to be angry with Meghann, to write her off for standing him up. When she had stepped into his arms and looked up at him with tears in her eyes, he'd wanted desperately to help her.

My sister has a brain tumour.

He closed his eyes, not wanting to remember, not wanting to feel the way he did.

He'd held Meghann for almost an hour. She'd cried until there were no tears left inside her, and then she'd fallen into a troubled sleep. He imagined that it was her first sleep in days. He knew. After a diagnosis like that, sleep either came to a person too much or not at all.

They hadn't spoken of anything that mattered. He'd simply stroked her hair and kissed her forehead and let her cry in his arms.

Behind him, the screen door screeched open and banged shut. He stiffened, unable to turn round and face her. When he did, he saw that she was embarrassed. Her cheeks were pink, and that gorgeous hair of hers was a fuzzy mess. She tried to smile, and the attempt tore at him. 'I'll put you in for a Purple Heart.'

He wanted to take her in his arms again, but he didn't dare. Things were different between them now, though she didn't know it. Hospitals. Tumours. Death and dying and disease.

He couldn't be a part of all that again. He had only just begun to survive his last round of it. 'There's nothing wrong with crying.'

'I suppose not. It doesn't help much, though.' She moved towards him; he wondered if she knew that she was wringing her hands. He got the sense that the time in his arms had both soothed and upset her. As if maybe she hated to admit a need. He'd been alone long enough to understand.

'I want to thank you for . . . I don't know. Being there. I shouldn't have busted in on you.'

He knew she was waiting for him to say 'I'm glad you're here'.

At his silence, she stepped back, frowning. 'Too much too soon, I guess. I completely understand. I hate needy people, too. Well. I better go. Claire starts radiation tomorrow.'

He couldn't help himself. 'Where?'

She paused, turned back towards him. 'Swedish Medical Center.'

'Did you get second opinions?'

'Are you kidding? We got opinions from the best people in the country. They didn't agree on everything, but *inoperable* was a favourite.'

'There's a guy. A neurosurgeon at University College, Los Angeles. Stu Weissman. He's good.'

Meghann was watching him. 'How do you know Weissman?'

'I went to school with him.'

'College?'

'Don't sound so surprised. Just because I live like this now doesn't mean I always did. I have a degree in American literature.'

'We know nothing about each other.'

'Maybe it's better that way.'

'Normally I'd have a funny comeback to that. But I'm a little slow today. Having a sister with a brain tumour will do that to a girl.' Her voice cracked a little. She turned and walked away.

With every step she took, he wanted to go after her, apologise and tell her the truth, who he was and what he'd been through. Then, perhaps, she'd understand why there were places he couldn't go. But he didn't move.

When he went back inside the house, he saw the last remaining picture of Diana staring at him from the end table. For the first time he noticed the accusing glint in her eyes.

'What?' he said. 'There's nothing I can do.'

Alison listened carefully to Claire's explanation of a golf-ball-sized 'owie' in her brain.

'A golf ball is little,' she said at last.

Claire nodded, smiling. 'Yes. Yes, it is.'

'And a special gun is gonna shoot magic rays at it until it disappears? Like rubbing Aladdin's lamp?'

'Exactly like that.'

'How come you hafta live with Aunt Meg?'

'It's a long drive to the hospital. I can't go back and forth every day.'

Finally Ali said, 'OK.' Then she got to her feet and ran upstairs. 'I'll be right back, Mommy!' she yelled down.

'You haven't looked at me,' Dad said when Ali was gone.

'I know.'

He got up and crossed the room, then sat down beside her. She felt the comforting, familiar heat of him as he put an arm round her, pulled her close. She rested her head on his shoulder and felt a splash of tears on her face. She knew he was crying.

He sighed heavily, wiping his eyes. 'Have you told Bobby?'

'Not yet.'

'But you will?'

'Of course. As soon as he's finished in Nashville. I won't make him give up his big break for me.'

'You can't make decisions for other people, Claire, especially not for people who love you.'

'But you can sacrifice for them. Isn't that what love is?'

'You see it as a sacrifice? What if he sees it as selfishness? If . . . the worst happens, you've denied him the one thing that matters. Time.'

Claire looked at him. 'I can't tell him, Dad. I can't.'

Before Dad could say anything else, Alison bounded into the room, dragging her worn, stained baby blanket, the one she'd slept with every single night of her life. 'Here, Mommy, you can have my wubbie till you get all better.'

Claire took the greyed pink blanket in her hands. She held it to her face and smelt the little-girl sweetness of it. 'Thanks, Ali,' she said in a throaty voice.

Alison crawled up into her arms and hugged her. 'It's OK, Mommy. Don't cry. I'm a big girl. I can sleep without my wubbie.'

The next morning Meghann sat in the radiation treatment waiting room at Swedish Medical Center, trying to read the newest issue of *People* magazine. Finally she tossed the magazine on the table beside her and went up to the desk again.

'It's been more than an hour. Are you sure everything is OK with my sister?'

'I spoke with radiology five minutes ago. She's almost finished.'

Meghann sighed heavily and went back to her seat. The only magazine left to read was *Field & Stream*. She ignored it.

Finally Claire came out. Meghann rose slowly. On the right side of her sister's head was a small area that had been shaved. Claire touched her bald spot, feeling it.

'They tattooed me. I feel like Damien—that kid from *The Omen*.'

Meg looked at the tiny black dots on the pale, shaved skin. 'I could fix your hair so you couldn't even see the . . . you know.'

'Bald spot? That would be great.'

They walked through the hospital and out to the parking lot.

On the drive home, Claire said, 'It didn't hurt.'

'Really? That's good.'

'I closed my eyes and imagined the rays were sunlight. Healing me. Like that article you gave me.'

Meg had given her sister a stack of literature on positive thinking and visualisation. 'I'm glad it helped.'

Claire leaned back in her seat and looked out of the window. Meghann wished she could say something that mattered; so much was unsaid between them. With a sigh she pulled into the underground garage and parked in her space. Still silent, they went upstairs.

In the apartment, Claire touched her sister briefly; her fingers were icy cold. 'Thanks for coming with me today. It helped not to be alone.'

Their gazes met. Again Meghann felt the weight of their distance.

'I think I'll lie down,' Claire said. 'I didn't sleep well last night.'

So they'd both been awake. 'Me neither.'

Claire nodded. She waited a second longer, then turned and headed for the bedroom.

Meg went to the apartment's in-home office. Once, files and briefs and depositions had cluttered the glass desk. Now it was buried beneath medical books, articles, and clinical trials literature. Every day boxes from Barnes & Noble.com and Amazon arrived.

Meghann sat down at her desk. Her current reading material was an article about the potential benefits of tamoxifen to shrink tumours. She opened a yellow legal pad and began to take notes. She worked furiously, writing, writing. Hours later, when she looked up, Claire was standing in the doorway, smiling at her. 'Why do I think you're planning to do the surgery yourself?'

'I already know more about your condition than that first idiot we saw.'

Claire came into the room, carefully stepping over the empty Amazon boxes and the magazines that had been discarded. 'I think I better read it for myself, don't you?'

'Some of it's . . . hard.'

Claire reached for a standing file on the left side of the desk. She picked up a manila file with HOPE emblazoned in red ink.

'Don't,' Meg said. 'I've just started.'

Claire opened the file. It was empty. 'This goes in it,' Meg said quickly, ripping several pages out of her notebook. 'Tamoxifen.'

'Drugs?'

'There must be people who beat brain tumours,' Meghann said fiercely. 'I'll find every damn one and put their stories in there.'

The doorbell rang.

'Who could that be?' Meghann sidled past Claire and walked to the door. By the time she got there, the bell had rung another eight times. 'Good doorman,' she muttered, opening the door.

Gina, Charlotte and Karen stood clustered together.

'Where's our girl?' Karen cried out.

Claire appeared, and the screaming began. Karen and Charlotte surged forwards, enfolding Claire in their arms.

'Sam called us,' Gina said when she and Meghann were alone in the hallway. 'How is she?'

'OK, I guess. The radiation went well.' At Gina's frightened look Meghann added, 'She didn't want to worry you guys.'

'Yeah, right. She can't be alone for a thing like this.'

'I'm here,' Meghann answered, stung.

Gina squeezed her arm. 'She'll need all of us.'

Meghann nodded. Then she and Gina looked at each other.

'You call me. Whenever,' Gina said quietly.

'Thanks.'

After that, Gina eased past Meg and went into the living room, saying loudly, 'OK, we've got spas-in-a-bucket, gooey popcorn balls, hilarious movies, and, of course, games.'

Meghann watched the four friends come together, all talking at once. She went back to her office and shut the door.

Though the radiation treatments themselves lasted only a few minutes a day, they monopolised Claire's life. By the fourth day she was tired and nauseated. But the side effects weren't half as bad as the phone calls.

Every day she called home at noon. Ali always asked if the owie was all better yet; then Dad got on the phone and asked the same question in a different way.

Meghann stood beside her for every call. She hardly went to the office any more. Maybe three hours a day, tops. The rest of the time she spent huddled over books and articles or glued to the Internet. She attacked the issue of a tumour the way she'd once gone after deadbeat dads.

The only time Meg seemed willing to disappear into the woodwork was at two o'clock. The designated Bobby Phone Call time.

Now, Claire was alone in the living room. In the kitchen, the two o'clock buzzer was beeping. Claire dialled Bobby's cellphone number.

He picked up on the first ring. 'Hey, baby, you're two minutes late.'

Claire leaned back into the sofa's downy cushions. 'Tell me about your day.' She'd found that it was easier to listen than to talk. Lately her mind was a little foggy. She wondered how long it would be before he noticed that she spent their conversations listening or that her voice always broke when she said, 'I love you.'

'I miss you, Claire.'

'I miss you, too. But it's only a few more weeks.'

'Kent thinks we should have all the songs chosen by next week. Then it's into the studio. Do you think you could come down for that? I'd love to sing the songs to you.'

'Maybe,' she said, wondering what lie she'd come up with when the time came. She was too exhausted to think of one now. 'Well, babe, I've got to run. Meg is taking me out to lunch, then we're getting manicures.'

'I thought you got a manicure yesterday.'

Claire winced. 'Uh, those were pedicures. I love you.'

'I love you, too, Claire. Is . . . is everything OK?'

She felt the sting of tears again. 'Everything's perfect.'

'I made us a picnic lunch,' Meghann said to Claire in the car the next morning after treatment. Within minutes they were on the freeway. To their left, Lake Union sparkled in the sunlight.

On Mercer Island, Meghann left the freeway and turned onto a tree-lined drive. At a beautiful, grey-shingled house, she parked. 'This is my partner's house. She said we were welcome to spend the afternoon here.'

Meghann helped Claire out of the car and down the grassy lawn to the silvery wooden dock that cut into the blue water. 'Remember Lake Winobee?' she said, guiding Claire to the end of the dock, helping her sit down without falling.

'The summer I got that pink bathing suit?'

Meghann set the picnic basket down, then sat beside her sister. They both dangled their feet over the edge. Water slapped against the pilings and a varnished wooden sailing boat bobbed easily from side to side.

'I stole that bikini,' Meghann said. 'From Fred Meyer. When I got home, I was so scared I threw up. Mama didn't care; she just looked up from *Variety* and said, "Sticky fingers will get a girl in trouble."'

Claire turned to her sister. 'I waited for you to come back, you know. Dad always said, "Don't worry, Claire-Bear. She's your sister; she'll be back." I waited and waited. What happened?'

Meghann sighed heavily, as if she'd known this conversation couldn't be avoided any more. 'Remember when Mama went down for the *Starbase IV* audition?'

'Yes.'

'She didn't come back. I was used to her being gone for a day or two, but after about five days I started to panic. There wasn't any money left. We were hungry. Then Social Services started sniffing around. I was scared they'd put us in the system. So I called Sam.'

'I know all this, Meg.'

'He said he'd take us both in.'

'And he did.'

'But he wasn't *my* father. I tried to fit in to Hayden; what a joke. I got in with a bad crowd and started screwing up. Every time I looked at you and Sam together, I felt left out. You were all I really had, and then I didn't have you. One night I came home drunk and Sam told me to shape up or get out.'

'So you got out. Where did you go?'

'I bummed around Seattle for a while. Then one day I remembered a teacher who'd taken an interest in me, Mr Earhart. He had convinced me that education was the way out of Mama's trailer-trash life. That's why I always got straight A's. Anyway, I gave him a call—thank God he was still at the same school. He arranged for me to graduate high school early and take the SAT, which I aced. Perfect score. The UW offered me a full scholarship. You know the rest.'

'My genius sister,' Claire said. For once, there was pride in her voice instead of bitterness.

'I told myself it was the best thing for you, that you didn't need your big sister any more. But I knew how much I'd hurt you. It was easier to keep my distance, I guess. I believed you'd never forgive me. So I didn't give you the chance.'

'The only thing you did wrong was stay away,' Claire said.

'I'm here now.'

'I know.' Claire looked out to the sparkling blue water. 'I couldn't have done all this without you.'

'That's not true. You're the bravest person I ever met.'

'I'm not so brave, believe me.'

Meghann leaned back to open the picnic basket. 'I've been waiting for just the right time to give you this.' She withdrew a manilla folder and handed it to Claire. 'Here.'

Claire took the folder with a sigh. It was the one labelled HOPE. Her hands trembled as she opened the file.

In it were almost a dozen personal accounts of people who had had glioblastoma multiforme tumours. Each of them had been given less than a year to live—at least seven years ago.

Claire squeezed her eyes shut, but the tears came anyway. 'I needed this today.'

'I thought so.'

She swallowed hard, then dared to look at her sister. 'I've been so afraid.' It felt good, finally admitting it.

'Me, too,' Meg answered quietly. Then she leaned forwards and took Claire in her arms.

For the first time since childhood Claire was held by her big sister. Meghann stroked her hair, the way she'd done when Claire was young. A handful of hair fell out at Meghann's touch.

Claire drew back, saw the pile of her pretty blonde hair in Meghann's hand. 'I didn't want to tell you it's been falling out. Every morning I wake up on a hairy pillow.'

'Maybe we should go home,' Meg said finally.

'I *am* tired.'

Meghann helped Claire to her feet. Slowly they made their way back to the car. Claire leaned heavily on Meg's arm.

Back in the apartment, Meghann helped Claire change into her flannel pyjamas and climb into bed.

'It's just hair,' Claire said. 'It'll grow back.'

'Yeah.' Meghann set the HOPE file on the nightstand and backed out of the room. At the doorway she stopped.

Her sister lay there, with her eyes closed. Tears leaked down the sides of her face, leaving tiny grey splotches on the pillow.

And Meghann knew what she had to do.

She closed the door and went to the phone. All of Claire's emergency numbers were on a notepad beside it. Including Bobby's.

In the past twenty-four hours Claire had lost almost half her hair. This morning, as she got ready for her appointment, she spent nearly thirty minutes wrapping a silk scarf round her head.

'Quit fussing,' Meghann said when they arrived at the nuclear medicine waiting room. 'You look fine.'

'I look like a Gypsy fortune teller. And I don't know why you made me wear make-up.'

Claire left for her treatment and was back in the waiting room thirty minutes later. She didn't bother putting the scarf back on.

'Let's go out for coffee,' she said when Meghann stood up.

'I have to go into the office. I've got a deposition scheduled.'

'Oh.' Claire followed Meghann down the hospital corridor, trying to keep up. Lately she was so tired, it was hard not to shuffle like an old woman. She practically fell asleep in the car.

At the apartment door, Meghann paused, key in hand, and looked at her. 'I'm trying to do what's right for you. What's best.'

'I know that.'

'Sometimes I screw up. I tend to think I know everything.'

Claire smiled. 'Are you waiting for an argument?'

'Just remember that I'm trying to do the right thing.'

'OK, Meg. I'll remember. Now go to work. I don't want to miss *Judge Judy*. She reminds me of you.'

'Smart-ass.' Meg opened the apartment door. 'Bye.'

Claire went into the apartment, closing the door behind her. Inside, the stereo was on: Dwight Yoakam's 'Pocket of a Clown'.

Claire turned the corner, and there he was. Bobby.

Her hand flew to her bald spot. She ran to the bathroom, flipped open the toilet lid and threw up.

He was behind her, holding what was left of her hair back, telling her it was OK. 'I'm here now, Claire. I'm here.'

She closed her eyes, holding back tears of humiliation one breath at a time. He rubbed her back.

Finally she went to the basin and brushed her teeth. When she turned to face him, she tried to smile. 'Welcome to my nightmare.'

He came towards her, and the love in his eyes made her want to weep. 'Our nightmare, Claire.'

She didn't know what to say. She was afraid that if she opened her mouth, she'd burst into tears.

'You had no right to keep this from me.'

'You'd dreamed of singing for so long.'

'I dreamed of being a star, yeah. I like singing, but I *love* you. I can't believe you'd hide this from me. What if . . .'

Claire caught her lip between her teeth. 'I'm sorry. I was just trying to love you.'

'I wonder if you even know what love is. "I'm in the hospital every day, honey, battling for my life, but don't you worry about it, just sing your stupid songs." What kind of man do you think I am?'

'I'm sorry, Bobby. I just . . .' She stared at him.

He pulled her towards him and held her so tightly, it made her gasp. 'I love you, Claire. I *love* you,' he said fiercely. 'When are you going to get that through your head?'

She wrapped her arms round him, clung to him. 'I guess my tumour got in the way, but I get it now, Bobby. I get it.'

Hours later, when Meghann returned to the apartment, the lights were off. She tiptoed through the darkness.

When she reached the living room, a light clicked on.

Claire and Bobby lay together on the sofa, their bodies entwined. He was snoring gently.

'I waited up for you,' Claire said.

Meghann tossed her briefcase on the chair. 'I had to call him, Claire.'

'This is the second time you've called a man to come and save me.'

'You're lucky to be so loved.'

Claire's gaze was steady. 'Yeah,' she said, smiling at her sister. 'I am.'

The days passed slowly; each new morning found Claire a little more tired than the night before. She strove to keep a positive attitude, but her health was deteriorating rapidly.

The Bluesers came down often, separately and together, doing their best to keep her spirits up. The hardest times were weekends, when they went to Hayden; Claire tried to pretend for Ali that everything was OK.

In the evenings, though, it was just the three of them—Claire, Meg and Bobby—in that too-quiet apartment. At first, when Bobby arrived, they'd tried to spend the evenings talking or playing cards, but that had proved difficult. Too many dangerous subjects. None of them could mention the future without thinking, Will there be a Christmas together? A Thanksgiving? So, by tacit agreement, they'd let the television become their night time soundtrack. Claire was grateful; it gave her several hours where she could sit quietly, without having to pretend.

Finally the radiation ended.

The following morning, Claire got up early. She dressed and drank her coffee out on the deck. It amazed her that so many people were already up, going about their ordinary lives on this day that would define her future.

'Today's the day,' Meg said, stepping out to join her.

Behind them, the glass door opened. 'Morning, ladies.' Bobby came up behind Claire and kissed the back of her neck.

They stood there a minute longer, no one speaking; then they turned together and left the apartment.

In no time they were at the hospital. As they entered the waiting room, Claire noticed the other patients who wore hats and scarves. When their gazes met, a sad understanding passed between them. They were members of a club you didn't want to join. Claire wished now that she hadn't bothered with the scarf. Baldness had a boldness to it that she wanted to embrace.

There was no waiting today, not on this day that would answer all the questions. She checked in and went to the MRI. Within moments she was pumped full of dye and stuck in the loud machine.

When she was finished, she returned to the waiting room and sat between Meghann and Bobby. She held their hands.

Finally they called her name.

Claire rose. Bobby steadied her. 'I'm right here, babe.'

The three of them began the long walk, ending finally in Dr Sussman's office. The plaque on the door read CHIEF OF NEUROLOGY. Dr McGrail, the chief of radiology, was also there.

'Hello, Claire. Meghann,' Dr Sussman said. 'Bobby.'

'Well?' Meghann demanded.

'The tumour responded to radiation. It's about twelve per cent smaller,' Dr McGrail reported.

'That's great,' Meg said.

The doctors exchanged a look. Dr Sussman went to the view box, switched it on, and there they were, the grey and white pictures of Claire's brain. He turned to Claire. 'The decrease has bought you some time. Unfortunately, the tumour is still inoperable. I'm sorry.'

Sorry.

Claire sat down in the leather chair. She didn't think her legs would hold her up. 'How long do I have?'

Dr Sussman's voice was gentle. 'The survival rates aren't good. Some patients live as long as a year. Perhaps a bit longer.'

'And the rest?'

'Six to nine months.'

Claire stared down at her brand-new wedding ring, the one Grandma Myrtle had worn for six decades.

Meghann went to Claire then, dropped to her knees in front of her. 'We won't believe it. The files—'

'Don't,' she said, shaking her head, thinking about Ali. She saw her baby's eyes and sunburst smile, Heard her say, 'Here, Mommy, you can have my wubbie till you get all better,' and tears ran down her cheeks. She felt Bobby beside her, and she knew he was crying, too. She wiped her eyes, looked up at the doctor. 'What's next?'

Meghann jerked to her feet and began pacing the room, studying the pictures and diplomas on the walls. Claire knew her sister was scared and, thus, angry.

Dr Sussman pulled a chair round and sat down opposite Claire.

'We have some options. None too good, I'm afraid, but—'

'Who is this?' Meghann's voice sounded shrill. She was holding a framed photograph she'd taken off the wall.

Dr Sussman frowned. 'That's a group of us from medical school.' He turned back to Claire.

Meghann slammed the photograph on the desk so hard, the glass cracked. She pointed at someone in the picture. 'Who's that guy?'

Dr Sussman leaned forwards. 'Joe Wyatt.'

'He's a *doctor*?'

Claire looked at her sister. 'You know Joe?'

'*You* know Joe?' Meghann said sharply.

'He's a radiologist, actually.' It was Dr McGrail who answered. 'One of the best in the country. At least he was. He was a legend with MRIs. He saw things—possibilities—no one else did.'

Claire frowned. 'Meghann, let go of it. We're long past the need for a radiologist. And believe me, Joe wouldn't be the one to ask for help. What I needed was a miracle.'

Meghann said to McGrail, 'What do you mean he *was* the best?'

'He quit. Disappeared, in fact.'

'Why?'

'He killed his wife.'

Chapter Ten

THE RIDE HOME seemed to last for ever. No one spoke. When they got to the apartment, Bobby held Claire so tightly she couldn't breathe, then stumbled back from her. 'I need to take a shower,' he said in a broken voice.

She let him go, knowing what he needed. She'd cried a few tears of her own in Meghann's expensive glass-block shower.

She went to the sofa, collapsed on it. She was tired and dizzy. There was a ringing in her ears and a tingling in her right hand, but she couldn't admit any of that to Meghann.

Meg sat down on the coffee table, angled towards her. 'There are all kinds of clinical trials going on—'

Claire held up a hand. 'Can we be real for just a minute?'

Meghann looked stricken. 'What?' she demanded.

'When I was little, I used to dream about getting some rare illness that would bring you and Mama to my bedside. I imagined you crying over my death.'

Meg stood up so abruptly, she banged her shin on the coffee table and swore harshly. 'I . . . can't talk about you dying. I can't.' She couldn't get out of the room fast enough.

'But I need you to,' Claire said to the empty room. A headache started behind her eyes again. It had been lurking nearby all day. She started to lean back into the sofa, when the pain hit. She gasped at it, tried to cry out. Her head felt as if it were exploding.

She couldn't move, couldn't breathe. Alison, she thought.

Then everything went dark.

Meghann stood by her sister's bed, holding on to the metal bed rails. 'Is the medication helping?'

Claire looked small in the hospital bed, delicate, with her pale, pale skin and patchy hair. Her attempt at a smile was heart-rending. 'Yeah. A grand mal seizure. Welcome to my new world. How long will I be here?'

'A few days.'

'It's time to call Mama.'

Meghann flinched. Her mouth trembled. 'OK.'

'Tell Dad, Ali and the Bluesers they can come to see me, too.'

Meghann heard the defeat in her sister's voice. She wanted to make her sister angry enough to fight, but her voice abandoned her.

'I'm going to go to sleep,' Claire said. 'I'm tired.'

'It's the meds.'

'Is it?' Claire smiled knowingly. 'Good night. And take care of Bobby tonight, OK? He's not as strong as he looks.'

A few minutes later Bobby walked into the room, looking haggard. His eyes were red and swollen.

'She woke up,' Meghann said. 'And went back to sleep.'

'Damn it.' He took Claire's hand in his. 'Hey, baby. I'm back. I just went for a cup of coffee.' He sighed. 'She's giving up.'

'I know. She wants me to call everyone. Tell them to come and see her. How do we tell Ali this?' Tears stung her eyes.

'I'll tell her,' Claire said quietly, opening her eyes. She smiled tiredly at her husband. 'Bobby,' she breathed, 'I love you.'

Meghann couldn't stand there another second. 'I've got phone calls to make. Bye.' She raced from the room.

It was late now, and the hallways were quiet. She went to the bank of payphones and dialled Mama's number.

'It's me, Mama. Meghann. Claire's sick.'

'She's on her honeymoon.'

'That was a month ago, Mama. Now she's in the hospital.'

'This better not be one of your stunts, Meggy. Like the time you called me at work 'cause Claire had fallen out of bed, and you thought she was paralysed.'

'She has a brain tumour, Mama. The radiation treatments didn't work and no one has the guts to operate on her.'

There was a long pause. Then, 'Will she be OK?'

'Yes,' Meghann said, because she couldn't imagine any other response. Then, very softly, she said, 'Maybe not. You should come and see her. Without your entourage, Mama. Alone.'

'I've got a *Starbase IV* event tomorrow at two, and a—'

'Be here tomorrow, or I call *People* magazine and tell them you didn't visit your daughter who has a brain tumour.'

'I'm no good with this sort of thing.'

'None of us are, Mama.' Meghann hung up, then punched in the 800 number on her calling card and dialled Sam. The phone rang, but she lost her nerve. She couldn't tell Sam this over the phone.

She slammed the receiver onto the hook and went back to her sister's room. Bobby stood by the bed, singing softly to Claire, who snored gently. It brought Meghann up short.

Bobby looked up at her. Tears glistened on his cheeks. 'She hasn't opened her eyes again.'

'She will. Keep singing. I'm sure she loves it.'

'Yeah.' His voice cracked.

Meg had never seen a man in so much pain. 'I'm going to go tell Sam. If Claire wakes up—' She caught herself. '*When* Claire wakes up, tell her I'll be back soon. Do you have your keys to my place?'

'I'll sleep here tonight.'

'OK.' Meghann left the room.

She practically ran for her car. Once inside, she headed north.

Ninety minutes later she reached Hayden. She slowed down through town, stopped at the light.

And there it was: the corrugated-iron hut.

Joe Wyatt.

Dr Joseph Wyatt. Of course. No wonder he'd looked familiar. His trial had been front-page news.

He's a radiologist. One of the best in the country. It came rushing back to her now, the stunning news that had been lost somehow, buried beneath a thick layer of grief.

Yet when she'd come to him, sobbing about her sick sister, he'd done nothing. Nothing. And he *knew* Claire.

'Son of a bitch.' She glanced sideways. The envelope containing copies of Claire's most recent MRI films was on the passenger seat.

Meghann turned the wheel hard and slammed on the brakes, parking along the kerb. Then she grabbed the envelope and marched towards the cabin. She pounded on the door, screaming, until she heard footsteps coming from inside.

When he opened the door, saw her, and said, 'What—' she shoved him in the chest so hard, he stumbled backwards.

'Hey, Joe. Invite me in.' She kicked the door shut behind her.

'It's practically midnight.'

'So it is, *Doctor* Wyatt.'

He sank onto the sofa and looked up at her.

'You held me. You let me cry in your arms.' Her voice trembled. 'And you offered *nothing*. What kind of man are you?'

'The kind who knows his hero days are behind him. If you know who I am, you know what I did.'

'You killed your wife.' At his flinch she went on. 'Your trial was a big deal in Seattle. The prosecution of the doctor who euthanised his dying wife.'

'Euthanasia is a prettier word than manslaughter.'

Some of the steam went out of her at the sadness in his voice. 'Look, Joe, in an ordinary world I'd talk to you about what you did. But it's not an ordinary world right now. My sister is dying.' She tossed the oversized manila envelope onto the coffee table in front of him. 'These are her MRI films. Maybe you can help her.'

'I let my licence lapse. I can't practise medicine any more. I'm sorry.'

'Sorry? *Sorry?* You have the power to save people's lives, and you hide out in this dump of a cabin feeling sorry for yourself?' She stared down at him, wanting to hate him, hurt him, but she couldn't imagine how to do either one. 'I *cared* about you.'

'I'm sorry,' he said again.

'I'll send you an invitation to the funeral.' She turned on her heel and headed for the door.

'Take this with you.'

She stopped, gave him one last withering look. 'No, Joe. You'll have to touch them. Throw them in the trash yourself.'

Then she left. She made it to her car before she started to cry.

Outside the trailer, Meg sat in her car, trying to compose herself. Every time she opened her compact to fix her make-up, she looked at her watery eyes and it made her cry all over again.

Finally she got out of the car and walked up to the trailer.

Sam opened the door before she knocked. He stood there, frowning, his eyes watery. 'I wondered how long you were going to sit out there.'

'I thought you didn't know I was here.'

He tried to smile. 'You always did think you were smarter than me.'

'Not just you, Sam. I think I'm smarter than everyone.' She wanted to smile but couldn't.

'How bad is it?'

'Bad.' When she said it, the tears came back. She wiped them away.

'Come here,' Sam said gently, opening his arms.

Meg hesitated.

'Come on.'

She surged forwards, let him hold her. She couldn't seem to stop crying. Then he was crying, too.

When they finally drew back, they stared at each other. Meg had no idea what to say.

Suddenly there were footsteps in the hallway. Ali came running out, dressed in pink pyjamas, carrying her Groovy Girl. She looked up at Meg. 'Do we get to go see Mommy now? Is she all better?'

Meg knelt down and pulled her niece into her arms, holding her tightly. 'Yeah,' she said in a throaty voice. 'You get to see Mommy tomorrow.'

Claire grew weaker. By her second day in the hospital she wanted simply to sleep.

Her friends and family had begun showing up religiously. All of them. Even Mama. The Bluesers had descended on her tiny hospital room, bringing life and laughter, flowers and fattening food. They talked and told jokes and remembered old times. Only Gina had had the guts to brave the harsh, icy landscape of Claire's fear.

'I'll always be there for Ali, you know,' she said when everyone else had gone to the cafeteria.

'Thank you,' was all Claire was able to say. Then, softly, 'I haven't been able to tell her yet.'

'How could you?'

Gina's eyes met hers, filling slowly with tears. They'd both been thinking about how a woman said goodbye to her five-year-old daughter. After a long pause Gina smiled. 'So what are we going to do about your hair?'

'I thought I'd cut it off. Dye what's left of it platinum.'

'Very chic. We'll all look like old housewives next to you.'

'That's my dream now,' Claire said, unable to help herself. 'Becoming an old housewife.'

Ultimately, as much as she loved to see her friends, she was glad when they went home. Late that night, in the quiet darkness, she gave in to the meds and fell asleep.

She woke with a start. Her heart was pounding too fast, skipping beats. She couldn't seem to breathe. Something was wrong.

'Claire, are you OK?' It was Bobby. He'd obviously been sleeping. Rubbing his eyes, he stood up, came to her bedside.

'Bobby,' she whispered, 'get into bed with me.'

He looked at all the machines, the IVs, the tubes and cords. 'Oh, baby . . .' He leaned down and kissed her instead.

She closed her eyes, feeling herself sinking into the pillows. 'Ali,' she whispered. 'I need my baby—'

Pain exploded behind her right eye.

Beside her bed an alarm went off.

There is no pain. No ache. The tubes that connect her to the machines are gone. She wants to shout out that she is better.

She realises suddenly that she is watching herself from above—watching the doctors work on her body. They've ripped open her gown and are ramming something on her chest.

'Clear!' one yells.

There is such relief in being above them, where there is no pain.

'Clear.'

Then she thinks of her daughter, her precious baby girl, who will have to be told that Mommy has gone away.

The doctor stepped back. 'She's gone.'

Meghann ran to the bed, screaming. 'Don't you do it, Claire. Come back. Come back, damn it.'

Someone tried to pull her away. She elbowed him hard. 'I mean it, Claire. You come back. You cannot run out on Alison this way.' She grabbed Claire's shoulders, shook her hard. 'Don't you dare.'

'We have a heartbeat,' someone cried out.

Meghann was pushed aside. She stumbled back into the corner of the room, watching, praying, as they stabilised her sister.

Finally the doctors left, dragging their crash cart with them. Meg stared at Claire's chest, watching it rise and fall.

'I heard you, you know.'

At Claire's voice Meg moved forwards.

There was Claire, pale as parchment, smiling up at her. 'I thought, "God, I'm dead, and she's still yelling at me."'

Joe had tried to throw out the damn envelope at least a dozen times. The problem was, he couldn't bring himself to touch it.

Coward.

He heard the word so clearly, he looked up. The cabin was empty. He stared at Diana, who looked back at him from the mantelpiece.

He didn't need to conjure up her image to know what her words would be right now. She would be as ashamed of him as he was of himself. She would remind him that he'd once taken an oath to help people. And not just anyone, either. This was Claire Cavenaugh, the woman who'd sat by Diana's bedside hour after hour when she was ill, playing dirty-word Scrabble and watching soap operas.

Now it was Claire in a bed like that, in a room that smelt of despair. If she were here right now, Diana would have told him that chances didn't come any plainer than this. It was one thing to run away from nothing. It was quite another to turn your back on a set of films with a friend's name in the corner.

He released a heavy breath and reached out, pretending not to notice that his hands were shaking. He pulled out the films and took them into the kitchen, where full sunlight streamed through the window above the sink. As he studied them, he knew why everyone had diagnosed this tumour as inoperable. The amount of skill needed to perform the surgery was almost unheard-of. It would require a neurosurgeon with godlike hands and an ego to match. But with a careful resection there might be a chance. It was possible—just possible—that this one thin shadow wasn't tumour, that it was tissue responding to the tumour.

Stu Weissman. The cowboy. Stu Weissman at UCLA might be able to do it. Joe glanced at the clock. He knew he couldn't reach Stu on the phone until the afternoon.

There was no doubt about what he had to do next.

He took a long, hot shower, then dressed in the blue shirt he'd recently bought and the new jeans, wishing he had better clothes, accepting that he didn't. Then he retrieved the film, put it back in the envelope and walked over to Smitty's house. Smitty was in the living room, watching TV. He looked up. 'Hey, Joe.'

'I know this is irregular, but could I borrow the truck? I need to drive to Seattle. I may have to stay overnight.'

Smitty dug in his pocket for the keys, then tossed them.

'Thanks.' Joe went to the rusty old '73 Ford pick-up and got inside. The door clanged shut behind him.

He stared at the dashboard. It had been years since he'd been in the driver's seat. He started the engine and hit the gas.

Two hours later he parked in the underground garage on Madison and Broadway and walked into the lobby of his old life.

When the elevator doors pinged open, he stepped inside. Two white-coated people crowded beside him, talking about lab results. They got off on the second floor—the floor that led to the sky bridge that connected this office building to Swedish Medical Center.

He couldn't help remembering when he'd walked through this building with his head held high.

On the thirteenth floor the doors opened. He stood there half a second too long, staring at the gilt-edged black letters on the glass doors across the hall: SEATTLE NUCLEAR SPECIALISTS. The business he'd started on his own. There were seven or eight doctors listed below. Joe's name wasn't there.

He walked past the row of women waiting for mammograms, then turned onto another hallway. At the far end he took a deep breath and knocked on a door.

'Come in,' said a familiar voice.

Joe entered the big corner office that had once been his. Li Chinn was at his desk, reading. At Joe's entrance he glanced up. An almost comical look of surprise overtook his face. 'I don't believe it.'

'Hey, Li.'

Li looked awkward, uncertain of how to proceed, what to say. 'It's been a long time, Joe.'

'Three years.'

'Where did you go?'

'Does it matter? I have some film I'd like you to look at.'

At Li's nod, Joe went to the view box and put the film up. Li came closer, studying it. For a long moment he said nothing. Then, 'You see something I do not?'

Joe pointed. 'There.'

Li crossed his arms, frowned. 'Not many surgeons would attempt such a thing. The risks are grave.'

'She's going to die without the surgery.'

'She may die because of the surgery.'

'You think it's worth a try?'

Li looked at him, his frown deepening. 'The old Joe Wyatt never asked for other men's opinions.'

'Things change,' he said simply.

'Do you know a surgeon who would do it? Who *could* do it?'

'Stu Weissman at UCLA.'

'Ah. The cowboy. Yes, maybe.'

'I can't practise. I've let my licence lapse. Could you send Stu the film? I'll call him.'

Li flicked off the light. 'I will. You know, it's an easy thing to reinstate your licence.'

'Yes.' Joe stood there a moment longer. Silence spread like a stain between the men. He started to leave.

'Wait.' Li moved towards him. 'Privately many of us would have wanted to do the same thing. Diana was in terrible pain. There was no hope. We thank God that we were not in your shoes.'

Joe had no answer to that.

'You have a gift, Joe,' Li said. 'Losing it would be a crime. When you're ready, come back to see me. This office is in the business of saving lives, not worrying about old gossip.'

'Thank you.' They were small words, too small to express his gratitude. Embarrassed by the depth of his emotion, Joe mumbled thanks again and left the office.

Down in the lobby, Joe found a payphone and called Stu Weissman.

'Joe Wyatt,' Stu said loudly. 'How are you? I thought you fell off the face of the earth. Damn shame, what you went through.'

Joe didn't want to waste time with the where-have-you-been stuff. He said, 'I have a surgery I want you to do. It's risky as hell. You're the only man I know who is good enough.'

'Talk to me.'

Joe explained what he knew of Claire's history, told him the current diagnosis, and outlined what he'd seen on the film.

'And you think there's something I can do?'

'Only you.'

'Well, Joe. Your eyes are the best in the business. Send me the film. If I see what you do, I'll be on the next plane. But you make sure the patient understands the risks.'

'You got it. Thanks, Stu.'

Joe replaced the receiver. Now he had to speak to Claire.

He went back to the elevators, then crossed the sky bridge and headed into Swedish Hospital. A few people frowned in recognition; a few more whispered behind him. But no one had the guts to speak to him until he reached the intensive-care unit. There someone said, 'Dr Wyatt?'

He turned slowly. It was Trish Bey, the head ICU nurse. She and Diana had become close friends at the end. 'Hello, Trish.'

She smiled. 'It's good to see you back here. We missed you.'

His shoulders relaxed. He almost smiled in return. 'Thanks.' They stood there, staring at each other for an awkward moment; then he headed for Claire's room. He knocked quietly and opened the door.

She was sitting up in bed, asleep, her head cocked to one side. He moved towards her, trying not to remember when Diana had looked like this. Pale and fragile, her hair thinning to the point where she looked like an antique doll that had been loved too hard and then discarded.

She blinked awake, stared at him. 'Joey,' she whispered, smiling tiredly, 'I heard you were home. Welcome back.'

He sat down beside her bed. 'Hey, Claire.'

'I know. I've looked better.'

'You're beautiful. You always have been.'

'Bless you, Joe. I'll tell Di hi for you.' She closed her eyes. 'I'm sorry, but I'm tired.'

'Don't be in such a hurry to see my wife.'

Slowly she opened her eyes. 'There's no hope, Joe. You of all people know what that's like. It hurts too much to pretend. OK?'

'I see it . . . differently.'

'Are you telling me I shouldn't give up?'

'Surgery might save you. But there could be bad side effects, Claire. Paralysis. Loss of motor skills. Brain damage.'

'Do you know what I was thinking just before you got here?'

'No.'

'About how to tell Ali Kat that Mommy is going to die. I'd take any risk, Joe. Anything so I don't have to kiss Ali goodbye.'

'I'm sending your films to a friend of mine. If he agrees with my diagnosis, he'll operate.'

'Thank you, Joe,' she said softly, then closed her eyes again.

He leaned down and kissed her forehead. 'Bye, Claire.'

He was almost to the door when she said, 'Joe?'

He turned. 'Yeah?'

'She shouldn't have asked it of you.'

'Who?' he asked, but he knew.

'Diana. I would never ask such a thing of Bobby. I know what it would do to him.'

Joe had no answer to that. It was the same thing Gina always said. He left the room and closed the door behind him. With a sigh, he leaned against the wall and closed his eyes. *She shouldn't have asked it of you.*

'Joe?'

He opened his eyes and stumbled away from the wall. Meghann stood a few feet away, her eyes reddened and moist.

She walked towards him. 'Tell me you found a way to help her.'

'I've spoken to a colleague at UCLA. If he agrees with me, he'll operate, but—'

Meghann launched herself at him, clung to him. 'Thank you.'

'It's risky as hell, Meg. She might not survive the surgery.'

Meghann drew back, blinked away her tears. 'We Sullivan girls would rather go down fighting. Thank you, Joe. And . . . I'm sorry for the things I said to you. I can be a real bitch.'

'The warning comes a little late.'

She smiled, wiped her eyes again. 'You should have told me about your wife, you know.'

'In one of our heart-to-heart talks?'

'Yeah, in one of those.'

'It's hardly good between-the-sheets conversation. How do you make love to a woman, then tell her that you killed your wife?'

'You didn't kill her. Cancer killed her. You ended her suffering.'

'And her breathing.'

Meghann looked up at him steadily. 'If Claire asked it of me, I'd do it. I'd be willing to go to prison for it, too.'

'Pray to God you never have to find out.' His voice broke.

'What do we do now?' she said. 'For Claire, I mean.'

'We wait to hear from Stu. And pray he agrees with my assessment.'

The next morning Stu Weissman called Claire. She was so groggy, it took her several seconds to understand him.

'Wait a minute,' she finally said, sitting up. 'Are you saying you'll do the surgery?'

'Yes. But there could be a bad outlook all the way round. You could end up paralysed or brain damaged or worse.'

'Worse sooner, you mean.'

He laughed at that. 'Yes.'

'I'll take the chance.'

'Then I will, too. I'll be there tonight. I've scheduled the surgery for eight a.m. tomorrow.' His voice softened. 'I don't mean to be negative, Claire. But you should put your affairs in order today. If you know what I mean.'

'I know what you mean. Thank you, Dr Weissman.'

All that day Claire said goodbye to her friends.

To Karen she joked about the grey hairs Willie was sure to cause in the upcoming years. To Charlotte she said, 'Don't give up on babies; they're the mark we leave in this world. If you can't have one of your own, find one to adopt.' Gina was more difficult. For almost an hour they were together, Claire dozing off now and then. 'Take care of my family,' she said at last.

They all pretended Claire would still be there tomorrow night. She left her friends with that faith, and though she wanted to own it for herself, hope felt like a borrowed sweater that didn't quite fit.

Time and again throughout the long day, she found herself wishing that she'd died already, simply floated from this world unexpectedly. The thought of the goodbyes she still had left was devastating. Bobby and Sam would hold her and cry, Meg would get angry and loud, and then there was Ali. How could Claire possibly get through *that*?

Claire must have fallen asleep again. When she woke, the sunlight outside had faded, leaving the room a soft, silvery colour.

'Mommy's awake.'

She saw her daughter clinging to Meghann like a little monkey, arms wrapped round her neck, feet locked round her waist.

Claire made a whimpering sound before she rallied and pulled out a tired smile. The only way to get through this moment was to pretend there would be another. For Ali, she had to believe in a miracle.

'Hey there, Ali Kat.' Claire opened her arms. 'Come here.'

Meg leaned forwards and gently deposited Ali into Claire's thin arms. She hugged her daughter tightly. She was battling tears and hanging on to her smile by a thread when she whispered into her daughter's tiny, shell-pink ear, 'You remember how much I love you.'

'I know, Mommy,' Ali said, burrowing closer. She lay still as a sleeping baby, quieter than she'd lain in years. That was when Claire knew that Ali understood. Her daughter leaned close to say, 'I told God I'd never ask for Cap'n Crunch again if He made you all better.' Claire clung to Ali for as long as she could. 'Take her home,' she said when the pain became more than she could bear.

Meghann was there instantly, pulling Ali into her arms again.

But Ali wiggled out of Meg's grasp and slithered to the moulded plastic chair beside the bed. She stood there on the wobbly chair, staring at Claire. 'I don't want you to die, Mommy,' she said.

It hurt too much even to cry. 'I know that, darling, and I love you more than all the stars in the sky. Now skedaddle on home with

Grandpa and Bobby. They're going to take you to see a movie.'

Meghann picked Ali up again. Claire could see that she was near tears, too. 'Make Bobby go home,' she said to her sister. 'Tell him I said Ali needs him tonight.'

Meg reached out, squeezed her hand. 'We need *you*.'

'I need to sleep now,' was all Claire could think of to say.

Hours later Claire came awake with a start. For a split second she didn't know where she was. Then she saw the flowers and the machines. If she squinted, she could make out the wall clock. Moonlight glinted on the domed glass face. It was four in the morning.

In a few hours they'd crack her skull open.

She started to panic, then saw Meg was in the corner, sprawled in one of those uncomfortable chairs, sleeping.

'Meg,' she whispered, hitting her control button; the bed tilted upwards. 'Meg,' she said in a louder voice.

Meghann sat upright and looked around. 'Is it time?'

'No. We have four more hours.'

Meghann dragged the chair over to the bed. 'Did you sleep?'

'Off and on.' Claire glanced out of the window at the moonlight. Suddenly she was so afraid, she was shaking. 'Do you remember what I used to do when I had a nightmare?'

'You used to crawl into bed with me.'

'Yeah. That old cot in the trailer's living room.' Claire smiled. 'When I got into bed and you hugged me, I thought nothing could hurt me.' She looked up at Meghann, then very gently peeled back the blanket.

Meghann hesitated, then climbed into bed with Claire, drawing her close.

'How come we forgot all the things that mattered?' Claire asked.

'I was an idiot.'

'We wasted a lot of time.'

'I'm sorry,' Meg said. 'I should have said that a long time ago.'

Claire reached for Meg's hand. 'I'm going to ask you something, Meg, and I can't ask this twice; saying each word is like swallowing broken glass. If the worst happens, I want you to be a part of Ali's life. She'll need a mother.'

Meg squeezed Claire's hand tightly. Long seconds passed before she answered, 'I'll make sure she always remembers you.'

Claire nodded; she couldn't speak.

After that, they lay in the darkness, each holding the other one together until dawn lit the room and the doctors took Claire away.

Meghann stood at the window staring out at the jumble of beige buildings across the street. In the three hours since they'd taken Claire to surgery, Meghann had counted every window.

Someone tugged on her sleeve. Meghann looked down. There was Alison, staring up at her.

'I'm thirsty.'

'OK, honey,' Meg said, scooping Ali into her arms. She carried her down to the cafeteria.

'I want a Pepsi Blue. That's what you got me last time.'

'It's only eleven in the morning. Juice is better for you.'

'You sound like Mommy.'

Meg swallowed hard. 'Did you know your mommy loved Tab when she was little? But I made her drink orange juice.'

Meghann paid for the juice, then carried Alison back to the waiting room. But when she leaned over to put Ali down, the girl squeezed harder.

'Oh, Ali,' Meg said, holding her niece. She wanted to promise that Mommy would be better, but the words caught in her throat. She sat down, still holding Ali, and stroked her hair. Within minutes the child was asleep.

From across the room Gina looked up, then went back to her crossword puzzle. Sam, Mama, Bobby, Karen and Charlotte were playing cards. Joe sat off in the corner reading a magazine. He hadn't looked up in hours, hadn't spoken to anyone.

Around noon the surgical nurse came out, told them all that it would be several more hours. 'You should get something to eat,' she said. 'It won't help Claire if you all pass out.'

Sam nodded, stood up. 'Come on,' he said to everyone. 'Let's get out of here for a while. Lunch is on me.'

'I'll stay here,' Meghann said. 'Ali needs the sleep.'

When they'd gone, Meghann leaned back in her chair, rested her head against the wall. It seemed like yesterday that Meg had held Claire this way, telling her baby sister everything would be OK.

'It's been four hours, damn it. What're they all doin' in there?'

Meg looked up. Mama stood there, holding an unlit cigarette. Her make-up had faded a little, smudged off in places, and without it she looked faded, too. 'I thought you went out for lunch with everyone.'

'Eat *cafeteria* food? I don't think so. I'll eat dinner in my hotel suite.'

'Have a seat, Mama.'

Her mother collapsed into the plastic chair beside her. 'This is the worst day of my life. And that's sayin' something.'

One hour bled into the next until finally, around four o'clock, Dr Weissman came into the waiting room. Meghann tightened her hold on Ali and got to her feet. Bobby stood up next; then Sam and Mama; then Joe, Gina, Karen and Charlotte. The doctor managed a tired smile.

'The surgery went well.'

'Thank God,' they whispered together.

'But she's not out of the woods. The tumour was more invasive than we thought.' He looked at Joe. 'The next few hours will tell us more.'

Chapter Eleven

CLAIRE WOKE UP in recovery feeling groggy and confused. A headache pounded behind her eyes. She was about to hit her call button and ask for some pain relief when it struck her: she was alive!

She tested her memory by trying to list all the towns she'd lived in as a child, but she'd only made it to Barstow when the first of the nurses came in. After that, she was poked and prodded and tested until she couldn't think.

By the second full post-op day Claire had become irritable. She hurt now; her body ached everywhere, and the bruises on her forehead from the iron halo had begun to throb like hell.

When it was time for her postoperative MRI, Claire visualised a clean, clear scan of her brain, saw it so clearly that by the time it was over, her cheeks were wet with tears.

Waiting for the results was unbearable. Meghann paced the small hospital room. Bobby squeezed Claire's hand so tightly, she lost all feeling in her fingers. Sam came in every few minutes.

Finally Claire's nurse returned. 'The docs are ready for you.'

Little things got Claire through the wheelchair ride—the warmth of Bobby's hand on her shoulder, the way Meghann stayed close.

When they entered the office where Claire's doctors were waiting, Dr Weissman was the first to speak. 'Good morning, Claire.'

'Good morning,' she answered. The men waited for Meghann to sit down. Eventually they realised that she wasn't going to.

Dr Weissman clicked on the view box. Claire studied the films of her brain, then looked up at the men. 'I don't see any tumour.'

Dr Weissman smiled. 'I think we got it all, Claire.'

'Oh my God.' She'd hoped for this, prayed for it.

'Initial lab reports indicate that it was a low-grade astrocytoma.'

'Not a glioblastoma multiforme? Thank God.'

'Yes. That was good news. Also, it was benign.'

One of the other doctors stepped forwards. 'You are a very lucky woman. Dr Weissman did an incredible job. However, as you know, most brain tumours will regenerate. Twenty-eight per cent—'

'Stop!' Claire didn't realise that she'd yelled out the word until she saw the startled looks on the doctors' faces. 'I don't want to hear your statistics. It was benign, right?'

'Yes, but benign in the brain is a rather misleading term. All brain tumours can ultimately be fatal, benign or not.'

'Yeah. Yeah,' Claire said. 'But it's not a cancer that's going to spread through my body, right?'

'Correct.'

'So it's gone now, and it was benign. That's all I want to hear. You can talk to me about treatments from here on, but not about survival rates.' She smiled at Meg. 'My future is sunny.'

Only Dr Weissman was smiling. He crossed the room and bent down to her ear. 'Good for you.'

She looked up at him. 'There are no words to thank you.'

'Joe Wyatt is the man you should thank. Good luck to you.'

As soon as she was back in her room, Claire broke down and cried. Bobby held her tightly, until finally she looked up at him. 'I love you, Bobby. Now go get our little girl.'

He hurried out.

'You were amazing in there,' Meg said when they were alone.

'My new motto is "Don't screw with Baldie".'

'I won't.' Meg grinned.

Claire reached for her sister's hand, held it. 'Thanks.'

Meg kissed Claire's forehead and whispered, 'We're sisters.' It was answer enough. 'I'll go get Mama now. She'll probably bring a film crew.' With a smile Meghann left the room.

'The tumour is gone,' Claire practised saying aloud to the empty room. Then she laughed.

Meghann found everyone in the cafeteria. Bobby was already there, talking to Sam. Mama was at the food line, signing autographs. The Bluesers and Alison were sitting in the corner, talking quietly among themselves. The only one missing was Joe.

'And there I was,' Mama was saying to a rapt audience, 'all ready to take the stage in a dress that wouldn't zip up. I am *not*,' she said, laughing, 'a flat-chested woman, so y'all can imagine—'

'Mama?' Meghann said, touching her arm.

Mama spun round. When she saw Meghann, her smile faded. For a moment she looked vulnerable. 'Well?' she whispered.

'Go on up, Mama. It's good news.'

Mama sighed heavily. 'Of *course* it is. Y'all were so dramatic.' She turned back to her audience. 'I hate to leave in the middle of a story, but it seems my daughter has made a miraculous recovery. I am reminded of a television movie I once did, where . . .'

Meghann walked away.

'Auntie Meg!' Alison said, jumping up, throwing herself at Meg, who scooped her up and kissed her. 'My mommy is all better!'

At that a whoop went up from the Bluesers. 'Come on,' Gina said to her friends. 'Let's go see Claire.'

Bobby walked up to Meghann. 'Come on, Ali Gator,' he said, pulling the little girl into his arms. 'Let's go kiss Mommy.' He started to walk away, then paused and turned back. Very gently he kissed Meghann's cheek, whispered, 'Thank you.'

Meghann closed her eyes, surprised by the depth of her emotion. When she looked up again through a blur of tears, Sam was coming towards her. He reached out, touched her cheek.

'You've been Claire's rock through this nightmare,' he said softly. 'You have the kind of heart that saves people. And I'm sorry I didn't see that when I was younger.'

'A lot of things have become clearer lately.'

'Yeah.' It was a moment before he said, 'I'll expect you at the house this Thanksgiving. None of your lame excuses. We're family.'

Meg thought of all the years she'd declined Claire's offer. Then she thought of last Thanksgiving, when she'd eaten raisin bran for dinner by herself. All that time she'd pretended that she wasn't lonely. No more pretending for her, and no more being alone when she had a family to be with. 'Just try to keep me away.'

Meghann went to the elevators and rode down to the lobby, then headed outside. It was a glorious sunny day. Everything about the city felt sharper, cleaner. She walked downhill, thinking about so many things—her life, her job, her family.

Maybe she'd change her career, practise a different kind of law. Or maybe she'd start a business, sort of an informational clearing-house for people with brain tumours. The world seemed wide open to her now, full of new possibilities.

It took her less than half an hour to walk home. She was just about to cross the street, when she saw him, standing outside the front door of her building.

When he saw her, Joe pulled away from the wall he'd been leaning against and crossed the street. 'Gina told me where you lived.'

'Stu told you about the MRI?'

'I spent the last hour with him. It looks good for Claire.'

'Yeah.'

He moved towards her. 'I'm tired of not caring, Meg,' he said softly. 'And I'm tired of pretending I died when Diana did.'

She looked up at him. They were close now, close enough for him to kiss her if he chose. 'What chance do we have, a couple like us?'

'We have a chance. It's all any of us gets.'

'We could get hurt.'

'We've survived it before.' He touched her face tenderly; it made her want to cry. 'And maybe we could fall in love.'

She gazed up into his eyes and saw a hope for the future. She saw a little of the love he was talking about, and for the first time she believed in it. If Claire could get well, anything was possible. She put her arms around him and pressed onto her toes. Just before she kissed him, she dared to whisper, 'Maybe we already have.'

Epilogue
One Year Later

THE NOISE WAS DEAFENING. The fairgrounds were packed with people—kids screaming from the carnival rides, parents yelling after them.

Alison was up ahead, dragging Joe from ride to ride. Meghann and Claire walked along behind, talking softly, carrying the collection of stuffed animals and cheap glass trinkets that Joe had won. Claire's limp was the only physical reminder of her ordeal, and it was getting less pronounced each day. Her hair had grown out; it was curlier and blonder than before.

'It's time,' Claire said, signalling to Joe. The four of them fell in line together, walking past the refreshment stand and turning left towards the fairgrounds' bleachers.

'There's a crowd already,' Claire said. She sounded nervous.

'Of course there is,' Meghann said.

'Hurry, Mommy, hurry!' Alison was bouncing up and down. At the special side door, Claire showed her backstage pass. They made their way through the staging area, past the musicians and singers who were warming up.

Bobby saw them coming and waved. Alison ran for him. He scooped her into his arms and twirled her round. 'My daddy's gonna sing tonight,' she said loud enough for everyone to hear.

'I sure am.' Bobby looped an arm round Claire and pulled her in for a kiss. 'Wish me luck.'

'You don't need it.'

They talked to him for a few more minutes, then left him to get ready. They climbed the bleachers and found their seats in the fourth row. Meghann helped Claire sit down; her sister was still unsteady sometimes.

'Kent Ames called last week,' Claire said. 'Mama ripped him a new one for cancelling Bobby's contract.'

'She's been cussing him out for months.'

'I know. It seems he wants to give Bobby another chance, after all. Said he hopes Bobby's *priorities* are straight this time.' Claire smiled.

A man took the stage and announced, 'Bob-by Jack Austin!'

The crowd applauded politely.

Alison jumped up and down, screaming, 'Yay, Daddy!'

Bobby leapt up onstage with his guitar. He scanned the audience, found Claire and blew her a kiss. 'This song is for my wife, who taught me about love and courage. I love you, baby.' He strummed the guitar and started to sing. His beautiful voice wrapped round the music and mesmerised the crowd. He sang about finding the woman of his dreams and falling in love with her, about standing by her side in dark times. In the final stanza his voice fell to a throaty whisper; the crowd leaned forwards to hear the words:

> 'When I saw you stumble
> over rocks along the way
> I learned the truth of real love
> and the gift of one more day.'

The applause this time was explosive. Half the women in the audience were weeping.

Meghann put an arm round her sister. 'I *told* you he'd make a great husband. I really liked that guy from the first moment I saw him.'

Claire laughed. 'Yeah, right. And what about you and Joe? You guys are practically living together. It looks to me like maybe there's a prenuptial agreement in your future.'

Meghann looked at Joe, who was on his feet, clapping. Alison was in his arms. Since he'd started practising medicine again, he said anything was possible. They'd taught each other to believe in love again. 'A prenup? Me? No way. We were thinking about a small wedding. Outside—'

'Where it rains? Where bugs breed? *That* outside?'

'Maybe with hamburgers and hot dogs and—'

'Gina's potato salad.'

They both said it at the same time and laughed.

'Yeah,' Meghann said, leaning against her sister. 'That kind of wedding.'

KRISTIN HANNAH

Like Meghann, the take-no-prisoners divorce attorney in *Between Sisters*, Kristin Hannah trained for a career in the law. In fact, she was at law school when she made her first attempt at writing fiction. At the time her mother was terminally ill with breast cancer and to occupy themselves during hospital visits, they began to write a historical romance together. It was set in Scotland, and every day Kristin would stop at the Seattle library to pick up piles and piles of research material with which to inspire their brainstormings. 'I showed neither the talent nor the inclination to be an author,' Kristin recalls. 'The first chapter, written in purple ink, was pretty bad, though my mother was sure I had a writing career ahead of me. And when she eventually turned out to be right . . . well, I know she sees it all and reads everything I write, even though she's not here.'

Kristin Hannah passed her law exams and was practising entertainment law when she became pregnant with her son. After going into premature labour, she had to spend the rest of the pregnancy in bed. 'Here I was, the classic law-school joke: practise for a year and then fall pregnant. I felt like a failure,' Kristin recalls. Her husband made the suggestion that while she had some free time, she might use it to write a novel. She took his advice, selling the novel to a publisher when her son was two. He's now fifteen— and Kristin has published eleven successful best sellers.

Kristin Hannah feels that her legal studies, and motherhood, have helped to give her the discipline she needs to be a writer. As a working mother she needs to be highly organised and motivated when she is writing. 'There never seems to be a typical day,' she admits. 'My writing schedule revolves around my real-life obligations: that endless list of ordinary chores that consume my time. However, I do try to write in school hours—then I take a great deal of time off in the summer and during the holidays so that I can be with my family. The tradeoff for that is long hours from September to June. In a perfect world, I begin writing at around nine in the morning. How long I spend at it is largely dependent on where I am in the book. In the first draft, which I write long hand, I can only work for four or five hours at a time. After that, as the novel begins to take shape, my ability to concentrate increases. By the end of the process, I am often working ten to twelve hour days. This is my favourite time. Scenes and chapters and characters often end up on the cutting-room floor, but I begin to see the end. By this time, I know my characters as well as I know myself. Things begin to simply feel right. It's normal to spend hours on a single page, looking for exactly the right turn of phrase. Honestly, I never believe I'm done, but sooner or later my deadline arrives and I'm forced to say "enough". I am so lucky —writing fiction is one of the joys of my life.'

Jane Eastgate

Janice Graham
Safe Harbour

The restoration of St John's, an American cathedral in the centre of Paris, is not proving an easy task for Father Crispin Wakefield. Just at a time when his home life, too, has become rather stormy. Then, on a misty autumn evening, as he contemplates his problems, a figure steps out of the shadows; a woman from his past, from a time when life was so very different . . .

❧ ONE ☙

IF YOU ARE IN PARIS in the late autumn you will notice how a sadness settles over the city. The air turns brittle cold and the drizzled grey sky becomes a spiritual force driving the soul inwards, just as the rain drives the sodden leaves into the damp earth. Things get buried in the autumn. Light diminishes. The clocks are rolled back, morning comes in a dull, heavy-lidded stupor, and night falls early.

It was nearly dark and the street lamps had already come up through the city when Father Crispin Wakefield set off from the cathedral on the Avenue George V. The broad avenue was beautiful and alive with light from hotels with grand names like the Prince de Galles and the King George, and all the boutiques and bistros seemed to swell with radiance. It was splendid the way the city sprang up in defiance of the darkness.

This time of year was always difficult for Father Wakefield. He shrank inwardly with the coming winter, and when Tuesday at 5 p.m. rolled round he dragged himself out of the warmth of his study, loaded up his motorcycle, fastened on his black and red helmet and struck out across the city. It was easy to pick him out as he wobbled through traffic in his yellow slicker, weaving recklessly down the avenue towards the river. The cathedral loomed behind him, a stationary and steadfast thing.

Father Wakefield knew where he could find the miserable ones, especially now with winter coming on. They wouldn't come into a place like the cathedral. They hated those images and icons. So he took himself out to them. He carried with him a little food and medicine, toothbrushes and soap, and he always wore his clerical collar.

There were times when he was greeted with hostility and times when they insulted him, and his French was good enough now to understand what they were saying. He was never offended, but that was his nature. He did what he could; he fed those who needed feeding and listened to what they had to say. If someone needed medical care he would get them to a hospital. Sometimes the best thing was just a little laughter and a smile.

On this afternoon the traffic along the *quai* in front of Châtelet was so dense even motorcycles couldn't advance. No one was moving and it had started to rain. Crispin noticed a girl—not much older than his daughter Megan—sitting on the kerb hugging her knees, her head down and face hidden, a cheap sports bag at her side. She looked up and he could tell by her eyes that she was in trouble.

Crispin was good at reading people and he believed she had made herself visible for a reason. He ran his motorcycle up onto the pavement, removed his helmet and knelt down beside her.

There was still that shock, and sometimes fear, when you came up against lives being lived so differently from your own. This is why Crispin always finished his goodwill tours with a drink—most often at Harry's Bar or the Cricketer. The Cricketer on the Rue des Mathurins was boisterous and inviting, and tonight Crispin needed cheering up. He stood a better chance of running into a familiar face at the Cricketer, so that's where he headed.

Rhoderic was standing at the end of the bar shovelling peanuts into his mouth. He was a barrister and very dignified-looking, and he would work for free for his friends.

The priest shook out his slicker and hung it on a hook, placing his helmet on the rack above. Rhoderic waved him over.

'Hey, Crispin! Good to see you. Tough day?'

'Yep.' Crispin wedged himself into a space at the bar, and Rhoderic slid the peanuts towards him. Crispin shook his head. 'Real sad. Found a sixteen-year-old girl who'd just tested positive for HIV.'

'Bloody hell.'

'That about sums it up.' Crispin ordered a Scotch on the rocks and then said, 'Poor kid just got the results and was wandering around.'

'No home?'

'Not around here. Some little village down near Nîmes, she said.'

'What did you do?'

'Oh, you know. A little counselling. Something hot to drink and a sandwich. I got her to call her folks at least. They're driving up to get her in the morning. I got her a hotel room for the night.'

Crispin reached for the Scotch as soon as it came. He took a long drink and it tasted good and burned away a little of the sadness.

'If I went around paying for hotel rooms for strange women, my wife would slay me,' Rhoderic said.

Crispin shrugged. 'I just slap it on a credit card.'

'Oh, that's right. You Americans all run around with your private lines of credit.'

'Middle-class welfare.'

'Damn nuisance, all this mess.'

'Yes, it is.' Crispin wasn't quite sure what he meant, but he got the general drift.

'We might do things differently if we didn't have our families.'

Rhoderic had six children from three different wives. Crispin only had three, all girls, and Paris had taught them a thing or two about spending money.

'Well, on a lighter note, I thought you might want to see this.' Rhoderic bent down to the briefcase between his feet and withdrew that day's *Herald Tribune*. 'Didn't you say you knew her?'

'Who?'

Rhoderic pointed to a name in bold-faced type: JULIA KRAMER.

Crispin took the paper from him and looked at the photograph of Julia standing between her husband and a British director who had shot one of the films that had brought her recognition. It showed them deep in conversation, and Julia, with that limpid smile of hers, had her eyes on Jona. The men were in tuxedos and Julia wore earrings that looked very expensive. Jona looked like he always did in the pictures Crispin had seen of him—a bald man with a satin-smooth smile and gimlet eyes obscured by thick, black-rimmed glasses. They were at a gala to celebrate the sale of the King George Hotel to a British hotel chain. The caption said that Jona was the new hotel president. It also mentioned that Julia was to begin shooting a new film with the director.

'The King George is right up the street from you.'

Crispin nodded.

'Didn't you say you grew up together?'

'Yeah. They were our closest neighbours. They farmed a little land.'

'You should look her up.'

Rhoderic stuffed the paper back into his briefcase and Crispin thought about it while he drained the last of his Scotch. Casting a glance at his reflection in the mirror behind the pretty bottles of rums and cognacs and gins, he wondered if there was anything in his face she might remember or even like.

'Oh, I don't know,' he answered Rhoderic. 'Been a long time.' He glanced at his watch. 'I've got to go. Got to find a birthday present.'

'Whose birthday?'

'Megan. My eldest.'

'How old is she?'

'Coming up to fourteen. An expensive age.'

'It only gets worse.'

The rain had stopped. Crispin unlocked the motorcycle and headed up Boulevard Haussmann towards the big department stores. Along the way he looked for a kiosk where he could buy a copy of the *Herald Tribune*. He found one and folded the paper tightly and slipped it inside his jacket pocket. He knew now why that lost girl on the kerb had wounded him so with her look. She had Julia's eyes.

As Canon of St John's, Crispin was given lodgings adjacent to the cathedral, as was the Dean, who had a spacious apartment with its own private entrance off Avenue George V. The rectory where the canon resided nestled in the shadow of the imposing cathedral walls. It was a stone cottage built in the Gothic style of the cathedral, with ornamented windows and pointed arched doorways that reminded Lola, Crispin's youngest daughter, of Sleeping Beauty's castle.

The cottage had suffered waves of renovation over the century, resulting in some curious fixtures. There was a deep square tub where you had to bathe in a seated position, and a toilet built into the top step of what used to be the stairway to the attic and appropriately referred to as the throne room. There were no fitted cupboards, only the wardrobes where Lola would hide to read her picture books by the light of her Tinker Bell torch. Her favourite wardrobe was the one in her parents' room because it held Phoebe's fox coat and she loved the smell of the warm furs and her mother's perfume. Secretly she believed that one day the back would open up and she would enter Narnia.

The only real disadvantage the Wakefields found with the rectory was that their front door opened onto the courtyard just opposite the cloisters that led to the offices and reception halls of the cathedral. Phoebe often complained that she could be overheard every time she raised her voice, and she was tired of jokes about her cooking ('My goodness, is Phoebe roasting lamb again?').

Tuesday was Phoebe's night out and Crispin always ordered pizza to be delivered to their door. Lola called it their American night, but as he glanced round the tiny kitchen for a place to set the boxes it looked like they had never left America. The work surface was cluttered with brand names like Old El Paso salsa and open bags of Doritos and Pringles.

'Who was that?' Phoebe shouted from the hallway. Her shoes made sharp clicking sounds on the hardwood floor.

'Pizza man,' he called back.

She appeared in the doorway with her earrings in her hand. Phoebe was tiny with sculpted features, but she was anything but fragile; she had been working as a personal trainer when Crispin met her.

'You called them already?'

'Lola said she was hungry.'

Crispin set down the pizzas and turned to look at his wife. She was stunning in a lizardskin-like jacket trimmed with chartreuse-tinted fur.

'You look nice.'

'Don't glare at me like that. I got it in a sale.'

'I wasn't aware that I was glaring.'

She had a way of tightening her jaw when she thought she was being unfairly accused, and she looked away while she worked an earring through her ear.

He said, 'I got a birthday present for Megan.'

She was having trouble with the earring. 'Oh, Cris, I told you I'd get her something tomorrow. You don't even know what she wants.'

'I got her a silver necklace. With a little horse on it.'

'I hope you can take it back. The French are so unreasonable about that.'

'Maybe she'll want to keep it.'

'I doubt it. She's very picky about her jewellery.'

Megan was passionate about horses and competed in shows every other Sunday. Crispin could never go, which was just one of many reasons why his eldest daughter was estranged from him.

Phoebe walked away from him to the bedroom, while she screwed the back on the other earring. You couldn't help but notice Phoebe's walk, and the high-heeled shoes. She wore black fishnet stockings that were quite the rage but reminded Crispin of Halloween. Everyone admired Phoebe's style, but for Crispin it had become a burden.

He found Lola in the living room watching *The Little Mermaid*, which is what she did when her sister Cat needed the bedroom to study. There were only three bedrooms in the cottage, so Lola shared a room with Cat. There was seven years' difference between the two sisters, and Crispin thought the arrangement was unfair to Cat, but Megan would no more consent to share her room than to carry a bucket of petrol into hell. It had been a workable solution because Lola was a quiet child and compliant, two character traits foreign to the rest of the family.

The five-year-old sat upright on the sofa, her thin little legs pointed at the television screen. She wore a Tigger dressing gown over her *Lion King* pyjamas, and *101 Dalmatians* slippers dangled from her toes.

'Hey, kiddo. Dinner's here. Where shall we eat?'

She turned her face up to him, but a response was not forthcoming.

'I thought we'd make it a picnic night. Spread out a tablecloth on the floor. That OK with you?'

She turned her attention back to Ariel, who was being chased through a sunken ship by a shark. Crispin interpreted her silence as agreement and opened the sideboard and took out a tablecloth. He spread it on the floor in front of the television.

'Shall we use a candle?'

Lola thought for a moment, then nodded her head.

'Go wash your hands,' he said, and she hit the pause button, then slid to the floor and dashed off towards the bathroom.

When she returned, the tablecloth was spread with cheese pizza and Coke and carrot sticks. Lola smiled, and Crispin imagined he saw a little of himself in her face, but he knew better. She sat crosslegged next to him, then folded her hands under her chin and tilted her face upwards where she imagined God to be. She pronounced a hasty grace, and Crispin sneaked a look at her while her eyes were shut.

They were interrupted by Caitlin's voice in the hallway. 'Is the pizza here already?'

'In the oven.'

'Somebody could've told me.' She sounded miffed.

'I didn't think you'd be hungry yet.'

The oven door squeaked open, there was a rustling of boxes, then Caitlin's voice rose in an exasperated cry.

'Dad, didn't you get pepperoni?'

'Last time nobody ate it.'

'We always get pepperoni!'

Caitlin was overweight—not excessively so, but along with her braces it was enough to make adolescence seem like a steep climb to Golgotha. Crispin had acquired a sensitivity to these issues and had learned patience.

'Sorry, Cat. I'll remember next time.'

She grumbled loudly while slamming a few kitchen cupboards and he let it pass, knowing that next week she would be on a diet again and would not touch the pepperoni.

Caitlin passed Megan in the hallway on her way back to her room and Crispin noted with relief that there was no exchange of words—their mutual silence signifying there were no current grievances to be aired.

344

He did not like to deal with Megan. She had acquired a sense of empow-erment no child should have, a problem that was Phoebe's doing. She was Phoebe's monster; and only Phoebe could contain her.

Megan stepped barefoot over their tablecloth, barely missing the bowl of carrot sticks, and leaned over the coffee table to rifle through a stack of magazines. Even at home, when she was lounging around or doing homework, Megan had an acute sense of fashion. At the moment she was wearing skimpy tartan boxer shorts slung low around her hips and Phoebe's black silk tank top. Only Megan dared enter her mother's wardrobe and help herself to whatever took her fancy, and Megan's fancy changed several times a day.

Crispin said, 'Pizza's in the oven if you want some.'

'I'm not hungry,' she mumbled, but then she looked up and showered them with an unexpected smile. 'You two look like you're having fun.'

'Sure you don't want to join us?'

'Right, like I'm just dying to watch *The Little Mermaid*.'

Her thick honey-blonde hair hung loose around her shoulders and she smiled again in an artless way that ensnared the heart. Just then Crispin felt in the pit of his stomach that raw love of parent for child. Wholly unsentimental and instinctive.

'Dad, you didn't take my magazine, did you?'

'What magazine?'

'The new *Teen People*. Mom just got it for me today.'

'Haven't seen it, honey.'

'Well, I can't find it. Cat!' she shouted. 'Did you take my magazine?'

Lola visibly flinched at her sister's raised voice. She covered her ears with her hands.

'Cat!' screamed Megan.

'No!' came the reply from down the hall. 'Why would I read your stupid magazines?'

'Well, it's not here!'

Crispin watched in awe as she vented her frustration on cover models and politicians and editorial reviews. Magazines and newspapers sailed to the floor.

'Shit,' she muttered.

'Megan!'

They were saved by the melodic jingle of Megan's mobile phone, which she carried with her from room to room.

'Hello?' she answered sweetly, and her face became all radiance and joy. 'Hey,' she said, and hurried from the room, leaving the magazines strewn around the floor.

'Saved by the bell,' Crispin said with a nudge to Lola and she looked up at him and giggled.

They were alone again with Ariel and her underwater friends. Megan and Caitlin never ate with them. He understood they needed a break from routine, but it hurt him that their hallowed family mealtime lost its sanctity whenever Phoebe was out. Only Lola enjoyed his company. He had concluded that five was a perfect age.

Crispin was in bed but still awake when Phoebe returned. He looked up from St Thomas Aquinas and removed his glasses as she kicked off her shoes.

'Did you have a good time?'

'The restaurant was awful.'

'Where'd you go?'

'This very chic place on top of the Pompidou Centre. Gerry recommended it.' She unbuttoned the lizard jacket revealing a beige and pink lace bra that Crispin had never seen before.

'How was the food?'

'Very mediocre and very expensive.'

Crispin took refuge behind St Thomas. He had repeatedly asked Phoebe to be sensitive to their financial situation, but she felt a certain appearance had to be maintained as wife of the Canon. The Dean's wife, Geraldine, was the self-appointed doyenne of an elite circle of churchwomen, who knew every bit of gossip worth knowing and many things Crispin would have liked to know. At best, he considered her dinners a necessary business expense; Phoebe was his intelligence operative, although he was not totally convinced of her loyalty.

She slid in next to him and clicked on her bedside lamp. 'Cris?'

'Yeah?'

'You know, at one time last year we talked about getting a horse for Megan. Can we think about it again?'

'Sure. Thinking doesn't cost me anything.'

'Is it totally out of the question?'

'Yes.'

He did not look up from his book; he did not want to meet her gaze.

'Isn't there any money at all left from the company?'

He took a deep breath and tried to focus his attention on the words of the saint. 'There hasn't been any money left in years.' She knew this, and he wondered why she was so stubborn about it, as if she suspected him of hoarding savings in a Swiss bank.

'I just can't believe it. What happened to all of it?'

'I can give you an exact account if you want. But it'll take me a few weeks.'

She answered in a peeved voice. 'It was a rhetorical question. You don't need to get sarcastic.'

'I wasn't being sarcastic. It would honestly take me that long.'

If there was anything Phoebe hated, it was accountability, particularly where money was concerned.

'Well, I just thought it would be a good idea. It's such a healthy sport.'

'And an expensive one.'

'They would get outdoors, Crispin. They miss the outdoors. And these schools are just hopeless when it comes to sports.'

'You're just talking about Megan, aren't you? Cat doesn't ride.'

'She might want to if we had a horse. There's one at the stables that's up for sale. A beautiful *selle française*.'

'We can't afford it, Phoebe.'

He waited tensely, trying to gauge her reaction. He would have liked to turn and read the look on her face, penetrate behind her eyes. Phoebe did not dissemble well and there were always clues. He closed his book and reached to turn out his light.

Phoebe got up and threw on her robe. 'I'll read downstairs,' she announced flatly as she flipped off her reading lamp.

After she had gone, Crispin threw back the blanket and dropped to his knees beside the bed. It was an old habit, but Phoebe found it annoying. She thought prayers must surely be as effective stretched out in a warm bed as on one's knees. Crispin was inclined to agree, but he did not kneel to make himself heard. He wanted to empty his mind and free his spirit, and he would have lain prostrate on the cold wood floor if it would have helped.

This night his mind did not want to settle down, and he took deep purging breaths to cleanse his brain. Moments passed and he was almost there, nearing that still place where he found his strength.

Into this vacuum swept Julia, not so much as thought but as image. He did not see her the way she appeared in the photograph in the paper, but as she was at the age of fifteen, the year she went away. The image was incomplete, eroded by time, but it left the unmistakable impression of Julia, the startling eyes and impish smile. Just as quickly as it appeared, the image faded from his mind, and he was left with an inexplicable heaviness of heart.

When Phoebe returned, he was still pondering the significance of this brief yet potent resurrection of his past. She crawled into bed without turning on the light. She did not even notice he was still on his knees.

⁂ TWO ⁂

SOMETIMES, IN THE EVENING, Crispin would slip across the courtyard and let himself in to the cathedral. His favourite spot was on the chancel steps below the altar, where he liked to sit and meditate. At times he would stretch out on his back on the floor behind the railing to study the vaulted ceiling; he found it so relaxing that on occasions he had been known to fall asleep.

The cathedral changed when empty like this, without the crowds of people, and much of the time he came here just to feel the cold draughts of her breath and listen to her silence. On cloudless nights, pale traces of moonlight filtered through her darkened glass windows and infused the air with opaque light, and Crispin imagined she was somehow impregnated with everything she had ever witnessed and heard, with all the vanity and prejudice and loneliness and hope that humanity had laid silently at her door.

On this Friday evening Crispin had come in to rehearse a sermon he was to give the following Sunday—a privilege Dean Noonan allowed his canons only when he was out of town. Public speaking still terrified Crispin. Back at his old church in Chicago he had taken to drinking a beer before the service each Sunday to steady his nerves, and here in Paris he kept a small reserve of Beaujolais in his study for such occasions. His phobia was aggravated by the fact that Dean Noonan's oratorical skills were far superior to his own.

During his initial interview four years ago, Crispin had sized up the Dean—a graduate of Princeton's school of theology who prided himself on his reputation as an intellectual powerhouse—as a man of ambition. That afternoon Dean Noonan had made it clear that all he really wanted was a self-effacing canon to perform weddings and carry the burden of pastoral care. It would fall to Crispin, were he to be so called, to oversee what the Dean felt privately to be the dullest work in his parish: ministering to the sick, the grieving, the troubled, the dying. It was a fact of life that pride and ambition ran rampant through the ranks of the clergy just as in secular sectors of society, but Crispin was vexed by the hubris of some of his brethren.

Crispin's role was greatly enhanced when his entrepreneurial experience became known and he was put in charge of the cathedral renovation project, but he still looked forward to those rare Sundays when he could stand in the pulpit and address his parish. He had spent two weeks writing what he hoped would be an enlightening sermon on the manifestation of the Holy Spirit. After running through it once from the pulpit he stepped down and stretched out on his back on a pew and recited it in his head.

It was six o'clock in the evening and the Dean's secretary was just leaving; she always left like clockwork because she had a train to catch. You always knew it was her because of the sharp clicking sound her heels made on the marble walk. When she had gone, Crispin felt a deep silence settle over the cathedral. The typed manuscript slid to the floor and he folded his hands over his chest and closed his eyes.

It wasn't always easy to recognise Julia Kramer, even if you knew her name and had seen her films. Julia's face had a mysterious way of transforming itself, which was one of the things directors found so intriguing. It changed dramatically when captured under a certain light or at a certain angle, or depending on how her hair was styled. Whether she wore it wild and loose or pulled back to reveal her wide forehead, slender arched brows and dreamy eyes.

This is why the Dean's secretary didn't recognise her when she passed her on the steps. Julia stopped her and asked for Father Wakefield and the secretary told her he was probably in the chancel.

Julia was not at home in churches. The cathedral was cold and eerily silent, and she was afraid to make the slightest sound. She took a few steps forwards and the echo of her footsteps in the great emptiness made her feel very small.

She had been trying to reconcile the image of a priest with her memories of Crispin Wakefield, and now she tried to imagine him behind the towering pulpit, hands gripping the lectern, looking down on the congregation. Strangely, she could picture him up there, the boy whose strength of character had remained so vividly in her memory.

At the same time she felt a little sad about it. Priests are celibate men, she thought. They do not marry and produce offspring and fight with their wives. She had always imagined Crispin would go on to live a conventional life.

She felt uncomfortable standing there with his note in her hand; the one he had left at the hotel just this morning. She could not imagine what they would have in common. It had been so long ago, and for so many years she had clung to the image of Crispin as her saviour. Then Jona had come along and there was no need to cling to memories.

She smiled to herself, stuffed the note into the pocket of her coat and approached the altar down the long central aisle. The chancel was roped off with a scarlet cordon, and after a moment's hesitation she unhooked it and went up the stairs past the choir and stopped in front of the altar.

She did not see Crispin, but she heard him; a faint rumbling snore that startled her. She gasped and whirled round just in time to see an equally startled priest rise from the pew where he had been sleeping and scurry to his feet.

It was his appearance that confused her; he seemed so very ordinary, a man of average height and build with longish hair greying at the temples, and a kind of eccentric disregard for appearance that you sense in people who have serious things to do in the world and who cannot be bothered with matching socks.

'Cris!'

She approached the choir and gazed up at him with her mouth open to form some kind of exclamation but she could only shake her head.

'Julia,' he pronounced in a low voice. 'I never imagined . . .'

'So you're a priest?'

'I'm a priest,' he nodded. 'I can't get over you. Standing here. All grown up.'

'And growing old.'

'Oh, no. You're in your prime.'

'Hollywood doesn't seem to think so.'

'So you got my message.'

She smiled. 'Read it about a dozen times since this morning.'

He climbed down to where she stood and when he reached her the smile faded and she said in a voice that ached with tenderness, 'I always hoped I'd see you again.'

'Hey,' he smiled, and took her hands in his. 'I'm glad to see you.'

They were interrupted by the sound of a girl's voice behind them.

'Dad?'

Crispin turned and smiled at Cat standing below the chancel steps. She wore a sweatshirt and jeans and looked very American. 'Come here, honey,' he motioned. 'I want you to meet somebody very special.'

Cat was unsettled by the sight of her father and this woman she had never seen before, and the way they stepped back from one another when she approached.

'Julia, this is my daughter, Caitlin.'

'Hello, Caitlin.'

'This is Julia Kramer.' Cat showed no recognition, only wary scrutiny.
'Hello,' said Cat.

Julia picked up on Crispin's embarrassment, and she crinkled up her
nose with a smile and said to him in a low voice, 'Not the same genera-
tion, Cris.'

'Hey, Cat's my film buff,' he defended.

But then Caitlin's eyes grew wide. 'Oh, you're Julia!' She smiled, and
the tension ebbed. 'Dad's got all your films.'

Julia looked pleased and said to him, 'Do you really?'

Cat interrupted to say, 'Hey, Mrs Fleming called. You have to call her
back right away. It's urgent, she said.'

'Oh, no,' Crispin muttered. 'It's probably her husband. He's been sick.'

He thanked Cat, but she remained there watching them. Finally,
Crispin said, 'Tell your mom I'll be right up.'

'OK.'

Unwillingly, she turned and left.

Julia whispered, 'You have a child?'

'Sure.'

'So you're not Catholic?'

'No. Episcopalian.'

'So you're a priest, but not a celibate one?'

'That's right.'

She looked genuinely relieved, and he laughed.

'I was trying to imagine you like that . . . and I just couldn't.'

'Good grief, neither could I. I have three daughters.'

'Three?'

'And a wife.'

She smiled, genuinely pleased. 'Then you must be very, very happy.'

It seemed such a strange assumption that she should equate the two.

'Well, I came to all this'—he gestured at the altar—'after my first two
were born. It was what you might call an early midlife crisis.'

'And you're happy,' she repeated. She seemed to want to believe this.

'I made the right choice. I have no doubts about that.' But then he
added in a low, somewhat drier voice, 'But I'm sure Phoebe does.'

'Phoebe?'

'My wife.'

'What a delightful name. I'll bet she's beautiful.'

'I hope you'll meet them all.'

'I'd love to.'

'Can you come for lunch on Sunday? With Jona, of course.'

'Jona's away. He's in New York.'

'Then come on your own. Come to the service. I'm giving the sermon.'

The smile froze on her face. Crispin added quickly and with a grin, 'It's not a long sermon. I try not to bore.'

'Oh, it's not that.' She reached out and touched his arm in a reassuring manner. 'I just haven't been to church for so long.' She glanced behind Crispin, and her eyes swept across the high altar to the triptych painting. 'I didn't know this was an American cathedral.'

'We're a very friendly bunch.'

She seemed to relax a little then, and said, 'Of course I'll come.'

'Eleven o'clock.'

She leaned forward and gave him a light kiss on the cheek, and he caught the sweet scent of her perfume. 'I look forward to it.'

He watched from the chancel as she disappeared into the shadows. Then he re-attached the scarlet cordon, gathered up the pages of his sermon and exited through the back, throwing the light switch on the wall and sending the cathedral into darkness.

He went home and straight to the kitchen, where he found Phoebe and Megan putting away groceries. The way both of them fell silent and turned their backs to him meant that Cat had told them. He drew a deep breath and then told Phoebe he had invited Julia Kramer to lunch on Sunday. It took Phoebe a moment to recover because she had not expected him to be so forthright and she had a suspicious mind.

Megan asked, 'Is this that actress? The one you grew up with?'

'Yep.'

'Cool.'

'Well, we'll go out,' Phoebe said. 'I don't want to cook.'

'I'd rather entertain here,' Crispin said.

'Cris, you know how I hate cooking Sunday lunch. There is absolutely no privacy here on Sunday—the kitchen window looks straight out onto the cloisters and I feel like I'm on display. And you're giving the sermon so I know you'll be a nervous wreck. Let's just go out.'

'Eating out's expensive.'

'We can leave the girls at home.'

Megan cried, 'No! I want to go!'

'That sort of defeats the whole purpose,' Crispin replied.

'I do not want to cook Sunday lunch.'

But Crispin wouldn't argue with her and Phoebe had learned that after a certain point it was useless so she just set her jaw and started thinking about the menu.

'We'll have lamb.' She said it like a threat.

'Lamb's fine. You do good lamb.'

'Lamb is what we always have when we invite guests for Sunday.'

'Then do something else.'

'Anything else is too much work.'

'Do roast beef.'

'I won't eat roast beef,' Megan cried. 'We'll get mad cow disease.'

Crispin sighed. 'Lamb is fine, Phoebe.'

He kissed her gently on the cheek and left the kitchen to call Mrs Fleming. What Phoebe didn't see was the turmoil in his chest and how badly he felt about not being able to afford to take them all out to lunch. In the end it was all about money.

Paris was not a bad spot for ambitious priests, and although Dean Noonan's French was not as good as it should have been, he was certainly fluent enough to sparkle in interviews with radio and television stations whenever they needed a spokesperson from the Anglican or American community. He was very dapper and his black hair and china-blue eyes looked good on television. He taught a class in theology at the American University, wrote scholarly papers that were published in journals, and travelled a lot. He never seemed to be around when you needed a definitive answer or some emergency erupted.

After a while everyone began to notice how Crispin could handle crises in a decisive and reassuring manner, so it was only a matter of time before the staff began to look to Crispin as the man who got things done. And although you quickly learned never to badmouth the Dean to Father Wakefield, you knew he would listen to legitimate complaints and try to handle them as best he could. Increasingly people left Dean Noonan to his scholarly pursuits, and questions and problems got rerouted to Crispin's desk. At first the Dean was only too happy to pass off all these annoying details but then he noticed the change.

When Crispin had arrived at the cathedral four years before, they were in the early stages of a government-mandated restoration and cleaning of the cathedral's façade and tower. They had already gathered estimates, obtained bids and managed a successful campaign to help cover the costs estimated at over four million francs. Tom Noonan was good at the fundraising and you could count on him to come back from Dallas and Washington, DC with his pockets full of pledges from American Friends of St John's.

The actual restoration and cleaning was a mammoth undertaking, and there wasn't really any one person overseeing it all, but committees, and within the committees were factions and some powerful personalities. After Crispin arrived they began coming to him to sort out their differences. He was always calm and level-headed and for some reason he didn't inspire jealousy, but most of all they saw how much he loved the cathedral. The first time he climbed up on the roof with the architect and the senior warden, and got down on his hands and knees and saw for himself the holes, crumbled the rotting wood between his fingers and caressed the broken stones the way a man would caress the woman he loved, they knew how he felt about it.

The *ravalement* was a massive undertaking, and the firm that had done the restoration of the Eiffel Tower was commissioned to do the job. Once the scaffolding went up and they had built a steel cocoon around the north façade and the tower, you could take the elevator up and walk along steel-girded corridors in the sky and look out at the city spread below. Crispin would go up whenever he could to watch the sculptors and masons as they worked. There were stones to be polished and stones to be sanded down to remove the calcite deposited by decades of heavy rains. There were stained-glass windows to be cleaned and grills to be repaired and ironwork to be regilded.

When the team cleaning the north façade discovered problems with the tower, Crispin made an initial inspection and then came to Tom Noonan with his file bulging with notes. The Dean tried to weasel out of a discussion, pleading that he was to leave the next morning for Washington, DC, and had much to do. But Crispin had cornered him just before noon, so Noonan said the only way he could handle bad news was over a rib steak and a bottle of good Bordeaux and they went out to lunch together to a place in the Rue Marbeuf. Crispin didn't like lunching with Tom Noonan because they would end up going halves on the bill even though Crispin only had roast chicken and chips.

They had a good table near the window and Tom was studying the menu with his reading glasses perched on the end of his nose; he looked at Crispin and said, 'You're not going to order *poulet frites* again I hope.'

'I sure am.' Crispin had laid aside the menu and was going over his notes. 'You know what they're going to have to do, don't you?'

'Who?'

Crispin glanced up. 'The cleaning crew.'

'Oh.' Noonan hid behind his menu again.

'Well, one of the pinnacles will have to be dismantled and repaired and remounted. That means we'll need another level of scaffolding and we'll have to hire a crane. But the pinnacle at the far right corner—'

Tom interrupted him to catch the waiter and they ordered. When the waiter had gone Tom took off his reading glasses, slid them into his breast pocket and fixed Crispin with an attentive look. 'Go on.'

'The pinnacle at the far right corner is so badly rotted they'll have to rebuild it. We're lucky it hasn't fallen down and killed someone.'

'How much is this going to cost?'

'I'm not finished.' Crispin closed the file and leaned back. 'The tower's leaning. We're going to have to call in an expert on this.'

'They said to expect surprises.'

'Yeah, but we didn't expect half a million francs' worth.'

'Half a million?' Tom let out a low whistle.

'I don't think we can get any more out of the Ministry of Culture,' Crispin said. 'We'll just have to raise it ourselves.'

'I don't know where.'

'We'll have to go back to our parishioners. Friends of the Cathedral. Everyone. Tell them what we've found and ask for their help.'

The waiter came over with their wine. He opened the bottle and Tom tasted it and declared it acceptable.

'You'll have a glass, won't you?'

'No, thanks.'

'Oh, you have to. It's a very nice Meursault,' he said and motioned for the waiter to pour Crispin a glass.

Tom was finding all this talk about leaning towers a little tedious, so he took advantage of the interruption to switch to one of his favourite topics of conversation—the reprobation of his brethren. His latest grievance was an Episcopalian rector in Rome who had been too lax on a priest tainted by scandalous rumours of homosexuality.

'The priest should have been fired,' the Dean said.

'Could they prove anything?' Crispin asked.

'Oh, I don't know. In some of these cases there's no way of proving a thing unless you want to have the guy trailed by a private eye. The priest denied everything. But where there's smoke there's fire.'

'Not necessarily,' Crispin said and helped himself to another glass of wine. He figured if he was going to pay for half the bottle he'd darn well drink his fair share. 'It's pretty easy for false rumours to get started. You know that as well as I do. Just listen to our wives.'

'Still, we must be above reproach.'

'You leave early tomorrow morning, right?' Crispin said, thinking it best to veer off in another direction.

'Flight's at eight a.m. You'll have to do morning prayer service.'

'I was planning on it.'

The wine was beginning to have an effect on Crispin and he said all of a sudden, 'You'd make a darn good bishop, Tom.'

Tom's eyes had that look of someone taken off guard, and right away Crispin knew he had hit upon a truth.

'What makes you say that?' Tom replied.

'You like being on the go, don't you?'

'Yes. I do. Bishops must go out. Out to the world.'

'Yes, yes, they must,' Crispin nodded.

'You see, Crispin,' and he threw back his shoulders and his chest swelled, 'the Bishop's mission is universal. He has his cathedral but you seldom see him there. His ministry embodies the unity of the church.'

'Absolutely,' Crispin cried, and he raised his glass in a toast. 'Should you ever become one, may you serve your mission well.'

'Well, thank you,' Tom nodded with studied humility.

The waiter brought Crispin's roast chicken and Tom's steak and they smiled congenially at one another and fell to eating. After a moment, Tom wiped his mouth with his napkin and cleared his throat. 'Well, I guess I might as well tell you. I'm one of three finalists being considered for the bishopry at the National Cathedral in Washington.'

Crispin's head cleared all of a sudden and he looked up.

'Tom! That's tremendous! Congratulations.'

'Actually my trip tomorrow is for the final interview. Of course you'll keep this under your hat, won't you?'

'If you want it that way.'

'Although I think maybe it wouldn't be a bad idea to get a search committee going to find a replacement. Discreetly, of course—until the decision is final.'

It was like announcing he knew he had the job. Washington, DC was the most powerful and influential diocese in America, and Crispin could only guess how many applicants he had been up against. His eyes fell on the file he had brought along. Noonan could read his thoughts.

'I admit the timing's bad, but I've brought in a lot of money for the cathedral,' Tom said. He folded his hands with a contemplative air, a pompous mannerism that never failed to irritate Crispin. 'Someone else is going to have to carry on. I think the search committee will see the necessity of bringing in someone with qualities similar to mine.'

'Assuming you are called to the bishopry, how much can we depend on you to help us raise these additional funds?'

'I can't answer that. I can't very well return to DC, to what will be my new diocese, and ask them to cough up more money for St John's. And I won't have the time to make many more trips.'

'When will you know for sure—if you have the seat?'

'Oh, it could take several months.'

'And then?'

'I'd have to be in DC on the first of June.' He folded his napkin and waved for the bill.

Crispin said, 'I wish you luck, Tom.'

He meant it sincerely. That's the kind of man he was. But Tom Noonan lacked the purity of heart to recognise this rare quality in others, so he only smiled that smug smile of his and saw envy where there was none, and contention where there was a desire for peace.

❧ THREE ❧

FOR A WHILE he lay there like he often did, guessing the time, but finally he groped for the alarm clock and pressed the button to light up the face. It was only 3.46 a.m., and he rolled over and sighed.

Phoebe mumbled, 'Please stop thrashing around.'

'I'm sorry. I didn't know I was thrashing.'

She batted at her pillow. 'If you can't sleep then get up.'

'All right.' He flung back his blanket but did not move.

She rolled over and through the darkness he could feel her eyes on him. 'Crispin, you've given hundreds of sermons over the years.'

'I'm out of practice.'

'You do a wedding almost every week.'

'That's not the same thing.'

He sat up on the edge of the bed and felt with his feet for his slippers. 'I'll get up so you can sleep.'

'You'll do fine,' she said and reached out and patted him on the back. Then she rolled away from him and nestled down in the bed.

The stairs were hardwood like the floors and they creaked all the way down. It was very cold downstairs and he thought about building a fire, but then there would not be enough wood to make a fire this afternoon when Julia came to visit, so he pulled the tartan blanket from the sofa, wrapped himself in it and sat in the dark. He was having doubts about the sermon. He rose and padded into his study with the blanket trailing on the floor behind, and he sat down behind his desk, flipped on his computer and began writing from the heart.

Just before dawn he completed an entirely new sermon. He printed it off and then lay down on the sofa in the living room and slept. He woke when he felt Lola standing over his head. He opened his eyes and saw her bending over him with her alert dark eyes on his face.

'Hi, muffin,' he mumbled.

'Will you make me some cinnamon toast?'

'Sure, sweetie.'

He rolled over to look at his watch and for a moment he thought he wasn't seeing clearly.

'Oh, good Lord!'

He flung off the blanket and stumbled towards the bathroom crying Phoebe's name. When she came down he was in the middle of shaving. She stood in the doorway yawning.

'Why didn't you wake me?' he said with a fierce glance in the mirror while he rinsed off his razor. 'Didn't you hear the alarm?'

'But you weren't in bed and I thought you were already up.'

'Do you realise what time it is? I've got fifteen minutes before the nine o'clock service.'

'I'll make you some coffee.'

'No, no coffee! Just bring me a glass of wine.'

She brought him a glass of wine and he drank it straight back like medicine, but his hand was still shaking while he shaved his upper lip.

The early Eucharist service went smoothly, and Crispin returned to his study afterwards and had another glass of wine while he made a few last-minute revisions to his sermon. By the eleven o'clock service he was loose and mellow and sang his heart out during the procession with the choir. During the scripture readings he searched the pews for Julia but it was too difficult to see the faces at the back, and he knew she wouldn't sit near the front. Nor could he find Phoebe and Megan, although Cat had come along with Lola, who had opted out of Sunday school in order to hear her father preach, and the two of them were sitting in the second row just beneath the pulpit.

In the end, Crispin gave one of the best sermons of his career. The congregation sat riveted to the pulpit in silence, and when Crispin sat back down, he let out a sigh of thanks and relief.

After the service, as he stood at the door, he was pleased and even a little surprised at the enthusiasm with which people greeted him. He mingled only briefly in the parish hall during coffee hour and sent Cat back to the rectory to take Lola home and to see if Julia had arrived, but Cat came back to tell him she was not there.

'I told Mom she missed a really good sermon,' she said, and she snatched two cookies from the tray on the coffee service table.

'You mean your mother wasn't there?'

Caitlin stuffed a cookie into her mouth and shook her head. Once she had fully swallowed the cookie she answered, 'Nope. Mom said she had to cook and Megan stayed home to help.'

'Good grief,' Crispin muttered. 'We're having one guest. Not an army.'

Finally, he disengaged himself and slipped through the back hall and up the stairs to his office, which was an enclosed loft built over the Dean's office. It had just one small lancet window that caught the light briefly in the late afternoon. There were quite a few books, but what really caught your attention were the photographs of Crispin's homeland—images of strange, treeless hills, cast in red by the light of the setting sun, with deep shadows sinking into the valleys; of an endless sea of tall grasses whipped into waves by the wind. Some were aerial photographs that Crispin had taken himself.

There were also photographs of his daughters and Phoebe, of Crispin on horseback with his father, and of his mother before she died. It didn't really look as you would imagine a priest's office to look. There was nothing particularly reverent or scholarly about it, but you knew from the moment you set foot inside that it was a good place to be.

Crispin closed the door, took off his jacket and hung it on the back of the door. Without turning, he began to unbutton his clerical collar. All of a sudden he heard a rustle and before he could turn to face the intruder, he felt her fingers at the back of his neck.

'Here, let me do that for you.'

But his hand caught hers and he turned with a look of astonishment. 'Julia!'

She wore her honey-coloured hair swept into a smooth French twist at the back, and her dramatic eyes were set off by the fur collar framing her face. For a moment Crispin's breath caught in his chest.

'Turn!' she commanded, and he did so, and she said lightly, 'I've always had this fantasy about defrocking a priest.'

'Shame on you.'

'Oh, I think it's just we all like to think a man would love us enough to give up even his soul. Isn't that it?' She smiled and dangled the collar in front of his nose and he snatched it from her.

'Where were you?'

'I'm so sorry,' she said, and there was honest contrition in her voice. 'I was carrying all these things'—she stepped back and gestured to the gift bags clustered on the floor—'and I asked the secretary if I could leave them in your office . . . and by then I was late and missed your sermon.'

'And for once I was darn good.'

'I'm so sorry, really I am. But I came up here and . . .' She walked round behind his desk to where the framed photographs hung and pointed to one of Crispin as a shirtless teenager in jeans and boots and dark glasses sitting on the bumper of an old pick-up.

'Do you remember who took that photograph?' she asked.

'Of course I do,' he grinned.

'I took it.'

'I know.'

'Did you take these?' she asked, pointing to the aerial shots.

'Yeah, from my plane.'

'Your plane?'

'Yeah. I had my own plane.'

'Oh, Crispin,' she cried. 'That was your dream, wasn't it? To fly.'

'Well, I finished my degree in engineering, but then the air force wouldn't take me. My eyesight wasn't good enough. I'd been selling aviation insurance to pay my way through college and I really enjoyed it—got to meet a lot of other guys like me. Farmers, ranchers, doctors, all with their own planes. It was a good business, so I stayed with it. Married Phoebe and bought us a big, big house, and filled it up first with furniture, then with kids, and then . . .' He shrugged, suddenly self-conscious, reluctant to continue.

'Go on, tell me the good part.'

'The good part?'

'Yeah. What makes a man give up all that for this?'

He liked the way she was watching him, that teasing smile of hers, and he was thinking how she had grown into her beauty.

'I don't tell many people.'

'Would you tell me sometime?'

'If you'd like to hear it.'

The teasing smile had faded, replaced by a softer look.

'I don't have anyone like you in my life, Crispin. I want to hear what's taken you down this path. You must have given up a lot.'

'And gained a lot.' Crispin bent to retrieve the gift bags. 'Let's go. The girls are dying to meet you.'

Even if you had never seen Julia act, you knew when she crossed a room that she was someone worth watching. Her mouth was too full perhaps, and her dark eyes nearly eclipsed her face, but when she smiled she was undeniably lovely and there was something real and good behind her eyes. Quite a few people recognised her on the way through the parish hall and along the cloisters. Heads turned and a ripple of silence passed through the crowd in her wake.

Clutching a shopping bag in each hand, Crispin led the way like a bulldozer, and Julia, close behind, found it touching the way he became all sober and grim like a bodyguard. Once they had entered the court-yard garden and Crispin had closed the gate behind them, he stopped.

'Are you all right?'

She had gone pale, and her eyes had taken on a glassy look.

'Just a little light-headed,' she smiled, dismissing it with a wave of her gloved hand.

'Here, sit down,' he commanded, and he lowered her onto a stone bench in front of the fountain.

She turned a smile on him. 'Thanks for getting me through that crowd. There are times when I'm just not up for playing the part, if you know what I mean.'

He sat down beside her and settled the shopping bags between his feet. 'Still playing the over-protective brother, aren't I?'

'I don't mind.'

She glanced across at the old stone rectory on the other side of the courtyard. 'Is that where you live?'

'That's home.'

She cocked her head to one side. 'It reminds me . . . what is it? I know. Sleeping Beauty's castle.'

'That's what Lola said when she first saw it.' His eyes swept up the wall to the spire extending beyond the top of the scaffolding, sur-rounded by the patch of slate grey sky overhead. 'What I like about this place is the feeling of being enclosed. Enclosure is one of the oldest meaningful forms in the history of architecture.' He was about to go on, but then he caught a glimpse of Julia's gently mocking eyes.

'There I go again,' he said, reprimanding himself with a slap on the knee. 'Another one of my lectures.'

She studied him quietly and said, 'You haven't changed, Crispin.'

'Is that good?' he grimaced.

'Yes. That's good,' she answered soberly.

Lola had climbed up onto the kitchen work surface and was on her knees peering through the window.

'Get down,' Megan said sharply and snapped her on the rear with a tea towel. Lola's wail brought Phoebe downstairs and by then Cat and Megan had pushed Lola out of the way and were standing over the kitchen sink peering through the curtains.

'Dad's talking to her about the cathedral,' Megan said.

'That could take a while,' Phoebe quipped.

'Did you see her handbag?' Megan whispered, pulling back a curtain panel. 'That's Dior.'

'I can't believe the things you notice,' Cat answered contemptuously.

'Well, she's a movie star, duh . . . It goes with the territory.'

Phoebe interceded and told them they'd all look like fools if Julia saw them peeking at her from behind the curtains. At that moment Crispin bolted noisily through the front door, announcing their arrival, and Phoebe herded the girls into the drawing room.

Much to Crispin's delight, Phoebe and Megan had set the table with their best china and the candy-coloured crystal wine glasses Phoebe had bought at the flea market. Megan had cut out star-shaped name cards and labelled them in gold ink, and Julia's was the largest and most elaborate. It was enough to melt Crispin's heart, and he caught Phoebe behind the kitchen door and pulled her into his arms and kissed her. She looked up at him with a pleased smile.

That afternoon, in the company of Crispin and his family, Julia felt as if all the years had never intervened. She was older, and Crispin was older, and here were his wife and children instead of his parents, and she felt the same contentment she had felt in his home as a child.

It was clear to all of them that Julia had taken more than a superficial interest in them. She had called the Dean's secretary to find out the girls' ages and tastes and there was a black hip-hugger belt with a rhinestone buckle for Megan, a silver charm bracelet for Caitlin, and a Pooh Bear child's tea set in real china for Lola. For Crispin and Phoebe there was a bottle of champagne and some caviar, which Jona acquired in quantity during his frequent trips to Russia. They started with the caviar and finished the champagne with their curried shrimp entrée. For Phoebe's lamb (succulent and pink to perfection) they opened a very nice Margaux for which Crispin had paid dearly.

Although Lola remained withdrawn and ate her meal in shy silence, Megan and Caitlin warmed quickly to Julia and asked her all manner of questions about how films were made—what it was like to kiss men she barely knew, and do it while dozens of strangers looked on, and didn't it make her husband jealous? Julia clearly loved playing up to their youthful curiosity, and told countless behind-the-scenes anecdotes that entertained them throughout the meal. She was particularly excited about her next film, which she would start shooting in the early spring in Yorkshire; she was to play the lead role of Charlotte Brontë.

When Cat heard this she sputtered, 'The *Jane Eyre* Charlotte Brontë?'

'Have you read the book?' Julia enquired.

She nodded enthusiastically and tucked a strand of dark hair behind her ear. 'Twice.'

'I'm impressed. That's heavy reading.'

Cat beamed and looked down at her plate. Megan threw her a bored look. 'Cat, don't hoard the salt.'

Cat slammed the salt shaker down in front of Megan.

'Girls,' warned Phoebe.

But Julia could not talk about herself without talking about Jona, and it seemed at times as if her pride in Jona surpassed all other things. He had started off as a journalist for the *Wall Street Journal*, she said, and then—seeing he had the instincts for corporate raiding—set himself up as a public relations consultant for hostile takeovers. By the time she met him, Jona had moved into commodities trading. He specialised in barter arrangements and currency exchange from countries without convertible currency, most specifically the USSR. Jona's grandmother was Russian and Jona spoke the language fluently. Back in the days of the Soviet empire he had been one of the few Americans to hold a permanent visa to Russia.

But she didn't dwell long on his business. She had a playfulness that bordered on the comic, and she'd squared her shoulders, gripped her fork between her fingers the way Jona held his cigars, and mimicked in a faultless Jimmy Cagney Brooklynese, 'You wanna feel the pulse of the world? You watch the little guy. The ones low on the food chain.'

Megan was so enraptured that she had hardly touched her lunch. 'It must be so cool,' she braved, 'owning a hotel.'

Caitlin piped up. 'She doesn't *own* the hotel, stupid.'

'That's what Dad said,' Megan shot back.

'Jona's the president,' Crispin corrected gently.

'Oh,' Megan said meekly, burning with embarrassment inside.

'Well, it's almost as good as owning it,' Julia said gently. She could feel for the girl. 'Actually, Jona really doesn't have to do much of anything. The managing director runs the place. But one of the perks that comes with the title is that we get to live there. And that's pretty cool. Come over and I'll give you a tour sometime.'

'That'd be neat,' Megan smiled, feeling vindicated.

'Or better yet, you girls come for lunch. Or maybe tea would be more fun. They serve tea in the gallery and it's a great place to people-watch.'

There was a sudden explosion of enthusiastic chatter while they ran through their schedules and tried to find an afternoon when they were all free. Only Lola remained quiet, although Julia had been careful to include her in the invitation, and while they were clearing the plates she slipped away from the table and disappeared to her bedroom.

Phoebe followed her roast lamb with a lavish cheese board and chilled tangerines, and she made coffee while Crispin built a fire. They settled into that late Sunday inertia, with Julia in an armchair, her hair falling loose round her face and her cheeks flushed from the heat and the wine, and Phoebe nestled up against Crispin on the worn sofa.

'We have dessert, you know,' Phoebe said, trying to stifle a yawn. 'I made a lemon tart.'

'Oh, Phoebe,' Julia smiled, 'it couldn't get any sweeter than this,' and Phoebe laughed and Crispin's heart swelled, for he could tell when Phoebe truly liked someone and he knew that Julia had won her over.

Julia sank back into the armchair with her coffee cup in her hands and let her eyes drift round the room. Portraits of past rectors and deans hung on cords against cherrywood panelling alongside sketches of Crispin's father's hunting dogs, and silk-fringed lamps shed their muted light on scarred mahogany tables cluttered with books and photographs. With its rumpled sofa and worn armchairs flanking the fireplace, the rectory had the feel of an old, slightly down-at-heel country house. It was a place that harboured a family in all its intimacy, promising them security, comfort and continuity.

'What a marvellous home,' Julia said. 'How lucky you are.'

'Oh!' Phoebe cried. 'It's a junk yard! Some of the things aren't ours but I'm embarrassed to say most of them are. Or rather they're Crispin's.'

'Some of the things were gifts, too,' Crispin pointed out, too content to rise to an argument. Then, with a lazy grin to Julia, 'Phoebe likes her places to be pretty.'

'We have a lovely little farmhouse up in Normandy and I'm trying to furnish it bit by bit. I refuse to put any of this junk up there. If it were up to me I'd throw all of this out and start from scratch.'

'You wouldn't!' Julia exclaimed.

'Oh, yes, I would. And another thing, living here is like living in a fishbowl. You can barely walk out the door without somebody starting a rumour.'

Crispin glanced at his watch and said he had hoped to take Lola to the Champ de Mars to ride her bike. 'If we hurry we can get in a short walk,' Crispin said.

Phoebe looked across at Julia. 'Julia, go with him if you want.'

'Let me help you with the dishes,' Julia offered.

'The girls will do the dishes. You two go. Lola needs to get out.'

Crispin brought the car round and they loaded Lola's bike into the back and drove across the Seine to the avenue de la Bourdonnais where they parked up a side street. The temperature had dropped and there was a dampness in the air that held a promise of snow. Their breath vaporised in the pale light and it felt good to both of them to be walking together like this in the cold at dusk. The queues at the Eiffel Tower were short because it was a Sunday in November and bitterly cold. Behind it stretched the wide green lawns of the Champ de Mars, once the parade grounds of the military school, but this too was nearly deserted. They took a gravelled side path that wound through the landscaped gardens. The leaves had been raked from their branches by the sharp wind, and the ground was a heavy blanket of butter-yellow maple, rusty chestnut and bronze elm. In the summer there would be hordes of children crowded noisily around the puppet shows and pony rides, but now there were only darkly-clothed figures hurrying briskly along and a scattering of children bundled up in scarves and gloves.

Lola walked alongside Crispin, holding his hand, but she was quiet. When they reached the wide gravel avenue Crispin set down her bike and she mounted it, then he trotted along behind her to steady the bike, but she pedalled away and wove shakily along the path on her own.

'Don't go too far!' Crispin called after her.

Julia had watched this from a distance, and she caught up with Crispin and said, 'Maybe I shouldn't have come along. I remember how I used to feel when my dad would come to visit me and he'd bring along a friend. I was so angry but I was afraid for him to see I was angry.' She stopped all of a sudden and dropped her head. 'Listen to me. This is terrible. I haven't even thought about them in so long. It's like I'd almost wiped them off my radar screen.'

'And then I came along.'

'Yeah.' She said it with a smile, but he knew she had not said it lightly.

'I always wondered why you took the name Kramer.'

'It was Jona's idea. He thought Julia Streiker sounded too much like Julius Streicher. He was some big bad Nazi.'

'So,' he said, 'Julia Streiker became Julia Kramer.'

'In more ways than just in name.' She hesitated. 'I got a contract to model, with this place in Kansas City, but then they sent me to New York. I never even finished high school. I met Jona a couple of years later.' She pulled her collar up round her ears and glanced down the path for Lola. 'He helped me reinvent myself. I couldn't have done it without him. He's my Pygmalion.'

At that moment the lights came on across the city and the tower appeared behind her, its pig-iron girders crisscrossed in perfect symmetry, narrowing to a slender needle at the top. It towered lambent gold against the blue-black sky and, despite its monumental size, it awed with a delicate beauty.

'Look,' Crispin said, spinning her round to see it.

His touch was brief and he quickly stuffed his hands back in his pockets, but she stood near him and felt his warmth at her back, and she was aware of a sense of well-being in his presence.

Suddenly a child's wail cut through the air.

'That's Lola!' Crispin said, quick as a heartbeat. Farther down the path they could make out a huddle of shadowed figures. Crispin broke into a run. Lola had lost control of her bike and collided with another child. It took Crispin a few minutes to get them untangled and to quieten her, then he picked Lola up in his arms and they all returned to the car.

Even while Crispin loaded the bike into the boot, Lola's little chest was still quaking with sobs, and so Julia asked if she might sit in the back seat with her on the way home, if Lola would permit it, and Lola nodded that she would. They descended Avenue de la Bourdonnais and followed the flow of cars. Crispin listened as Julia told Lola stories about Crispin when he was a boy and they were growing up together. As they waited in traffic Crispin turned and glanced over his shoulder at them. Lola's sobs had ceased, and her face was transformed. Julia had entranced her.

As they were nearing the hotel, Julia said to Lola, 'Now, when you get home, your daddy'll make you some magic healing potion, won't he?'

Lola glanced warily at her father. 'Does it taste bad?'

'Bad?' Julia said. 'Hot chocolate? I've never heard of hot chocolate tasting bad. But I do know there's a secret recipe for a very special kind of hot chocolate that has great healing powers. Your Grandma Wakefield used to make it for me whenever I got hurt real bad.'

'You knew Gigi?'

'She was like a mother to me.'

'I don't remember her. She died.'

'Well, I'm sure she taught your daddy her secret recipe.' Julia tapped him lightly on the shoulder. 'She did, didn't she?'

'Sure,' nodded Crispin and he caught her eye in the rear-view mirror and grinned.

'But it only works on big kids,' Julia hastened to add. 'You have to be at least five, I think. Isn't that it, Crispin?'

'That's right.'

Lola jumped in then. 'I'm five,' she said brightly.

'Well, then, he can make it for you.'

Lola fell into a contented silence, and when they dropped Julia in front of the hotel, Crispin came round to open the car door but the doorman was already there in his black top hat and tailcoat.

Lola stared wide-eyed at the man and Julia bent down and politely said good night to her, the way you would to a real person, and then she turned to Crispin and reached for his hand.

'It was a beautiful day,' she said in a low voice, kissing him lightly on the cheek.

Crispin watched as she passed through the revolving glass doors into a lobby bursting with light from crystal chandeliers, and he felt as if she had suddenly separated from him and gone back to her own world. The last image he had of her was of the honey-coloured hair streaked with gold and her coat unfurling in a blur of ambient light.

The King George Hotel was a grand palace from another era, and like an old crank settled in its ways, it had resisted change. It was synonymous with Paris and Paris was in love with its past, and the city's history of decadence, turbulence and pride was distilled in the ageing beauty of the hotel's rooms.

As part of the deal he struck when he negotiated the sale of the King George to its British buyers, along with the title of president, Jona was given a small suite on the top floor. He had benefited from the same arrangement at the Westchester Hotel in London, where he and Julia had lived for nearly eleven years. They had never owned a home of their own, and Julia felt the impermanence of their lives very deeply. But there were reasons for this choice of lifestyle, and Julia could not dispute them. Here everything was within her radius of safety, for the entire hotel became her home, and she felt secure within it.

She had learned to feel comfortable in these places, and she had learned how to dress the part, but she had not grown up in this world, and it would never be hers. She felt this even more acutely as she left Crispin and walked through the doors of the King George, along the hall and past the bar, down the long splendid gallery towards the Prince's Staircase. If Jona had been there she would have taken the elevator, but she would not take it on her own. She could still remember times when even stairs had been impossible for her. Once, many years ago in London, while at Harrods, she had only been able to get out of the store by inching backwards down three flights of stairs on her hands and knees, oblivious to the stares of passers-by. Twenty minutes of sheer terror that had seemed like an eternity to her. She could always feel it coming, like a black cloud, a sentiment of impending doom when fear emerged from its hiding place within her.

At other times reality seemed to shift to another dimension and she could not function, could not even name the thing she held in her hand, let alone know what to do with it, even if it was only her keys and she was standing in a car park next to her car, and all she had to do was insert the key into the lock.

That very morning she had lied to Crispin. She had arrived only a few minutes late at the cathedral, then she had paused in the vestibule with the gift bags in her hands, watching the tail end of the procession through the glass door. A greeter stood on the inside with a handful of Sunday bulletins and, seeing Julia hesitate, she had smiled and reached to open the door. The stirring echoes of the organ and choir had swept into the cold entrance, and that's when the panic had seized her. It had hit her so rapidly that she had been totally unprepared. The intensity of it nearly smothered her and she could not breathe, so she spun round and fled down the cloisters, taking refuge in the Dean's office, from where the secretary had directed her to Crispin's office. Humiliated, she had waited there, worrying about how to explain her absence.

God knows how she had battled to hide it from all of them. Throughout her career, directors had labelled her capricious and demanding when she had been unable to come out of her dressing room, when she had sent the make-up artists and hair stylists away and sat paralysed in front of her mirror with a pounding heart, praying for the fear to pass.

Once they were shooting a small scene at the top of an escalator; she was to ride it down and then try to race back up. But when they called for action, she had shrunk back and grabbed the arm of the gaffer who had just checked the lighting on her face, then crumpled into a ball on the floor. She had covered up, making them think it was violent stomach pains, but she was sweating so badly her make-up was ruined and a doctor was called in. She didn't make a film for two years after that.

She learned later to accept roles that were far removed from her own personality: courageous, strong-willed women or women of another era. She would stay in character even after the cameras stopped rolling, and this enabled her to function without fear, for then she would not be Julia, she would be someone else. If she had her own dressing room she asked the set designer to decorate it with props from the set. She read books and listened to music according to her character's tastes. All these things made it easier for her, and no one thought much of it, for all these techniques were part of an actor's craft.

Julia often joked lightly about her little idiosyncrasies, but no one apart from Jona and Susannah Rich, her New York publicist, knew how extreme her distress was and how fear ruled her life. Whenever Julia was tempted to put her trust in a particular director or a producer, Jona would caution her. He warned that if the truth about her debilitating anxieties became known, she would never make another film.

Papa Jo, she called him in private. It was the name she had given him seventeen years ago when they first met in New York. She had been modelling for two years but the work was still sporadic, and once, when she was desperate for cash, she had gone for an interview with an escort agency. They had sent her out that same evening to the Pierre Hotel for drinks and dinner with an executive who was entertaining overseas clients and needed pretty young women to jazz up the party. The agency made it clear that the escort's obligations did not go beyond dinner. Julia had arrived an hour early, hoping to get familiar with the place and calm her nerves with a glass of wine at the bar.

It was a little before six in the evening and the lounge was filling up. Julia sidled up to an empty bar stool next to a well-dressed man with a sleek, bald head and Coke-bottle glasses, who was hunched over his mobile phone. The television above the bar was tuned to the evening news and he would occasionally glance up and squint at the screen while he scribbled notes on a napkin with a silver pen; it was hard to tell if the notes had anything to do with his conversation, which was in a language Julia had never heard before. He felt Julia's attentiveness, turned a bemused look on her and gave her a wry grin. Then he covered the telephone with his hand and said, 'I've got some Russian friends lost in FAO Schwarz.' A few seconds later he covered the mouthpiece again and landed a witty little quip that made her smile. He kept up a running commentary, and Julia could picture it all, the Russian and his wife wandering in a daze past Barbies looking for Tomb Raider, while this man next to her tried to guide them through the maze over the telephone. The stranger was so hilarious that her nervousness finally broke like a bubble and she was seized with a fit of laughter that she was helpless to control. Everyone in the bar turned to stare at her, and the bartender brought her a glass of water, but she just kept on laughing. She fully expected the stranger to get up and move away; instead he handed her napkins to blot her eyes and urged her to take deep breaths and relax.

When it was all over and she had grown calm, she confessed to him why she was there, and that she had been very nervous having never done this kind of thing before, and now that she had had such a good laugh she would pay for her wine and go home and to hell with the escort agency. And she had him to thank for it.

But she did not go home. Instead they spent the entire evening at the bar eating oysters and drinking champagne, and Julia thought she had never met a man like Jona Wahlberg. He was a ruthless wit and a bewitching storyteller, but what Julia really appreciated was the earthiness hovering just beneath the impeccably groomed exterior, and he never once made an unseemly move. All she was wondering was if he was married, and if he would walk away and she would never see him again. Neither proved to be true. When they made love for the first time it was at her place one evening when her roommate was out of town, and afterwards he wrapped his suit jacket round her and held her in his arms and recited a long passage in Russian from *Anna Karenina* about beauty. A week later she packed everything she owned into her big blue Samsonite suitcase and three cardboard boxes and moved in with Jona.

In the early days of their relationship they were rarely out of each other's sight. Jona shifted the focus of his prodigious energy to Julia's career, and within a year she was in Hollywood with a contract for a daytime soap. All the major decisions of their lives were left to Jona. He decided where they would live and if they should move; what roles Julia should solicit or turn down; and where they should travel on holiday. He read her scripts and reviewed her contracts. Her trust in him was absolute, like that of a child's. He negotiated her fees, invested her money and paid her bills; he told her what she was making on each film but Julia rarely remembered. Somehow the figures blurred in her mind.

Despite her insecurities, Julia was a born actress; she was emotional and dramatic and had a great sense of fun. Julia gave Jona all the credit for recognising her hidden talent, but all he had done was simply to follow the natural impulses of a middle-aged man at a crossroads in life, who had had the good fortune to stumble across a sylph-like creature with dreamy dark eyes.

He had taken her by the hand and propelled her into the spotlight, and she had eventually earned the respect of critics, producers and directors for her fine portrayals in less than inspiring films. But as far as Julia was concerned, her most challenging role was the one she played every day off screen—that of a normal, independent woman.

The idea of having tea with Julia at the King George delighted Crispin's daughters. Phoebe was hurt that she hadn't been included and, when Julia called to set a date, she weaselled an invitation for herself. When Crispin found this out, he told Phoebe that the occasion was the girls' special treat, and he insisted that they go alone. It never took much to spark jealousy in Phoebe, and it struck her straight away that Julia was in a special category of her own, more than friend but not blood family.

It was raining heavily that afternoon as the girls walked up the street from the rectory together, the three of them jostling for centre under Crispin's lopsided umbrella and bickering over who was getting wetter. They were late because Lola had insisted on wearing the Cinderella costume Crispin had bought her at the Disney store for her birthday that summer, and neither sister could dissuade the child. Now they dragged her along and arrived at the hotel out of sorts and wet from the knees down. Megan came through the door first, having abandoned Cat to deal with the dripping umbrella, and then Cat followed her in with a disgruntled look on her face and Lola in tow.

Only Lola seemed unperturbed. She stood in the lobby in her winter coat with her sodden blue tulle skirt drooping down around her ankles, gazing up at the crystal chandelier, believing she was a princess.

It was not only the King George itself that overwhelmed them, but the reception they were given. Julia had sent the hotel's assistant manager to greet them, and he welcomed them graciously before ushering them down the carpeted hall and into the gallery, where he seated them at a round table laid with starched linen and a sprig of orchids in the centre.

Julia appeared just a few minutes later. They watched her descending the grand Prince's Staircase and thought she was the most glamorous thing they had ever seen. She was not dressed in anything remarkable—a polo-neck sweater and fitted black trousers—but she moved with a dancer's grace. She put them at ease immediately, and, seeing that they were wet and bedraggled, bundled them off to the powder room where Megan restyled her hair and Julia dried Lola's skirt with a hair dryer.

They ordered a full cream tea, with rich hot chocolate for the girls and delicate sandwiches: egg salad, smoked salmon and cream cheese and cucumber. Lola sat on the edge of her chair with her plate balanced on her knees and her blue tulle skirt spread around her, looking very pleased with herself.

As well as sandwiches, there were also bite-sized chocolate tarts, pistachio and chocolate and raspberry macaroons, and pretty petits fours, and Julia could see how Cat was trying to restrain herself. She kept eyeing the last remaining chocolate tart, and she bristled when Megan snatched it up and popped it into her mouth.

'You shouldn't take the last one,' Cat scolded.

'Nobody else wanted it,' Megan snapped. 'Get off my case.'

Julia quickly intervened. 'We'll ask for more,' she said.

'No,' Cat insisted, 'I don't want any.'

'Maybe Lola does,' Julia said.

'Lola doesn't like sweets.'

'*J'aime celui-là*,' Lola said, pointing to an egg salad sandwich.

'Speak English, Lola,' whispered Cat.

'Let's order more,' Julia repeated.

'Not for Lola,' Cat said. 'She's a bottomless pit.' She asked her, 'Lola, are you still hungry?' But Lola was watching the piano player who had just sat down at the keyboard. 'Lola, *tu as faim*?' repeated Cat. Lola shook her head. 'See, she's not hungry.'

Megan added, 'She was only one when we moved here. She speaks better French than English.'

'I think we'll probably go back next year,' said Cat.

Julia looked surprised. 'Really? Your dad didn't tell me that.'

'Dad says it costs too much to live here,' shrugged Cat.

'Don't tell people that,' Megan whispered.

'Do you girls like it here?' Julia asked.

'I do,' Cat nodded.

'I can't wait to go back home,' said Megan.

'Only 'cause you won't have to work so hard at school,' Cat said.

Julia glanced at her watch and reminded them that Megan had to get back for her riding lesson, and she left them to make a call from the hotel phone to arrange for a car to take the girls home.

'At least you'll arrive home dry,' Julia said when she returned, smiling at Lola who was brushing crumbs off her skirt.

'Is it a limo?' Megan said all breathy-voiced.

'Megan!' scolded Cat. 'You are *so* rude.'

'It's Jona's car,' Julia explained. 'A Mercedes.'

'Oh, cool!' Megan exclaimed. Even Cat couldn't suppress her pleasure.

Megan stood up and put on her coat, taking a final glance around. 'I was thinking maybe I'll have my birthday party here instead of at Planet Hollywood. That'd be cool.'

'Who said you could have it at Planet Hollywood?' Cat shot back.

'Mom did.'

'I don't think Dad'll let you have it there.'

'Why not?'

'Because it's expensive, that's why.'

'Since when are you Little Miss Penny-pincher?'

'You're not the only one in the family with a birthday, you know.'

'Well, I'm the only one who has any friends to invite to their party! '

That's when Cat crumpled, just broke into tears in front of them all. She tugged her coat on quickly and ran off down the hall.

Julia glanced at Megan who was now looking guilty, then she turned and hurried after Cat. She found her standing outside under the porch, crying. She turned wretched eyes to Julia and sobbed, 'She is so mean!'

Julia tried to find something reasonable to say, but in the end she just said, 'That was very cruel of her.' She slipped her arm round Cat and said quietly, 'But you don't know how lucky you are to have your two sisters. Even if you fight and hurt each other.'

Cat's mouth trembled, and she muttered, 'I hate her.'

'Of course you do. But you're still lucky.'

'Sometimes I wish she were dead.'

'No, you don't.'

'Oh, yes, I do,' she pronounced bitterly.

Julia stood with her arm around the shivering child. 'I had four brothers,' Julia said in a voice barely louder than a whisper. 'But they all died.'

Cat went very still, and looked up at Julia.

'They drowned. I would have drowned too if your dad hadn't found me.'

At that moment the car drove up, and Julia went back inside to get Lola and Megan. A doorman held a huge umbrella over their heads while they all bundled into the back seat, and Julia waved them off. She did not see the look in Cat's eyes.

❧ FOUR ❧

Tom Noonan had just returned from a round of informal sessions in Washington, DC, where laymen and clergy were given the opportunity to get acquainted with the three candidates for bishop, of which Tom was one. In his own words the visit had been a 'splendid success' and now he was finding it hard to focus on the day-to-day business of his own cathedral, which was in the untidy throes of renovation. But regardless of his inclination to flee at any given opportunity, he never missed a monthly vestry meeting. The vestry, the cathedral's governing body, was charged with the financial and material responsibility of the cathedral, and the thought of that board of fifteen men and women making decisions without the weight of his influence struck fear into an otherwise iron-clad heart.

To compensate for his gross neglect and downright ignorance of some issues, he turned to Crispin for regular briefings. It had become a tacit understanding between them that it was Crispin's job to make the Dean look good before the vestry, and Crispin did his job well, but it rankled him. However, he also knew that Tom's love affair with his own image had given the cathedral enormous visibility and brought in considerable money, and this was something Crispin knew he would never be able to do on the same scale. Whether he liked it or not, they complemented one another. Crispin laboured tirelessly in the Dean's towering shadow, and Tom Noonan reaped the praise in return.

This month the Dean had insisted they meet at his apartment on a Saturday, and Crispin had felt very imposed upon. He'd had to leave the girls to walk to their tea with Julia in the pouring rain, while he had dashed to the Dean's building, lugging his heavy briefcase.

The subject of the deanery came up while Crispin was providing the background information on the renovation of the courtyard garden.

'You are aware of the incident that took place last summer, aren't you?' Crispin asked. He looked across the low coffee table to where Tom sat in his armchair.

'I don't recall . . .'

'The little Romanian boy.'

Tom's eyes widened. 'Romanian boy?'

'The immigrant family we sponsor.'

'Oh, yes,' he nodded, but Crispin knew he didn't have the faintest idea who they were.

'He was playing on one of the old stone planters. The thing toppled over on him and broke the kid's shoulder.'

'We weren't sued . . .'

'Thank goodness no, but we do need to address some safety issues. We need to look at some long-term planning here, maybe—'

'Crispin,' Tom broke in, 'tell me, what are *your* long-term plans?'

Crispin seemed not to hear him; he was jotting down a note. But Noonan waited, refraining from revealing what he had heard from his wife, Geraldine, about how difficult the Wakefields' financial situation had become.

Finally, Crispin laid down his pencil and looked up thoughtfully at Tom. 'We haven't made any decisions yet. Though I'll make sure to let you know when we do, of course.'

'Well, in the case of my being called to the bishopry, it would certainly be helpful to have you here while we look for a new dean. It would be hard to lose a dean and a canon in the same year.'

'It would.'

'Have you been looking elsewhere?'

'Absolutely not.' Crispin scowled. 'I love this place. I can't imagine being anywhere else.' He removed his glasses and massaged his eyes, then put the glasses back on and said matter-of-factly, 'It's a matter of money, Tom. I've got myself a pretty high-maintenance family.'

Tom leaned forward and took a pistachio from a bowl on the table. 'If I can be of any help . . .' He prised open a nut and popped it into his mouth. 'We're on good terms with the Banque Populaire, if you need to do any refinancing.'

There was nothing to refinance, thought Crispin. They owned nothing except the little farmhouse in Normandy.

'Thanks,' Crispin replied flatly. 'I'll bear that in mind.'

'You know, several years ago we had a fellow here to do a seminar on budgeting. You might want to check into something like that.'

'Yeah, thanks for the tip.' Crispin's smile was stretched thin as he picked through the pistachios, selected one and bit it open.

'Well, not that it's much of a pay rise, but you might like to know there are several members on the vestry who would like to see you elected dean.' He hurried to add, 'Should the position become vacant.'

Crispin dropped the shell into an ashtray and brushed off his hands. 'I wasn't aware my name had come up.'

'It hasn't officially.'

'Official or unofficial, I'm honoured.'

'But others think we need a different kind of personality.'

With a trace of dry humour, Crispin replied, 'Well now, our vestry is never unanimous on anything, is it, Tom?'

Tom picked up his glass and stared soulfully into his wine. 'There are some—quite a few to be honest—who think the cathedral needs someone charismatic. Someone who can inspire with words. But that's only part of it,' he continued, sinking back into his armchair. 'We need someone who can bring in the big bucks we need to keep this place running. That's where I've been able to put my talents to work.'

Crispin sat still for a moment, riding the silence. 'I'll tell you what,' he began, leaning back into his chair, and fixing Tom with a direct gaze. 'How about a little contest?'

'A contest?'

'If you are called to the bishopry . . . and I'm assuming you'll know within the next few weeks . . .'

'At the most,' answered Tom, reaching for another pistachio.

'From that day on I'll match every penny you raise for the restoration. And I don't mean money that's just been pledged. I mean money that's cleared the bank. If I succeed, you back me for the deanship.'

Tom's jaw stopped working.

'Look at it this way,' Crispin continued. 'Whatever the outcome, the cathedral's the winner—right? So, are we on?'

Tom dumped a pistachio shell back in the dish and dusted off his hands. 'Fair enough,' he said, but he wasn't looking Crispin in the eye.

'Good.' Crispin glanced at his watch and began to gather up his files. 'Vestry meeting's not till Thursday,' he said, rising. 'If you have any more questions we can finish up early in the week.'

The rain was coming down hard when he stepped out onto the pavement. Up and down the street a few umbrellas bobbed along, but Avenue George V was nearly deserted. Crispin was in no mind to wait out the downpour and so he turned up his collar and hunkered down against the pelting rain. But the possibility of being called to the deanship of St John's sent a thrill of exaltation rushing through his body. He threw back his head and took the full force of the wind and rain in his face, and bounded on up the street swinging his briefcase and muttering under his breath, 'Yes! Yes! Yes!'

Phoebe was home but the girls had not yet returned, and she was in a state because Megan had to get ready for her riding lesson and they were going to be late, so Crispin dropped off his briefcase and hurried up the street in the rain to get them.

The twirling glass doors of the hotel spun him into the lobby, where he caught sight of Julia in a trench coat in the middle of the foyer, fiddling with an umbrella that did not want to open.

'Crispin!' she exclaimed as he approached.

'Hi, Julia. Where are the girls?' he asked, slicking back his wet hair.

'On a joy ride. I sent them home in Jona's Mercedes. They should be there any minute. Claude just called me from the car. He said the girls had talked him into taking them for another run around the block.' She was still struggling with the umbrella.

'Here,' he said, taking it from her.

'It's jammed,' she said with an exasperated sigh.

He said, turning it over, 'This looks just like mine.'

'It is. The girls forgot it, and I was sort of in a hurry.'

While Crispin fiddled with the catch, Julia fished a piece of paper out of her pocket and unfolded it.

'Where are you going?' he asked.

'Here,' she said, holding out the list for Crispin, and he noticed that her hand was trembling.

Crispin stopped fiddling with the umbrella and his eyes darted down the list.

'Silicon lubricant? Spark plug gappers?'

'Where can I find that kind of thing?'

'The BHV's probably your best bet.'

'Is it big?'

'Your usual department store. Big enough. Why?'

'Oh.' She became silent, folded up the list and slipped it into her bag.

'Something wrong?' He said it softly, and she lifted her eyes to meet his. For a split second he forgot where he was. 'What do you need all this for?'

'For them.' He followed her gaze to where two men in business suits stood in the recess of a bay window. 'That's Jona with the cigar,' she said.

The first thing that struck Crispin was the man's powerful physique, something the photographs he'd seen had not captured. Then there was the nice suit, and those Coke-bottle glasses, and the way his baldness gleamed in the light of the chandelier. All together it was a very smooth package, but Crispin felt an immediate dislike for the man.

'I'd introduce you, but I'm afraid it's not a good time. That's Boris Tarazov he's talking to. His business partner.'

'That's Boris Tarazov?'

'You've heard of him?'

'Sure I've heard of him. He owns that very controversial independent television station in Moscow.'

A third man, a dour-looking fellow in a grey bargain-basement suit and a permanent scowl, scanned the room with narrow eyes.

'Who's the thug?' Crispin asked.

'Sergei. He used to be head of the KGB's foreign counterintelligence. Now he works for Tarazov. Half of Moscow works for Tarazov.'

'What's Jona involved in?'

'Some kind of defence conversion thing. I don't understand it, to tell you the truth. And I don't really want to.'

'And what do these guys want with spark plug gappers?'

'They're gifts. You know, things that are hard to find over there.'

'Why can't you send someone from the hotel? I imagine these hotel employees have been sent after much more titillating things than spark plug gappers.'

'Jona doesn't want the King George business mixed up with his own.' She glanced over Crispin's shoulder. 'I think Claude's back.'

'Here,' Crispin said, slipping the now-functioning umbrella into her hands. 'It's a very devout umbrella. You have to recite a bit of liturgy.'

She gave him a sheepish look. 'I don't remember much.'

'Oh, anything will do. Abracadabra is fine.'

Julia wrinkled her nose in reply, the way she used to do when she was a kid, and it made him smile.

'But now you don't have an umbrella,' she said.

'I'm already soaked.'

'Can we drop you off at the cathedral?'

'You want me to come with you to the BHV?'

Her face lit up. 'Would you?'

'One advantage to having me along is that I know what a spark plug gapper looks like.'

'Don't you have to get back home?'

'Everyone'll be out this evening except for Cat, and she'll be in her room with her headphones on.' He shrugged matter-of-factly. 'I doubt anyone'll miss me.'

Traffic was barely moving because of the rain. The windscreen wipers thumped back and forth, and Julia stared out of the window without seeing anything and kept telling herself all would be fine. They were both quiet and Crispin was enjoying the silence, but she was listening and waiting for the signs of the dragon, as she called it, waiting to feel the heat of its breath. That's how it began, a burning like her brain was on fire and then it moved in to devour her. She would try to run to get away, to make it stop, but there was never anywhere to go. It would sit on her and asphyxiate her and she would be wide-eyed and screaming inside but she couldn't let anyone hear. Once she had dug a nail file into the palm of her hand, hoping the pain would chase the thing away. It left only when it pleased, just as it came, unpredictably and capriciously, slinking away into darkness and leaving her sweating and shaking, wondering why this was happening and how long it would be until it came again.

They were moving along the *quai* now, heading into a tunnel. Breathe, she said to herself, breathe and become someone else.

'You haven't told me about your new film,' said Crispin.

'Fabulous role,' she said. 'I've been waiting all my life to play a character like this.'

'I always thought of Charlotte Brontë as very short and unattractive,' he said, turning to her with a smile.

'Oh, but she had these great big beautiful eyes, and a voracious appetite to see the world.' As she spoke she felt the weight on her chest slowly lift.

'Tell me about her,' he said, and he leaned slightly towards her.

'Such a tragic story,' she said. 'She lost all of her family, one after the other. Everyone died except her father . . .' She went on to explain how Charlotte, in her late thirties and well past the marrying age, had received an offer of marriage from a curate who had fallen madly in love with her. 'But her father wouldn't let her go. He was a stubborn old tyrant but Charlotte was devoted to him. Finally, they got it all resolved and Charlotte and her dear Reverend Nicholls got married. Six months later Charlotte got pregnant, but she became very ill and died.'

'Seriously?'

'It's a true story, Cris. Nobody had to fiddle with it to make it tragic.'

He didn't say anything, but reached for her hand, and pressed it.

A moment passed before Julia said, 'I wanted this part so badly. But nobody thought I could do it. I had to fight tooth and nail for it.'

'When do you start filming?'

'Not until March.'

'Good. Then you'll be around for a while.'

Claude turned round then, and pointed out the BHV. 'I wait here.'

'Are you OK?' Crispin asked. 'You look a little pale around the gills.'

'I have a shameful confession to make,' she said, pasting on a smile. 'I hate to shop. Especially in big department stores. It's just such a . . .' She looked past him towards the throng of shoppers.

'We'll be fine. Just hold on to me. We'll make it through.'

He opened the car door. Her ears began buzzing again and the heat rose to her cheeks. She managed to get herself through the front door and follow him inside, although she felt her chest constricting. She grabbed Crispin's coat and gripped it tightly, keeping her eyes on his shoulders as they rode the escalator down to the basement. They bought gaskets and a tune-up kit, which was not on the list, but Crispin thought it would be appreciated by the anonymous Russian recipient of Jona Wahlberg's gift. Lipstick was also on the list so they went upstairs to cosmetics, and to Julia's astonishment Crispin set the heavy bag of automotive supplies between his feet and withdrew a tester tube of lipstick from the counter display.

'Rose Nu,' he said, scrutinising the label. 'Think this would go over big in Moscow?'

He was a man undistinguished by any notable physical traits with the exception of the clerical collar he wore, and yet when he spoke and moved, his eyes and mouth and face were animated by something beautiful. Julia felt there wasn't a more remarkable man on the face of the Earth than Crispin. Through some mysterious charisma he surpassed even Jona.

'No,' he frowned without waiting for her reply. 'Too subtle.' He returned the tube to its slot and picked up another. 'Here we go. Red

Tango.' He sniffed it. 'Smells nice too.' He held out the tester to Julia. 'What do you think?'

She sniffed it and said, 'I've never known a man to take such an interest in lipsticks.'

'I've got girls, remember? You've got to relate on their level.'

'You're marvellous,' she said. Such blunt admiration took him off guard and for a moment she wished she hadn't said it because he might misunderstand. 'They're lucky to have you,' she added hurriedly.

'I think I'm the lucky one,' he said.

They bought a dozen each of Fauve Nu and Red Tango and Frivolité. Jona didn't like the Russians to have too much choice, Julia said; it led to disputes and jealousies and it was better if they all had the same.

From the car Crispin called home and Cat told him that Mia, the cathedral's youth director, had dropped by and that the two of them were heading up the Champs Elysées to McDonald's and maybe to a movie, so when Julia told him that Jona was dining with the Russians he asked if she'd like to have dinner with him. 'I'd like to show you my favourite restaurant,' he said with an inviting smile.

'Oh, Crispin . . .' She stammered to a halt, her eyes averted. 'I'd rather not. Not tonight. Some other time, I'd love to.'

'Is it this?' he asked, laying a hand on his clerical collar. 'You want me to take it off?'

'Oh, no,' she cried warmly, and her hand flew out to touch his. 'That's not it at all.' She was aware of the intense warmth of that touch and she withdrew her hand quickly.

'Not many priests wear it. Especially here.' He was unbuttoning the collar as he spoke. In her eyes it was a transformation; the spiritual man fell away and the carnal man emerged. He removed the clerical collar and then unbuttoned the top button on his shirt and loosened the neck. 'But mostly it's my choice,' he continued. 'I love the formality of it. We live in such informal times, so I love things that remove us from the street. Sometimes I even wear my cassock around the church. There's meaning behind the tradition of those garments and the altar dressings. Just like all those flying buttresses and pointed arches. They have a structural purpose of course, but there's meaning in the architecture. The place is full of symbols. I love coming in from off the street and going in there. Even if you don't understand any of it, if you let it it will wrap you up and hoist you out of despair. Despair is our greatest enemy, Julia. We must never despair.'

He came to these last words and then fell silent; his eyes were fixed on hers with a burning intensity, and his words struck home.

When Julia returned to the hotel, she went up to her room, pulled out a suitcase and packed the things they had bought at the BHV. Jona was leaving in the morning for Moscow. He'd be happy to see she had managed so well. Pleasing Jona was very important to her and she tried hard, even though it had been terrifying to leave London.

She knew how to handle new places but it was never easy. When they had first arrived, she had established a morning ritual. She would kneel on the floor of the suite and unfold maps of Paris and plot her daily walks along the streets outside the King George, each day a little longer, a little different. On the maps, the twenty *arrondissements* of Paris were shaded in different colours; the eighth *arrondissement* where she lived was canary yellow, the *métro* lines in ruby red, and seeing it like this made it nicely circumscribed and less terrifying. Now that Crispin was just down the street, it seemed to her that a door had been opened, and Paris was a different, accessible world.

Julia had the habit of working in bed, and tonight the floor and the bed were strewn with books on Victorian social history, along with biographies of the Brontës and pictorial books on Haworth where they had lived. Anything visual that would bring their world to life. Jona rarely slept beside her. Even when he was not travelling he would be up most of the night. His work schedule was daunting.

When Jona came back from dinner it was late but she was still reading, and they talked while he undressed. Jona was obsessive about his appearance. The cufflinks he wore were solid gold and he had many pairs of them, and all his shirts were custom-made. Even his pyjamas had to be ironed and he was compulsive about his nails.

Jona sat down on a chair and loosened the laces on his shoes and told her how Tarazov had lined up some meetings the next day in Moscow which he was happy about. Jona was a maverick and he didn't like doing business in America any more because there it was the lawyers who played the game; it was dull and not at all like doing business with the Russians. The Russians were in thrall to his American-style efficiency. They loved Jona's disregard for hierarchy and position, those very things they held in respect, because he got things done. Russians had little use for lengthy legal documents and Jona liked that about them; trust was built on personal relationships, not legalities.

Julia listened to him, but she wasn't in awe of him any more. She had reached the age where she wanted an equal but Jona couldn't see her like that, and so she listened.

Tonight he was not working but got into his pyjamas and she had to clear her books off his side of the bed. He climbed into bed next to her and she told him about the trip to the BHV and what they had purchased. She told him Crispin's idea about the tune-up kit and Jona was pleased.

'It's too bad you didn't meet Crispin.'

'Was that him I saw you with in the lobby?'

'Yes.'

Jona started to read a magazine for a while, but after a few minutes Julia asked him, 'Do we ever give money away to charities?'

'Sure we do. Every year. We donate to a couple of foundations.'

'I want to give some money to St John's.'

'What's St John's?'

'Crispin's cathedral. It's the one just down the street. The one with all the scaffolding out front.'

'Sure. Why not?'

'I was thinking maybe twenty-five thousand.'

He closed the magazine. 'You want to go into real estate, is that it? You want to buy the church?'

'They have to totally renovate the front façade of the building.'

'Give him a grand,' said Jona and he picked up the magazine again.

'Surely I can afford more than that?'

'Baby, you throw away money like that, you'll be back waiting tables.'

She waited a while before she said anything else. It offended him when she asked him about her money, about how her investments were doing, how much she had. He would say she didn't trust him.

She kept her voice submissive. 'If I can afford it, I'd like to do something really special for him. He cares so much about that cathedral. I think it would make him very happy.'

'You don't need to make him *that* happy,' he replied, flinging the magazine on the floor. He removed his glasses and his watch and laid them on the bedside table.

'Can't I do more than a thousand?' she said, still meek.

'You don't owe him anything. That's in the past.'

She had already thought about that, but she didn't really think it was a gesture premised on the past. If anything it was a renewal. She lifted his arm to burrow underneath it and laid her head on his chest.

'Jona,' she whispered, drawing the fingers of his hand around her breast, 'what would you say if I told you I was ready to have a baby?'

'You got your baby already, honey,' he said drowsily, and gave her a gentle hug. 'I'm your baby. And don't you forget it.'

She lifted his hand and kissed it, and his fingers smelt of his cigars.

'But I want more,' she whispered. She rose on her elbows with her face close to his. 'Talk to me, Jona. Don't dismiss me like you always do.'

His eyes flashed open, and they were as dark as deep cauldrons.

'Don't be angry,' she said quickly.

'What brought all this on? Charity. Babies.'

'Crispin and his family, I guess.'

'Hey, kid, don't go comparing yourself to conventional people. That's a good way to make yourself miserable.'

'But what if I want to be like other people?'

'It's too late for that, baby,' he said. His eyes had fallen shut again. 'Turn off the light and go to sleep.'

Julia did as he asked. She reached across and turned out the light.

Jona travelled frequently that winter, to London and Moscow, but mostly to New York, and Julia turned to Crispin and his family during Jona's absence. Crispin was within the radius of her safe world and the rectory became her second home. She spent Christmas with them, and after that she was frequently invited for dinner. Sometimes she came by with deli food from the Lebanese *traiteur* round the corner, or some gourmet pasta, or sushi, which pleased Phoebe immensely because she wouldn't have to cook. Cat particularly enjoyed Julia's presence. She and Julia would talk about the Brontë sisters, their novels and their poetry.

Knowing Megan's interest in fashion, Julia brought over the costume designer sketches of Victorian dresses she was to wear in her film, but Megan kept the actress at a distance. Megan's instincts were firmly on her mother's side, and Julia, for all her innocence, was an intruder, another woman. So Cat became the favoured one, and a real friendship began between the self-conscious girl with braces and the movie star. As preparation for her film, Julia worked every day with a phonetics coach to learn the Yorkshire accent, and when Cat showed an interest, she invited her to the hotel one afternoon to observe a session. Cat came home that evening and entertained them throughout the entire meal with her Yorkshire accent, and for the first time in her life this sensitive and complex child knew what it felt like to shine.

Phoebe latched on to Julia like a trophy, used her in her conversations like a sprinkle of glitter. But Julia would not attend any of the guild meetings, nor would she speak at their luncheons. It baffled Phoebe, and she would grumble about it to Crispin.

'She's very snobbish.'

'I don't think that's it at all.'

'Then what is it?'

'She's very focused right now. Preparing for her film.'

'I don't think she likes women very much.'

'She's just reclusive.'

Then Julia stunned them all. She invited Crispin for drinks at the King George and told him she wanted to do something for St John's. 'I've wanted to do something for a long time, but I didn't know what. And then Phoebe told me you have this annual fundraiser coming up.'

'Our annual chicken and noodle dinner.'

'I thought, maybe, if you wanted to do something a little grander, I could get you a reception room here—at no cost.'

Crispin leaned forwards and set down his drink. 'If you're going to donate anything I'd like it to be yourself.'

'Myself?'

'Of course. You're an attraction, Julia. People will come to see you.'

She sank back a little in her chair and a dark look fell over her face.

'You don't like the idea?'

She peered at him from beneath lowered eyes. 'I just get a little nervous at those things.'

'You mean fundraisers?'

'Oh, anything where . . .' She sat up straight and crossed her legs and tucked her hands into her lap. She gave him a probing look. 'You really think it would help if I made some kind of an appearance . . .'

'Well, you'd have to do more than that. You'd have to attend the dinner. Maybe announce the winners of a silent auction. Something like that.' Her hands moved nervously, and it seemed to him she was looking pale. He reached out to touch her knee. 'Hey, are you OK?'

She smiled at him, 'It's the Scotch,' she said, reaching for an olive. 'I should know better than to drink on an empty stomach.'

'Order yourself something to eat.' He sounded concerned and he looked up to find a waiter.

'No,' she said, 'I'm fine. I'll do it.' He looked back to see her stabbing at an olive with a toothpick. Her hand was shaking. She gave up chasing the olive and laid down the toothpick, folding her hands back into her lap. 'I'll go to the dinner and I'll do whatever I can to make it a success.'

Geraldine Noonan, who was chairing the event, loved the idea, but it took some arm-twisting to convince some committee members that they should replace their annual chicken and noodle dinner with a sophisticated gala orchestrated around the participation of a film star. But Geraldine Noonan prevailed in the end, and the gala was held in February in the ballroom of the King George Hotel.

The men grumbled a lot about putting on a tuxedo, but the women loved a formal occasion. Gerry Noonan came dressed in something black, expensive and unremarkable, but Phoebe shimmered in a strapless lime-green satin cocktail dress and pink shoes encrusted with tiny rhinestones. She wore her short hair spiked and gelled and sprinkled with a touch of pink rose petals and looked very young and flirtatious.

Rhoderic arrived looking as elegant in a tuxedo as in a wig and robes.

'You made it,' Crispin said, handing him a glass of champagne.

'Of course I did. I'm not totally void of philanthropic impulses.' He glanced around. 'Julia Kramer here?'

'Not yet.'

They were interrupted by a clerk from reception who approached Crispin and said in a low voice that Mr Wahlberg needed to see him in his office. He led Crispin down a flight of carpeted stairs and knocked on a door. A voice answered, and Crispin was shown into Jona's office.

Jona came round his desk and greeted Crispin with a handshake.

'I wanted to speak to you alone,' he said.

'Is everything all right?' Crispin asked.

'It will be. But Julia's got a little problem.'

Crispin felt as if a sledgehammer had caught him in the stomach. There were 180 people buzzing around upstairs waiting to meet her.

'What kind of problem?' Crispin asked.

'Julia's never talked to you about her agoraphobia, has she?'

'What?'

'She has severe panic attacks. You never noticed?'

Crispin was struck dumb; he could only shake his head.

'She hides it well. But she's had a panic attack this evening. Once the medication kicks in, she'll mellow out a bit. She doesn't like to take the stuff—has some unpleasant side effects. But she didn't want to let you down.' Jona laid a hand on Crispin's shoulder and led him to the door. 'Now,' he said, 'the game plan's this. I'm gonna bring the kid down and mingle a bit with her, but I can't stay. I've got some business to take care of. After I leave, you need to stay as close to her as possible.'

'Of course.'

'She does OK if she's near somebody she trusts.' He flipped off the light and closed the office door.

'How long has she suffered from this?'

'It started a couple of years after we met. When we were in London she was better. But the move to Paris was tough on her.'

'Where is she now?' Crispin asked.

'Upstairs in the flat. Try to delay dinner for half an hour. I'll get her down there as soon as I can.'

Crispin nodded.

'You won't mention this to anyone, will you? It'd kill her career if it ever got out.'

'I understand.'

On the way back to the ballroom, Crispin began to put together the pieces of Julia's behaviour, and it all made sense. He remembered the afternoon they met for a drink and talked about this event, and how painful it had been for her to commit to an appearance. He remembered her discomfort shopping in the department store, and her refusal to have dinner with him. And the morning he had delivered the sermon and she had not appeared, and he had found her in his office and later she had felt faint when they passed through the crowded parish hall. Phoebe and Gerry Noonan had pestered her to speak at their luncheons, and when Julia had refused, they had accused her of snobbery. It made him wonder how often she had been misjudged.

Finally, a little past nine thirty, the doors of the mirrored reception hall were swung open by scarlet-coated waiters and the guests caught a glimpse of the candlelit room. At that very moment, Julia and Jona entered from the opposite side. They made a striking couple—Jona sleek and preened in his tuxedo and Julia a head taller than him, with her cognac-blonde hair swept into a smooth French twist. Her enigmatic smile was a lovely and deceptive mask. Crispin tried to appear casual as he approached, smiling, and kissed her on both cheeks, but he could feel her tremble and she breathed quietly in his ear, 'Thank you.'

Crispin murmured, 'Everything's going to be fine.'

He took her free arm and folded it into his, pressing her hand tightly. With Jona and Crispin on each side they entered the room; heads turned like a ripple through the crowd and the chatter died as it does at the sound of glass breaking.

Phoebe broke the ice by rushing to greet Julia with a kiss on the cheek. Crispin gave her a grateful wink and thought again how pretty his wife looked and how proud of her he was.

It never occurred to Crispin that anyone would misread his attentiveness towards Julia on the night of the gala, certainly not with Phoebe present and seated on his other side. No one would have known that Crispin had, several times throughout the dinner, discreetly reached for Phoebe's hand under the table and given it an affectionate squeeze, nor would they have known that, while refilling her wineglass, he had whispered in her ear that she was the most beautiful woman there. People would say he spent most of the evening turned attentively, almost anxiously, towards Julia. Some commented on the obvious intimacy between them, and believed that kind of thing was only possible between lovers.

The rumours most likely originated with the Ribbeys—Tom and Gerry Noonan's closest friends. The Ribbeys were well-meaning, but religion had made them self-righteous, parenting left them self-involved, and Synthia's promotion to *Time* magazine's bureau chief and Edward's Pulitzer prize for journalism had confirmed them in their self-importance. Neither of them were any fun, and Crispin and Phoebe had always avoided them as much as possible.

After everyone had been seated and the waiters were serving the *Confit de Pigeon de Racan*, Crispin caught the Ribbeys observing Julia, each with a hard, blinkless stare of one passing judgment.

It had not worried him at the time, but on Sunday afternoon Cat came home from the cinema in tears after Florence, the Ribbeys' fifteen-year-old daughter, had asked if it was true that her parents were getting a divorce because of Julia. Crispin sat with her for a long time trying to reassure her, and it disturbed him a lot although he tried not to let it show. He explained that she would have to get used to this kind of thing if the vestry voted him dean, because Crispin was convinced the malicious rumour had less to do with Julia than with Tom Noonan's determination to block Crispin's rise to the deanship.

Cat kept the rumour to herself, said nothing to her sisters or her mother. She had grown very attached to Julia, who she felt seemed to see something worthwhile in her that the others didn't see.

If the rumours reached Phoebe's ears, Crispin hoped she would dismiss them. But then, on Monday evening, he was in his study when she arrived home in a foul mood. She dumped the groceries on the kitchen work surface, raced up to their bedroom and slammed the door. Crispin waited a moment, then got up from his desk and ventured upstairs.

But it was not about the rumour at all.

She was sitting up on the bed with a box of tissues in her lap.

'Do you know what you've just put me through?' she said in a quivering, high-pitched voice.

Crispin took a deep, bracing breath.

'I tried four cards!' The tears broke forth then, and she blubbered, 'Four different credit cards! All of them were turned down! Every one! I was absolutely humiliated! All these French people lined up to pay for their groceries and I had to put nearly everything back and walk out with just what I could pay for in cash!' She yanked a tissue out and blew her nose, and when she looked up at him her eyes were full of contempt.

Crispin had never seen her so bitter, and it stunned him. 'I didn't know we'd maxed out the Barclay's Visa,' he said calmly and sat down on the edge of the bed next to her.

'I give you my receipts every week,' she said with an air of grievance.

'I haven't had time to look at anything. Not for months.'

'Months?' she cried indignantly.

'I've just had so much going on,' he said quietly. 'I'll get online this evening to have a look at the accounts.'

It sickened him, all of it, the constant struggles to accommodate them all, and his own weaknesses.

He started to reach for her hand but caught himself. His gesture would only meet with scorn. He settled his glasses on his nose. 'But face it, there are some things we're going to have to do without.'

Her reaction was always the same. She grew closed and tight and hard. She looked away.

'Phoebe, be my partner in this,' he urged.

She turned an astonished look on him. 'A partner in poverty? Is that what you mean?'

'You know, I'm proud of the decision I made. You knew we'd have to make a change in our standard of living and you were behind me then.'

'But we didn't!' she cried, sitting forwards with a pleading look. 'That's just it! Things went on just like they always had. We had all that money from the sale of your company . . .'

'I know. I'd planned on easing us into a different lifestyle, but we just spent it all. And now we're miserably in debt.'

She turned away again, her jaw set hard.

'Look, I admit, I didn't manage it like I should have. I gave in too often, and now the girls expect things like expensive birthday parties and horseback riding and—'

Her head shot round. 'You can't stop Megan's riding lessons!'

'I'm stopping a lot of things, Phoebe,' he said. You could hear the regret, but behind it was stone-cold resolve. It chilled Phoebe's blood.

Crispin stood up and walked out. He returned to his study and closed the door. It was a cramped little room, with barely enough space for an old leather armchair, a small computer desk and a scratched, ink-stained escritoire. But he preferred being here in the evenings, near his family, rather than up in his office. The noises they made never disturbed him. It was only silence that disturbed him. He didn't know what he'd do in a silent house, without them.

He sank into his armchair, dropped his head into his hands and wondered why he was suddenly so afraid of losing them.

⚘ FIVE ⚘

CRISPIN WAS A STUBBORN MAN about some things, and he was stubborn about Julia. He wanted people at the cathedral to see her the way he did, not the Julia framed by stardom and sketched by the overheated pens of critics. He had no intention of hiding their friendship; to conceal something implied guilt. But he had been very concerned about the rumours, even though he hadn't let on to Cat. His immediate concern had been for Julia. Following Jona's revelation, he saw her in a new light, and he had to make an effort not to appear overly protective.

Julia had always brought out that side in him even when they were young, which was strange because as a girl there were so few things that had frightened her. They had waded through murky ponds at night hunting bullfrogs with their torches and dip nets, and huddled together at the bottom of a dry gully as they waited out a summer thunderstorm.

The Julia of his childhood had been tough, a scrappy little kid who walked with a swagger and didn't talk much. Her father had gone to Alaska to work the offshore oilfields, and Julia had taken over for her mother who cried all the time and never came out of her room. Julia cooked for them all and cleaned up after her four younger brothers, and taught them to read and write, because that's what her father wanted.

She never let anyone in Cottonwood Falls know how hard things were at home and refused to talk about her mother's depression, although people had their suspicions. She loved her father, but when he arrived the house had to be immaculate, the children well behaved and the meals ready on time. He only came home for a few days every month, and these visits weighed on Julia. He did not approve of unhappiness and thought badly of his wife when she cried. He was not around to see his wife break down. When Julia was fourteen her mother walked out of the door and disappeared for five days.

And then the next spring the flood came. It rained for days and nights without stopping. They were holding prayer groups on the top floor of the Presbyterian church. They even gave Redbird Banks permission to hold a native American ceremony in the school gymnasium to pray to the gods to dry up the skies.

It was a place where, in times of trouble, everyone depended on their neighbours. But when the river ripped away the trees at its banks and then crept over the fields and advanced on their homes, then people had to rely on themselves to manage the best they could. In part that was why things happened the way they did, because nobody was there to know the truth except Julia.

With only the two women and the little boys they hadn't been able to move much out of the way of the water, just the food, toys and books, as well as a silver butter dish and coffee service and the hand-painted porcelain that had belonged to Julia's grandmother.

Timothy and Samuel, who were seven and eight, shared a room; three-year-old Danny slept with Julia; and the baby, Hank, slept with their mother. When the flood came Danny started wetting the bed again, and Julia would wake up in the middle of the night to find the bed drenched in his warm urine. She would have to get up and change his pyjamas as well as her own, and cover the wet place with a towel before trying to get back to sleep. But that night her mother had taken Danny to bed with her so that Julia could get some sleep. Later Julia discovered why she had done it, and that made it worse because she realised how planned it had all been.

Julia had been sleeping deeply, and when she woke it was to the sound of whimpers and feet in the hall outside her door, but she could not shake off the groggy feeling and she had fallen back asleep again. She woke again to find her mother looking down at her, her hair wet from the rain. It was dripping onto Julia's shoulder.

'Mama?' Julia sat up immediately. 'What's wrong?'

Her mother did not answer but stood gazing down at her daughter with a ghostly solemnness.

'Mama, what have you been doing? You're all wet.'

'I'm hollow,' her mother whispered. 'There's nothing in me. I'm empty.' She turned shivering towards the mirror over Julia's dresser and gazed at her own reflection. 'I can see myself,' she said, 'but I'm not there.' Then she gave a violent shudder.

Julia noticed that her mother's nightdress was muddy at the hem and the damp nylon clung to her hips and legs. She sat on the edge of her bed feeling for her slippers with her feet.

'Mama, let's get you a dry nightgown,' she said soothingly. 'Then you go back to bed.' She stood up and pulled her dressing gown from the back of her wardrobe door. The door to the boys' room was open and, as she peered in to check on them, she saw that their beds were empty.

Julia knew then that something terrible had happened. She raced into her mother's room and flung back the sheets on the bed, but she knew before doing it that her younger brothers would not be there.

Julia spun round to find her mother in the doorway watching her.

'You mustn't ever tell your father,' she said in a frightened whisper.

'Where are they? Oh, Mama! What have you done?'

When her mother did not answer, Julia pushed past her, raced down the stairs and threw open the front door. She ran out onto the front lawn and stood in the rain shouting their names. Then her mother came out of the house, and Julia followed her round the side of the house to the cellar entrance. She watched in horror as her mother pointed down into the dark pit. The cellar was flooded up to the top step, and as she peered over the edge she saw a tiny white hand floating in the murky water below. She began to scream and her mother grabbed her and shook her, told her to be quiet, but Julia shoved her away and dropped onto her knees. She reached down into the hole for the hand but it was too far down, so she swung her legs round, scrambled down the first few steps and waded into the water. Her heart was racing with terror and the icy-cold water knocked the breath out of her. She grabbed the pale hand—by the size she knew that it was the baby—and she pulled him up into her arms and crawled out of the cellar. She sat rocking on her knees with Hank in her arms, and then raised her eyes to her mother. 'Where are the others?' Julia cried. 'Where's Danny? And Timmy and Samuel? Oh God, what have you done?'

'They weren't good enough for your father,' her mother said with a trembling voice. 'None of them were good enough.'

'Are they all down there?' Julia nearly gagged on the words.

'Put him back, Julia. Your father likes things tidy. Put him back where he belongs.' She flew at Julia and tried to wrestle the limp body from her grasp, but Julia clutched Hank tightly, rolled on her side and kicked at her mother, while her mother screamed at her. Julia fought hard but the ground was slippery and her dressing gown was covered with mud and it dragged her down. Suddenly her mother backed away and, as Julia raised herself on her knees and struggled to stand, she felt herself shoved from behind. She fell down the concrete steps and into the dark water, with Hank's body in her arms. While she floundered, trying to find her footing and to get her head above water, she heard the cellar door squeaking on its hinges and then a thundering crash as it fell shut, and she was immersed in total darkness.

The water rose that night, and all the next day. Light seeped through the cracks in the rotted planks of the cellar door, and Julia tried not to look at what was in the water around her. Somewhere in the pit of the house's foundations floated her three brothers. She cradled Hank while she crouched on the top step, immersed in water up to her waist. From time to time she would shout, but there were only the sounds of the rain outside, and the wind that had turned blustery, and the water around her, lapping at her waist. After a while hypothermia set in and she stopped shivering and grew sleepy. She was afraid she would fall asleep and drown, and she tried to think of things to do that would keep her awake. She sang all the church hymns she could recall, and Christmas carols, and she recited Bible verses she had memorised, and then she could not feel her body any more. Hank had drifted away from her and she grew weary of trying to save herself.

That was the spring Crispin turned seventeen. He had grown to be good-looking and muscular like his father. He played football and wrestled for his school, taking home awards and trophies, and girls liked him a lot. Things had begun to change for him that year, and he had not seen as much of Julia.

Crispin's father was a vet, and when the flood came and the river made its advance on their homes, he took Crispin with him before dawn to help neighbours move their livestock to high pasture, and to help him on his rounds. The nights were long and Crispin and his dad were weary and sad. They were worried about the flood and they had a lot to keep them busy, but Crispin felt bad that he had not taken the time to drop by Julia's and give them a hand.

Crispin came home late and went straight to bed that night, too exhausted to eat his dinner or take off his clothes. But, tired as he was, he kept thinking about Julia and her family. Finally, he dragged himself out of bed and stumbled downstairs to the phone and called. It was after midnight but there was no answer. It worried him because it was late and there was always somebody to answer.

Finally, he got up, took the keys to the truck and slipped out of the house. He didn't tell his parents where he was going. He knew they'd tell him to go back to bed and get some sleep, that they'd check things out in the morning. But Crispin didn't want to wait.

From a distance the Streiker house looked dark; he could see no lights, and he began to think they must have gone away and left the place to the rising water. Nonetheless, he knew he'd feel better if he could see for himself. The driveway was flooded, so he parked on the road, got out of the truck and slogged through the shin-deep water towards the house. He noticed the family's truck was still parked near the shed, but their Toyota was not in sight. And then he noticed the front door was wide open.

Inside, the house was quiet; he tried the light switch in the hall but it wasn't working. He called Julia's name and then her mother's name, and when there was no answer he climbed the stairs. Stacked along the hall-way upstairs were boxes and paper bags filled with things they had emptied out of the kitchen cabinets, and it seemed odd to him that they had gone away and left everything like this. Julia's bedroom was the first on the left: it struck him as strange that the room had been left with the bed unmade, her tennis shoes on the floor and her jeans hanging over the footboard of her bed. The boys' room and her mother's room were the same. The beds were unmade and clothing had been left as if they had simply vanished in the middle of the night.

Crispin walked back downstairs and out onto the front porch. The wind had come up and was chasing the clouds across the sky, and the moon lit the hills with a dappled light. He thought he might check the stables but he didn't know what he was looking for. When Julia's father had gone to Alaska, they had sold their two horses and the few cattle they owned, and leased their land, so now there was no live-stock to tend. There was no reason for anyone to be out there.

This is silly, he thought. You're being paranoid. They've gone, that's all. They would have called if they needed help. He was cold now, and he tugged the collar of his jacket up around his neck and trudged down the front steps through the flooded front lawn towards his truck. But then he hesitated and looked back. Come on, he thought, coaxing him-self into action. Just take a walk round the house. Then you can go back home and rest easy.

How slight and insignificant his decision had seemed at the time. He had acted more in response to his own feelings of guilt than any cosmic sense of fate. But his hesitation had saved Julia's life.

And then, had there been no moonlight, he might never have noticed the curious object protruding from the cellar door. As he drew near and bent down to look, he heard a faint whimper from below, and then realised what he was examining: a fabric belt had been wound round a flat stick and rammed upwards between the slats from below.

'Julia!' he cried as he crouched and struggled to raise the cellar door, but it would not open and he saw with horror that the latch had been secured with a padlock. He found a pair of hedging shears in the shed and then splashed back to the cellar and used the long metal blades to prise the latch loose from the wood. The wood splintered easily, and it didn't take him long. The cellar door was unusually heavy and he could only lift it a foot or two. It was dark below, but as he peered into the pit he realised something was attached to the door. Suddenly the stick pulled loose and there was the muffled splash of a body falling into the water. He was able to lift the cellar door then, and he looked down to see Julia's white face sinking below the water.

As he lowered himself through the opening and grabbed for her, he saw that she had tied the belt from her dressing gown round her chest, securing it underneath her armpits. She'd then wound the other end round the stick and jammed the stick between the wooden slats, thus fashioning a kind of harness to keep her head out of the water.

She was like ice when he dragged her out and laid her on the ground. She groaned and her eyes fluttered. 'What happened?' he cried. 'Where's your mom? Where're your brothers?'

Finally, convinced there was no one else alive in the cellar, he lifted her into his arms, carried her up the front steps and into the house and lowered her onto the sofa. He called his father and told him what he'd found, and his father said he'd call an ambulance and then he'd be right over.

Crispin knew Julia couldn't survive the loss of any more body heat, so he ran upstairs to her room, tore the blankets from her bed and dragged them back to the sofa. He hesitated only momentarily, then he slipped the wet nightdress over her head. As she lay there naked, pale and cold, it was not a sexual longing he felt, although she was beautiful and no longer a child; it was anguish and rage that anyone could do this to her. He wrapped her in the blankets but he knew that was not enough, so he began to rub her bare arms and her face and hands, even her feet, until he heard his father's truck pull up outside.

Julia could not face what her mother had done. She retreated into silence and would not speak to anyone; not the doctors nor the psychiatrists, nor the detectives investigating the case. Crispin was the only visitor allowed in her hospital room, and he would sit in the corner doing his homework after school while Julia slept. Her father flew back from Alaska and went to visit her at the hospital, but when he walked into her room she became hysterical and they had to make him leave.

Eventually she talked to Crispin, and through him revealed what had happened that night. Her mother's mutilated body was discovered in a tunnel in a Colorado mountain pass where she had thrown herself down on the railroad tracks.

Trying to change his family's spending habits was by far the greatest challenge of Crispin's adult life. For two weeks after Phoebe's outburst over the rejected credit cards, Crispin was barraged with a heavy, sullen silence. But he held out against the assault. He treated Phoebe with cheerful civility, and nothing she did could break his resolve.

One evening he took Megan into his study and told her that he would not be able to pay for her to ride on the competition team the following year, and there would be no more purchases of expensive tack, of bridles and special bits and monogrammed saddle cloths.

Megan sat quietly, staring at him with vengeful eyes, and then rose and started out the door. But she stopped, and finally gave in to the impulse. 'You know what?' she said, her eyes full of rage. 'As a dad, you suck.'

Next he called Cat into his study. Cat would adapt—if for no other reason than to spite her older sister. What hurt Cat the most was that they wouldn't be able to return to their grandparents' home at Santa Barbara for their summer holiday. Cat had made close friends there, and the friendships were renewed each summer.

'I'm so sorry, Cat, but four round-trip tickets to Los Angeles . . . Honey, we just don't have the money.'

'Mom said maybe Grandma and Grandpa would pay.'

Crispin reminded her that they had a great country house in Normandy, and suggested she invite her friends to fly over for a long visit in the summer.

'They're old enough to travel on their own now, Cat. They'd love it,' he urged. But Cat didn't see it like that, and she left his study in tears.

Later, when he was trying to focus on his work, Lola came in, barefoot in her dressing gown, and stood and stared at him until he looked up. He asked her what was wrong, and she said it was her turn, that she didn't want to be left out.

Only one thing boosted his morale these days, and that was his documentary about the cathedral. It had been Julia's idea; she came up with the plan after Crispin told her about his wager with Tom Noonan. She jumped at the opportunity to champion Crispin in his fight for the deanship. They collaborated on the text, which Julia would narrate, and together they combed the cathedral for the best interior shots; Julia even consented to put on a hard hat and take the elevator up to the scaffolding to get some footage of the restoration in process. She brought in a director who offered to donate his time to the project—at least that's what she told Crispin; in reality, she was paying the director's fees out of her own pocket.

The morning before the shoot, Crispin arrived at his office to find Julia waiting for him.

'There you are,' she said.

'This does not bode well,' he said as he dropped a handful of message slips onto his desk.

'What makes you say that?'

'Just my antennae talking. What's up?'

'It's my schedule. They moved up the shoot by two weeks.' She gave him a pained look. 'I'm sorry. I don't have any say about it. I have to leave for London tomorrow. I have a week of make-up and costume tests and then I have to go directly on to Haworth. I'm so sorry.'

Crispin sank into the chair behind his desk and his eyes fell on the script they had written together.

'Oh, Crispin,' Julia said. She was standing there with her eyes squeezed shut and her brow tightly furrowed, and when he looked up and saw this he couldn't suppress a grin.

'Does it hurt?' he asked.

'Yes,' she whined.

'Good. This is a huge disappointment.'

'I know, but listen.' She pulled up a chair and leaned across the desk towards him, all earnestness. 'I've got it all figured out. I'll find someone else to fill in for me. I've already got somebody in mind. And I talked to the director and he's still available next week.'

'Hey, Jules, whoa. You don't have to do all this. You've already given so much.'

She unsnapped her handbag, pulled out an envelope and laid it on his desk. 'Here. This is for you.' She sat before him, smiling and clutching her bag, wearing the glow of a child at Christmas.

He picked up the envelope and turned it over. 'What's this?'

'Open it.'

He tore it open and took out a cheque, and his mouth dropped open. 'Twenty-five thousand dollars?' he breathed.

She leaned forwards, laid her hand on his arm and looked at him with pleading eyes. 'For the *ravalement*. You won't refuse it, will you?'

'Of course I won't.'

'I didn't know for sure who to make it out to, so I made it out to you directly . . .' She jabbed a finger in the direction of Tom's office below. 'That's so it's perfectly clear as to who's bringing in this money.' Then she pointed to the cheque. 'But there's a note at the bottom indicating it's for the cathedral renovation.'

He looked up from the cheque and saw the delight on her face.

'Julia,' he murmured. 'You never cease to amaze me.' His eyes kept returning to the cheque, and then up to her radiant face. He stood up, walked round the desk and pulled her to her feet. He took her in his arms and held her.

'Don't,' she said gruffly, pushing him away. 'I'll start crying.' She rubbed at her eyes with the back of her hands.

'Is this your money?' he asked, still a little stunned.

'Yes.'

'My goodness . . .'

'It's OK. Jona takes care of me. I know how much the cathedral means to you. And since I can't do the video, it's the least I can do.'

'Do you have time to go and get a coffee?' he asked. 'I could use a bit of caffeine.'

'I'll make time.'

They found a booth at the rear of a scruffy little workers' *café tabac* squeezed between a gaudy Cantonese restaurant and a stationer's on the Rue Marbeuf. The café was narrow and deep and there was little room to navigate between the tables and the counter, but Crispin liked the place because the young *patronne* smiled and made an effort to talk to you even if you didn't speak French very well. Crispin came in a couple of times a week and had a coffee at the counter, and from time to time he came by at lunch and had the daily special.

Crispin had never brought anyone to his café before. Not Phoebe or Tom Noonan or any of the people he worked with all day long. He had never given much thought as to why this was so. And he didn't give much thought to it that morning when he opened the door for Julia.

'This OK with you?' asked Crispin as they seated themselves and Julia unbuttoned her coat.

'This is fine,' she answered.

Crispin ordered coffee for both of them and a croissant for himself and when the waiter had gone he said, 'So, you're off to England.'

'I'm off to England.'

'Jona going with you?'

She shook her head. 'He's not even in town. He's in New York.'

'How will you handle the flight?' he asked.

The waiter brought their coffee then, and there was a silence before she said, 'I have methods, techniques I've learned.' She dropped a lump of sugar into her coffee and looked up with a broad smile. 'Then, once I get to England I'll be Charlotte Brontë and I'll be this complex little woman with a gargantuan appetite for life, and I won't be myself at all.'

She stirred her coffee while Crispin waited for her to continue.

'I'll transform myself into someone else. The clothes always help. I'll be wearing Victorian silk dresses with petticoats and bonnets and tiny pointed shoes.' She raised her coffee cup to her lips. 'Have you ever been to Yorkshire?'

'Nope.'

'Neither have I. But the photographs I've seen remind me a little of home. It's not so vast, but you get this sense of isolation. It really comes through in Emily's poetry.'

She set down her cup and, in a Yorkshire accent she began to recite:

'In all the lonely landscape round
I see no sight and hear no sound,
Except the wind that far away
Comes sighing o'er the heathy sea.'

She looked up at Crispin with glowing eyes. 'Doesn't that remind you of the hills?'

He had never seen her quite like this. She was often animated and expressive, but something in her mannerisms when she spoke of her work hinted of a passion he had never witnessed.

'So you memorised her poetry?'

'Emily's. Charlotte's poetry wasn't nearly as good.' She smiled broadly at him. 'I remember how I felt when I got the script. I knew there was something in that story that spoke to me at some profound level. These passionate, obstinate children isolated on harsh moorland and cut off from normal social interaction. They were so intellectually refined, so different from the rest of the villagers. Charlotte was always dreadfully nervous and shy with strangers, to the point of offending people sometimes. But she had such a passion for life and adventure.'

'Reminds me a little of someone I know,' he grinned.

'It's sort of the same soup, isn't it?'

'Yep.'

She sighed, and she seemed to unwind a little. 'I knew you'd get it. Jona doesn't, though. He didn't want me to take the role.'

'Why?'

'He says audiences like films with cute, wacky heroines or sexy, power-house kind of women, and the last thing they're going to flock to see is a film about two English clergymen fighting over a middle-aged Victorian spinster. And he's right. It's not likely to be a blockbuster.'

'Do you care?'

'I do. I want it to be seen. But that's not a reason to turn it down.'

He was watching her intently and with such earnest compassion that it made her smile.

'I bet you do a lot of this, don't you?' she said.

'What's that?'

'Don't you Anglicans have confession?'

'This isn't confession.'

'No, but you're such a good listener.'

Crispin shrugged in that self-conscious way he had when good things were said about him. 'I do listen a lot. People tell me things. I've always thought it was a bit of a curse,' he continued. 'When you see things from somebody else's point of view, it can weaken your own perspective. Sometimes I envy people with really rigid mindsets.'

'Jona's like that. He never seems to doubt who he is. He's tone deaf to anything that challenges his authority.'

Crispin raised a dubious brow. 'And you married this man?'

'Actually, we never married.' She studied him to see his reaction. He only dipped the last of his croissant in his coffee and cocked his head and replied, 'Could've fooled me.'

'We almost did. Years ago. Jona wanted to get married. Do the family thing. I couldn't. I was so afraid I'd end up just like my mother. Jona made me go through therapy. I guess it helped a little.' She shrugged with a smile of resignation. 'Meanwhile, as far as I'm concerned, what Jona and I have is as sound and committed as anything on paper.' She reached out and laid her hand on his arm. 'Oh, Crispin,' she whispered, 'you are *so* where you're supposed to be.'

He stared at her a little stunned. 'I'm glad you think so. It does me good to hear it.'

'Why? You mean others don't agree.'

He was a long time replying, and she withdrew her hand and gently asked, 'Is it Phoebe?'

'It's difficult sometimes,' he replied. 'It's been a radical change in lifestyle from what we used to have.' He drank down the last of his coffee. 'I spoiled them rotten, when I had the money to do it.'

'Crispin, don't ever doubt what you're doing with your life. You have a gift for it.'

He was a little taken aback. 'What makes you say that?'

'I don't know. Something about the way you respond to people. It's like you just knock your ego out of the way and love them.'

There was a long and solemn pause. At the next booth, the waiter was setting the table for lunch.

Crispin replied, 'Thanks, Julia. I needed to hear that.'

The first thing Julia did when she got back home was to call Phil, their accountant. She told him she had written a cheque on her New York bank account for $25,000. She told him to sell whatever he needed to in the way of stocks or bonds to make the cheque good.

When she had finished speaking, there was a long silence on the other end of the line. Julia waited anxiously, knowing she was defying Jona, and that Jona would know about it before the end of the day. When Phil finally replied he asked if Jona had authorised this.

'It's my account, Phil. It's my money. I'll do what I please with it. Just cover the cheque.'

She hung up then, and she was glad she was already sitting down because she felt light-headed. She took a few deep breaths to calm her nerves and then she got up and turned on the radio. She was smiling to herself, and was feeling light and giddy, and free.

৶ SIX ৶

JULIA FELL IN LOVE with the moors at first sight. She found in the bleak little village of Haworth, with its dramatic sweep of rugged moorland, a wrenching beauty that tugged at her heart in much the same way the Kansas grasslands had once done. It was a landscape of shifting moods; one moment luminous and drenched in colour, the next thunderous and grey, and always with clouds wrestling overhead. And then there was the wind; a wind so ever-prevailing that the lack of it was cause for comment.

The landscape moved Julia deeply, and she had been in Haworth less than a week when she wrote the first of a series of letters to Crispin in which she expressed these sentiments. She wrote nothing of this nature to Jona; the idea of writing all this to Jona never even crossed her mind.

March 12th

My dearest Crispin,

How I wish you could see Haworth Moor. It would not appeal in the slightest to the sophisticate but rather to the mystic, and although we have never spoken of those things I assume a priest must have some kind of inclination in that respect, and therefore I conclude this is a place for you. Only now, being here, do I fully grasp Emily's poetry.

I'm staying in a cottage in Haworth just down the street from the parsonage where the Brontës lived. My assistant finds it depressing and wishes I'd move into the hotel in Bradford with the rest of the cast. It's true the cottage is cramped, the ceiling low, and the windows narrow.

Every sound can be heard, the floor creaking above (Fiona's room), or the housekeeper setting the table for dinner downstairs. But I feel so much better here than in big places.

I am sitting here in a very Victorian nightdress, similar to something I imagine Charlotte might have worn, with a shawl over my shoulders and a coal fire in the grate, writing to you in period fashion—by hand.

When the spring break comes around, would Phoebe like to bring the girls over to visit the set?

Much love,
Julia

March 28th

Dear Crispin,

Your letter warmed me so. Jona has not been able to visit; he has spent a lot of time in Moscow recently trying to salvage some deals, and although he tells me very little, I sense he is worried. I am so thankful for my work just now. I would be terribly anxious if I were back at the King George in Paris waiting to hear from him.

I'm getting along fabulously. I knew once I threw myself into the character I would shed my anxieties, and so far so good. I do so love exploring Charlotte's mind. She was such a romantic. And Mr Nicholls—the clergyman she finally married—I've concluded he was really a remarkable man beneath all his conventionality.

I am disappointed with the actor playing Arthur Nicholls, however. Heath McEwan is a fine British stage actor, but so lacking in subtlety (he has done very little film). He plays Nicholls as a bit of an arrogant twerp which is so wrong. Actually I envisioned Arthur as more like you in nature. Michael Langham (the director) keeps having to tone down Heath's performance.

Must get to bed and get some sleep. I'm up at five for make-up.

Love to the girls and Phoebe,
Julia

April 12th

Dearest C,

Got your email. My assistant prints out my emails and I read hard copies.

So, Tom Noonan will soon be bishop. Washington, DC, right? This means the way is clear for you, and I do hope you will charge ahead. You never say an unkind thing about Noonan, but I sense this is only because of your generosity of spirit. I'm sure he is plotting behind your back to keep you out of the Dean's chair, even in his own absence. What does Phoebe think of all this?

Going out to dinner this evening. Pub up the road. Yorkshire pudding and roast beef. Very English. I have fun speaking to the locals in my Yorkshire accent. Have fooled a few of them.

Must go,
Love, J

PS I can't tell you how much your encouragement means to me. You are a great support. I just hope I'm not burdening your life too much these days. You already give so much of yourself to so many people.

Crispin was trying to love his children and his wife without indulging them, but they did not understand what he was trying to do and they were bitter. For the first time in his life he felt prepared to do whatever it took, and the battle was as much with himself as with his family. He traded their new SAAB for a Renault with 70,000 kilometres on the clock. Phoebe was appalled and Megan said she'd rather take the bus or walk all the way to the Bois de Boulogne for her riding lessons than embarrass herself in that car. Crispin pointed out that the difference in car payments and insurance might permit him to continue paying for her riding lessons, but this fact did nothing to mitigate her indignation.

Cat countered her sister's petulance with a Herculean effort at cheerfulness, and it hurt Crispin to see her act like the little mother at dinner, attempting to hold up the conversation with tales of her school day. You could see Megan itching with impatience to start a row with her, but it seemed part of her mother's strategy to withdraw into silence, to freeze Crispin into compliance, and with just a look or a pat on the knee, Phoebe brought her eldest daughter under control.

Lola ate her meals in silence, obediently, without prodding, although at times Crispin thought he saw tears in her eyes. Then he would tell her she didn't have to finish, that she could leave the table if she wished, and she would immediately carry her plate to the kitchen, then scamper off to her room. She got into the habit of changing into one of her play dresses as soon as she came home from school. She would become Cinderella or Ariel, or Sleeping Beauty, wearing the dress through dinner, until it was time to change for bed. Crispin knew it meant something, and that she must feel the tension in the family.

As his domestic life slid into decline, his esteem among his parishioners rose. The news of Julia's generous donation on top of the success of the fundraiser had given Crispin the cachet he needed, establishing him as a viable successor to Tom Noonan. The Dean was too consumed by his status as Bishop-elect to bother challenging Crispin's candidacy for the deanship, and although the vestry would interview other candidates out of necessity, it was common knowledge that Crispin was already assured the majority of their votes.

During this time, he took mental refuge in his ongoing exchange with Julia. He never saw any danger in his attachment to her. When he had first met Phoebe, she had dazzled him with her physical charms, and this was the experience of love to which he compared all others. His loyalty to his wife and his firm belief in the sanctity of marriage had always acted like a firewall to physical temptation. But a love affair of the mind and spirit is another thing altogether. He was a man open to intimacies of the heart, open to beauty of the soul, and this was how Julia came to him, filling him even when he did not know he was empty.

No one in their narrowly proscribed world could have foreseen the events that followed, and yet they were all connected, linked through people and time to a place where other dramas were unfolding, centred on people they never knew and would never meet. The time was early that spring, and the place was a noisy street in central Moscow, an office in a concrete monolith of a building hidden in a yellow haze of smog and dust. There were only two men—a General Streletsky who had consented to meet an Oleg Yavlinsky, a man the General neither liked nor respected, and who he greeted with barely concealed contempt. There was something weak about Oleg Yavlinsky, an unsavoury hint of perversion.

The General knew why he was here. For over a year Yavlinsky had been discomforted by the rising success of his competitors Boris Tarazov and Tarazov's American partner, Jona Wahlberg.

'Tarazov is scum,' Yavlinsky said, his hands tightening around the briefcase balanced on his knees. 'We can't let men like him rule Moscow. We have to eliminate him.'

'Oleg Alexandravich, my good friend, our security forces were not created just to eliminate your competition.'

'Tarazov's no threat to me!' Yavlinsky cried, as if he had been personally insulted. 'His television station is no competition for mine! But the man's dangerous. He's out of control. Tarazov must be eliminated. And I'll show you why.' Yavlinsky opened the briefcase and with fumbling fingers withdrew a slim document and laid it carefully under the General's eyes.

'Here,' he said, jabbing a finger at the document. 'That's what the Americans call a position paper. That's what Jona Wahlberg drew up and presented to the American Federal Aviation Authority. He's been Tarazov's partner for a long time. They've done a lot of business together.'

General Streletsky was skimming through the paper. His brow knotted and his face went pale.

Yavlinsky nodded eagerly. 'Yes, it's worrisome, isn't it? They're talking with your deputy defence minister about converting our Typhoon nuclear subs into oil drill subs.'

'We have other plans for those subs,' Streletsky said in a steely voice.

'Of course you do. But wherever you go, Tarazov and Wahlberg will follow. When I formed my joint venture with the Americans, Tarazov did the same. Then, when I established my bank, Tarazov opened his and stole our most lucrative accounts. Then it was the television network. And now this. Tarazov and Wahlberg undermine everything we do. As long as they're around, all our efforts are useless.'

Again the General glanced through the proposal Yavlinsky had set before him, and his face hardened into a deep scowl. Yavlinsky knew he was getting close to the mark.

'We're losing time.' Yavlinsky pressed on and his voice modulated into a whine. 'If Tarazov and Wahlberg go ahead with this, do you realise the opportunity we'll have lost? And not just this one. Tarazov starts with this, and soon he'll be doing all the defence conversion. And all the money will go into his pockets, not ours.' Yavlinsky leaned back and slapped his briefcase. 'Time doesn't stand still. For things to move ahead we need certain decisions to be made on your part.'

'You'll have them,' the General replied, and he closed the proposal with a determined and final gesture.

Tarazov knew it was coming. Streletsky had given him ample notice. First there were attempts on his life by snipers or drive-by assassins, but Tarazov always escaped. Finally, Tarazov's enemies grew tired of being subtle; they crammed explosives under the seats and in the boot of a Volvo estate, parked it near Tarazov's television station and then detonated the bomb by remote control when his car passed by.

News of Tarazov's death was brought to Jona that night as he dined with two American venture capitalists in the Marriott Grand Hotel. He quietly laid down his napkin beside his plate and excused himself, then he went up to his room and made a call on his mobile phone. When his secretary called back half an hour later to confirm he was booked on a morning flight back to New York, Jona's suitcase was already packed.

He left before dawn for Sheremetyevo International Airport and passed unnoticed through the security and passport control. As he sat in the airport lounge waiting for his flight to be announced, he was approached by two men in uniform. A French banker waiting for the same flight who witnessed the encounter told the embassy officials that the American seemed perfectly calm and the uniformed men treated him quite respectfully.

Two days later a taxi driver feeling an urgent need to relieve himself pulled over to the side of the motorway a few kilometres south of the airport. He crept a little ways into the woods, and as he unzipped his fly and casually glanced around, his gaze settled on a muddy heap sprawled at the foot of a tree. The body was identified as Jona's. He had been stabbed numerous times.

It was midafternoon the following day when Susannah Rich, Julia's New York publicist, arrived in the village of Haworth to break the news to Julia. Susannah sent word to the director that she would wait for him in the Black Bull Inn, and then holed up in a back room making calls and taking care of business.

To her dismay the producer was also visiting the set, and although her plan had been to consult Michael Langham, the film's director, before she took any action, Larry Turman's presence meant she would have to bring him into the picture. Susannah dreaded the idea of confiding in Turman. He was a crass and notoriously underhand man, and Turman's name was synonymous with sleaze. Susannah knew that the only reason he had bought the Brontë script was to lure an A-list director like Michael Langham into working with him in the hope of transforming his image. They arrived together a little after six o'clock. Langham was on the heavy side, a little bald, slightly rumpled. Turman had the suntan and didn't look sixty, which he was. He wore a sports jacket, black polo-neck sweater and sunglasses although the sky was a mist-filled grey.

Susannah closed her Filofax and stood up. She had the well-groomed appearance and perfectly scripted responses of a television broadcaster, which she had once been, and she commanded considerable respect in the business. Both men greeted her with a kiss on each cheek.

Langham sat down with a heavy sigh and searched his pockets for his cigarettes. 'This can't be good news if you've flown all the way across the Atlantic to deliver it,' he said as he tapped a Marlboro out of the pack.

Susannah told him about Jona's assassination and Tarazov's car bombing. 'Geez,' whistled Turman.

Langham listened, absolutely motionless, the lighter halfway to the cigarette between his lips. 'Oh God,' he said, shaking his head. 'What a bloody awful thing.' Finally he lit up his cigarette. 'Bloody awful timing too,' he groaned.

Turman asked, 'Who is this guy of hers? Some Russian *mafiya*?'

'That's an inaccurate description,' Susannah answered, feeling suddenly defensive of Jona, a man she had never much liked. 'Jona Wahlberg's been doing business with the Russians for decades.'

'So, do we have an image problem here? Is our star a mob moll?' Turman said, smiling at his own twist of humour.

Susannah levelled a look at him. 'Image isn't really what I'm worried about just now,' she answered with composure. 'When the press makes the connection between Jona and Julia, then we'll do what we need to.'

Michael took a long drag on his cigarette. He knew Susannah hadn't come all this way just to discuss image.

Susannah leaned towards Langham, ignoring Turman. 'I'm very concerned about what will happen to Julia when she hears the news.'

'So, she takes a few days off for the funeral, you shoot around her,' Turman said callously. 'These things happen.'

He leaned back in his chair to flag down a waitress and Susannah took advantage of the moment to throw a meaningful glance at Michael. 'I doubt if it'll be as easy as that.'

'She's got a contract. She's a professional, isn't she?' Turman answered.

'She was very dependent on Jona. It'll be tough for her.'

Turman was craning backwards in his chair to see the bar in the adjoining room. 'What does it take to get service here?'

'This is a pub,' Langham told him. 'You go up to the bar to order.'

'Christ,' he groaned, sounding miffed. 'Well, I'm gonna go get a beer. You two want something to drink?'

Susannah shook her head.

'Sure, I'll have a pint,' answered Langham. 'Thanks.'

As soon as he was out of earshot, Susannah turned to the director and whispered furtively, 'There's something you need to know. I'm really risking it by taking you into my confidence, and if I do you have to swear you'll keep this strictly between us. And above all, don't tell Turman. I could lose Julia as a client if this gets out.'

'Is this something other people will have to know?'

'Absolutely not. You can work around it. Trust me.'

'All right. Go ahead.'

'Julia's got a severe anxiety problem. She's agoraphobic. She has absolutely crippling panic attacks.'

Langham screwed up his brow in disbelief. 'But she's been fine. Shows up on time for make-up and costume. Always prepared. The first week I could see her shifting around a little, testing herself and testing me, but then one day she walked on the set and there was Charlotte

Brontë. Sometimes when I watch her I forget who she is . . . I forget she's my actress. Hell, I even forget I'm directing. She's totally relaxed. It's like she isn't even working at it any more. She *is* Charlotte Brontë. It's spooky. If she doesn't get an Oscar nomination for this . . .'

'Of course she'll get a nomination.' It was Turman, back with their beers and a bowl of peanuts. 'We'll all get Oscars. Peanuts anyone?'

Susannah shook her head.

'No. Thanks,' Michael answered, taking a drink of the beer Turman had put in front of him. He turned back to Susannah. 'So, you think Jona's death might . . .' he prodded, without finishing the sentence.

'Yes, I do,' she replied cryptically. 'She'll need support. Someone she's close to.'

Turman butted in. 'Get her a therapist. They've got people specialised in dealing with these things.'

'Has she developed a close relationship with anyone on the set?' Susannah put the question discreetly.

'She's strictly professional,' Langham answered. 'Doesn't go out much.'

'How about her assistant?'

'Fiona gets along with her well enough. But I don't think they're particularly close.'

'Does she ever talk about Jona?'

'All the time. Like he's her North Pole.'

Susannah nodded knowingly.

Turman was beginning to get a little nervous. He said, 'Hey, look, if you think this guy getting himself murdered is gonna jeopardise the production, then just don't tell her. Simple as that.'

'We can't do that,' Susannah said.

'Why not?'

Susannah looked at him with unconcealed contempt. After a cool pause, she said, 'Because we don't operate by the same rules.'

'What rules?' Turman replied indignantly. 'I'm a producer. That means my goal is a marketable product. Not a bunch of celluloid in the trash.'

You're a shit, thought Susannah, but she only stared at him impassively.

'Look,' Turman said, 'how many more weeks of shooting do we have left? Two? Three?'

'For Julia, about that,' Langham answered.

'What are you suggesting, Larry?' Susannah probed, sensing where he was going with this.

'Michael just said she doesn't go out much. Hell, let's just hide it from her. Screen her calls. Limit her contacts.'

'You can't hide that kind of news from someone,' she answered, seriously alarmed. 'This is her husband we're talking about.'

'I didn't think they were married,' Turman replied.

Susannah spoke quietly, struggling to remain composed. 'They've been together for seventeen years. That's longer than all your little bimbos put together.' She punctuated it with a smile.

Turman's jaw hardened. He quietly edged his chair back from the table and rose stiffly, pausing only to give Langham a fraternal pat on the shoulder. 'Call me tonight, Mike,' he said, and strode out.

Susannah's fair cheeks were burning. 'Forgive me,' she apologised quietly. 'I'm short on sleep.'

'Don't worry about it. He'll get over it.'

She brushed a dark curl back behind her ear and said, 'Look, Michael, I want Julia to finish this film as badly as you do, but I don't know what will happen when she finds out about Jona's death. All I'm saying is you'd better be prepared.'

'I'll look over the production schedule this evening. See how we can work around her for a few days.' He ground out his cigarette and looked up at her hopefully. 'Are you going to stay on?'

'I can't,' she answered firmly. 'I'm supposed to be in LA right now. I'm flying out tomorrow. I can break the news to her, but you'll need some kind of support after I leave.'

'So you'll tell her?'

'That's why I flew over here.'

'I appreciate that.'

'I'm just terrified she'll find out from somebody else before I get to her.' Susannah unzipped her bag and dropped her Filofax inside. Then she headed for the door with her face set in a look of grim resolve.

On either side of the village's steep, cobbled main street stood soot-blackened stone cottages that had once housed combers and weavers of the wool trade, where Victorian women had sat dawn to dusk over their hand looms, their livelihood dependent upon the meagre light cast by a grizzled sky through rows of narrow stone-mullioned windows. There were fresh lace curtains at the lower windows of Heather Cottage and pansies in brightly painted window boxes, which relieved the bleakness all around. Susannah rapped upon the door, and after a moment there was the sound of hurried footsteps and the door was opened by Julia's assistant, Fiona, who announced in an exaggerated hush that Julia was napping and she was not to be disturbed. Susannah dropped her bag onto the stone floor and, unknotting the belt of her trench coat, summarily informed the young woman that she had flown all the way from New York with a message that could not wait, and would she please show her to Julia's room and then bring up some tea.

Fiona led the way up the narrow wooden stairs. The floral curtains had been drawn and Julia was sleeping, sprawled on her back in her dressing gown. She stirred as the door opened.

'Fiona?' she said groggily, rising on her elbows and squinting at the light from the doorway. 'Is it time to get up?'

'Julia, it's me,' Susannah replied, drawing back the curtains. Julia sat up and blinked. Her hair was coloured brown now, and it made her seem unfamiliar.

'Susannah?'

'None other.' Susannah leaned down and hugged her. Julia could tell then, by the way that she clung to her, that something was wrong.

'What is it?' Julia said anxiously. 'Is something wrong?'

Susannah reached for her hand. 'I have some very sad news for you . . .'

Julia did not expect it to be Jona. She thought it had something to do with the film, and she had that terrible anguish in her stomach at the anticipation of some great disappointment.

'What's happened?'

Susannah sat down on the bed. 'Jona's been killed,' she said softly.

Julia's first reaction was a nervous laugh. 'You're kidding.'

'No, honey, I'm not.'

'Jona? Papa Jo?'

In the twilight Susannah could see the confusion on Julia's face. She told her everything she knew, about Tarazov's murder and about how Jona had tried to escape the country; how he had made it to the airport, then been lured away and killed.

Julia listened but there was disbelief in her eyes and she responded with soft utterances of denial. 'They killed him?' she muttered. 'I don't believe it! No. They wouldn't have done that. Not Jona. They all knew him. He helped them. He did so much for them.' She rambled on like this for a while, but then came the moment when realisation hit her, stripping the disbelief from her face. Susannah touched her but Julia recoiled. The pain was too private and powerful. She turned her head away and, curled in a ball, she wept.

After a while she wiped her face with the sleeve of her dressing gown. 'Where is he? Where's my Jona? What did they do with him?'

'The embassy's returning his body to Paris. We'll have to get you back there.'

'Oh, no. Not again.' She took another deep, shuddering breath.

'I'll send someone with you.'

'You can't come?'

'I'm sorry, sweetie. I have to be in LA tomorrow.'

'Oh my God, the film . . .' Julia rushed to say, anxiety creeping into her voice. 'I can't leave it . . .'

'They'll shoot around you. I've already spoken to Turman and Langham.'

It came sweeping back over her again. She could be distracted for only a few seconds, and then it returned like a keen blast of cold wind.

'Oh God,' she muttered, struggling to halt a new flood of tears. 'Stay with me,' she begged softly as she pressed Susannah's hand.

'Of course I will. I'm not going to leave your side until we put you on that plane tomorrow. Are you taking any medication? For your anxiety?'

Julia shook her head. 'I haven't needed any. I've been doing so well.'

'If you need to start again, let me know. I can get it in New York and send it overnight express.'

Julia gave her a grateful smile. Susannah knew exactly where to situate herself in the chaos of crisis. 'I'm so glad you're here.'

'You'll pull through this.'

'I have to finish this film. I have to come back. I have to finish.'

'That's what Jona would have wanted.'

Julia nodded, but she knew better. Jona had never encouraged her to take this role. But Crispin had; he had understood its significance, how it resonated with her past. Crispin had always understood her. This realisation brought a brief moment of serenity. Dear Crispin, she thought. If she kept him in her mind, she could get through it all.

The return trip to Paris exhausted Julia, but she was relieved to be back at the King George where she was received with kindness.

She wasn't quite sure of the order of things, how to handle death and burying the dead. She spent the morning with the concierge of the King George and a rabbi, going over the funeral arrangements. Fiona, the assistant who had accompanied her from England, was kept busy answering the telephone and keeping track of the extravagant arrangements of flowers that poured in. Julia felt adrift, and she longed for something or someone to anchor her. Most of all, she longed for a quiet moment to call Crispin.

Then in the afternoon Maître Albert arrived, and the others left. Maître Albert had come to read the will. He was a small man with a moustache that covered his upper lip. Today, he was nervous, but Julia didn't notice this. Now, dressed in a sober black dress, with her hands curled into a ball on her lap, she sat stiffly in the corner of the leather sofa while he searched his inside pocket for his glasses, settled them on his nose and began to read.

At first she tried to follow, but the legal language bored her, and Maître Albert spoke English with a marked accent that made him diffi-cult to understand. First there was the will, but the will bequeathed his entire estate to his trust. Maître Albert finished reading and asked if he might have something to drink. He downed the water that Fiona brought him, then put the glass down gently, delicately, on the table. He picked up a copy of the trust with shaking hands. Julia noticed this, and in that brief second she knew something terrible was about to happen.

In the time it took to read the trust agreement whereby the majority of Jona's assets would be distributed to his legal wife, one Raza Lichovich, and his son by said wife, Alexander, the world Julia had created for her-self was utterly and completely eradicated. The pallid little man read through to the end of the lengthy trust, and then Julia excused herself and went to the bathroom and vomited. Fiona tapped meekly on the door, asking if she was all right, and Julia replied that Maître Albert mustn't leave, that she would be out in a minute. She splashed her face with cool water, rinsed her mouth and brushed her teeth, and then went back into the living room.

Maître Albert stood near the door ready to leave, his briefcase weigh-ing him down, looking very formal and awkward. He bowed slightly.

'Who is this woman?' Julia asked with an unsteady voice. 'You can't walk out of this room until you tell me who she is. You must know. You're the executor of his estate.'

He set down his case. 'She is a Russian lady. She lives in New York.'

'How long have they known each other?'

'I only know that they were married last summer, just before the birth of the child. I believe he felt it was his obligation.'

'I don't believe this! Not for one minute do I believe this. Jona didn't want children. She must have tricked him into it.'

He hesitated, then replied with a slight air of apology. 'Monsieur Wahlberg was a Jew. The mother is Jewish. He gave me the impression that he was very proud of being a father.'

'*How can you say that?*' Julia screeched, and the sound of her voice startled both of them. 'Jona always tried to hide his Jewishness! All the years we were together he never once set foot in a synagogue!'

The little man was clearly embarrassed by Julia's outburst. 'The child is not inheriting very much,' he added with a twitch of his moustache, as if this resolved the matter.

'He left him his entire estate!'

'There will not be much left, Madame, once all is settled.'

To Julia's stunned silence he replied with a shrug of the shoulders, and leaned down to pick up his briefcase. 'After the funeral you must call his financial manager and discuss it with him. There may be certain limits imposed on your expenditures until after the estate issues are finalised. He will explain all this to you.'

'Are you telling me I don't have any money?'

His hand was on the doorknob. 'I cannot answer that, Madame.'

He opened the door and fled.

Julia picked up the telephone and called the front desk. She asked them to hold all her calls and to make no more deliveries to her suite, and then she sent Fiona away. She needed to be alone now, she explained. When Fiona had gone she disconnected the telephone and hung a DO NOT DISTURB sign on her door.

She opened the door to the balcony and stepped outside. The clouds had turned the day grey and dim and there was a chill in the air. Piano music drifted up from the lounge below. Across the courtyard were other suites, as opulent as her own. This was Jona's world. She kept seeing him before her eyes, strutting into a room wearing an iron-clad arrogance that suited him so well; a barrel of a man with a heart-bending smile and infectious laugh that swept you up and never let you go.

A light rain began to fall but she did not go back inside. For a long time she stood there, feeling the rain penetrate her hair and trickle onto her scalp, down her neck and into her eyes. She focused on the edge of the balcony, willing herself to approach it. Then the spire of Crispin's cathedral rising above the skyline caught her attention. Suddenly she heard his voice, as clearly as if he were standing beside her. *Don't ever despair, Julia. Don't ever despair.*

Suddenly panic seized her. Her heart pounded mercilessly in her chest, and the marble floor beneath her feet seemed to give way. The thought of taking a step in any direction terrified her. Unable to move, she sank to her knees. If she stayed close to the ground, she would not fall. Her heart still racing, she crawled back inside on her hands and knees. She was able to close the door and then, still on hands and knees, she inched to her bedroom. She stripped off her dress, then crawled back to her bed clutching a vial of sleeping tablets in her hand. But she could not sleep in the bed. Jona was still there. He was everywhere.

She pulled a blanket and a pillow from the bed, crawled into her dressing room and closed the door. With a trembling hand, Julia counted out just enough capsules to make her sleep.

During the hours that passed, Julia's grief turned to rage, and her rage was titanic. But she did not know how to hate Jona without hating herself, and when she awoke late that night, she set about shredding each and every strip of her clothing. She cried while she ripped the beautiful dresses from their hangers and hacked away at them. Jona had been with her when she bought these things; his taste had moulded hers and with time she had grown into the clothes and the image, learned how to walk with attitude, her head high. She never saw others stare at her but Jona did and it gave him enormous pleasure. Her clothes were an erotic pleasure for him as well as a totem of status.

And so that night she whittled away at herself. When she had purged some of her anger, she began to feel guilty, realising that she could have given the clothes away to one of Crispin's charities. Jona had always criticised her impulsive generosity to strangers, saying, with a scowl, that it was a sign of weak sentimentality.

She saw that scowl now, as she wrestled trunks out of wardrobes and suitcases down from the top shelves and packed up all her remaining clothes, along with her alligator shoes and Prada and Dior handbags. She felt his disapproval weighing down on her, but she battled with it, and tried to see Crispin's face instead and Crispin's joy. She knew now what she would do. She would go back to Haworth, alone, and finish the film. The greatest struggle would be to get out of town. Shedding Jona's image of her was not the same as shedding her fears but she wanted desperately to make her way on her own.

Once she had emptied her wardrobe, saving only a few pairs of shoes and some sweaters and jeans, she sat down at her desk and made a list of what needed to be done and how she would do it. She called Air France and made a reservation for the next morning, billing the ticket to her account at the hotel. When it was done she put down the telephone and felt a rush of elation.

She bathed and dressed, and brushed her hair back into a simple ponytail, then she sat down and wrote a note to Crispin and told him what had happened and what she was doing. She would send the letter over to the cathedral in the morning along with the trunks and suitcases of clothes. By then she would be gone.

It was much easier to leave at night. She instructed the porter to take her holdall and call her when he had loaded it into a taxi. When she went downstairs, there was no one in reception but the desk clerk, who nodded respectfully and then went back to reading his newspaper.

As the taxi left the hotel, she sat in the back, gripping her bag as if it were an anchor. She instructed the driver to cruise slowly past the

413

cathedral, and she rolled down her window and looked up at the now dark spire and thought with sudden lucidity how this place had entered into her life. How Crispin was now at the centre of it. She rolled up the window, then pulled her bag closer, hugging it to her breast.

'Oh, my goodness,' Phoebe cried as she read Julia's letter over her husband's shoulder. The letter had been addressed to both of them, and had been delivered to the rectory that morning, along with the trunks and cases of clothes. Phoebe had not dared to open the envelope, but had called Crispin out of his study to see what it was all about.

The letter told of Jona's betrayal, and Julia's need to cleanse herself of him and his influence. Crispin was baffled that she had not called, but he knew she must have been reeling from shock and humiliation. In her innocence she had chosen to include Phoebe in her confidence. But Crispin took one look at his wife's face and realised that he should have opened the letter in private. 'Don't you breathe a word of this to anyone, Phoebe,' he warned.

'Of course I won't.'

'Can I trust you?'

'Of course you can!'

Crispin wasn't so sure. During the early years of his ministry in Kansas City and Chicago she had been a true helpmate. But she had changed. There were many extraordinary women at the cathedral, but Phoebe had chosen to make friends with women much like herself, women whose only interests were the petty struggles of power within an insular world.

'Can I open them?'

Phoebe was referring to the luggage the porter from the King George had deposited in their living room.

'No,' he replied curtly, stuffing the letter back into its envelope. 'I think we should just leave them alone until she gets back. She's overreacted. I'm sure she'll want them back.'

'Well, if she doesn't, don't you dare give anything away until I've had a chance to look.'

'If she doesn't want the clothes, then they're to be a gift to one of our charities.'

'Oh, come on, Crispin. Don't be so stubborn.'

'Don't you have enough clothes as it is?' he shouted.

Crispin never raised his voice and Phoebe was stunned. She spun round and marched out.

He stuffed Julia's letter into his jacket pocket. It was raining as he dashed across the courtyard. He needed to be alone, away from eyes and ears. He was hating Jona Wahlberg just then. It was such a violent, disturbing sensation, and he didn't like having it inside him. He could only imagine what Julia must have gone through when she had learned of his betrayal. She hadn't deserved this.

He stormed down the street, rain pouring down his neck, stomping through puddles like they were Wahlberg's face. Rarely had Crispin been angered to the point of physical violence, but he was now. He wanted to slam his fist into something, or kick something, or knock someone down. Finally, he stopped halfway up the Rue Marbeuf and turned to stare at a window display. People were bustling down the street with their heads down because of the rain, so no one could see he was fighting back tears.

That evening after the rest of his family had gone to bed and he could be alone, he sat up late in his study and sent Julia a long email. He was just closing down his computer when he heard Phoebe coming down from their bedroom. She opened the door and gave him a sweet smile.

'You're working late,' she said, and crossed to him and laid her hands on his shoulders as if she cared, but he knew she was just reading the screen over his shoulder.

'I was just sending an email to Julia.'

'That's all so sad,' Phoebe said, and Crispin could almost believe she meant it. And then she ruined it all by adding, 'We should have taken her up on her offer to visit the set. Now it's too late. I don't imagine she'll want us up there now.'

Crispin hid his dismay. 'I agree with you there.'

'I know she's a glamorous film actress and all that, but frankly I always felt a little sorry for her. I think she wanted what we have.' She gave Crispin's shoulders an affectionate squeeze.

There was a frozen silence, and Crispin was tempted to say, 'Just what do we have, Phoebe?'

Then she said, 'Why didn't she have any children?'

'I suppose that was their decision. I don't know.'

'She's such a needy person, isn't she?'

'Did you want me for something?' he asked a little sharply.

'I was thinking about the girls' Easter holidays. I thought I'd take them back to Santa Barbara to visit my parents.'

'That's out of the question.'

'Let me finish,' she said with strained patience. 'I already talked to Daddy. He'll pay for our tickets.'

The news hit hard, and it hurt. He turned round in his chair and looked at her. 'But I thought we were going to our house in Normandy,' he said. 'That's what we do every year after Easter.'

'That place depresses me.'

'You liked it when we bought it.'

'I saw its potential. But you've never let me do a darn thing with it.'

'It's simple. And cosy.'

'Oh, for goodness' sake!' she cried in exasperation. 'Spare me, will you?' She stormed off with her dressing gown billowing behind her.

Days passed and Crispin received no answer to his email. It had wounded him that Julia had returned to England without calling or trying to see him. Perhaps he had assumed too much, imagined himself to be more important to her than he really was. He wanted very much to hear her voice, to know she was all right. He missed her.

The girls' Easter holidays were upon them and Phoebe seemed determined to inflict her anger and disappointment upon him, which in turn only heightened his sense of failure as a husband and father. He had the feeling something was being asked of him, and the fear that hovered deep down in the darkness of his thoughts told him the sacrifice might be more than he was willing to pay.

❧ SEVEN ❧

THE VESTRY WAS NOW interviewing candidates for the deanship. Three of them, two from the US and one from Malaysia, were flying in for interviews, and Tom Noonan had repeatedly commented to Crispin that they all seemed to be exceptional. It needled Crispin, and Maddy Cartwright, the senior warden, picked up on this and invited Crispin out to lunch the day after the first candidate had come and gone, with the intention of reassuring him. She asked Crispin where he'd like to go, and Crispin took her to the café on the Rue Marbeuf where he had taken Julia.

Maddy was a woman in love with the things Crispin loved: the ritual and the beauty of the cathedral. But she also loved the people, and when her husband died she had turned her benevolent spirit towards the good of others. She did anything anyone asked of her, and on occasions she went with Crispin on his Tuesday rounds when he ventured out into the city, ministering to the sick and the destitute. She always brought along Piaf, her tiny Yorkshire terrier. Sometimes people they talked to on the street would want to hold the little dog, and she'd go to them and sit in their arms and sort of loosened their tongues. They'd stroke her and suddenly it would become easy to talk about their troubles, and there would be this priest and this large, bosomy old lady with angel-white hair and this Yorkshire terrier all willing to listen.

Piaf had that effect on Crispin now, as he sat opposite Maddy in a booth at the rear of the café, lunching on home-made *hachis parmentier*.

'I appreciate this gesture, Maddy. Your support means a lot to me.'

'Tom hasn't given up the battle yet, you know.'

Crispin raised his eyes from his plate. 'You think not?' he said.

'I know not. He's got his bloodhound going through the restoration expenses as we speak, seeing if he can find the slightest trace of an irregularity.' The 'bloodhound' was Maddy's nickname for Edward Ribbey.

'Waste of his time.'

'Oh, we all know that. Everybody knows it doesn't have a darn thing to do with anything, except that Tom'd rather see the devil himself up there on his little throne than cede the deanship to you. You're his Achilles heel, you know. You succeed where he fails.'

'I always thought it was the other way around.'

'That's what he wants you to think. But you're what we need. You're exemplary, Crispin. Really you are.'

'Thank you.'

'But there is something you'll have to be on the watch for.'

'What's that?'

'We have a lot of unhappy women among our parishioners. A man with your qualities could easily find himself the subject of controversy.'

The way she said it put Crispin on the alert. He laid down his knife and fork and gave her a long querying look before he spoke. 'Are you hearing rumours?' Crispin asked.

'You don't know who I'm talking about?' she leaned towards him.

'I assume it's Julia.'

'It's just jealousy,' she said. 'You're a lot cuter than you like to think you are.'

'Damn them,' mumbled Crispin. He picked up his fork and poked at a sprig of parsley. 'They better leave her alone.'

'You two go way back, don't you?'

'I didn't have any brothers or sisters, you know. Julia was like a sister to me. We had this thing. We always seemed to find each other. Like needles in a haystack.' A look of reminiscence passed over his face and he gave a light laugh, but then the smile faded. He picked up the parsley and twirled it between his fingers. 'Julia had four brothers.' There was a long pause, and then he said quietly, 'Her mother drowned them all. Julia was the only one who survived.' Crispin dropped the parsley and wiped his hands on his napkin.

Maddy let out a soft gasp. 'Oh, my goodness,' she whispered.

'Yeah,' said Crispin. 'I was the one who found Julia. She still thinks she owes me her life. I don't feel it that way. Sometimes I think I owe her mine. Don't ask why. I can't explain.'

Maddy had become perfectly still. After a while Crispin threw off the heavy silence and looked up at her with that beguiling grin of his.

'You should get to know her, Maddy. You'd like her a lot.'

'I'm sure I would.'

'And besides, if I left my wife for anyone—which I won't—it'd be for you, Maddy.'

For some unknown reason, Piaf squirmed at their feet and emitted a slow and unexpectedly deep growl.

Crispin drove Phoebe and the girls to the airport, and stayed to see them off to California. He came back a little lighter in spirit, feeling as if he could get a lot of work done.

After everyone had left for the day, he went into the cathedral and knelt at the altar of St Paul the Traveller for a good half-hour. Afterwards he returned to the rectory, and was nosing around in the refrigerator for something to eat when the telephone rang. He picked up the receiver and heard a woman introduce herself as Susannah Rich. She said she was Julia's publicist, calling from New York.

'I understand you're a close friend of Julia's,' she said. The line was crystal clear, and it sounded like she was in the same room. 'You're a priest, right?'

'Yes, I am.'

'You know about Jona's death?'

'Yes. I got a letter from Julia about five days ago.'

'Could you make a trip up to northern England to visit her?'

'When?'

'As soon as possible. She's locked herself in her room and hasn't come out for four days.'

'Did she ask for me?'

'She won't talk to anyone. But her assistant remembered you'd been corresponding during the shoot . . . before Jona's death.'

'Yes. That's right.'

'Well, we took the liberty of pulling up your emails, and we thought, given the nature of your friendship, she might open up to you.' Susannah's voice became less controlled. 'I'm really worried about her.'

Crispin slammed the refrigerator door shut and said, 'Look, I'll get the first train up there in the morning. Tell her I'm coming.'

He called Eurostar and found there was a train that night at 21.13; he booked a seat even though it meant he'd have to spend the night in a hotel somewhere in London. The train was nearly empty, and he tried to read a little but he couldn't concentrate, so he spent most of the journey drinking coffee in the buffet car. In London he had to pay an exorbitant rate for a hotel, where he got only four hours' sleep, and then he was back at King's Cross Station at six the next morning buying a ticket for Leeds.

At Leeds he changed for Keighley, and from there took a steam train on to Haworth, arriving in the village centre at noon. From the train he had caught a glimpse of the moors that Julia had described for him, but he was disenchanted by the grim blocks of houses and flats that obscured the land, and the beauty of the morning was lost in a dull industrial haze.

In the village the narrow cobblestone high street was swarming with tourists. Crispin found Heather Cottage and knocked on the door. Mrs Ingilby, the proprietor, had been expecting him, and she opened the door and welcomed him inside.

'You can go up in a moment, Father,' she said, 'after you've had a cup of tea.' She told him to have a seat at the small table in the living room.

When she came back from the kitchen with a pot of hot tea, Crispin asked, 'How is she?'

'She's been crying a lot.' She poured his tea and then set the teapot down. 'I went up last night and talked to her through the door. I told her you were coming. I think it upset her. She said we shouldn't have bothered you.'

'No. It was the right thing to do.'

'I thought so too.'

'Where can I stay? I'd like to freshen up.'

'The room at the top is yours. No one else is here except me. They sent that young woman who was her assistant back to London.'

Crispin finished his tea and carted his bag up the squeaking stairs to his room on the top floor, where he had a quick shave and changed his shirt, then went down one floor to Julia's room.

'It's me, Julia,' he said. 'May I come in?'

There was a long silence, and then he heard a quiet tread and the door opened slightly.

'I can't believe they called you,' she whispered from behind the door. She sounded very tired.

'I'd cross mountains for you,' he said. He reached through the opening in the doorway. 'Give me your hand,' he said. She took his hand, and hers was warm and damp. 'Why don't you want to let me in?'

'I don't want anybody to see me,' she said. She lifted his hand and ran his fingers over her cheek, and whispered, 'See what I did?'

Gently, he pushed open the door. The room was dark; the heavy curtains were drawn, blocking out the light. She had recently taken a shower and the room was humid and smelt faintly of perfume.

'Let me see,' he said. He drew her towards the dressing table and switched on a small bronze lamp.

'Here,' he said, lifting her face. There were long inflamed gashes down each cheek. 'Did you do this to yourself?'

She nodded, unable to look him in the eyes.

He reached for her, and she buried her face in his chest, clinging tightly to him.

'You take it all out on yourself, don't you?' he whispered, and she nodded, her face buried in his shoulder.

'I'm so humiliated,' she muttered. 'That's why I never called.' It was so much easier to talk about it like this, with Crispin's arms round her. 'I still can't believe it. It's just not like Jona to do something like this. But he did. So I'm a fool. And I guess, in a way, he was protecting me, because he knew if he left me I'd fall apart.'

'No, you would've grown up. And that's what's going to happen now. And I promise you, you won't fall apart. The Julia I know has courage like no one else I've ever met.'

She shook her head, a vague, hopeless gesture.

'And don't ever despair,' he pressed. 'Ever.'

She grew very still, and lifted her eyes to his.

It takes a strong soul to bear the weaknesses of others without despising them. Not many people had that gift of seeing with love, but Crispin did. Julia knew this; she had known it since they were young, although it had not yet been formulated in her mind then, as it was now.

'Oh, my,' he teased lightly, touching a lock of her hair, 'they've turned you into a brunette.'

She tried to smile but couldn't. He folded her back into his arms and held her. He had cradled many people in his arms, women who had lost children, husbands who had lost wives, but he had never felt his heart so full of sorrow as he did when he listened to Julia cry.

After a while he helped her back into bed. He covered her with a blanket and then pulled a chair up beside the bed.

'Don't leave me yet,' she whispered.

'I won't leave you at all.'

He stroked her hair, and gradually she relaxed, and soon she was asleep. Crispin thought about going up to his room. He needed sleep badly, but he didn't want to leave her. Quietly, so as not to wake her, he stretched out on the bed beside her. He was careful not to even touch her, but he could not sleep. He lay there listening to her breathe, praying that the proximity would not arouse passion, because he knew he could feel that for her, and he didn't want to feel it. Not now. Not ever.

Mrs Ingilby knew things would be all right. She had faith in Father Wakefield from the first moment she laid eyes on him, and she went to a good deal of trouble to prepare a special dinner, hoping he would coax Julia into eating. So when Crispin appeared in the kitchen later that afternoon, and asked if they could have dinner upstairs that evening, Mrs Ingilby felt greatly relieved.

Crispin's arrival had revived Julia's appetite, and she ate a small portion of Mrs Ingilby's rabbit stew and drank some wine. He could tell when she was thinking about Jona and did not press her to talk. After clearing their plates, Mrs Ingilby lit a fire for them, and Crispin sat in an armchair and read *The Times*. His silent presence, his undemanding acceptance of her, brought her reassurance in a way no one else could have done. She sat opposite him, watching him and marvelling at his patience and the way he fitted into her life.

Crispin lowered the paper and caught her gaze, and then she began to talk. At first she didn't speak about Jona but about her fears, because it somehow seemed to her that they were at the root of her failure.

She told him how everything beyond the walls of Heather Cottage terrified her, but her greatest fear was that she wouldn't be able to finish the film. All the techniques that had worked for her before, everything she had learned to do to reduce her anxiety, had all failed her once she had arrived back in Haworth. It was as if she had used up every last ounce of courage, and she was doomed to be a prisoner within these walls for ever. Daily, even hourly, she fought against despair, against the urge to take her own life. At times her despair turned to rage, and she imagined herself confronting Jona with his lies; she'd scream at him and dream up ways to hurt him, but then the grief would return.

Since Jona's death, she had begun to re-examine her relationship with him, and was slowly coming to grips with the disastrous consequences of relying so completely upon his guidance. She confided in Crispin how, when she was younger, and had yearned for an adult to care for her, she had willingly given him control over her finances. He had asked her to sign entire chequebooks, and Julia had never questioned how the money was being spent. Years later, when she asked him to explain how their investments worked, he had made a ruthless game out of it, purposely confounding her with rhetoric far beyond her grasp.

Eventually she had stopped asking him to explain anything, and had relinquished her hopes of self-reliance. Nevertheless, if she was still under his influence after all these years, it was because she had thought he was the best man in the world—the best lover, the best friend. He had been everything to her.

The hours swept by, until finally, around eleven, Crispin began showing signs of drowsiness and Julia urged him off to his room.

'How long are you staying?' she asked.

'As long as you need me. Phoebe's back in California with the girls, visiting her folks. It's the Easter holidays.'

'What about the cathedral? All those people who rely on you?'

'Why are you worrying about others? You think you're not important? I want you to be safe. I don't want anything to happen to you. I don't want anyone to hurt you, not ever again.' He touched her swollen cheek gently with the back of his hand, and he felt himself suddenly aroused. He tore his hand away. 'Don't hurt yourself again, Julia. You must be good to yourself.'

'I know,' she said, her hand rising to her cheek where he had touched her. 'What I did was terrible.'

He leaned forwards and kissed her on the forehead. 'Try to sleep.'

He turned and headed for the door. Then he turned and said, 'I was thinking maybe I'd get up early and go for a walk.'

'Oh, you should. It's so beautiful. Even if it rains, you should go. Mrs Ingilby has a lot of old hiking boots lying around. She'll have your size, I'm sure. And anything else you'll need.'

'Good. I'll see you when I get back.'

But in the morning, when he went downstairs, he found her waiting in the sitting room. She was dressed in a period costume she had worn during the first week of shooting, a grey muslin dress with wide sleeves and white lace collar, and her hair was pinned back in a tight bun. She smiled at Crispin's surprise.

'I'm coming with you,' she announced. She pointed to some boots and a hunter's all-weather coat on a bench. 'Those are for you. Mrs Ingilby's still asleep, so I pulled out some things we're using for the film.'

'Good,' he said with a restrained smile, trying to conceal the immense joy he felt.

'I suppose you think I'm being very dramatic, going out like this. But . . .' She faltered.

'Don't explain. I understand. You told me. Back in Paris.'

'It's the only way I can handle it.'

As he was lacing up his boots he said, 'It's odd, but I can see what you mean. You're not Julia any more.'

'You look very Victorian in Reverend Nicholls's coat.'

'Do I?' he grinned, glancing at her dress. 'You're sure you'll be warm enough?'

'I have a cloak. And I packed us breakfast. Some cheese and bread. And some beer.'

They set out under the pale mist of dawn, with the cottages huddled in shadow, the streets quiet and the windows dark. The hill was steep and the wet cobblestones slippery, and Julia clung to Crispin's arm, gripping her skirts with her free hand while they climbed. At the head of the village the street levelled out, and they followed it past the Black Bull Inn and round the church, turning into a lane. Here Julia picked up her pace, her skirts raised above her ankles. Once she stumbled, and Crispin caught her and looked down into her face. He could see the anxiety building in her eyes.

'Are you OK? Do you want to go back?'

She shook off his hand. 'I'll be OK once we're out of the village,' she replied, hurrying past him.

They turned off the lane onto a footpath beside an avenue of trees, and finally, with the morning light filtering through a grey-cast sky onto the moors, Crispin caught his first glimpse of the distant hills. They rose in great rolling sweeps, one horizon beyond another, receding into paler, mistier shades of blue.

Crispin and Julia had been raised in a place not unlike this, but here there were no extremes, no floods or droughts or plagues. The hills were steep and the moorland wild and uncultivated, but there was in this bleak and dramatic landscape a heart-wrenching beauty that gripped their souls. It was a land of ever-prevailing winds, of sudden, violent rains, of winter snow and starry nights. They had never outgrown their love for these things, and they became like children again, delighting in every aspect of nature around them. Every turn or rise opened up a new vista, and when at last they reached Top Withens, Julia led Crispin to a high slope behind a ruined farmhouse and its lone, gnarled tree, and they stood side by side and gazed out at the dim blue chain of mountains surrounding them.

They spread Julia's cloak on a grassy knoll and ate the picnic breakfast she had brought along. It was late morning by then, and the sun was warm, and after they had eaten they stretched out beside one another, Julia with her head resting on Crispin's arm. The beer and the meal had made them drowsy, and they both fell asleep and slept until the sun disappeared behind dark clouds, and they were woken by the wind rising from the north and drops of cold rain. They gathered up their belongings and hurried down the slope to the farmhouse ruins. The roof and the upper storey had collapsed long ago, and they took shelter in a corner and watched the dark sky and the wind-driven rain.

Crispin said, 'Maybe it wasn't too wise. Coming this far.'

'It'll pass. It won't stay like this for long.'

'You're cold,' he said. 'Put this back on.' He threw her cloak over her shoulders.

'This doesn't frighten me, you know,' she said earnestly. 'It feels good, not being afraid.'

'You can finish the film now.'

'Not until my face heals up.'

He took her chin between his fingers, and turned her face towards him and studied it. 'It will heal quickly.'

Her eyes were wide like liquid moons, and tendrils of her hair hung around her face. She had unbuttoned the collar of her dress, revealing the hollow at the base of her throat, and he had a sudden desire to kiss her there. He looked away quickly, and withdrew his hand.

Julia stared quietly at him. Suddenly the clouds separated and a shaft of sunlight fell upon the moorland. The storm was passing. 'See,' she said. 'I told you it wouldn't last.'

They were both still for a moment, and then she whispered, 'You should go back home tomorrow, Crispin.'

He knew she was right, but he was sad, and for the rest of the day he carried that sadness around like a stone on his chest.

They returned to the village midafternoon, and the tourists on Main Street gawked at them. Julia hid her face with the hood of her cloak. Someone stopped Crispin and asked if they were making a film, but he only hurried past, trying to shield Julia from their curious stares. Someone else snapped photographs of them as they entered Heather Cottage.

They had dinner downstairs that night, in the dining room, and you could tell subtle things had changed between them. Finally, halfway through their meal, Julia laid down her knife and fork and buried her face in her hands and cried out softly, 'Oh, Crispin, let's not ruin this, please. I couldn't bear to lose you too. When you're beside me, I feel like I can take on the world.'

It was the first time he knew that she felt the same way that he did, although he couldn't say so, because it would sound like a betrayal.

'Where will you go when you finish the film?'

'I don't know.'

'You can have our farmhouse. The place up in Normandy. It's not very glamorous . . . and it's not Paris, of course . . .'

Her eyes lit up. 'Phoebe wouldn't mind?'

'Hardly. She doesn't like the place.'

Julia reflected on the idea in silence, then sat back with tears glistening in her eyes. 'But there's no money for me, Crispin.'

'What?'

'That's what he meant.'

'Who?'

'That little geek of a lawyer. He said the estate didn't amount to much. I don't know. I'm supposed to be meeting with some financial adviser.'

'Would you like me to handle it?'

'Oh, Crispin . . .'

'I have a buddy who's a lawyer. He'll take care of it. He'll do it as a favour.' He was thinking of Rhoderic. 'Let him meet the guy.'

She nodded, relieved. 'I'd like that, if you could arrange it. I can't trust anyone we knew. They were all Jona's advisers. They must have known about this all along.'

'You have to build your own world, but you can do it.'

His encouragement put a glimmer of a smile on her face.

'And I never thanked you,' he said.

Startled, she replied, 'What on earth for?'

'For your donation. All your clothes.'

She laughed lightly. 'Oh, that.'

'You've got a heart, girl.'

She reflected for a moment, and then said quietly, 'That's funny. Nobody's ever said that about me. They tell me how great I look, or how much they like some film I've done . . .'

'That's because they don't know you. You were trying to protect yourself, so you built walls. Walls aren't always a bad thing. They're necessary to survive. And you're a survivor.'

'Not without you,' she said, unabashed, and her eyes locked on his.

Crispin couldn't look away but Julia did, and it made her want to cry because she recognised in that brief instant all the beauty life could hold with a man like him, and she knew it could never happen.

'Do you want me to go back for you?' he said quickly, to cover the awkwardness.

'Go back?'

'To the King George. Pick up the things you left behind. Anything personal you might want later.'

'You don't have time to do that.'

'I do now. With the girls gone. I could box up your things. You could keep them at the place in Normandy. We've got a big empty attic. You don't want to just abandon everything.'

'You're the voice of reason speaking.'

'Then call the concierge. Tell him to let me in.'

'If it'll make you feel better,' she mocked with a grin.

He left early the next morning, took the train back to Leeds, then on to London. He caught the Eurostar to Paris and was back in his office just after five in the afternoon. He had been gone a little over forty-eight hours but it felt like he had been gone for weeks. The next day, people teased him about disappearing as soon as Phoebe had left town. He didn't take it seriously. And then word got round that he had gone to England to see Julia, and the rumours spread like wildfire, growing in intensity and consuming and destroying, so that when the flames were finally extinguished, it was too late, and the landscape of his life had been disfigured beyond recognition.

After Crispin's visit to England, he and Julia frequently exchanged calls. He always spoke to her in private, behind closed doors, and sometimes the conversations were long. He also took calls from lawyers and financial advisers. Unmarked cardboard boxes appeared in his office, stacked behind his desk, and when asked what they were, he replied evasively. There was nothing to indicate an intimate liaison, but to Tom Noonan and his supporters it all added up like a simple mathematical operation with only one possible solution.

If Maddy Cartwright had been around she could have controlled the damage; she would have alerted Crispin and he could have addressed the rumours. But Maddy was in Atlanta attending her granddaughter's wedding, and his other supporters, of which there were many, were too embarrassed to approach him on the subject. To confront Crispin with suspicions of something as serious as adultery was a mission none of them wanted to undertake.

You didn't need to do much sleuthing to deduce who was spreading the slander. Gerry Noonan and Synthia Ribbey led the campaign, although everyone knew that Tom Noonan was behind it all. Gerry was truly fond of Phoebe and she meant her no harm, but she was fonder still of her husband. She never saw it as slander or gossip-mongering, but as upholding her husband's ideals.

Tom had put it to her quite clearly one night after dinner when they were discussing Crispin's hasty flight to England.

'It just reeks of deceit,' Tom had said sourly. He was knotting a big plastic bag full of kitchen rubbish while Gerry scoured out the sink.

'But he didn't really try to cover it up, Tom,' she reasoned. 'He didn't lie about where he was going.'

'All the same, the whole thing's just got out of control. I've heard too much from too many parishioners to ignore it. It's been very damaging for the cathedral. All these salacious innuendos whenever his name comes up. It's all anyone wants to talk about.'

'Do you think it's true?' Gerry asked. 'That they're having an affair?'

'The fact that he's given so many people reason to suspect an affair is what matters.' He straightened and stood there tall and righteous. 'I'm just afraid he's going to slide into the deanship on his personal popularity, and that would be a downright calamity.'

'You really think the vestry will vote him in?'

'I do. Unless something catastrophic happens.'

'Like what?'

'Like Phoebe leaving him.'

'I doubt if Phoebe knows a thing,' Gerry said. 'She's still in California. They won't be back for another week yet.'

'Maybe she should,' he said with a smile of satisfaction. 'Yes. Maybe she *should* know.' Then he went to take the rubbish out.

Phoebe loved her visits to her parents' home in Santa Barbara, even more so after she and Crispin had left Chicago and moved the family into the cramped rectory in Paris. So when the girls grumbled about the weather, which was unseasonably cool and rainy that spring, and moaned that this was no different from the Easter holidays they spent at their farmhouse in Normandy, Phoebe was quick to point out that their farmhouse had rotting wood beams, slanted floors and creaking steps, and that when there was no sun in Normandy they always ended up spending their days working on the house.

Hilary and Richard Darrs' home was a splendid Palladian villa, set deep in the interior of a vast maze of separate gardens, where there were vine-covered pergolas and terraces, fountains and streams, and even a Tuscan-style grotto. There was a turquoise pool for swimming and a reflection pool for reflecting and palm trees for the sound they made.

Phoebe had never tried to hide Crispin's financial difficulties from her parents, but on this visit she began to voice her complaints openly, and she gave the story a new spin. Phoebe had a gift for manipulating perceptions, and the husband she portrayed to her parents was an infuriatingly unreasonable man who was taking self-denial to the extreme and forcing them to live a life not of their own choosing.

Phoebe took to spending her mornings at a local health club where she ran into Cecilia Glass, an old friend from university in Los Angeles, who was now living in Santa Barbara. Their morning workouts were generally followed by fruit drinks and long chats at the bar. Cecilia had been through three divorces and each husband had been wealthier than the last, so she had all sorts of sound advice for Phoebe, who listened with interest. She did not really want to divorce her husband, but she was very discontent. Being back in Santa Barbara, surrounded by a level of luxury of which she had long been deprived, only heightened her discontent.

Phoebe was sunbathing by the pool that morning. The weather had turned again, and it was a fine, warm morning with only a thin haze in a brilliant blue sky. Then the housekeeper came out and handed her the telephone; it was Gerry Noonan.

Gerry approached the subject obliquely. She enquired about the children and Phoebe's parents and declared how much they were missed. Then she talked about Crispin, emphasising how busy he was and how little they were seeing of him around the cathedral. Only towards the end of the conversation did she mention Julia.

'Isn't it awful about Julia Kramer? That man of hers dying?' Gerry said.

'I know!' Phoebe exclaimed, lowering her voice. All of a sudden the conversation took on real interest. 'He was murdered!'

'Is that true?'

'Absolutely! Did you hear about the clothes she left?'

'No . . .'

'She sent over these trunks full of her clothes and asked Crispin to donate them to a charity.'

'Why on earth would she do that?'

'I can't tell you. Crispin doesn't want any of it to get out.'

'You mean about his murder?'

'Oh, Gerry, there's a lot more to it than that,' Phoebe said with tantalising secrecy. 'It was mind-boggling what Jona pulled on her.'

Gerry lowered her voice. 'Oh, Phoebe, I won't tell a soul. You know I can keep a secret.'

So Phoebe told all. She explained how Jona had led a double life, marrying another woman and having a child, all the while living with Julia. And that he had left his entire estate to the child.

'So I suppose all those clothes were things he'd bought her?' Gerry surmised.

'I'm sure of it. And I don't know for certain, but from the letter she wrote us, I got the impression she may have tried to kill herself.'

'Oh, my goodness!' Gerry exclaimed. 'So that's what all the urgency was about. Of course, no one had any idea she was threatening suicide, but it makes sense now. The way Crispin just raced off to England overnight. Right after you left.' Gerry paused, taking in Phoebe's stunned silence on the other end of the line. Then she said, in a low, confidential tone, 'You didn't know, did you, Phoebe?'

'Didn't know what?'

'That he went to see her.'

A long tentative silence hung in the air. Finally she replied, 'We haven't talked in a while. We've been missing each other. He's called but we've been out. It's difficult, with nine hours' time difference.'

'Well, of course,' Gerry said.

There was another awkward silence, and then Gerry said, 'Look, I'm sure he would have told you. It's just, well, you need to be prepared for all the rumours. They're flying all over the place. I didn't want you to come back with all this going on behind your back, and not know what everyone has been saying. There's nothing worse than being the last to know.'

Phoebe started to speak, but her voice broke.

Gerry said then, 'Oh, Phoebe, I'm so sorry. But don't "shoot the messenger". Please. I'm your friend. Somebody had to tell you.'

Phoebe was crying now. 'Oh, Gerry, I'm so glad you did. She won't ever set foot in my home again, I promise you that much.'

'But I heard she's moving into your house up in Normandy, after the film's finished.'

'What?' Phoebe cried.

After she hung up, Phoebe sat at the edge of the pool with her pretty brown feet dangling in the water, hating her husband for something she wasn't even sure he had done. It didn't matter that she herself was most clearly guilty of infidelity, that she had once, years ago, indulged in that very same behaviour. The affair had lasted five months. It had been an immediate and intense attraction, something wild and inexplicable. Day after day she had drowned in illicit pleasure, aroused to extremes she had never imagined possible, until she found out she was pregnant with Lola. She had never loved the man, she had not even liked him. But she never really felt ashamed of what she had done. Her betrayal sat in a tightly sealed little cubicle at the back of her mind, far removed from the rest of her life.

When Phoebe told her mother about Gerry's call, Hilary's maternal heart sank in her chest. 'Oh Lord,' she said, 'I think I'm going to be sick.' Her hand flew to her mouth. 'What are you going to do?'

'I don't know, Mama.'

'Oh, honey. How awful. Will you run into her?'

'Crispin told her she could move into our house in Normandy,' Phoebe sobbed. 'He didn't even ask me,' she said, tugging a tissue from a box beside her bed. 'Can you believe it?'

'I'm sure this isn't the first time he's rushed off to console some poor unfortunate woman. And I can see how they might fall for him. He has such a good heart, and he is such a good-looking man. You just need to go back and get this sorted out,' Hilary soothed, stroking her daughter's hair. She had always been fond of Crispin and had found his decision to enter the priesthood an admirable one, but now she felt betrayed.

Phoebe shot up. 'I can't stand the thought of going back there.' She blew her nose. 'It's all too awful. I hate that place!'

'I thought you loved Paris.'

Phoebe heaved a long sigh. 'I do. But I'd love it a lot more if it we weren't always fighting over money. It's such a struggle, Mama. Being married to a priest. It was so different when he had his business.'

'But I remember, even when he was making a lot of money, he wasn't really attached to it. He just wanted to see all of you girls happy.'

'He doesn't seem to give a damn now. He seems to think there's some kind of virtue in being poor. I wasn't made for that kind of life.'

'What are you saying, sweetie?'

'I don't want to go back there, that's what I'm saying.'

'Honey, the girls have to go back to school.'

'There are schools here, you know, Mama.'

'How would the girls feel about that?'

'They'd love it.' At least Megan would. And Megan was the only one she'd really have to deal with.

'Are you sure about this?'

'Mama, if he wants to sort this out, he can come here. After all the misery he's brought down on me, he can damn well come here and explain himself.'

❧ EIGHT ❧

THERE WERE SOME at the cathedral who were close observers and reasonable people, and all of them noted later that Crispin did not act like a guilty man, but rather like a man burdened with responsibilities. There was the *ravalement* and critical decisions to be made with the chief architect and engineers, and his ongoing efforts at fundraising. He performed weddings and visited the sick and the dying, and lent his comforting ways to the families of the bereaved, as well as meeting those who just came looking for someone to listen to them. He did all of these things because he loved the people, and he thought that if he did his job well, he might briefly uncover the face of God so they could get a glimpse of a world he had once seen himself.

As promised, he met Jona's lawyer and brought in Rhoderic to represent Julia's interests and find out all he could about Raza Lichovich and her son, Alexander. He looked over financial statements and spoke to bank trustees to try to unravel the whole mess, but he could see right away that no one person knew all there was to know about Jona Wahlberg's business matters.

Phoebe and the girls were due to return on Saturday morning, on a direct flight from Los Angeles, and Crispin was at the airport early. He had not spoken directly to Phoebe since the beginning of her holiday, but he had spoken to the girls several times and to Phoebe's father once, and everything was fine. Nevertheless, he had been feeling guilty that he had sent Phoebe off to California with a modest amount of cash and no credit cards, and she had been furious.

He dwelt on these thoughts while he waited in an airport café, staring at the crowded hall where family and friends waited for arriving passengers, when he heard his name paged over the loudspeaker. He sprang out of his chair and rushed from the café. At the airport information counter there was a young man dressed in motorcycle leathers waiting for him. He opened a courier pouch, handed Crispin an envelope, and waited while he signed for it.

Crispin's hands were shaking when he opened the envelope and read the letter. Suddenly he felt dizzy, and he knew he was going to have to

431

sit down. He found another café and went to a table at the back and sat down to read the letter again. And then he felt it, the whole crushing weight of what was happening. On the way home he had a sudden deep ache for Lola, and he had to pull over to the side of the motorway because he couldn't see to drive any more.

When he got back to the rectory he called Santa Barbara even though it was one o'clock in the morning. He got the answering machine and this fuelled his anger, because they must have known he would call.

The rest of the day he tried to keep busy, but he couldn't concentrate. Whoever asked about Phoebe and the kids was told they'd been delayed. He called Santa Barbara every hour, but no one answered the telephone.

Finally, in an act of desperation, he called Air France. There was a seat available on a flight to Los Angeles the next morning. He paid for the ticket over the telephone with a credit card he had saved for emergencies. It was a day flight and very long, and although there was plenty of room to stretch out he wasn't able to sleep. By the time he picked up his rental car at Los Angeles International, he was feeling like he'd been drugged, and he stopped at a gas station to get some coffee, but it wasn't strong enough to do any good.

It was dark when Crispin arrived in Santa Barbara and he drove straight up into the hills to the Darrs' home. The property was hidden behind high white walls and he parked at the gate, got out of the car and pressed the buzzer. Hilary, Phoebe's mother, answered the intercom. If she was surprised at his unannounced arrival, she hid it well. But he had to wait for several minutes before the gates opened and he figured she had gone to tell Phoebe he was there.

A regiment of perfect foxtail palms, as refined as Greek columns, lined the reflecting pool that led to the pool house. Hilary Darr had told him that Phoebe would be waiting for him there. He came up the path and saw her and stopped at the opposite end of the pool. She wore shorts and a scoop-necked sleeveless shirt and she was very brown.

She was contrite, but only just. 'Obviously you got my letter.'

He waited for her to go on, but she just stood there with her arms folded across her chest. He was angry and wanted to kick something but he paced instead. 'What is this all about?'

It was quiet in the garden and his voice carried on the night air.

'Keep your voice down, Crispin, please.'

He answered just a shade lower, but you could still hear the anger.

'Look, I flew nearly halfway around the world, you can damn well walk the length of this pool to meet me.'

She came sulkily towards him. It was a walk he had found sexy at one time, but not now. 'Come with me,' she said, and he followed her down a gravel path with more palms. He could smell lavender somewhere. She kept walking until finally he stopped her.

'I just wanted to get away from the house,' she said, turning to face him. 'So they wouldn't hear us.'

'What did you tell them?'

She tried to look him in the face but she couldn't. 'I told them the truth. The reason why we're not going back to Paris.'

'Which is?'

'You know why.'

'Phoebe, I flew over here to talk to you face to face because you didn't have the decency to come back home. Now talk to me! Tell me what this is all about!'

'Don't yell at me, Crispin!' she said. 'How do you think I felt? Getting that awful call from Gerry telling me that as soon as we were gone, you went to see her.'

'Gerry called to tell you that? You make it sound like it was a planned tryst,' he sputtered, trying to control his rage. 'Julia's publicist in New York called and asked me if I'd go to see her.'

'Why you?'

'Because I'm a priest.'

'Doesn't England have any priests? Do they have to import them from Paris? Why are you so special?'

There was a pause, and then he answered quietly, 'Some people think I am. Apparently you don't.'

She looked down, knowing she had hurt him. 'Everybody thinks you're having an affair with her.'

'They were saying that way back at the beginning. You didn't believe it then.'

She fixed him with a probing look. 'Where did you stay when you were there?'

'At Heather Cottage. Where she was staying.'

'That looks real good,' she quipped.

'Her publicist and the director made the arrangements. They were afraid she might do something . . .' He faltered. 'For heaven's sake, this isn't the first time I've intervened in a crisis like this.'

'Why didn't you tell me?'

'I would have if you'd returned my calls.'

'I did return your calls!' she flung back. It was a bold lie, but Crispin ignored it.

'Phoebe, you and I both know that Julia has nothing to do with this.'

'Well, it just pushed me over the edge. And it was a pretty big shove.'

'I think you had this planned all along.'

'That's not true!'

'You don't just break up a family overnight.'

'*You* broke it up!' she snapped. 'You! Not me.'

He stared at her. What she was doing was incomprehensible. He couldn't get inside her head to figure it out.

All of a sudden, he wasn't sure that he wanted to figure it out any more. Hardened, he said, 'You're going to believe what you want to. You always have. You never could think rationally.'

She slapped him then, and he grabbed her wrist and squeezed it so hard that she winced, 'You do what you want, but don't you dare take my girls away from me.'

He flung her hand away and she rubbed her wrist. 'That hurt,' she said, looking at him warily.

'That's nothing compared to what you're doing to me.' He glanced towards the house. 'I want to see them.'

'You can see them tomorrow. Come around four o'clock. They'll be back from school then.'

Crispin was stunned. 'You enrolled them in school over here?'

'Of course. I didn't want them to get behind.'

After he had gone, Phoebe sat outside and cried. Crispin sat up most of the night in his motel room, flipping through television stations. Neither one of them had expected things to go the way they had. She had expected him to put up more of a fight. He had expected to feel differently. Both of them had wanted something else out of the encounter.

The next day, they decided that Phoebe would send the girls down one by one to meet their father on the terrace behind the reflecting pool. This had been where Phoebe and Crispin used to sip margaritas and watch sunsets when they were first married and visiting her parents. They had even made love there, and it was a bitter reminder to both of them. But it was also a secluded place, removed from the main house.

Crispin wanted to see Lola first. She came skipping barefoot down the steps in white shorts, with her legs all brown from the sun, and she jumped up into his arms and wrapped herself round him like a little tree frog. It was tough on him, and a sob broke from his chest, involuntarily, but he hid it with a whoop of laughter.

'I'll bet you had a good time at school, didn't you?' Crispin asked.

She nodded warily, looking to him for the right answer.

'School's fun here, isn't it?' he said.

Her face exploded into a big smile. And she went on to tell him about her first days in an American school. Watching her, he could see she was different here and happy in a way she had not been back in Paris.

What really hurt was that Cat refused to see him. Megan came down, and they talked a little. He could tell she'd been crying. She didn't want to talk about herself, but about Cat.

'She said she saw you and Julia in the cathedral way back last autumn, and she said you two had been kissing.'

'She said what?' Crispin exclaimed.

'Well, something like that. Kissing or almost.'

'That time in the cathedral was the first time Julia and I had seen each other in . . . I don't know how many years. Since I was seventeen. It was a pretty emotional thing.'

'She said you were touching.'

'If we were, it was the way old friends touch when they meet.'

She was sitting back in the patio chair, her eyes fixed on the floor, legs stretched out before her, scratching at the metal armrest with a finger-nail. He was surprised at her. She seemed mellow and contemplative.

'And then,' she went on, still not daring to look up, 'Cat said there was a time after that big fundraiser when all the girls at church started talking about the two of you.'

'Did they say anything directly to you?'

She gave him a fiery look from beneath her long lashes. 'They wouldn't dare,' she snapped. 'Cat's so gullible. She believes anything.'

'The rumours aren't true. I've never been unfaithful to your mother. And I don't want a divorce.'

She sat there, refusing to meet his look, a tear rolling down her cheek. She brushed it away, and he wanted to reach out and hug her, but that would be too much. So he took her hand, and she responded by squeezing it; it was the only way she could tell him she loved him. Abruptly, she shoved out of the chair and shot past him up the stone steps.

Crispin ate dinner alone, at a plain Mexican restaurant recommended by the locals. When he returned to his motel he found a message from Phoebe asking him to meet her at the bar of a beachfront restaurant.

She slid up onto the bar stool he'd been saving for her, and ordered a Perrier water. She wore a hooded sweatshirt over her shorts and her hair was tangled and windswept. She'd been walking on the beach.

'I've reconsidered,' she said. 'You're right, Cris,' she confessed, finger-ing the bottle. 'There was a lot more to it than Julia.'

'I'm not having an affair with her.'

'I believe you.'

He took a drink of Scotch, then turned away to watch a wave break over the shore. He wasn't sure where to go with this now. He wasn't even sure if he cared. But there were the girls to consider.

He said, 'Then let's cut straight to the heart of it. I haven't taken any vows of poverty, but I'm a priest, and I'm sure not about to get rich. I thought you could adjust. You certainly made me believe you could—'

'I did think . . .' she interrupted, but he raised his hand.

'Let me finish, please.' He turned towards her with a clear gaze, and he was detached in a way he had never been before. 'If you decide to stick it out, and for the sake of our daughters I hope you do, let me warn you, it'll probably get worse before it gets better. I mean financially. But the deanship is something . . .' All of a sudden his eyes burned and he dropped his gaze to his glass because he didn't want her to see him get emotional. 'The deanship of St John's Cathedral . . . that's an incredible honour. And you're my wife, and that's something to be proud of. There's a certain status in that, Phoebe. If that's any help. The money won't make that much difference. But there are other benefits.'

'Such as the Noonans' apartment,' she teased.

'That too,' he said and returned her smile. The lightness should have been a sign of encouragement, but he couldn't be sure. He was trying to negotiate his future with a partner he no longer trusted.

She brushed a tangled wisp of hair out of her face.

'OK,' she said. 'I'll call Dad's travel agent. See if she can get us on a flight within the next few days.'

The first thing he did upon his return to Paris, even before a shower and shave, was to track down Tom Noonan. The Dean was in his office leafing through a catalogue of liturgical wear.

'Crispin. Come in,' he said. He leaned back in his chair.

'We need to talk,' Crispin said as he stepped inside and started to close the door.

'Yes. We do. But I don't have time right now.' He glanced at his watch and said, 'Got an appointment to get my hair cut in a few minutes.' He rose from his desk. 'How about this afternoon?'

But Crispin closed the door anyway. 'This can't wait, Tom,' he said. 'Sit down. Please.'

Tom smiled pleasantly, but he was peeved. He sat down all the same.

Crispin pulled up a chair to face his desk and said, 'We've got to put an end to these rumours.'

'If you're talking about yourself and Ms Kramer—'

'They're slanderous and they're false.'

Tom disowned any responsibility with a graceful gesture of his long hands, lifting them into the air in much the same way he blessed the chalice on Sunday mornings.

'I certainly never believed them myself. But it's what our parishioners believe that counts. They're the ones you minister to. You've lost their trust. Adultery is no light matter.'

'The rumours are false.'

'Appearances matter in these things.'

'Appearances are what you make of them.'

'What are we supposed to make of your wife leaving you?'

'Who said she's left me?'

Tom's expression curdled.

'Who said she's left me?' Crispin repeated.

'The sources are many.'

'The sources are misinformed. Intentionally so.'

Tom caught the implication. He stiffened a little. 'I certainly hope you're not implying that I had anything to do with it.'

'Phoebe and the girls will be back next Tuesday.'

There was a taut silence, and then Tom foiled with a dazzling smile.

'I'm very glad to hear that, Crispin. I hope you've got things ironed out.' He rose to signal the end of their conversation.

Crispin remained seated. 'There's another thing you need to understand, Tom. Julia Kramer cares very much about my family. I don't want her to think she's the source of any of my problems. She's gone through enough tragedy as it is. If she should decide to seek consolation here in our cathedral, I trust she'll be welcomed—by all of us.'

He rose and strode deliberately out of the office.

Julia called that evening. Just the sound of her voice lifted his spirits.

'Hold on,' he said, groping for the remote control underneath the sofa cushions. 'Let me turn this thing down.' He muted the television and sat up. 'Hey. What's up?'

'I'm finished! I got through it! Shot my last scene today!'

She was bubbling and he thought how good it felt to hear her voice. 'Congratulations,' he said.

'I couldn't have done it without you. You gave me hope.'

'You found it in yourself.'

'You can take a little credit.'

'You need to start taking credit yourself, for what you've accomplished. Without Jona. Without me.'

437

He came off a shade churlish, and he wanted to blurt out an apology, but he didn't. He had crushed her enthusiasm, and when she spoke again her voice had lost the bounce.

'I think we've made a beautiful film. I don't know if anyone will go to see it, but it's a beautiful film. And my work is good.'

'You made the right choice, didn't you? To make it.'

'I guess I did.'

'The house is waiting for you.'

'Your offer's still good?'

'Of course it is.'

'Is tomorrow too soon?'

'I can get away around noon. I'll meet you up there. Go through the place with you.'

'Crispin, remember, if Phoebe and the girls or anyone else wants to come up for a weekend, I can move into a hotel.'

'Hey, there are plenty of rooms. Having friends and family around is what that place is all about.'

'I'm really sorry they never got the opportunity to visit the set. You'll tell them for me, won't you? Tell them I'll make it up to them?'

'Of course I will. Now, you'll need directions . . .'

After they hung up, Crispin turned the television up, lay back on the sofa and tried to focus on the news, but he ached inside.

Julia took the train back to France. At Waterloo Station there was a moment when she was afraid she wouldn't be able to go through with it, but Michael Langham had accompanied her and brought along a burly chauffeur who carted her bags to the platform and loaded them into her compartment. They kept a constant watch on her, like guards transporting a convict, waiting until the train pulled out of the station to make sure she didn't jump off and make a run for it. She would have found it funny if she hadn't been so sick, and for the first fifteen minutes of the train ride she locked herself in the lavatory and sat shivering through a horrendous panic attack. After it had passed she dragged herself back to her seat and fell into a hard sleep. When she woke they were already through the tunnel and arriving in Calais.

She hired a taxi to take her to the village of St Yvoi. The driver had to get out and enquire at a *tabac* because they couldn't find the house, but eventually they found it off a narrow street up the hill from the priory. It was composed of a generous two-storey stone central structure with a half-timber wing on one side and a barn on the other, and larger than she'd imagined. Built in the nineteenth century in the Norman Revival style, it had languished for decades. The roof over the barn had collapsed and there were broken panes in the windows of the half-timber wing. Nature had reclaimed the place; gulls were nesting in the chimneys and creeping vines had overrun the barn.

Julia found bicycles in the barn, and while she waited for Crispin to arrive she rode one round the courtyard, and then summoned the courage to press on into the village. If she had succeeded in taking the train all the way from London, then she could darn well make it into the village centre. The sun was warm and the breeze sweet, and she felt brave and good about life. The local bakery was open, so she went in and bought some bread. On the way back she passed a lilac tree, and she broke off some blooms and put them in the basket and raced back to the house before anyone could catch her. She was so pleased with herself that she cycled round the courtyard singing loudly. This was the way that Crispin and Maddy found her when they pulled in.

Crispin had asked Maddy to come up with him.

'I need to open up the house for her,' he had explained. 'And I don't think it would be wise for me to go up there alone.'

'So you want a chaperone, is that it?' she asked.

He answered, 'No. An eye witness.'

When they pulled into the drive, Julia came wobbling towards them, guiding the bike with her knees, arms outstretched with the wind, the lilacs and a baguette crammed into the basket on the handlebars. She had lost weight since Jona's death and her arms were thin. Her brown hair had been cut, and she looked very young and artless. She pedalled up alongside the car and grabbed the wing mirror to steady herself. As Crispin rolled down his window, Maddy watched them together. There was unguarded joy on Crispin's face, but if he was in love, he didn't know it or wouldn't believe it. Maddy was sure about that.

Julia and Maddy had met briefly at the fundraiser and once Maddy had dropped by the rectory when Julia was there, but they had never had an opportunity to get to know one another. Julia, who loved dogs, made much ado about Piaf. She nestled the dog into the bicycle basket amid the lilacs and took her for a spin round the courtyard while Crispin unloaded bags from the boot of the car.

This house was special to Crispin. It was the only piece of property he owned, and he had wanted it to be special to his family too. He had wanted a family retreat for their holidays, a place they could make their own and return to year after year. Its renovation had been a family affair. When they came to Normandy, if the weather was too cold or rainy to go to the beach, Crispin always put them to work with a paintbrush or spade. In exchange for their labour the girls had the right to choose their room (there were seven bedrooms) and they were given free rein in decorating it. Megan splashed pink on the walls and then pasted together fashion ads to make a ceiling-to-floor collage; Cat chose a more subdued effect with glow-in-the-dark stars upon a midnight blue ceiling and posters of unicorns and magical beasts. Lola, who had just turned three when they bought the house, had been too frightened to sleep in a room by herself. Then one day Crispin came home with an antique wardrobe. On the inside back panel he painted a winter landscape, and he lit it from within so that when the doors were opened it appeared as if you were entering Narnia. The effect was magical. He positioned the wardrobe against the wall at the foot of her bed, and Lola would lay there and gaze into the wardrobe and dream her way to sleep.

Over the three years that they had owned the house, they had worked hard to make it comfortable. And yet, for all their work, after the first year their family visits had become fewer and shorter in duration, and as soon as school was out in the summer, Phoebe took the girls back to California. Crispin would go up to Normandy by himself during the months that they were away, driving up on Sunday after service and returning on Tuesday morning. He had wanted someone to attach themselves to it the way he had done, but that had not happened.

Now, the idea that Julia would be staying there made him a little self-conscious. He hesitated in the doorway with Maddy's bag in his hand, seeing it with a freshly critical eye, but then Maddy nudged past him with Piaf's bed under her arm and trudged up the stairs. Crispin didn't notice Julia step up behind him. He was lost in his thoughts for a moment and then she prodded him with the baguette.

'May I come in?'

He moved aside and she swept past, bringing the smell of dog and lilacs with her.

'I love it!' she cried. She set Piaf down and stood in the hall with the flowers dangling from one hand.

'Can't see a thing until we get some light in here,' he said and he stepped past her into the sitting room. She followed him and watched as he opened the double doors and folded back the louvred shutters, and light flooded into the room.

'I love it! Nothing matches!'

'You're pulling my leg.'

'Absolutely not. I'm so fed up with places done by decorators.'

'Well, then, you'll feel at home here.'

'I already do,' she said, and while he went around the dining room throwing back the shutters, she rummaged through a cupboard and found a vase and took it into the kitchen to fill with water. When he came into the room, she glanced up and said, 'You know, I was so worried. I was wondering how I'd manage. But I'll be fine. I can tell.'

'The neighbours are good people. Madame Cristophani loves to talk to you from her window. But I am worried about your being too isolated.'

'I'll get along.'

At that moment, Maddy burst in on them to suggest they drive in to Deauville for dinner. Crispin made excuses, saying he thought it might be nice to have dinner at home. He and Maddy could drive into town to pick up some fish, and if the weather held they could eat outside.

Julia could see that Maddy was disappointed. She turned to her and said, 'Maddy, if Crispin doesn't want to go out to eat, it's because of me. He knows I have panic attacks in public places. I'm agoraphobic.' She gave Maddy an apologetic smile and left the room carrying the vase.

Maddy stood mouth agape. 'She's agoraphobic?'

Crispin nodded. 'At times she's completely debilitated by it.'

'So that's why you went to England.'

'She wasn't able to work. She was afraid she couldn't finish the film.'

'Oh, goodness gracious,' Maddy muttered, and she pulled out a chair from the kitchen table and lowered herself into it. 'How's she going to manage up here all alone?'

'She thinks she'll be OK.'

'Do people know about this?'

'Only a few. Me. Her publicist. Jona did, of course.'

'Phoebe?'

Crispin shook his head. 'It mustn't get around.'

'I understand.'

'Obviously, she trusts you, Maddy.'

Maddy thought about how so many people had been wrong about Julia, and the injustice of it all struck her hard.

'I'm glad she trusts me,' she said, putting a reassuring hand on Crispin's arm.

Crispin lowered his voice and said, 'Something else you should know. I've never said a word about the problems Phoebe and I have been having. I don't confide in her like that. She thinks . . .' He hesitated. 'She thinks my marriage is doing just fine. And if she knew people thought we were having an affair . . .' He took a long breath. 'She wouldn't see me again. She wouldn't stay here. And she doesn't have anywhere else to go.' He levelled a tough gaze on Maddy. 'She needs me, Maddy. She needs you. She needs all the stability she can get.'

When Maddy and Crispin returned from Deauville, Julia had set the table outside with some dishes, a few half-burnt candles and the vase of lilacs. Crispin had bought champagne to celebrate Julia's successful completion of her film, but he felt like celebrating anyway. It was an evening where everything was good. Maddy did the fish very simply but it was fresh and tasty and they had good wine. When they finally went inside, Crispin lit a fire and Maddy and Julia sat together on the sofa while Crispin poked at the burning logs. After a while Maddy went off to bed, but Julia stayed.

She smiled at Crispin. 'You know, it looks like my career's taking off again. The word's out that the film is good, and I'm getting some offers.'

'That's wonderful.'

'It's exciting.'

'How are you getting along?'

She gazed into the fire, gave it some thought and then said, 'The worst thing is the confusion. I'm either aching for him to come back or wanting to kill him.'

'I have a little more information for you.'

'About the woman?'

'She was a journalist in Moscow. She wrote for a Russian economic review. Apparently, they met when she interviewed him.'

'When was that?'

'The first time was about three years ago.'

She let out a soft cry. 'Three years? That long?'

Julia curled up into a ball in the corner of the sofa and stared sadly into the fire. Crispin hated to see her hurt like that, and he wished then he hadn't brought it up. 'We don't have to talk about this right now.'

'That's all right. I'm OK.'

'Then shall I go on?'

'Yes.'

'She's forty-one. Born and raised in Leningrad. Studied at the London School of Economics then went back to Moscow to teach at the university. Married a mathematics professor. They got divorced and he emigrated to Israel. No kids. After the Soviet collapse she went to work for Tarazov's television station. It seems Jona pulled strings to get her a green card. She moved to New York and they were married last summer.'

'And the baby?'

'He was born in September. Jona's name is on the birth certificate.'

'Wow,' she said with a sad smile. 'Can't beat that for legitimacy.'

'Rhoderic thinks you should fight it in court.'

'For what? What am I going to win? His estate? That's nearly worthless.

What's left? His loyalty? His love? I sure can't contest that now, can I?' She sat up and brushed her hair back with a tired gesture. 'I have to reconstruct myself. And I'll do it with my own money.'

Crispin said, 'Hey, that's the spunky kid I used to know. You could be so rebellious. I liked that about you.'

She turned to him and an easy smile passed between them.

'In the morning I'll do some shopping before Maddy and I leave. You can make me a list. I'll get what you need.'

'No. You let me take care of that. I need to take my life back.'

She checked her watch and saw it was late, and she rose. She was thinking about giving him a good-night kiss, but decided against it.

A little before eight o'clock in the morning, Crispin was woken by a pounding on his door. He was stumbling blindly into his jeans when the door flew open and Julia barged in. She waved a tabloid newspaper under his nose.

'Look at this! Look at this! I cannot believe them . . .'

'OK, hold on. Just a minute . . .' Crispin had been sound asleep and dreaming something very pleasant. He sat down on the edge of the bed.

Maddy appeared at the door looking as sleep-rumpled as Crispin and asking what on earth had happened.

'*Look!*' Julia cried, and she spun round and held the tabloid open.

Maddy took the newspaper from her and Julia pointed to the headline: JULIA KRAMER'S REAL-LIFE LOVER-PRIEST. Below it was a photograph of Crispin herding Julia down Main Street in Haworth with a protective arm round her shoulders. Julia was in a hooded cloak, attempting to hide her face from the gawking tourists; Crispin was wearing the Victorian overcoat she had loaned him, his white priest's collar starkly visible at his neck. Next to this picture was another photograph revealing Julia in costume embracing a man dressed in the same Victorian overcoat. The hood of Julia's cloak had been thrown back and her hair was loose, and you saw on her face a look of absolute abandon, the look of a woman's resolve overthrown by passion. But the man's face was obscured by the brim of his hat. Only his hand cradling her head was visible.

Crispin peered over Julia's shoulder. 'What's this all about?'

But then he saw the photographs, and before Maddy had a chance to read the article, Crispin snatched the newspaper out of her hands.

'What on earth—?'

'That's not you wearing the hat,' Julia said to him.

'I know it's not.'

'That's Heath McEwan.'

'Wearing the same coat that I'm wearing in the other photograph. Someone must have taken this on the day we went up to Top Withens,' Crispin said.

'Heath left the coat in my cottage,' Julia explained to Maddy. 'That's where we rehearsed. I loaned it to Crispin the day we went for a walk.'

'Where'd you get this paper?' Crispin asked.

'Heath sent it to me. He called and said he was sending me something very amusing. I didn't bother opening it until this morning.'

Crispin passed the paper back to Maddy, who couldn't help but notice the troubled look on his face.

'At least it wasn't front page,' she interjected.

'Nobody's going to believe it,' Julia said. 'Phoebe won't believe it. She knows you too well. But you should tell her anyway. I learned that with Jona. These tabloids splash around such trash. You need to explain what they did.'

Maddy looked up. 'She's right. You should do that.' It seemed that Julia believed in his marriage more than Crispin did, and Maddy's heart sank at her innocence. There was a beautiful earnestness in Julia's face, a true love and concern for Crispin. No guilt. Nothing to conceal.

Julia was looking again at the photograph of herself and Heath McEwan, and she said to Crispin, 'You know, Heath's hands do look a little like yours.'

Crispin broke away from them and headed downstairs. 'I need some coffee,' he mumbled.

Maddy called to him, 'Make some for me too. I'll be down in a minute.' She passed the newspaper back to Julia and headed back to her room. Julia followed her.

'You don't think Phoebe will believe this, do you?'

Maddy stopped at her door and turned, trying to avoid Julia's probing look. 'I don't know. But I do know that a scandal like this could ruin his chances for the deanship.'

She saw the devastation on Julia's face and she reached for Julia and gave her a big hug, before going into her room.

When Crispin returned to the cathedral that Monday afternoon, he closed himself in his office and reviewed his diary. To his horror he had forgotten an appointment, and there were messages and mail piled high on his desk that needed his attention.

There were two voicemails and an urgent note that Irène Bourdin, the cathedral's finance director, had left for him. The first message was dated over a week ago, while he had been in Santa Barbara. He thought he'd better find her and apologise for not returning her calls. On the way downstairs he ran into Edward Ribbey.

'Crispin,' Edward said. 'Just coming up to find you. Tom would like to see you.'

Crispin followed him into Tom's office. Irène was there, perched on the edge of a chair in front of Tom's desk. She was an older woman, very no-nonsense and competent. She was meticulous, and watched over the cathedral's accounts as if her salvation depended upon it.

Crispin greeted her warmly, and she gave him a fond smile but quickly turned away. Edward closed the door behind them and stationed himself next to Tom like a centurion.

'How was Deauville?' Tom asked, addressing Crispin over the top of rimless reading glasses.

'Nice. Had some sun this morning.'

'Good.' Tom removed his glasses slowly, carefully folding the arms and laying them on top of a leather blotter. Then he rubbed his eyes. It was the meditative gesture of a man weighing his next words.

'How much did Julia Kramer donate to the restoration fund?'

The question took Crispin by surprise. He glanced towards Irène. 'Twenty-five thousand,' he answered, turning back to Tom. 'Why?'

Edward spoke up. 'The cheque was made out to you, is that right?'

'Yes,' Crispin answered.

Tom asked, 'Was part of it intended as a personal gift?'

'Absolutely not. It was all for the renovation. Why?'

'Why did she make the cheque out to you?'

Irène interrupted. 'I told you about that.'

But Edward cut her off. 'Irène, we know how it was handled, but we thought it might help if Crispin explained why she made it out to him in the first place.'

The 'we' added a disturbing note to what was already sounding like an inquisition.

Crispin would not give Edward the satisfaction of recognition. He addressed his reply to Tom, without so much as a glance at Ribbey.

'Julia wanted to make sure it went to the renovation,' Crispin explained. 'She knew I'd channel the money where she wanted.'

'And can you explain exactly how the money was passed on to the church?' Tom asked.

'Irène and I discussed how to clear the cheque. Instead of my endorsing it over to the cathedral and putting it in the French account, then waiting a month to six weeks for it to clear, I deposited it into my savings account in Chicago and gave instructions to have the money cabled back here as soon as the cheque cleared.'

'And how long did that take?'

Crispin looked at Irène. 'What did it take? A week? Ten days?'

'About that.'

Edward asked, 'Irène, what was the exact balance that was transferred back to us?'

Irène slipped on the reading glasses hanging from a chain around her neck. Her hands shook ever so slightly as she opened the file in her lap and read from a bank statement. 'Eighteen thousand, seven hundred and twelve dollars and thirty one cents.'

Crispin looked puzzled. 'What?'

'That's not twenty-five thousand,' Edward piped in.

Crispin reached for the file. 'May I see that?'

She eagerly passed him the statement. Her tone was apologetic. 'That's all we ever got.'

Crispin examined the statement. He looked up at Irène, baffled. 'Why didn't you tell me?'

'It was your money coming from your account, and Ms Kramer was your friend. I just thought . . .'

'That I'd skimmed a little off for myself?'

Attempting an avuncular, caring tone which came out strained, since it was not at all in line with his character, Tom said, 'Crispin, it's no secret that you've been having financial problems.'

'You're accusing me of embezzlement!' Crispin countered hotly, and Tom leaned forward with his hands folded on his desk.

'No, Crispin, we're not. We just want to know where the rest of the money went.'

And then it occurred to Crispin that Phoebe had access to that account, and he grew bright red at the thought of it.

He asked Irène, 'Did you talk to anyone at the bank about this?'

'I did, but they wouldn't give me any transaction history. They just said they were following instructions.'

Edward started to speak again, but Tom shot him down with a sharp look, and then said to Crispin, 'You haven't checked your own account?'

Crispin thought of the unopened mail piled in the corner of his desk. 'Let me look into this,' he said, rising from his chair with the file in his hand and marching solemnly from the room.

Irène caught up with him as he was heading for his office. 'I have been trying to speak to you about this for weeks, Father. I left several messages,' she explained.

'It's OK. It's my fault. I should have got back to you.'

'I really didn't think it was urgent, and then Edward comes and puts his nose in my books. He says he is doing an internal audit. *Quel farceur celui-là*,' she fumed, her chin lifted in typical Gaulish disdain. 'I knew what he was up to. But I couldn't hide the facts.'

'I didn't expect you to.'

'I'm very sorry.'

'You've done your job well, Irène,' he said, trying to absolve her with a reassuring smile.

He went into his office, and his heart knocked into his chest like a battering ram as he sat down at his desk and switched on the lamp. The bank statements were buried somewhere among his papers. He found the one from the Chicago bank and slit it open. When he unfolded the statement, a wire transfer notice slid out, sending waves of sickness through his stomach. Phoebe had cabled money directly to the equestrian outfitter where she bought Megan's tack and the riding gear she needed to participate in the horse shows. The cable was dated one day before the remaining balance was transferred out to the cathedral.

There was a good, healthy crowd at the Cricketer, and the place hummed with pleasant conversation. Crispin slung his helmet on the rack and unzipped his jacket, and the barman greeted him by name. He ordered a beer and looked up to see Rhoderic blow in.

'Am I off a day?' Rhoderic quipped as he set his briefcase on the floor and loosened his tie. 'Is this Tuesday?'

'Phoebe's still in California. I'm a free man. Until tomorrow morning.'

'You're not wearing your priest's collar,' Rhoderic commented after he had ordered.

'Nope,' Crispin replied, watching the barman pulling their beers.

Rhoderic pried a little, which was inevitable given the mood Crispin was in, and Crispin told him about the money Phoebe had taken. 'What I can't figure out is how on earth she managed to find out it was there and spend it. She knew about Julia donating that money, but she didn't know where I was depositing it.'

Rhoderic gave a sympathetic grunt.

Crispin looked up and caught a glimpse of himself in the mirror behind the bar. His unruly hair was looking distinctly shaggy, and he hadn't shaved this morning. 'I'm in deep trouble,' Crispin said wearily.

'You'll pay it back,' Rhoderic said.

'I can't. I don't have it. It's embezzlement.'

'A judge wouldn't think so. It wasn't intentional.'

'I can't be sure of that.'

'You don't think Phoebe knew it was the cathedral's money, do you?'
'I don't know. Maybe she did.'
'Well, ask her.'
'I can't do that.'
'Why not?'

It was painful for him, but finally he confessed. He told Rhoderic everything, about Phoebe's desertion and her accusations, and the rumours about Julia. It was going to be a week from hell, he said. Phoebe was due back the next morning and the vestry would be meeting the following Sunday to vote for the next dean, and he was just trying to keep a lid on the thing until after the vote.

Rhoderic listened, and grimaced and groaned in all the right places, and Crispin felt a lot better when he'd finished. Then Rhoderic drained his glass and said, 'That's bloody awful. Being innocent of something most men out there would love to be guilty of.'

Crispin had not thought of it in quite that light, and he concurred that the dilemma was not without humour. He smiled for the first time since he had waved goodbye to Julia.

⊛ NINE ⊛

CRISPIN DIDN'T KNOW what to expect when Phoebe and the girls returned. He did expect awkwardness and there was plenty of that on the drive from the airport back to Paris, but then they all went to bed and slept through the day. That night he made the girls' favourite tuna casserole from his mother's recipe; it was the only thing he could make that tasted as good as when Phoebe made it. He woke the girls so that they could eat, but he let Phoebe sleep on. He was glad to have them to himself for a change.

At the beginning of the meal Cat was sullen, but the tuna casserole softened her up and by the second helping she was talking about her classes and looking forward to going back to their school. The idea of returning to the French *lycée* had Megan totally depressed, and she sat at the table with the calendar counting the number of days until they would return to Santa Barbara.

'Is it true we might move back to California?' she asked her father, forking aside a chunk of celery that was thicker than the accepted norm.

Crispin was cutting Lola's noodles. He handed the fork over to the child and sat back. Cat was watching him with troubled eyes.

'Well, you all know I'm hoping to be elected Dean of St John's.' Lola had stopped chewing, but her mouth was full like her eyes. He went on. 'But if that doesn't happen, then who knows? Maybe I'll stay on here, maybe not. But one thing's certain: whatever decision we make, we make it for the family. Just like we did when we came here.'

'Well, what about Santa Barbara?' Megan pressed.

'I don't have a job there, Megan. I have to go where the job is.'

Twirling her noodles round her fork, Cat said, 'I think it'd be cool.'

'Moving back to Santa Barbara?' he asked.

'No. I mean you being Dean. I think that'd be cool.' She didn't look him in the eye, and you knew she was still hurting and feeling betrayed, but there was forgiveness there too.

'Thanks, honey,' Crispin said.

Over the next few days, Phoebe used jet lag as a way of avoiding a confrontation with Crispin, sleeping until noon and coming to bed late when he was sound asleep. As for Crispin, his pastoral duties that week kept him away most evenings, and when he was at home he kept to his study. He had decided not to confront Phoebe about the money she had misappropriated from their Chicago account, but he gave a full account of the situation, in writing, to Tom Noonan, with a copy to Irène and Maddy, along with a proposal to repay the money over the next six months. His proposal drew no comment from Tom, but Maddy found it perfectly workable and honourable. She said the fact that Noonan had not responded to it meant that there was nothing more to be said.

But at home, the silences between husband and wife were indicative of strain and confusion. Throughout all their years together, even after he had joined the priesthood, Crispin had always done whatever had to be done to give Phoebe what she wanted. But that wasn't the case any more. He was emerging from the crisis toughened and Phoebe found this unsettling.

On Thursday, Phoebe lunched with Gerry Noonan and their circle of friends. She got back late in the afternoon, opened the door of Crispin's study and stood waiting for him to look up. Crispin was thinking, This is it. She's seen that miserable photo. But then he looked up and she smiled, and astonished him by telling him how she had come to his defence that afternoon. 'I told them there was absolutely nothing going on between you and Julia,' she said.

'Good.'

'I could tell Gerry didn't believe me, though,' she said, reaching down to take off her shoes.

'It's a political thing. You know that.'

'I think they want to see you fail.'

'Of course they do.'

She stared at the floor for a moment, and then asked, 'Are you sure you really want this?'

'You mean the deanship?'

She nodded.

He gave her a long, hard look. 'You mean you don't know?'

'I just thought . . .' But she didn't finish her sentence. She walked out with her shoes in her hand, closing the door behind her.

Phoebe's support, wavering though it might be, had sufficient impact to silence the rumours of infidelity, thus avoiding a full-blown scandal. On Sunday, after the Eucharist service, the names of the final candidates would be set before the cathedral vestry for a vote. Crispin was adamant that the entire family should attend the ten-thirty service. This meant that Megan was forced to drop out of a regional dressage event, and for once Phoebe sided with her husband. Throughout the coffee hour after the service, she stood resolutely by her husband's side. After coffee, they went to the Chinese restaurant across the street to wait for the election results. Around one thirty, Maddy came to report the results. Crispin saw her coming through the door but she was backlit and the lounge was dark, so he couldn't read her face until she got closer.

'Congratulations, Dean Wakefield,' she said with a smile. The girls squealed and Phoebe reached for his hand, looking honestly moved and proud. Cat jumped to her feet and hugged her father hard, and Lola crawled up on top of him and hung round his neck. Megan's pout was eclipsed by that stunning smile of hers. Crispin was glad for all the enthusiasm because he wanted to cry.

Afterwards they went back home and everyone had something to do, and for the first time in months it seemed like an ordinary Sunday afternoon. He made two calls, first to Rhoderic and then to Julia. Julia was ecstatic and relieved. After that, he just went to bed.

When he awoke, it was slowly, and he had the feeling that there was someone in the room with him. As he rolled over, he felt a sheet of paper crackle underneath his shoulder. He brushed it onto the floor without opening his eyes.

'Look at it,' Phoebe said.

He knew by her voice, in that one split second, what it was about.

He sat up and swung his legs over the side of the bed and yawned.

'Hold on,' he said, shaking his head. 'Let me wake up here.'

She jumped up from the armchair, picked up the paper and flung it at him. '*Look at this!*' she cried. The paper floated to the floor.

'I've seen it,' he said calmly.

'You've seen it?'

'It's faked.'

'You lying bastard.'

'Call the tabloid and ask them. I am not the man embracing Julia.'

Phoebe was stung. It was hitting her a lot harder this time than it did before, because now she was believing it.

Crispin retrieved the sheet of printer paper; it had been printed from the tabloid's website. 'How'd you get this?'

'Florence Ribbey saw it on the Internet and emailed it to Megan.'

That's what had worried him more than anything else, that one of the girls would hear about it.

'Have Megan come in here,' he said firmly. 'She needs to hear the truth. The man embracing Julia is the actor who plays opposite her in the Brontë film.' He held it out for her to examine. 'Come on, Phoebe, look at it closely. He's wearing a hat. You can't see his face.'

'That's your hand. I'd recognise your hands anywhere.'

'That's not my hand. That hand belongs to Heath McEwan.'

'How do you know about it?'

'Julia showed it to us when Maddy and I were up in Normandy.'

'Julia's seen this?'

'I told you. She brought it in and showed it to Maddy and me. She was worried. She even encouraged me to tell you about it. But I didn't. Because I was afraid you wouldn't believe me.'

'You're a liar.'

'I'm not a liar,' he said. All this defending himself was making him tired.

'And she's a husband-stealing bitch!'

He sat there on the edge of the bed in his T-shirt and trousers, staring down at his socks and weighing up his next words. There was so much he could say, and it all depended on what he wanted in the end.

'Don't say anything else like that, Phoebe. It's not right.'

She had started to cry. '*Right?*' she screamed.

Crispin rose from the bed. She was doubled over in the chair with her head in her hands, and he knelt in front of her and tried to prise her hands away from her face but she shook him off.

'Don't touch me, you bastard!'

'That's not me in that photograph, and if I have to, I'll get Julia to get

Heath McEwan on the phone and he'll tell you it's him.'

'Of course he'll say it, because Julia will tell him to and she'll do anything to get you away from me!'

'Phoebe, Julia doesn't want me,' he said gently. 'She wants a man who's dead and who's never going to come back.'

Phoebe grew very still, and the hot tears cooled to a look that was more menacing than threats and screams. 'You're going to lose everything, Crispin. You just wait. You'll lose me, and the girls, and your job, and I won't be sorry one damn bit!'

She gave him a shove and bolted to the wardrobe, where she began ripping his clothes off the hangers and flinging them onto the floor.

'Stop it, Phoebe.'

'I want you out of here tonight. You can go up to Normandy and live with your little actress whore.'

'Don't talk like that.'

'I'm taking the girls back to Santa Barbara.'

Then he stopped her. He took her by the arm and stopped her in mid-stride and she squirmed to get out of his grasp.

'Don't you dare take my daughters away from me. I told you that in Santa Barbara.'

'I'm getting out of here. I'm not staying here one day longer than I have to.' She pointed to the crumpled paper on the floor. 'That'll be all over the cathedral tomorrow. You think I can bear to show my face around here after what I've been through these past few weeks?'

'We've all been through it. Not just you.'

'Yeah. And you've made me out to look like a stupid fool!'

'Not if you stand by me like you did this week.'

'The next time I stand by you, it'll be in a court of law!' She was pulling down suitcases now. 'I'm leaving. I'll take the girls and we'll move into a hotel.'

'I can't afford to pay for a hotel.'

'*Screw you!*'

'Phoebe . . . Phoebe, take it easy. Just calm down. At least let the girls finish their school year here. You can't move them again.'

'I hate this place! This damn cathedral! Everything around here reminds me of you and'—she knew she had already said too much, but she couldn't control herself any more—'you don't deserve me, Crispin! You never did! I deserve somebody who can give me what I need. I'm still young and beautiful and I'm not about to waste my last good years counting every penny and not being able to pay for pretty things and living in homes that'll never be mine, with this godawful furniture . . .'

Sobbing, she collapsed to her knees in the middle of the mess of clothes strewn on the floor. Crispin stepped over a wool jacket and stooped down and pulled her to her feet. As awful as it had been, all he could feel was pity. She looked pathetic and hopelessly miserable, so he took her in his arms and held her while she cried. She lifted her tear-streaked face to him and whispered, 'Don't think I never loved you. I did. But I can't be your wife any more.'

Even as he comforted her, Crispin knew it was the end. Phoebe didn't know it herself until those words spilled out, bringing the truth along with them. The saddest thing was that there was no one there for him. He had stalwart friends at the cathedral who believed in his innocence, but even those who were very fond of him had heard too much for their liking. In the end, Tom Noonan's subtle campaign had succeeded in undermining Crispin's bedrock popularity.

Although the vestry had voted, there still remained the Bishop's final approval of their recommendation before Crispin could be confirmed as Dean of St John's. In a telephone call early on Monday, Crispin requested an urgent meeting with him, and by the time they met that afternoon in the Bishop's home on the Avenue du Maréchal-Lyautey, the Bishop had been shown the damning evidence.

It was a sweet spring day and Crispin found Bishop Stroup out on his balcony elbow-deep in potting soil.

'Hope you don't mind if I continue with this while we talk,' the Bishop said.

'Not at all.'

'Should have finished it yesterday.' The Bishop poked a red geranium down into the window box and patted earth around it. He looked up at Crispin. 'I suppose you've come here to offer me your resignation.'

'Yes.'

'I've spent a lot of time in thought and prayer about all that's gone on.'

'None of it's true. I didn't think people would see my friendship with her in that light.'

'A lot of people love dirt, Father,' the Bishop said, removing his gardening gloves. 'In one form or another.'

'This is breaking my heart, you know. But even if you went ahead and confirmed me, I couldn't stay. I couldn't put an ocean between me and my children.'

'What do you plan on doing?'

'I'll look for a parish in California, not too far from Santa Barbara. That's where the girls will be living.'

'So you're divorcing?'

'I'm afraid so. Phoebe's agreed to do it amicably.'

'Let's hope it continues like that.'

He said it as if he knew Phoebe well, and Crispin couldn't refrain from smiling. 'I could use your prayers on that one.'

'You'll have them. Every day. Even when you're far away in some thriving California parish and have forgotten all about us.'

'I could never forget this place.'

Crispin insisted that he and Phoebe confront the girls together, and on Monday evening, after Crispin had formally withdrawn his candidacy for the deanship, they sat the girls down in the living room and told them they had decided to separate. From the very beginning, Crispin set the tone, and it was gentle and non-confrontational. He took Lola onto his lap and talked about mothers and fathers and husbands and wives in a language he hoped she could understand, and Cat and Megan listened to their father with raw, red-rimmed eyes full of disbelief. He explained that this had nothing to do with Julia, and once again affirmed Julia's and his own innocence. He talked to them about tabloids and the things they did to sell their papers, and how the stories implied falsehoods through trickery and deceit. Then he gave them the choice—to finish the school year in Paris or to return immediately to Santa Barbara. But at that point the whole thing broke down because Cat jumped up and ran sobbing to her room and slammed the door, and Lola buried her face in her father's chest and covered her ears with both hands. Megan sat on the edge of the sofa with her hands wedged between her knees, tears flowing from her cheeks. Phoebe moved over and sat down next to her and tried to take her in her arms, but to Crispin's astonishment she wrenched free of her mother's embrace.

'I'd rather just go back to Santa Barbara. I don't want to face anybody here. They're already making fun of us. Florence told me this evening that they were firing you.'

'I've given my resignation. I'm resigning so that I can go back to California to be near all of you.'

This took her by surprise, and she met his gaze with a curious look. 'You'd do that?'

'Of course I would.'

'But you love it here.'

'I love you more.'

So it was agreed that the girls would return immediately to Santa Barbara to Phoebe's parents' home to finish the school year in California, and Phoebe would join them as soon as she had packed up their things.

The night before her departure, Crispin went up to their bedroom, where Phoebe was packing her suitcase.

'We need to get a few things clear before you leave,' he said, noticing the bareness of the room without her things.

She put down her cosmetic bag and sat on the bed to listen.

'I know how lawyers can be,' he said. 'They feel like they've got to get the best possible deal for their client, and the only thing I have left to lose are my kids.'

'I'm not going to take the girls away from you.'

'You did it once. I don't trust you.'

'This is different.'

'I suggest you come to full disclosure with your lawyer before you put him up to anything.'

'What do you mean?'

'I'm talking about Lola.'

It was like he had slapped her. For a few seconds she stopped breathing.

'If you make it hard for me, I swear I'll ask for a paternity test.'

Her jaw went slack with astonishment. 'You what?'

'Just remember that.'

'You wouldn't . . .'

'Lola's my child because I've raised her. And I'd cut off both hands before I'd tell her any different. But your lawyer might be a little more flexible if he knew the truth.'

They didn't talk much after that. He took her to the airport and helped with all the luggage. He even waited until she had checked in. But he resented the way she turned to him with watering eyes, as if there were still some lingering regret. It sickened him so much that he couldn't even kiss her goodbye. He set down her bag and wished her a good flight, and then strode away without looking back.

In order to avoid offending those who were sensitive to his alleged transgression, Crispin thought it best that he no longer officiate at matins or Sunday Eucharist, nor did he perform weddings during his final weeks as Canon. The cathedral was losing both its canon and its dean, and there was much name-calling, and many accusations were tossed about. But most of all there was a sense of great loss. Many people felt his coming departure deeply, and believed, as did their bishop, that a great injustice had been done to a remarkable man.

He'd been exhausted by all that had to be done at such short notice— not the least of which was trying to find a new parish—and there were many goodbyes to be said. Maddy hosted a party one evening, and Crispin left that night fighting back tears, overwhelmed by the generosity and warm wishes of those who had seen him through to the end.

Then came the tedious job of packing up all of his personal belongings. What disturbed him most was not what Phoebe had taken, but what she had chosen to leave behind. Small things he thought might hold some sentimental value had been passed over, so Crispin wrapped them up in packing paper and stuffed them into boxes. Stacks of boxes grew up around the house like cubicles of his past to be stored away and forgotten. He had nowhere to take them, except to Normandy. He had decided to keep the house there, no matter how tough things got.

On the morning of his departure, he made one last visit to the cathedral. As he walked through the aisles he felt himself already detached from it. He had loved this place, with its vaults and domes and frescoes, but it was already slipping into the past. He closed the door, strode through the cloister and outside to his car, and drove quietly away.

He had always loved the stretch of road leading northwest to the sea; it passed through countryside where the remains of once-great forests rose on distant hills, and in the spring the orchards burst forth pink with apple blossom. But this morning, after weeks of waiting, Crispin drove with reckless speed, ignoring the beauty. His mind was already there. He even timed himself, and arrived at the village one hour and fifty-three minutes from the time he sped away from the cathedral.

When he pulled into the courtyard it was still early and the shutters were all closed. He noticed that Julia had set terracotta pots of pink geraniums around the perimeter of the courtyard. He thought she would still be sleeping, and he imagined what it would be like to see her come down the stairs in the morning. He shut off the engine and sat for a moment, bowed over the steering wheel. He had not called to tell her that he was coming. He hadn't even made up his mind until last night. He had a few days before his plane left, but he wasn't sure how to handle saying goodbye to Julia.

The day after his meeting with Bishop Stroup, Crispin had written to Julia to say that he was turning down the deanship and returning to the States. He had been deliberately vague, saying only that it was the best solution for the family, and he hadn't mentioned a word about his separation from Phoebe. He thanked Julia for her support and encouragement. He knew she would be disappointed, he said, but he felt that he was doing the right thing, painful as it was for him. He explained he was keeping the house in Normandy, and assured her she would be welcome to stay as long as she wished.

Now, sitting in the car in the early morning, while the mist still hung over the village, and looking up at the window of the room where she slept, he wondered if it wouldn't be better if he just drove away without ever seeing her again. There was no longer any doubt in his mind that he was in love with her, but he had buried it deep in a solid and well-fortified heart. He would never know for sure if Julia shared the same feelings; if she had responded to him so tenderly in Haworth, it was because he had been acting in the role of friend and priest. If it was something more, he didn't want to know. He had sworn their innocence to his wife and his daughters as well as his many friends and supporters at the cathedral. It was their innocence that had helped him to bear the unjust accusations. To give in to his feelings for Julia would make a mockery out of his denial.

It was quiet in the house, and he started some coffee brewing while he stored his boxes in the basement. When he went back up to the kitchen, he startled a big, scruffy-looking man in a bathrobe pouring himself a cup of coffee.

'I heard someone drive up. I assume you're Crispin,' he said as he extended his hand. 'Michael Langham. Julia's director.' He moved over to the table and sat down.

'Yes. Sorry about the intrusion,' Crispin replied, trying his best to conceal his astonishment at having a strange man in his house. He had to remind himself that it was Julia's home at the moment.

'You're the bloke who bloody well saved my film,' Michael said.

'I'm glad I could help.'

Crispin poured himself some of the coffee and joined Michael at the table. He eyed him warily over the rim of his mug, while the director rambled on about his film and how Julia had given such an astonishing performance. Crispin wasn't paying much attention. He was too busy wondering if Michael Langham had just crawled out of Julia's bed.

'Are you two talking about me?'

Julia stood in the doorway in white socks, tying a rumpled floral-print robe around her waist. She was smiling at Crispin.

'You sneaky thing,' she said, coming up to him and bending over to hug him. He could feel the curves of her breasts through the light robe.

'Sorry,' he said in a low voice. 'I should have called first.'

'I was so afraid you'd leave without coming to see me,' she whispered.

'I wouldn't do that,' he smiled back.

Just then a stunning, Medusa-like creature with black hair snaking down her shoulders in crisp tight curls bounced into the kitchen in black jogging pants and running shoes.

'Is this the morning-after party?' she asked.

'Susannah, this is Crispin,' Julia announced proudly.

'Oh, my goodness,' Susannah exclaimed. 'So you're Crispin!' She leaned down and gave him a hug, burying him in a cascade of curls.

'This is my publicist, Susannah Rich,' Julia said. 'From New York. You spoke to her on the phone.'

'Of course,' Crispin said. 'I remember.'

'I'm so pleased to meet you. That was so marvellous, what you did for Julia. Actually, for all of us.'

Crispin mumbled an acknowledgment, but he was more interested in the way Susannah had slipped her arm over Michael's shoulder, and the way he slid his hand along her hip. She bent down and they kissed briefly, and it was sexual. Relief flooded through Crispin.

It seemed they had made plans to go into Deauville that morning to the open-air market, to shop for dinner. But now Julia insisted the dinner be in honour of Crispin, something very special, a thank-you and going-away celebration all in one.

After breakfast Crispin drove them into Deauville, and while Susannah and Michael worked their way along the chain of stalls, Crispin and Julia finally had a moment to themselves.

'Are you OK with this?' he asked, gesturing to the crowd.

'I'm always more courageous with you around.' She said it lightly, and laughed and linked her arm through his. 'I know you don't like me to say it. You don't want to be a crutch . . .'

'It's not that.'

'But you're right. I've been using you like that.' Then she caught herself and said, 'That didn't come out right. That wasn't what I meant.'

'I know,' Crispin assured her, but he wondered if maybe there was truth in it, that this was the extent of her affection.

They came upon Michael at the fish stall, where he was stumbling through a conversation with the fishmonger about recipes for monkfish, and Susannah was over in the cheeses. Julia stopped Crispin in front of a vegetable stall and said, 'So, you're moving back to California?'

He nodded.

'You gave it up?'

'It's best. For all of us.'

Julia could read the look on his face. 'Oh, Crispin,' she whispered, and she reached out for his hand and squeezed it.

'It just wasn't going to work out. I was getting carried away with my ambitions and ignoring everyone else.'

'Don't you think it's OK to do that sometimes?' She said it gently.

'You have to make decisions for the family. Sometimes it means no one individual really gets what they want, but the family as a whole is better off.'

'I know,' she said, a shade apologetically, and she gave his hand another tender squeeze, 'I've always lived such a self-absorbed life. I don't have any experience with making those kinds of decisions. But it must be the right thing, if that's what you've decided to do.'

'I think it is.'

'Oh, goodness,' she said, 'that means there will be a whole ocean and a continent between us.' She tried to make it sound carefree and teasing, but she couldn't hide the sadness in her voice.

'The house is your home as long as you want it. And I'm hoping that maybe at some point the girls will want to come back for a holiday.'

She tried to sound happy. 'Then we won't be completely out of touch.'

He wanted to say something then, say something that would let her know how he felt, but there was no point in it.

'You're scowling,' she said.

'I am?'

'Crispin,' she whispered, and amid the blur of vendors and shoppers with their bags and wicker baskets, amid the crates of fat creamy cauliflowers and beds of spinach, she locked her eyes on his and said, 'You're hiding something, and I don't know what.'

'I'm not . . .' he started to deny, but then he stopped, and looked down into her sweet eyes. 'I'm worried about you. I truly am. I don't want anything to happen to you. I feel like I've let you down.'

'You haven't let me down,' she assured him. 'You've helped me through the most difficult time of my life.' She caught herself and said, with a grin, 'Actually, you've done it twice. You've taught me so much, just being here in my life. You've reminded me of all the things that are important.'

'Oh, Julia.' He smiled, full of gratitude.

'I'll get along fine, I promise. I won't let you down. I won't fail you.'

'Fail me?'

She nodded emphatically, and said, 'I don't know what brought us together again, but I do know that after all that's happened, a lot of good has come out of it. At least for me.'

He hadn't been able to tear himself away from her eyes, and when she said that, he took her face between his hands. The gesture was almost ferocious, and so full of passion it took her by surprise. She gasped, and then he closed her mouth with a kiss. Her lips were soft and heavenly but that kiss scorched his soul. When their lips parted, it seemed a violent thing, separating one breath into two. She let out a soft exclamation.

In the stunned silence that followed, the world pounded its way back into their consciousness, and they heard the clamour of vendors and the sounds of the market. There were tears in Julia's eyes, and he took her hand and held it as they searched the crowd for Susannah and Michael. But not long after that Julia began feeling light-headed and anxious, so they completed their shopping and drove home.

Julia stayed in her room most of the afternoon while Crispin took care of things around the house, and even when Michael and Susannah went for a walk, Crispin would not go to her room. He kept thinking about what she had said to him: 'A lot of good has come out of it,' she had said, and her innocence had left him burning with shame. If anyone had been deceived, it was Julia. He had led her to believe his marriage was strong and healthy. That he was returning to California with his wife and children, where they would all be the happy family. It made him sick to think how monstrous had been his deception. He had told himself that he was misleading her in order to protect her, that he was putting on a front of family unity for the sake of Julia's mental stability. But it wasn't Julia who was the weak one; it was him. When he was away from her, he could manage to keep their friendship locked into its narrow chamber; but in her presence, he felt his will unravel.

The kiss had been so unexpected, and it had confused Julia. For a long time she had been reluctant to try to sort out her feelings for Crispin for fear of what she might discover. Ever since their days together in Haworth, there was never a doubt in her mind that he was much more to her than friend and priest. She lived in his home and every day she went into his room and sat on the bed; sometimes she napped there in the afternoon, although she would never sleep in his bed at night. She searched the house for things that bore his mark, wore his old sweaters and coats, and read his books. She became intimate with him in this way, furtively, because there was no danger in it.

His kiss had changed all that, but she knew what was best for Crispin. Regardless of his motives or intentions, any real involvement would destroy him. And if he should ever guess how she felt, it would make the burden more difficult for him to bear. She recalled the way he had looked when he had kissed her, the warmth of his mouth, the touch of his hands. He excited her and she knew how easy it would be to respond to him, and she relived that kiss a hundred times.

When she came down and went into the kitchen to help Susannah with the dinner, she appeared serene and untroubled. She had changed into more sophisticated clothes, and styled her hair and wore a little make-up. Julia knew her craft well. She knew it so well that Crispin didn't recognise it as craft at all. He mistook it for something real. She was light-hearted but distant, and when he tried to connect with a look, she returned a sweet, almost apologetic and purely dispassionate smile.

During dinner they talked about Crispin's decision to move to California, and Julia teased him about it. She warned him about the land of temptation, and predicted that he would leave the clergy and return to a secular vocation, make tons of money and live happily ever after. Her prescience unsettled Crispin, and he felt dull and tongue-tied.

'But, honestly, if that's what makes Phoebe and the girls happy, then you should do it,' she urged, with a sincerely candid smile. 'Your family should come first. Always. You're so lucky to have them.' She went on, addressing Susannah and Michael, 'Crispin has the most incredible family,' she said. 'Phoebe is gorgeous and fun, and a very good mother to the three most entertaining girls I've ever met.'

She looked to Crispin for confirmation. Fortunately his mouth was full of monkfish and he got away with a tight smile and a nod. He didn't have her acting skills, and he covered his discomfort by reaching for the bottle of wine. He emptied the last of it into Susannah's glass, then went into the kitchen for another bottle. When he returned, the conversation had changed; it seemed Michael was urging Julia to move to Los Angeles for the sake of her film career.

'Crispin,' Michael said, 'what do you think?'

'I don't think I should try to influence her,' he answered, as he refilled Julia's glass.

Julia said, 'But I'd like to know what you think. Truly, I would.'

'I don't think you'd be happy there.'

For just a moment, her composure slipped. A wounded look flashed across her face, but Crispin was pouring wine for Michael and didn't notice. Julia recovered, then turned to Michael and said, 'So, there. He knows me better than anyone else.'

'But sometimes our own personal happiness has to take a back seat,' Crispin added. 'You need to earn a living and, like Michael said, this film has put you out there. Made you visible. You need to seize the moment. You may not have another chance.'

Susannah jumped in. 'The man's wise, Julia. You should listen to him.'

'I suppose if you want to go back to London, you could do theatre,' Crispin said.

'You know I can't do theatre. I couldn't stand up on a stage in front of a live audience every night.'

'Then what will you do when you get older? Find another Jona?'

A stunned silence fell over them. Susannah shot Crispin a horrified look. Julia slowly lay down her fork and folded her hands in her lap. When she looked up at him, there were tears in her eyes.

Crispin was furious with himself. It was the only time in his life that he had ever willingly caused her pain.

'I'm sorry,' he murmured. 'Forgive me.'

Susannah rose then and began to clear the table, and Michael followed her lead. When they had gone into the kitchen, Crispin said again, 'I'm so sorry.'

Julia brushed away a tear and said softly, 'But you're right. I do have to think about these things.'

'You'll be OK. You'll find someone to take care of you.'

'*That's not what I want, damn it!*' she lashed out, flinging her napkin onto the table and rising from her chair. 'That's the very thing you've been warning me against! And I listen to what you say because you always get it right!' She gave him a wounded look and then marched up the stairs to her room.

Later, Susannah and Michael drove into Deauville, and Crispin sat by the fire, trying to concentrate on a book. For a long while he debated whether or not he should go up to her room. He would be leaving early the next morning, and it struck him that he might never see her again. For a while he heard her footsteps creaking on the old floorboards overhead. Then the house grew silent. Crispin put out the fire and went to bed.

In the morning he rose before dawn, and before he left the house he went back upstairs and stood in front of her bedroom door with his heart pounding. Finally, he summoned the courage to knock softly, and when there was no answer, he opened the door and looked in.

She was awake, and she rolled over and sat up, and in the deep shadows you could see only the faint outline of her head and shoulders against the white pillows. 'Crispin?' she whispered.

'Did I wake you?'

'No. I've been awake. I was going to get up to see you off.'

'You don't have to.'

'Don't you want some coffee?'

'I'll stop in Deauville. Not to worry.'

'It's raining, isn't it?'

'Yes.'

'Drive safely.'

'I will.'

There was just a moment of silence while Crispin stood in the doorway gripping his keys in his hand.

'I couldn't go without an apology,' he said. 'I'm sorry for the way I spoke to you. I was suffering from wounded pride.'

He wanted very badly then to stay and explain everything. All it would take was a small gesture on her part, a tiny indication of what she felt for him, and all the barriers would come down.

Julia looked at him, standing in the dark doorway with the collar of his raincoat turned up around his ears, and the thought of expelling him from her life terrified her. But she would have to rise above her fears and love him the way he needed to be loved.

'Could you come in?' she asked. 'For just a second?'

He approached the bed and she reached out and took him by the hand. Her hand was warm.

'Sit down here,' she said, patting the edge of the bed.

He sat down next to her.

She spoke quietly and her voice was cool and controlled. 'You're a very special friend,' she began. 'My most special of friends. You always will be. And I'm so sorry if I ever led you to think I felt anything for you other than deep affection.' She paused, and Crispin withdrew his hand. 'I don't want you leaving this morning thinking there may be something between us other than friendship. At least not for me.' She smiled, and then scolded gently, 'You took me a little by surprise, you know.'

'I'm sorry for that.'

'No, you shouldn't be. It was good. That way we got it out in the open. It's been haunting us a little, hasn't it?'

Crispin nodded, feeling like a chastised schoolboy.

'I will see you again, won't I?' she asked gently.

'Of course. Nothing's changed,' he said. It was such a bold-faced lie. It would never be the same between them again.

He drew her hand to his lips and kissed it.

'God bless you, Julia.' He rose from her bed and went out, quietly closing the door behind him.

Crispin's warning about the future of her career had a harrowing impact on Julia's outlook. To work again, and as soon as possible, became a clear priority. In June she flew to London to audition for a role in a Hollywood studio production with a big budget, and the next day her agent called and announced she had the part. It was a major departure from anything she had done before—the story of a single mother who struggles to guide her teenage rock star daughter through the tumultuous corridors of early fame and wealth.

'I can't believe they wanted me!' she cried to Susannah over the phone.

'You underestimate yourself.'

'I thought the audition was dreadful.'

'If they cast you it's because they know you've got the emotional range to do it. Don't start doubting yourself.'

'It's a fabulous script. And doing this right on the heels of the Brontë film really breaks me out of the mould.'

'Look, Julia, I know this is delicate, and I don't want you to take it the wrong way. I know Jona's death was a tragedy for you, but he had you trussed up like a Thanksgiving turkey. And I think this is just the first glimmer of the silver lining in that cloud of yours. Now, having said my piece, tell me, where will they shoot the movie?'

'Los Angeles.'

'Good. Maybe this will be the kick in the butt you need to get you over there. Once you're there, maybe you'll stay. And Crispin's there, isn't he?'

'He's up in Santa Barbara.'

'Close enough. Are you still in love with him?'

Julia was struck silent.

'Aha,' Susannah teased. 'I hit a nerve, didn't I?'

'You're wrong,' Julia said in a controlled voice. 'I was never in love with him.'

'Ha!'

'We're friends. That's all.'

'That fight you two had at dinner that night was not the kind of fight friends have. That was a lovers' quarrel.'

'He's married, Susannah.'

'Yeah. And a priest. I suppose you're right to go into denial. You shouldn't mess with that combination.'

'He did me a favour that night. What he said was cruel, but it worked.'

'I've been trying to send you the same message for years. You just wouldn't listen. When Crispin talks, you listen.'

'Well, we don't talk much any more.'

'That's too bad. Because you two sure had something extraordinary.'

Although determined, Julia had little experience in fending for herself, and she questioned her every decision, praying she was doing things for the right reasons. Behind every move she made was the hope that Crispin would approve, and beneath that was a constant struggle to free herself from the need for approbation. Confusion and indecision bogged her down at every turn, until finally she plunged in and signed a one-year lease on a bungalow apartment in the hills north of Sunset in west Los Angeles.

In Crispin's absence, Maddy Cartwright had become caretaker of the house in Normandy. With Julia leaving, the house would be rented, and in July Maddy drove up to take a look. Together they went from room to room, discussing what should be done to ready the place for rental.

Maddy opened the door to Lola's room and poked her head in.

'Oh, my goodness. He'll never be able to rent it like this.'

'I think it's absolutely fabulous!' Julia smiled. 'What little girl wouldn't love a room like this?'

'I don't know. I just hope we'll find someone so he can keep up the mortgage payments,' Maddy sighed.

Julia sank down on the bed. 'Sit down, Maddy,' she urged, sweeping aside a few old stuffed toys. 'Tell me about him. How's he doing? Has he found a new parish yet?'

Maddy lowered her heavy frame onto the squeaking bed. 'No,' she answered. 'He hasn't.'

'Why? He's such a marvellous priest.'

'Indeed he is. The best.'

'Then why won't anyone take him?'

Maddy fixed her with a steady gaze. 'He's been blackballed, at least that's what the Bishop told me.'

'Oh, no,' Julia cried. 'Why?'

Maddy stretched out her legs and stared down at her swollen ankles. 'Phoebe left him back in April. Right after he was elected Dean.'

'*What?*'

'He was essentially blackmailed. Tom Noonan took his devotion to you and twisted it into something lascivious and lurid, and did such a good job that just about everybody, including Phoebe, believed it.'

Julia's hand flew to her mouth and she suddenly felt sick to her stomach. She jumped up from the bed and ran to the bathroom. When she returned she was a little pale. She sat down next to Maddy, who reached out and patted her hands. They were cold and she was trembling.

'You're in love with him, aren't you?'

Reluctantly, Julia nodded. Tears glistened in her eyes. 'But he doesn't know it. As a matter of fact, I told him just the opposite.'

'When was this?'

'The last time I saw him.'

'Phoebe had left him by then. She'd gone back to the States.'

'So they were already separated?'

'Yes.'

'I had no idea. He never told me.'

Julia reflected in silence for a moment, and then she said, 'Even if he knew how I really felt, Maddy, nothing could ever happen between us.'

'Why do you say that?'

'Because it would prove them right. It would seem like we'd been having an affair all along.'

'It doesn't make any difference now. The damage is done.'

'Oh, no,' Julia contradicted. 'It would make all the difference in the world to his daughters. Those girls are the backbone of his soul. It's what they believe that matters to him.'

Julia took a deep breath and rose, then helped Maddy to her feet.

'What colour shall we have them paint this room?' Maddy asked.

'Something neutral,' Julia replied.

ঞ TEN ৯

PHOEBE HAD LOVED CRISPIN, but over the years, and since his calling, he had matured into a man with values starkly different from hers, and she returned to Santa Barbara resolved to find a new husband more suited to her material needs, if not her heart. Santa Barbara was the Promised Land for Megan, who had always dreamed of living the California life. Lola missed Crispin too much to be happy, although he saw the girls every weekend. Perhaps Caitlin suffered most from the upheaval; she was like her father, a combination of sobriety and passion that had truly blossomed in Paris. She had lived there at an impressionable age when attitudes and opinions are formed. She had always been proud to be the daughter of a priest, and her father had been Canon, and nearly Dean, of that most beautiful cathedral, and she had hoped to grow up there. She deeply resented her parents' separation and the sweeping changes it had provoked, and she had begun to see the role her mother had played in the destruction of her father's life.

Phoebe urged Crispin to relocate to Santa Monica, a beach resort community on the west boundary of Los Angeles and reasonably close to Santa Barbara. Crispin acquiesced, although he felt pretty much a misfit. Santa Monica's population consisted primarily of hardcore high-achievers with sophisticated needs and tastes.

He took Phoebe's advice and, swallowing his pride, accepted a generous loan from her parents to enable him to sign a lease on a two-bedroom apartment overlooking the ocean. It was furnished in taupe leather and chrome and glass with soothing neutral colours throughout. The girls loved it because it was thoroughly modern, although Crispin found it impersonal and was very lonely there during the week when they were away.

Numerous churches had initially shown keen interest in his candidacy only to suddenly cool for no apparent reason, and after several promising positions had fallen through, Crispin made a call to Bishop Stroup in Paris and confirmed what he had suspected: a certain clergyman, highly placed in the Los Angeles diocese, had been blocking Crispin's candidacy. It did not come as a surprise to learn that the man was a friend of Tom Noonan's.

The interviews were a struggle for Crispin because he felt obliged to be candid about the scandal with Julia and the misappropriated church funds. He grew tired of defending himself and reasserting his innocence time after time.

There was an Episcopal church near his apartment that he attended weekly, but it only underscored his own sense of loss, for he was a priest, and he had no parish. He missed performing Holy Eucharist and all the ritual surrounding it—the weight of the cross, the silver chalice cool to the touch, richly worked vestments in vivid hues of greens and purples according to the seasons, the crack of the thin wafer echoing through the silence of the great cathedral. No one kneeled before him now with expectant eyes lifted to his, waiting for him to deliver grace, and no one trusted him with their conscience or their soul.

Even though he was living among tribes of displaced people like himself, Crispin didn't reach out to any of them. There was misery all around him—Santa Monica was a retreat for the homeless as well as the affluent—but he felt he had nothing special to offer them.

At first he took up aviation insurance again, just to make a little income while waiting for a calling. But right away it felt good to be back in the secular world where no one was judging him. His reputation grew by word of mouth and his client base expanded quickly. It was just a temporary measure, but then the commissions started to come in, and it was a relief to be able to reimburse Phoebe's parents and pay off some of the debt that had smothered him for so long.

Crispin was firmly resolved to conceal his unhappiness from his daughters, and when they came to visit he took them rollerblading along Venice beach, or to the zoo, or on a whale-watching excursion. But there were weekends when they just wanted to stay in, and they would rent videos and Crispin would sit with Lola curled up on his lap and her head on his chest, and no one would say much throughout the evening.

Despite Crispin's attempts at stoicism, the girls could see their father was not the same man he used to be; he'd lost something invisible and vital, like he'd lost the fire in his belly. Megan and Caitlin, who had little in common, were united in their desire to see their father happy. They often talked about it when they were alone, and they began to forge a new closeness. They almost never argued when they visited him.

On special occasions, Crispin would take them out to their favourite restaurant, the Ivy, a bistro where movie stars in dark glasses lunched elbow to elbow on the terrace. It was great entertainment for the girls but nerve-racking for Crispin, because there was always the chance that he might run into Julia at a place like that. He knew she was in Los Angeles now—Maddy had kept him informed—but Maddy had never said exactly where she was living and Crispin had never asked.

It was late on a Thursday afternoon in March, and Crispin had just walked in the door of his apartment, when Megan called. She was so excited that Crispin had to make her repeat herself several times. Even then he could only understand enough to know that she was talking about Julia.

'Dad,' Megan said breathlessly. 'It's this really big deal and it's formal.'

'What's formal?'

'The party, and we get to ride in a limousine . . .'

'What party?'

'For her movie! Julia's movie!' Megan was losing patience.

'You mean the Brontë film she made last year?'

'Yes! She invited us!'

'You mean she's invited you to the premiere of her film?'

'Not just me, all of us! She said she wanted to make up for not inviting us to the set. It's OK, isn't it?'

'How does your mom feel about it?'

'She's not home.'

'You mean you haven't talked to her about it yet?'

'Look, you want to talk to Caitlin? She's here.'

'Yeah, pass me to Caitlin.'

Caitlin's mind worked a little more like Crispin's, less of the shotgun effect, more of the blanks filled in.

He could hear excited chatter in the background, and then Caitlin came on the line. 'Dad?'

'Hi, sweetie.'

'It'll be OK, won't it?'

'Of course.'

'You think Mom will go for it?'

'Why wouldn't she?'

'Well, you know, it's Julia . . .'

'Your mother has no reason to bear any grudges against Julia. We're all pretty clear about that now, aren't we?'

'Yeah,' Caitlin answered. 'At least I am.' There was a shade of resentment in her voice. Caitlin and her mother did not get along very well now that Crispin wasn't around.

'It all sounds pretty cool to me.'

'Dad, don't talk like that. I hate it when you try to talk young.'

'What? Cool isn't cool vernacular?'

'Here's Megan.'

The telephone was passed back again, and Megan said, 'I'll have Mom call you when she gets back.'

Crispin had planned on running to the store that evening but he put it off to wait for Phoebe's call. At eight thirty, he was watching CNN when the phone rang.

'Problem is, there are just five tickets,' Phoebe said.

'You talked to Julia?' Crispin asked.

'Yeah. I called her back.'

Crispin was too stunned to reply.

Phoebe said, 'She was very gracious. She wrote us a thank-you note for letting her stay at the house in Normandy.'

'You didn't tell me you'd heard from her.'

'Well, anyway, she said since we didn't ever get a chance to visit her on the set when they were making the movie, maybe we'd like to attend the premiere. Apparently it's a big formal thing. She said the studio think they might get some Oscar nominations.'

'Hey, that's great.'

There was a pause, underlining the awkwardness they both tried to fly around all the time. Then Phoebe said, 'But with just five tickets . . .'

'We don't have to sit together, Phoebe. You can go with the girls.'

'But the girls get to ride with Julia in her limousine. And apparently she's got special seats for them in the row right behind her.'

'You mean it's like a reserved seating thing?'

'Yeah. The other two seats are together.'

There was silence, then Crispin said, 'You have somebody you'd like to take?'

She took a moment to reply, and then said gently, 'Well, yes, I do.'

'Then take my ticket.'

He would have liked to see her face just then. 'Are you sure?'

'I'm sure. And do me a favour. Check out Heath McEwan's hands.'

It took a second for it to sink in, and then she laughed. It was sweet, bell-like laughter that he hadn't heard in a long time, and he wondered if she had been really miserable for the last years of their marriage.

The invitation to Julia's premiere gave Crispin the opportunity to appear to his daughters in a new light. As soon as they arrived the next Saturday morning, Crispin hauled them off to shop for the event. In the Beverly Center he watched them spray perfumes on one another, test eyeliners and eyeshadows and open box after box of shoes. Phoebe had always assumed a certain pre-eminence in her daughters' lives by reason of gender, and pleasures such as this were her prerogative. But Crispin enjoyed himself thoroughly, and that weekend the girls found much to appreciate in their father

Since the premiere was in Los Angeles and fell on a Saturday night, it was understood that the girls would be picked up at Crispin's place. He brought in a hairdresser to style their hair, and he sat around that afternoon with the television tuned to a basketball game and tried to stay clear of their bedrooms. The girls were so excited that they refused to eat the sandwiches he had made for them, so he gave in and ordered pizza. All afternoon there were squeals and squabbles and singing to bass-heavy music, and the constant roar of the hair dryer, and the smell of bubble bath and hairspray and perfumes, and he loved every minute of it.

He took pictures of the girls, and watched from the balcony as they appeared on the stairs below, a little wobbly in their high heels, with beaded bags dangling from their wrists, making their way to the waiting limousine. He was hoping to catch a glimpse of Julia, but the chauffeur closed the door and the car pulled away, leaving Crispin feeling very empty. He went round the apartment tidying up, and had an armload of wet towels when the phone rang. It was Caitlin.

'Hey,' she said, sounding very adult. He could hear excited chatter in the background.

'You three looked so gorgeous walking out of here.'

'Thanks for everything, Dad,' she said.

'Hey, don't thank me. This is Julia's doing.'

'Not entirely,' she said, and it felt like everything in his chest froze up on him. It was Julia's voice.

'Hi there,' he answered. He had to clear his throat, and he hoped she didn't notice.

'These girls look so beautiful. I may need a bodyguard for them.'

'Hey, a great big thanks,' he said. 'I hope you know how much this means to them.'

'It's my pleasure, I promise you.'

'I'm sorry I'm not getting to see your film tonight.'

'Yes. So am I.' He sensed she wanted to say more.

'I understand there's a party afterwards,' Crispin said.

'Yes, but I'll have them home whenever you say. What's their curfew?'

'You can have them as long as you want.'

'Then they can stay for as long as they can keep their eyes open.'

Excited cheers erupted in the background.

The woman who arrived at the entrance to the Mann's Chinese Theater that evening to give brief interviews to the press and pose for photographs alongside her director and leading man, had all the appearances of perfection—the dress, the hair, the style, the smile. No one would guess by looking at her how difficult it had been for Julia to get here tonight. Michael Langham remained at her side, reassuring her throughout the event, and she was doing beautifully until just around midnight, at the post-screening party, when she began to experience a familiar smothering sensation. Then, all of a sudden, her heartbeat surged. She excused herself and hurried outside to the limousine parked in the lot behind the restaurant where the party was being held. The chauffeur waited outside to give her a little privacy as she huddled in the back, trying to control her breathing so she wouldn't pass out. Finally, the rapid pounding ceased, and, hands still shaking, she opened a bottle of water from the bar and poured a little into her hand to cool her face. The attack left her trembling, and she pressed a button to open the sunroof. She sat breathing the night air, trying to summon up the courage to return to the party, when she heard the chauffeur speaking to someone. She looked out and saw that it was Caitlin.

Julia opened the door and called to her, and Caitlin turned towards her. 'It's OK,' Julia said. 'Come on. Get in.'

Cat climbed in and shut the door. She had tried to look sophisticated and glamorous like Megan, but her blue velvet dress—chosen for its slimming effect—seemed dull beside Megan's teal chiffon. But her eyes were dancing this evening.

'How's it going?' Julia asked. 'Having a good time?'

'Oh, yes,' Caitlin enthused. 'I just came out to tell you that Mom's leaving, and she wanted to know if you wanted her to take us.'

'Are you ready to go home?'

'Not really,' she replied.

'Then you don't have to go. I'll have the driver take you back whenever you're ready.'

It was very unlike Cat to do what she did just then, for she was a reserved child. She threw her arms around Julia and hugged her.

'Thank you so much for tonight,' she muttered into Julia's shoulder.

'Oh, honey,' Julia said, returning the hug. 'It's so good to see you again.'

'I sort of missed you,' Cat said shyly. 'It was cool, being your friend.'

'I liked being your friend, too. Did you enjoy the film?'

'Oh, yes. Very much,' Caitlin answered. She sat back and looked up at Julia with a shy smile. 'It made me think I might want to be a writer when I grow up.'

'I bet you'd be very talented.'

'Why?'

'For a start, because you're very sensitive. Your father's like that.'

'You don't see Dad any more, do you?'

'No,' Julia replied. Then, after a pause, 'How is he?'

Cat shrugged. 'He's OK, I guess. He's changed a lot.'

'How?'

Cat shrugged. 'I think he really misses being a priest.'

'I'm sure he does. It was very unfair, what happened to him. He didn't deserve any of it.' Julia looked down at Cat's hand resting in her own. 'It's too bad he didn't come this evening. That was very good of him, to give up his ticket to your mother.'

'Yeah. He wanted to come.'

'Maybe we could have lunch sometime. All of us together. You think you could handle that?'

'With Dad, you mean?'

'Yes.'

'That'd be cool.'

'You wouldn't be uncomfortable?'

'Not me.'

'How about Megan? And Lola?'

Cat shrugged. 'I think they'd be OK with it. They like you.'

'Then we'll do it.'

The girls returned home in the early hours of the morning. Lola, who had fallen asleep in the car, was carried upstairs by the chauffeur and delivered to Crispin, who carried her off to bed while Megan and Caitlin staggered to their room, leaving a trail of shoes and handbags on the carpet. Crispin had Lola propped on the edge of her bed and was stuffing an arm into her pyjamas when Cat came in to kiss him good night.

'Had a good time, huh?'

'Oh, yeah,' she said, and she watched while Crispin pulled back the covers and rolled Lola into bed.

'What is it?' he asked, sensing there was something on her mind.

'Oh, I'll tell you in the morning.'

'What? Your mom's new boyfriend?' Phoebe had finally told him that she was dating a surgeon introduced to her by her tennis instructor.

'No. It's about Julia.'

Crispin switched on the Dalmatian nightlight beside Lola's bed, then turned off the table lamp. 'How's she doing?' he said in a whisper, hoping his voice sounded normal.

'Do you like her?'

'Of course I do.'

'I mean, like a girlfriend. Could you like her like that?'

'Honey, Julia thinks of me like a brother. A friend. Nothing more,' he replied, closing the bedroom door. Cat followed him around the living room as he tidied up.

'I think it's more than that,' she said.

Crispin straightened, shoes in each hand. 'Oh?'

'That's just the feeling I got, from the way she talks about you.'

'Well, I think you're misreading it. Everybody always did.'

'Maybe things have changed.'

'I don't think so. I'm pretty sure I know how Julia feels about me.'

'What about you? How do you feel about her?'

He stood there, his heart pounding, and then said, 'Do you want the honest truth, honey?'

'Yeah. I do.'

'I think if ever I gave my heart to anyone again, it would be to Julia.'

'I think that'd be pretty cool,' Cat smiled.

'Do you, now?' Crispin replied lightly, but tears were burning his eyes.

'I'd like it if Julia came around. I think Julia'd be good for you.' She gave him a kiss on the cheek. 'Good night, Daddy,' she said, and she turned and went off to bed.

On Monday Crispin got a call from a secretary saying Ms Kramer deeply regretted that he hadn't been able to make it to the premiere, and that she was calling to invite him to a private screening of her film on Thursday evening at the Warner Brothers lot in Burbank.

'Just a few intimate friends,' the secretary said.

Crispin didn't have high expectations of the evening. He didn't think he'd have a chance to speak to Julia alone. On Thursday evening he drove to the Burbank lot and gave his name to the security guard. A receptionist directed him to the screening room, but when he arrived the theatre was empty. He found a seat and waited impatiently, checking his watch, convinced he had the wrong place or the wrong time, but a few minutes later a man entered and unlocked the projection booth, and then Julia arrived.

Crispin got to his feet as she came down the aisle towards him. She slipped into his row and hurried up to him, a little out of breath.

'Hi,' she said. 'Sorry I'm late.' Her eyes betrayed a certain wariness, but there was warmth in her voice and her smile.

'Hello, Julia,' he said softly.

It had been a year, and neither of them knew how to begin. For the moment, there was no superficial chatter, only a silence both awkward and sweet.

'Gosh,' she said, cutting through the nervousness with a grin. 'I don't think I've ever been tongue-tied with you.'

Crispin laughed, and it broke a little of the ice, although he was wary too. 'Yeah. Pretty strange for us, isn't it?' He shifted his eyes towards the back. 'Who else are you expecting?'

'Crispin,' she said gently, laying her hand on his arm. 'I need to tell you something before anything else is said between us.' She took a deep breath to steady herself. 'I lied to you. What I said to you that morning in your house in Normandy, when you came to my room, when you were leaving. Do you remember what I said?'

'I remember.'

'It wasn't true.'

He hesitated. He wanted to make sure he understood her correctly. 'What part wasn't true?'

'About being just friends. I said that my feelings for you were strictly those of a friend. Nothing more. But I lied. I feel so much more, Crispin,' she confessed, her eyes locked onto his with a pleading intensity. 'So much more.'

It took a moment for it to sink in, and then a boyish grin slowly spread over his face. 'You're kidding me.'

'No,' she insisted. 'It was all an act.'

Crispin took a deep cleansing breath. He was feeling a little giddy.

She went on, 'I don't have any idea what your situation is now, if you're dating someone, or what, but . . .'

He silenced her with a kiss.

This time, Julia returned the kiss.

'There,' she murmured. 'That's what I really wanted to do last year, but I couldn't. I couldn't let that happen.'

'I know.'

'You didn't tell me about Phoebe. You led me to believe everything was fine.'

'I thought it was best.'

'I understand,' she said, pressing her fingers to his lips. 'You don't need to explain. I understand.'

He leaned forwards to kiss her again.

'Crispin,' she whispered, slipping her hands round his neck, 'we can work it out, can't we? With the girls, I mean.'

'I think so,' he smiled, and kissed her eyelid and then her ear. 'I hope no one else shows up,' he whispered.

'They won't,' she answered with a teasing smile.

'I thought this was for a small group of intimate friends.'

'It is,' she replied. 'You and me.'

He threw back his head and laughed.

'Oh, Cris,' she said as he enfolded her in his arms. 'It's been so hard keeping away from you all this time. But there was just so much confusion in my life, and I wanted to be sure I was in love with you for the right reasons.'

'And are you?' he asked, kissing the top of her head.

'Most definitely.' She sighed deeply. 'But are you sure you want me?'

'I'm sure.'

'But I come with so much baggage.'

'I know, Jules. I was there when you packed it.'

'I guess you were.'

They were interrupted just then by the projectionist who came out from the booth to ask if Ms Kramer was ready to begin. Julia looked up at Crispin.

'Any time,' he mumbled, his face so close she could feel the words on his lips.

'You know,' she said, slipping an arm round his waist and pulling him closer. 'Maybe we should reschedule this.'

'You mean the screening?'

'Yes,' she said.

'Would you rather do something else?' he whispered, sliding his hand down her hip.

'I'd rather do more of this,' she whispered in his ear.

'Well, if it's just the two of us . . .' he suggested with a smile.

'It is.'

Crispin signalled to the projectionist. 'You can start any time,' he called. The projectionist disappeared into the booth and the lights dropped.

'Sit,' Julia ordered. 'I'll be right back.'

'Where are you going?' He was holding on to her, but she slipped out of his grasp.

'Stay there,' she called to him as she hurried up the aisle to the booth.

The studio logos flashed by on the screen, and then the music came up. Crispin looked over to see Julia coming towards him down the row.

'Come here,' he said to her, pulling her across his lap.

Julia settled onto him and wrapped her arms round his neck. 'I don't really think I need to see this film,' she said with her mouth against his ear. 'You can watch it. I'd much rather look at you.'

'I think I might have a hard time paying attention.'

'There are a couple of scenes where I was imagining Heath was you . . .'

'Now that's a cute little twist,' he muttered. She was doing things to his ear that took his breath away. 'Can I ask him to leave?' Crispin asked, with a nod towards the projection booth.

'He's already gone,' she replied softly, and she raised herself slightly and tugged at the zip on her jeans. 'I told him not to come back until the end,' she said as she squirmed out of her trousers.

'How long is that?' Crispin asked, as she straddled him.

'Exactly two hours and twelve minutes.'

'That's not long enough,' he murmured as he unbuttoned her blouse.

Eyes closed, she whispered, 'How long do you need?'

It was a little awkward at first, being lovers and being free. They were self-conscious, furtively glancing over their shoulders, but eventually they relaxed and behaved like others did. They walked hand in hand down the street, and kissed in parking lots and looked very much in love. The girls could see they were in love, and they accepted it, not because it was easy, but because they needed their father to be happy again.

Julia believed in Crispin the way he needed a woman to believe in him. She refused to let him give up the life they both believed he had been called to lead. Eventually, armed with a letter signed by hundreds of parishioners of St John's, Crispin went directly to the Bishop of the

Los Angeles diocese and stated his case. An enquiry brought to light unethical procedures practised by certain powerful clergy, and Tom Noonan's friend in the diocese was dismissed. Tom himself received an official reprimand for his conduct.

Then came an opening with a church in the Hollywood Hills, a struggling parish that served widely disparate needs—young families on welfare and young professionals, a number of homeless and elderly and unemployed—and the fact that Julia encouraged him to go for the interview was an indication of how well she understood him. As part of the interview process, it was customary for a candidate to give a Sunday sermon as a visiting priest. Crispin arrived early, and Julia slipped into a pew with Caitlin to wait for the service to begin. But the waiting made her nervous and so she went searching for Crispin and found him in the vestment room, putting on his purple stole.

Her hands were shaking when she reached up to adjust his collar, and he snatched one of them and kissed it. She was radiant, despite her nerves, and dressed in a crisp spring dress.

'Why are you so nervous?' he asked. 'I'm the one giving the sermon.'

'I'm sorry,' she said, and he could see she was taking it all so earnestly. 'I just want this so badly for you.'

'Honey,' he said, 'if it's right, then it'll happen.' He kissed her on the cheek. 'Go and get yourself a seat.'

'Cat's saving me a place.'

'You're on the end, I hope?'

'Yes.'

'If you feel an attack coming on, you just slide out of there. Don't worry about what people will think.'

'Crispin,' she said with a look that stilled him, 'even if I had a heart attack right there in the pew, I wouldn't so much as squirm.' She kissed him again. 'I'll be fine. We'll both be fine.'

'I have you to thank for this,' he said.

'I love you, Crispin Wakefield.'

'I love you too, the soon-to-be Mrs Wakefield.'

'Oh,' she exclaimed. 'I do so like the sound of that.'

They stood there holding hands and beaming at one another as the organ prelude concluded with a blast of trumpets.

She kissed him on the cheek. 'Go,' she said. 'I'll put your things away.'

He swept out, looking all priestly and wonderful. In all the ways that she loved him, she loved him best like this.

The processional hymn began, and Julia hurried to hang his jacket in the locker reserved for visiting priests. As she was closing the door, she noticed something sticking out of his pocket. She knew what it was; Crispin carried it around with him like people carry pictures of their children and spouses and dogs. She pulled it out and took a look at it again. It had been handled a lot and was a little dog-eared.

It was a postcard that she had sent him from Haworth just after his visit. The greeting was short and unsentimental, but he hadn't kept it for the words. He had kept it for the photograph.

The image was that of heathery moorland bathed in mist-filtered light and, in the distance, at the highest point of the hills receding into a hazy blue horizon, there stood a gnarly wind-bent tree beside the stone ruins of an old Yorkshire farmhouse. It was a striking image, because of the vast emptiness all around and the solidarity of those two surviving creations, one natural and one man-made. They represented everything that is common and ordinary in life. A weathered tree and a crumbling stone house. And it seemed as if, over time, they had fused together in a state of perfect symbiosis.

Julia knew exactly why he kept it.

JANICE GRAHAM

Remarkably, for someone raised in a small town in Kansas, on the seemingly endless prairies, Janice Graham has travelled widely and built a very international career. She completed her French studies at Kansas University and then moved to Paris, where she worked in a variety of jobs. She then went travelling in Greece and Israel, before returning to the United States to enroll in a film studies course at the University of California. It was here that she discovered her passion for writing, and her second script, *Until September*, was produced and released as a feature film in 1984.

Yet even as she was writing that screenplay—the first of many successes—she knew that her real desire was to become a novelist. 'It is a passionate and arduous process and requires enormous discipline and perseverance. But when I reach the point where the characters are so well developed that they take over on the page, it is absolute sheer delight. Writing is an all-consuming thing, and what's so marvellous is that it allows you to stretch yourself to enter worlds and ways of thinking that are so different from you own.'

So why did Janice Graham, so keen to explore life, create the agorophobic Julia in *Safe Harbour*? 'Since I've always been an intrepid traveller myself, I thought it would be interesting to write from the point of view of a character who was exactly the opposite; someone whose entire life was circumscribed by fear. I researched the disease thoroughly and, by talking about it, I discovered one of my neighbour's friends suffered from it.'

Janice Graham is currently hard at work on a new novel, set in Victorian times, in London, and on the same dramatic Yorkshire Moors that provide the backdrop for some of the powerful scenes in *Safe Harbour*. 'Several years ago, I read all the works of the three Brontë sisters, and I was so fascinated by their family that I thought I'd like to do a screenplay about them. I travelled to Haworth and spent several days in the village with my young daughter. We hiked through the moors, where the landscape is open and ancient and has the feeling of something that goes on to eternity. I haven't had time to write my screenplay yet, but I find I keep returning to the moors!'

The author is very close to her sixteen-year-old daughter, and values her insight and judgment. 'Gabrielle has yet to read any of my published novels, but she serves as a good sounding board during the writing process.' With Crispin Wakefield's three young daughters in mind, is she concerned about the choices that girls face these days? 'Yes, I have strong feelings about the way our children, particularly our girls, are bombarded with such overwhelming messages pushing sex and greed. I have handled it by keeping an open dialogue with Gabrielle, and I've been lucky so far.'

Anne Jenkins

THE QUEEN'S FOOL. Original full-length edition © 2003 by Philippa Gregory Ltd. British condensed edition © The Reader's Digest Association Limited, 2004.

BETWEEN SISTERS. Original full-length edition © 2003 by Kristin Hannah. US condensed edition © The Reader's Digest Association, Inc, 2003. British condensed edition © The Reader's Digest Association Limited, 2004.

SAFE HARBOUR. Original full-length edition © 2003 by Janice Graham. British condensed edition © The Reader's Digest Association Limited, 2004.

The right to be identified as authors has been asserted by the following in accordance with sections 77 and 78 of the Copyright, Designs and Patents Act, 1988: Philippa Gregory, Kristin Hannah and Janice Graham.

PICTURE CREDITS: COVER: © Imagebank/Getty Images. Philippa Gregory photograph, and page 199 © Robin Matthews. Kristin Hannah photograph, and page 335 © Sigrid Estrada. THE QUEEN'S FOOL: pages 6 & 7: woman: © Jeff Cottenden. BETWEEN SISTERS: pages 200 & 201: illustration: Claire Rankin; sisters image: Thinkstock/Getty Images. SAFE HARBOUR: pages 336 & 337: coffee table: Photographers Choice/Getty Images.

Reader's Digest, The Digest and the Pegasus logo
are registered trademarks of The Reader's Digest Association, Inc.

Printed and bound by Maury Imprimeur SA, Malesherbes, France

601-024-1